TELL US WHAT HAPPENED IN...

HARROWDEAN MANOR

THE COMPLETE DUET

J ROSE

Copyright © 2025 J Rose

Published by Wilted Rose Publishing Limited
Edited and Proofread by Kim BookJunkie
Cover Design by The Pretty Little Design Co

All rights reserved. This is a work of fiction. Any names, characters and events are used fictitiously. Any resemblance to persons living or dead, establishments or events is coincidental.

This book or any portion thereof may not be reproduced or used without the express permission of the author, except for the use of brief quotations in the context of a book review or article.

ISBN (eBook): 978-1-915987-33-4
ISBN (Paperback): 978-1-915987-34-1

www.jroseauthor.com

J ROSE SHARED UNIVERSE

All of J Rose's contemporary, dark romance books are set in the same shared universe. From the walls of Blackwood Institute and Harrowdean Manor, to Sabre Security's HQ and the small town of Briar Valley, all of the characters inhabit the same world and feature in Easter egg cameos in each other's books.

You can read these books in any order, dipping in and out of different series and stories, but here is the recommended order for the full effect of the shared universe and the ties between the books.

More Information:
www.jroseauthor.com/readingorder

AUTHOR'S NOTE

Thank you for picking up Harrowdean Manor.

For housekeeping purposes, this duet begins during Sacrificial Sinners (Blackwood Institute #2) and spans some of Desecrated Saints (Blackwood Institute #3). However, you do not have to read Blackwood Institute first, though I would strongly recommend it.

Next, I'm going to issue a warning. I don't usually hand hold in this way, but this is an enemies-to-lovers romance, through and through. Please read the TW and enter with caution.

Our leading lady is a morally corrupt antihero who has made a lot of controversial choices. Because why should only the male love interests be antiheroes? Let's give our women the chance to be baddies too.

Speaking of which—the male love interests. This is a complicated story fuelled by hatred and revenge. The guys aren't here to be heroes. They're broken, traumatised and make very ethically questionable decisions.

I don't write straightforward romance. This shared universe is sinister. Imperfect. Flawed. It explores humanity in all its most disturbing forms. If you're up for a challenge, read on. But don't expect redemption to come quickly or easily.

Thank you for being here. Grab a blanket, make an iced coffee, and look after your mental health while reading dark romance.

Love always,

J Rose

HARROWDEAN TOOK EVERYTHING FROM US. BUT IT DIDN'T TAKE OUR FAMILY.

SIN LIKE THE DEVIL

HARROWDEAN MANOR #1

TRIGGER WARNING

Sin Like The Devil (Harrowdean Manor #1) is a why choose, reverse harem romance, so the main character will have multiple love interests that she will not have to choose between.

This book is very dark and contains scenes that may be triggering for some readers. These include strong mental health themes, drug addiction and overdose, graphic violence, attempted murder, psychological torture, mentions of self-harm, allusions to childhood sexual abuse, and suicide.

There is explicit language throughout and sexual scenes involving dubious consent, blood play, breath play, knife play and orgasm denial.

If you are easily offended or triggered by any of this content, please do not read this book. This is dark romance, and therefore, not for the faint of heart.

Additionally, this book is written for entertainment and is not intended to accurately represent the treatment of mental health issues.

"Maybe we feel empty because we leave pieces of ourselves in everything we used to love."

- R.M. Drake

Established in 1984, a world-first experimental program pioneered by global investment group, Incendia Corporation, founded six private psychiatric institutes across the United Kingdom.

Blackwood Institute
Harrowdean Manor
Priory Lane
Compton Hall
Hazelthorn House
Kirkwood Lodge

Hidden behind multimillion pound, state-of-the-art facilities and slick marketing campaigns, these institutes hide a far more harrowing reality. To find the truth, you must enter the gates of hell with the other patients assigned to Incendia's care.

These are their stories.

PROLOGUE
1121 – HALSEY

RIPLEY

Present Day

Did you survive a tragedy if you never speak about it?

Some people would argue not. Well, they're assholes. The lot of them.

Personally, I don't give a fuck whether you want to air your dirty laundry for the entire world to pick apart or not. That's your call. We all survive the aftermath of total self-destruction in our own ways.

But we've been programmed to view survival as being contingent on our later success—the capitalistic drive to monetise your demons and sell them to the highest bidder in the name of bullshit self-improvement.

There are survivors out there who remain silent. Invisible. Slipped through the cracks of society's broken fringes, watching the parade of inspirational figureheads championing their own resilience.

We don't all talk about our pasts. Nor do we all want to remember the struggle. The fight. The breaking. The cost of survival. These things are left unsaid in the shadows while the loud ones toot their own horns.

I've spent my life running from cameras and film crews, bloodthirsty reporters and foolhardy journalists, all determined to get the scoop on what happened ten years ago when the whole country burned. The fuse was lit inside the country's psychiatric institutes. I had the honour of being incarcerated in one.

Harrowdean Manor.

It's the last unsolved mystery.

When the biggest failed experiment in modern medical history was dismantled and exposed, the six private institutes embroiled in the conspiracy fell into ruinous violence.

Some made it out alive.

Others didn't survive.

Already uncomfortable, I shift my short, barely five feet body in the stiff leather armchair that I've been assigned to after having my hair and makeup done. The blinking eye of the camera set up catches every sharp breath I suck into my lungs.

Tucked off to the side, Elliot O'Hare—the eagle-eyed investigative journalist who's spent the best part of a decade harassing me—is fiddling with the microphone attached to his grey lapel.

Any sane person would be nervous for this interview. But any sane person wouldn't have survived what I did. Perhaps that's what shielded us from harm—the poisonous cloak of our insanity.

It protected us from the horrors we endured because we were already broken in the first place. That's the whole reason we were all trapped inside of Harrowdean Manor. Society deemed us all unfit for their picture-perfect world of falsehoods.

"Okay, then." Elliot straightens his narrow frame, an overflowing notebook clasped in his wrinkle-lined hands. "Are you ready to start, Miss Bennet?"

Staring down at the oil paint-stained tips of my fingers, I absently pick at my chipped purple nail varnish. "As ready as I'll ever be."

"If you'd like to stop for a break at any time, please let me know. I understand this will be difficult for you. We'll go at your own pace."

Difficult.

The word weighs heavy on my tongue like acrid cigarette ash. Escaping Harrowdean wasn't difficult. It wasn't even hard. In the end, it extracted a simple toll. I left one thing behind.

My broken heart.

The splintered remains... *they* took with them.

"Three... Two... One. The camera is rolling."

When the blinking red light of the camera begins to strike its deathly knoll, I sit up straighter, attempting to conceal my anxiety. My heart has been trying to tear free from my ribcage ever since I arrived.

After spending hours trawling through my meagre wardrobe this morning, looking for something other than my studio clothes, I shed my usual sweatpants in favour of plain black jeans and an off-white blouse that complements my tawny hair and pale complexion.

It's rare that I emerge from my combined apartment and art studio. The real world is unpalatable to me. I prefer the safety of my canvases and the slick of oil paint wielded as a weapon by my brush. No one can ever get close enough to hurt me as long as I live in isolation.

"Please state your name and age for the record," Elliot prompts.

I clear my scratchy throat. "Ripley Bennet. Thirty-six years old."

"Thank you for agreeing to speak to me, Miss Bennet. We've spoken to many ex-detainees of this cruel regime, but your story in particular has always fascinated us."

Summoning a lifeless nod, I remain silent.

"We've been working on this documentary series for several years now." Elliot tells the viewers what I already know. "Incendia Corporation was officially disbanded a decade ago by the prestigious security firm, Sabre Security."

The London-based, private security company has become a household name. It was taken over by ex-inmates of Blackwood Institute four years ago. I choked on a mouthful of cereal when I read that headline. Now there's a hell of a story.

"We're releasing this documentary series to commemorate the anniversary of the disbandment," Elliot continues. "This is our chance to give the victims back their voices."

The past echoes inside my head. *Drip, drip.* Bloodstained corridors stretch out around me. *Slash, slash.* The knife is cold in my grip. *Stab, stab.* The cries of death and agony compose a sinister soundtrack. I'm still caught in Harrowdean's web of contradictions.

Illusion and distortion.

Patient and exploiter.

Innocent and culpable.

"Miss Bennet." Elliot's professional voice draws me back.

Shaking the rising haze from my head, I stuff the memories back into their internal prison. My therapist says they're safer in there. *Safe, Ripley. You're safe.* Harrowdean is long gone. Even on those dark days when a twisted part of me wishes it still existed.

"Sorry," I mutter.

"It's quite alright. I understand this must be a difficult subject for you, even after all these years. You lost people in Harrowdean, correct?"

All I can manage is another jerky nod that ruffles my unruly, jaw-length mop of curly hair. The words are caught in a barbed wire trap in my throat, unable to tear themselves free.

Fingers twisting together, I focus on the layers of ink that wrap around my arms in intricate tattoo sleeves. But even that isn't a distraction—the tattoos on my left arm are disfigured by puckered scarring. Another reminder of my time inside.

"We've spoken to many ex-detainees and heard shocking stories of medical malpractice, psychological torture and abuse."

"That's what they kept us in there for." I shrug. "We were never meant to be more than their playthings, all for the sake of medical experimentation."

"Quite," he hums.

That's the thing most people don't get. Not what happened inside of Harrowdean Manor and the other institutes—that's a matter of public record now. But the involvement of the patients themselves in the abuse. And those of us who enabled it.

The infamous story that's printed in the history books is only half of the truth. The other half lies buried in our broken minds, waiting to eventually see the light of day. That's why I'm here. After a decade, the time has come for me to reveal mine.

"Perhaps, you'll tell us about how you came to be incarcerated in Harrowdean, one of six experimental institutes owned by Incendia Corporation that were shut down and demolished—"

"Harrowdean wasn't just an institute," I interrupt.

Elliot taps his pen against his chin thoughtfully. "How so?"

"Well, that's just what the world wanted to see. It made it easier to ignore the truth that was staring them in the face for so many years."

My eyes stray back to the blinking camera, capturing every last traitorous syllable. In the years since Harrowdean, I swore I'd never tell. As long as I kept Harrowdean's secrets, my life was safe. But that didn't protect those I sacrificed for my own selfish purposes.

"We're here for the truth," Elliot states simply.

"I'm not sure the world is ready to hear it."

"But are you ready to tell it?"

Hesitating, years of silence hold my tongue hostage. I've never told my story before, and for good reason. The world feels no sympathy for people like me. Speaking up now will unleash hell upon me, but after years of torment, I've finally taken my therapist's advice. I can no longer live my life in the shadows. This is how I'll heal.

I need to exist.

I need to speak up.

I need... salvation.

Nodding cautiously, I refocus on my clenched fists. "Yes."

"Then tell us, Ripley. What was Harrowdean?"

"For me?"

Elliot's mouth lifts into a kind smile. "Yes."

Trawling back through years of torrid memories, dipped in spilt blood and dusted in the substances I peddled for my own benefit, the truth is a simple admittance of guilt. I find the awful words far too easily.

"Harrowdean Manor was my kingdom to rule."

CHAPTER 1
RIPLEY
PUNCHING BAG – SET IT OFF

Ten Years Earlier

BIPOLAR DISORDER IS A FUCKING BITCH.

Shit, sorry. I meant that to come out better. More hopeful, maybe? But you don't need me to do that. There are plenty of others who write articles for mental health blogs and wear their stability as a badge of honour.

Fuck. Okay, too dark.

Let me start again. My brain has zero filter before a minimum of three macchiatos, and I haven't had caffeine since the day I was taken into custody. Like a simple fucking coffee is going to make us any crazier? I've never heard such crap.

Anyway, I'll amend my statement since we're just talking between friends here. You can handle God's honest truth, right?

Bipolar disorder is a motherfucking cunt.

Better?

Awesome.

Don't get me wrong... The highs are high. Feverishly so. In those bright, otherworldly periods, you become a deity-like figure of supreme power and excellence. A god with all the power and almighty importance such a role would entail.

Those are the good times that doctors don't like to advertise. When they talk about bipolar, they make it sound bad to be so high, you believe that your eyeballs are two giant marshmallows in your head, just waiting to be melted over a campfire.

But the lows?

They're the real kicker.

I once read that when technical divers go deep into the ocean, they have to take several decompression stops on the way back up to prevent themselves from being paralysed by the pressure that's built within their body. That's what the lows feel like to me.

Total paralysis.

The weight of the whole world is pressing down on you—crushing, splintering, overtaking every breath until it feels like you're attempting to breathe fire rather than air. When that pressure builds, it's impossible to avoid the depressive stasis that follows.

I was always an odd child. The lonely orphan, rattling around her absent uncle's cold, impersonal four-story townhouse. I've been on antipsychotics and mood stabilisers ever since the housekeeper found me having a midnight birthday party for my friends on the balcony.

The overpaid London doctors said I was hallucinating my fourteen-year-old ass off and too manic to realise that my so-called friends weren't even real. My horrified uncle, Jonathan, swept me off to an expensive psychiatrist who slapped a nice, neat label on my forehead.

That was it.

Bipolar.

End of story.

From that day forward, a handful of brightly coloured pills converted me into a semi-functional human being who graduated from art school at twenty-one and established her own life. And it worked for several years, until I relapsed and had an episode so bad, I landed myself in here.

After thinking that Martians were attempting to take me away, and if I left my two-bedroom flat in Hackney, I'd break an air lock that surrounded my apartment, Uncle Jonathan signed off on a generous donation to ensure I'd be dealt with quietly.

He easily handed me over to avoid any damage to his public image. Being a prolific financier and investor in the city might have afforded him a luxurious lifestyle that I benefited from growing up, but it didn't allow for a batshit crazy niece, assaulting the pizza delivery guy while manic.

Leaning against an oak tree located off the green quad at the centre of Harrowdean Manor, I await the gaggle of patients making their way towards me. Right on time, as per usual. Everyone knows what day it is. I run a tight ship and never stray from the schedule.

Wednesday afternoon is our designated time slot for contraband collection. Santa Claus is here with gifts, and someone is about to get shit-rich on their self-destructive tendencies. Being the self-proclaimed queen of Harrowdean has its benefits, but I'm just an intermediary. My payment for the illegal crap I peddle comes in other forms.

"Hi, Ripley." Santos reaches me first, his bleary eyes downturned. "My usual, please."

Reaching into my sock, I pull the small plastic wrapper of cocaine from its hiding place. He checks in for more every day or two, and as long as my contraband lines hold steady, I regularly fulfil his order.

"Usual price."

"Uh, well…" He avoids eye contact, shuffling his worn shoes.

"Come on, man. Don't give me that."

"My girlfriend's behind on rent," he rushes to explain. "She's gonna smuggle the cash in at tomorrow afternoon's visitation after she gets paid. Can I settle up then?"

"Tomorrow?" I raise an eyebrow.

His washed-out eyes finally meet mine, brimming with panic. "Please, Ripley."

"You know the deal."

"It's just one day—"

"No payment, no coke."

"No!" he begs again, dragging his palms down his face. "I need to re-up."

"I'm not a charity. Pay up or fuck off."

Hands trembling, he seizes a handful of my oversized anime t-shirt. "All I'm asking for is twenty-four hours."

Unbothered, I inspect my cuticles. "Not going to happen."

"What is wrong with you, bitch?"

Now he's pissing me off.

Sliding a hand into the waistband of my worn grey sweats, I grasp the metal switchblade I keep stashed at all times for my own protection. Santos's eyes widen as I draw the weapon free and flick out the blade, gesturing with a wave. He quickly releases my shirt.

"Back off or I'll happily paint the ground with your innards and let the guards find your body. They'll take great pleasure in covering it up to avoid filing the damn paperwork."

Cursing under his breath, he raises his hands in surrender, taking several large steps backwards. My blade remains drawn until he slinks away, muttering his displeasure.

I squash the faintest crack of pity trying to grow roots in my heart. Nothing is free in this world. Not even illegal contraband passed between patients like we're fucking prisoners trapped on death row.

My regulars slowly appear over the course of the next hour. Requests vary, week by week. Harrowdean is small enough for me to know all the other patients by name with a maximum occupancy of just sixty people spread across two floors of private bedrooms.

Rae requests blades. Always. She cuts herself until the razors turn blunt then barters for whatever cash she can scrounge in here to buy herself more. Usually by sucking dicks.

We're on friendly terms, but I keep her at arm's length after what happened before I came here. I learned that lesson the day the last person I cared about met a grisly end. Finding my best friend swinging from the ceiling was the worst day of my life.

I've been haunted ever since.

For most patients, it's drugs. Cigarettes. Alcohol. Sometimes weird shit, like the time our resident nympho, Tania, paid me in stolen jewellery for a nine-inch pink dildo complete with ribbed veins. Like I said, weird shit. That isn't even the half of it.

Taking a pack of cigarettes from me, Rick hands over a crumpled ten-pound note while unashamedly checking me out. He's a douchebag, through and through. I hate his guts, but he's a good customer. I'll tolerate his sleaziness for the repeat business his nicotine addiction provides.

"Eyes up, pal."

"You're looking good, Ripley. Nice t-shirt."

Eyes narrowed, I don't take the bait. Unlike some who attempt to escape the reality of being locked in here by dressing fancy as fuck, I'm rarely caught out of my favourite well-washed t-shirts or paint-splattered sweats. I'm not here to impress anyone.

"You hear about Priory Lane?" he asks conversationally.

A deathly chill races down my spine. "What about it?"

Rick tucks the cigarettes into his jeans pocket. "It's under official investigation. Everyone's being relocated until the heat dies down."

The mention of a place I'd love to forget is enough to sour my stomach. I spent twelve months in Priory Lane before being transferred here to live out the rest of my three-year psychiatric sentence. Not even leaving that hellhole scrubbed away the memory of finding Holly's corpse there.

"Priory Lane will be open again by the end of the week." I huff in derision. "These investigations never last."

"You're not interested in what the authorities may find?"

Suppressing a laugh, I can't help but find his optimism entertaining. We all know these institutes are corrupt as hell and more about profit than the treatment of the unwell.

But they'll never find any dirt in Priory Lane. Hush money shuffled in all the right places will see to that. The truth about our dire circumstances is more known here at Harrowdean, but if anything, the situation is bleaker. No one ever comes here or asks questions.

"I couldn't give a shit." Irritation leaks into my tone.

He lowers his voice. "Scared?"

"Fuck off, Rick."

Feet spread, he eyes me with amusement. I hate the way his tongue skates over his teeth as if he's deep in thought, contemplating how best to get in my head. The dickhead loves to play mind games.

"If these places go under, your little reign of terror comes to an end. You don't mean shit out there in the real world. We all know you're just the warden's bitch."

"Feel free to source your ciggies elsewhere if you have a problem with me."

He straightens, a nasty sneer painted across his lips. "Like where? You own us all."

Damn straight, I do. Everyone in this place belongs to me. Even the ones who don't buy contraband fear the power I have.

"You know, I hope when the police do come knocking to tear this hellhole down, you're the first one they throw under the bus for enabling it all."

"You chose to come here. I heard about what you did." I scan him up and down in disgust. "Did it feel good? Beating that guy to death?"

"Like you're so innocent, psycho."

Humiliation curdles in my gut. "I didn't kill anyone."

"Not for a lack of trying, though. I've heard the gossip. Besides, I'd rather be locked inside a real prison than this twisted shit show."

"You took the deal," I point out.

"If I could go back, I'd never agree to come here. None of us would."

I'm sure Rick and so many of his criminal pals spew the same shit. It makes them feel better, like they can forget they signed up for Harrowdean's glittering rehabilitation program. Duped like the rest of us.

"You committed a crime. It's not my fault you're doing the time."

"People come here to be helped," he argues, two red splotches forming on his cheeks. "This is supposed to be a treatment program. We all know that's a sham, though. Soon, the world will too."

Cruel laughter bubbles out of me. Now he's really starting to piss me off. I'm not above kicking his ass in front of everyone to teach him a lesson about respect.

"Whatever, man." I dismiss him with a wave. "Get out of my face."

"Watch your back, Ripley. I wouldn't want a knife to slip into it."

With a wink, he disappears to smoke and join his friends. I school a perfectly blank expression into place. No one can know the effect his words really have on me. I hate to admit it, but Rick's right.

I've spent the last year building a reputation for myself. Doling out contraband and inflicting a beating where necessary has earned me this hard-ass image. But I can lose it just as quickly. Perhaps it's time I taught these sheep a lesson to remind them who's in charge.

My eyes connect with Noah's pale brown orbs from across the lawn. He's slumped over at his usual picnic bench, mouthing the words *half an hour* with a raised brow.

I shoot him a thumb's up, anticipation already rolling down my spine. This new friends with benefits arrangement is working nicely. What? A girl's gotta eat. Especially when the excess energy grows too unbearable, inching its way into mania-territory.

Noah is a gangly, fellow manic depressive who got transferred here less than a month ago. He's tolerable for now. The others all want to fuck me too, I'm not denying that. But only to score themselves some free gear.

Noah's different. Lengthy periods of depression will do that to you. He's far too numb to mastermind an elaborate scheme to win me over to score himself a free spliff or whatever shit he's into.

I like that about him. The brokenness hidden behind his sad eyes and slumped shoulders is its own safety net. He's incapable of feeling anything too deeply. Therefore, he can't get attached. This arrangement is only temporary.

By the time I've offloaded this week's deliveries with no further incident, it's almost time for my dick appointment. I cast Elon—my least favourite grunt and assigned guard—a nod as I pass him on the way to my room on the fifth floor.

"Any problems?" he queries.

There's no sense lying to him. His gunmetal eyes catch everything. He's stocky and well-built, his closely cropped hair accentuating the harshness of his features. The man is as ugly and rough around the edges as they come.

"Nothing I can't handle."

"What does that mean?" His voice is a lazy drawl.

"It's been taken care of."

"You're supposed to keep them under control, inmate. Fail to do that and alternative arrangements can be made."

"That won't be necessary." I swallow the trepidation bubbling in my throat.

"For your sake, I hope not."

Grinning creepily, he gestures for me to continue up the winding, mahogany staircase that services the east wing. The beady, painted eyes of countless original paintings follow me, denoting various long-dead old bastards in white wigs and frilly suits.

Harrowdean Manor is the smallest of six privately-owned institutes spread across the United Kingdom. Nestled in the quiet, inconspicuous countryside of the rural midlands, it's a sprawling, Victoria-era manor house straight off the pages of history books that tell the tale of long-gone asylums.

Only, this one isn't long gone.

Far from it.

Hidden in a secretive forest of juniper and willow trees, Harrowdean is a gothic monster split across four huge wings—dorms, classes, therapy rooms and utilities like the cafeteria and library. It's a whole world locked behind dramatic stained glass, tall archways and crisscrossed bay windows.

Decades ago, it was converted into a home for the mentally unstable, including those deemed too fucked for prison.

Most people end up here one of two ways. Some are criminals, offered a shiny lifeline that enables them to escape jail time by agreeing to a three-year sentence in the experimental program.

But the rest of us? We're genuinely insane.

And I'm talking fucking *clinical.*

I didn't joyride in a celebrity's limo or burn a handsy relative alive. Yes, both true stories I've heard. I wish my story was that interesting. Instead, my manic ramblings were silenced, and I was shipped off to avoid causing my uncle more bad press.

Harrowdean wasn't even my first stop on the crazy train. Sedated and restrained, I was taken to the bigger, northern branch first—the infamous, and apparently under threat, Priory Lane. Fuck, how I'd love to see that slice of hell burn along with everyone in it.

Passing other patients in the carpet-lined halls, most avert their eyes. They all know I'm top dog. If you want anything illegal in here, I'm the girl to speak to. And that role grants me the respect, and more importantly, the fear, that I relish in without shame.

"Rip!"

Sighing, I halt outside my bedroom door, *Room Seventeen.* Rae is several doors down on the same floor. Dark-brown, almost black eyes lined with thick kohl, she flashes me a toothy smile from beneath her voluminous auburn curls.

"You know my name," I drone back, gripping the door handle. "At least bother to finish it."

With an eye roll, she lays her deep, raspy voice on thick. "Ripley. Satisfied?"

"Overjoyed." I begrudgingly release the knob and turn to face her. "What do you want?"

"I'm out. The last pack you gave me were dull."

"It's not like I can just nip down to the drug store and find the good, sharp razor blades for you to slice yourself up with. I'm beholden to others too."

"Yeah, whatever. I want the good ones."

Darkness creeps in. It blooms in the pits of my mind, metastasising with the weight of my guilt. I prefer the days when I'm too fucking high —or even better, too fucking depressed—to give a shit what she does with those razors.

But those in-between periods of lucidity as I wait for the bipolar roller coaster to regain speed are the most destructive. The days when I have to contend with the consequences of my decisions. At least when I'm off my head on imbalanced dopamine, I don't care who gets hurt.

Semi-sane Ripley cares.

Way too much.

"Ripley?" she whines. "You with me?"

Licking my lips, I force moisture into my mouth. "Fine, I'll figure it out. Now fuck off, Rae."

She grins back. "Love you too, doll face."

"Uh-huh."

Flipping her off, I quickly scan the keycard that unlocks my bedroom door and escape into the cool comfort. Early January daylight barely penetrates the darkness inside.

I keep the curtains drawn over the barred window. The dark drapes rest on an anti-ligature rack, held up by magnets. I keep minimal personal effects around, but the folding photo frame depicting the last family trip with my parents rests at my bedside.

Safely hidden, my eyes burn, but I refuse to release the moisture swelling inside. Looking at that photograph, I can still remember when the social worker sat me down and told me my mum wasn't coming home.

It was a hit and run. Dead on collision. I didn't discover those details until years later when I was old enough to pry into her death. Dad had passed a little over a year earlier from heart failure. Faster than blinking, I became an orphan.

Don't think, don't feel.

That's how to survive, Ripley.

I've lived by those words since my childhood. But part of me wonders how liberating it would be to let all the pain and grief I've been quelling since I stared at that social worker overwhelm me.

If I was consumed by that wave, perhaps I wouldn't float back to the surface again. Perhaps I'd finally be free of Holly's ghost still haunting me. I may rule this kingdom, but I built it for her.

Finding her dead ruined me.

They ruined me.

CHAPTER 2
LENNOX
HATEFUL – POST MALONE

"ARE WE THERE YET?"

Jerked out of my simmering anger that's built over the hours-long drive through the midlands, I focus on the view outside the window. Concrete motorways and impoverished cities have been swallowed by empty countryside.

We're surrounded by frost-bitten fields, dotted with the occasional livestock. Even the sheep look miserable. It's a little more built up than the north of the country, but we're far from the nearest town or city.

"Not yet," I grunt back.

"We've been driving for hours."

"Just be grateful we're being transferred together."

Sighing through his nostrils, Raine tilts his head back and lets it hit the chair cushion. His long fingers are tangled together, wringing and twisting. He'd never admit to it, but I know he's nervous as hell.

It fucking pisses me off. I hate that everything he knows, the safety systems he's put in place that allow him to function, have all been torn away.

Priory Lane is being ripped apart as we speak. Some ex-patient talked, probably thinking they were doing us a favour. That couldn't be further from the truth. Our files were stamped for immediate relocation when the institute's doors closed.

Glancing across the narrow aisle that separates the transfer van, I try to catch my best friend's eye. Xander stares straight ahead, a bored look on his face.

He's utterly unfazed, as per usual. Some days, I'd happily beat him black and blue just to elicit a hint of emotion. His lack of concern or even annoyance is infuriating.

The handful of others all cuffed and shoved onto this rattling piece of scrap emblazoned with Priory Lane's coat of arms don't dare speak in our presence. It's good to see that our authority is upheld even outside our territory.

We'll need that dog-like obedience to continue if we're to survive whatever lays ahead. If it's anything like the last place, this institute is just another torture chamber hidden by slick marketing and the public's disinterest in the mentally ill.

We will take it just like we took Priory Lane—hard, fast and with force.

Cuffed hands gripping the back of the chair in front of me, I clench the cheap plastic until it creaks and splits. That gains Xander's attention. He spares me a cold glance, his midnight-blue eyes devoid of understanding. My emotions run hot, much to his disdain.

"Don't say it," I bark at him.

"Pull yourself together, Nox."

"How are you not freaking out about this transfer?"

He shrugs nonchalantly. "I'm not concerned."

"You should be!"

Nothing rattles Xander. Not after what we endured together, months before Raine came along. Xander has always had little empathy, but the slivers of human vulnerability that remained were quickly beaten out of him in Priory Lane.

Returning his attention to the mist-soaked scenery outside the window, Xander ignores me. I didn't actually expect a response. But fuck if it wouldn't feel good to see his airtight control falter, even for a second.

Silence reigns until the winding road ends at the entrance to the rural estate. We drive through a huge, wrought-iron archway sandwiched between brick pillars.

Adorned with twisted vines and perfectly formed roses, the garish crest at the apex of the gate denotes two letters: HM. A signed death warrant that's stamped on our thick case files.

Harrowdean Manor.

"We're here," I whisper to Raine.

Adjusting the round, blacked-out glasses balancing on his straight nose, he nods detachedly. His hands are trembling, despite his poor attempts to hide it by forming fists. A thin sheen of sweat coats his forehead too.

With the long journey and constant supervision, he hasn't been able to get high today. I should've known this would happen. But dealing with his inevitable withdrawals is low on my list of concerns right now.

This is our new home.

The kingdom we must conquer to survive.

Along the winding, cobblestone driveway, weeping willows sway in the cool winter air. Up ahead, Harrowdean looks pretty small in comparison to the institute we've unwillingly left behind.

Relief momentarily extinguishes the furious fire that's constantly burning in my veins. Hell, this will be easy. It's tiny in comparison to Priory Lane's sprawling compound of buildings.

"Small," Xander comments.

"Good news for us. We can figure shit out fast and get back on top."

Quickly counting six floors marked by dark windows and glossy ivy strangling the red-brick exterior, a smile tugs at my mouth. This will be even easier than I thought.

The whole institute appears to be based in one huge manor house with the odd smaller building dotted around. Most of the offshoots look abandoned. If everyone is housed inside, we can take control of such a small population easily.

Parking outside the wide-set entrance steps flanked by more pillars, a tall, narrow-shouldered man awaits with the usual black-clad security presence. His fine suit and prominent gold tie pin betray his identity.

I recognise him from those expensive brochures that always seem to be floating around in the institutes. This guy features in all the phony marketing materials.

The warden's here to greet his newest arrivals.

"Hold onto me," I mutter.

"I'm fine," Raine murmurs back.

"Jesus, man. Just hold my fucking sleeve or something."

"I said I'm fine."

Biting back the urge to cave his head in, I grab his hand and move it to my arm, forcing him to grip my coat sleeve. His lips are pressed in a tight line as I guide him down from the van with Xander leading the way.

The others fall behind us without a single word uttered. No one dares move before we do. After disembarking, we're quickly scanned with wands to search for weapons, and our bags are confiscated to be searched.

I play close attention to Raine's violin case as it's scanned and combed through. If anyone dares cause trouble for him, it'll be the last thing they do. I don't let anyone give Raine shit.

The warden plasters on a smile that doesn't reach his eyes. "Morning all. I'm Mr Abbott Davis, the warden here at Harrowdean."

There's a murmur of greetings.

"So who do we have here?"

"Xander Beck, *Warden*."

Davis studies Xander with an appraising look. "Mr Beck."

Lifting his slim wrists to be un-cuffed, Xander doesn't flinch beneath Davis's watchful stare. The warden's lip curls at the power move. He knows exactly who we are and what we were to Priory Lane's regime.

"Sir." A blonde-haired guard approaches with a clipboard. "All inmates accounted for. These six complete our arrivals from Priory Lane."

Davis nods, still staring down Xander's icy glare. "Excellent. Please show our new arrivals inside."

Gritting my teeth hard enough to physically hurt, I swallow down the barrage of abuse that wants to escape. Being cuffed and dragged about like sacks of meat feels fucking degrading after all we've done for the powers that be behind our captors.

"What's happening?" Raine grunts.

"Stick with me."

"I can walk alone."

"Doesn't mean you have to."

Awkwardly gripping his guide stick in one cuffed hand, he purses his lips. He's at a disadvantage without the gift of sight, but no matter his pride, Raine knows we'd never let anyone set a damn hand on him. Not while I'm breathing. I've lost enough people I care about.

We all follow the guards inside. Xander will have a plan. I trust his judgement. The tap of Raine's stick against the interior's hardwood floors breaks the oppressive silence as he searches for obstacles.

Harrowdean is as lush as expected. It's all dark, stained wood, glinting crystal chandeliers and panelled walls covered in fancy as fuck artwork. The well-lit reception is small and leads to a grand staircase, splitting off in different directions.

CCTV cameras are fixed at multiple strategic angles, of course. Heaven forbid management fail to capture the material they're so desperately seeking. That's another dark secret, though. One of many.

"Stick." A guard stops at Raine's side.

He tilts his head. "Nope."

"Not a request, little freak."

Forcing Raine behind me, I move to block the guard's approach. "You really gonna stoop that low?"

The asshole sneers at me. "Just doin' my job. Lord knows what illegal contraband he's got stashed in that thing."

"There's nothing in it," Raine defends.

"Hand it over, inmate."

Meeting Xander's eyes, his mouth is a flat line, the only hint at his underlying emotions. The fucking robot isn't going to intervene? Fine. He may wield his words as a bloodless weapon, but these wankers don't listen to reason.

"Nox," Raine warns, doing his weird, mind-reading perceptive shit.

How he somehow manages to read us despite not being able to see our bodies or facial expressions, I'll never know. Raine's perceptive by necessity and highly attuned to other people's emotions.

He sees beyond the usual social cues the rest of us are so easily distracted by. But I don't need analysing right now. Ignoring him, I seize a handful of the guard's black t-shirt and wrench him closer.

My movements are limited with the cuffs cinched tight around my wrists, but I can still smash my forehead into his nose to elicit a delicious *crack* that makes me drool with satisfaction.

"Leave him the fuck alone," I threaten.

The guard's wail of pain is music to my ears. I manage to lift my hands quickly enough to get two awkward punches in, causing him to fall flat on his ass, blood dribbling down his chin.

Tackled from the side by another guard, I'm soon eating a faceful of the polished wood floor. My entire body hums with electric rage, setting my nerves alight and incinerating all sense of reason.

I buck and thrash, attempting to throw off whoever is pinning me to the floor. I'll kill them all. If we're not gonna rule this place, then we'll burn it to the ground instead. I won't go back to being a specimen.

"Ah. Mr Nash, I presume?" Davis crouches down on my left. "Your reputation precedes you."

"Gee, thanks." I turn my head to look at him.

"It isn't a compliment. Are you that determined to spend your first night here in solitary confinement?"

"You wouldn't dare. Don't you know who we are?"

He casts a critical eye over me. "I think it's quite clear that I do."

"Then why the hell are we still here?"

"Because you are my patient like anyone else now. Your previous arrangement is null. We run our own operations at Harrowdean Manor."

"Warden Aldrich assured us this would be a smooth transition." Xander hasn't moved an inch, still wearing that inscrutable look. "We had an *agreement* after the events of last year."

Davis scoffs in genuine amusement. "I don't care how Aldrich ruled his patients. He's under investigation now, isn't he? This is my institute, and you are under my care. Fall in line or face the repercussions."

Fuck, fuck, fuck.

After losing everything, we survived Priory Lane by taking the lifeline we were offered. A chance to escape the clinician's sadistic program and serve a greater purpose. Without that, we're as vulnerable as the rest of these lunatics.

Gaze connecting with Xander's dead eyes, he offers the tiniest shake of his head. *Fucking fine, dickhead.* He wants to play this smart instead of smashing shit. We'll see how well that strategy works.

"Sure," I grit out. "Care to call your attack dog off?"

Smiling thinly, Davis stands and smooths his charcoal suit trousers. "At ease, Langley. Our angry friend here will keep a lid on his temper."

The heavy weight on my back vanishes. I'm free to awkwardly stand. Hands white-knuckled on his guide stick, Raine is staring straight ahead behind his black lenses, appearing checked out.

I know he's hanging on to every verbal clue to decipher what's happening. Most assume he's zoned out when he does this, but he's actually picking apart every last sound and scent.

"Let's get this show on the road, shall we?" Davis looks between us all. "Much like Priory Lane, classes and weekly therapy are mandatory. Your previously chosen educational subjects will be accommodated."

"Where are the dorms?" a quieter patient asks.

"The east wing is assigned for residential use. Utilities can be found in the west wing, with classes and therapy rooms spread between the north and south. Other buildings are off-limits."

The urge to ask sizzles through me. What about the rest? We know from first-hand experience what he's deliberately omitting from his explanation. More lies beyond this whistle-stop tour. The real purpose behind this institute.

"Your previous IDs will suffice," Davis continues. "Keycards will be issued for your assigned rooms along with schedules. Some of you will have to bunk up."

Our bags, now searched and declared clear of any contraband, are dumped back at our feet by more of Davis's obedient lapdogs. Scooping up mine and Raine's bags, I touch his hand to guide it back to his violin case. He wouldn't dare entrust anyone else with his precious baby's safety.

Sparing us all an authoritative glower, Davis adjusts his silk tie. "Heed the lessons learned from your last incarceration. I won't tolerate any trouble."

I swear, the corner of Xander's mouth twitches infinitesimally. But it's gone so quickly; I have to wonder if I imagined it. Beneath his iceman persona, we all know that trouble is his fucking middle name.

"Follow the rules, complete your sentence and go home." Davis nods like it's that easy. "Welcome to Harrowdean Manor."

Yeah… Fucking welcome.

CHAPTER 3
RIPLEY
DEAD OR ALIVE – STILETO & MADALEN DUKE

QUAKING WITH ANXIETY, *I tentatively step out of the dorms and peer around the quad. It's my first day here. Priory Lane is truly massive. Countless antiquated Victorian buildings are dotted around, looming and oppressive in the frigid winter air.*

Curious eyes stray my way from other patients lingering nearby, chatting and basking in a rare blast of cold sunshine. It's colder here than I'm used to. London usually retains some of its sweatbox status in the winter. I think it may actually snow here.

"Hey! Newbie. Over here."

Squinting, I catch a flash of bouncy hair. A tall, willowy woman is waving at me from across the grass. Her oval-shaped face is pretty in a fairy-like way. She's rugged, visibly several years older than me. When she sees me hesitating, she rolls her eyes.

"I don't bite. Just saying hey, neighbour."

"Neighbour?" I inch down the stone steps.

"Your room's across from mine."

"Oh."

Another patient sidles up to the woman, eyes nervously darting from side to side. She reaches out a hand, and they exchange a quick, perfunctory shake. Something is passed between them before the other patient scuttles away with a muttered, "Thank you."

I'm shocked to silence. I thought this place was meant to be some kind of rehabilitation program, yet here this chick is, dealing drugs in broad daylight without a single care. It's hard not to be impressed.

"Can I get ya something?"

I stop at the edge of the grass, close enough to see the calculating gleam in her eyes. "Like what?"

"Anything you want."

The relentless itching in my veins forces me to ask, despite my determination to remain invisible for the next three years. If I don't paint or sketch soon, I'll be staring down the barrel of yet another manic episode.

"Charcoal pencils? And a sketchpad?"

Snorting, she doubles over with a short laugh. "Do I look like a fucking art supply store?"

"You said anything I want."

"People usually ask for stuff that's a little more... irregular."

I shrug dismissively. "I'll pass on the hard stuff, thanks. I didn't get time to pack all my supplies before they took me away, and my useless uncle has pretty much disowned me. So pencils it is."

"What did you do?" she chortles.

Biting my lip, a smile breaks free. "Might've accused the pizza guy of being a Martian and gone on a rampage that made the news. You know, the usual world-ending stuff for prissy family members."

"Clearly." Considering for a moment, she looks me over. "Fuck your family. I can get your damn pencils."

"How much?"

"Consider it a welcome gift. You got a name?"

"It's Ripley."

She outstretches her wrinkled hand for me to clasp. "Holly. Stick with me, kid. You'll be alright."

Quickly shaking her hand, I catch sight of two other patients hanging nearby in the shadows of the tree line. Rather than approaching to strike up a deal with her, they're silent, creepily watching us.

Two pairs of contrasting eyes track our every move—one belonging to an over-muscled boulder of a man. His eyes are filled with burning anger that corrupts his pale seafoam irises visible beneath his mop of tousled, chocolate hair.

The other is a stark comparison. Where his companion is all muscles and rage, he's slim and birdlike, his platinum hair paler than fresh snow. He wears his midnight-blue eyes with absolute detachment. Not a single hint of emotion belies his intense stare.

"Friends of yours?" I whisper, unnerved by the attention.

When Holly tracks my line of sight back to the pair, her easy-going persona *falters, showing a glimpse of something darker. It flickers across her features like bubbling storm clouds, casting a foreboding shadow that promises retribution.*

The broad mountain with fiery eyes offers a smirk before walking away, his ghostly pale friend following behind. Nothing that passes between them and Holly could be classed as friendly; I feel like I've inadvertently stepped into a minefield between two enemy lines.

"Hell no," Holly mutters curtly. "If you know what's good for you, kid, you'll stay the fuck away from those two."

Jerking upright, a cold sweat clings to my skin. I'm shaking so hard, it feels like my body is vibrating. The memory rests at the forefront of my mind after clawing its way out of my mental lockbox while I fitfully slept.

My nightmares are usually reserved for high-definition retellings of my parents' deaths. Not so much Dad's heart attack. My mind prefers to imagine how Mum's car crash unfolded while I was safely at home with a babysitter as she travelled back from a girls' night.

But not tonight.

Instead, Holly is haunting me.

I can feel salty droplets clinging to my body in the darkness of my bedroom. Scrubbing my face, I drag in a breath. She isn't here. I'm alone in my room at Harrowdean, far from the clinging horrors of last year.

Being turned over to the care of Priory Lane was the most terrifying moment I've ever experienced. Far scarier than losing my family, being confronted by my own delusions or even the resignation in my uncle's eyes as I shared my diagnosis.

It was the moment I lost all control.

My life no longer belonged to me.

The moment I stepped out of Uncle Jonathan's town car and into the northern chill, I knew my life was over. Three-year rehabilitative program or not. There was no coming back from being practically disowned by your only remaining family and forcibly confined to a psych ward.

Shoving back the bedsheets, I try to sit up but waver. My limbs are heavy and feel like they're wrapped in cotton wool. Numbing paralysis pumps through my veins, cutting off feeling to my extremities.

Depression is a silent but deadly weight that I know all too well. It's been a few weeks since my last down episode, but I recognise my own warning signs. The ups and downs are a regular part of my life now.

While others may feel the darkness creeping into their minds, the first thing to go is my ability to move like a normal human being. It's the technical diving effect playing out in real time.

Just get up, Ripley.

Fucking move.

You're in control of your own body.

But the awful truth is... I'm not. I haven't been for a long time. My brain doesn't belong to me; it belongs to my illness. That cruel bitch calls all the shots around here. I'm just along for the ride. Powerless to the rising tide approaching to decimate my self-control all over again.

"Come on," I whisper weakly. "Please, just move."

By the time I've worked up the will to move my leaden limbs, the sun is almost threatening to rise. I struggle to remain upright as I stumble through scattered art supplies to the attached ensuite, hands outstretched to stop myself from falling.

The plastic surface of the mirror above the sink distorts my reflection as I wait for the shower to heat up. I've always kept my hair short. More often than not, half the tight curls are shoved up in a sloppy knot and secured with a paintbrush, leaving stray, tawny-brown ringlets to tickle my jawline.

My wide, round, hazel eyes are more green than brown, framed by thick lashes that cast shadows across my lightly freckled cheeks and slightly upturned button nose. I straighten my silver septum ring with a sigh then step into the shower.

It takes scrubbing my ink-swirled skin to within an inch of its life with my favourite papaya body wash to remove the remnants of my nightmare. Holly sometimes infiltrates my dreams, but those two demons haven't shown their faces for a while.

Teeth gritted, I scrub hard enough to leave dark purple lines from my nails. *Bastards. Bastards. Bastards.* My mental chant accompanies my scrubbing, on and on, until I'm bright-red and aching from my own bodily assault. But at least I can feel my limbs again.

Making myself step out of the spray, I wince at the sting of cool air against my abused skin. I'm not like Rae. Pain isn't my thing. But hating every inch of myself sure as hell is, and a violent shower helps tame the thoughts of self-loathing long enough to reconstruct my mask each day.

I've convinced myself that if one day I scrub hard enough, I'll be able to rip the very skin from my bones and tear free from this carcass holding me prisoner. If I leave this body behind, perhaps I can leave my sins with it.

Until then, I must live with the monstrous person I've become. Some days that's easier than others. I can slip into a human skin suit and play the role I've been given. But other times, it's excruciating.

After drying off, I grab my discarded grey sweatpants from the floor and throw on a loose, acid-wash t-shirt. With each breath, I piece my careful façade back together. Another section of my armour is replaced, layer by layer, until the vulnerable version of Ripley is safely hidden.

The world can never know she exists.

Weakness would be my downfall.

By the time I grab my keycard and throw on a hoodie, my familiar, hard-faced scowl is safely back in place. I've got a date with a to-go breakfast and the unfinished canvas sitting in Harrowdean's studio. Aside from the weekly art therapy sessions, I usually get the place to myself.

It's early enough for only the non-sedated patients to be braving the cafeteria. The usual breakfast rush doesn't hit until at least nine o'clock when the previous night's court-sanctioned sedation inevitably wears off for everyone else.

Down the winding staircase that descends from the fifth floor of the east wing, the lavish decor and glimmering chandeliers fail to impress me. That's how they suck you in—a luxurious, well-polished exterior, crafted to conceal the truth.

That doesn't stop the private sponsors from lavishing the institute with donations so they can proudly pronounce themselves as mental health advocates. It's all shallow. Performative. No one actually cares if we're rehabilitated or not, as long as we're safely out of sight, and therefore, out of mind.

"Langley," I greet stiffly.

One foot propped behind him, the usual morning guard spares me a glance. He's tall and well-built, his tanned biceps straining against the soft material of his black shirt.

He's always been friendly to me. Sometimes suspiciously so. He's cute in a boyish way with his dark hair and fuzz-covered jawline.

"Morning, Rip. You're up early."

"Got a project calling my name in the studio."

Bright-blue eyes scanning over me, he frowns slightly. "Anyone causing ya trouble?"

"Nothing I can't handle on my own."

When his aquamarine eyes soften, I cast a cursory look around, ensuring no one is watching. I like Langley. Unlike some of the warden's well-paid thugs, he has a heart. Shame I can't afford to have any form of attachment in this place.

But in here, I don't get to have friends. Connections. *Weaknesses*. There's a reason why I keep everyone at arm's length. I'm here to do one thing. Survive. And I'll take myself out long before I let anyone break me again.

"Anyone gives you shit, I want to know about it." He moves to rest a hand on the baton strapped to his hip. "Contrary to what you may think, you're not alone in here."

"I've been alone for a long time," I say matter-of-factly. "It has nothing to do with this damn place. Do me a favour and mind your fucking business."

Waiting for the hurt to fill his eyes, I stare for a second longer before walking away. The sooner he stops seeing me as some tragic experiment that's somehow his to protect—from his employer no less—the better.

The cafeteria is located on the ground floor of the west wing. Traipsing down plush corridors adorned with more priceless artwork, I force my exhausted body to obey. Food. Paint. Forget. That's how I'll get through today.

With freshly waxed hardwood floors, cream walls and several long, rectangular tables to house the small patient population, it's practically empty at this hour.

Food awaits on the service line in the uppermost corner. I bypass the hot option and grab some fruit to take away. As I'm grabbing a juice box in lieu of the macchiato I'd rather be drinking, something hard shoves into my shoulder.

I trip and stumble, catching myself on the service line before I faceplant on the floor. Rick offers me an innocent smirk before he turns away with his breakfast tray in hand.

"Sorry, didn't see you there," he coos over his shoulder.

"Seriously?"

"What's up, Rip? No guard dog to kiss your ass today?"

Placing my food down, I snatch the back of his loose blue shirt and yank. He's dragged to a halt long enough for me to slip a foot around his ankle and shove his shoulder, causing him to go flying.

Food splatters across the floor as he lands unceremoniously on his ass. Rick bellows in shock and pain. I stare down at him pathetically rolling around.

"Sorry," I snap angrily. "Didn't see you there either."

"Motherfucker!" he screeches.

"You seem to have egg on your shirt."

Swiping spilt milk from his face, Rick eyes me furiously. "You have a fucking death wish or what?"

"I was perfectly happy minding my own business until you showed up." I tilt my head to stare down at him. "You're cut off. I don't sell to assholes. Spread the word."

Before he can respond, I grab my apple and saunter away with a wink delivered to an open-mouthed Langley, watching everything unfold from his post. He shakes his head at me, lips quirked up as he fights his amusement. What? I told him I could handle myself. Maybe next time, he'll believe me.

The art studio is located in the deserted south wing, at the end of another seemingly endless corridor surrounded by locked classrooms. I swipe my keycard to let myself into the large, shaded space.

Flicking the lights on, the comforting surroundings of my happy place are revealed. No one touches my canvases or supplies—not even Lena, the resident hippy art therapist—so I have a whole corner all to myself.

Everyone knows better than to fuck with my artwork. Like Rick said, being the warden's bitch has its perks. It only cost my soul.

Pulling out my oil paints, I begin to set up. My paintbrushes are clean and waiting for me. The only exception to people touching my shit is when I use my leverage to get someone to clean up after me. Again, *perks*.

The canvas I'm working on is a disturbing sight. Violent sprays of black, dark-green and crimson form the bleak landscape I'm crafting. It's a horrifying scene, and in the eye of the storm, a single shadowy figure stands.

She's alone. Trapped. Powerless to escape the endless tragedy all around her. My hand flicks, bends and swoops, splattering paint in an unrestrained torrent of previously suppressed rage.

All the emotions I spent my shower time shoving down come rushing back to the surface. I'm not sure where the two additional shadow figures come from in the background, but my hand soon creates them.

Throat parched and stomach rumbling, I barely stop to shove an apple into my mouth. Once I slip into that trance-like state of deep focus, it's impossible to come back to reality. Not until the painting is done and I've spilled my guts onto the canvas.

The lights in the art studio seem to grow brighter, and I distractedly register the sun setting through the room's bay windows. Not even the promise of dinner is enough to release me from my frenzy. It's pitch-black outside by the time I add the final flick of paint and deflate.

Jesus.

Fucking.

Christ.

It takes a lot to scare me after all I've seen, but even I can admit that what I've created is downright terrifying. It looks like a scene from Dante's inferno. The final layer of saturated flames on top of the greyscale shadows completes the hellish landscape.

Bleak.

Apocalyptic.

Beautiful.

Studying my work, I realise that I've been gently swaying to the rhythm of haunting violin music this entire time. Glancing around trying to gauge the source, it sounds distant, leaking through the partially open door leading to the corridor.

My stiff body protests as I move close to the doorway, following the melody. As it's a Sunday, there are no classes taking place. This wing should be deserted. But a few doors down, I can see that one of the classrooms is unlocked, the door slightly ajar.

I've only been into the music room once. A long since discharged patient bent me over the piano and fucked me senseless during one of my hypersexual manic episodes. He was a good lay.

Curiosity drives me to walk towards the classroom. Peeking around the door, I find the room in almost darkness. The only light is from the moon, a waxing crescent spilling through the arched window and illuminating a single figure sat alone in the shadows.

The violinist.

It's… a guy.

With an exquisite instrument tucked beneath his chin, he stares straight ahead into nothingness while playing with masterful control. I have no idea how he can see what he's playing with such dim lighting, but the notes spilling from his fingertips are pure perfection.

I can't make out much beyond the golden sheen of his hair that's illuminated by the moonlight, the strands long on top and roughly shoved back from his lowered face. He's slim but built, his limbs poised to strum the next note. I'm certain that he's new—I don't recognise him and Harrowdean is small enough for me to know everyone.

When the newbie hits a bad note and softly curses, I study his nimble fingers, realising his hands are shaking. It's a familiar tremble. I've seen it enough in my customers when they can't afford to re-up for a few days and go through withdrawals.

Is that why his music is so hauntingly sad?

Am I hearing the ache to shoot himself full of poison?

Hands freezing on the instrument, he tilts his head ever so slightly. It's a subtle cocking motion, like he's listening for the patter of approaching prey, inching closer to his hunting trap.

My heart is beating so loud, I can hear it roaring in my ears. When he speaks, his rough voice slices into my skin like razor blades. There's a delicious raspiness to his intonation.

"Hear something you like?"

Inhaling sharply, I look around like a complete idiot, convinced he's talking to someone else. How the hell does he know I'm listening? I've barely poked my head around the door.

Before I can offer a smart remark, my throat closes up. I don't know if it's the deep, gut-wrenching pain entangled in his music or the raw tenor of his voice, but any clever response I had dries up in my mouth.

"Well?" the violinist prompts.

He still hasn't lifted his head. Not even a glance in my direction. Hands scrunched, my nails dig into my palms. I want to yell at him for breaking my peace when I banked on this wing being empty. Yet not a single syllable spills from my tongue.

"If you're here to gawp, feel free to fuck off." His voice is resigned as he resumes playing the violin. "Your breathing is ruining my concentration."

My... breathing?

"Sorry," I mutter.

Disturbed by this strange creature, I turn on my heel and race away without a second glance. The sound of his crooning instrument hitting every last chord with finesse follows my retreating footsteps.

I return to my canvas to finish up, the sound of his music continuing. Lilting. Anguished. Hitting every note with well-timed perfection. If I wanted to, I could get a guard to heave him away for distracting me.

But I don't.

Instead, I find myself swaying again.

Although we are both lost in our own worlds, we're only metres apart, separated by the thin walls between us. The evocative violin music continues late into the night, long after I've tidied up, stacked the canvas and run out of unnecessary jobs to do.

I mentally scold myself and leave the art studio. As I pass the music room, the door left ajar, I catch another glimpse. The violinist has paused briefly, his instrument in his lap. I watch him lift the back of his hand to his nose.

He snorts up whatever is there, a relieved sigh slipping out of him. His bowed shoulders seem to perk up, and when he returns to his violin, the melody has lightened to a more joyful rhythm. I quickly turn and walk away.

Survival is a personal thing.

Sometimes, it looks a whole lot like self-destruction.

CHAPTER 4
RIPLEY
I'M NOT YOURS – THE HAUNT

"RIPLEY BENNET!"

Startled out of my numb daze at the sound of my name being called, I shuffle forward. The line is moving at a snail's pace this morning. It's always the same on Mondays, when classes and therapy sessions resume.

Harrowdean runs like any other secure unit—relying on a tried and tested combination of regimen, strict order and regular poking and prodding by the on-site clinical staff. All the usual day-to-day banalities of life on a psych ward, at least to the average Joe.

What goes on behind closed doors is a whole other ball game. One that not everyone has to bear witness to. They're blissfully unaware of their privileged position as one of the protected. Patients too risky to be targeted, often with families and loved ones who would notice their turmoil. Not all of us have that benefit.

"Rip." Rae nudges my shoulder. "Hurry the fuck up, would ya?"

"Alright. Don't get your panties in a bunch."

I force myself to approach the nurse's station to collect my meds. The swaying, zombified line of patients behind me all watch with varying degrees of interest.

Some are desperate for their daily dose of sanity, while others are dragged into line by the ever-present guards. The nurse slides a small paper cup brimming with tablets through the hole in the metal grate to me.

They have to keep the pharmacy strictly under lock and key, for obvious reasons. I've lost count of the number of attempted break-ins I've witnessed. Not everyone can afford my services.

One thing Harrowdean has no shortage of are desperate bastards searching for any way to remove themselves from the chess board of life. Pills. Blades. Rope. It's all the same to them.

A quick fix. An easy escape.

Who wouldn't want that?

Hell, everyone heard the story about Blackwood Institute's incident a few months ago. Gossip gets around, even behind bars. From what I hear, some asshole threw himself off the roof.

Bang.

Splat.

Goodnight.

One scrambled set of brains on the hard concrete, and it's game over. They must've been well-connected to even get access to a rooftop. Hearing that news brought my precarious arrangement into sharp focus.

The power my position provides may be keeping me alive right now, but I'm not the only one feeding this toxic machine of exploitation and abuse. Every institute has one of me.

Have you figured out what I am yet?

No spoilers...

Studying the lurid selection of pills in the paper cup, I quickly swallow them down then stick out my tongue to be inspected. The nurse dismisses me with a waved hand.

"Next!"

I'm not on their radar. If I wanted to kill myself, I could do it a lot more quickly and efficiently than by stashing my meds. I haven't lasted this long only to go and throw it all away now. Annihilation isn't my end game here. Survival is, plain and simple.

Watching Rae take her medication, it's obvious the staff are keeping a keen eye on her. I'm pretty sure that she wound up in here after a serious attempt on her life. And here I am, wilfully arming her with more ammunition to continue harming herself.

You can hate me.

It still won't compare to how much I hate myself.

"Gross." Rae shudders, sparing me a puzzled look. "What are you staring at?"

I roll my eyes at her. "None of your business."

"Weirdo. You eat already?"

"Yeah, I've got my session with Doctor Galloway. You off to class?"

Flicking fiery auburn hair over her shoulder, she shrugs. "Maybe. You get my next shipment?"

Shame curling around my internal organs like a poisonous cancer that I'll never hope to cure, I nod back.

"Slipped under your door."

"Sweet. What do I owe you?"

"The usual."

Bouncing on her feet, she's eager to escape. "Can I get you later?"

Glancing around, I ensure no one is listening. Rae is the only exception I'll make to my own personal rules. Call it sentiment or stupidity, but I care about her. Even if I'd never admit it out loud.

"Not like I'm going anywhere."

"You're the best, Rip."

Trust me, I'm really fucking not.

At the promise of a fresh stash of razor blades, her face has transformed. The heavy weight of defeat has evaporated, like darkness lifting after a solar eclipse to reveal the cold light of day once more.

My coping mechanism is detachment. But Rae's? It's the power to inflict pain so great, it offers a twisted form of relief. We are night and day yet bound by the same infallible sickness that trapped us in this purgatory together.

Rushing away to skip class and lock herself in the bathroom until she blunts her newest toys, I'm left with the gut-punching pain of knowing whatever damage she inflicts, I shall forever bear the responsibility. Everything I've done is at the expense of her slow death along with all the others I've armed to destroy themselves.

Walking past the remaining patients picking up their morning meds, I meet a few eyes, taking note of their visible fear and respect. Both emotions inextricably entwined. Luka, an anorexic from the sixth floor, even steps out of line to open the exit door for me.

Doctor Galloway's office is located on the left side of the north wing, past admin rooms filled with dull-eyed staff and the heavy guard presence lingering in the reception area. I'm early as usual.

Leaning against the wall, I'm lost in the intricate swirls of ink that make up the landscape canvas mounted outside her office when the door clicks open. Her familiar lilting voice leaks out from inside.

"You know where to find me if you require additional assistance settling into life here at Harrowdean."

"That won't be necessary," a rough drawl responds.

"We can make adjustments to accommodate your specific needs."

"I managed fine in the last place. I'll be alright here."

"Well, as you wish."

When the door swings open, Doctor Galloway spots me lingering outside. She's mid-fifties at best, her wrinkled face usually pulled taut in a grimace that deepens her crow's feet. Wearing her silver-streaked hair in a slicked back bun does her ageing appearance no favours.

Today's outfit is another ill-fitting pantsuit and tweed blazer. This woman needs to hire a stylist already. Harrowdean must pay her enough to afford one. Silence is expensive, after all.

"Be right with you, Ripley."

"Sure, doc."

Summoning a tight smile of acknowledgement, she holds open the door to release her last patient. The moment he's unveiled, my heart spasms in my chest. As he makes his way out into the corridor, the bright chandeliers overhead reveal all the details I couldn't make out last night.

His haunting violin music has played on a loop in my mind ever since I found him in the music room. Staring at my mystery violinist, my breath falters. Goddamn, what a sight he is.

Golden hair slicked back, his perfectly proportioned nose and full, thick lips are front and centre. The razor-edge of his jawline is sharp enough to cut metal like it's butter and covered in a light blonde scruff.

A pair of blacked-out glasses on the tip of his nose, his caramel-coloured eyes flick upwards for a brief moment. They're unfocused. Darting around the corridor without ever daring to grace me with their honeyed magnificence.

He rushes to slide the glasses back into place and takes a deep inhale. I don't know why I bite my lip and hold my breath, like somehow if I don't dare steal a single inhale for myself, he won't recognise me.

"No live performance today, babe." The corner of his mouth quirks in an amused smirk. "You'll have to gawp elsewhere."

Eyes hidden from sight, he unclips a folded, plastic stick that was clasped in one hand. It reaches mid-chest, and the tip is red, extended to reach the floor. That's when the penny drops.

The comforting darkness.

His unfocused gaze.

A strange awareness of my breathing.

He's *blind*.

"See you next week for your next session, Mr Starling."

"Raine is fine."

Doctor Galloway continues to prop the door open for him. "Okay, Raine. Do you need assistance finding the exit?"

"I'll manage," he responds easily. "My friend is meeting me."

"Oh, good. I'm glad you were all transferred together."

"We got lucky," he comments vaguely.

The unusual name befits everything I find weirdly fascinating about this golden-haired man. His seemingly perfect, almost angelic appearance tempered by the memory of his anguished music, played alone and in the shadows. Nothing but his violin and loneliness to hold his hand.

My curiosity is only heightened by the fact that he played like fucking Vivaldi without being able to even see where to place his fingertips. But as I scrutinise him, silently berating myself for being foolish enough to show an ounce of interest, I realise he *can* see.

Perhaps more than I can.

Perhaps more than any of us can.

"Hmm." Raine tilts his head again in that strange, calculating way as he stares in my general direction. "Is it guava?"

"I'm sorry?" I splutter.

His mouth twitches again. "Your body wash. I couldn't place it last night."

I watch his tongue dart out to wet his full lips, almost like he's tasting the air. Brain still short-circuiting, I mentally slap myself hard enough to knock myself back into gear.

"So?" he presses.

"I'm not sure how my choice of body wash is any concern of yours."

Doctor Galloway is watching us like we're some fascinating car crash unfolding. That doesn't stop Raine from studying me with every sense available to him from behind those odd glasses.

"When you disturb my violin practise smelling like a walking smoothie, it becomes my business."

Cocky son of a bitch.

"Then find somewhere else to practise," I snap back.

Steeling my shoulders, I'm about to push past him when footsteps march down the corridor towards us. My back is turned to whoever is approaching as I move to escape into the therapy room.

I can't see the newcomer—I only hear a sonorous, low-pitched bark.

"Raine! You done, man?"

No.

It can't be.

"Yes," Raine replies.

With the creeping agony of ice filling my veins, I'm forced to slowly turn to confirm the nightmare I'm living. As soon as I look, I'll know it's just my imagination.

Wake the fuck up, Ripley.

He isn't here. He can't be here.

I made sure of it the day I left Priory Lane and all its bad memories behind. Those two demons showing up in my dreams can't have been an omen. I made sure they'd never see the light of day again for what they did.

The son of a bitch I buried alive is walking right towards me, those muscle-carved shoulders as broad as ever, bearing the weight of his sadistic cruelty. My demons have escaped their state-funded prison.

I'm staring at Lennox Nash.

Gorgeous.

Insane.

Categorically evil.

When his pale, seafoam eyes land on me, I have the pleasure of seeing his utter shock. Clearly, he also didn't expect to be running into a ghost this morning. I have a split second to summon a perfectly blank expression.

"Lennox." My voice is flat and emotionless. "It's been a long time."

We've played this game before. It doesn't take long for his shock to vanish, replaced with his ever-present rage. Lennox is the definition of angry man syndrome.

He's furious with the whole fucking world and out to solve all his problems with his fists. Those muscles weren't made in the gym, though he spends most of his time in it. Lennox's strength comes from a lifetime of fist fights.

Long overdue for a shave, his round jaw is smothered in dark-chocolate hair. Those furious, deep-lidded eyes sit above a slightly upturned nose, marred by a small bump above the bridge. No doubt cracked beneath knuckles during one of his countless fights.

A small silver ring glints in his left ear, matching the silver chains peeking out of his white t-shirt. The fitted sweatpants that hug his tight ass and bulging thighs should be prohibited. I hate that he's so goddamn attractive.

"Tell me this is a joke." He halts several metres away. "For your sake, I better be imagining this shit."

My hands curl into balls at my sides. I'll fight my way out of this if I have to. Make no mistake, Lennox isn't the kind of man to allow his enemies to escape unscathed.

I went for the jugular the day I left Priory Lane behind, uncaring of the consequences of my actions. If he didn't hate me before, he sure as fuck does now. I made sure they knew who arranged their misfortune.

"Shouldn't you be dead by now?" I clip out.

Lennox's lip curls, baring his perfect teeth in a snarl. "Was that your plan?"

"I'm disappointed that you thought I intended anything else."

Our audience looks as bemused as I feel by his sudden appearance. Doctor Galloway is lingering in the doorway to her office, seeming conflicted as to whether she should intervene or not. Raine's head swivels back and forth, tracking the sound of our voices.

Arms folded across his barrel chest, Lennox glares at me with enough fury to melt the skin from my bones. I can almost feel the individual skin cells catching alight and turning to liquid mulch.

Those light-green eyes once terrified me. But I needn't have feared him or his best friend. In the end, it wasn't my blood they wanted. They settled for stealing my soul and trampling it to pathetic, irreparable pieces.

"We were almost killed!" he yells.

"Well, Nox..." I unleash a sadistic smile. "*You* killed *me* first."

"Clearly, I didn't do a good enough job of it." Nostrils flaring, his voice is a spine-chilling warning.

"Clearly."

"Don't worry, Rip. I won't make the same mistake again."

It happens so fast, Doctor Galloway is powerless to intervene. He closes the distance between us in a flash. Raine is shoved aside as Lennox lunges forward to attack, his huge hands easily finding my throat.

Slammed against the wall, pain radiates through my skull when the back of my head connects with the hard brick. His scarred hands are two huge clamps squeezing the very air from my windpipe, worsened by the sharp bite of his nails digging into my flesh.

I grab his wrists, attempting to wrestle myself free. My lungs are on fire. Burning. Smouldering. A scorching torrent blazing ever stronger behind my ribcage. He's actually going to kill me this time.

Maybe I'll enjoy it.

My empire of sin will die with me.

"Nox!" Raine yells.

At the same time, Doctor Galloway speaks up. "Stop it!"

But still, my attacker refuses to relent. He's determined to choke me to death for every last ounce of pain I arranged to be inflicted upon him. I doubt any achievement of mine will ever compare.

"Do you have any idea what they did to us?" Lennox spits, his saliva hitting my face. "Or the twisted shit I had to watch them do to my best friend?"

Abandoning my futile attempts to overpower him, I settle for kneeing him in the dick instead. Thankfully, it's far more effective, causing him to finally release me so I can breathe. Each inhale is an excruciating wheeze.

"He d-deserved to have his insides p-plucked out and examined!" I huff between gulps of air. "I h-hope they tore him apart and m-made you watch the show."

Cupping his sore Crown Jewels, Lennox shoots me a glare. "I'm going to enjoy doing the exact same thing to you."

The old Ripley would've run away screaming and locked herself in her dorm room. She would've let Holly protect her from the Big Bad Wolf and comforted herself with falsehoods like *it'll be okay*.

But not this Ripley.

She isn't the victim.

She's the fucking predator now.

Catching my breath, I force my voice to steady. "I'm not a scared girl anymore. That person died alongside her best friend. But you'd know all about that, wouldn't you?"

The smug grin that overtakes his expression is yet another kick in the teeth. I'll surrender every ounce of power I've carefully cultivated here for the chance to wipe it from his goddamn face.

"How is your precious friend?" Lennox taunts as he straightens. "What was her name again?"

Not even the distant sound of Doctor Galloway calling for security stops me. Hurling myself at him, I'm determined to drain every last drop of life from his veins.

Just like he did to me.

Just like he did to *her*.

"You know her name!" I tackle him to the thickly carpeted floor. "I hope her memory haunts you both!"

The sound of Raine's shouts doesn't stop us from battling. We tangle together and roll, both grappling for the upper hand. I know he won't go down without a fight, but any ounce of self-preservation I had has been obliterated.

I don't care about survival right now. Fuck the countless lives I've sacrificed to protect my own worthless hide. I'll give it all up for the chance to draw blood. To repay him for the life he so cruelly stole.

Lennox Nash deserves to die.

And I want the privilege of claiming the kill.

Knuckles crunching and skin splitting, I inflict as many blows as I can before the thunder of security approaching causes me to falter. Lennox is beneath me, a stunning curtain of blood pouring from his split eyebrow.

"You're in my institute now." I lean close to whisper menacingly. "This time, I'll be the one to take everything from you."

"Like hell!" he roars.

"Be afraid, Nox. Be fucking afraid."

With my parting shot fired, I let my body go limp. I'm easily plucked off him and dragged backwards by two guards. A bubble of hysterical laughter inches up my throat, and I gladly release it.

"Take her to the warden's office!" Doctor Galloway demands. "Now!"

"She's a psychopath." Lennox swipes dribbles of blood from his face. "Put her in solitary and throw away the damn key."

"You'll be joining her for inciting violence, Mr Nash!"

Poor, foolish Galloway.

She has no idea what she's dealing with. Lennox and his sadistic best friend only speak the language of violence, and a night in a padded cell won't ever change that.

A pair of hands loop under my arms, then my ankles are seized.

Lifted into the air, I don't even fight it. Trying to run from Harrowdean is futile. Its irrevocable sickness gets us all in the end.

As I'm carried away to whatever punishment lies ahead, all I can see is the slight upturn of Raine's lips. It isn't happiness contorting his features. Not even amusement. He just heard me attempt to kill his friend.

And somehow...

He looks impressed.

CHAPTER 5
RAINE
ALL THE WAYS I COULD DIE – ARROWS IN ACTION

TAP. *Tap. Tap.*

Lost in the vast expanse of blackness that paints my vision, I rely on the ever-present beat of my guide stick. My life has been reduced to that incessant, steering tap, counting out each pace to be committed to memory.

Fourteen steps forward. Five left. Rough cotton bedsheets. Three steps right. The sleek metal of a built-in lamp. Six steps back. Smooth wooden wardrobe doors. More cotton folded neatly inside.

That's how I know Xander unpacked my shit for me. The obsessively folded piles. He's as meticulous about his space as he is his carefully chosen words.

Tap. Tap. Tap.

You know, "experts" say that eighty percent of human perception comes from the eyes. Vision. It's by far the most important sense of the five. When our other senses fail us, our eyes will always protect us from danger.

But who can see the incoming threat, the approaching tiger salivating over its prospective prey, when your eyeballs are two useless lumps of meat in your skull? I may as well be walking around with two empty sockets where my eyes should be.

Fingertips gliding over stacked clothing, I explore the over-washed fabric, searching for signs of my favourite t-shirt. It's a remnant of a past life. The memory of its charcoal-grey colour and neon band slogan are fuzzy in my memory after five years of nothingness.

There.

I can feel the frayed edges and smattering of holes in the fabric. Unlike some, I couldn't give a fuck what I look like to others. You quickly stop caring about being judged when your whole existence is ripped away by a doctor in a white coat that you can no longer see.

Tugging the t-shirt over my head, I smooth my mop of hair away from my eyes. I keep it longer on top but shoved back as the strands distract me when they tickle my face. It used to be golden-blonde, brighter than the sun, but I haven't seen my reflection since I was eighteen.

I'm sure for a lot of people, losing their vision two days after coming of age would be the end of their life. And in some ways, it was for me. But the narcotic abuse I put my body through, and continue to do, started long before a dirty needle stole my entire basis for existence.

"Raine? You up?" A fist thumps on the door.

Quickly yanking a pair of skinny jeans into place, I fumble my way back towards the bedroom door. This room is smaller than the last one I had. It'll take some time to remember the correct paces to cross the space. I've already stubbed my toe twice.

Swiping under my nose, I make sure any remnants of the pill I awkwardly crushed and snorted in the bathroom are gone. I'm sure Lennox has already noticed the shakes and cold sweats.

I'm trying to stretch out the last of my stash for as long as possible. After my morning hit, I feel all warm and tingly. Navigating a pitch-black world is just a little less terrifying when my mind is swimming in happy chemicals.

"Password?" I drone.

There's a pissed-off exhale.

"How about open the fucking door before I break it down?"

I feel for the handle then swing the door open. "You're such a morning person, Nox."

I don't know what my friend looks like. We shared a particularly awkward encounter early on in our friendship when I requested to run my hands all over him to produce a mental picture of his appearance.

I know he's big. Burly. Grumpy. And a certified, grade A asshole. Except to me and maybe Xander. Lennox doesn't care about anyone or anything but those he considers family. It's his modus operandi.

Thunderous footsteps thumping past me, he barges into my bedroom with a low growl. I slam the door shut behind him then resume fastening my jeans. Though he's seen me in far less.

"To what do I owe the pleasure?"

"Family meeting," he grumbles. "The almighty one is on his way."

"Now, now. Don't go inflating Xander's ego any more than it already is."

I hear the creak of expanding bedsprings as Lennox takes a seat. "Hardly."

"Does this family meeting have something to do with your guava-scented girlfriend?"

"Jesus, Raine. Do you know how weird it is to hear how you categorise us in your head?"

I drop my shoulder against the wall and unleash a smirk. "Alright, Mr…" I take a deep inhale. "Hm. Burning wood? Campfires, maybe? Or is that tobacco? I thought you quit smoking."

Lennox softly curses. "Trust us to pick the weirdest fucking stray out there to adopt."

"No backsies. So what's the deal with guava girl?"

"It's papaya, genius."

I feel my eyebrows raise to my hairline as surprise washes over me. "How do you know what kind of body wash she uses? Feels like more than an educated guess."

"Xander." His tone is thick with amusement. "And believe me, you don't want to know how he got that information."

"Why not?"

"Leave it, Raine."

It's not like the infamous Lennox Nash to keep secrets from me. He may be a knucklehead with the world's shortest fuse, but he's loyal to a fault and never shies away from telling you exactly what he thinks. If Lennox hates your guts, you'll damn well know it.

"You get taken to the warden too, then?"

"Nah," he rumbles. "They just wanted her. Haven't seen the bitch since."

Ignoring the way that makes my insides twist uncomfortably, I retrace my careful steps across the room. *Tap. Tap. Tap.* When my guide stick connects with what I think is the desk, I feel for the chair then spin it around to sit down.

"Technically, you started it."

"How would you know?"

"My ears work perfectly fine." I flip him the bird, hoping it's in the right direction. "You gonna fill me in on this little feud?"

"Little." He laughs, but it's bitter and strained. "There's nothing *little* about the purgatory that evil cunt left us in. She wanted us dead."

"It obviously didn't work."

"Obviously," he mutters.

"What happened before I came to Priory Lane?"

Before he can respond, there's a terse, all-business knock on the door. I hear Lennox move to open it, letting Xander step inside. I'd recognise his trademark spearmint scent from a mile off without needing to see his face.

Our fearless leader has to be the most cold-hearted bastard I've ever had the displeasure of meeting. Xander is the kind of person to stop next to a car wreck just to take photos rather than call the police.

Last time I touched him, his features felt narrow and bird-like. I bet the iceman looks like a breakable China doll. Pair that with his short, cropped hair, so soft I'd wonder if he bought shares in a hair product company, and he's the full picture of elegance.

"Where have you been?" Lennox demands angrily.

Xander silently pads into the room, the rustling of paper being unwrapped telling me he's pulling out a stick of gum. Oh, yes. The iceman is always minty fresh.

"Have you seen her?" Lennox asks. "Xan?"

After a long beat of silence, his flat response comes. "No. Are you sure it's her?"

"You think I'd forget?" Lennox hurls back. "She kicked me in the fucking ball sack."

"Doesn't sound much like her," Xander challenges coldly, his voice as lifeless as ever. "I think you're seeing ghosts, Nox."

"It. Was. Fucking. Her."

I can just imagine the pair of them glaring daggers at each other right now. For two men who claim to be best friends, family even, they fight just as hard as they love. Though Xander would never admit such a thing. He shows love in far more violent and sadistic ways.

I wave a finger in the air. "If it helps, I witnessed the whole thing. This chick knew who Lennox was and sure didn't sound happy to see him."

"You hear her name?" Xander asks in a loud exhale.

"Yeah. Ripley."

He hesitates before his voice changes, almost like he's speaking around a smile. "So she's here, then. And the little toy has found a backbone."

"Ripley ran off here to hide after she fed us to the wolves!" Lennox explodes.

They lapse into loaded silence, though I can hear someone cracking their knuckles. I like to think I'm a patient guy—I have to be to simply communicate these days—but being left out of non-verbal conversations drives me fucking insane.

"Still waiting for my debriefing." I clear my throat pointedly.

My bed protests beneath the weight of someone sitting down. By the sounds of the groaning springs, it's Lennox's over-muscled frame. I'm surprised the bed supports him.

"Ripley Bennet was a patient in Priory Lane before you arrived." He speaks in a clipped tone.

"So what? You guys fucked her?"

Xander tsks. "It's hardly something so juvenile."

That's not an outright denial. Seems like Lennox isn't the only one keeping secrets.

"Is that a yes?" I push.

"Why do you care?" Lennox fires back.

Mouth clicking shut, I shrug it off. "Just want to know what we're dealing with."

"Trust me, Raine. Stay far away from Ripley," Lennox warns. "She's psycho with a capital P, and not in a cute way."

She smelled pretty damn cute to me.

"We earned our place in Priory Lane through brute force." Xander states matter-of-factly. "But the contraband lines that flowed through the institute once belonged to someone else."

"Someone else?" I repeat. "Her?"

"No."

The question of who hangs between us. I caught on quick when I arrived in Priory Lane, realising Lennox and Xander were the fucking kingpins of the institute.

"We did what we had to do to survive. Plain and simple," Lennox justifies. "Not everyone sees it that way."

Several pieces of the puzzle simultaneously click together. Whatever you wanted—smack, booze, blades—they could get it for you. It's how we met in the first place.

I was on my fifth stint in rehab after showing up to a scheduled gig too incoherent to remember my own name. The ultimatum came from my manager... Get clean, or my career in the music industry would be over.

After rehab failed, he dangled this golden lifeline instead. That same day, I walked straight into Priory Lane's arms. It seemed like a sweet deal to escape more rehab and appease the bastard profiting off the one thing that makes my life worth living.

My violin.

Of course, I didn't get clean. Lennox refused to sell to me at first. But when I made it pretty clear that I'd find a way to get high with or without their help, Xander was the one who caved. At least that way they could keep an eye on me.

"What did you do to her?"

"Ripley?" Lennox scoffs. "Not a damn thing."

"No, asshole. Her friend. Whoever the hell she accused you of hurting."

Lennox hesitates before answering. "Absolutely nothing. She did it to herself."

There's another beat of awkward silence, broken by the sound of feet shuffling. I can feel the tension skyrocketing between them.

"With enough encouragement," Xander adds.

"Wow. Fuck." I knead the back of my neck, which is feeling tighter the more they speak.

"It's really not how it sounds," Lennox protests.

"Isn't it?"

"Yes," Xander interjects. "It's exactly how it sounds."

Processing that, I wish I could say that I'm surprised. Out of us all, I'm generally the most level-headed. Even for a smackhead. These two have a list of issues longer than my arm that not even my penchant for opiates can compete with.

Grumbling to himself, Lennox moves again to begin pacing the room. I know it's him—his footsteps are heavy and furious. The man has fucking ants in his pants today, this Ripley chick has him all riled up.

"What exactly did she do to you?" I ask carefully. "For you to hate her so much, I mean. I sure as hell get why she hates both of y—"

"Ripley Bennet must be dealt with." Xander cuts over me, completely ignoring the question.

Lennox's pacing halts. "I don't think it's that simple."

"And why not?"

"She said something after she kicked my ass." Lennox pauses, presumably reaching for the memory. "*You're in my institute now.*"

"What does that mean?" I lift and drop a hand.

Neither responds for a loaded second, filled with enough tension for me to taste its cloying bitterness on the tip of my tongue. Someone huffs, while another taps their feet. It's weird as fuck to see my friends so unnerved. Well, not see. More like sense.

I've taught myself to recognise their emotional cues—even Xander, who barely has any. Spend enough time with someone and their tells become like clockwork. Sighing. Pacing. Huffing. This is the eighty percent of my perception now.

"It means… she thinks she's untouchable." Xander makes a small, almost amused noise in the back of his throat.

"So?" Lennox sighs.

"So that will be her downfall."

CHAPTER 6
RIPLEY
MISFITS – MAGNOLIA PARK & TAYLOR ACORN

LAYING on my back with my feet above me, resting on the padded interior of the cell, I toss the apple I was given for breakfast up in the air. Do they seriously expect this pointless, solitary shit to work on me?

I get it. *Bad Ripley*. My role here is simple. Incite violence, addiction, fights—whatever the fuck I want—and supply all these worthless sons of bitches with enough self-destructive shit to fan the flames, but do not get involved. I'm supposed to remain neutral.

The perfect inside man.

An inconspicuous weapon.

My role definitely doesn't entail beating the crap out of someone and almost revealing my hand. Secrets and subterfuge, remember? That's the name of the game. Instead, I ran my mouth and threatened to kick Lennox's well-toned ass.

In front of a clinician, no less.

Real fucking clever.

Catching the apple, my hand stills mid-throw when a loud shriek lances through the morning's peace. Even through the walls of my padded cell, I can hear it. The terror. Fear so horrifying in its intensity, it would make a grown man run like a scared puppy.

Taking a big bite of the apple, I crunch through the sharp tartness, unfazed by whatever is unfolding around me. Better them than me. You don't get far in a place like this by having an ounce of sympathy.

But as the shrieks continue to grow in pitch and intensity, feeling soon slinks back in. Ever the deadly assassin. What if it were Rae in there? Or Holly? Everyone is somebody to someone.

A brother. Lover.

Father. Sister.

Just because I don't give a shit about the screamer one cell over doesn't mean they don't have family out there, praying for their safe return from the brink of insanity.

How different would this world be if we all cared a little bit more? Or allowed ourselves to admit that we give a shit about other people, even when they refuse to care about us?

No, Ripley.

I cared before.

Look where that got me.

To pass the time, I imagine Lennox in there instead. Screaming like a red-faced toddler begging for a snack. Hmm, nope. What about Lennox attached to electrodes, convulsing as he's shocked repeatedly?

Much better.

Add in some bulging eyes and wet sweats too. What an awesome image. I'd pay to see that motherfucker torn apart for someone else's entertainment. I don't even want the leftover pieces. I just want to see him suffer while his limbs are removed.

I've yet to see the almighty keeper of his short leash. Xander was the only person who could ever keep that rabid dog in check. If Lennox is here, then his psychopathic overlord won't be far behind.

I meant what I said.

This time, I will be the one to take everything from them. As soon as they let me out of this goddamned cell, I'll plaster on a pretty smile to get myself back in management's good books, then let the games begin.

A sharp rap on the steel door is my only warning before it's unlocked and clanks open. I jut out my bottom lip, pouting like a child at Elon's displeased glower.

"Poor, Elon. Sent to babysit the naughty patient."

"Get the fuck up, Ripley."

"Maybe I quite like it here."

"You wanna stay another night?" he snorts. "Be my guest."

Turning his back to leave me here, I quickly scramble, finding my feet. He tosses my confiscated shoes at me to put on. They took them when I was dragged here, like I'd attempt to use the laces to string myself up or something.

"That wasn't so hard, was it?" he sneers.

Shoes slid on, I surrender my wrists to be cuffed. "Whatever."

He easily restrains me, then I'm dragged from the padded cell, out into a well-lit corridor surrounded by other occupied cells. This is the wing rolled out for clinical inspections and investors' tours.

Trust me—if you're taken into the *other* wing, you don't walk out. Cuffed or not. And that circle of hell sure doesn't make it into the fancy brochures laid out in the reception area.

"I thought you were smart enough to keep your head down," Elon says disdainfully. "You want to lose the privileges you've been given, inmate?"

"Nothing about this life is fucking privileged."

With a hiss, he spins and slams me up against the white-painted wall. I squeak in shock as his hand clenches around my already sore throat, squeezing on top of the fresh bruising inflicted by Lennox.

"You want to see the real horror show, Ripley? Don't think for a second that you have it hard here. Watch your goddamn mouth, or you'll lose it all."

He tightens his grip until I nod, admitting defeat. I slump forward when he releases me, rubbing my aching throat. I'm going to be walking around like some kind of bruised up sex doll at the rate I'm pissing people off.

"Come on. The warden wants a word."

"Fabulous," I rasp.

He flashes me another warning look. "Attitude, inmate."

This time, I have the sense of mind to keep my mouth shut.

I'm towed onwards, past the solitary confinement wing to the offices beyond. Warden Davis prefers to keep to himself far from the clinicians and patients alike. He's paid far too much to lower himself to our level.

Gleaming linoleum turns to thick carpet as we enter the administrative side of the wing. At the third door to the left, marked with a small bronze plaque, Elon knocks politely then waits to be called in.

"Enter," Davis calls out.

Inside, it's as lush and pretentious as you'd imagine. Hardwood floors and thick, patterned rugs. A sprawling dark-wood desk littered with organised paperwork and framed photographs. Not to mention the middle-aged man of the hour in his fine grey suit and usual gold tie pin.

With salt-and-pepper hair, a neatly trimmed beard and deep set, coal-black eyes, Abbott Davis is the corporate dream. I'm sure Harrowdean's PR team popped a fat boner the day he walked in. He's the perfect poster boy for their pet project.

"Ah, Miss Bennet." Davis's usually professional tone is marked with annoyance today. "Take a seat."

I have to bite back a sardonic response. "Warden."

"I hear there has been some commotion." His incisive gaze sweeps over me. "Care to explain yourself?"

Taking a seat opposite the desk, I wait for Elon to find his place in the corner of the room before responding. "It was nothing."

"By Doctor Galloway's account, you had an altercation with one of our new arrivals."

Glancing out the window behind him, I try to act unaffected. I don't want him to know how much power he holds over me. The fear he can so easily provoke. Before long, my eyes stray back to him though.

"Just... a little misunderstanding."

"Is that so?" he hums with a slightly quirked lip. "Perhaps you're also misunderstanding your role here, Miss Bennet."

My heart hammers behind my ribcage. "No, sir."

"When you transferred to Harrowdean Manor, I saw an opportunity for you. Has your time here not been... productive?"

The urge to scream in his picture-perfect face almost overwhelms me. Productive. I doubt the bereaved families of patients I've sold gear to would care for that choice of word. Frankly, I don't either.

"Yes... sir," I choke out.

"I'd hate to have to report back to one of my best investors that his niece isn't behaving."

I swallow hard, forcing down the hot ball of nausea making its way up my throat. Most days, I can forget that my uncle is the one who put me here. Or rather, his money did. He may be an investment banker by name, but that doesn't mean all his enterprises feature on the FTSE 100.

Harrowdean and its sister branches run off the dirty money bankrolling their depravity and the carelessness of those splashing the cash while turning a blind eye. I just so happen to be related to one such piece of shit.

"If it wasn't for Jonathan's generous donation to facilitate your transfer, I doubt we would've accommodated such a volatile subject in this position." Davis continues to study me. "I need someone I can count on."

Panic takes root. I can feel my carefully laid plan unfolding. After losing Holly, I knew I had to do something. Anything to escape Priory Lane and the demons who took it from her. Begging my uncle for a quick transfer was a level I felt willing to stoop to.

Priory Lane could keep its new kings. I didn't care enough to stop their ascension. But I wanted them broken, smashed to pieces and ground to a paste before they took their thrones. Then the world would see them as I did.

"I understand," I reply.

"Do you?" He inclines his head, eyes narrowing.

"Yes, sir."

"Then remind me. What is the purpose of a stooge?"

Lacing his fingers together, he props his chin on top and gives me his undivided attention. Does he want me to lay it out for him? Every last way I've corrupted my soul to avoid the torture I've seen inflicted on others?

If you haven't figured it out yet, grab the fucking popcorn. How far does the depravity go? The answer would take far longer to explain than even I think I have left on this godforsaken planet.

And it starts right here. At the top.

"To be a secret participant."

"In what?" Davis asks pointedly.

I lick my suddenly dry lips. "In a psychological experiment."

He smiles slyly. "The stooge acts like one of the patients, but their loyalties lie elsewhere. To further the aims of the research team and perform whatever task they may require of them."

Tasks like selling drugs. Blades. Contraband. Whatever volatile elements the clinicians fancy throwing into the mix to elicit a new result. The more accelerant, the hotter the flames. That's good for research and good for business. As long as it remains a secret. That's why it's all controlled from within by surveillance and the placement of a stooge to gain the patients' trust.

I choose the perfect candidates.

Then sell to them so the clinicians can study the result.

I'm not just allowing them to hurt the vulnerable people in here for their own scientific purposes. No. Far worse. I'm the one hurting the patients here, people just like me, to avoid being hurt myself. Their pain is my protection.

The ultimate selfishness.

But don't the selfish ones always survive the longest?

"You've been given a very comfortable life here, Miss Bennet. A lot of allowances have been made."

"I understand that."

"Then tell me why you're attacking other patients and threatening Lord knows what?" Davis frowns like this whole conversation is an inconvenience. "When you've been explicitly told to keep your nose clean?"

I don't respond. He doesn't want to hear anything I have to say. It'll only buy me a one-way ticket back into that padded cell. Or somewhere far worse. A useless stooge is a dead stooge. Rich uncle or not.

"We have to keep the program running as discreetly as possible. You signed yourself over to us the day you agreed to work for us."

"Yes, sir," I repeat monotonously.

What I wouldn't give to puppeteer him the same way that I do every other crazed, medicated patient in this place. I'm their God. But management? They're mine.

"No more fighting." He straightens, palms landing on his desk. "Do your job. I don't want to see you in here again. Do you understand?"

His harsh tone brooks no argument. And fuck, do I want to argue. That broken, pitiful part of me, still convinced that we can piece the jagged shards of our morality back together, wants to stop this once and for all.

But I won't walk away from Harrowdean if I do. This job offers me protection from the sickness the others must face. The truth behind the story everyone else is told about these institutes.

This isn't just an experiment.

It's far more sinister than that.

Behind the façade—a successful, rehabilitative regimen for criminals and the insane alike—lies its true purpose. Camouflage for the program. An experiment of the sickest sort. The same torture I signed Xander and Lennox up for as a parting gift.

"Miss Bennet," he barks, jerking me from my thoughts.

Nodding, I bite my tongue hard enough to draw blood.

"Good. One more strike and I'll be forced to re-evaluate your place here."

It takes all of my self-control to summon a pretty fucking smile and plaster it in place. If I'm removed by management and subjected to God knows what, Lennox and Xander won't hesitate to take my place.

It wouldn't be the first time they've grabbed power. They saw what Holly was, the control she had. She didn't stand a chance against them once they decided to take it from her. To become the stooges themselves.

"Get out of my sight." Davis dismisses me with a terse nod. "And heed my warning, Miss Bennet."

Keeping my lips sealed, I stand then scuttle from the room. He has to think that he's subjugated me. That the threat of punishment is far greater than my desire for revenge. Little does he know, I'd sacrifice it all to taste blood.

The lives I've traded for my own mean nothing while those monsters continue to breathe air. I thought they were gone. Lost in the system. Broken by whatever the fuck Priory Lane's *special wing* decided to do with them once I arranged their induction.

Yet they live.

But not for long.

I'll have to do it myself. Tear them apart, chunk by blood slick chunk, until they beg to return to the purgatory they crawled out of. It will look like paradise in comparison to what I spent my night in solitary planning for them.

Leading me back out to the reception, Elon pauses to unlock my handcuffs. The handful of patients floating around avert their eyes when I glower at them.

"See something that interests you?"

The onlookers quickly dissipate.

Elon snickers at the fear that fills their expressions as they scurry away. Rubbing my sore wrists, I spare him a nod then leave before he can change his mind.

The stairs leading up towards the residential floors feel endless. My legs are two concrete-filled pillars attached to my body after a sleepless night. Halfway up to the second floor, I hear their voices descending.

Familiarity is another sharp and unwelcome slap in the face. After a year spent trying to erase the memories that haunt me, hearing them so close feels like living a nightmare.

"The dickhead started it." Lennox's voice is a low grumble. "Who takes five minutes to decide which damn cereal to eat?"

"You can't just go around punching people, Nox."

"Says who?"

"Erm, the fucking law?" I recognise the raspy tenor of Raine responding. "Are you looking for trouble?"

"He doesn't even have to look for it," a voice responds.

The third voice causes a chill to break out across my skin. As if a snowstorm has swept over the staircase, the air is laced with frigid anticipation of his arrival. I knew he was here. But hearing him takes me right back to that night.

It was before my entire world changed. His cool, clinical touch brought me to life. A lash of pain. Soft, wet swipes of his tongue soothing the sting. Limbs pinned and spreadeagled. Powerless. At his utter, irrevocable mercy.

Fuck!

I turn and bolt back down the stairs before they can spot me. I'm no coward, but I have to play this smart. Facing off against Xander fucking Beck in this state will win me no awards. Plotting how to take down the king of cold calculation already took me several hours of pondering.

Ducking behind a tall potted plant at the bottom of the staircase, I hold my breath and wait. It doesn't take long for them to descend. Xander walks at the head of the group. Lennox stomps behind, a hand grasping the cute violinist's elbow.

"You know," Raine begins. "If she—"

"Not here," Xander clips out.

Lennox steers his friend towards the south wing where the daily classes are located. They trade conspiratorial whispers that I can't make out, and I keep my breath held until they disappear.

Shit.

I'll never get close enough to inflict any amount of damage when they're all together. Lennox has already had his hands around my throat. And I have no doubt Xander would happily give him another chance to choke me to death. As long as he could watch.

Breaking outside into the quad, it's a bright but freezing cold January day. Those not in therapy or classes mill about, wrapped in wool scarves and bobble hats. Guards bounce on their feet, red hands cupped over their mouths in attempts to warm up.

I have a plan.

All I need is a sacrificial lamb.

Scanning the smattering of picnic benches, he's in his usual spot. Noah likes the bite of cold air. He once told me it makes him feel something, if only for a second. His depressive episodes come more frequently than mine.

"Look alive," I greet wearily.

His head snaps up as I approach. "Ripley. Heard you got taken to the hole."

"News travels fast, huh?"

"In this place?" He lifts a shoulder in a shrug. "Nothing much else to do than gossip."

"Well, people better not get too excited. I'm back now."

"They were probably more concerned about where to source their shit from than excited."

I loop a leg over the bench seat. "Were you concerned about that too?"

"I'm not a junkie." Noah sighs. "I have no interest in buying drugs."

"Well, I don't just sell drugs. Interested in a trade?"

A sparkle briefly lights his sad, lifeless eyes. Everyone has that one thing. A pressure point. Find it and you'll own them, head to fucking toe. I just need to know what Noah's crutch is beyond meaningless one-night stands with batshit crazy drug dealers.

"I have a job that needs doing." I lower my voice, subtly glancing around. "You see the newbie yet?"

"Which one?" he replies. "I counted several."

"Big. Bulky. A sour-faced bastard with a bad attitude."

Noah snorts. "Saw him punch someone in the breakfast line this morning. That your guy?"

Fucking Lennox.

"Bingo."

"What about him?"

"I want you to pick a fight. Make it look like he started it. You're gonna get hurt, enough to get him thrown into the hole for a good while."

His brow line raises. "Why would I do that?"

"Name the price. It's yours."

Noah's mouth opens and closes several times before he finally responds. "You're serious?"

One day, people will stop underestimating me. Until then, I have to justify myself to idiots like Noah who see nothing but a mousy girl playing a game she doesn't understand.

"Do I look like I'm kidding around?" I gesture angrily.

While he chews over my proposal, I feel my plan begin to solidify. I can't get to Xander while his rabid pet is around. He serves his master too well. Remove Lennox from the picture, and Xander is free game.

That is how I'll win.

Break their family, and I break them.

"Well?" I push anxiously. "What'll it be?"

Gnawing on his lip, Noah seems to decide something. He nods to himself, not quite in defeat but with a look of satisfied resignation. I tap my fingers against the wooden bench and sigh.

"Noah?"

"I don't care what it is, but I want enough of it to OD. That's my price."

Taken aback, I feel my spine stiffen as shock coils within me. "To overdose?"

He watches me stoically. "Yes. In exchange, I'll let him fuck me up so bad, he never sees the light of day again."

My mind whirls. "So this OD... We talking hospitalisation or... you know, night-night?"

The corner of his mouth lifts in what is almost a smile. "Well, let's just say we better make our next booty call the last."

With icy dread pulsating through me, I simply stare. Not at my hook-up. Not even at my fellow patient. He's just another human, another sufferer, without an ounce more to give to this world. He wants me to kill him.

A life for a life.

Is revenge worth that price?

"Noah..."

"Whatever you're going to say, don't bother."

"But—"

"No." Noah holds up a hand. "I know you've been where I am."

"Look, this isn't—"

"I said no. I'm done, Rip."

"I can get you anything. Just... not that."

"That's what I want," he reiterates.

Taking a moment to consider, I stare at him. Every last telling detail. Who am I to tell him what he should do? I'm nothing to him. Not really.

Only someone who's been at the bottom of that black pit, the crushing weight of the earth pulverising their bones to ash as it bears down on them can understand how truly bleak it feels.

Like I said, doctors don't want to advertise the benefits of being high, and feeling invincible, like the whole world is your oyster. But at least when you're manic as fuck, you don't want to kill yourself. I'll take that sweet deal any day.

If I take his life, am I depriving him of the chance to feel that euphoria again? To find hope, peace or even a life without all this misery? Can I live with myself knowing that he'll never have the chance to find out?

Yes.

Yes, I can.

Because I told you... I'm not the good guy. I'm not even the misunderstood but morally redeemable fuck-up. The troubled kid with a good heart. There are enough stories out there about that person—go to the damn library and see for yourself.

I'm the monster they made me. Born from blood and thirsty for revenge, enough to sacrifice an innocent to achieve that goal. For some, redemption isn't realistic. All we have is our rage to keep us warm at night.

"If we do this... I can't have it lead back to me."

"I'm sure you can figure out the details," he replies in a bored tone. "Not like I'm gonna be here to deal with the repercussions."

"Yeah, hilarious."

But Noah isn't laughing. He holds out his hand towards me. Would you hate me less if I say I hesitate? Because I don't. Not even for a second. Our hands link as we seal the deal.

It'll take a while to sneak enough of what he needs from incoming batches of contraband. I can't exactly request a nice little cocktail on his behalf. Even Harrowdean has its standards, and typically, test subjects have to be alive to be helpful.

"I'll need a while to source everything. When it's go time, you better be ready."

"Not like I'm going anywhere, is it?" he counters.

"I guess not." Feeling like I need to say more, I dare to allow a sliver of emotion into my voice. "I'll remember you."

Lips thinning, he shakes his head.

"Please don't. Not like this."

CHAPTER 7
RIPLEY

MEET YOU AT THE GRAVEYARD –
CLEFFY

ONE HAND TRAILING along the staircase's balustrade, I will my body to respond. It's another down day, but this one feels different. Not even the paper cup of coloured pills from the nurse's station alleviated the weight bearing down on me.

I tried to sleep the feeling away this morning, but this isn't physical exhaustion. No amount of sleep will cure the crashing chemicals in my brain dragging me back down. More often than not, it only makes me feel worse.

What is it my old psychiatrist used to say to me? *Each step is a small victory.* Even if that's only to the bathroom and back. I suppose he wanted to make me feel better about ending up with a UTI when in the height of a depressive episode, I didn't move for three days.

"Ripley!"

Internally groaning, I ignore Langley abandoning his post to follow me as I reach the bottom of the staircase.

"Hey, Rip. Wait up."

"Not today," I reply tersely.

"Are you okay?" Langley's hand hovers just above my arm.

"Fucking brilliant. Leave me alone."

"Just doing my job." He scowls.

"Are you?" I look up into his baby blues.

After my brief stint in solitary, I'm keenly aware of every eye laser-focused on me. If the warden even suspects that Langley is overstepping his duties, a dismissal is the best-case scenario. I dare not think of the worst.

His gaze is soft with concern. "I'm trying to look out for you."

"And I told you—"

"It's alright, Jayden," a sneering voice interrupts. "I can take it from here."

Thick-soled boots stopping next to us, Elon's ever-present, phony grin is firmly in place. His blue eyes narrowed suspiciously, I can tell that not even Langley is convinced by it. He has no choice but to step aside.

Elon takes his place next to me, tightly clutching my wrist. "Shouldn't you be in class, inmate?"

Asshole. He knows I don't attend classes like everyone else. Yet another perk. If only my privileges could get me out of weekly therapy too.

"Just off to the studio," I force out.

"How opportune. I can escort you."

"Oh, fabulous."

Ignoring the sarcasm dripping from my voice, Elon frogmarches me through reception and towards the south wing. I don't bother looking back at Langley. That man needs to learn when to give up.

Once we're in an empty corridor, Elon drops his voice. "You're late on inventory."

"Yeah."

"That's it? Yeah? Unacceptable."

Wrangling my wrist from his crushing grip, I pull a folded piece of paper from my sweatpants. Elon quickly takes it from me, his thin lips pursed. He scans over the neatly scribed lines of items with his steely gunmetal gaze.

Folding my arms below my chest, I don't let my apprehension show. I've only added a few extras to my usual contraband order, small quantities I can sneak into a stockpile for my arrangement with Noah. Anything in large amounts would rouse suspicion.

Elon quickly refolds and pockets the list. "Don't be late again. We say jump, you say how high. Got that?"

"It was a couple of days. Cool off, will you?"

Grey eyes hardening, he takes a step closer. "Did you not learn your lesson? I've got a padded cell with your name on it if not."

I should be playing this smart, but fuck it. Today is not the day to be all up in my business. I'm already struggling to stay afloat.

"If you lock me up in solitary, who is gonna sell your shit?"

His nose wrinkles in disgust. "You think we can't find another desperate bitch to do our bidding?"

"I imagine you'd only have to look in the mirror to find that."

"You little—"

Tap. Tap. Tap.

"Is there a problem here?"

That raspy voice, filled with palpable self-assurance, apparently shocks Elon out of his rage. He glances over his shoulder to find Raine in the middle of the corridor, one hand holding a violin case, the other wrapped around the guide stick clasped in front of him.

Gleaming blonde hair slicked back, his blacked-out glasses rest above his full lips, stretched in a smirk. I don't know who puts his outfits together, but between the glasses, ripped grey jeans and loose tee, he looks every part the violin-toting rockstar.

"Keep moving," Elon barks.

Raine readjusts his grip on the guide stick. "I was actually on my way to see Ripley here."

"You were?" I gape at him.

His grin widens at my surprised tone. "Still got time to help me with that art project? It's uh, rather urgent."

The subtle cocking of his brow would be humorous if I didn't know who this guy is friends with. I don't know what's worse… a run in with Elon or accepting help from Lennox's latest puppet.

"Sure," I say uneasily. "I have some time."

"Great. Lead the way."

Sauntering up to me with his stick tapping away, he offers his elbow. I quickly step out of Elon's reach and take the proffered arm. Raine follows without question, letting me guide him down the thick carpet towards the classrooms.

Out the corner of my eye, I see Elon ball his fists and glower at Raine. He quickly abandons any plan to follow us, probably disappearing to take care of his list. When he vanishes, I breathe a sigh of relief.

"You're welcome, guava girl," Raine whispers.

I quickly release his elbow. "My body wash is papaya, alright?"

"Oh, I've been made aware. Doesn't have quite the same ring to it though, does it?"

"You've been discussing my choice of body wash?" I ask incredulously.

Raine chuckles, deep and throaty. "Gotta pass the time somehow."

"Sounds thrilling."

"A conversation with me?" he replies slyly. "It always is."

Avoiding the arc of his stick clacking out a clear path, I fight to keep my eyes off him. Something about Raine intrigues me. He's full of conflicts—vulnerable yet confident, a silver-tongued flirt hiding behind glasses and scruffy t-shirts.

Nothing about him makes sense. Yet nothing can erase the memory of him caressing his violin's strings alone in the music room. I've found my mind replaying that scene over several times, attempting to comprehend what I saw.

"Well, thanks for the save," I begrudgingly admit. "Feel free to go back to whatever you were doing."

"Actually, we're going in the same direction." He lifts his violin case. "Can you tolerate me for a bit longer?"

Fighting a smile, I keep my voice disinterested. "Suppose I'll have to."

"Promise I'm a lot more civilised than the company I keep. Though if you want to tackle me like you did Lennox, you have my full consent. It sounded hot."

"Your *friend* deserved what he got."

Raine snorts. "Of that I have no doubt."

Keeping his elbow to himself, he follows me at a leisurely pace. I sneak glances at him every few steps, but his slight grin remains sealed in place. How can someone capable of such mournful music have such a normal outward appearance?

"Did you know that your breathing changes every time you're about to ask something?" Raine enquires conversationally.

"I wasn't going to ask anything."

"But everyone always wants to. Stop hesitating, it's annoying. Ask."

I suck in my bottom lip, nibbling on it as we pass several classrooms. "I suppose everyone wants to know the same, right?"

"More often than not." An amused chuff bursts from him. "Short answer? No, I wasn't born blind."

When a door opens and patients begin to spill out in search of lunch, the first cracks in Raine's exterior begin to show. His jaw clenches, betraying a slight tic. Each tap of his guide stick becomes a little more forceful, like firing warning shots.

Someone rushes out with their head down, focused on a sheath of papers. Before they can collide with Raine, I quickly grasp his wrist and tug him aside. His skin is hot to the touch, almost feverishly so, and silky-soft beneath golden fuzz.

His hard body brushes mine, head tilted downwards and turned towards me like he's seeking safety. For a brief second, I savour the warmth of him pressed right up against my side.

He's surprisingly firm. Chiselled. Muscular beneath his revolving door of frayed t-shirts and skinny jeans. A lump forms in my throat at his sudden close proximity.

"Now we're even."

He releases a short breath. "You keeping count?"

"I don't like owing people."

I'm close enough to get a waft of his scent. The intoxicating combination of freshly squeezed orange juice and salty seawater overwhelms my senses. He smells like lazy mornings on the beach, sharing breakfast picnics before catching the next surf.

"Get a good sniff?" Raine snickers.

I flinch away, releasing him once more. "Your good hearing is creepy."

"Oh, I've been told. But it comes in handy."

Feeling exposed, I train my gaze on the art studio at the end of the corridor and move faster. Somehow, Raine is able to see far past the tactics I've long since perfected to portray my indifference.

He doesn't need his sight to read me like a book. That's a scary realisation. Even my breathing can betray the lie I live to him. No amount of bravado will stop him from discovering the version of myself that I refuse to let the world see.

"Music room is on your right." I deliberately don't stop for him. "Door's open."

Entering the art studio—deserted as usual on a Thursday—I'm flustered as I approach my covered canvas from last week which still needs signing and varnishing. I'm gathering my supplies when the sound of a stool scraping against the wooden floor fractures the peace.

After placing his violin case on a workbench, Raine hops up onto the stool and crosses his jean-clad legs at the ankles. He's facing the window, so I clear my throat and watch his head turn towards me.

"Why are you following me?"

Tilting his body, he repositions himself to face my direction. "We're supposed to be working on an art project."

"There is no project."

"And if your friendly resident stalker returns, looking to continue your conversation?" he counters. "You're going to need that alibi."

Slamming down my tin of varnish and brushes, I brace my hands on my hips. "What's your deal? Did Lennox or Xander put you up to this?"

"Nope." He pops the P exaggeratedly. "And I doubt they'd approve."

"Then what's the motive here?"

"Does there have to be one?" Rolling his lips, Raine looks like he's fighting laughter. "Sounds like people give you a wide berth. Maybe I just want some peace and quiet."

Despite by brimming curiosity for this mysterious man, I keep my voice level. "You're disturbing mine right now."

"Say no more." He mimes locking his mouth and tossing the key. "Pretend I'm not here."

Staring at him incredulously for several seconds, I quickly realise he isn't going to move. I'm keenly aware of his presence mere metres away as I suppress a growl, turning back to my canvas. I'm not used to sharing my personal space.

Beneath the paint-flecked white sheet, my finished canvas sits untouched. I sign it off with my signature in the bottom right corner then methodically begin varnishing, quickly becoming engrossed in my task.

Not even the sound of Raine unlatching his violin case and setting up his instrument disturbs me. I'm lost to the swirls of oil paint and varnish, sucking me back into the terrifying landscape that poured from my brush.

By the end of the first coat, my body has started to sway along to the muted chords Raine is plucking out as he tunes his violin. It's a stripped-back rhythm, light and oddly reticent, never quite betraying the raw emotion I heard him perform in private.

I still, laying down my brush. "When did you learn to play?"

"Before I lost my vision. I was around nine." The plucking continues. "My school's music program was wildly unpopular. Just like me. I fit right in."

"You were unpopular?"

"No one likes the junkies' son. I didn't have the latest clothes or mobile phone like everyone else. Everyone knew my folks were crackheads."

Still staring at my canvas, I wrestle with my conflicting emotions. "Why the violin?"

"I stumbled into the classroom one day while running from some bullies and found this ancient, battered violin. The rest is history."

"How old are you now?"

"What's with the third degree, guava girl?"

"You're the one who followed me in here."

"I guess that's fair. I'm twenty-three."

Turning on my stool, I allow myself another glimpse. He's a year younger than Lennox, while Xander is twenty-six, the same as me. That makes Raine the baby of their friendship group.

"You continued to play after you lost your vision?"

Raine nods hesitantly. "Took some practise, but I never stopped playing after it happened. Music gave me something to focus on."

I bite back the urge to ask what happened to him. No wonder he can play the chords by heart without the need for a single glance. Those wound metal strings are an extension of him, and he strokes them like it's second nature. Easier than breathing, almost.

"When was that?"

"This?" He gestures towards his eyes. "A little over five years ago."

An internal voice is telling me to stop asking rapid-fire questions, but he's like a puzzle I can't help piecing together. I want to know how this smooth-talking violinist with the filthiest smile ended up becoming friends with people like Lennox or Xander.

I hear him inhale before he speaks. "My turn. Do you always work with... Is that oil paint I can smell?"

"Yes it is, and that depends," I answer honestly.

"On what?"

"Sometimes, I prefer the richness of this medium and its saturated colours. Other times, the piece requires a lighter touch. Pastels, watercolour, sometimes pencil."

"What is it that you paint?" His head tilts in interest.

"Mostly landscapes or abstracts. But I dabble."

Fingertips still dancing over the neck of his violin, his pale brows knit together, like he's willing his mind to conjure some clue as to what I've painted.

"Can you describe it to me?"

Despite his confidence, there's a slight, almost unnoticeable crack in his voice. A hint of vulnerability. Something tells me that he wouldn't let it show by accident.

Ignoring every last warning bell telling me to put distance between us, I shift my stool to the left.

"Come closer."

Raine places his violin back in its velvet-lined case then walks towards me. After abandoning his guide stick, his steps are slow and hesitant. Another snippet of the person behind the mask. The same mask that I find myself wearing every day too.

We both put on a show. Play pretend. Bury any hints of weakness to survive in a world that doesn't allow for fragility. Perhaps Lennox and Xander are part of that show. Even monsters make good allies when it's convenient.

I reach out and snag his shirt sleeve. Raine lets me steer him into place, standing directly in front of the still-wet canvas. His lips are parted, breathing slightly unsteadily. He feels it too, then. The fear of flaws being exposed to another person.

"The canvas is about three feet in front of you," I explain, my voice breathless. "Imagine the ocean. Raging, wild, uncontrollable. There are sprays of deep forest-green and hints of crimson against the waves."

His throat bobs, the muscles in his neck tensing, but he remains silent. Despite feeling exposed by the emotion passing between us, I decide to continue.

"In the eye of the storm, shadows form a solitary figure. Trapped. Powerless. She's unaware of the others behind her, two larger silhouettes lurking in the background. They're all imprisoned by saturated flames, eating up the ocean."

Still holding his shirt sleeve, my hand grasps his bicep, feeling that same burning heat emanating from his skin. He isn't trembling like last time, but I know a withdrawal fever when I see one. He's in the early stages.

"Why is she trapped?" he asks quietly.

I consider the varnished canvas. "Because who isn't trapped by something? None of us are free. Especially not from ourselves."

After a long beat of silence, Raine replies in a thick voice. "What about the others in the painting?"

"They're trapped too."

"So they aren't the bad guys?"

Unnamed pain lashes against my breastbone. "Being trapped by the same evil doesn't automatically make them good people. Victims can still be monsters."

"Doesn't make them bad either."

"Circumstance excuses nothing," I reply hotly, irritation bleeding from my words.

"Sorry, Ripley." His tone lacks its usual playful lilt. "Circumstance is everything, isn't it? You don't blame soldiers for the price they paid to survive the battlefield."

For a split second, I almost give him the benefit of doubt. Part of me actually thought that we were the same. But anyone willing to condone their friends' violence is cut from the same fucked up cloth. He's just like them.

You're a hypocrite, Ripley.
Stop lying to yourself.

If I follow through and help Noah end his life, will I be any better than them? Willing to shed blood, to sacrifice another living, breathing human being, simply to achieve my own goal?

If they're the villains in my story… am I the villain in theirs?

Circumstance. It's a real bitch.

"Well, it's a good thing that it's just a painting." My voice trembles with the torment clawing at my insides.

"Is it?" Raine challenges.

When I shift, trying to put a safe distance between us again, he manages to blindly snag my wrist. His thumb presses above the furious pounding of my pulse. Even I can feel it's going wild.

"You're angry." He gently runs his calloused thumb across the thick veins protruding beneath my skin.

"You needed to feel my pulse to figure that out?"

"Look, I don't know what happened between you and the guys, but—"

"No. You don't know what they did." The words escape my gritted teeth. "To me. To *her*."

"I know." Raine's chest rises with his inhale. "They hurt someone you cared about."

My heart is a dead lump, entombed behind my ribcage. "They destroyed someone I cared about."

"And? Isn't what you did to them payback enough?"

"Someone's been gossiping."

Raine shrugs dismissively. "I know shit went down before I showed up. Xander doesn't talk about it. Lennox punches a wall if I bring it up."

Huh. Perhaps they didn't escape as unscathed as I thought. I'd still like to know how the pair of them wrangled their way out of the deadly trap I laid for them.

"I'm going to hurt your friends, Raine. If you don't want to get hurt too, keep your distance from them and me."

Head dipping lower, his salty, citrus scent assaults me. "Is that a warning?"

"It's a threat."

"I'm not the type to abandon my friends. So you'll have to hurt me too."

Is he grinning at the mere thought?

Staring into the black depths of his lenses, I can't decide if I want to punch this cocky shit or find out if the taste of sunshine also dances on his tongue. I must've finally lost it to even be contemplating the latter.

"I think I'm starting to understand why you're here."

Chuckling, he resumes stroking the sensitive skin of my tattooed inner wrist, causing the hairs on my arms to lift. I internally scold myself for enjoying the featherlight touch.

"This place is a hell of a lot more interesting than rehab ever was."

I feel the hum of his rising fever once more. "You were in rehab?"

"Spent more time in than out. Five stints."

"That wasn't enough to keep you out of this place?"

"Apparently not." He laughs humourlessly.

I never give a shit about customers. It's the price of doing business. Yet I find my heart cracking open and bleeding for this broken boy, hiding a deadly addiction behind smirks and over-exaggerated bravado.

Does anyone else see how hard he's faking it?

This Raine isn't real.

His entire act is an illusion.

"This isn't a game." I push away the empathy trying to gnaw through my resolve, redirecting us back to safe ground. "I meant what I said. If I have to kill you to get to them, that's exactly what I'll do."

"We've progressed to killing?"

"I won't let them hurt anyone else."

Rough fingertips dancing upwards from my wrist, he traverses my ink-covered forearm, leaving a blazing trail in his wake. I find my breath stuttering. Luckily, he can't see me biting my lip hard enough to sting.

Those sure fingertips feel like tasers against my flushed skin. His thumb tugs my shirt sleeve, testing the rough cotton before he moves higher and wraps my loose, brown curls around his digits.

"What are you doing?" I ask nervously.

He fingers the coarse strands of hair. "What colour is it?"

"Um, dark-brown."

"The curls are natural?"

His laser focus is making nervous sweat bead on my forehead. I feel like I'm being inspected. He lightly tugs on a strand, measuring the length against my jawline like he's taking mental notes to better construct an idea of my appearance.

"Yes," I squeak.

"What about your eyes? Colour?"

"Uh, hazel."

Releasing the ringlet clasped in his fingers, Raine's hand hovers close to my face. "Do you mind? It helps me to form a mental picture of who I'm talking to."

"I bet you say that to all the girls."

"Most don't complain about me wanting to touch them." He sighs in a long-suffering way.

I want to tell him to get lost. Instead, I find myself suppressing a snort.

"I should've known the whole blind thing was a flirting tactic."

"You caught me." Chest rumbling with laughter, Raine seems to consider me behind those blacked-out lenses. "Feel free to do whatever you'd like in return. I'm an open book."

"Um." My throat seizes. "I don't kn…"

An invisible hand wraps tight around my windpipe before I can say no. That damn curiosity is too strong to ignore. As my voice trails off, Raine waits expectantly. Not daring to touch my face yet, his hand hangs in limbo as I deliberate.

For once, I don't want to run. Those violin-toughened fingertips promise salvation, and the smirking man bulldozing my self-imposed boundaries knows it.

Instead of answering, I lift an unsteady hand and grasp his glasses. Raine's throat spasms as I carefully slide them from his face. All I want is another glimpse of the honeycomb jewels he keeps hidden.

If it wasn't for them or the telltale bouncing of his eyes from side to side, never finding a target to land on, I wouldn't know he's blind. His irises are golden pools of treacle.

It isn't always dramatic like how it's shown in the movies—clouded over eyeballs or obvious, gnarly scarring. Even his pupils still dilate, untouched by whatever stole his eyesight. They're a regular size. He must've run out of whatever I caught him snorting the other night. That explains the lack of intoxication.

"Satisfied?" Raine murmurs.

Gently placing his glasses down, I stare into his unfocused eyes. "Seems only fair."

"Agreed. Now, hold still."

Fingers connecting with my left cheek, he gingerly caresses my skin, following the slope of my features. His index finger traces the outline of my jaw, while his thumb swipes over my lips, tugging the bottom one down ever so slightly.

Travelling upwards, Raine strokes beneath my eye, as if feeling for the sunken ravines that provide evidence of my exhaustion. My heart gallops painfully when he traces my eyebrows and cupid's bow before following my narrow, upturned nose.

"What do you see?" I breathe out.

Inspection complete, he brushes the backs of his knuckles against my cheek. "Well, I can hazard a guess why Lennox and Xander are so obsessed with you."

"I could've told you that. They hate my guts."

His hand falls away. "Even if they hadn't told me the bitch who set them up is hot as fuck, I would've guessed so. But it doesn't matter to me either way. I have a different concept of beauty now."

I'm not sure what's more entertaining—the fact that pair of assholes willingly said something semi-nice about me or Raine's back-handed compliment. The feel of my face tells him I'm hot. People have said a lot worse to me, so I'll take it.

"What do you find attractive?"

Tongue darting out to wet his lips, those honeyed orbs dart around, searching for the forever out of reach.

"Conversation. Laughter, but only the genuine kind. The way someone breathes. Footsteps. Nervous tics like teeth grinding or fidgeting. The slightest change in tone or intonation."

"You pick up on all of that?"

Raine hesitates, the corners of his eyes crinkling in thought, before he answers. "I have to. I live my life in the margins of a full page. All I've got is subtext."

Hand searching the nearby table for his glasses, Raine locates them, then his gaze vanishes once more. Retreating back behind the relative safety of his lenses and a scripted persona.

"Thanks for the art lesson." He changes the subject.

"Raine—"

"I should go."

Fumbling back to his abandoned violin case and guide stick, he gathers his belongings to leave. My muscles twitch with the urge to chase after him and break those fucking glasses so he has no ability to hide anymore. Not from me, at least.

"And good luck with the grand revenge plan," he adds. "Perhaps you'll feel differently about circumstance when your so-called enemies are dead and you're left to deal with the consequences."

Tap. Tap. Tap.

I'm left staring after him, my face still tingling from the tender caress of his fingers mapping its topography.

CHAPTER 8
RIPLEY
DEVIL – LOWBORN

"OI! BITCH!"

I release Luka's hand, a small bundle of laxatives passed between us. He takes one look at the impending hothead barrelling towards us then books it with a muttered *thank you*.

"Welcome," I grumble.

My Wednesday deliveries are almost complete. The usual suspects have scuttled up to accept their packages and deliver payment or hopelessly barter for a grace period they should know I'll never give.

Blowing out a long breath, my skin prickles with pins and needles. It feels too tight. Stretched thin over my bones, like the groaning, rusted springs of a used trampoline being pummelled by an overexcited child. Mania always begins physically for me.

Another warning sign.

The upward swing is coming.

After my intense encounter with Raine, I spent a two-day stint in bed. Leaden and immovable. I only moved to use the bathroom and drink water from the tap. Not even my stomach could fight the weight of depression and force me to eat this time.

Tossing and turning, his words tormented me on a sleep-deprived loop. *You don't blame soldiers for the price they paid to survive the battlefield.* Maybe not. But shouldn't the survivor feel some remorse? Shouldn't they mourn the blood on their hands?

Lennox and Xander don't feel remorse. They have no regret for their cruelty, only pride at the position they stole in the most heinous of ways. Some villains cannot be redeemed. Especially those who refuse to acknowledge their own crimes.

"Ripley!" the voice hollers again.

Sighing, I scratch at my irritated inner arms beneath my jacket. I should've known that Rick would send one of his lackeys to fetch his usual smokes, like I'd somehow surrender the goods if he didn't show his face again.

The poor bastard looked scared shitless when I told him to trot back to his friend to deliver the bad news. I ain't selling shit to Rick ever again. Not after the stunt he pulled. But apparently, he's going down swinging.

"Morning to you too," I greet cheerily.

Stopping short, Rick holds back a snarl. "Where the fuck are my smokes?"

"As I told your little pet, Carlos, I have nothing for you."

His hands curl into fists at his sides. I don't give a shit about the lines of olive-toned muscle bulging beneath his t-shirt. If he makes a single move, I'll unleash hell on him.

"We have a standing order!" he insists, nostrils flaring.

"Like I explained in the cafeteria, I don't sell to assholes. Clearly, you didn't heed my words."

"You cannot be serious."

"People keep doubting me." I lay on an exaggerated pout. "Am I not being clear enough?"

Rick's face is slowly turning a beetroot shade of red. It's not an attractive look. No one's here to pay attention to us in the abandoned quad, it's too cold to brace the icy wind and impending snowstorm today.

I'd prefer an audience; I can't have people thinking they can talk to me like I owe them shit. Rick's been inching ever closer to crossing that line for a while now. My authority over the patient population can't be challenged without consequence.

"You don't want to do this," he warns in what I'm sure he thinks is a threatening tone. "I don't care what people here think of you. I'll bury you all the same."

"For refusing to sell you some cigarettes?" I laugh at him.

"For disrespecting me!" His lips curl back in a grimace. "And for being a bitch!"

Laughter dying, I let him see exactly how pathetic I think he is. "Tell me who the hell would respect someone like you?"

"Back off, Ripley. Final warning."

"Or what?" I challenge. "You gonna teach me a lesson, tough guy?"

His shoulders hunch in preparation. "Maybe I will."

I see the blow coming from a mile away, ducking before his fist can connect. However, a punch to my stomach comes too soon after for me to avoid. Pain flaring in my midsection, I wheeze through a choked breath.

"Still wanna laugh at me, bitch?" he shouts.

Rick takes advantage of my momentary surprise and goes for another hit. This one connects with my left cheekbone. My head whips to the side, a delicious sizzle of agony racing through my extremities.

But there's no satisfaction to give him.

Pain doesn't shut me down.

It wakes me up like a lightning bolt to the heart, reminding me why I've spent years fighting to survive in the first place. To hurt. To feel pain. To be unequivocally alive. I'm living for Holly too, and every ounce of agony I can secure further repays my debt to her ghost.

It's no less than I deserve. A life of immeasurable pain and suffering. Perhaps then, when I ascend the steep slopes into the devil's lair, he'll take pity on me and send me straight back up. Doesn't seem likely though, does it?

"You walk around this place like you own it, but I see through you," Rick hisses, his spit flying. "You're worthless."

Shaking the dizziness from my head, I glare up at him. "You're right. I'm nothing."

"Too right!"

"But you know what?" My feet spread into an even stance. "That also means I have nothing to lose."

When I lunge, Rick tracks the move and attempts to block the blow. Exactly as I knew he would. I pivot at the last second, my Converse-covered feet sliding on the lawn as I land a low punch to his kidney instead.

The air whooshes out of him, choked off by a second punch to his ribcage. As he attempts to cover himself, I switch stances and hit upwards, clipping him straight in his square jaw.

Pain cracks across my knuckles, but he stumbles backwards, a second from falling flat on his backside. I take a moment to enjoy the show. Watching him flail about is fucking hilarious after all his bravado.

"You asked for this!" he bellows.

I shrug nonchalantly. "Do your worst, hot shot."

With an angry scream, he barrels towards me. I won't tackle him like I did Lennox. That would be too easy. I want to enjoy this oh-so sweet victory before I bury this son of a bitch once and for all.

Down we go.

Twisting, punching, we're a violent tangle of limbs. Rick's legs find my waist, and as I make impact with the ground, he manoeuvres himself on top to straddle me. His triumphant grin only makes me even more giddy.

I feel a hot slick of blood trailing from my mouth, the ache sharpening my awareness. His eyes latch on to the sticky ribbon. As he inspects his handiwork, I fight the urge to buck him off.

"Wasn't so hard, was it?" he leers. "Whores like you belong on their backs."

"I suppose this is the only way you can get a girl to touch you, huh?"

Fingertips sliding over cold grass, I inch my hand down my oversized tee and into my waistband. He's far too distracted by peacocking his fragile masculinity to pay any attention to my movements.

"Believe me, I'd need a hell of an incentive to touch you." He looks over my face with exaggerated disgust. "Who could ever want you?"

"Is that supposed to hurt my precious, girly feelings? Fuck off, Rick."

He grips my biceps, keeping me pinned. "Not until you learn some damn respect!"

As I'm wrapping my fingers around the handle of my switchblade with full intent to stab him in the liver and be done with this already, the weight pressing into me instantly vanishes.

"Argh!" Rick screeches.

He's tossed aside like little more than a sack of potatoes, tumbling before landing on the ground with a pained curse. In his place, a slim but wiry shadow blots out the winter sun beaming through snow-filled clouds.

The shadow crouches, bringing his midnight-blue, almost black gaze level with mine. His appearance steals the oxygen from my lungs. Such devilishly familiar eyes. A frozen wasteland, bereft of all human emotion and empathy. Nothing but cruelty stares back at me.

I'm sucked into that desolate black hole without warning, despite the years since I first found myself caught in his spider's web. I couldn't help it back then; his savagery intrigued me. But now, I know what kind of monster I'm up against.

I won't survive a second round.

One already broke my soul in half.

"This guy bothering you?" he asks crisply.

"Xander."

"Hello, Ripley."

Nothing escapes his all-consuming orbit. Not even the promises I made to myself that if we ever came face to face again, I'd be more than the submissive toy he saw me to be, standing in the way of his grand master plan.

A mere obstacle.

And one he could destroy.

That's what put me in Xander's line of fire. It was never personal. Not even sexual. He wanted power, and to get to Holly, he had to eliminate me. Even if that meant reaping my soul and devouring it whole, like a fucking appetiser.

It was just one night.

One fateful, agonising, fucking *liberating* night.

That's all it took to leave her exposed.

"Cat got your tongue, little toy?" He raises a single, platinum-blonde eyebrow. "I wondered when our paths would cross."

Unable to stand the sight of him looming over me, I ignore Rick's pained whimpering and clamber to my feet. "I hoped they never would."

"I bet you did. Have you been hiding from me?"

Yes.

"Don't flatter yourself," I grind out instead.

Tall and compact, Xander doesn't pack his threatening prowess in bulk like Lennox does. He's still ripped beneath his starched polo shirt and jeans, but he could raze entire armies with nothing more than his intelligence and sharp tongue.

Those soulless orbs are framed by long, luscious lashes, a stark contrast to his spotless alabaster skin pulled taut over exaggerated cheekbones and thin lips. He's beautiful in that ethereal, masculine way only those blessed by the DNA lottery can be.

His hair, kept neat and short, is the purest shade of snow-white. It gleams like pale moonlight. Oh, the fucking irony. How can this walking, talking incarnation of the devil so closely resemble an angel?

And he knows it.

But his victims never do.

"Back off." I force some steel into my voice. "He's mine."

Xander's brow is still raised. "Were you under the impression that anyone but myself is allowed to steal those exquisite sounds of pain from your tongue?"

Goddamn. Fucking. Psychopath.

"I'll be giving you no such thing," I snap back. "Exquisite or otherwise."

"It seems you're mistaking me for giving you a choice in the matter."

It takes all of my willpower to force back a barrage of desire-tinged memories. Wrists throbbing beneath the tight constrict of restraints. Shoulders burning from being pinned, powerless and vulnerable during the hours of torment he inflicted.

I wish I could say that he forced me. But even as I protested and writhed, terrified by his clinical, sadistic approach to sex, a traitorous part of me wanted the pain he was so fascinated by inflicting.

"I'm rather busy right now." I brush myself off. "Find another time to annoy me."

Casting Rick's still-slumped form a disdainful look, Xander lowers his voice. "As enjoyable as watching you bleed is, I don't take too kindly to others playing with my toys."

Wiping my split lip with the back of my hand, I narrow my eyes in challenge. Xander stares back for several seconds like he's waiting for me to cower and obey. Not this time. When I don't back down, he gestures for me to go ahead.

"But by all means."

"That's what I thought," I mumble.

Turning, I find Rick still on the ground, struggling to catch his breath. Xander may not look the part, but I know how strong he is. Even if he feels no need to advertise it like other men do, he could've broken Rick's back without a smidge of remorse.

Conscious of the iceman himself still watching, I finish pulling my switchblade from its hiding place and flick out the knife. It's sharp. Glinting. Begging for a drop of blood to embellish its metallic surface. Rick's eyes widen as he sees me approach.

"Listen, Rip."

"So where do I belong?" I gesture wildly with the blade. "What was it, hmm? On my back?"

"You can't do this to me!"

With a cursory glance around, I note the nearby CCTV camera. We're just out of shot in my usual delivery spot. No one will ever know if I rough him up, especially if I can scare Rick enough to keep his mouth shut.

I place a foot either side of his waist. "No one is coming to save you."

When he begins to tremble in fear at the blade moving ever closer to him, I lift a foot and smash it down on his face. The satisfying crunch of his nose smashing beneath my shoe is truly a glorious thing.

Blood is a riotous explosion pouring from his busted nose as I peer down at him. Still, it doesn't sate me. I usually tame this side of myself with the violent outpouring of artistic rage that I inflict upon my canvases. But not today.

Knees bending, I hover over his torso, dragging the sharpened tip of my blade along his clavicle. His t-shirt is flecked with blood beneath the grass stains and mud from his fall. Digging a little deeper, I slice into his skin.

"The only one who needs to learn respect here is you," I whisper sweetly. "You've forgotten who's in charge here."

"That's what y-you th-think," he splutters. "You're d-deluded, Ripley."

Digging it in deeper, I watch his eyes blow wide with pain. "Want to say that again?"

"This... isn't your institute. You're just an experiment... Fuck!" He yelps in pain. "Just like the rest of us."

Hearing Xander shift on his feet behind me, I refuse to let even a crack of concern for Rick's words show. I'm more than that. Harrowdean needs me. I'm valued here. Important. In control. They'd never successfully run their program without me.

Would they?

"You're... replaceable," Rick spits out. "We all are."

"Shut the fuck up, Rick."

"No. Like you, I also have nothing to lose." He smiles through the blood running down his chin.

Repositioning my grip on the switchblade, I stab it down into the earth an inch away from his head. He flinches, his eyes darting to the cool kiss of steel so close to impaling his face.

"Stay away from my business, and keep your mouth shut. Or next time, I won't miss. Understood?"

"It's only a matter of time until this whole thing is exposed to the world." His teeth are stained bright-red. "Priory Lane's already under investigation. Who will they blame for Harrowdean?"

I hang over him. "Stop. Fucking. Talking."

"The corporate masks hiding behind their fancy lawyers, or the unhinged nutcase on the ground, peddling drugs for profit?"

Patience expired, I yank the knife from the ground and raise it above my head. Rick yells as it swooshes towards him, burying handle-deep in the soft flesh of his thigh.

"I am not deluded," I hiss in his face as his screams reach a fever pitch. "This is my kingdom, my institute, and you belong to me."

"Fucking lunatic! My leg!"

Grasping the switchblade, I drag it out of his thigh with a sick pop. "You slipped and fell, right? Better go and get stitched up. I'd hate for you to bleed out and fail to spread the word that I'm still in charge here."

After wiping the blade on his t-shirt, I climb off him and inch backwards. Rick presses a shaking hand to the wound in his leg as he wobbles to his feet. With a final filthy glare, he limps away towards the west wing.

My entire body is vibrating with vehement rage. Seeing the trails of blood left in his wake does little to appease me. I rebuilt my life after Holly's death on pillars of control—choosing Harrowdean, becoming their stooge, discarding everything I believed in for the same job she once did.

I took the deal.

I sacrificed it all.

But am I the one to blame?

Hands clamp down on my shoulders from behind, two steely traps preventing me from fleeing the scene of the crime. The scent of spearmint brushes over me as a soft, cold pair of lips teases the shell of my ear.

"Old Ripley was a delight to break," Xander murmurs. "But you, little toy? You're going to be my favourite project of all."

A sick shiver curls down my spine. "Let go of me, Xan."

"You know, it was quite the surprise to hear who arranged for us to be admitted into the program before vanishing from Priory Lane. I didn't think you had it in you."

Fury boils in my gut. "It clearly didn't work."

"Oh, but it did." His tongue flicks out to tease my fluttering pulse point. "They broke us, dearest Ripley. Every day for months. But that's what you wanted, right?"

"I dreamed about it every night," I spit, acutely aware of his tongue lashing my skin. "I imagined you bleeding and in pain. Locked in a cell. Cold. Alone. Maybe dead."

He sucks in a breath at my words. "Did you enjoy your revenge?"

When his teeth scratch my earlobe, sinking in with a sharp bite that feels deep enough to draw blood, I gasp. He'd tear my throat out with his bare teeth if he felt so inclined. Probably without blinking.

"Answer me," he demands.

My body still remembers its ordeal. Obeying his every command to obtain even an ounce of relief. I'm powerless to stop it from surrendering once more.

"Yes."

"There's a good girl," he purrs.

Slipping a hand into my short hair, he grasps the messy strands then tugs so hard, it causes tears to burn in my eyes. My head is pulled back, exposing my throat to his fingertips. He trails them over my skin, a gentle caress yet full of threat.

"Then you know why I must now repay the favour," Xander says coolly. "I'm going to enjoy breaking you all over again. And I won't stop until you're begging for death."

"I don't beg for anything. Not anymore."

"But you will for me."

I hate him so fucking much, it's searing my insides like I've swallowed acid. Yet I can't convince my body to respond. Nor does it stop the hot flush of want from curling in my core. I know just how it feels to be broken by him.

"Your institute won't protect you from me, Ripley. I'll take everything you've built here and burn it all to the ground long before I let you escape again."

Releasing my hair and throat, his hot breath vanishes from my ear. I stand stock-still, paralysed by too many conflicting emotions to make any logical decisions.

"Run. You know I love the chase."

As much as I want to stand my ground, defend the life I've spent rebuilding to never be that weak, submissive girl again, she never truly left me. Not beneath the shields and defences I've constructed.

So I run.

CHAPTER 9
XANDER
RAIN – GRANDSON & JESSIE REYEZ

PEN TAPPING against her leather-bound notebook, Doctor Chesterfield stares. She looks frustrated. Even a little bemused. I drag a single fingertip up and down the soft velvet of the armchair I've spent an hour sitting in.

"Your notes from Priory Lane were... enlightening."

I simply stare back.

"You're in the final nine months of your sentence now. How do you feel about that?"

Stare. Blink. Wait.

She'll have to admit defeat eventually. Baiting me to speak has never worked before, and it certainly won't now. I vowed to never again allow a shrink into my head after the third round of hydrotherapy in Priory Lane's *special wing*.

Admittedly, I was curious to know how long it would take for frostbite to set in. A twelve-hour session chained in sub-zero water finally did the trick. I carried around a toe of dead tissue for a week before they did me the kindness of removing it.

Can't have a product limping, can they?

That wouldn't appeal to buyers.

Doctor Chesterfield leafs through a thick binder of notes. "Have you enjoyed studying maths in our program? I know you like computers."

Now she's really fishing. When that doesn't work, the doc decides to get personal instead. It never takes them long to reach for that old line of attack.

"Seventeen is a young age to be diagnosed with antisocial personality disorder, clinically speaking. It's noted that your childhood symptoms worsened with age."

Gazing straight through her, I burrow into the cold emptiness that flows through me. For as long as I can remember, it's been there. Not even the abhorrent depths of foster care awakened anything within me.

"No father listed, I see." Her watery-grey eyes flick over the scrawled notes. "Your last contact with your mother was at eight-years-old, correct?"

With a sigh, I cross my legs at the ankles then lean back.

"She made no attempts to contact you once social services intervened?" Doctor Chesterfield presses. "That must have been difficult to process as a child."

Little does she know, I've long since filed away the memories of my alcoholic mother. She's as good as dead. Abandonment is easier to accept when for all intents and purposes, the parent in question is deceased to you.

"I see there was an investigation after you were taken into care." She spares me a searching glance. "You refused to testify against her partner."

Waiting, she frowns at my continued lack of response. Bringing him into this isn't going to work. Worse people have tried. We never would've survived Priory Lane's program if we broke that easily.

"He was prosecuted though, wasn't he?" she asks in a gentler tone.

Jaw aching from grinding down on my molars so hard, I straighten in the armchair and speak for the first time. "I believe our sixty minutes are up."

"Xander—"

"Until next week, Doctor."

The weight of her eyes follows me out of the therapy room. I slam the door, perhaps a little harder than necessary, and glower at the wall for several seconds. Processing. Compartmentalising. Burying.

In the subterranean hellscape where we were held after everything with Ripley went down, memories were worth their weight in gold. The clinicians loved to pluck them free then parade them in front of us, desperate to elicit a response.

When we refused to crack, their determination increased. As did their torture techniques. The knowledge that our precious Ripley somehow arranged our admittance to that wasteland was a hateful twist they quickly used against us.

The innocent, vulnerable lamb.

But with a hell of a bite.

She's not the broken, unstable girl we last saw, screaming and sobbing as they took the body bag away, wheeled past her bedroom that was directly across the hall. The moment she turned and saw us admiring our success, she knew what we'd done.

I thought we'd scared her to silence. If the night she spent in my room didn't do the trick, then what Lennox did while I kept Ripley occupied should've sealed the deal. Instead, we set alight something I never knew lived within her.

A fighting spirit.

I was fascinated by her loneliness and vulnerability before, but the bloodstained creature I found mid-brawl in the quad intrigues me even more. Breaking her won't be easy this time around.

That thought excites me more than any small distraction I've found since I last tasted her. I'll need to do my due diligence. Study her. Discover who this new Ripley is—her proclivities, vulnerabilities, pressure points.

Broken out of my plotting by my phone demanding attention, I fish it from my pocket. Like Priory Lane, we're allowed mobile phones here, but internet access is strictly limited.

That's how they do it—give you just enough freedom to feel grateful so you don't ask questions. If you give a death-row inmate a small length of rope, they'll make do and hang themselves without asking for an inch more.

"Yeah?" I snap.

"Xan. Code red."

My spine stiffens. "An OD?"

"No!" Lennox rushes out. "Fuck... I forgot the goddamn colours."

"You're useless," I mutter. "Where?"

"Music room. South wing."

Hanging up, I pocket my phone and move fast. The carpet-lined corridors are a blur around me. Harrowdean is small and easy enough to navigate, allowing me to quickly find the wing where the classrooms are located.

Classes are in progress, humming with voices as lessons take place.

The educational aspect of these institutes is yet another tactic. Offer the sick or uneducated a nice, dangling carrot to keep them satisfied. All people want is a distraction from their misery.

Scanning the doors, I follow the signage to the music room. It's one of the less popular choices here from what I've heard. The instrument-filled space is cast in low light as thickly falling rain batters the bay window outside.

"Nox?"

"Down here," his voice echoes.

Picking through scattered chairs and sheet music stands, I search the polished hardwood floors for a body. Though we tried to avoid that by controlling his supply ourselves, it wouldn't be the first time we've found Raine passed out and incoherent.

"Here, Xan."

The broad set of Lennox's shoulders hunched over someone guides me to the farthest corner. He's kneeling down next to Raine, who rests against the wall with his glasses set aside and his blonde head lolling forwards.

Concern causes my pulse to spike as I join them on the floor. "What happened?"

"I'm fine," Raine mumbles.

"He's not," Lennox rebukes.

Resting the back of my hand against his forehead, he's blazing hot to the touch. Clammy sweat coats his face. He's breathing rapidly and shivering uncontrollably too. Sharing a glance with Lennox, we communicate silently.

I knew he'd run out soon enough, though he promised me he'd ration his stash until we could assess the situation. Ripley's presence in Harrowdean—as the clinicians' stooge, no less—has sent all our plans up in smoke.

"You guys know I hate it when you don't talk out loud." Raine winces at some invisible pain. "I'm f-fine. Just need another b-bump."

"So why haven't you?" I question as Raine weakly shoves my hand away from his face.

"He's run out," Lennox growls.

"Everything we brought with us?" I press the heels of my palms into my weary eyes. "Goddammit, Raine."

"I'll figure it out," Raine says in a frail voice. "Leave me alone."

This won't even be the worst of it. He's in for a world of misery if he doesn't re-up. Keeping him jacked enough to function but sober enough to avoid overdosing has occupied a lot of the last year.

Lennox usually handles him solo. He's the protective type, and ever the bleeding heart beneath his aggression, he took Raine under his wing last year when he arrived.

"What do we do?" Lennox worries his lip with his canine.

"We've got nothing and no supply routes in here." I watch as Raine's teeth start chattering, his entire body still trembling. "You know who controls contraband in Harrowdean."

"Motherfuck!" Lennox slams a clenched fist against the floor. "I refuse to ask that whore for help."

"Then Raine will have to detox."

"Without medical supervision? He could fucking die!"

And knowing the shit that Raine's spent his life snorting, popping and once upon a time even injecting, that's a very real possibility. He ended up here for a good reason. Five failed stints in rehab and now this place.

"Can we buy from another patient?" Lennox suggests.

"Who? We don't know these people."

"You're not being very helpful, Xan." Lennox moves to grip Raine's shoulder. "Come on, let's move first."

Sliding a hand under his arm, I help Lennox manoeuvre Raine between us. He's limper than a strand of cooked spaghetti and groans in pain at even the slightest movements. This is going to be a nightmare.

"How do we do this?" Lennox mutters to himself.

"There's no discreet way to do it."

"We have to try. He can't stay here, anyone could walk in."

"Medical wing?"

Raine jerks in our arms. "B-Better leave m-me. No doctors."

"He's right," Lennox agrees unhappily. "I don't trust these assholes. Not after what they did to us."

"Let's just get somewhere private."

Half-carrying, half-dragging Raine across the room, even with our strength, we stumble several times. He's a dead weight between us.

We get close to the door before falling into a music stand, causing a loud clatter. Lennox trips and knocks over several chairs on the way down.

"Shit!" he groans.

Grasping Raine's waist, I hold him upright. "Good job."

"Fuck off, Xan."

Lennox makes even more noise, detangling his limbs and awkwardly lumbering to his feet. No one could ever accuse him of being graceful at his size. The lump of meat is deadly in his own right, but subtlety isn't his forte. It's why we make such an excellent team.

Just as he's brushing off his form-fitting sweats to retake his position, the door to the music room crashes open.

"Raine?"

Sweetheart-shaped face dappled with flecks of paint, Ripley's wild curls are pinned on top of her head by two paintbrushes. She's in her usual *I don't give a fuck* outfit, complete with a slashed black t-shirt depicting some obscure anime show I've never heard of.

"Did you fall?"

Stopping short when she sees us, I watch the concern melt from her lightly freckled features. It's quickly replaced by my new favourite look on her. Rage. Hatred emanates from her that is so palpable, I'd be surprised if she can even think straight in our presence. I know I certainly can't.

Hatred and obsession.

It's a fine line.

"What the fuck did you do to him?" she snarls, venom practically dripping from her words.

"What did we do?" Lennox hisses back. "What the fuck did *you* do?"

"He was fine!" Ripley defends angrily. "Raine's been practising in here while I paint every day this week."

"Has he now?" I clip out.

Lennox looks equally as surprised. I don't expect Raine to hate her the way we do; she didn't ruin his life. But some damn loyalty wouldn't go amiss after all we've done for him. My sick fascination aside, Ripley Bennet is bad news for us all.

Eyeing us warily, Ripley approaches then ducks to look at Raine's slumped form. "I thought his fever had broken."

"You knew he was like this?" Lennox glowers at her.

"You didn't know that your friend was going through withdrawal?" she hits back. "Maybe he'd be better off without you."

Moaning under his breath, I watch as Raine leans into her touch. She's cupping his cheek, brushing sweat aside as she inspects him.

Last I'd heard, Raine stood by while Ripley and Lennox beat the shit out of each other. Seems I'm working on outdated information.

"Take your filthy fucking hands off him," Lennox warns in a low voice.

Ripley straightens and steps back. "What has he been taking?"

"Raine isn't your concern."

"Because you're taking such good care of him?" she replies dryly.

"He never went through this shit when we were in charge!"

Lennox is a hair's breadth from choking her to death. I can see his palms twitching with the urge to close the kill while he has a chance. I'd enjoy seeing him try, but since he adopted Raine into our ranks, the kid is my responsibility.

"H," I answer. "That's his thing."

"He shoots up?" Surprise pulls at her features.

"Used to. Now just pills."

Rubbing her bottom lip, she seems to do some mental math. "Anything else?"

"How long have you got?" Lennox grumbles. "If it feels good, he'll pop it or snort it."

Enraged storm clouds invade her gaze. "You used to sell to him."

"We were just doing our jobs," Lennox combats. "I controlled his intake personally. We're the only reason he hasn't overdosed and killed himself already."

Ripley shakes her head, setting loose several tight curls. "One day, you're going to feel every ounce of pain you've inflicted. I'll damn well make sure of it."

"Who supplies Harrowdean's drug market?" I point out.

Her brown and green eyes dart up to me, narrowed defensively. "I haven't sold to Raine."

"But you have others. How much pain has precious, perfect Ripley inflicted, I wonder?"

From the gritting of her teeth, I know I've found a sore spot. How fascinating. Old Ripley never would've had the stomach for the role she now plays. That mousy, scared little thing was happy to hide behind her friend from the moment she arrived.

It gives me a pleasant thrill to imagine that we made her into this person—selfish, monstrous, capable of such cruel indifference. For every last drop of blood she's shed, our memories must have haunted her. The torture never ceased, no matter how far she ran.

"I can help him," she eventually announces. "But not here."

"He doesn't need your kind of help." Lennox puts a defensive hand on Raine's chest. "We need to get him clean, once and for all."

"The doctors are more likely to get rid of him than waste their time on a detox." Ripley quickly dismisses him. "He'll be discharged back to rehab."

"No!" Raine whimpers.

"Or end up somewhere worse." Her hazel eyes darken. "I've seen nuisance patients be admitted to the Z wing before."

Tales of the Z wing are told in whispers between the few who know about it. Even then, what happens there remains a myth. I don't know if Harrowdean works the same as Priory Lane, but from what I've heard, every institute under the care of Incendia Corporation has a Zimbardo wing.

Though few of us have actually seen it and lived to tell the tale. The Z wing program is a well-kept secret, hidden in the shadows that engulf the institute. Flashes of disjointed memories quickly overwhelm me.

The sharp bite of hypodermic needles. Chafing handcuffs. Ice-cold bathtubs of water. Padded cells. Scratch marks. Bloodstains. Screams and pleas for mercy. The Z wing is no place for humans. I suppose that's why none ever come out.

"P-Please," Raine begs, lifting his head long enough to look at her. "I'll take… anything."

Ignoring Lennox's violent cursing, Ripley locks eyes with me. Her visible anguish is so enticing, I'm actually hard at the sight of how much this decision is fucking with her head.

She doesn't want to hurt Raine, but in this fucked up world, all any of us know is pain. The suffering we inflict on others to lessen our own anguish. Love exchanged in droplets of spilt blood.

Jaw locked, I nod once.

She purses her lips and nods back.

"Let's get him to his room," I instruct, shifting his weight back onto me. "Take his other arm, Nox."

"We are not working with this cunt!" he seethes.

"Then go. I'll do it myself."

"Xan." Lennox drops his voice. "She cannot be trusted."

"You think I don't know that? You adopted the fucker. He's our responsibility. Right now, she's a temporary solution."

"She wants to punish us! For all we know, she'll poison Raine to do it."

"If it's any reassurance." Ripley's snarky voice chips in. "I did warn Raine that I'd kill him to get to you. But that doesn't mean I plan to do it like this. I have some tact."

Thick brows raising, Lennox stares at me as if to say *see?*

"Better the devil you know than the devil you don't." I pin the devil in question with a long, hard stare. "Harm him and you'll join your pathetic friend in the afterlife."

With an eye roll, she gestures for us to follow her. Lennox winds Raine's arm around his shoulders. We move slowly, towing him out of the music room. Thankfully, classes are still in full swing. There's no one to witness our predicament.

As we approach the reception, other patients start to appear. Most avert their eyes when they see Ripley leading us, not daring to question the semi-conscious patient we're dragging along.

"Guard," Lennox warns under his breath.

Ripley doesn't even hesitate. "It's fine."

Aiming for the staircase that leads to the residential wing, we quickly gain the attention of the guard standing watch. His blue eyes widen as he takes in the scene, a hand moving to rest atop the baton strapped to his hip.

"Ripley? What's going on?"

She stops at the foot of the stairs, waving for us to pass. "It's fine, Langley."

"But—"

"Everything is under control."

Some silent message passes between them. Who the fuck is this guy? I don't like the way he's looking at Ripley like she's his to protect from us. I'll gladly rip out his spine and shove it down his throat.

Grumbling, Langley backs off and returns to his post. He refuses to take his eyes off Ripley though, even as she passes us and resumes leading the way upstairs. Definitely some spine ripping needed to wipe that puppy dog look off his face.

"Friend of yours?" I snark coldly.

She tosses a glower over her shoulder. "I don't have any of those."

"How much did he pay you to fuck him, then?" Lennox laughs.

"Not everyone is desperate like you."

"You little bi—"

His next word cut off by the sound of Raine groaning, Lennox settles for a death glare instead. We fall into stony silence until we reach the sixth floor.

"Where is your room?" I ask curtly.

Ripley scoffs. "Like I'd tell you that. I'll bring the goods to you."

"What do you think we're going to do? Break in and smother you in your sleep?" Lennox asks incredulously.

"I wouldn't put it past you. And frankly, it wouldn't be the first time you've eliminated the competition."

"Fine," I cut in. "Room forty-four."

She rushes off to head back down the stairs. Lennox turns his displeased stare on me as I watch her go, that tight ass shaking with each step, begging for the privilege of my handprint.

"You need to get a fucking grip, Xan. She isn't some little experiment for you to toy with and discard when you're done. That woman wants our heads on stakes, and she has the means to do it."

"I'm aware."

"You're aware? The fuck does that mean?"

Wrestling Raine towards his room, I huff out a breath. "Let me worry about Ripley."

"Let you fuck her into submission, right?" he snorts. "If that's what you call whatever you do with people."

"By the time I'm done with her, she will no longer be a concern. Let's leave it at that."

"Jesus. Sometimes you're legitimately insane."

Lennox fishes the keycard from Raine's jeans pocket then unlocks the door so we can escape inside. His room is neatly organised by necessity. Nothing is out of place or in disarray.

Raine has to know exactly where everything is, down to the precise steps it takes to reach furniture or doors. We deposit him on the bed then study our violently shaking friend.

This is the worst he's been in a long time. Supply issues are inevitable, but we've never let him get this far into the withdrawal process before.

"Here." Lennox returns from the bathroom with a wet washcloth. "Come on, Raine. Head up."

Grumbling unintelligibly, Raine doesn't even open his eyes. Lennox is forced to lift his chin for him to clean the sweat from his face. I watch on, lips pursed.

"You could help," Lennox mutters. "This is your idea."

"I warned you not to get attached to him. Look where it's brought you."

"Attached?" He shakes his head. "Raine is one of us."

"Which is why we're not leaving him to die on the floor. That doesn't mean we should care."

Balling up the washcloth, Lennox tosses it aside and rises. He gets in my face, every shred of rage that's bound tight at the core of his being on full display in those seafoam eyes.

"What they did to us in the Z wing broke something inside you, Xan. Something that I don't think can ever be fixed."

"What's your point?"

"You've always been a heartless bastard, but never cruel."

"Cruel?" I repeat flatly.

"This right here is fucking cruelty!" He gestures at me. "You used to care. You used to *feel*. Even if it was only a little bit."

Staring back into his eyes, I don't feel even a hint of remorse.

"I think you're confusing tolerance for caring."

Lennox recoils like I've punched him square in the teeth. Seeing his shock and confusion so viscerally carved into his expression almost summons an ounce of emotion. Almost. But the embers soon flicker out again.

"My best friend died in that dungeon," he accuses acerbically. "I don't know who the fuck I escaped with, but I don't know him."

The sound of knocking on the door breaks our stare off. Lennox turns his back to me, returning to Raine's side. I exhale loudly and move to let Ripley inside.

"This is all I can spare." She pulls a clear bag of slightly off-white pills from her pocket. "Should last a few days."

I reach out to clasp the plastic baggie. "I've seen purer."

Her brows pull together into a frown. "How do you see anything from the high pedestal you've put yourself on?"

Ignoring her sass, I tear open the bag and tip a couple pills out into my palm. They have a slightly vinegary scent, the only sign that she isn't dealing tabs of paracetamol to migraine sufferers.

"I expect an extra ten percent," she blurts. "Rush fee."

Lennox barks a laugh. "You're un-fucking-believable."

"This isn't a charity." She briefly lifts one shoulder. "I wouldn't give this shit to a friend for free, and you guys sure as fuck aren't that. Be glad I'm helping at all."

"Why are you helping?" I can't help but ask.

Wringing her fingers together, Ripley can't hide the subtle glance she takes in Raine's direction. I spent months studying this woman. I know all her tells. The minute details that allowed me to create a profile as we plotted our moves.

I thought she was an easy target. Her fear called out to me like a siren's song that slipped beneath my skin and metastasised into something more. Something far more pervasive and deadly. But I never expected that night to come to mean something to me.

Once wasn't enough.

Not with her.

I want to tear apart the very fabric of her soul and keep the shredded remains for myself, like organs preserved in jars for the world to admire. Her carcass in my collection will be my finest achievement.

"My motivations are not your concern." She clears whatever strange glimmer was present in her gaze. "Tell him to pay up, or withdrawals will be the least of his concerns."

Keeping her eyes averted, she turns and leaves. Clasping Raine's pills in my hand, I stare after Ripley, wondering how the fuck my silent little lamb found the courage to make such threats.

And why it's so fucking hot.

CHAPTER 10
RIPLEY

THNKS FR TH MMRS – FALL OUT BOY

"SO? HOW WAS IT?"

Munching on a carrot stick, I consider Holly's question. "What's there to discuss? It's therapy. Same shit, different doctor."

Her eyes twinkle with amusement. "I'm not sure that's the best attitude."

"You're telling me you seriously buy into their crap?"

Stabbing a limp French fry on her plastic tray, Holly sticks it in her mouth and chews as she thinks. I'm so glad she took a shine to me and hasn't let go in the months since I arrived. I was dreading lonely mealtimes in here like the new kid on the block.

"You're not getting out of here unless you get better," she explains with a shrug. "Not gonna do it on your own, are you?"

"Some of the world's greatest minds had bipolar." I gesture with my fork. "Van Gogh. Churchill. Hemingway. Maybe I don't need to be fixed. It's the rest of you norms who are the problem."

"Would your traumatised pizza delivery guy say the same thing?"

Wincing, I fight off a memory of screaming at the poor, terrified teenager. It made perfect sense in the moment—that he was a Martian attempting to invade my apartment. Like I hadn't ordered the pizza half an hour before and forgotten in my manic state.

He barely fled with his life after I attacked him with the baseball bat that any young woman living alone hides behind her front door. I'm not saying I would've cracked his skull open with it, but the broken bones he received got me arrested nonetheless.

The news story quickly broke when the kid started posting online about his ordeal.

Uncle Jonathan's name, along with the company he works for, were splashed all over the press.

"Sure, he'd agree." I wave dismissively.

"Uh-huh. Nothing to do with the buttload of money your uncle paid him off with to shut up, right?"

"Bringing me that pizza was the luckiest day of his life. He can pay off the motorcycle he was riding and brag to all his friends about surviving the crazy chick with the baseball bat. I did him a favour."

"Is a broken collarbone a favour?"

"It is in my books."

Glancing up, we lock eyes then both burst out laughing. I've never told anyone about my complicated relationship with my uncle before, but I trust Holly not to judge me. She doesn't react like other people do when they hear my story.

Most people assume that money equals happiness, but for the orphaned girl in need of love, cash doesn't excuse the absence of a real parent. I would've taken a warm, loving uncle who took his role seriously over the shining gold credit card he offered up instead.

The sound of our laughter draws the attention of patients scattered around us. Like circling sharks, two rise from their seats and prowl over. I watch Holly's hand tense around the plastic cutlery she's holding.

"What exactly have you two got to laugh about?" Lennox slides into the seat next to Holly.

"Nox," Holly warns.

"You're running a sinking ship, Hol. We've heard all about your supply issues recently."

"Back off."

Running a hand over his messy chocolate locks, Lennox wears his signature, cruel smirk. "Why? Afraid that your new little friend will see you for what you really are?"

The bite of cold daggers piercing my skin forces me to look beyond Holly's tormentor. Standing behind Lennox, I find the source of my discomfort. Xander is staring right at me, those bottomless pits of blue harshness burrowing into my flesh.

I stare back, transfixed by his attention. It's not the first time I've caught him watching me like I'm some fascinating scientific experiment. A curiosity to be dissected and documented. If I couldn't see his chest rising, I'd think he's a statue carved from ice.

"Final warning." Holly calmly places her plastic fork down. "I'm in no mood to take your shit today."

With malice sparkling in his eyes, Lennox leans close to whisper something in her ear. The chain around his neck gapes from his collar but doesn't quite slip out. I wonder, not for the first time, what he carries on that necklace.

Watching with bated breath as Holly's face sinks, she quickly smooths her business mask back into place. But for that brief moment, she looked so exhausted. Enough to give in.

Holly would never be defeated by a pair of bullies, right? She's the strongest person I know. A take-no-shit badass with a heart of gold beneath her steely exterior.

Lennox pulls back, his necklace disappearing. "Think about it."

"Not a chance in hell," Holly replies tersely.

"This doesn't have to get ugly."

"Then learn your fucking place, and back off," she snarls.

"Well… suit yourself. What happens next is on you."

Hands scrunching into fists, Lennox stares at her for another second, as if he can decapitate her with a mere glance. She doesn't deign to offer him another moment of her time, her complete lack of fear seeming to only piss him off more.

"Nox," Xander finally speaks. "We have somewhere to be."

His voice is a whip flaying every exposed nerve-ending, the flat tenor dragging down my spine like sharpened fingernails on a chalkboard. The man terrifies me. At least with Lennox, his rage is predictable. He hates Holly, and she hates him.

But with his best friend, it's different. Hatred would demand far too much of Xander's precious time and attention. He stalks around the institute like we're all beneath him, only lowering himself to our level when he needs a new specimen to toy with.

"You'll regret this," Lennox hisses.

Holly spares him the briefest of looks, utterly unfazed. "Threaten me again, and you'll regret it. Priory Lane is mine."

"For now." He storms off before she can respond.

Head cocked, Xander studies me for a moment longer. I'm flustered and sweat-slick beneath his rapt attention for reasons I don't want to analyse. When Holly lays a possessive hand on my arm, the corners of his mouth quirk.

"Challenge accepted," he murmurs, barely audible.

Vanishing after his friend, we're left in peace. The breath I didn't realise I was holding whooshes out of me.

"What the hell was that about?" I whisper furiously.

Holly's hand doesn't release my arm. "They want power and control. We're not going to give it to them."

"We?"

She meets my eyes. "We. You're in this with me now, kid. We're sticking together."

Her voice floats through my mind, accompanying the repetitive beat of my feet on the treadmill. Harrowdean's gym is deserted around me. No one would dare interrupt my private time for fear of the consequences.

Punching the buttons on the screen in front of me, I increase the speed, my legs pumping like firing pistons. I've been running for nearly two hours, and despite being drenched in sweat, the swarm of angry wasps eating at my insides refuse to abate.

You're in this with me now, kid.

"Get out of my head," I pant.

We're sticking together.

Head buzzing with dizziness, I urge my legs faster, determined to exhaust myself. I should be dead on my feet after two sleepless nights, but when these manic episodes hit, not even sleep-deprivation can slow me down.

On a scheduled patrol, a female guard pokes her head inside the gym to scan the equipment-laden room. When she spots me glowering at her, she nods briefly then disappears again.

Not even Elon dared to comment or harass me when I rushed past him earlier, practically vibrating with the need to expel some energy before I incinerate like a supernova. He merely watched me go with that annoying-as-fuck smile.

They want power and control.

"You said we wouldn't give it to them," I hiss out between breaths. "You promised to fight."

She isn't real. I'm hearing nothing but mania-fuelled whispers of a long-dead ghost. I wish I could ignore the voices when they speak to me —it's been a while since I've had that symptom. My medication usually keeps the worst of it at bay.

We're not going to give it to them.

"Leave me alone!" I scream to the thin air.

The vows Holly once made didn't stop the inevitable. Their cruel taunts tore apart the woman who took me in, gave me a home in the most terrifying of places, and taught me how to survive. In the end, she couldn't save herself.

But that's what they wanted, right?

To slowly splinter the formidable badass who'd once opposed them. Rip her into breakable pieces then scatter the remains behind them as they strolled into their new notoriety. Taking her life wasn't hard—it was a convenience.

In the game of survival, it's dog eat dog. Holly was a mere speck on their non-existent moral landscape. An annoying fly buzzing around, forever eluding the hand of its swatter until that fateful moment arrives.

Splat.

You're left with an empty dorm room, a hurriedly cut noose and a zipped body bag. Taking a life should be harder than that. It should leave a deeper scar. So where the fuck are their scars? Why did they get to walk away and forget, but I never could?

Lost in the unstable frenzy of my grief, I don't hear the soft *tap, tap, tap* of Raine's guide stick until it's too late. The golden-haired angel appears, leaning against the handlebars of the treadmill as he draws to a halt beside me.

"Really hoping no other girl in this shithole uses papaya body wash, or I've tracked down the wrong person."

I use my tattooed forearm to wipe sweat from my face. "Don't act like you just sniffed your way down here to find me."

"What? It sounds way more impressive than me asking Xander where you're hiding."

Honestly, I'm not even surprised that Xander's keeping an eye on me. I spotted him lingering outside my therapy session one morning too. This is how he prowls. Silently. From afar. Plotting and instigating until the right time to pounce presents itself.

"Tell your psycho buddy to stop fucking following me."

Swiping a hand over his sleek blonde mop, Raine braces an elbow on the treadmill. "Like he'd listen to me."

Inspecting him out the corner of my eye, I search for any signs of the wreck I left behind the other night. Dressed in jeans and ratty t-shirt, he seems loose, relaxed.

I can see past the act he puts on though. His grin is a tad too wide and voice a little high. I wasn't sure how long that bag would last him. He must be nearly out.

"Listen, Ripley. I need to say thank—"

"Don't mention it," I interrupt.

"Can't even accept a simple thank you?" His mouth curls into a grin.

"For enabling you to continue ruining your life? I'll pass."

He pauses for a beat, appearing surprised.

"Wow. Someone left their filter in bed this morning."

I want to bark out a laugh, but I'm too overwhelmed. Exhausted yet agitated. My body is buzzing like a live wire, and the brutal run has done little to abate the feeling. I've already scrubbed myself to the point of bleeding in the shower. This was my last resort to get the swarming energy out of my system.

I've learned the hard way that unless managed, manic episodes can turn bad. Fast. These days, I recognise my warning signs and act to stabilise myself. I don't want to ever get to the point where I lose control again. That's what landed me in here in the first place.

"Ripley?" Raine prompts. "You okay?"

Slamming a hand on the stop button, I wait for the track to slow. "Look, Raine. I'm glad you're alright. But me giving you those pills doesn't mean we're friends."

"Ouch." He chuckles.

"Leave me alone."

"I was hoping we could talk," Raine offers placatingly. "About you taking on a new customer."

A fresh burst of anger shoots through me. I'm here, battling tooth and nail to get control of myself, while he's sniffing around for more gear. The painful fizzing in my limbs only heightens my disgruntlement.

"Hey, Ripley," I mimic his deep, rattling voice. "You wanna take pity on me and help me continue to kill myself?" I return my voice to normal. "Sure, Raine. Why not? I have no morals and don't care. Give me your money."

Head tilting, it almost feels like his covered eyes are following me as I shakily climb off the treadmill. My entire body is drenched with sweat, and my legs can barely hold my weight. But still, it isn't enough.

I've pushed way past my comfort zone. I know this isn't a healthy way to cope with these emotional spikes, but it was this or do something truly destructive like hurl myself down the staircase, convinced that if I want it enough, I'll be able to fly. The intrusive thought did cross my mind.

"Did I hit a nerve?" Raine asks.

"You know, I used to be more than this." I scoff at my own bitterness. "I had a life. An apartment and studio. Friends. What the fuck would they think of the person I've become?"

Suddenly furious, I don't care that he's getting a front row seat to witness my unravelling. The cocky son of a bitch has never had much trouble reading me anyway. Maybe if he gets to know the real me, he'll stay away. We can forget this weird kinship ever happened.

"I'm so sick of being the person people call when they want to kill themselves. My survival isn't worth it."

Raine's head shifts as though his eyes are brushing over me. "Like it or not, you've survived. Haven't you?"

"What if I don't deserve to?" I counter.

He shrugs. "Few of us rarely get what we deserve. At some point, you have to stop caring, and just take what you're given."

Tears mix with the sweat still dripping down my face. The floodgates are down, and any scrap of self-preservation has deserted me. Right now, I want to give in to every last reckless thought racing through my mind at lightning speed.

"Is that what you do? Take what you're given?"

He gestures towards his eyes. "Like I've had any other choice."

Memories bubble to the surface. Being sat down by the social worker as a terrified child and told that my mum was dead, not even a year after we lost Dad. Leaving an empty house full of packed boxes behind. News reports. Sympathy cards. Bereavement therapy and child counsellors.

None of them ever cracked through the lake of ice I quickly erected around my heart. Losing people hurt less that way. Until Holly came along with her sharp tongue and possessive friendship, refusing to let me tread water alone for a moment longer. Somehow, she tunnelled through the trenches surrounding my heart and set up camp.

It changed nothing.

Death stole her from me too.

"Well, I refuse to live like that," I deadpan.

"Rip—"

"No! All I've done is take what I'm given! My parents left me. I have an uncle who incarcerated me the moment I embarrassed him. My best friend was bullied to death. And if I don't do as the warden says, I won't be far behind her."

Chest heaving, my feet carry me over to Raine of their own volition. I stop directly in front of him, shaking with fury, exhaustion and the fiery riptide of emotion that's loosened my tongue.

He's one of them. An enemy. So why does the sound of his heartbroken violin keep me awake at night? Why did I sacrifice my own supply to fund his addiction? Why the fuck do I care about this person?

Because despite all the shit I've seen, I still wasn't strong enough to plug the final cracks in my heart. Raine has managed to sneak in too with those damned smirks and snippets of vulnerability hidden behind a cocky demeanour. He found my weakness.

Well, *fuck him.*

I'll do the exact same bullshit to him.

"I don't want to take what I'm given." My voice drops lower as mania turns to blood-laced desire. "I want to take what I *want.*"

Raine hesitates, silently taking in the details he can sense beyond his non-existent line of sight. I wonder if the drugs in his veins feel like the poisonous sickness in mine. If we'd be here, together, without either of those things drawing us together.

"What do you want?" he asks breathily.

Salvation. Plain and simple. No matter the pain I must inflict to reach that ethereal paradise, beyond the demons dragging me back to reality every goddamn time.

"The same as you." Hand trembling, I slide the glasses from his face to reveal his pinprick pupils. "To feel alive."

His throat undulates. "It's been a long time since I've felt that."

"Alive?"

Raine's habitual smirk reveals itself. "You're talking to a self-proclaimed junkie, babe. We shoot up to feel everything… Or nothing at all."

Tossing his glasses aside, I close the final gap between us. My heartbeat roars in my ears as I grab a handful of the loose grey t-shirt he wears over his ripped jeans and drag him closer, until our chests slam together with an audible *thwack.*

"Then feel something with me."

Raine's plump lips part on a sharp inhale. I could gaze into the molten caramel depths of his distant eyes all day long, not caring for a single second that he'll never be able to gaze back. I exist in his mind. That's a far greater privilege than many get.

Need overwhelms me. Need to be loved. To be wanted. To exist for someone in a far greater capacity than their dealer or destroyer. I want Raine to see me for the girl I used to be, not the girl I am now.

My mouth slants over his, sealing our twisted exchange with a hard, painful kiss. Eyes closing, I join him in the blackness. Our lips collide like two gamblers engaged in a ruthless battle of Russian roulette.

It doesn't take long for Raine to respond and move his mouth against mine. My breathing falters with the violent onslaught of his lips attacking mine. He's far too fucking good at this. One hand moves to clasp my hip as the other rises, searching blindly until he cups the back of my head.

The soft growl in the back of his throat causes warmth to flood my throbbing core. I thrust my tongue into his mouth, searching for a silent commitment to our shared need for an escape. I don't care if he's high and I'm on the verge of a manic meltdown.

I need his tongue.

His touch.

A reason to exist.

Dragging a hand over the rough scruff on his face, I clutch his chin and deepen the kiss. I want to suck the used oxygen from his lungs and let it poison my airways. Then he can offer his friends the victory of my death, and perhaps, I'll finally know peace.

His hips rock forward, revealing the hard press of his erection as it grinds against my centre. A moan rumbles from my chest with the movement, and Raine thrusts again, making his intentions crystal fucking clear.

I'm a second from letting him fuck me on the treadmill to give me the release I crave when an ear-shattering alarm breaks out, causing us to jump apart. It's excruciatingly loud, blaring relentlessly as the emergency lights begin to flash.

"What the hell is that noise?" Raine covers his ears.

"It's the panic alarm," I shout over the clamour, licking my now-swollen lips. "We're supposed to get on the floor."

"Screw that. We're not done here."

His hands find their way back to my head and hip. Fingers fisting in my sweat-drenched hair, he pulls hard until his lips meet mine with cataclysmic finality. Not even the painful shriek of the alarm can stop me from falling victim to his hot mouth on mine.

I know we only have a matter of minutes before a guard arrives to escort us to our rooms. That alarm signals the institute going into lockdown. An incident must be unfolding, but for the life of me, I couldn't care less.

Releasing my hip, Raine's fingertips search the stretchy material of my workout leggings. He's moving lower, feeling a path to the heat that's burning between my thighs. I gasp into his mouth as he cups my mound.

"Fuck, Rip. I can feel how soaking wet you are through your clothes."

"You gonna do something about it?" I challenge.

Lips equally swollen, he grins at my boldness. "Like I'd ever leave a girl wanting."

"We're going to have company very soon."

Finding my waistband, he eases his hand inside. "Then you'd better come all over my fingers fast, shouldn't you?"

Returning his lips to mine, he shoves his tongue back into my mouth at the same time his hand breaches the soaked cotton of my panties. I can't help rocking my hips, guiding him to exactly where I want his touch. The frenzy within me is begging for an outlet.

Even if this is a bad idea.

My unstable brain couldn't care less right now.

Raine's tongue is a bulldozing force of nature, claiming every available inch of my mouth and stealing it for himself. It feels like he's taking the time to catalogue every last corner, filing it away in his ever-expanding portfolio of information beyond his lack of sight.

I moan loudly when his fingers slip inside my panties and glide down towards my humming cunt. He easily parts my folds, his thumb circling my sensitive bud as he slides a digit through my heat.

"Fucking hell," he mutters into my ear. "I can't wait to feel this sweet cunt clenching around my cock."

Delivering his filthy words with a sharp thrust from his fingers, he pushes inside my slit. My back arches, a hot sizzle of need pulsating through me. I want nothing more than to feel him stretching my walls and filling every desperate inch of me.

"Are you always this wet, babe?" Raine murmurs.

I'm so not going to explain my hypersexual state when I'm mid-episode. We may be using each other right now, but there's no need to underline the truth.

"I don't know," I gasp.

"Well, I'm looking forward to finding out."

A second finger pushes into me, stretching me even wider. I'm a panting mess of sensation, grinding against his palm as my legs begin to tremble. Raine finds a steady pace, finger-fucking me into a breathless wreck.

"That's it," he coos. "Ride my hand, Rip."

Each time I circle my hips, he thrusts back into me, pushing his fingers in and out of my entrance at a maddening tempo. I can feel how coarse his fingers are from a lifetime of violin playing. It gives me a twisted thrill to have them buried deep inside me.

Just as the cusp of my orgasm begins to rise, the sound of footsteps approaching registers. I grab a handful of Raine's t-shirt to stop him.

"Hear that?"

"Yeah," he grunts.

"We have to stop."

"Not yet, babe. I'm not done."

Curling his finger inside me, he touches a mind-blowing spot that swallows whatever protest I was about to muster next. Raine grins at my loud mewling, rubbing his finger up against my inner walls to tease more moans free.

"Raine," I groan.

"I want to hear those pretty sounds as you soak my fingers. Screw whoever's coming."

"We can't—"

"Shut the fuck up," he instructs.

Skating his hand up my body, he clamps his palm over my mouth. Well, that's hot. Each flick of his wrist causes his fingers to slam deeper into me, his speed gradually increasing as I moan and pant into his hand.

With my sounds muffled, the feeling of euphoria washes over me. I'm so close. When Raine dares to slide a third finger into my sopping core, the coiled band of tension inside me explodes.

"That's it," he says triumphantly.

I scream into his palm, my eyes clenched shut as I detonate. Bolts of lightning crackles down my spine, and my knees weaken with the force of my climax. I'm suddenly adrift, but vaguely aware of the doors slamming open and boots stomping into the gym.

"You two!"

Aw, shit.

Not even the displeased boom of Langley's voice can shatter my post-orgasm high. I manage to peel an eyelid open to look over Raine's shoulder, finding Langley standing in the entrance, hands braced on his hips.

"What on earth are you doing?" he interrogates.

Not a single decent excuse manifests.

"Getting off?" I blurt instead.

His mouth drops open. "There's a brawl going on outside!"

"Well, shit." Raine grins lopsidedly at me. "Sounds like we're missing the fun."

"Both of you out!" Langley yells. "Right now."

Keeping his back to the displeased guard, Raine pulls his glistening hand from my leggings. I'm mesmerised and totally unembarrassed as he pops his fingers into his mouth and sucks enthusiastically.

"Now!" Langley adds.

Raine releases his now-clean digits then leans closer to speak into my ear. "Next time, I want you to spread these heavenly juices all over my face. Got it?"

Holy. Freaking. Shit.

"Got it."

His smirks deepens. "Good. Let's go before we get our asses kicked."

Quickly righting my clothes, I hand Raine his guide stick. We reluctantly walk over to where Langley waits. He turns and stalks out, muttering something I can't hear over the shrilling alarm. I bite my lip to hold in a laugh as Raine chuckles.

"Worth it," he declares.

"Eh. If you say so."

"Well, shit. Thanks for the glowing review, guava girl."

"We all have room to improve. I don't want to overinflate your ego."

"Something tells me that would be impossible in your company," Raine quips back.

When his spare hand connects with my arm and slides down to find my hand, our fingers somehow end up intertwined. I don't know if I'm exhilarated or terrified by how right it feels to be held by him.

CHAPTER 11
RIPLEY
BIPOLAR RHAPSODY – KID BRUNSWICK

PATIENTS MARCH towards the cafeteria in regimented lines, trapped under the watchful gaze of stony-faced guards. Everyone's on edge. A sleepless night of shouting and constant alarms blaring has left us all haggard.

When we were escorted back to our rooms, no one on the fifth or sixth floor knew what had happened. Rumours circled, but I don't believe the ramblings of Joshua—our resident schizophrenic. He once claimed to have seen Santa Claus dancing naked in the quad.

Rae slips between several patients to sidle up to me. "What's the stink?"

"You didn't see what happened either?"

"Nah." She glances around at the heavier than usual security presence. "Just heard about it through the grapevine. Did someone get their ass kicked?"

"I guess so."

Fights in Harrowdean aren't uncommon, but most people lack the energy to start shit here. They're far too concerned with the messy business of surviving day to day. But when scuffles happen, they get violent fast.

"That's unlike you," Rae comments.

"Huh?" I shoot her a look.

Waggling her auburn brows, she grins at me. "You're usually the first to know everyone's business around here. What had you so busy that you missed a fight?"

Cheeks heating, I avert my eyes. The memory of Raine and his sordid whispers making me come so hard I saw stars fills my mind. Fuck, does he know how to get a girl off.

It was a shame that we were forced apart afterwards, or I would've happily returned the favour. I'm dying to get my hands on that man's body. I'd like to see if he'll live up to all his filthy promises.

"Oh," she says knowingly. "It's like that, is it?"

"I have no idea what you're talking about."

"Sure." Rae nudges my shoulder as she walks beside me. "I had no idea that you could blush. Must've been a hell of a show."

"We are so not discussing this."

Jogging to catch up to us despite the grumblings of disgruntled guards, Noah stands on my other side. I don't miss the way he scans over me, checking for any signs of harm.

"You both alright?"

"We didn't see anything," Rae answers.

His throat contracts as he skims a hand over his mouth. "Someone went berserk last night. Guards dragged 'em outside, and a bunch of others followed. A full-blown mob fight broke out."

Rae gawps at him. "Seriously?"

I know this place is a fair comparison to hell on earth, but seriously, what the fuck? The guards abuse their authority more often than not. The sedatives and restraints usually come out long before this kind of thing happens, though.

"You saw the fight?" I clarify.

He nods solemnly. "It was chaos with all these idiots joining in, but I saw who the three guards dragged outside. Carlos started it."

Well, double shit. Carlos is Rick's lapdog. If what Noah says is true, the resident asshole is going to be out for blood. No wonder several others joined in. No one messes with his friends and gets away with it.

"Where were you last night?" Noah frowns.

"The gym."

His eyes scan over me, cataloguing the bruise-like smudges beneath my eyes and the still-present trembling of my body on overdrive. The gruelling run and fooling around with Raine hasn't quite taken the edge off.

I only bother going to work out when I'm struggling to hold it together. I've also been known to seek Noah out for a quick fuck when those episodes hit. But not this time. I haven't even considered approaching him since my attention moved elsewhere.

"You didn't call."

"I didn't need to," I answer impassively.

Rae's gaze bounces between the two of us, caught somewhere between confusion and amusement. Great. It's painfully obvious that I wasn't with my usual go-to hook-up last night. I can see she's desperate for details about where I was.

"What about that… other thing?" Noah asks quietly.

"What other thing?" Rae looks between us.

"I need more time." I ignore her, pitching my voice low. "But be ready."

He nods in understanding. "I will be."

Before Rae can continue fishing for information, a harsh voice barks, startling us all.

"Silence!"

The guard, Kieran, is one of Elon's scowling sycophants. He pierces the three of us with a glare until we're forced to shut up. I catch Noah's gaze, and he shakes his head, warning me off talking back to this wanker.

"What crawled up your ass and forgot to die?" I snap, disregarding Noah.

Several nearby patients sneak us nervous looks, waiting to see Kieran's reaction. It's clear that even the guards are on edge this morning.

"You want to say that again?" Kieran returns, hands on his hips.

"Why? Are you deaf as well as stupid now?"

Laughing under her breath, Rae catches his attention next. His lips curl in a derisive sneer as he takes a step closer to her. She can't stop laughing at him.

"That's insubordination, inmate. Let's go."

"Go where?" Rae giggles.

"A night in solitary ought to shut you up."

The colour drains from her face as her laughter dies off. Rae hasn't experienced that delight yet, and I have no doubt a night in a cell with nothing but her own mind for company will truly end her.

"She's just laughing," I defend.

"Enough," he snaps at me. "You were told to be silent!"

"You're threatening my friend."

"Then she should've kept her goddamn mouth shut, shouldn't she?"

Seeing the visceral terror on Rae's face is the final straw. Regardless of the awful things I've enabled her to do to herself, I still care about her. I'll take this dick's wrath before letting her suffer.

"You can't talk to us like that," I chide. "We still have rights."

"Not that I noticed," Kieran sneers.

Consequences or not, I want to beat the shit-eating smile off this bastard's face. Whatever happened last night has nothing to do with us. He can take his bad attitude elsewhere.

"You all need to learn who is in charge around here!" he rages loudly, his voice causing several patients to startle. "Disrespect will not be tolerated."

"I'm s-sorry." Rae is now trembling, her eyes filling with tears. "Please don't make me go to the hole."

"I don't give a shit, inmate. You're coming with me."

"No!"

"Enough! You're out of here!"

When Kieran reaches out to restrain her, I leap into action and step in front of Rae. She ducks behind my shoulder, her cheeks stained with tears.

"Leave her alone. She's done nothing wrong."

"You both wanna go down there instead?" His spit flies angrily.

"Gladly!" I shout back. "If it'll mean I don't have to look at your ugly mug for a second longer."

His narrowed eyes fill with discontent. "You little…"

Drawing his baton from the belt around his waist, he raises it high. I try to move to protect myself from the blow, but sandwiched between the tight press of patients, I'm too late to avoid it swinging towards me.

"Rip!" Noah bellows.

Pain blooms in my abdomen from the hard strike. I double over, coughing and wheezing as I fight to avoid hurling. I feel an arm wrap around me as I blink aside tears. I won't give him the satisfaction.

"That fucking hurt," I grit out.

"Now, now." Elon's smarmy voice nears. "What's going on here?"

With my head lowered, I can see his shining black boots approaching our huddle. He easily parts the crowd around us before stopping next to his dickhead colleague.

"Nothing to worry about," Kieran responds.

"Then let's not make a scene."

"But sir, she—"

"Move along, everyone," Elon commands. "Nothing to see here."

Surrounding patients begin to shuffle away, resuming their trudge into the cafeteria. I hear Elon move closer, his knees bending so he can lower himself to my level.

"When will you learn to keep that loud mouth of yours shut?" he hisses.

"Fuck off," I croak.

"Get your ass inside, Ripley. My patience for you is wearing very thin."

Returning to his full height, I hear Elon clap his pal on the shoulder before he saunters away. Kieran reluctantly follows him, still complaining to himself about tossing our asses in solitary.

"Jesus Christ," Noah grunts. "They've lost their minds."

"Can you stand?" Rae touches my shoulder.

Nodding, I straighten my spine, despite the fierce agony curling around my midsection. Rae backs off at my cursing, giving me some space to breathe.

My eyes catch a pair of seafoam orbs amidst the crowd. Lennox isn't even fighting to hold back his grin. He shifts to murmur something in Xander's ear, the pair of them watching me struggle. Raine is nowhere in sight.

Teeth bared, I flip them off.

Xander slips back into the crowd with his buddy. I've caught him silently following me several times recently, never once saying a word, but keeping me within his sights at all times. Stalking. Hunting. Studying.

I'd very much like to take that baton from Kieran and shove it up Xander's asshole. Perhaps he'd learn then that I'm not some scientific curiosity for him to tear apart. I don't even want to consider what he's planning.

"Come on." Rae grips my elbow. "Let's go before we get in more trouble."

"Yeah."

"Um, Rip?" A rush of breath shoots from between her lips. "Thanks for sticking up for me."

I study her tear-streaked cheeks and glassy, kohl-lined eyes. Emotion claws at my throat. Thick. Cloying. A bittersweet concoction that I usually shove down as deep as possible when I fulfil her regular orders.

"You deserve better, Rae."

"Than what?"

The backs of my eyes burn. "Than any of this."

Arm curled around my aching waist, I turn away and follow the moving flow of patients. Noah accompanies us through the packed reception and into the awaiting cafeteria where long tables are slowly filling up.

At the head of the room, Davis watches over us all with cold calculation. His salt-and-pepper hair is slicked back today, perfectly matching his impeccably tailored suit.

We approach an almost full table, the few patients spread across the seats quickly scattering when I cast an eye over them. A couple even mumble apologies without daring to look up at me.

Rae takes the seat opposite. "What does the warden want?"

I shrug, easing myself into the chair with a wince. Before Noah can sit down next to me, a huge, scarred hand clamps down on his shoulder. He's roughly shoved aside so someone else can take his place.

"Seat's taken," Lennox growls roughly.

I glower up at his smiling mug. "Like fuck it is."

Despite his smirk, the predatory gleam in Lennox's eyes is pure malice. He ignores Noah's put-out expression and slides in next to me, the overwhelming bulk of his shoulders brushing against mine.

"What are you doing?" I snarl under my breath.

Lennox fiddles with the silver chain tucked into his neckline. "That beating was a hell of a sight."

"Show's over, Nox."

He chuckles throatily, the sonorous sound rumbling from his chest. "I think it's just beginning."

Beneath the table, my fingers curl until I feel the sting of my nails piercing my palms. "I saved your friend. Leave me alone."

"You think that makes us even somehow?" he huffs. "We need to get a few things straight."

Determined to ignore him, I focus on the small scuffles and shows of aggression unfolding around us. Several patients are being shoved and manhandled. The tension is racketing up more with each second.

I don't recognise several of the additional guards that have been called in to beef up security. They seem even more overzealous, positioning their sheathed weapons clearly on display and barking at everyone who dares to scuttle past.

"Listen, bitch," Lennox demands.

"What?" I hiss back. "Get on with it, then fuck off."

He leans close, his tone frigid. "Raine was high this morning."

I don't respond at first. Wrestling with my decision to sell to him after what happened in the gym has relentlessly occupied my thoughts. But when the trembles returned, I had no choice but to cave.

"I won't watch you deal drugs to Raine and screw him up even more."

"You'd rather poison him yourself, huh?" I retort.

"We protected him," Lennox grinds out.

"And benefitted from every drop of goodwill, no doubt."

"You won't keep him safe." His shoulders hunch, lined with determination. "I refuse to watch someone I care about get hurt because you're too greedy to regulate his intake."

"Is it hard?" I peer deep into his pale-green irises. "Seeing someone you care about get hurt? I wouldn't know what that's like, would I?"

Ignoring my snark, his hard gaze cuts into me. "We will take control of Harrowdean, one way or another. Why don't you just give it up now?"

"Because, almighty Lennox, men like you are the reason why places like this exist."

At my words, he recoils like I've stabbed him in the gut. I can feel the rage and indignation pouring off him in waves. I almost laugh out loud at his visceral reaction. Drilling into Lennox's ceaseless vein of fury will never stop being entertaining.

Beneath the anger he wields as a deadly weapon, Lennox likes to think that he has this strict moral code. Some pathetic justification for the horrors he's inflicted in the name of keeping those he cares about safe.

Lennox isn't just an angry man; he's a broken one. And that particular brand of twisted love is the reason so many of us walk around with holes in our hearts through which our sanity escapes.

"If anything happens to Raine because of you—"

No longer able to stifle it, laughter tears free from my throat.

"What? You gonna kill me? Or perhaps another one of my friends?"

Casting a quick glance around the bustling room, Lennox moves fast for a man of his stature. I gasp as he seizes a handful of my short curls and slams my face down into the solid tabletop. Hard.

"Argh!"

Wrenching my hair in his grip, he lifts my head to inspect the blood that's exploded from my now-throbbing nose. I breathe raggedly, swallowing the river streaming down my throat.

Lennox's lips touch my ear. "I'll make what I did to Holly look like a walk in the park compared to your death."

"So you keep threatening," I choke wetly. "Yet… I'm still alive."

"Careful what you wish for, cunt."

Releasing my hair, he rises and quickly blends back into the crowd of patients. I straighten my septum piercing and pinch the bridge of my nose to staunch the blood. Today is not my fucking day.

"Here." With eyes the size of dinner plates, Noah pulls a crumpled tissue from his jeans pocket as he sits down. "Your face is covered in blood."

I quickly plug my nose. "Thanks."

"What the hell is his problem?" Rae gawps after the giant.

Watching Lennox's broad shadow part the crowd, I can't even answer her. If Holly were here, she wouldn't take this laying down. She'd know what to do. But with each passing day, I feel like I'm losing more control. Just like she did.

"Attention all." Davis's voice booms over the low conversation. "Be seated."

His authoritative tone matches the terrifying coldness in his gaze. The walls of the cafeteria are crawling with guards, shoulder to shoulder, all watching with the same frigid glares.

"Last night's violence was deeply unfortunate and will not be tolerated." Davis casts a look around the packed room. "A full investigation will be taking place to determine what unfolded."

"Where is Carlos?" someone shouts.

Glancing to my left, I spot Rick and his gaggle of buddies. They're all glaring and visibly bruised, like they spent the night plotting the institute's demise after getting their asses handed to them.

Davis clears his throat. "We have a zero-tolerance policy for violence here at Harrowdean."

"Violence?" Rick yells, breaking his silence. "What have you done to him?"

"Enough!" Davis shouts back with a rare flash of temper. "Inciting group violence against our staff is unacceptable. We have rules that must be followed."

"Fuck the rules!" another person calls out.

"Where is Carlos?"

"You can't keep shoving us around!"

With each voice that adds to the melee, more and more patients are speaking up. Guards close in around us, pushing and shoving, but their intimidation isn't working. Not when we have strength in numbers.

Davis gestures for the guards to halt. "Our number one priority here at Harrowdean is your safety. Action was taken last night to preserve the peace."

"Bullshit!"

More enraged shouting ensues. Rick and his friends are at the heart of it, spitting and raging, despite the tight press of security attempting to contain them. Seeing their outburst sets off others until Davis's voice is no longer audible.

"This is going to turn bad, fast." I glance around at the advancing guards. "With all that extra muscle."

"We need to get out of here," Noah agrees.

Pulling the wad of wet tissue from my nose, I shove it in my pocket before offering Rae a bloodstained hand. She smiles gratefully then links our fingers so we can stand up together.

"Let's go."

"What if they stop us?" she worries.

"The guards are gonna have bigger things to worry about if this goes south." Scanning the crowd, I search for Langley. "Besides, I can get us out."

Seeing us rise, several other nervous patients begin to follow, seeking a safe route out of the increasingly unstable situation. How I became a symbol of safety, I'll never know. It's laughable, really.

Winding a path through the crowd, we're halfway to the doorway when there's a loud crackling noise. I glance over my shoulder in time to see one of Rick's friends—Owen, I think—thrashing on the cafeteria floor.

"Tasers?" Noah gasps. "Move!"

A cacophony of screams fuels the rising panic. There's another loud crack. Thudding batons. Crying. Barked orders to disperse. Now there's a tsunami of people trying to do exactly the same as us—escape.

We're being half-carried by the shoving crowd. Sounds of violence echo all around us, adding to the carnage. All it took was a tiny spark to ignite.

"Ripley!"

Waving above his head, Langley motions for us to go to him. Clenching Rae's hand tight, I tow her along, hoping that whoever is behind me can fend for themselves. We have to fight to get over to Langley as it is.

Snagging his shirt sleeve, I drag us the final steps. Langley clears the rest of the path. He has a reputation for being one of the good ones, so he doesn't seem to be attracting the attention of those looking to fight.

"What happened to your face?" He winces.

"Just help us!"

Langley pushes open the exit doors then ushers us outside into the welcome safety of the corridor. As soon as we're free, I can drag in a full breath. It's short-lived, though. There's a whole ass stampede hot on our heels.

"Get out of here," Langley instructs. "Go!"

Still holding Rae tight, I break into a run. Only this time, it isn't a crazed fellow patient posing a threat. It's the very forces hired to protect us who want to harm us.

My kingdom is crumbling.

Harrowdean isn't safe anymore.

CHAPTER 12
LENNOX
MONSTER – FIGHT THE FADE

ARMS FOLDED ACROSS MY CHEST, I lean against the corridor wall. My room is being thoroughly ripped apart by two guards, leaving no item of clothing or possession untouched. I don't know what they're hoping to find.

Down the entire hall, similar scenes of destruction are replicated. Why bother asserting their control when they know full well who supplies contraband in this place? Well, for exactly that reason.

It's all about control. Scare the herd enough, and they'll stay contained in their self-enclosed pen. The clinicians may be feeding this experiment to elicit the juicy results they desire, but the chaos must be strictly governed.

They want us to suffer. Self-destruct. Barter and bicker our way to dominance over each other. Those are the fascinating situations they want to see play out. But when the guinea pigs start to bite their masters? The chaos isn't so measurable then.

"Nox."

Tapping his way towards me with his stick outstretched, Raine whisper-shouts my name. I take a final glance at the guards ripping apart my mattress to check for stashed weapons and approach him.

"You alright?"

"I heard my room's next," he says in a panic. "I've got shit they can't find."

"Fuck, Raine!"

"I know. Help me, man."

Shaking my head, I snag his long shirt sleeve and frogmarch him towards his room. Raine hands me his keycard so I can unlock the door quickly. We step inside, hoping no one has spotted us.

"Where is it?" I sigh tiredly.

"Bottom drawer in the nightstand has a false bottom." He anxiously chews his lip. "And there's a loose floorboard behind the desk."

"Go stand near the door. If you hear them coming, shout."

Quickly nodding, he taps a path back towards the door then presses his ear against it. I set to work investigating the nightstand and quickly find a notch in the smooth, dark wood that I prise open.

He's been better since the night we begrudgingly enlisted Ripley's help. Regardless of my feelings about that soulless bitch, I know we couldn't let him stay like that. It was far too risky to let him detox there and then.

But the idea of her supplying him on the regular is making me want to demolish this whole damn room to ensure he has none of her pills to snort. I don't know how he convinced her to sell to him, but there's nowhere else he's getting this stuff from.

"Got it?" Raine asks.

I scoop up two baggies of pills in a variety of colours. "What is this shit, Raine?"

"Just get the rest. They're coming."

Slotting the false bottom back into place, I duck beneath the nearby desk next. It takes several seconds to locate the loose floorboard underneath. I have to dig my nails into the edges to wriggle it free.

More pills.

These ones are that weird, off-white shade and clearly the same as the ones in the baggie Ripley previously supplied. I gather his stash in a pile then shove it into the waistband of my sweatpants, tightening the drawstring to hold it all in place.

"We good?" Raine's voice is strained.

I slot the floorboard back. "All clear."

His shoulders sag with relief just as the lock on the door buzzes. It's flung open, narrowly missing him. The two assholes who were tearing apart my room order us outside before they begin obliterating Raine's neatly organised space.

"Fucking hell." He winces at the sounds of destruction. "There goes my system."

"We'll put it all back," I try to reassure him.

"The bastards aren't even pretending to be gentle." The sound of crashing punctuates his words. "Do they really think this tactic works?"

As I peer up and down the corridor full of terrified patients, seeing what Raine cannot, I hate to admit that it does work. Everyone knows where to get their illegal shit from in here, but few know the sinister secret behind the program's existence.

Most assume that Ripley has some pretty impressive connections to get her hands on anything that's requested. If the entire institute knew the clinicians are feeding this toxic machine of mental illness in the name of experimentation, they'd kill themselves or try to escape.

Few are doomed to know the truth.

Including us.

Those who remain clueless are petrified of raids like this. They scuttle around, obeying the rules and hoping their sentence will pass without incident. Forever ignorant to the fact that management wants the exact opposite.

Clasping Raine's elbow, I slowly guide him down the staircase and out into the windswept quad. Winter is rolling on, dousing the Victorian institute in frost and ice.

I have a maths class to get to before some anger management crap later on with my assigned therapist, but the surprise search threw everyone off. Even Harrowdean's precise routine seems to be breaking down.

"Pass me the stuff." Raine shrugs his elbow free.

"Not a chance. I'm holding this for you."

"Wait, what?" he splutters.

"You've got at least two weeks' worth here. I don't trust you not to take the whole lot at once."

"Nox!" Raine exclaims. "I don't want to kill myself."

"Yet you seem determined to try. Who needs to sit on this many pills at once?"

"I don't wanna run out again. That's all."

"Yeah, right," I scoff.

He tries to make a grab for me, but I easily duck out of the way, escaping his off-target hands. Raine growls in annoyance, unable to sense where I've moved out of reach with his stash.

"Lennox! This isn't funny!"

"Do you hear me laughing?" I fire back.

Giving up, he huffs, his lips pressed into a harsh line. "I think I preferred it when you didn't give a shit about me."

Jaw clenching, I battle the urge to grab him by the scruff of his t-shirt and punch the stupid out of him. I'm not a fucking idiot. I know I have some serious issues. But they've never included a lack of caring. Quite the opposite.

"If you think that's true, you don't know me at all."

"Stop pretending like I'm your problem to fix then!" Raine stomps his foot like a toddler. "I survived long enough on my own before I rocked up at Priory Lane."

"I'm trying to help you."

"Maybe I don't want your help!"

Staring at my stubborn as fuck friend, all I can see is the dark-green eyes of another staring back at me. My sister. She looked more like our mother, though. Daintier. Light-footed. Always dancing and practising her ballet.

Our coarse, often messy brown hair and big toothy grins were the same, despite the several years between us. She was always smiling too. I remember that detail.

Until… she stopped.

Breath seizing, I have to fight back the onslaught of memories that usually only visit me at night. I can't hold on to the cloak of my protective anger then. That's when she sneaks in to torment me about all the red flags I failed to see.

Even at her tiny height, she had the presence of a motherfucking giant when she yelled. It breaks my goddamn heart to hear these words from Raine now as much as it did hearing it from my sister then.

Just stop fussing over me, Nox!

I don't want your help.

Yet she needed it. Far more than I ever realised. I only knew just how much she needed her big brother to protect her when it was too fucking late.

By then, all I had left were ashes to scatter and belongings to pack. *He* wanted any memories of her existence scrubbed away. I'll never know if it was his guilty conscience or covering his tracks.

"Lennox?" Raine's voice drags me back. "Look, I'm sorry. I didn't mean that."

"Yeah," I say flatly. "Whatever."

Pulling the bags full of pills from my waistband, I don't care who sees us. Raine squeaks in shock as I grab his hands and deposit the stash there.

"Do what you want with these," I snarl. "Better than me trying to help, right?"

"Nox—"

"Just don't call me next time you're stuck."

For once, I don't have the desire to shout and rave. I've punched my way through life since Daisy died and fought off any threats against those I care about with fists and blood. But what has that left me with?

No living family.

Two messed-up friends.

And a whole lot of dysfunction.

I couldn't protect Xander from the fucked up shit they did to us in the Z wing. The deep freeze bathtubs that made him lose a toe. Electrocutions. Sensory overload. Sleep deprivation.

Every last medieval torture tactic designed to strip a person's soul away was tried at least once. After all that, they thought we were unbreakable. That we were in fact the perfect stooges to run their operation because we refused to crack.

But little did those sadistic doctors know, we did break. Just in ways we allowed our pain to escape undetected. Those moments happened when the machines were turned off and cell doors locked.

Breaking isn't always a loud, cataclysmic implosion of a person. Sometimes it's silent. Imperceptible. I took my hatred and stoked those righteous flames to keep myself warm at night. Xander wrapped his ice-cold detachment around himself for comfort instead.

"Later."

"Nox!" Raine shouts after me.

I'm already storming away, unable to look at him for a second longer. Seeing Daisy's sweet, teenage face superimposed over his is harrowing. I let her down. I couldn't save her from evil or even herself. Stopping Raine from slowly poisoning himself isn't going to bring her back.

The heavens open, sending silvery bullets of rain hammering to the ground. It doesn't stop me from storming into the thick tree line, needing an escape. I'm soaked through in seconds, but I keep walking into the underbrush.

I soon find the perimeter fence. Harrowdean is small and self-enclosed, a clandestine bubble of pure evil, tucked into the fringes of society. Grasping the slick chain-links that hold us all captive, I stare into the forest beyond.

If Daisy hadn't died, I never would've ended up here. That monster didn't just kill my sister, he killed us both in one fell swoop. I ruined my own life in a torrent of rage and grief, hoping that revenge would somehow ease the agony of finding my baby sister's corpse.

It didn't ease the guilt. The grief.

Instead, my anger only grew.

"You shouldn't be here," a familiar voice calls out.

Startled, I glance to the side. Ripley is blurry through the thick rainfall, but her mass of sopping wet curls is unmistakable. She sits at the base of a tall juniper tree, her knees pulled tight to her chest.

Even in the rain, I can see the purple bruising on her face where I slammed it into the table. Knowing I inflicted those bruises should be satisfying, but the usual fury that fills me at the sight of this bitch doesn't come.

All I can muster is sadness. If things had been different, perhaps I wouldn't have ruined her life. And she wouldn't have ruined mine. We're both caught in this ceaseless cycle of violence.

"Are you following me?" Ripley asks in her usual disinterested tone.

I bark out a bitter laugh. "Believe it or not, my life doesn't revolve around you."

"Well, shucks. Isn't that a disappointment."

I shouldn't enjoy the heavy sarcasm dripping from her tone. This short, curvy wisp of a woman is responsible for some of the bleakest months of my life. Unimaginable agony and desolation.

All in the name of some bullshit revenge. At least I can understand her motivations. The shit I've done all in the name of revenge would be newsworthy too. But what if she'd killed Raine? Or Xander?

Would I have done the same to her?

I don't know who the villain is anymore.

"It's raining," I point out the obvious.

Ripley hugs her knees tighter, keeping her eyes averted. "I'm aware."

"Then what are you doing here?"

Her gaze is stuck on the same impenetrable forest I was just studying. Yearning. Reaching. Perhaps even imagining a life beyond these chain-link fences. I hate how entrancing her big, hazel eyes are, brimming with so much grief right now, it's making me doubt myself.

I hate her.

I'm *supposed* to hate her.

But part of me still wonders what she'd be like out there—beyond the roles we've constructed for ourselves. Or rather, we've forced ourselves into, slicing apart and re-stitching our souls to fit into an unrecognisable caricature of our former selves.

"Having a fucking shower. Leave, Lennox."

With the rain pouring down on her, she looks lost and broken. I see the same gaping wound in her that I feel tugging at my insides. A black hole sucking in all light and hope. Neither can survive this place.

I despise the fact that the only one who could ever understand how I feel is the one person I hate more than anything. Ripley knows better than anyone the price we must pay to rule in this world.

She's sacrificed her own soul along the way too.

Are we so different?

"Go!" Her voice cracks a little.

I lick my dry lips, an alien sensation swarming in my gut. "She didn't deserve what we did to her, you know."

Swiping dripping hair from her face, Ripley peers up at me. Chapped lips parted, those devilish eyes are blown wider than usual. She gapes at me like Bigfoot has just stomped through the woods to greet her.

"I know that," she cuts back.

"But we did it anyway."

"Yeah," Ripley deadpans. "You did."

"I'd be lying if I said I was sorry." My eyes bore into hers. "Holly had something I wanted. So I took it from her. That was a price I was willing to pay."

Her stare shimmering with unshed tears, she doesn't even flinch at my confession. I'm sure she already knows that I feel no remorse for our actions. Not anymore. It's a luxury I cannot afford.

"Why are you telling me this, Lennox?"

"It's just that we have good reason to hate each other."

"Too right. I've never hated anyone or anything as much as I hate you."

"Not even Xander?" I can't help but ask.

Ripley scoffs. "Xander is an animal wrapped in human skin. But only one of you walked out of that bedroom and left my best friend swinging from a noose."

Yeah. Me.

I'd never admit it to her, but I still think about that night. The cruel words of encouragement I whispered to Holly. Threats I made. Hell, even the sound of her choked, gurgling sounds. She didn't achieve a clean neck break.

The makeshift rope cinched around her throat instead. All while I stood there, chanting to myself that it had to be done. Only the powerful survive these institutes. She had the key to our survival.

I refused to lose the family I'd found in Xander—the second chance that caring for him, another victim just like Daisy, gave me. It didn't take much to see the same brokenness in him that I never spotted in Daisy. Not until it was too late.

"I did what I had to do to survive."

"Killing an innocent did that?" Ripley's nose wrinkles in disgust. "You make me sick."

"Tell me. Have the innocents you've hurt allowed you to survive?"

This time, my words find their mark and she recoils. Her mouth opens and shuts several times, but nothing comes out. Not a single line of defence.

"Are you sorry, Ripley?"

"Why do you care?"

"Answer the damn question."

Shuffling my feet, I have no clue why I'm doing this. I have the perfect opportunity to choke the stubborn bitch to death without a single person witnessing it.

But seeing the broken, pissed-off, beautiful fucking disaster I've created, I need to know the truth. Does she feel the same bottomless pit of despair where her heart used to be that I do? Does it drive her to the brink of insanity, knowing she's irredeemable?

Her face contorts, riddled with so much pain, I don't know whether to relish in it or take the question back. The latter option shocks the shit out of me. Since when do I give a fuck about her pain?

"Yes," she admits. "Every day."

"Then you're a better person than me."

"I know exactly what kind of person you are." Ripley slowly clambers to her feet, her sweats soaked and mud stained. "Holly was my friend. My *family*. You took that from me, and all for what? Power?"

"Power. Protection. Control." I shrug dismissively. "All the things you're looking for too."

Her small, paint-flecked hands scrunch into fists. "Then when I tie the noose around your neck and make it look like a suicide, you'll understand why I will never, ever be sorry either."

Stopping in front of me, she's a small but fearsome dot beneath my towering height. Raindrops cling to her eyelashes, framing tear-filled, mottled eyes that brim with such fury, it's formidable. I've never seen anger like it beyond my own.

I want her to hate me.

I want to feel every drop of her wrath.

The rage that found its home within me the day I lost Daisy has never found a fair competitor. Anger is a lonely road to madness, and staring at Ripley now, I know she's trodden that same path. We both have.

"What do you really want?" she deadpans. "Because if you think I'm going to break like Holly did, you're in for a long wait."

Head cocked, I consider her. Every steely, unterrified inch. She saw the very worst in us, the depths that we will sink to in order to achieve our goals, yet she's still standing. If Holly's death didn't kill her, nothing will.

"I know you won't break."

She rears her head back in surprise. "Why?"

"Because you're stronger than she ever was." I scan over her features, loathing the way I want to trace each dimple. "That's why I fucking hate you."

"I really don't understand you."

"Why aren't you broken like the rest of us? Why did you walk away unscathed when we didn't?"

"Unscathed?" Ripley repeats incredulously. "Do I look bloody *unscathed* to you?"

"I just had to confiscate a kilo of drugs from one of my best friends!" I explode. "I don't even recognise the other one these days, he's so far gone. Yet here you are, enjoying your luxurious life."

The more I speak, the more her outrage grows. Her face is practically shadowed with it—twisting, contorting, brows scrunched and gaze seething. I love it. So goddamn much. I want her to be as angry as I am.

"Nothing about Harrowdean is a luxury!" she shouts.

"Could've fooled me."

"You son of a…"

I see her clenched fist coming from a mile off and easily duck to avoid being punched. Ripley curses as I move to grip her balled hand, blocking another attempted blow.

Tugging on her arm, I drag her close enough for our wet chests to crash together. She slips through the grass and collides with me. I strangle the rush of appreciation that feeling her tight curves pressing into me provokes.

"Perfect Ripley, huh?" I taunt. "Can't even punch right."

"You're fucking dead!"

Relishing the acidic lash of her voice, I lean close. "Wrong again, little Miss Perfect. I already died a very long time ago."

Grabbing her other wrist, I hold them both, pinned against her chest. I know just how scrappy she can be, but I still have a couple hundred pounds of muscle on her.

"Struggle all you want. I may enjoy it."

"Sick bastard!" she screams.

"I never claimed to be anything else."

Twisting and writhing, she's a panting blur of rage. I narrowly dodge a swift knee in the balls, whirling us around so I can shove her into a nearby tree trunk. Ripley gasps in pain at the hard collision.

Sliding a knee between her thighs, I spread her legs wide. Our hips are glued together, and with her wrists still pinned to her chest, she doesn't have a single inch of space to move.

"Much better." I appraise her prone form.

Still, the fear I'm searching for refuses to enter her eyes. Nothing penetrates her hatred. It burns hotter than any other emotion I hoped to elicit, and as her lips poise, I can guess what's coming.

"Fuck you." She hawks a mouthful of saliva right in my face.

I let her spit trickle down my cheek, unflinching. "Is that all you've got?"

"You don't want to see the best I've got."

"Enlighten me, then."

Grimacing, she tries to twist her wrists to escape my bondage. It's futile. I've got her pinned too tightly. With a growl, Ripley slumps, giving the impression that she's given up.

"You're so weak an—"

Crack.

Her head suddenly snaps forward, slamming so hard into my nose, I see stars. My grip on her wrists slackens. I stumble back, cupping my nose as it pulses in time with the pain thrumming through me.

"Call me weak again," she seethes. "I'll skin you alive."

Spitting out the blood that's filled my throat, I cast her a glower. "Nice shot. Now we'll match."

"It's the least you deserve."

When she moves to strike again, I abandon my aching face and grab her. She grapples with me as we wrestle, both vying to gain control of the other until our knees give out, and we hit the forest floor.

Rolling and bucking, we're a rain-soaked tangle in the mud. Ripley snarls beneath me, semi-crushed by my weight. I grab a handful of her hair then yank hard, causing her to hiss in pain.

"Can't escape, Rip?"

"Don't call me that! You piece of shit!"

"Well, damn. Now you're hurting my precious feelings."

"You don't fucking have any."

Each shift of her writhing limbs beneath me sends blood pumping to my crotch. Apparently, my dick didn't get the memo that we're supposed to hate this whore. Not enjoy the feel of her battling to escape.

Antagonising her shouldn't be so goddamn hot. I have the perfect opportunity to choke the life from her lungs right here in the mud. There are no guards. And I don't give a fuck about the CCTV cameras positioned on the perimeter fence.

What can they do to me now?

I've already lost everything.

"Just stop," she cries angrily. "If you're going to kill me, do it. Fucking do it, Nox!"

"Why? Because you think that you deserve it?"

"Yes!"

With that confession, she stills. Her anger is fizzling out. I can see the despair I found her drowning in returning. Spreading with each second she spends trapped in the dirt.

No. I don't want her defeated.

Not anymore.

I want her so enraged, she can't breathe without thinking of her hatred for me. She wants to fade away? I won't fucking let her. She doesn't get to escape so easily. Her punishment is living with her own self-loathing.

Every bit of rational thought flies from my mind. With my pelvis pinning her to the slick ground, I shove her wrists above her head then trap them there. Utterly exposed, she can't stop my approach.

"Death would be too easy for you," I croon. "Torturing you will be far sweeter."

She blinks rapidly, a brief, fleeting whisper of delicious fear finally entering her gaze. Fanning those flames, I decide to hell with it. My lips slam against hers, swallowing her sounds of protest.

If this is the only way to truly hurt her, I'll cross the invisible line between us. But at the first touch, any thought of revenge flies out of my mind.

Fuck. Me.

I never expected her lips to be velvet soft and laced with such tantalising sweetness that I lose all sight of my plan. My need to destroy her by any means necessary is overtaken by the heat suddenly pumping through my veins.

She's rigid against my touch. That escaping fury comes roaring back as her teeth clamp down on my bottom lip, sinking in deep enough to break the skin. I rear back with a sharp hiss.

"Y-You…" Ripley splutters. "How dare you—"

"Shut the fuck up."

Crashing my mouth back on hers, I don't know if I'm punishing her or myself. This is just about hurting her, right? I know she hates me. I know my touch has to be damn repulsive to her. This is the only way to make her break.

So why the ever-loving fuck does her tiny, perfectly curved body feel so good against mine? Why do I want her to scream, shout, bite and kick? Why do I want her hatred and not her defeat?

Her sounds of protest die out. I'm not sure if I imagine the moan emanating from her throat. I'm not sure if I imagine the way it makes my heart pound, cock twitch, and skin prickle with arousal either.

Is the fucking bitch enjoying this?

Am I enjoying this?

I'm not sure when her mouth begins to move against mine. Hard. Wet. Undeniably passionate. Lips sliding in a spiteful rhythm, she kisses me like she hopes to torture the truth out of me.

Hips grinding, I thrust into her core, seeking any amount of friction against the painful pressure gathering in my cock. Fuck, the way I want to fill her up and hear every last vindictive word spew from her lips as I do. I want her to despise how much she loves the feel of my cock inside her.

Shoving my tongue into her mouth, I relish in the way she responds.

Enraged and thrashing. Invading my mouth with the same wrath that's fuelled the furious dance we've spent the last year locked in.

She's fighting it with every second our mouths are locked, but that doesn't stop her hips from lifting to press into mine. The woman is grinding against me. Pressing her core into my cock, silently pleading for more. That realisation shatters my lusty haze.

I abruptly break the kiss. "What are you doing?"

Her mouth is swollen and red. "What are *you* doing? Why are you kissing me?"

"Why are you kissing me back?"

Pupils dilated, she licks her inflamed lips. "You… This… What the fuck, Nox?"

I'm practically dizzy with the adrenaline and desire pumping through my system. Confusion only adds to the blur of emotions causing my control to falter. I wanted to provoke her. I didn't expect to want to fuck her too.

Scrambling for an excuse, I plaster on the smirk I know she detests. "I just wanted to see if you're as much of a whore as everyone says."

Before I can react, her knee collides with my still-hard cock. She knees me dead centre in the bollocks, easily shoving me off her body as I choke out a wheeze. I crumple onto the ground, panting through tightly gritted teeth.

"I will never be your whore, Lennox Nash." Ripley sits up and brushes herself off. "This changes absolutely nothing between us."

All I can do is lay here in the dirt while she stands up, casting me a final derisive look. Watching her stalk off, those devilish hips swaying and tight ass shaking with each step, I wonder when the fuck this parasite invaded my brain.

We're sworn enemies. She'll destroy me, my family, the life I've tried to create since taking that plea deal to avoid prosecution. I thought I'd be safe in Priory Lane. Even in Harrowdean. Better than prison, right?

But nowhere is safe.

Not with Ripley Bennet around.

CHAPTER 13
RIPLEY
HERO – DAVID KUSHNER

PICKING at the dry flakes of paint on my hand, I cast a final look at my wet canvas. It's a pathetic effort. My mind is unfocused, agitated. With each swoop of the paintbrush, I get more and more frustrated

"Stupid fucking thing!" I hurl it across the art room.

Storming out of the room, the door slams shut behind me. I'm dead set on stomping back to my bedroom and scrubbing myself in the shower to remove the ghost of Lennox's touch. His hands. Lips. Roughened stubble. Hard length grinding into me.

But no amount of angrily showering multiple times a day has diminished the pure ecstasy that him pinning me down and forcibly inflicting his rage on me created. It's all I've been able to think about.

The anger. Mutual hatred. Battling for control. Power. The right to punish. Even admitting it in my head is fucking unbearable, but I was getting off to a literal monster paying me even an ounce of attention.

I'm a piece of shit.

Holly would be ashamed.

"Ripley? You good?"

The sound of Raine's gentle, melancholic violin halts. I'm tempted to rush past the half-open door to the adjacent music room, but I know he already heard me. He'd only follow. I asked him to practise in there today, needing some headspace.

"Yeah," I shout back.

"What's going on?"

Stopping in the doorway, I study his slim but well-honed frame. He's dressed in light-washed, grey jeans today with a loose, V-neck, black shirt that shows off his razor-like clavicles.

His soft blonde hair is smoothed back like usual, round glasses in place. He looks as tempting and mysterious as ever, but as I spot the empty plastic bag peeking from his jeans pocket, my inner contempt intensifies.

"Rip?"

I clear my throat. "Nothing. I'm fine."

His head cocks. "Are you staring at me?"

"No, jackass."

"Well, don't just stand there. It creeps me out."

"I'm done. I need some air."

Raine pulls the violin from beneath his chin. "Wait up."

"You're busy," I protest.

He shrugs, searching for his violin case. "Sure. My schedule is crammed. How will I ever spare a moment?"

Fighting a smile, I step into the room to help him. He'd never surrender his baby to me; that violin is practically his left arm. But I quickly locate the velvet-lined case then touch his wrist, guiding him to it.

"Why exactly are you still following me around?"

Raine lovingly packs his violin away. "This place is boring and lonely as fuck. I'm the only one taking music classes, so the teacher doesn't even turn up, meaning it's always deserted."

"You just want company? Is that it?" I laugh.

"I've had worse company than you."

"Oh, thanks. You do compliment me."

Clicking the case shut, he unfolds his guide stick next. "You told me off for flirting last week. This is me keeping myself in check."

If I'd known that fooling around with Raine would lead to him stalking me like a lovesick puppy, I wouldn't have given in to temptation. Well, maybe. Hell, who am I kidding? I was done for the moment I saw those warm, butterscotch eyes.

We haven't kissed since, though. Part of me is terrified the attraction I felt was just the mania talking. I needed an outlet. A quick fix. Raine was there to provide that.

But a bigger part of me is scared that the feelings I have for him are real and can't be excused as some semi-psychotic fluke. That would be bad. Deadly, in fact.

"You hungry?" he asks.

"Nope."

"Cool. I'd rather avoid the cafeteria."

Come to think of it, I haven't seen his two bodyguards lurking around like usual. Lennox has made himself scarce since our tangle in the mud, and Xander is still being invisible. But I know his eyes are always on me.

"Trouble in paradise?"

"Something like that," he mumbles.

"I'm shocked. You're friends with such good men."

"Don't start, Rip." His voice is oddly defensive. "Shit is complicated."

I blow out a frustrated breath. "Don't I know it."

Clasping his violin case, he stretches out his guide stick to begin tapping a path to the exit. I automatically take his elbow, helping steer the way. He's a little unsteady, but for a drug addict, I'd say he's high-functioning.

I'm not sure when we fell into such a familiar routine. Somehow, trying to keep my distance has had the opposite effect. Raine refuses to let me go.

Out in the corridor, classes are breaking for lunch. It's chaos. Patients make a beeline for food or therapy, wrapped up in their own little worlds. I have to manoeuvre Raine through the crowd so he doesn't get clattered.

"It's like they're pretending they can't even see the stick," I complain. "I'm gonna fucking deck one of these idiots in a minute."

"Chill out, guava girl."

"You could get hurt!"

Raine's chuckle is smooth like honeyed whiskey. "It wasn't so long ago that you were the one threatening to hurt me."

"I haven't taken it off the table."

The sound of his gravelly laughter is a soothing balm to the soul. Nothing is over-complicated with Raine, despite the disaster zone that surrounds us.

When we're alone, we don't discuss the drugs I've sold him. Xander and Lennox. Harrowdean... None of it. Instead, it's just my paint palette and his soft, crooning violin strokes keeping me company.

Silence and companionship. A mutual understanding for the art of escapism. I hadn't realised how lonely my own coping mechanisms had become.

When someone shoves my shoulder and doesn't bother to apologise, my patience snaps.

"Let's get out of here."

"You wanna catch a flight to Paris?" Raine suggests sultrily. "Or perhaps Venice? Little romantic getaway?"

"Sure, *darling*. Let me just pack my suitcase and call the driver, shall I?"

"Don't forget the bottle of champagne." He sighs in a wistful manner. "I remember those days. My manager used to bring me a glass of Dom Perignon after every show I performed."

I almost trip over my own feet. "Your manager?"

"You thought I just played violin for my own benefit?"

Mouth closing, I feel like an idiot. It never occurred to me that his talent went beyond mere passion. Being incarcerated in a place like this doesn't exactly line up with some luxurious celebrity lifestyle.

"I played professionally for several years. Four world tours. Things exploded after I recovered from losing my vision. Everyone wants to see the blind violinist play, right?"

"I guess. How did you end up here then?"

Raine rakes his teeth over his bottom lip. "Not a pretty story. I'm an open book, but let's talk somewhere else."

"Come on. I know a place."

Tightening my grip on his arm, I guide him through the reception and out into the quad. There are a few people filtering around, taking wrapped sandwiches and juice boxes outside to enjoy the rare blast of winter sun.

We walk towards the gym—a large, cinderblock building in the uppermost corner of the institute. Most don't bother to look behind it, though.

There are several abandoned buildings across Harrowdean with day-to-day operations now taking place in the manor itself. Tucked far behind the gym, a thick tangle of bushes almost entirely covers a second, smaller building.

This one is part of the original architecture with ornate, shuttered windows, moss-covered pillars and cracked entrance steps. We have to wrestle through the brambles to see any of that though, slicing our hands on sharp thorns.

Raine curses several times as he struggles to navigate the path, attempting not to trip. I do my best to hold the worst of the roughage out of his way. Eventually, we emerge through the building's sarcophagus.

"Watch your step," I advise. "There are five."

Raine nods gratefully. "Are you taking me to a quiet corner to kill me? I can't hear anyone out here."

"Well, I don't want any witnesses."

"Aw, shit. I wish you'd told me. I could've gotten high one last time."

"You've had enough."

He sniffs. "Not for my own funeral, I haven't."

There's a rusted combination lock on the door, preventing any unruly patients from escaping inside to fuck or shoot up in privacy. Though I doubt anyone could ever find this place without knowing where it is.

After quickly inputting the combination, the lock slides off in my hand.

"Is there anything you don't know about Harrowdean?" Raine asks.

"Doubt it. I make it my business to know everyone else's business."

"Sounds exhausting."

Surprised, I chuckle. "Yeah, it is."

Stepping inside the building, the scents of mould and disuse wash over us. Nobody comes here. Not even the guards. Harrowdean's dark dealings take place elsewhere, but I've kept this bolthole on my radar for those days when privacy is needed.

"Smells delightful." Raine scrunches up his nose.

"The original institute was built in 1843. I found some dusty, old documents in the library last summer. It was an asylum for decades, then a rich kids' boarding school."

"Smells like this place hasn't been used since 1843. What the hell is here?"

"You'll see."

Feet creaking over rotten floorboards and smashed tiles, we creep through the shadows. On the right side of the building, vintage changing rooms lie behind rusty shower curtains and clinking brass hooks.

The left side of the building contains a cavernous room marked by signage pointing towards what once was a huge swimming pool. Now it's merely an empty, mouldy basin filled with discarded trash.

Anything the previous owners deemed worthless ended up in this concrete pit. Broken bed frames. Smashed chairs. Old, rotting books.

The first time I stumbled across this place, it was like discovering Atlantis. I felt more at home surrounded by destruction and decay than anywhere else.

Raine sniffs the air. "Chlorine?"

"You'd struggle to take a dip in this pool."

"Yeah, it's faint. How big was the pool?"

I steer him around a pile of collapsed bookshelves. "It's full size. No idea how long it's been empty for."

The ceiling is high and domed, peppered with small windows that have long since caved in or been smashed by extreme weather. Part of the roof is gone too. The wind whistles in, carrying a hint of winter sun into the murkiness.

On the other side of the empty swimming pool sit a couple of ripped, sagging armchairs I found while poking around. Sometimes, I escape here with my sketchbook and charcoals, needing the silence.

"Three steps in front of you," I direct him.

Poking the armchair with his guide stick, Raine strokes a hand over the ancient fabric. "Gotcha."

We both take seats facing the desolate pool house after Raine places his violin case and guide stick on the ground.

"What do you want to know?"

I twist in my armchair to face him. "How does a professional violinist end up somewhere like this?"

He snorts. "By being a total fuck-up?"

"Can't he get you out? Your... uh, manager?"

Mouth twisting into a grimace, his fingers tap out a staccato rhythm on the armrest. "He's the reason I'm here. The asshole sold it to me as a sweet deal."

"I mean... this is pretty sweet."

Raine's head moves on a swivel, his glasses-covered eyes casting around the swimming pool like he can actually see the opulence.

"Smells sweet to me."

"Don't complain about my choice of location for our first date."

"This is our first date?" He grins, waggling his eyebrows.

Smooth, Ripley.

"Back to the topic at hand." I shake my head, glad he can't see my embarrassment. "Why did your dickhead manager lock you up in a psych ward?"

He smothers his grin, straightening his posture. "Several trips through rehab failed. I kept messing up my shows, and my reputation was trashed. Calvin intervened. He sits on his ass and lives off my tidy salary now."

"Intervened... by getting you interred?"

"I mean, he acted like Priory Lane was some award-winning, state of the art shit. Far better than the hellish rehabs I'd spent years failing at. Stupid me thought this was my chance to get clean."

A beam of weak sunlight illuminates his face. The golden boy. Nimble fingers and perfect smiles. He's the full package, but beneath the act, Raine's just as broken as the rest of us. Perhaps even more so.

"When was your first trip to rehab?"

He smacks his lips together. "Fifteen, I think."

"Jesus. Really?"

"I grew up with addicts for parents. It wasn't hard to get curious about what they were snorting and shooting on a daily basis. The fear of drugs that most kids have was never instilled in me."

"They still alive? Your parents?"

"Apparently." Raine smooths back a loose strand of hair. "Haven't seen them since I lost my vision. They bailed real fast when I couldn't work and bring in money for them to snort anymore."

"Fucking hell."

"Yeah, they were shit. Tried to come crawling back when my music became popular. I told them I never wanted to see them again."

Working up the courage to dig deeper, I try to keep my voice light. Even though he said he's an open book, it still feels rude to ask. I've wanted to know what happened to him since the moment we met.

"You were eighteen when you lost your vision, right? What happened?"

He nods. "Dirty needles."

"You used to shoot up?"

"Yeah, until I developed Endophthalmitis. Left the infection untreated for too long. By the time I got to the hospital, the doctors could only do damage control. My retinas were destroyed by scarring."

My heart squeezes, picturing a younger, terrified version of him curled up in a hospital bed. Alone and exploited. Paying the price of shitty parenting and a lifetime of bad decisions. He deserved so much better.

"Christ, Raine."

Curling lashes frame his caramel-hued eyes. I don't know how he can imbue his gaze with such emotion when he lives in perpetual blackness, but it's there. Fear embroiled in curiosity. A hint of challenge coiled around his pinprick pupils.

"If I'd never picked up a needle, I would still have my vision." He folds the glasses then places them on his violin case. "I wouldn't be trapped here. My life… it could've been so different."

"I'm sorry," I reply with empathy.

"It's not so bad, I guess." Raine smirks in his typically confident way. "I'm in an abandoned pool house with a beautiful girl. My life could definitely be worse."

"You still have no idea what I look like."

He wiggles his fingers. "I got a good feel."

I snort in amusement. "Uh-huh."

"Besides, I've already told you what I find attractive. And it has nothing to do with the way you look."

A hot blush races across my cheeks. Compliments don't usually mean a damn thing to me. But from him, it feels genuine. He sees beyond what everyone else does. There's no bullshit or games.

"Now I feel like an even bigger asshole for dealing to you," I groan.

"Yeah. You're the worst."

"Raine!"

Belting out a laugh, he shakes his head. "It's not a big deal. Just a business transaction, right? Nothing more."

"Is that what I am?" I retort. "A business transaction?"

"You're a damn sight more than that. But we can separate business and pleasure."

Can we?

"I don't know when I've ever been more than a business transaction." Even to my own ears, my voice is pained. "Not even my uncle saw me as more than that when my parents died."

Raine fixes his attention on me. It's a different kind of active listening to when others pay attention. His chin is tucked down, left ear tilted in my direction as he thoughtfully strokes the blonde scruff on his face.

"You said they left… but I didn't know you were orphaned. I'm sorry."

"It's fine." I brush him off. "Shit happens."

"How old were you?"

"Dad died just before I turned eight. Then my mum passed almost a year later."

I sound weirdly detached, even to my own ears. Anyone would think that I don't mourn my parents, though that couldn't be further from the truth. But if I allow myself to think of Mum's tight, floral-scented hugs or Dad's terrible jokes, I couldn't bear to live.

We were normal. Picturesque, even. A modest, working-class family living in the British countryside. Mum worked in a nursery, and my dad owned a butcher shop in the local village. Our lives were quiet but perfect.

But isn't that always the case?

Tragedy strikes without impunity or mercy. It takes whatever victims it desires, regardless of who deserves it. If we could collectively line up every bad person in the world to assign them to lives full of evil instead, don't you think we'd all do it?

I'd sacrifice a million souls if it bought my parents' lives. Hell, I probably belong in that queue of sinners now myself. Lining up to be fed to the devil's jaws to buy another innocent life back. My parents wouldn't recognise me now if they were alive.

"Your uncle adopted you?" Raine drags me back to the present.

"Yeah, my mum's younger brother. They weren't very close though, so he kinda got lumped with me as my last living relative. I moved to London and was basically raised by his housekeeper."

"He's rich, then?" he guesses.

"Investment banker. Unmarried, no kids."

Seeming thoughtful, Raine nods as he catalogues this new information. I haven't shared this much with anyone since I met Holly. She was the only one I trusted enough to share my life with. I don't know why I'm doing it now.

"I started painting at a young age. I was lonely and needed an outlet, I guess. Set up a business to sell my art, and after a few years, I bought my own flat. I moved out the first chance I got."

"That must've been hard," Raine muses. "Going out on your own like that."

I shrug, forgetting he can't see the gesture. "Like you, I grew up fast. Just in a different way."

"How so?" His head tilts.

It's not lost on me that we come from opposite worlds. I had wealth and comfort, while Raine struggled in poverty, turning over every penny he earned to fund his parents' addiction. Two polar opposites.

But we still turned out the same. Trapped in the same broken system. Equally forgotten by society and discarded by those who are supposed to love us. Left to pick up the pieces and find our own makeshift families.

"Uncle Jonathan didn't like having a bipolar niece. Bad for his reputation. It was easier to get far away from him and fend for myself than deal with his disgust when I had a bad episode."

Cursing, Raine shakes his head. "What an asshole. You didn't choose to have this illness."

I pick at my nail bed. "He didn't see it that way. The burden he got stuck with suddenly became a far bigger job to look after than he banked on."

"You still talk to him?"

"Nah. Only once since I started my three years. I was desperate when I called him. He got me out of Priory Lane and transferred here instead."

"Birthdays? Christmas?" Raine pushes expectantly.

"That would require too much effort."

He looks pissed off on my behalf, but honestly, I don't feel anything anymore. Not even disappointment. I already lost my parents, and when I realised that Jonathan wouldn't replace them, I lowered my expectations.

Being alone is far easier that way.

I rely on myself, no one else.

"Rip," Raine whispers. "Come here."

"Hmm?"

Crooking his finger, he gestures for me to approach. As vulnerable as I should feel after revealing all that, a broken part of me wants his comfort. I want to feel arms around me. Warmth. Familiarity. It's been so long since anyone gave an actual shit about me.

Walking over to his armchair, I tentatively crawl onto his lap. Raine grips my hips, pulling me closer so I have to spread my legs either side of his waist to straddle him. My arms wind around his neck, bringing us flush together.

His freshly squeezed orange and sea salt scent infiltrates my nostrils. I greedily breathe it in. Everything about him is vibrant, fresh, alive. For someone who struggles to perceive the world and numbs himself to escape it, he burns so goddamn bright.

I rest my head on his firm chest, the sound of his steady heartbeat pounding in my ear. *Budum. Budum. Budum.* The sound is an anchor, holding me in the moment. I'm savouring the feel of being held so fucking tight, tears prickle my eyes.

"You act like nothing ever hurts you," he murmurs, tenderly brushing my cheek with his knuckles. "Being abandoned is easier to handle that way, right? When no one cares in the first place?"

Thick, bitter emotion clogs my throat. "I…"

"Don't pretend like it isn't true. I see you, Ripley Bennet. You're a fierce, terrifying spitfire, but beneath this untouchable act you've got going on, I know deep down there's someone who cares far too much."

"Only about those worthy of being cared about."

"So do I make the cut?" His chest vibrates beneath my ear.

"I'm scared, Raine," I admit in a tiny whisper. "I'm scared of caring about you. I'm scared of what that will mean. I'm scared of losing another person who matters to me."

"You wanna know what I'm scared of?"

I fist my fingers in the longer lengths of hair at the back of his head. "Yes."

"When I'm with you—listening to the flick of your paintbrush, mumbling to yourself, the way your breathing speeds up when you apply that last drop of paint—I feel so fucking alive."

His voice is so soft, it feels like a butterfly is dancing across my skin. I don't know whether to swat at the damn thing or cup it in my palms, keeping it safe and secure from a world determined to crush its wings.

"I've never found that feeling from a person before. That's what scares the shit out of me. But hell if I'm gonna let that fear take this chance away from me."

"Raine—"

"Don't tell me not to get attached, Rip, because it's already too late. I want to peel back these bullshit defences you've wrapped yourself in and get close enough to matter to you. I want that honour."

"Trust me, it isn't an honour. I'm nobody."

He moves me to sit upright, smoothing a hand over my loose curls. "You're somebody to me."

I lift my head, staring into his mesmerizing, sightless eyes. Letting the liquefied honey seep over me, thick and glutenous, until I'm trapped in a depthless pool and unable to tread water for a moment longer.

I'm drowning in Raine.

His confusingly fascinating contradictions.

His mutual search for meaning.

"I… feel alive around you too," I make myself admit. "More than I have in a long time. But I'm not ready for a commitment."

The corner of his mouth quirks, that goddamn confident smirk forever serving to drive me insane.

"I'm not asking for one. But does that mean we can't chase this feeling?"

"Of course not," I reply on a breath.

"Then run with it, Rip. I don't need a label."

Clumsily bringing his forehead to mine, his lips fumble. After he catches the corner of my mouth, I tilt my head enough to seal our lips together. Raine threads a hand in my hair to hold me still.

We kiss slowly, gently, meaningfully. A silent exchange. A promise. Both agreeing to drop the act around each other and run headfirst into the inevitable disaster that lies ahead of us.

He's chasing the high that no pill or needle could ever give him. I shouldn't want to be someone's drug, or even their escape, but I need this too. I want to be cared for. I want to fucking belong for once.

His tongue swipes against mine, velvet soft and exploratory. It's nothing like the violent lash of Lennox's kiss, attempting to punish me. I swiftly shove that psycho from my mind before I can contemplate the ethics of kissing Raine too.

Stroking the back of his head, I tease the strands of spun silk. The kiss intensifies. Growing deeper and more passionate, our teeth clash and lips smack together. He even tastes like sunshine.

The golden boy, but with a dark, fractured soul. Seeing past his playful pretence feels like a big deal. I shouldn't take it for granted.

Sliding a hand up my spine, he teases a path around my waist to find the swell of my left breast. Squeezing it over my oversized tee, his thumb strokes the hardened pebble pushing against my bra.

I press my chest into his hands, a whine crawling up my throat.

Everything aches. I want him to relieve the need that's built within me with each whispered touch between us over several weeks.

"Rip," he says throatily.

"Yes?" I moan into his lips.

"I need you so fucking badly, it's driving me insane. I'm not asking for exclusivity or whatever, but I don't just want to be one of your regrets."

Peeling his hands off me, I quickly stand. He looks panicked for a moment as my weight disappears from his lap, but the rustle of me sliding my sweats over my hips seems to reach him.

"I'd never regret you, Raine."

Uncaring of our surroundings, I push my panties down and let them join the puddle of fabric on the ground. Cold air kisses my thighs. I rush to retake my place in Raine's lap where denim brushes against my bare pussy.

Searching out my naked ass, he grabs a handful. "That's so hot."

Retaking his lips, I grind against him. Each brush of his jeans on my core is a painful tease, the rough fabric feeling amazing against my throbbing clit. I'm practically trembling with my desire to feel him.

"I need you too," I whisper. "I haven't needed anyone for a long time."

Circling my hips, his lips peck mine in a fervent beat. "It's okay to be vulnerable around me. You're safe."

One hand splayed across my pelvis, his hand dips between my legs to reach for my pussy. I arch my back, sighing against his lips when he finds my sensitive bundle of nerves. His thumb bears down on my clit in small, teasing circles.

I move my hips in time to his rotations. Each flick of his thumb is a tiny firework display deep inside my core, setting alight nerves that beg for more. Reaching for his wrist, I take control, encouraging him to ease a finger inside me.

"So impatient," he mumbles.

"Yes."

With his finger sliding inside me, that impatience only grows. All of the anger and infuriation that prevented me from being able to paint earlier comes rushing back. I'm so sick of feeling like I'm losing control.

I reach beneath my careful perch on his lap to find his waistband. His jeans button pops open, allowing me to push the flaps of fabric down and expose his tight, black boxer shorts. His stomach is hard and flat, marked by a hint of abs.

Curling his finger, Raine smiles at the needy moan I release. My urgency to feel him around me causes me to fumble with his boxers, desperate to release the steel sheath trapped inside. He lifts his ass high so I can nudge them down low enough.

Finally, his long, hard cock is revealed. It's generous in my hand, studded with thick veins that beg to be licked. Wrapping a hand around his shaft, I work it over, familiarising myself with his proportions.

"Fuck, Rip," Raine hisses.

"Be quiet."

He fights back a grin. "You've got it, boss."

I'm soaked just imagining his long length pressing inside me. I want to feel every inch with nothing between us. Thank God for contraceptive implants.

Raine slides a second digit into my slit as I spread the bead of precome over his cock's velvet head. Our surroundings don't hold me back. We're alone here with no cameras, guards or prying eyes. Nothing but the lost. The broken. The abandoned. We fit right in.

Placing a steadying hand on Raine's shoulder, I can't wait any longer. I clasp his wrist to ease his fingers from between my legs then position his cock at my entrance.

Every muscle is shaking in anticipation of the sweet, euphoric relief I'm chasing. Fortunately, Raine doesn't offer a single complaint at my dominance.

Pinned beneath me, he lets me hold him in place as I slowly, torturously sink down on his length. We both groan at the same time, the feeling of being joined washing over us.

I wouldn't normally have the presence of mind to care in these situations, but knowing he can't even see me as we share this moment, I feel a burst of fear.

"This okay?" I check.

"Fuck yes, beautiful girl." His throat rumbles with a growl. "You feel incredible wrapped around me."

Vindicated, I lift my hips and rise on his lap. The next downward thrust takes him deep into my cunt, my pleasure increasing with each steely inch. Raine returns his hands to my hips, tracking each move as I rise and fall at a successive pace.

Riding him feels so good. Knowing that he's surrendering himself to me, giving me the gift of his control and pleasure, intensifies the hunger already consuming me. The trust is staggering. More than any meaningless hook-up.

Hand slotting beneath my t-shirt, he cruises a path over my stomach and to my bra line. Raine tugs the cup aside to free my breast, his fingers finding my nipple and gently rolling it. The brief pinch sends electricity sparking up my spinal cord.

"You feel alive now?" I laugh breathlessly.

Raine squeezes my breast playfully. "Do you?"

A sudden upward thrust of his hips causes him to surge into me at a deep angle. I mewl loudly, gripping his shoulders so tight, I'm sure he'll have fingertip-sized bruises tomorrow.

"God, yes," I admit.

"That feeling right there is what I'm chasing."

And I get it. Lord, do I get it. This place is designed to strip you down, remove your free will and leave you with nothing but rules and regimen. It's where souls are sent to die. But this right here is fucking nirvana.

He begins to move in time with me, surging upwards to seek out that aching spot. Each time he nudges it, my vision fuzzes over, unable to withstand the relentless waves of pleasure he's battering into me.

A morbid part of me wonders how intense this must feel to him with all his remaining senses dialled to ten. Each stroke must be overwhelming. Fuzz-covered jaw clenched, I can see that he's fighting to hold on.

Burying my face in his orange-scented neck, I work myself on him, hunting for the release I know will finally quiet my mind. Even if only temporarily. My lips pucker against his smooth skin, and I can't resist biting down to leave a mark.

No one would dare touch what's mine. Not in this place. And right now, I don't give a fuck who knows it. I want to trap his sunshine inside my chest and allow it to thaw my soul. Even if it sucks the life out of him.

That's what love is, right?

A mutual agreement to destroy each other.

I'll give him the gift of feeling alive in return.

Moving upward, Raine's fingertips dance over my clavicles before rising to clasp my jaw. It's a tight, bruising clamp that allows him to pull my mouth back to his. I surrender to the hot swipe of his tongue.

Suddenly, a loud clatter causes us to break apart. Raine bands a protective arm around me, still sheathed deep inside.

"What is that?" he urges.

I frantically look around the room, sucking in a relieved breath to see it's just a crow, entering through a broken window to find a perch.

"Rip?"

"Bird," I moan. "Don't stop."

"I wouldn't dare."

When he sucks my bottom lip into his mouth and bites down, the burst of pain throws me straight back into my upward climb. I'm getting closer to the edge. That tight, taut feeling inside me is getting stronger.

"Come on, babe," he coaxes into my ear, causing chills to stipple my skin. "I want to feel you come for me."

"Raine," I whimper.

"Let go. I promise I'll catch you."

Eyes squeezed shut, I follow that coiled thread. Deeper. Darker. It's a poised spring in my centre, waiting for the chance to snap. Mouth still locked on mine, Raine's thumb resumes its assault on my clit.

I'm done for.

I feel myself clamp tight around him. I'm exploding, thrown into the abyss and swallowed whole by ecstasy. He groans as he joins me in falling apart, his cock jerking inside me with each hot burst of his release.

Still moving on him, I drag out every second. I'm greedy. I don't want this moment to end. The raw satisfaction of warmth spreading between us is too damn good.

My limbs slowly turn to liquid. With a final sigh, I slump onto his chest. Raine braces me against him, stroking up and down my t-shirt clad back. His face buries in my hair, inhaling sharply.

Snuggled into him, we don't speak for a long time. Words would only burst our safe, temporary bubble. Even surrounded by junk, we're at peace. We can pretend like the rest of the institute doesn't exist.

I can't bring myself to consider the consequences of what we've done. The path to ruin I've set us upon. This man is best friends with the assholes I've vowed to destroy. And here I am, screwing him. A lot.

I'm fucked.

Utterly, utterly fucked.

My scalp prickles. Subtly looking around the room, I search for a pair of eyes. Nothing. But I know he's here, just like every other day I've felt him skulking. Xander's mastered the art of the silent prowl.

I'm surprised it took him this long to find us. He's never far away. While he doesn't feel the need to speak to me right now, he's made his presence known over the past couple of weeks. I want to ignore him, but I hate the thought of him seeing me exposed like this.

"Come on." I nudge Raine. "We need to go."

He groans in protest. "Don't wanna."

"Move it."

Before I can clamber off him and deal with our mess, Raine tries to grab my arm. He narrowly misses and swears, seizing a handful of my t-shirt instead.

"Rip." The note of vulnerability in his voice is unmistakable. "I don't care if we're friends or whatever you want to call it, but don't shut me out like everyone else."

"You don't need me, Raine."

"I do. You make me feel less alone."

Any signs of his swagger and confidence are non-existent. Deep down, Raine is petrified of being left alone in his own head. He'll pop, snort or cling to anything that offers a reprieve from the loneliness.

But I can't be his life raft.

Not when I'm drowning too.

CHAPTER 14
XANDER
N/A – BRING ME THE HORIZON

BRIGHT, *clinical lights sear my eyeballs. The screech of incessant white noise rages on, hour after hour, never once offering a reprieve. The pain in my skull has dulled to a low ache. I wonder, distantly, if my brain has finally liquified.*

Cold water submersion didn't work. Beatings didn't work. Psychological torture didn't work. Isolation didn't work. Now the clinicians have resorted to over-stimulation on all fronts. It's impossible to rest with the ceaseless light and sound in the cell.

They want us to break.
Bend.
Reform.

It's rare that I see Lennox now. At first, we were held side by side. As if seeing the other in pain would somehow ignite the process. When that failed, they soon split us apart, each assigned to our own personal cell in the Z wing.

I've seen others. Ghosts. Skeletal and pale-skinned, their eyes stripped of all human awareness. That's the whole point. They don't want traumatised patients; they want mindless machines. The Z wing's true purpose is to create exactly that.

Vessels for the rich. Malleable and capable of inflicting whatever force is required to further their buyer's aims. Murder. Extortion. Torture. Anything deemed too dirty for the spotless hands of the powerful one percent.

But power isn't free.
Not in this world.

After months of wondering why the corporation that owns six private institutes across the country would risk everything by engaging in such horrific abuse, I understand. These aren't treatment facilities. That's just a cover story.

They're factories.

Manufacturers of machines.

We were always bought and paid for. The moment we signed ourselves over to the rehabilitative program, accepting a three-year sentence to avoid something worse, our souls were marked for exploitation.

Not everyone is admitted to the Z wing. Hell, most patients don't know it exists. Evil always lurks in the periphery. Formless and invisible until the secrets finally break open and the truth comes spilling out.

Will we live long enough to see that day?

I took this sentence with the same nonchalance I had while embezzling disgusting sums of money from the rich and stupid all from behind a computer screen. Child's play. I didn't even want their cash.

I just wanted to make them hurt for the entertainment value.

Own their cash, and I owned them.

The lawyers thought they were doing me a favour when they rolled out my so-called 'traumatic childhood' and personality disorder diagnosis to argue against decades of jail time. They offered up Priory Lane like some goddamn wonderland.

When the screeching white noise abruptly shuts off, it takes several moments for it to even register. My ears are ringing so violently. I don't bother shifting from my curled-up ball on the cold floor. They can drag me to whatever they have planned next for all I care.

The cell door swings open, emitting my favourite sadist, Doctor Farnsworth. He's an old, ugly son of a bitch. Only this time, he isn't alone. I don't recognise the other elderly, silver-haired man practically dripping with wealth and self-importance.

"This is one of our troublemakers." Doctor Farnsworth gestures towards me like I'm a plant that refuses to grow. "No progress despite following our usual methods."

The second old bastard casts a critical eye over me. "We haven't had one this stubborn since Patient Seven in Blackwood. He was a tough nut to crack."

"Unfortunately, sir, there are no signs of cracking here. I believe this subject has an extreme tolerance to our physical and psychological methods. His history is already extensive."

If I could move a muscle, I'd laugh. These assholes don't scare me. They haven't quite clocked the extent of my indifference yet. Their pain is no motivator. I cherish it. Lavish in it. The agony is a warm, soft blanket that will never compare to the horrors I've already survived.

Pain is my fascination. Other people's suffering. Fuck, even my own. For years, I *carved pieces off myself, layering scar upon scar to see how much blood it would take for me to break. When that failed, my attention shifted to the agony of others instead.*

"Cease all activities with this one."

"But, Sir Bancroft—"

"We've wasted enough resources." Old Bastard looks thoughtful, his wrinkled mouth pulled taut.

"Should we dispose of him?" Doctor Farnsworth asks.

"That would be wasteful. I can think of far better uses for such promising resilience. It is rare these days. Your last stooge met an unfortunate end, isn't that so?"

"Yes, sir. This one and his friend saw to it."

"Then allow them to clean up the mess they made. Make him your stooge along with the other one." Bancroft approaches then crouches down to address me. *"Do you want out of this cell, son?"*

I summon the energy to barely nod.

"You know the price for defying us now. Your freedom isn't free."

With a final lingering look, he straightens.

"You work for Incendia Corporation now."

I don't wake up screaming like most who suffer with night terrors. It's more like lucid dreaming. I'm often aware that the hell I'm trapped in isn't real, but that doesn't make the memories any less horrifying.

Sitting upright in the twin bed, soaked covers pool around my waist, letting cold air lash against my bare, sweat-slick chest. A shiver threatens to wrack over me as I cool down. Lennox is snoring his head off in the adjacent bed—unperturbed, as usual.

We had the luxury of separate rooms in Priory Lane. Being in close quarters isn't my favourite thing. I like silence. Invisibility. Some of my best work is done in the shadows, far from the distraction of those with more morals.

Your freedom isn't free.

I didn't give a fuck what price I had to pay. I would've done the damn job for free. Bargaining our release from the Z wing was a mere bonus.

Rising from the bed, my steps are light and barely audible. Lennox doesn't stir as I shut myself in the small, attached bathroom and set the shower to cold. Funny how the mind craves what once traumatised it.

Ice-cold water sluices over my body. Goosebumps dapple across scar-striped skin. Most of the marks are white and shiny, softened by time. It's been several years since I took a blade to my own skin.

The thin stripes of raised tissue cover both arms up to my biceps. When I ran out of room, I moved to my stomach, then thighs. Once every inch had been tested, I grew tired of my own pain and looked elsewhere.

Then the real fun began.

By the time I've imprisoned the dreams back in their mental confines, Lennox is sitting upright in bed. I tuck a towel around my hips and comb a hand through my wet, snow-white hair.

"Another dream?" he asks.

I hum noncommittally.

"What was it this time?"

Ignoring him, I rifle through the cupboard tucked into the corner of the room that houses my selection of polo shirts and jeans.

"Xan. Don't shut me out."

"There's nothing to discuss."

"Has it been like this every night since we got out?" Lennox presses despite my clipped tone. "If I had known—"

"What, Nox?" I whirl to face him. "What could you have possibly done?"

Lennox dealt with what we went through differently. His survival was out of sheer stubborn will and rage. Nothing can break a man who has already lost his whole world. He quickly bounced back once we were released.

He sighs, though it lacks his usual anger. "I should've burned that goddamn place to the ground when I had the chance."

"That's your solution to everything," I point out.

"Do you have to be such an asshole?"

Admittedly, that was a low blow. Lennox's history is a matter of public record. First-degree murder has a way of making the news, especially the cases involving petrol and a well-aimed match.

It's what impressed me so much in the first place. His vengeance wasn't quiet or dignified. He didn't even care that he got caught. All Lennox wanted was to snuff out the life that killed his sister.

"Whatever." He lays back down then angrily stuffs his pillow. "Go skulk around somewhere and leave me alone."

Quickly getting dressed, I don't spare him another look, let alone an apology. He should know better than to expect that from me. Grabbing my ID, I slip out of the bedroom and head downstairs.

It's early enough to beat the morning rush. We've been taking mathematics classes together, much like we did during our last incarceration. Numbers were an easy choice for me. Simple and mind-numbing, allowing me to continue plotting in the background.

When I met Lennox, he didn't give a fuck about anyone or anything. It was sheer chance that landed us in the same class together in Priory Lane. I'm not sure what he saw in me that made him latch on so tight.

I'm queuing for a breakfast tray when I catch the first rumblings. The handful of early risers in the line are whispering amongst themselves, and it's easy to tune in to their low conversation.

"You hear about some riot over the weekend?"

"I heard there were fatalities."

"Where?" someone replies.

"Blackwood, apparently. The patients escaped then practically destroyed the place on the way out. I've got a friend on the outside. He said it's all over the news."

"Are they on the run now?" another voice chimes in. "The people who escaped."

"I guess so. This fancy private security company is investigating. Not the patients—the institute."

"Blackwood is under investigation?"

"That's what I hear. They've been doing messed-up shit to their patients."

Sounds like Priory Lane was only the first to fall. Investigations come and go, but usually, nothing ever sticks. That's what money can buy. Complete and utter impunity. But a riot is far harder to cover up, and it seems to have loosened a few tongues too.

"You think that's why they've stepped up security here?" a female patient wonders. "If a breakout happened at Blackwood, it could happen here."

"Yeah, dream on."

"I'm serious!"

Tuning them back out, I stifle an eye roll. They're all so desperate to escape. And for what? Like the outside world will offer them anything more than rejection and disgust. None of us can ever go back to our former lives.

Especially me. I don't even have a life to return to. My existence was a solitary one, and at least in here, there's plenty of fresh meat for my machinations. Endless targets. Curiosities. And the one victim I can't seem to take my eyes off.

Ripley's routine is loosely set. Her moods rise and fall like the tide, and with it, her day-to-day activities. It's taken me a few weeks of careful observation to familiarise myself with her habits.

One of those habits was an eyebrow raiser. I doubt Lennox has clocked that his adopted stray is fucking the girl he loathes. Raine has been a little distant, but given his new Velcro-attachment to Ripley, it isn't surprising.

Right on time, she stalks into the cafeteria. Today, her loose, tawny curls are pinned back by a crisscrossed pair of paintbrushes, leaving those fierce, mottled brown and green eyes to take centre stage.

They'd look better filled with tears.

I can still remember the magnificent sight.

Absently fiddling with the silver ring slotted into her septum, she pauses to snag an apple and shove it into her pocket. The sweats she wears are ripped and paint stained. Apparently, she couldn't care less about her appearance or what anyone thinks.

It's one of the things that makes her so enticing. Previously, I would've gone for the weak, insecure ones. Their fear always tasted the sweetest. But getting Ripley to break with her newfound backbone is a far sweeter challenge.

I follow her out, my breakfast long abandoned. Rather than heading for her scheduled therapy session, she stops outside, where the early signs of spring are beginning to reveal themselves.

Ripley pauses at a picnic bench occupied by that sullen, auburn-haired girl she's often with. Something exchanges between them. The glint of blades, I think. Leaning against the exterior wall, I can just hear them.

"Make these last a bit longer this time?"

The girl shrugs. "You know I'm good for it."

"That's not the point, Rae."

"You going soft on me? What's with the sour face?"

I watch Ripley's hands fist. How interesting. She usually wields her authority with complete detachment. It's enough to make me proud. But right there is a hint, a mere snippet of a different reality within.

The prospect is intriguing. I can work with that. The more I watch her, the more I uncover the chinks in her armour. It's why I'm doing my due diligence. This time, when I ensnare my little toy, I have no intention of her walking away after.

"Just... Fuck, Rae. Whatever. Forget it."

"Rip!"

But Ripley is already storming away, her lips clenched tight. Fascinating. I could stay and torment her frowning friend—she seems practically begging for an excuse to splinter apart—but Ripley has my sole attention.

I follow her, tucked out of sight as she scales a small staircase in the west wing, above the therapy rooms. She's detouring from her schedule. My intrigue spirals. With her all-access pass, obstacles like the locked, staff-only doors are no issue.

Lunging through each door before it can click shut, I follow her ascension to the top floor then prop a shoulder against the wall, hanging back in an empty corridor.

Ripley punches in a short, six-digit code on the door's keypad. I let her go ahead, the numbers already committed to memory. Though it will be disappointing if she's resolved to toss her pretty ass off the building before the fun has begun.

When enough time has passed, I tap in the code, finding a narrow service staircase on the other side. Cool morning air beckons me upwards, a silent footstep at a time, until I emerge on the manor's rooftop.

"Took you long enough."

Ripley's voice is flat, resigned.

I step out of the shadows. "Secret hiding place?"

"More like testing how far you'd be willing to follow me. How many more weeks are you going to keep up the stalking for?"

"I prefer the term enthusiastic observation."

The rooftop is slanted on either side with a flat strip down the centre. She's tiptoed her way down that platform to find a safe perch, her legs hanging over the edge to rest against slatted roof tiles.

"I prefer the term fucking sociopath." She flashes me a cold look.

I click my tongue, sensing that I should be offended, if I were capable of feeling such emotion. Enough psychiatrists have explained the difference to me.

"Sociopaths are violent, impulsive creatures with no self-control," I point out, leaning against the wall before shoving my hands in my pockets. "I'd prefer not to be compared to such recklessness."

Ripley's lips purse. "Are you giving me a psychology lesson?"

"If you're going to insult me, then at least use the accurate term."

"You're right," she scoffs. "You are a fucking psychopath."

"Much better."

Her shoulders stiffen at my slow approach. From up here, we have a limitless view of the surrounding woodland. Nothing but trees, rolling hills and the winding road that services the institute.

"Now that we've cleared that up." I crouch down next to her, my head tilted. "Let's discuss your little excursion with our friend, Raine."

"You're real sick for watching, you know?"

"There's an argument to be made for you continuing despite knowing I was there."

"I only realised afterwards," she spits back. "Why are you following me?"

I summon a loose shrug.

"This isn't like before, Xander. Whatever you're hoping to achieve with these mind games, it isn't going to work."

My, what a sharp tongue.

"There was a time when you quivered at the sight of me," I muse aloud. "Whatever happened to that scared little mouse?"

"She grew teeth and learned how to bite back."

Smiling, I slowly reach out to trail a single fingertip down her cheek. I'd forgotten the fascinating pattern of light freckles that blemish her skin. Each mark detailing its own tale. Ripley's jaw clenches tight.

"Do. Not. Touch. Me."

"Or?"

Her head turns, pinning two livid eyes on me. "Or this time, I really will kill you."

"Oh, dearest Ripley." I lean close to breathe her familiar, oil paint scent in. "I'd like to see you try."

Brushing the back of my knuckles along her silky-soft cheek, I watch each micro-expression. Nostrils flaring. Muscles locking. Eyes narrowing. Although her mind repels me, her body remembers our time together.

The sad, abandoned child. Desperate for love and attention, even as she cuts the world off with walls thrown so high, she thinks no one will ever dare climb them.

But I did.

She willingly shredded herself for the pleasure of my touch. The relief I drove her to the edge of insanity to achieve did not come easily.

Only once I'd conditioned her body to the extremes of ecstasy earned through pain.

"Xander," she breathes out.

"Hmm?"

Fingers sliding down to her lips, I stroke the chapped swell. She's been biting her bottom lip again. I've seen her do it when she's anxious or overwhelmed. How very telling. The infallible image displays a few more cracks.

"Get the fuck away from me." Her voice is strained, telling me she's forcing this attempt at showing strength.

If only her cowering clique could see her now. The way she trembles with each minuscule touch, her breathing becoming shallow, knuckles slowly turning white. I've seen her bravado around Lennox.

But not with me.

My scared little toy is still in there.

"There's nowhere in this world you can hide from me," I warn in a low tone. "Not even your little party trick in Priory Lane got rid of me."

Pushing my thumb past her open lips, I brush the pad against her soft, wet tongue. She shudders, her eyes smouldering, caught somewhere between defeat and hatred. I don't mind either. But her fight is what I really want.

"Did you think all this power would protect you?" I push my thumb deeper into her mouth. "That I wouldn't come back for what I'm owed?"

The shift is instantaneous. Her gaze sharpens as her teeth suddenly clamp down on my thumb. Biting hard, she waits for the yelp that never comes. Instead, I force her teeth apart again by shoving my index finger into her mouth for good measure.

"Nice try."

With droplets of saliva trailing down her chin, I push deeper into her mouth until my index finger is touching her throat. She gags a little, those smouldering eyes now covered in a wet sheen.

My other hand circles her neck, finding a loose grip. I squeeze incrementally, feeling for the erratic pulse of her jugular vein, pumping fear in the form of spillable blood. All it would take is one precise slash.

But what would be the fun in that?

We have plenty of time.

"Tell me, did you fuck him to prove a point?"

Her eyes widen, followed by an almost imperceptible shake of her head.

"Has the self-proclaimed Queen of Harrowdean gone and caught *feelings*?" I speak the word distastefully. "How predictable."

I can only imagine how much she'll plead when my cock's in her throat instead. Nothing compares to the thrill of tasting her inner conflict. Desiring humiliation when she demands compliance from the rest of the world.

Tightening my grip, I can almost feel the struggling flow of oxygen attempting to penetrate her trachea. What I wouldn't give to have her limbs tied and spreadeagled for me right now so that I can do as I please.

I'd tarnish each inch of her body. She bruises so beautifully. Perhaps bloody the rest. Carve my mark into her delicate flesh in case she ever forgets her place again. When the pain becomes unbearable, I'd make that sweet cunt sing.

Sliding my fingers from her mouth, I smear her own saliva over her lips. A single, defiant tear has escaped and rolls down her cheek to join the silvery smear. Capturing it, I bring the salty droplet to my tongue. I'd bottle it if I could.

"I don't want your throne anymore." I shake my head. "Instead I want the satisfaction of breaking this body and owning every single move you make while you sit atop your empire."

She'll own the world.

And I'll own her.

My hand loosens enough to grant her several deep gulps. She sucks in air, frenzied and desperate. When she speaks, her voice is a raw rasp.

"You will never, ever control me."

Vision going red, I release her throat to roughly grab the swell of her right breast. Her tits are as pert and shapely as I remember, the soft mound filling my palm.

"Then what is this if not control?" I counter. "Look at these hard buds threatening to break free."

I seize the sharp nipple poking my palm through the thin material of her t-shirt. Generous without being too big, her breasts can get away with no support beneath the baggy shirts she insists on wearing.

She whimpers when I twist, her tongue sneaking out to swipe her lips. "Please…"

"Yes, little toy? Please?"

Waiting for the next words to pass her lips, I'm hanging on a deadly precipice.

"Please… tell me." Her lips curl into a small, defiant smile. "Who hurt you so badly that you have to harm the rest of us to feel even remotely in control?"

It's a sharp slap to the senses. A bucket of frigid water. I feel my lips thin, the mental bars slamming into place and concrete walls hastily rising to hold back any weakness she may sense.

"Better yet… was his name Daddy?" Ripley gibes.

My mouth goes desert dry.

Her smile expands. "Gotcha."

Before I can attack, she seizes her advantage. Ripley throws her arms around my neck and flings her entire body to one side. I'm carried with her, rolling and twisting, down the side of the roof.

Jagged tiles slice into my back and sides, but I can't find purchase to break our tumble. She doesn't care that she's risking her own life to end mine. Ripley's arms remain resolutely locked around my neck.

The world is a blur. Trees, sky, an approaching ledge. It's all a dizzying muddle. Crying out, Ripley abruptly releases me and throws out her limbs. We reach the industrial-strength gutter at the same time.

Falling.

Thin air.

Biting panic.

Pain slices into my fingers as I catch the edge of the gutter before it's too late. My hold breaks, but I quickly recapture the thick metal and hold on for dear life. My entire body is hanging on the verge of a fifty-foot drop.

Is this what fear tastes like?

Head whipping from side to side, it takes a moment to register that Ripley isn't hanging with me. The image of her splattered brains several stories beneath me is a mental assault. Then her voice reaches me.

"What is this if not control?" she taunts.

The bitch is sprawled a few feet above me, her fall halted by an upturned roof tile. Panting and wild-eyed, she shifts to a safer position, preventing herself from slipping towards me.

Ripley eyes my precarious hold from her safe perch. "Falling from that height… you'd be dead on impact, I'd imagine."

"Help me!" I shout.

She huffs out a cold laugh. "Help? Oh, Xander. I didn't know you had a sense of humour."

Arms burning fiercely, I have to watch as she finds her feet then starts a slow crab-crawl back up the sloped roof. Never once looking back to see if I'm still fucking dangling.

"Get back here!"

Her laughter echoes. "The almighty Xander Beck doesn't need my help."

"Ripley!" I bellow.

It doesn't stop her from leapfrogging back onto the central platform and strolling away like she just deposited a parcel at the damn post office. The sound of the exterior door slamming matches my ragged breathing.

Fucking perfect.

CHAPTER 15
RIPLEY

.INTOODEEP. – DEAD POET SOCIETY

I CAST an apprehensive eye around the deserted loading bay. I'm in my usual spot behind the back of an abandoned storage building, one of many scattered across Harrowdean's estate. All off-limits, of course.

Elon is late. Every Wednesday morning, we have a standing appointment. He delivers the shit I've ordered, then I peddle it to the poor fucks paying top dollar for their personal vices. It's clockwork. He's never late.

Sighing, I study the rough gravel surrounding the dock. Sleep has been rough going. Given recent disturbances, the guards have taken to performing hourly checks. Our doors are thrown open, lights blazing and covers ripped back.

It's just another psychological game. Another tactic. Any way they can dehumanise us further. The ones brave enough to oppose the recent crackdown are being singled out and targeted. Pull a stick out of a bundle, and it's easier to break, right?

Rumours have been swirling for days about what's happening beyond Harrowdean's walls. Our internet access is meagre, but they can't silence word of mouth. And everyone's abuzz about Blackwood.

The escaped patients haven't been caught. More and more fatalities are being confirmed with each passing day too. I heard from someone that bodies are being pulled out of the institute's ruins by authorities every hour.

Some shit definitely went down. No one knows exactly what, but we will all feel the repercussions if the situation escalates. Secrecy and subterfuge have kept this program intact for decades, and Harrowdean is no friend to the spotlight.

Finally, the crunch of footsteps approaches. I look over my shoulder in time to see Elon arrive, his backpack slung over his shoulder. He glances at the CCTV camera—switched off, naturally—before pinning his sour gaze on me.

"You're late," I call out.

He scowls. "You adhere to my schedule, inmate. I'm not your fucking lapdog."

"Sure. I have nothing better to do than sit here and wait for you."

Stopping at the edge of the dock, he dumps the backpack. "I am in no mood for your lip today."

Tempted to poke the bear a little more, I decide to relent. The last thing I want is to pack myself off to solitary again. With the mood management's been in of late, I doubt it'll be a fun experience.

After surrendering this week's cash, I unzip the backpack and take a cursory glance. It's half-empty. Only a few baggies of the usuals, but none of this week's special requests. Glancing up, I find Elon even more stony-faced than usual, his grey eyes lit with frustration.

"You're also light."

"Deal with it," he snaps.

"Letting customers down is bad for business. I have orders to fulfil."

"You think I give a shit?"

Biting my tongue, I rifle through everything, mentally taking stock. This is barely half of the list. I'm going to have a lot of pissed-off patients on my case if I rock up with this load to sell.

"What gives?" I glance at him.

Elon rubs a hand over his cropped hair. "We're being closely monitored. I have to be cautious."

"This got something to do with Blackwood?"

Shutters immediately fall over his expression. "Why do you ask?"

"Come on. Everyone knows what's happening."

"You don't know shit, inmate."

"Who the hell died?" I gesture towards the backpack. "Because this haul is pathetic."

"The fucking warden did!" he erupts.

Not expecting an honest answer, I reel back. The gossip I've heard made it sound like unsuspecting patients lost their lives in whatever chaos engulfed Harrowdean's sister branch. Not the bloody warden.

"You're... serious?"

"The entire corporation is under investigation by some fancy assholes from London. All our asses are on the line."

Holy. Freaking. Shit.

Mind spinning, I try to pin down the ramifications, but I can't wrap my head around them. How does the perfect business model go so horribly wrong? What kind of courage did it take for patients to take down Blackwood?

"I still need the rest of the items on my list. I have requests to fulfil."

Towering over me, Elon's face is a stormy landscape. "Just go out there, do your job and keep your mouth shut. This place is a powder keg. You really wanna be striking that match?"

"Maybe," I retort without thinking.

He grimaces. "If this shit explodes, we're all going down with it. You think everyone will just forgive and forget what you've done here?"

"I... I haven't—"

"Sold drugs? Needles? Knives?" Elon laughs coldly. "How about you tell me why a patient was spotted dangling off the goddamn roof the other morning?"

I duck my gaze. "Not a clue."

"Your pass was used to unlock the doors. I checked."

"Nothing to do with me."

He snorts derisively. "I hear the bastard hauled himself up. Did you even care to check he hadn't crashed to the ground below?"

I didn't care to or need to. If Xander had fallen to his death and splatted like a broken egg, it would've been big news. And let's face it, I'm not that fucking lucky. The son of a bitch isn't that easy to kill.

"You were warned," Elon continues. "One more slip-up, and it's night-night for Ripley. You're on thin ice."

"Then it's a good thing he's alive, isn't it?"

Done with this pointless conversation, I occupy myself by picking up the backpack and slinging it over my shoulder. The rooftop showdown was reckless, but the psychopath needed a warning. These silent mind games have to stop.

"It doesn't matter who you're related to." Elon turns, calling over his shoulder. "You're evidence. They'll dispose of you like the rest of the problems that disappear in here."

I watch him swagger off with a lead weight curling in my stomach. Less than a year. That's all I've got left. I'll soon be free to return to my life. I have to survive that long.

But what if it's true?

What if this crumbling system is going to bury me too?

One hand gripping the strap, I suddenly feel like I'm being crushed by the insubstantial weight of drugs slung over my shoulder. A few handfuls feels like several kilos. I couldn't begin to guess how much I've sold since transferring.

How many overdoses is that?

How many deaths?

All written off as the price of business. Justified. Filed away in the jam-packed drawers I keep in the darkest recesses of my mind. I locked those drawers then set them alight for good measure.

Looking over my shoulder, I check the loading bay one last time. Still empty. Yet it feels like something is snapping at my heels. And I'm not talking about Xander. This is something invisible. Perhaps it's not even real. But it's catching up to me nonetheless.

I walk fast, a painfully tight grip on the backpack. It's still early for deliveries, but the sooner I can offload this shit and hide from the inevitable disgruntlement of those who will go without, the better.

Finding my usual CCTV blind spot, I rest against the tree's thick trunk and place the backpack at my feet after removing what I need to add to Noah's stock. It's taken several weeks to build a decent pile.

I'm deep in thought and attempting to calm myself when the *tap, tap, tap* of Raine's approach startles me. He's wearing different jeans today, these ones boasting a rip in the left knee that adds to his edgy vibe.

"Different shampoo?" he offers in greeting.

Weirdo.

"It's Rae's. I'm out."

Nodding, he continues towards me. "Just don't change the papaya body wash. I'll never be able to find you."

"Good to know. I may need to disappear sometime soon."

I try for a joke, but the words come out all wrong. Raine's blonde brows knit together as he reaches for me, snagging my t-shirt's hem then moving higher to touch my arm.

"What's wrong?"

"Shit's going down." I drop my voice. "I'm missing half my stock, and all the rumours that have been circulating are true."

"About that riot?"

"Yeah. People are dead."

Raine curses softly. "That's fucked up."

"It's gonna blow back on Harrowdean soon. Sounds like authorities are involved."

Humming, he releases me then rolls his guide stick between his hands. "Isn't that a good thing? The world may actually pay attention to the bullshit that's under the radar for once."

How do I tell him that my neck is on the chopping block too? Raine knows what I do. Hell, he buys from me on a weekly basis now. But that doesn't mean I want to spell it out for him.

"It'll be alright, Rip." He tries to comfort me. "No matter what happens."

"You don't know that."

"Worst case scenario, all the institutes are shut down. We can get the fuck out of here."

"And go where? Somewhere worse?"

"I was thinking somewhere far away from any psych ward or rehab centre. Hell, the fucking wilderness if that's what it takes."

Just the thought of him managing in the damn wilderness causes laughter to burst out of me. Raine quickly catches on to my line of thought and joins in.

"Okay, perhaps not a jungle. I need good ground clearance. There's nothing to trip over on a beach though, right?"

"You're ridiculous. We're not going anywhere."

His shoulders slump. "You are. I've got two more years of this."

My chest spasms at his palpable defeat. His assumption that me getting out first would be an issue is both heart-warming and petrifying. Criminal or not, everyone signs up for the same three years just to get accepted into Harrowdean's rehabilitative program.

Raine must sense my unease because he quickly drops the subject. "What are you gonna do with this lot, then? You can't fulfil half their orders and half not."

"Shift what I can, then haul ass. People will be mad."

"It's not your fault everything's going to shit."

"But I can't exactly tell them that, can I? I have appearances to maintain."

Catching sight of Luka lingering nearby, early like normal, I beckon him over. Raine remains silent as we exchange pills and payment. He shuffles off to gobble his laxatives, and I quickly re-zip the backpack.

"What will you do once you get out?"

Raine fiddles with the nylon strap attached to his stick. "Not a clue."

"You have a career waiting for you."

"Pretty sure I drove it off a cliff long before I wound up here. I honestly don't know what's waiting for me now."

I bite back what I want to say. *I will be.* I've known him for little more than a few months and spoken to him for less than that. I don't know what's waiting for me either, and I won't make promises I can't keep.

"Maybe you'll need some kind of musician in residence at your studio," he suggests with a smirk. "Free performances for the lady."

"If I go back."

"Where else would you go?" he asks.

I close my eyes, giving myself a brief moment to dream. "Somewhere no one knows my name."

"You want a fresh start."

"I want to forget."

He tilts his head back to rest on the tree. "Does this forgetting plan include erasing me? Your maybe platonic, maybe not, casual hook-up?"

Hesitating, I weigh my response. We haven't discussed what this is. There's no formal label and no need to assign one. But I've long since discovered that Raine's confidence conceals bone-deep insecurities. I won't hurt him with a lie.

"I doubt I could if I tried."

"I can't figure out if you're happy or mad about that," he admits. "But I'll take it."

"Things aren't so black and white, Raine. You know that. I'm glad you're here. Isn't that enough?"

"It'll always be enough, guava girl. I just…" He trails off with a sigh. "I just wanna know if this means something to you too."

Turning to face him, I ball the fabric of his shirt in my hand and pull him close. The cool surface of his blacked-out lenses touches my face as my lips peck his.

I'm shitty at this emotional stuff. Any ability I had to be vulnerable was long ago wiped out. But with Raine, when the jokes fall flat and we both turn serious, I want to try. I know he needs that reassurance.

Maybe I do too.

We're both just afraid.

"This means something to me," I murmur.

"Entertainment?"

"Well, I wouldn't want to blow smoke up your ass. But you were pretty good."

He guffaws. "You weren't so bad yourself."

The tension broken, I toy with his t-shirt.

"So... round two?"

"Aren't you working?"

"Self-employed," I joke.

"Well, fuck. Little Miss Entrepreneur. Anyone ever tell you how sexy that is?"

"Surprisingly not."

Several raised voices interrupt our banter. I cast a subtle glance over my shoulder and groan. Rick and a handful of his friends are wandering closer, exchanging heated, angry whispers. Yeah, no thanks.

"Come on." I release Raine and grab the backpack. "We've got company."

He cocks his head slightly. "Is it that asshole?"

"Rick. Five others too."

His hand clenches tight around mine as soon as I seize it. Raine's stick swings from side to side, but he lets me steer our path away from my delivery point and deeper into the institute's grounds.

At this hour, most patients are in classes, therapy or sleeping. Guards are peppered around, though. I try to ignore the prickle of unease I feel as Rick and his entourage remain on our tail.

"They're following," Raine mumbles.

"I know. Keep walking."

"Oi! Freaks!" One heckles.

Fingers tightening on Raine's hand, I attempt to slow down to clap back at the son of a bitch, but he tugs me onwards to keep walking.

"Don't bite back."

"But—"

"Rip," Raine warns. "There are six of them."

"So? What do you think they'll do?"

"I don't fancy finding out. Do you?"

Relenting, we continue walking. Our pace slowly increases, passing the red-brick exterior of the west wing. Shit. It's quieter at this end of the grounds. No guards to stop Rick if he decides to pounce. The library isn't far from here, but it's often deserted.

"Where are we?" Raine asks.

"Near the library."

"Is there a door leading inside?"

"Yeah." I pull Raine to the right. "But it's around the other side."

Their footsteps are still following. I hate giving the impression that we're afraid, but if Raine doesn't want drama, I'll attempt to keep myself leashed. If I were alone, I wouldn't be so restrained.

"We want to fucking talk to you!"

I recognise Owen's voice. He's a bulky, obsessive compulsive from the fifth floor. A recent addition to Rick's little gang and desperate to prove his worth. I'm sure he'd benefit from a good punching.

With the rear door to the library in sight, we're almost there when the first hands reach us. Raine is ripped away from me as someone's arms band around my middle, causing me to drop the backpack.

"Get off!" I shout.

"Voice down, Ripley."

Fucking Rick.

Owen and some other sneering dickhead whose name I haven't cared to memorise have hold of Raine. They kick his guide stick aside then hold an arm each, keeping him trapped in place. All while he curses and fights against them to no avail.

Rick's strong arms around my waist hold me against his chest. "It's rude to ignore people."

His breath is hot in my ear, making my skin crawl. I haven't sold cigarettes to him for a while now. His breath has certainly benefited from the detox.

"You think I give a shit about hurt feelings?"

"Come on, Rip. I wanna have a little chat with you."

Two of his friends go ahead, holding the doors to the library open so they can wrestle us inside. My heart sinks when I see that Linda, the on-site librarian, isn't at her desk like usual. Must be her lunch break.

"Get out!" Rick roars.

The handful of patients browsing the towering rows of books scatter.

"Go watch the doors," he barks at his two pals. "Don't let anyone in."

They dispatch to follow his command. Raine thrashes, trying to peel Owen's hands off, but his arms are wrenched backwards to hold him prone.

"Here's how this is going to work." Rick's hips press into me from behind. "Tell us a lie, and we'll fuck with your new boyfriend. Got it?"

Oh, hell no.

Desperately wishing that Raine could see the pointed look I want to give him, I force a nonchalant voice. I can't let them have this leverage over me.

"Do what you want to him. He's worthless to me."

"Is that so?" Rick chuckles in amusement. "You won't mind if we test that theory, then."

Drawing back a cocked first, Owen slams it into Raine's midsection. Air whooshes out his mouth as he doubles over, coughing and spluttering.

I grit my teeth. "Test away."

"Damn, bitch. You're cold. Hit him again."

This time, the other dickhead punches him square in the face. I wince at the sound of Raine's glasses cracking and flying off his face. Blood spills from the corner of his mouth as his eyes are unveiled.

Owen leans closer to get a good look. "Huh. Figured you'd have some ugly, gaping holes beneath those things."

"Fuck you," Raine spits.

Punching him in the gut again, a thick globule of blood flies from Raine's mouth. His breathing is laboured through the pain, teeth bared and spine curved to absorb each hit.

"Still nothing?" Rick taunts. "Alright then. Again."

It's the brief flash of fear on Raine's face that breaks my resolve. Before Owen's fist can crush his nose, I scream out.

"Wait!"

Chuckling again, Rick squeezes my waist. "There we go. That wasn't so hard, was it?"

"Leave him alone, for fuck's sake. What do you want from me?"

"I want to know where Carlos is."

Laughter rips free. "Seriously? All this for that idiot?"

"Hit him," Rick instructs.

Owen slams his fist into Raine's face again. Blood explodes from his nose and mouth, the crimson splatter staining his golden hair red. I battle harder against Rick's restraint.

"You asshole!"

"Watch your damn mouth, then. Where is Carlos?"

"How the hell should I know?" I yell in panic.

"You're Harrowdean's whore. Don't pretend like you don't know."

"I have no idea!"

"Another lie. Again."

This time, it's a throat punch. Owen releases Raine's arm as his friend does the deed, leaving Raine to crumple, his knees hitting the polished parquet floor. The strangled gasp coming from his throat makes me see red.

"I'll rip you apart for hurting him!" I scream.

"Where is Carlos?" Rick asks calmly.

"I told you that I don't know!"

He sighs, the stickiness of his breath stirring my hair. "Perhaps you need a different motivation. Selfish cunts can't be controlled by hurting others, right?"

Raine tries to sit up at that, but Owen draws back his foot and boots him firmly in the kidney. He lands flat on his back, unable to contain his heart-rending howl. There's blood splattered all over him.

"Ease off," Rick drones. "Come hold the bitch down. Watch him, Ant."

Stomping and kicking, I do my best to break free as I'm forced to the floor. Owen positions himself over me, seizing my wrists then stretching them high so I'm pinned with my arms above my head.

Taking the lower half of my body, Rick casts an eye over my predicament. He looks far too fucking smug. When he gets close enough, I quickly snap out my leg and kick him right in the face.

"Ow!" he screeches.

Removing his hand from his face, I'm awarded with the sight of blood trickling from the corner of his mouth. Damn, I got him good. He moves to sit on my legs, his disgusting weight bearing down on me.

"That wasn't very nice, Rip."

"I don't know where Carlos is!"

Rick shakes his head, now straddling my thighs. "He steps one foot out of line, and he's gone. No parents or siblings to worry about him. Just us. Convenient, huh?"

"He was probably transferred or some shit!"

"You think I'm fucking stupid?"

Striking me hard, the hit causes my head to snap to the side. I feel my lip split and blood begin to ooze from the stinging cut.

"Where is he?"

When I don't respond, he repeats the same move. My neck and head ache as I blink back tears. Doesn't mean I'm gonna give him shit, though. His friend is probably dead.

"How do you live with yourself, huh?" he seethes. "Selling for the goddamn enemy?"

"Wait—"

"You make me sick."

Raine's distant shouting doesn't stop Rick from striking again. Again. Again. Each hit harder than the last. Slaps turn to punches until I can feel the blood drenching my battered face. Everything is spinning and ticking.

"Stop it!" Raine yells. "She doesn't know!"

"Bullshit," Rick rages.

Boneless, I cough up blood. "Probably dead."

His next blow halts. "What was that?"

"They just... remove troublemakers. He'd be easy to erase."

The festering fury in Rick's eyes amplifies. Owen holds my wrists tight as he grabs my jaw, his grip bruising, causing teeth and bone to creak like old wooden beams. I'm surprised nothing has broken yet.

"Where do they take them? The people they want to erase?"

It isn't worth my life to reveal that information. Of the tiny minority who know about the Z wing, no one knows its location. Only me. If I reveal it, I'll face a far worse fate than this.

"Don't know."

"Liar!" He squeezes my jaw hard enough to grind. "Where?"

"Don't... know!"

"You're lying!"

Releasing my jaw, he takes my wrist from Owen. I try to scratch him, but Rick slams it on the floor to hold me still. His spare hand grasps my index finger tight.

"I've spent the last year watching you swan around this place like you own it. Hurting people. Mouthing off. Throwing your weight around. I know you're a lying piece of shit."

My gut boils with anger. Everything he hates about me is everything I fucking hate about me. And I don't care how mad it'll make him, I want him to pay for voicing my biggest shames out loud.

"Even if I knew where he is... I wouldn't tell you." I lick warm blood from my mouth. "Imagine what they're doing to him right now."

"Rip," Raine hisses.

"You wanna know what they do to disposable patients?" I continue regardless of the possible consequences. "Your stupid friend won't even know his own name by the time they're done."

I know I'm in for a world of pain when Rick begins to overextend my finger joint. He forcefully pulls until I feel something pop, followed by a sharp, intense burning that sets my whole left hand alight.

"You will tell me," he orders through gritted teeth. "Or I'll dislocate every single finger you have."

"Do it! I don't care!"

Moving on to the next finger, he wrenches it from the socket with a low growl. The pain is even more intense. This time, I can't hold back a wail. It feels like my fingers are being dipped in acid and corroded down to the bone.

"Shut her up," Rick barks at his friend. "We don't need company."

Clamping his sweaty palm over my mouth, Owen silences my cries. I continue to shriek into his damp skin as Rick dislocates two more fingers, each wrenching motion as merciless as the last.

Raine's yelling and frantic battling to escape barely register. He's still being held down, unable to throw his captor off in his weakened state. All I can feel is the steady pounding in my burning hand.

"Well?" Rick prompts.

Owen lifts his hand from my mouth long enough for me to respond. I pant roughly, my entire body slick with sweat and trembling all over.

"I h-hope you never find him."

"You stupid, stupid cunt."

Smiling through the pain, I scream myself hoarse when he moves to the last victim—my thumb. It's snapped out of place with a sick clicking sound. But Rick doesn't seem in the least bit satisfied by my escaping sobs.

"Maybe we should do him again?" Owen nods to Raine.

"I want the little bitch to hurt, not him!"

"Just an idea, man."

"Well I have a better one."

Reaching around the back of his waist, Rick tugs something free from his jeans. A switchblade, not unlike the one I stabbed him with, reveals itself with a distinctive flicking sound.

"It took eight stitches to patch me up after our last tangle." Rick studies the glinting blade. "So I owe you at least double that, right?"

Raine must clock the soft flick of the blade unlatching because he goes wild. Bucking. Bellowing. Promising death. Ant—the other dickhead—grabs a handful of his sandy locks and slams his skull into the floor with a crack.

He goes limp, limbs splayed and mouth lolling open. With that distraction taken care of, Rick kneels on my wrist and shoves the sleeve of my long t-shirt up past my elbow, despite my vicious cursing.

He holds the blade poised between his fingers. The curved tip almost resembles the bristles of my paintbrush, I think distantly. But I'm not the manipulator behind it this time. Pain is going to be inflicted on the canvas of my body instead.

"Hold her. I need to get close."

Owen places his hand on my mouth again then clamps the other one on my shoulder to stop me from struggling. I shout behind his gag as Rick leans closer, inspecting the intricate ribbons of inked vines wrapped around my forearm.

"Damn. These are good." He runs a finger over the painstakingly realistic tattoo. "Almost a shame to ruin it."

When the tip of the blade presses into my elbow crease, I feel a piece of me shatter. Something internal. Irreversible. A part of me I never thought I'd have to lose. Confirming that nothing stays safe forever.

The blade slices in deep, precise slashes. I can feel letters being carved into my skin. Each scrawled letter is a white-hot poker on my skin. When he curves the blade to cut each swoop and twist, my frantic cries die out.

"Fucking hell," Owen mutters in disgust. "That's sick."

"Shut up," Rick snaps. "She deserves this!"

"I dunno, dude. This is fucked up."

Frowning hard in concentration, Rick curses when his hand slips. My throat is too raw to wail at the sudden stabbing sensation of the switchblade sliding in too deep. He blanches when he realises his mistake.

Owen leans down to look. "Is it meant to bleed that much?"

"I fucking slipped."

"I didn't sign up for this shit!"

"She isn't gonna die, asshole! Shut up already."

Warmth trickles down my arm. I can feel a pool gathering. A twisted part of me wants to drag this out for as long as possible—without medical attention soon, I'll bleed out. That's freedom, right?

No.

I didn't come this far just to die at the hands of some power-tripping son of a bitch. If nothing else, the horror show I've created here must amount to more than that.

I won't die on the library floor. Even if this brings the wrath of Harrowdean's management raining down on me, at least I can accept that fate and go down swinging. Letting Rick bleed me out will be far more pathetic.

Mumbling weakly behind Owen's hand, it takes him a moment to notice. When he does, he grumbles for Rick's attention and releases my mouth once more.

"Yes?" Rick cocks a brow.

"K-Kingsman."

"What?"

"The disused dorms… B-Behind the storage buildings. Go to the basement."

"Carlos is there?"

"If… he's alive."

Triumphant, he nods at Owen. "Go get the others."

I'm quickly released. Relief is a misty cloud sinking into my pores, but it's short-lived. With Raine beginning to stir, Rick pinches his chin, considering me for a moment longer.

"You should've started with that."

Returning his blade to my flesh, he resumes carving, this time careless and hurried. There must be a final reservoir of adrenaline left inside me because I manage a choked screech as he completes his work.

The sound of my agony rouses Raine from his semi-awake daze. Lifting a hand to his head, he groans in pain. Ant doesn't bother knocking him out again. They already got what they wanted.

Owen returns with the two others. "Let's move!"

"Almost done," Rick murmurs.

With a final, few flicks, his artwork is complete. He wipes the blade off on my t-shirt then closes it, staring down at my arm with a weird look of pride.

"You'll never forget this place now, Ripley. No matter how far you run. I hope the memory of the evil you've inflicted follows you to your deathbed."

With that parting shot, he stands and follows his grunts out. None of them spare us a second glance. I don't bother to warn them about the impenetrable layers of security they'll face. No one enters the Z wing. Not successfully. But more importantly, no one gets out. If their asshole friend is down there, it's a suicide mission to even attempt to find him.

"Ripley?" Raine grunts.

I can't move my lips or tongue to respond. Everything is heavy. Numb. Powering down. All I can feel is the expanding puddle of blood growing around me from whatever the fuck Rick's nicked.

"Jesus... I can smell your blood. Where are you?"

Manoeuvring himself up, he resorts to haphazard crawl. His head collides with several bookcases before he touches the slick, warm trail of blood leading back to me. All I can summon is a whimper.

"Fuck! Rip, stay with me."

Raine collapses next to me, desperately feeling his way over my limbs.

"Where are you bleeding?"

It takes all my energy to prise my lips apart. "Arm."

Still cursing, he locates the mess that Rick's made and applies pressure. The weight of him pressing down on my shredded skin feels like live electrodes have been wired into my nerve cells and set to fucking vibrate.

"I'm sorry... I'm sorry..." he chants. "Forgive me, babe."

"S-Stop..."

"I can't, Rip. You've lost too much blood. Did he hit a damn vein?"

I'm so cold. Exhausted. My eyes feel far too weighty to bother trying to hold them open. When I don't respond, Raine presses down harder on my wounds, causing my spine to arch as I screech hoarsely.

"Stay awake! Please!"

Eyes blurred with coursing tears, I watch him fumble to pull off his shirt. I get a glance of my arm before he quickly wraps it up and ties the shirt as tight as possible, freeing up his hands to locate his phone.

It's a slightly chunkier smartphone with a tinny voice that speaks to him each time he presses the screen. I remember the laughter we shared the first time I saw him use it. The voice's faux-British accent is ridiculous.

Scrolling through his contacts, the limited list of names are read aloud. I want to scream *no* at the name he lands on. I don't want him to see me like this. Let alone someone far, far worse.

The line quickly connects.

"What, Raine?"

"Library. Bring medical help."

"Code red?"

"Just hurry."

There's a growling curse.

"We're coming."

Dropping the phone, Raine quickly shifts his attention back to me. Even through my fuzzy vision, I can see those limitless, maple pools darting around. His face is already swelling beneath the fresh blood and bruises.

"I d-didn't mean it," I struggle out.

"Mean what?"

"What I told them... You're not worthless."

He looks stricken, his frown lines pronounced and toffee eyes watering. "I couldn't protect you. If I could see—"

"No. Not your fault."

"But—"

"No."

The sound of incoming shouting reaches us. Thudding footsteps. Several guards, no doubt. Raine doesn't stop holding pressure on my arm, though he looks ready to keel over himself.

Everything fades out in the flurry of noise. I feel Raine being pulled away from me and replaced by someone else. Questions are barked. That familiar, sonorous voice sounds even angrier than usual. Now there's an achievement.

"Who the fuck did this?"

"I'm fine, Nox. I need to help Ripley!"

"Forget her! She deserves this."

"She's bleeding!" Raine shouts loudly. "You can't—"

There's a scuffle. More pained moaning. Through slitted eyes, I can see Raine clutching his head, like he tried to struggle but couldn't escape the muscled boulder pulling him from my side.

Lennox actually spares me an uncertain glance. Our eyes meet, hazel on seafoam. Hatred on disdain. Only neither of us can muster either emotion in the midst of such destructive violence.

The evil bastard should be enjoying the satisfaction right now. But instead, he looks physically sick as he studies my bruises, swelling and finally, my haphazardly bandaged forearm that's steadily leaking blood.

"Fuck," he splutters. "Xan?"

"Yeah. I've got her."

Kneeling in my blood, I can just about distinguish Xander's

spearmint scent in the copper-laced air. A pair of scarred arms slide beneath me and lift, half-pulling me against his body.

My head is cradled in his lap. I have no choice but to stare straight up into those midnight globes, filled with endless nothingness. The dark-blue hue is a mere breath away from murderous black right now.

"Who did this to you?" he whispers in a dangerously low voice.

"Why… do you… care?"

Those terrifying, onyx eyes catch on my dislocated fingers. I watch his throat bob up and down. Jaw muscles tightening. So many silent tells told in the smallest of reactions. Xander can't strangle all his emotions.

"Hold still," he orders.

Picking up my hand, Xander studies each traumatised joint in a clinical way. Cataloguing and assessing. I don't have time to wonder how he knows what to do with them.

"Breathe in."

He swiftly clicks the first finger back into place. The pain is intense but short-lived. Numbness resurfaces, filling me instead. It seems I've reached my threshold for the time being.

Xander is unperturbed by each swollen, misshapen finger he finds. Not even blinking, he deftly shifts them back into place, working efficiently despite my continued whimpers. Only experience can teach that perfect motion.

"This must make you h-happy."

His eyebrows knit together as he works. "Do I look happy?"

No. He doesn't.

Not even a little bit.

With more voices arriving all around us, I break eye contact with the devil watching over me. I don't need him to see my humiliation as the final chunk in the dam holding my emotions at bay breaks.

Xander's grip tautens when a sob bursts from my chest, though it sounds weak and lacklustre. He's holding me so tight; it feels like he's trying to stop me from slipping from his grasp and drowning.

I know what mess now decorates my body. I caught that brief glimpse. The scribbled craftsmanship inked in my own blood. Disfiguring my tattoos with the path of his blade. Rick left me a message.

Harrowdean's whore.

CHAPTER 16
RIPLEY
START A WAR – KLERGY & VALERIE BROUSSARD

Present Day

DROPPING my eyes from the camera lens, I look down at the lace-detailed cuffs of my off-white blouse. The beautiful foliage on my right arm is still intact, swirling upwards from my wrist to cover my whole forearm.

The left tattoo sleeve used to be an identical match. I got them done on my nineteenth birthday after spending months saving up from every piece of artwork I sold. I thoroughly researched the artist and even illustrated my own design.

Now the design is distorted by old, jagged scarring. It's faded a little over the last decade, but the skin is still puckered and shiny against dark spirals of ink, making the words easy enough to read. I should know. I trace them every day.

Harrowdean's whore.

"You never considered tattooing back over it?" Elliot asks me.

"Why? So I could forget? Pretend like Harrowdean never happened?"

Wisely, he keeps quiet. I've long hated journalists and their impertinent questions. Every single one of them who's attempted to buy my story has been out for one thing—blame.

They see me as an easy target, a place to put the world's rage, now that Incendia is gone. Even all these years later, unanswered questions remain. The scars left by our psychiatric sentences have never truly faded.

"Everything changed after Rick's attack." I look back up at Elliot. "Things were already shifting at Harrowdean, but that was the turning point."

"How so?"

"Wars often start silently. Pieces were sliding into place to precipitate what happened next, but even if we'd known… we couldn't have stopped it."

Flicking through his notebook, he studies lines of scrawled handwriting. "You've mentioned the rumours circling about what was also happening at Blackwood Institute."

"News travelled fast. Even when management didn't want us to hear it."

Elliot nods thoughtfully. "It was a national scandal at the time. We've attempted to interview several Blackwood inmates, including Brooklyn West, on a few occasions. But no such luck."

I suppress a snort. Brooklyn wouldn't waste a single second of her time on something like this. She's never played well with the media and doesn't care to revisit her past.

For a long time, I felt the same way. Like talking about what happened inside Harrowdean Manor would somehow drag me back there, into the clutches of evil beyond comparison.

"Incendia left many victims, Miss Bennet. I'm sure you know that better than most."

Because they're my victims too.

Feeling flushed all of a sudden, I tug at the collar of my blouse. All of the air in the room has vanished. It's like I've stepped into an airlock. I take a sip from the glass of water on the table, but it does little to calm me.

This is precisely why I never leave my safe bubble. When the panic attacks hit, they're intense and ugly. Old Ripley would laugh at the mess of a person I am now. Traumatised and haunted by all she's seen.

She'd eye me with disdain and keep walking, unwilling to spare a drop of empathy. I cared less back then. All I cared about was survival; nothing else mattered to me.

"I… need a moment," I choke out.

"Of course." Elliot gestures for his cameraman to stop rolling. "Would you like some more water?"

"Just… air. I need air."

Tugging the clip-on microphone from my lapel, I toss the handful of wires onto my chair then flee. The doors to the soundproof studio slam shut behind me.

Several startled employees working for the production company look up as I run past, though none look surprised. I bet I'm not the only interviewee who's ran from that damn camera.

The elevator ride is a painfully long wait that only adds to the pressure squeezing my throat tight. Finally breaking outside, the hustle and bustle of Central London is an unwelcome slap in the face.

I'm almost mowed over by a distracted commuter when a strong hand clamps around my bicep. Dragged out of the way, I'm propped against the wall of the huge glass skyscraper.

"You promised to let me do this alone," I pant raggedly. "I don't need a private security team."

"No, we promised not to follow you inside."

Tall, muscled and coated head to toe in tattoos, Hudson Knight is an intimidating force of nature. He's never caught out of black clothing, and there's an earpiece tucked beneath his chaotic mop of raven hair.

A few paces behind him, two others stand at ease. I stare into Warner's familiar baby blues. Along with Hyland, his number two, they're both members of Sabre Security's ruthless Anaconda Team.

"Ripley?" Hudson prompts.

When I turn back to him, his gaze is boring into me, a pierced eyebrow quirked in challenge. I should've known Kade would send his brother to hold the perimeter. He got all uptight and stressed when I mentioned that I'd accepted this interview request.

"I don't need the head of Sabre Security here to keep me safe."

"Technically, I'm only one half." He smirks at me. "Nobody would put me in charge of the company on my own."

"You're right about that. The place would crumble."

"Precisely," Hudson drawls. "So where's the fire?"

Pulling a pack of cigarettes from his pocket, he lights up and takes a long drag. I eye the tempting little death stick. Never been much of a smoker, but right now, I'd take a stiff shot of vodka and a fucking sedative.

Hudson rolls his eyes and surrenders the cigarette to me. "You don't smoke."

"I don't do a lot of things."

My hands tremble violently as I hold it between my lips and inhale deeply. Smoke fills my struggling lungs, causing me to splutter. The amused look on Hudson's face is gonna get him punched in a moment.

"Not sure smoking is the answer," he comments.

"Please leave the therapy shit to Jude. You're no good at it."

Hudson snorts. "Fair enough."

With Hyland and Warner keeping a close eye on us, we stand in silence. It's a welcome reprieve after hours of relentless questioning and reliving the past. I tune the hustle and bustle of England's capital city out.

Although I feel less trapped outside the confines of the blacked-out TV studio, it takes time for me to calm down. We've been talking nonstop. I'm exhausted and we've still barely scratched the surface of the story.

"I don't know why you're even doing this interview." Hudson lights his own cigarette. "These producers have been trying to pin us all down for years. It isn't worth the hassle."

"Not all of us have been able to move on, Hud."

"You think we're not still haunted by the shit that went down?" He shakes his head, pulling in a long draw of nicotine. "You're not the only one who can't forget. But that doesn't mean I'd entertain some clickbait interview."

Shrugging, I take another drag. I'm not going to judge how he's chosen to cope—how any of them have. We've all managed in our own ways. But this is my decision, and I made it for a reason.

"My point is, you don't have to do this."

"No." Feeling steadier, I drop the cigarette and stomp on it. "I don't have to do it. I *need* to do it."

"What about the backlash? You ready for that?"

"Well, it's a good thing I know the country's top private security company then, isn't it?"

Hudson drops a strong hand on my shoulder. "We can handle threats to your safety. I'm more worried about the impact the shit people will say about what we all did to survive will have."

"I don't care what people think."

"Then why put yourself through this?"

Placing my hand on top of his, I lightly squeeze. "I'm not looking for their forgiveness, Hud. I'm looking for my own."

He sighs, blowing out a cloud of smoke. "Then I'm not letting you do this alone."

"I can take care of myself."

"It's not for your benefit." Hudson puts out his cigarette then gestures for me to head back inside. "If Brooke heard that I'd sent you back up there alone, she'd serve my fucking balls for breakfast."

With a nod to Hyland and Warner, remaining on guard outside, we head back inside the building. Hudson's scruffy jaw is set in a hard line as he follows me into the elevator and back upstairs.

"You know the interviewer is going to shit himself when he sees you're with me. He's been fishing for the scoop on Blackwood for hours."

Hudson chuckles. "He can dream on."

"Just play nice, alright?"

"I'm always nice."

"Sure. You're a fluffy fucking teddy bear."

"Damn straight," he echoes.

Walking back into the studio, several assistants do a comical double take at the wall of glowering, inked muscle escorting me. Sabre Security has had many high-profile cases in recent years. Hudson's scowl is well known, much to his chagrin.

"Ripley." Elliot stands as I walk back into the interview room. "Is everything okay?"

"Fine. I just needed a moment."

"Of cou…"

He trails off as Hudson stalks in behind me, his trademark intimidating glower in place. This was a fucking terrible idea. The man is incapable of playing nice, and I don't trust him to keep a cool head if he sticks around to listen.

"My security detail wishes to be present," I try to explain.

Elliot sticks out a hand to be shaken. "Perhaps your security detail would care for a microphone too? I've been following your story for a long time, Mr Knight."

Lip curled, Hudson eyes Elliot's hand with disgust and doesn't take it. "No doubt."

Clearing his throat, Elliot drops his hand.

"I'll be right over here, Rip." Hudson takes his position in the corner of the room.

I pick up the microphone and reclip it to my lapel. Warily eyeing Hudson, Elliot sits back down and picks his notebook up. Once I'm comfortable, he instructs the cameraman to resume rolling.

"Where were we?" I sigh.

"What happened after the attack?"

I wring my fingers together, letting the past drag me back.

"I thought all I wanted was revenge. But what do you do when you're led to slaughter with no chance of escape? When your enemies are in fact your only allies?"

Heart pounding, I touch the scars on my arm again. They aren't the only marks I left Harrowdean with. Some scars I hate less than others. Some were made by force, and others I took willingly. My hand lifts to my throat, absently tracing the thin knife line there.

Hatred breeds insanity.

And all we had in hell was each other.

CHAPTER 17
RIPLEY
STREET SPIRIT (FADE OUT) – RADIOHEAD

Ten Years Earlier

I DON'T REMEMBER MUCH about my mother. Even the memory of her scent is vague—a generic, floral fingerprint, but I couldn't say what perfume she wore or her preferred bouquet for Valentine's day.

Over time, those details faded. Whether by choice or design, it's hard to say. Eight-year-old Ripley wanted to lock her pain in a box and bury it at the bottom of the ocean. To do that, she scrubbed her memories too.

I tried painting Mum once. My uncle never kept photos of his sister around. All my parents' belongings were either sold or put into storage after I moved, so I had to use nothing but memory alone.

Reaching for the image of my mother, I found an empty cavern instead. I'm not sure I could even tell you the colour of her eyes. Brown? Green? Blue? Grey? Whatever hue, they still turned to mulch beneath the ground she was buried in.

But I do remember one thing.

A few months before Dad's heart attack, I had to have my tonsils removed. I was always getting throat infections, spending whole months living off ice cream. My dad kept the freezer well-stocked.

When I woke up in hospital after the surgery, Mum was there. Curled up in the bed next to me, her body lined up against mine, that nameless flowery scent wrapped all around me. I remember how safe I felt. How loved.

She never let me go through the scary stuff alone. Splinters stuck in fingers. Grazed knees. Failed spellings tests. Dad's funeral. Mum was always there. Until the day she didn't come home.

I have no one left now.

Not for the hard stuff.

A tickle in my nostrils rouses me. The scent of hospital-grade bleach is an unpleasant stench. It sneaks into my awareness and pulls me from the hazy shroud of my mother's perfume, still floating in my mind.

"Come on. You've been discharged."

"No! I'm not leaving her."

"Who is she to you, Raine? What's going on here?"

"I care about her! Back off."

An incredulous scoff. "You know what she's done! This is where she belongs."

"I don't give a fuck about this feud between you two. It has nothing to do with me. I'm not leaving her."

This time, there's an irritated groan.

"She'll break your heart then walk all over the broken pieces. Don't come crawling back to me the moment she does. I'm not gonna be the one to fix it."

Imposing footsteps thump away. Each whack of the heavy soles on what sounds like tile or linoleum is a thunderclap. I want to cover my ears, but moving doesn't seem like a possibility. Not even my eyelids will lift.

"Your friend's an asshole."

Huh. Rae.

"Yeah," Raine responds tiredly. "That he is."

"You can go. I've got her."

"No, I want to be here."

"At least sit down. You look half-dead."

Chair legs scrape across the floor. Plastic cushions creak. I think I hear Rae sigh. They don't talk, their silence allowing me to hear the sounds of the medical wing. I'm certain that's where I am. It's a tiny corner of the institute.

I don't know how long it is before Rae speaks again.

"The guards track those bastards down?"

"I don't know." Raine sounds so exhausted, his voice raspier than usual. "I'm not sure what wild goose chase Ripley sent them on."

"We'll hear soon enough. I hope they're all transferred or sent to prison."

"That seem likely to you?"

Rae definitely sighs this time. "Nothing does anymore."

Lapsing back into silence, it's a long time before I hear Raine's rough voice again. It's thick with emotion now.

"I let her down."

"Come on," Rae sympathises. "That isn't true."

"I was passed out while that lunatic carved her up like a piece of meat. Ripley needed me. I'm fucking useless."

"Ripley would never admit to needing anyone, even if it meant life or death. She doesn't let anyone get close."

"What about you?" Raine asks.

Her pained chuckle hurts my soul. "Not for a lack of trying. I think she needs a friend. But after a year of back and forth, she still holds me at arm's length."

"I thought you were her friend."

"I'm not sure she has any of those. That would give her too much to lose."

Their murmurs are interrupted by a door creaking open. Shoes squeak across the floor, and from the swish of hospital scrubs, I'd guess it's a member of staff.

"Alright. Time to go."

"We're staying," Raine replies firmly.

I hear Rae hum in agreement.

"She's on strong pain medication. The blood transfusion will go on for a few more hours. Go get cleaned up."

"But—"

"Go on. Scram."

At the sounds of their reluctant retreat, I feel the warmth embrace me again, darkness creeping back in. With whatever magical drugs they're pumping into me, I can't say that I even want to wake up.

I float on a pharmaceutical cloud until the tug of someone pulling a needle from my arm drags me back to the surface. This time, the soft warmth of drugs has faded, pain exploding from every cell in my body.

My entire body pulses in time with each fresh wave of agony. Ribs burning, fingers aching, nose stuffy and sore. Excruciating pain emanates from my entire left arm. I'm convinced it's on fire.

"Here she is, Warden. We're easing her off the pain medication."

What sounds like dress shoes tap closer.

"What have you done this time, Miss Bennet?" There's a weary sigh. "Alright, lead him in."

A door clicks then more footsteps approach. I must still be high. I'm imagining talking, dismembered legs hovering around my bedside with no bodies attached to them. Until another voice forces me to discard that hairbrained theory.

"Christ."

"Jonathan," Davis greets politely. "I hope we didn't disturb you. How was the helicopter ride?"

"Fine. I was in a board meeting when you called. What's the situation?"

"Your niece will recover with time. She took a severe beating."

"Obviously," he quips. "Unprovoked?"

"Unclear. Though as far as Miss Bennet is concerned, she would not struggle to provoke someone. It's unlikely this was a motiveless attack."

"Sounds about right."

Yeah, definitely high. There isn't a chance in hell that my uncle is here having a nice little chat with the goddamn warden. I haven't seen Uncle Jonathan in years. He wouldn't trouble himself.

"This role was supposed to keep her safe from further trouble." Jonathan's voice is matter-of-fact. "That was the agreement when her transfer was arranged."

"Indeed it was."

"Then what's the issue here? Was my donation not sufficient?"

"Your niece has proven to be a difficult beast to tame. She steps beyond the bounds of her role on a daily basis. We can't risk our operations with such a loose cannon anymore."

Another longer, wearier sigh comes from my uncle. "These are precarious times for all of us."

"Then you understand our predicament."

"Of course, Abbott. I'll deal with my niece. I'd appreciate your discretion in removing the threat against her while I do so."

"On this occasion," Davis agrees. "Any further conflict or disruption, and I'm afraid not even your investment in the corporation will keep her safe."

"Naturally. You have a business to run."

My uncle's voice drips with detachment as he casually discusses my fate. Not even a moment's hesitation before so quickly washing his hands of me all in the name of fucking *business*.

Betrayal is a silent knife in the gut, tearing past intestines and kidneys to reach something deeper. Something that was broken to begin with, but I hadn't wanted to admit that sad reality.

He isn't my family.

He doesn't love me.

Maybe he never did.

I think I hear a shoulder being clapped before a set of footsteps fade away. Someone sits down close by. Tapping loudly on a phone screen, their breathing is even. Calm. I know it's him. He isn't leaving.

There's no avoiding this shitty conversation. With a lot of willpower, I wrench my eyes open. I have to blink rapidly to get the cubicle to settle. I am indeed in Harrowdean's small but functional medical wing. Curtains are drawn to offer my bay some privacy.

With white sheets pulled up to my chin, my right arm is resting on a pillow off to the side, a thin rubber tube leading into the crook of my elbow. I watch the dark, gloopy droplets of borrowed blood feed into me.

Thick swathes of bandages are twined around my other arm from elbow to wrist. Lower still, each finger has been splinted with black Velcro, holding the throbbing digits in place.

"Ripley."

Jonathan has what my mum called a *business meeting* voice on the rare occasion that she mentioned her baby brother. I remember that detail clearly. It's one of the first things I noticed when I was forced down to London as a kid.

He's ten years younger, now in his mid-forties, but he wears his age with well-pampered youthfulness. His dark-brown hair is an expensive dye job that covers the silver wisps he was developing when I last saw him.

With smooth, tanned skin, a well-trimmed beard and clear eyes that both captivate and terrify, it's no wonder he's a formidable opponent in the boardroom. Capable of negotiating even the trickiest of business deals or investments.

Elbows braced on his knees, his broad shoulders strain against his perfectly fitted, pinstripe suit. It probably costs more than the yearly salary of his multiple personal assistants. He has a whole walk-in wardrobe full of designer clothes.

"What are you doing here?" I manage to croak out.

He casts an eye over me. "Perhaps you'd like to answer that question. What am I doing here, Ripley?"

"You didn't have to come."

"When I get a phone call saying my niece has been half-beaten to death and sliced up by some punk, I'm forced to find out what she's gotten herself into."

Wincing, I try to sit up to see him better. He doesn't bother to help or offer to fluff my pillow. The needle feeding into my arm tugs, forcing me to give up and slump back on the lumpy mattress.

"It was a misunderstanding."

"A misunderstanding?" he echoes coolly.

"This idiot has it out for me. Thought I knew where his friend got shipped off to. People assume I know stuff… for obvious reasons."

Jonathan exhales through his nose. "The whole point of this role was to offer you protection. Do you have any idea what strings I had to pull to sort this safe haven for you?"

Safe haven?

For a man who's used his intelligence to amass a multimillion-pound fortune, he can be so fucking obtuse. Harrowdean isn't safe for anyone— patient, stooge or otherwise.

"You asked to be transferred from Priory Lane," he continues smoothly. "I made all the arrangements and ensured you'd have a comfortable life here. Perks included."

In my exhausted state, I can't hold my tongue.

"Do you think it's comfortable to be management's bitch?"

"You asked for this position!"

"I asked to be saved! Not sacrificed!"

Folding his arms, he leans back in the chair. "And what about the sacrifices I've made for you?"

My eyes prickle with furious tears. I've dealt with too much today to hold them back or plaster on a brave face. My mum isn't tucked into this hospital bed with me, holding me tight. In fact, no one is.

I'm alone.

Eternally.

Years of frustration and pain come rushing out. All the times I've wanted to scream and rave at him, but have managed to hold it back with a shoestring of control. I hate the pathetic tremble in my voice.

"The only thing you sacrificed was another dusty, unused room in your mansion. You never wanted to get stuck with me. If we had any other living family, you soon would've shirked the responsibility."

He shakes his head. "You're so ungrateful."

"Tell me what I should be grateful for, then. The missed birthdays? Weeks left in the care of your staff? Being stuffed with medication? Or packed off to the first place you could find to keep your batshit-crazy niece quiet?"

"I've taken care of you for all these years."

"No. You've tolerated me. Sometimes even that was too much to expect. I'm another business transaction to you like everything else in your life."

I wonder if I see a flicker of regret. Or even sadness. But his clear grey eyes don't reveal any such weakness, and the perfect poker face he's used on me for my entire life never once falters.

I wish I cared as little as he does. I've spent a year trying to emulate that same business-minded detachment. And where has it got me? To this goddamn hospital bed.

"I don't know why Mum left me in your care. Perhaps she thought the day she wouldn't be around anymore would never come. You were nothing more than a last resort to her."

Not even a flinch. It's like my words bounce right off him and roll back into the ocean without pulling him under. He straightens his cuffs before sweeping his gaze around the clinical room.

"Do you even care?" I feel more tears spill over.

"About what?" He sighs.

"Me!"

Jonathan clicks his tongue. "I care about the investment you've squandered by getting into pointless fights with your peers. Your place here is hanging by a thread."

"And it would be so inconvenient if I wasn't quiet and off your radar, right? Do you even want me to go home?"

His lips purse. Not even a nod. He can't muster the smallest amount of energy it would take to make me feel the slightest bit better. Is it any wonder that I've turned out like this? I learned from the best.

My cheeks sting with the lash of salty tears over deep bruises and swelling. But it still doesn't compare to the pain writhing in my chest, right about where my heart should be. Where nothing but a black hole resides.

"You've tied my hands, Ripley. There is nothing more I can do for you."

"What does that mean?"

Jonathan shrugs. "I can't risk myself any further."

"We're supposed to be family." My vision blurs with torrential tears.

He spares me another detached glance.

"Why couldn't you have been normal?"

His words are the final kick in the gut. Years of abandonment slam down on me. The unwanted niece who became the disastrous situation. That's all he sees me as. That's all I will ever be.

"Next time you find yourself in a mess, don't call my office. I can't help you anymore. I suggest you tread very carefully from here on out."

My hospital gown soaked from fierce sobs, I watch him stand up. Jonathan brushes off his tailored suit and turns away without another glance.

Tears gather in a pool at the base of my throat as I watch him walk away. My last remaining relative abandons me without any pomp or circumstance. It's a quiet retreat. The pinnacle of his slow withdrawal from my life—as limited as his presence has been.

And once again, I'm left alone.

It's been a long time since I allowed myself to completely fall apart without holding anything back. I've done everything in my power to hold that inevitable, cataclysmic breakdown at bay.

Hundreds of long, scrubbing showers. Hours spent on the treadmill. Countless splattered canvases. Brawls. Threats. Mask after mask, slotting my bravado in place. Avoiding friendship and intimacy at all costs. These things kept me safe.

Safe from caring.

Safe from getting hurt.

Safe from being abandoned again.

Hurting other people, supplying them with the means to hurt themselves, it's all allowed me to maintain a cobbled-together image of self-control. Broken shards duct taped together in a haphazard puzzle.

I hate the words that sneak out.

"Please come back," I whisper brokenly.

But he doesn't.

Nor does the person I always wished he'd be. The illusion I've clung to. Now both versions are gone. All that's left is an empty hospital room and the steady drip of someone else's blood feeding into me.

Not even the sound of the partition curtain scraping back halts my sobbing. It's peeled aside to reveal the unlikeliest of alabaster faces studying me. The midnight-blue in his eyes has returned to the surface.

Circling the bed, seeming as uncertain to his presence in my room as I am, Xander sinks into the vacated chair. He doesn't utter a word. But my dry blood still staining his polo shirt is telling enough.

He hasn't left me once.

Just remained tucked out of sight.

Face blank, his gaze slides down to my splinted fingers. The same ones he snapped back into place like he's been doing it since before he could talk. His eyes remain there.

It shouldn't be funny. None of this is. But the despairing laughter comes anyway. All I have left in the world is the man who hates me more than life itself. The iceman with his secret obsession.

"Go!" I shriek.

But he doesn't.

So I fall apart some more.

What feels like hours later, I stare back up at the popcorn ceiling. There's nothing left inside me. Not even defeat. My swollen, gritty eyes screw shut, too painful to hold open for a second longer. Oblivion is beckoning.

I must imagine it before I drop off.

But I swear, Xander takes my hand and squeezes.

CHAPTER 18
RAINE
PRETTY LITTLE DEVIL – SHAYA ZAMORA

I WAIT against the smooth trunk of a tree in our usual spot. After resting for as long as my limited patience would allow, I dragged my bruised and aching body down here for our usual weekly deal.

I don't want drugs right now, though.

Just Ripley.

Ears straining and senses dialled to ten, I listen for her approach. Ripley's footsteps are always soft and light, in total contrast to her fierce spirit and wickedly sharp tongue. She seems too small to hold such spunk.

Inhaling deeply, I can't smell her body wash. The scents of juniper and birch trees linger in the air instead. Spring is in full-swing, and the world is thawing, bringing with it a new miasma of stimuli to paint my internal world.

The scents I'd usually spend hours dissecting hold no interest today. She has to come. I was turned away from the medical wing at every opportunity, forced to wait for her discharge to smell her again.

But that was three days ago now and still nothing. She isn't at mealtimes. Not in the corridors nor the art room. Not so much as a passing encounter. I'm not going another bloody day without catching her.

So I wait.

Foot tapping and nose twitching.

I don't know how long I stand here, looking like a total fucking idiot.

I feel completely exposed without the comforting weight of my glasses resting on my nose, but until I can locate a replacement pair, I have no choice.

Right now, it's probably a good thing I can't see the likely pitying stares of all who shuffle past. God knows what I look like, but I don't give a shit what anyone thinks.

What're a few bruises and a nice egg on the back of my head after what they did to her? I don't give a shit what Ripley's weird non-friend says. I did fail her. When she needed me, I couldn't stop them from hurting her.

"What are you doing?"

I stifle a groan. "Go away, Nox."

Ignoring me, his heavy weight thuds closer. "You're waiting for her, aren't you?"

"I don't see how it's any of your business."

"Anything involving Ripley Bennet is my business."

A morbid smile tugs at my mouth. He really doesn't hear it. The way his anger and disdain sound a whole lot like something else. No one can feel that amount of hatred without passion too.

"Do I detect a hint of jealousy?"

Lennox's laughter is a rumbling earthquake. "I wouldn't touch that whore with a fucking ten-foot pole."

"Then we don't have a problem. Do we?"

I sense him stopping in front of me, his enraged teeth grinding audible. Even when she isn't around, Ripley still manages to get under his skin like nothing else. His hatred for her is borderline obsessive.

"Look what happened to you because of her!" he booms. "You're lucky those bastards didn't kill you to get whatever the hell they wanted."

I've kept tight-lipped about what went down. The last thing Ripley needs is for me to give Lennox or Xander more ammunition to use against her. Sure, those thugs beat the shit out of me to provoke her. But it wasn't her fault.

With the overnight disappearance of Rick and his trigger-happy posse, no one but myself and Ripley knows what happened in the library. I need to ask her where she sent them.

Part of me is afraid to know. I blacked out the moment my head cracked against the floor and woke up to them hauling ass. They didn't leave us without good reason. She sent them on a hunt.

"Raine." Lennox's voice softens, almost sounding like a plea. "Don't let her get in your head. You don't know what she's capable of."

"Like you're any better?" I scoff.

"What's that supposed to mean?"

"Come on, Nox. We all know why you're in here. What about the shit you're capable of?"

He gulps hard, the gurgling sound painting a mental picture of his throat bobbing up and down. With darkness all around, I have to piece together countless jigsaw puzzles. Thankfully, he's never hard to read.

"If I have to remove her from your life to keep you safe, I will," he redirects.

"Stay away from Ripley. I mean it, Nox."

"Listen to me! She's bad news!"

"Go." My voice is steady despite the ire seizing my muscles. "Don't talk to me again until you've learned to respect my fucking privacy. What I do with her is none of your concern."

He hisses out a loud breath. I can already sense the cogs in his mind whirling. Plotting. Scheming some great, heroic gesture to save the poor charity case he took pity on. The problem is, Lennox only knows how to use violence to achieve his aims.

Fuck that.

He isn't my damn bodyguard.

"Have it your way," Lennox declares.

Sighing, I rub the back of my neck as his stomping feet disappear. I just hope to God I haven't painted an even bigger target on Ripley's back by defending whatever the hell we are to each other.

When I feel my cheeks and nose starting to burn from sitting in the sun for too long, I know she's far past late. Ripley isn't coming. If she thinks she can scare me off with this hiding act, she's in for a shock.

I didn't want to resort to this.

But she's left me no choice.

Moving slowly and deliberately is the first step to getting around when I'm not being escorted. I struggled to use my guide stick for a long time—terrified of walking face-first into an obstacle despite swinging it around.

Now that instinctual fear has faded. Collisions still happen, but I have a deeper sense of spatial awareness than most people. Even on the days I'm high as a kite or blissfully numbed. Survival instincts kick in.

Climbing the stairs is another matter. It takes precise concentration. Mentally measuring each incline, feeling for the perfect height to place my foot down. After a couple of months here, I've sussed it out.

Regardless, it still takes longer than I'd care to admit to reach the sixth floor. I have to count each time the staircase curves around another corner, taking me farther upward.

Dragging my spare hand down the corridor's papered wall, I bear left and check every door. Metal numbers are screwed into each one, allowing me to fumble my way to my destination.

"Xan?" I rap on door thirty-seven.

It's a long moment before he swings it open. "Lennox went looking for you."

"Yeah, he found me. Listen, I need that favour."

He's silent for a moment. "What for?"

"I just want to borrow it quickly."

I briefly worry that Xander has developed a conscience. But when he mutters for me to wait, I know he's not going to ask any questions. I'm relieved to have at least one semi-uncomplicated friend.

Returning, Xander tugs my wrist then slaps the cool, plastic keycard into it. "Don't get caught with that. It's an all-access one."

"How did you manage to steal it anyway?"

"Probably best that you don't know."

With that, he slams the door in my face. Ever the charmer. I slide the keycard into my back pocket and painstakingly make my way back down to the fifth floor, searching for room seventeen next.

I want to respect Ripley's privacy, but what we just went through together is all kinds of fucked up. She must've gotten it in her head that it's changed something between us. But I won't let that stand.

With a cursory listen for any guards lingering nearby, I double check the metal numbers on her door before knocking twice. Tapping my foot, I wait. Then I knock again. When there's still nothing, I pull out the keycard and scan it.

Her door clicks open with a buzz. Stepping inside feels like a gross violation, but I quickly crush the feeling. I don't have time for ethics right now. Though I do call out her name.

"Ripley? It's me."

Silence.

"You in here? We need to talk."

Not a single whisper.

I'm about to curse up a storm and step outside to formulate a new plan when I hear it. The faint sound of breathing floating from deeper in the bedroom. Tuning everything else out, I can smell the fruity richness of papaya lingering in the air beneath the scents of human hibernation.

She's in here.

"Come on, Rip. You can't hide forever."

Her breathing changes—seizing on an inhale, like words are begging to be set free, but she's biting her tongue. Stick extended and one hand out, I tentatively step farther into the unknown space.

"If you think this hiding crap is going to work, we need to have a serious conversation. I'm shit at hide and seek."

Not even my terrible joke rouses a response. I curse when I stub my toe on something that feels a lot like a dresser. Bloody thing was jutting out from around the corner. I must be getting closer.

"Talk to me, guava girl. Tell me you're okay."

The tip of my stick meets something that isn't solid wood nor wall. I bend to feel what it is, my fingers depressing into fabric. Her mattress. I've located her bed. Her breathing sounds close too.

"You having a pity party without me?" I try again.

A sigh whistles from her. "Go, Raine."

"Ah, she speaks. I was starting to worry that I'm invading some random girl's bedroom."

Stopping next to the bed, I place a hand on the stiff cotton sheets. Warmth radiates from her curled-up form beneath the duvet, tucked into the top corner of the small twin bed. She's cocooned in a tiny ball and doesn't react to my touch.

"Thanks for making room for me. Did you hear me coming?"

"Please," she whispers. "I want to be alone."

"What you want and what you need are two different things. I know what this is. And I'm not going to leave you in here all alone."

"Why not? Everyone else does."

My stomach twists. "Because I'm not everyone else, alright?"

Propping my guide stick against the wall, I easily kick off my shoes. The laces are never tightly fastened to avoid struggling when I dress. Ripley doesn't protest as I slide back the covers and lower myself into her bed.

With her tiny body tucked against the cold wall, there's enough room for me to stretch out next to her. But I don't touch her. Not yet. It's like those early days after I lost my vision and couldn't lift myself from the despair I'd sunk into.

Like a terrified animal trapped in a cage, she has to be coaxed out of this state. Nothing but words will work. Ripley thinks she has my number, but I also have hers. She's always expecting abandonment.

As hot as I find her violent sass and strong headed will, I can see what pain lies beneath it. The way she holds the entire world at arm's length, so it doesn't get close enough to matter. She avoids any opportunity for vulnerability.

Until me.

What she gave me was precious.

I'm selfish enough to admit that I chased her for the thrill of it. The way her attitude made my endorphins spike better than any other drug. She makes me feel alive in a world determined to lock me in the darkness.

But more than that, I like her. More than I've ever liked anyone. This isn't just about feeling alive, it's about feeling whole. And when I'm with her, I don't feel lacking. I'm complete and present in the world just like everyone else.

"Are you asleep?" I murmur.

"No."

"Then you can listen." I moisten my suddenly dry lips. "I'm so, so sorry."

"I told you it wasn't your fault."

"They almost killed you."

She exhales loudly. "I wish they had."

Her broken admission is another brick on the heavy pile I'm being crushed beneath.

"Don't say that, Rip."

"Why not? There would be no one left to mourn me. No parents. No uncle. Not a single family member."

"You have friends," I argue.

"No. I don't."

The pressure in my chest expands. "You have me."

She's silent for several agonising seconds.

"You got hurt because of me, Raine. Because of what I know. They used you to get to me. How can I ever risk letting that happen again?"

"Rick and those shitheads are gone. No one has seen them for days."

"You think that matters? There's a long list of people who hate this place and hate me by extension. I can't say I blame them for wanting a pop at *Harrowdean's whore*."

Ripley spits the last words out with such hate-filled emotion, I can almost hear a flicker of the spitfire I've come to adore. When I overheard the onsite medic, Doctor Hall, discussing what Rick carved into her, I wanted to punch a fucking wall.

"He didn't even say goodbye," she mutters.

"Who?"

In the stillness, I can practically hear her chest seize. "My uncle came to visit me in the hospital."

"Shit. What did he say?"

"Nothing I didn't already know." Her voice wobbles. "I'm on my own now."

Oh, fuck this. She doesn't need coaxing. She needs someone to pick her up, wrap her in love and tell her that she's worthy of receiving it. I don't care if she has to hurt me in the process of accepting that.

Reaching across the bed, I band my arms around her tightly-balled form. She complains at first, but as I drag her into the shell of my body, her whispers die out.

I hold her against my chest, tucking her head beneath my chin and stroking my hand along the ridges of her spine. I can tell that she hasn't showered for a few days, but it doesn't bother me. We've all been there.

Holding her tight, I give her the safe space to break apart. Wet warmth soaks into my skin as she hides her face. I wonder if anyone has held her and given her permission to be weak since she lost her parents.

"Just leave me alone, Raine," she cries.

"Not a chance, guava girl."

"I'm tired of being the bad guy." She hiccups into my throat. "I don't want to be the reason anyone else gets hurt."

"That isn't your choice," I say gently.

"Why not?"

"Because we all get hurt in life. The trick is to find the person you care about enough to let them hurt you."

"I've never had that," she confesses after a long pause.

In the darkness that has long represented fear to me but now feels like home, I can admit the truth.

"Me neither. I guess we both just want to belong somewhere."

Ripley's lips brush against my pulse point. "Or to someone."

With her tears soaking into me and our breath mingling, I can feel our essences dancing hand in hand. There's something intimate about seeing someone at their lowest point. It's not just a milestone, it's a privilege.

I didn't have anyone to hold me when I needed it the most. I was alone. Afraid. Abandoned. Everything she's feeling right now. I won't let her go through it alone.

No one held me.

But I can hold her.

"Your uncle didn't deserve you as a niece."

I can practically hear the gears in her head grinding. It's a long time before she responds mournfully.

"He set this whole thing up for me. Gave me the fucking keys to the kingdom. But if I wasn't this awful person, perhaps I wouldn't be alone. Instead, I have nothing."

My hand moves higher to slide into her hair, gently massaging. "You're not a bad person, Rip. You're just a survivor."

"And a monster."

"This place has a way of making even the best people into monsters."

"Then why are you here?" She lifts her head, and I can imagine her staring down at me. "Why are you still humouring whatever this is?"

"Because I don't judge people on their worst mistakes. We've all made enough of them. And I'm not going to let you ruin this based on some whacked opinion of what you think you deserve."

"Damn. Say it how it is, huh?" An invisible smile peppers her words.

"Always, babe." I dramatically sniff the air. "On that topic… You're cute as fuck, but when was the last time you stopped moping around and showered?"

"Raine!"

"I don't have to be blind to smell that ripeness."

Her laughter fading, Ripley sighs. "It's hard for me to do basic stuff when these episodes hit. Even moving is difficult."

"In the future, we need a signal."

"Huh?"

"I've been sitting around like a chump for days waiting for you to show up. I just need to know you're safe, even if functioning is too much."

"What kind of signal?" she asks.

"A code word. A hand squeeze. Hell, I'll take anything. But on those days when your limbs are too heavy to move and everything is unbearable, I need to know so I can come hold you close."

Her legs slowly uncurl, like she's preparing for the long, tiresome walk to the attached bathroom. It's invasive that I can also hear the empty gurgling of her stomach, but my dialled-up senses didn't get that message.

"I guess I'm just used to dealing with my illness alone."

"That changes today. I'm making the decision for both of us."

Ripley snickers. "Then I guess a code word will do. Aren't they usually reserved for sex, though?"

"You wanna have one for that too? This friends with benefits arrangement just got interesting."

The bed springs creak with her standing up. "You're incorrigible."

"Like you'd want me any other way."

"I guess not." Her hand snags my arm then tugs. "Come and wash my back."

Letting her pull me out of the bed, I'm guided through the bedroom. The sound of the light clicking on and the shower starting are my first clues that we've reached the bathroom.

Ripley hisses in pain as she peels off whatever clothes she's wearing. My hands hover mid-air, looking to help, but she doesn't ask. So I work on unfastening my jeans and pulling off my t-shirt instead.

My body feels awkward and stiff. They did a real number on me. Nothing permanent, but I was lucky to avoid a concussion. The pain will fade soon enough.

"Christ," she gasps.

"How's it looking?"

"Well, your ribs and stomach look like an elephant stomped all over them. Matches your pretty purple face, though."

"You think I'm pretty?" I cup my own cheeks.

"Get in the fucking shower, Raine."

"You know that you have the advantage here. I've got no idea how rough you're looking right now."

I hear her step into the shower. Feeling for the entrance, I join her beneath the spray, the door sliding shut behind me. It's a tight squeeze, forcing her bare frame to press up against me in the steam.

"Shit." Ripley's body leaves mine. "I'm not supposed to get my stitches wet."

"Hold your arm above me and away from the spray."

Shifting, her breasts push into my chest as she finds the right position. My hands locate her hips, perfectly curved and slippery with warm water. Anyone would think that I'm dead inside not to be turned-on right now.

But this isn't about fooling around. As tempting as the slick heat of her body moving against mine is, I just want to take care of her. Beyond anything physical, I need her to know that she's going to be okay.

We both will be.

I'll make sure of it.

"Looks like I'm on cleaning duty. Pass the body wash?"

After twisting away from me again, Ripley curls my hand to place a plastic bottle in it. "I'm an arm down. Sorry."

"It is a hardship, having to lather you up."

The familiar, heady scent of papaya fills the shower as I spread body wash between my palms. Ripley holds still, letting me slowly run my hands all over her generous curves, ensuring every inch I locate is thoroughly lathered.

What feels like her forehead rests on my chest, just below my clavicles. I can tell by the wet tickle of her hair on my pectorals. My cock twitches, suddenly paying attention. She lets me massage every part of her before I begin to sluice the bubbles off.

"Feel good?"

"Mmm," she groans unintelligibly.

"Don't fall asleep on me. Where's your shampoo?"

Her head briefly lifts. "Here."

Once she's slumped back onto my chest, I move my attention to her hair. Washing someone else without a visual frame of reference takes a lot of trial and error. Ripley doesn't complain when I attempt to shampoo her face twice before eventually finding her hair.

The wet curls slide between my fingertips like reams of fine silk. I've been a scents and textures kinda guy since losing my vision. The details that are insignificant to everyone else can hold all of my attention.

Without any distractions, I can take my time memorising every inch of Ripley's topography. The small, rounded peaks of her ears. How her curls spring back even when wet. Her slim shoulders and the pronounced divots in her spine.

She lets me drink my fill, content to rest against me and enjoy the attention I'm lavishing her body with. Proportionally, she's everything

I find attractive in a woman. But it's her spirit that makes her stunning.

Once she's thoroughly washed, I hold her close beneath the spray. I'm debating how I'll wrestle her sleepy body out of the shower without us both faceplanting when she sighs, her lips puckering against my throat.

Small, open-mouthed kisses spread across my collarbones. Exploring and leaving a static charge in their wake, her lips retreat before pushing against mine. I return the kiss, magnetised by the draw of her skin against mine, holding me steady in the world.

"Rip," I murmur. "You're hurt."

Breaking the kiss, she touches the back of my hand then guides it down to cup her tight ass. Well, shit.

"Please," she whispers. "I… need to feel you, Raine."

"I can't… we're not—"

"I don't want to feel their fists anymore," she insists, cutting me off. "I've spent days reliving the feeling of his body weighing me down, his breath on my face, his knife slicing me up. Please make it go away."

"They won't hurt you again. I promise. No one will."

"Doesn't erase the memories." Her whispered voice catches.

My other hand clasping the back of her head, I plant kisses across her mouth. "I know you're feeling alone and scared right now. But you're going to get past this."

"How?"

"Because falling down is a part of life, Rip. Getting back up? That's living."

Mouth crushing against mine, she replies with a hard, almost frantic kiss. Like she's desperately kicking her legs, trying to tread water, and I'm her last source of oxygen.

Screw this.

Needing reassurance of my own, I kiss her back with every ounce of fear that's been eating away at me since I blacked out. The terror of not being able to defend myself or help. Then the silence of the past few days, all the while wondering if she's ever coming back to me.

This isn't the time or place. Sex was the last thing on my mind as I marched here, determined to find the woman I was told to hate, but I'm learning to… *Fuck.* Learning to what?

Like?

Maybe even love?

The realisation that she's wormed her way far deeper than I ever thought possible only spurs me on to seize this moment before it's ripped away from me like everything else.

Nothing good ever lasts, but I'm not ready to let go of this feeling yet.

Releasing her hair, I find the dripping swell of her breast and squeeze. She moans into my mouth, hips shifting with each kiss, pressing her centre up against my growing hardness.

When she abruptly pulls her lips from mine, I panic.

"Shit. Did I hurt you?"

"No."

Skimming her hand down my abdominals, she makes her intentions clear. Now unbandaged fingers wrap around my swollen cock, sliding up and down the shaft with a delicious application of pressure.

I grit my teeth, feeling a surge of heat deep within. Her hand feels far too fucking good wrapped around my dick. I hear her shift, feet squeaking against the shower floor, before the feeling of pleasure intensifies.

"Fuck, Rip!"

Her lips have found their way to my cock, taking it into the warm, welcome prison of her mouth. She must've kneeled down. I quickly locate her lowered head then retake a handful of her hair.

Beginning to suck, she bobs up and down on my length, her tongue sliding against my shaft with each movement. The loud shower and absence of sight forces me to focus on nothing but her mouth fucking me.

Lips tighten. Teeth graze. Her hands move to cup my balls and lightly play, causing me to jerk inside her mouth. Holding her hair, I let my hips thrust, working in time to her sucking.

She lets me slide deeper and deeper each time, until I can feel her throat nudging against my tip. Despite the quiet gagging sounds, Ripley doesn't stop sucking. I'm soon riding her mouth and battling to hold on.

"You're so perfect," I hum.

Her mouth cinches around me in response, teasing another surge of pleasure free. Those devilish lips know just how to imprison a guy and demand ransom in return.

What began as a small collection of embers is now a raging blaze inside me. I need to be balls deep inside her right now. She's turning me into some kind of primitive caveman.

Pulling her head back, I slide out before I can spill my load down her throat. As tempting as that is, my girl deserves a thorough fucking, and I'm not the kind of man to disappoint.

"Turn around and bend over," I instruct roughly. "Spread yourself open for me, babe."

Reaching behind me, I fumble to turn off the shower. The last thing I want is to soak her stitches. By the time I've twisted the knob, I can sense that she's moved. Her tight rear butting up against my erection confirms it.

Placing a hand on her lower back, I push down to make her bend even farther. I want to slide deep into her in one brisk thrust and feel her contract around me. She's breathing hard in anticipation, waiting for relief to come.

What I wouldn't give to have a view of her perfect cunt glistening with desire right now. Even a fucking glimpse. Instead, I have to slide two fingers over her ass then lower to locate my target.

Her moans intensify as I find her entrance and breach it, too impatient to tease her with featherlight touches. Her pussy responds immediately, pulling my fingers into its heat. She's so damn tight.

"Raine," she whimpers.

"I've got you, babe."

Working her over several times, I know she's good and ready. Her moans have dissolved into needy wails, and I can feel the silkiness of her juices on my fingertips.

Holding a thumb just above her cunt, I fist my cock and line it up with her slit. The euphoric cry that spills out of her as I piston inside is music to my ears. She cries out so loud, it reverberates around us.

I'm already buried deep in her, but shifting my hips back, I drive into her once more. She stretches around me, her walls hugging my dick in a vice. I already want to fill her up.

"This is going to be hard and fast," I warn her.

"Yes," she moans. "Please... Yes."

Gripping her waist, I pull out again only to surge back in. Faster with each pump. Harder with each slam. She takes me so well, I don't care how long this is going to last. Taking her like this feels better than mainlining fucking heroine.

Her escalating cries spur me on. Each time I advance into her, Ripley makes the most incredible sounds. The woman who stripped off and rode me like a goddamn pro in an abandoned building is roaring back to life.

Each plunge reignites the sore bruises that I can feel littering me, but the pain is inconsequential. It sharpens my senses until I can practically taste her sweet arousal dancing in the lingering steam.

"Raine," she pants. "I'm so close."

"Let go then, babe."

Driving into her hard and fast, I feel her clench tight. The increased pressure is pushing me to the finish line too quickly. I'm happy to go fast, but I still need to satisfy her first.

Ripley cries out again, her moans reaching a fever-pitch. I can feel her climaxing as every muscle tightens, holding her on the verge of a steep plummet before letting her freefall.

She isn't allowed to come down from that high. Not yet. I want her limp and boneless by the time she leaves this shower. Maybe then she'll think twice before hiding from me again.

Collecting moisture by gliding my thumb over her clit, I search for the tight ring of muscle I used as a compass earlier. She's a gasping wreck, but the moment my thumb locates her asshole, Ripley jerks back to life.

"Oh God!"

"Hold still. You're okay."

Her voice takes a hot as fuck, guttural note as my thumb pushes into her backside. I'm still sheathed inside her, and with both holes now filled, she's trembling so hard it feels like vibrations.

"Do you like it when I play with your asshole, dirty girl?"

"Yes," she whines.

"Are you going to come all over my cock again?"

"I can't… I'm…"

"That's the wrong answer."

Pushing deeper into her rear, I resume thrusting at the same time, adopting a brutal pace. My own climax is threatening. I'm tight with tension, and my balls feel ready to explode.

She's so wet and spent, it doesn't take much to push her to the edge again. Folded over, Ripley lets me fuck her raw like a man possessed. I have no idea how we're both still standing as my release finally crests.

Ripley calls out my name, her second orgasm milking me of every last drop. I spill into her with an uncharacteristic roar, letting pure instinct take over. My body is calling the shots.

When she wobbles against me, I move fast, sliding an arm beneath her folded-over body before she can crumple. Ripley lets me pull her upright, and her back meets my chest, our pants for breath filling the shower.

"Well." I suck in a lungful of air. "Next time you're in this state, my plan is to fuck the sadness out of you. Seems like it works pretty well."

Her breathless laugh is all the agreement I need.

CHAPTER 19
RIPLEY
HARDER TO BREATHE – LETDOWN

I STARE out the window at the storm clouds. Thick, pyroclastic swarms of dark-grey cover the sky, swallowing the sunlight and bathing the institute's grounds in melancholy. There's an almighty storm brewing.

Attending therapy like usual was the last thing on my list of priorities this morning. It covered taking medication, having a check-up and figuring out how the fuck I'm going to stay alive. But then Langley intervened.

I've never been escorted to a therapy session before. The clinicians don't usually pay that much attention to my so-called rehabilitation. So being marched to the north wing after he finished fussing was a new experience.

"Ripley. Please answer the question."

I cast Doctor Galloway a half-hearted glance. "I don't know what happened."

"This is a safe space."

"Really?" I drawl.

"Of course. You can tell me what's going on."

If I had the energy, I'd laugh in her face. I doubt my lies will make any difference now. If Rick and his friends found the Z wing, it'll be obvious who sent them searching. I'm surprised I haven't been cuffed already.

She exhales, studying me over her notes. I'd usually stare back.

Defiant and unfazed. But the fight that once drove me forward hasn't reappeared. So I return my gaze to the billowing storm clouds instead.

"You don't have much time left in this program," she attempts again. "I understand that recent events have been difficult, but don't allow them to set you back."

"Why do you care?" I quip.

"You're my patient, Ripley."

"And what about your other patients? What about the people in here with no one to vouch for them? Or the ones who will never complete their sentence and go home? Do you care about them?"

"We're getting off topic."

Indignation sprints through me. "How much do they pay you to keep your mouth shut? To sign off falsified medical notes and turn the other cheek?"

Looking back at her, I wait for a response. An ugly flush is spreading up her throat like a bad allergic reaction. Slowly, she stacks her paperwork then caps her fountain pen.

"Perhaps we should leave it here."

"Do you think about the people you've hurt when your head hits the pillow at night like I do?" I finger the edge of the bandage covering my arm. "Or does the promise of your next payday soothe the sting?"

She doesn't go as far as to call me a hypocrite, but I can see the accusation boiling in her eyes. That's precisely how I know she's full of shit. When my head hits the pillow, it's all I can think about. She has to feel the same torment.

I may be equally as guilty, but I didn't take an oath to do no harm like her. Though it makes me no less culpable, it sure damns her alongside me. She's supposed to be a doctor, yet she's in on the big lie too.

"You want to know what happened?" I lean forward in the armchair. "All the shitty decisions I've made finally caught up to me. And I hope the day comes when the same thing happens to you."

I stand and head for the door. I'm not going to sit here and be lectured about the benefits of opening up and sharing my pain. Not from a power-hungry opportunist who wants to package it with a fancy label and sell my sickness to the highest bidder.

When I open the door, it isn't Langley waiting outside. Although he surely thought that he was being helpful by bringing me to therapy today, it infuriated me to no end. I'd gladly take his meddling ways over the displeased mug staring back at me now.

"Ah, Ripley." Elon's thin lips pull into a grin as he looks me over. "Good to see you back on your feet."

"Is it?" I respond blandly.

"Nice bruises. You look like a punching bag."

"Spare me the small talk. What do you want?"

Flashing teeth, he beckons me into the corridor. "Let's take a walk."

The command feels like being offered a steep cliff to hurl myself off. I don't trust the sadistic gleam in his eyes. Between more of Doctor Galloway's torture fest or whatever trap Elon's sprung for me, I should've just stayed in bed.

"No cuffs?"

"Will they be necessary?" He cocks an overgrown brow. "I can assure you that declining or running isn't advisable. I'll simply return with a friend or two."

"You'll need more than that to drag me anywhere."

"I'm aware. But they will be able to carry you after I've jammed a sedative in your thigh. So, care to take that walk?"

Considering my options, I see no alternative. He nods in satisfaction when I fall into step beside him, keeping a safe gap between us. I don't fancy getting stabbed with a hypodermic needle.

When he doesn't lead me to the warden's office or the solitary floor, the first flickers of panic set in. I look around the reception, fruitlessly searching for a means of escape.

"Don't even think about it," he warns.

"Think about what?"

Elon looms over me. "Starting any shit. This place is locked down tighter than Fort Knox right now. You'll only get your ass kicked."

Now that he mentions it, there's an array of blank-faced guards manning every wall, corner and doorway. At least triple the usual fanfare. Their weapons are no longer carefully concealed—batons, tasers and glinting cuffs hang on every belt loop.

Biting my lip, I watch the show over my shoulder as Taylor, a loud-mouthed girl whose room is a few doors down from mine, gets pulled aside for a random pat down.

"Are you serious? I was just walking!" she shouts.

"Up against the wall, inmate."

"No! This is such horseshit."

When she doesn't comply, Kieran, the wanker who struck me with his baton, shoves her hard. She slams into the wall with a pained squeak, her hands forced to flatten and legs spread apart by his foot.

"You asshole!" she screeches.

Tension is at an all-time high. Some patients don't raise their heads as they scuttle past. Whatever fire filled Harrowdean's population before, recent displays of force seem to have tamped a lot of it down.

But others like Taylor? They're openly defiant. Bickering and shouting. Fists swinging and arms getting pinned. It doesn't take much to provoke a guard into getting handsy. They seem determined to prove their point.

We're still their puppets to control.

And puppets don't have any rights.

Her head turned to the side and cheek smashed up against the wall, Taylor's gaze connects with mine. I'm unnerved by the venom directed towards me churning there.

This overzealous shithead is running his hands all over her, but she's staring at me like it's my goddamn fault. Maybe she's right. I didn't make this world, but I sure as hell benefited from it.

Thinking no one's looking, Kieran skates a hand over her ass. She hisses a selection of insults, but it doesn't deter him from grabbing between her legs next. I watch the horrified tears stream down her cheeks.

"You're clean," he declares.

Taylor pushes off from the wall, her wagging tongue now silenced. I look away as she leaves, her arms wrapped tight around midsection. The guard saunters off, smirking to himself like he hasn't just committed a crime.

"Ripley," Elon snaps.

I catch up to him with a sickening weight curling in my stomach. It's never been hard to find examples of abuse in Harrowdean. But never has it been so blatant and relished in. Something has shifted.

"Did you see what he did?" I demand.

Elon rolls his eyes. "Just move it, inmate."

He grabs my bicep and tows me across the quad. My scalp prickles when I spot a familiar headful of ash-white hair. At least his vantage points are getting more creative.

Xander sits on the grass, back against a tree trunk. He's pretending to be occupied by the thickly bound maths textbook in his lap, but instead, his narrowed eyes follow me across the quad.

We stare at each other for a brief, tension-laden second. Just the sight of him causes my heart to speed up to a traitorous gallop. Whether in fear or some twisted sense of anticipation, I don't even want to know.

The memory of him sitting at my bedside in his bloodstained clothing rushes to the forefront along with the ghost of his hand grasping mine. As my world fell apart, he ensured I wasn't suffering alone.

Was it real?

Does the infamous iceman… care?

That can't be right.

Xander doesn't know how to care. That would require far too much emotional range. I don't know what he feels for me—hatred, fascination, a desire to torture and maim—but caring isn't a remote possibility.

His perched form disappears as we descend farther into the institute's grounds. The stirrings in my chest morph into a nausea-inducing pitter-patter of anxiety. Blood pounds in my ears with each step towards what I know is coming.

It's unassuming. Nondescript. An abandoned façade coated in ivy, cracked brick and signs of disuse. Even the once sparkling stained glass windows have been boarded over and eaten alive by overgrown shrubbery.

To the untrained eye, it's another relic of Harrowdean's colourful past as an asylum in the nineteenth century. Most of the unrestored buildings scattered across the grounds hail back to that sombre period of time.

"Wait—"

"Shut it," Elon snips.

"Please. I can't go in there."

"I said shut it, inmate. That sedative can still be arranged."

Tucked out of sight in a cluster of glossy ivy leaves, I recognise the blinking eyes of several CCTV cameras. Why protect an empty husk? It can't be for the cobwebs and ghosts of inmates long past that live inside.

The most sinister of evils always hide in plain sight. Hidden behind politicians' smiles and their empty promises. Glossy brochures with photos of therapy rooms, green forests and happy, smiling patients.

As I stare up at the disused exterior of Kingsman dorms, I

understand how this place and so many like it have operated under the radar for all this time. Even those who pay attention fail to see the truth that's right in front of them.

Harrowdean isn't real.

It's just a well-crafted disguise.

"You don't have to do this." My voice trembles pathetically.

"Scared, Ripley?" Elon laughs. "Come and see where you sent your little friends."

I send a silent prayer into the unknown as Elon tugs me up the crumbling stone steps, his head swivelling to ensure no one has followed us.

There isn't even a padlock on the door. They want it to look inconspicuous and blend in with the other worthless ruins. These people are truly shameless.

"We've had plenty of curious inmates wander in here over the years," he explains conversationally. "Most get bored though. There isn't much to see upstairs."

The interior of Kingsman dorms, once a lavish oasis for upper-class, privileged kids packed off by their parents to receive an extortionate education, is now an abandoned wreck.

Sagging wallpaper lines the corridor, yellowing and water-damaged. Bare, cobweb-covered bulbs hang from the ceiling, though they aren't lit right now. The early afternoon sunlight illuminates the dusty old signage denoting the different floors.

Elon heads in the direction of the basement, causing more dread to bubble inside me. It takes several twists and turns to reach a wrought-iron door protected by a security system. He scans a black keycard, unlike any I've seen before.

"Down we go," he announces jubilantly.

I stare down at the aged, concrete staircase. No fucking chance. People who go down there do not come back up. The fine hairs on the back of my neck stand up, while my skin suddenly feels too tight for my body.

"Please, Elon. Let's talk about this."

"Now she wants to talk." He snickers to himself. "The time for cooperation has passed."

"No! I'm not going down there!"

"I was hoping you'd make this difficult."

With a sinister grin fixed in place, he bends his knees and wraps his arms around my legs. I squawk as I'm lifted off my feet and slung over his shoulder like a sack of potatoes.

"Get off me!" I howl.

"Make as much noise as you want."

Battering my fists against his back, I thrash and shout, trying anything to break his hold. The bruising across my ribcage and stomach screams in protest at his shoulder digging into me.

After slamming the heavy-set door shut behind him, Elon begins to descend. The temperature plummets as we're devoured by darkness. It's like all the warmth has been sucked from the world and spat back out as clear, freezing fog.

Thick concrete swallows all sound and light until it feels like we're following Dante on his quest deeper into the seven circles of hell. I start to shiver violently, trapped by his arm banded across my legs.

"No! Stop!"

"Come now, Ripley," Elon croons. "You don't want to see what all your hard work is for?"

The terrain levels out, and I'm yanked back over his shoulder. My joints ache with the force of being dropped back on my feet. All around me, locked cells line a seemingly endless, subterranean hallway.

"Welcome to the Zimbardo wing."

I spin to face him. "Let me go. I'll keep my mouth shut, I swear."

He smothers a chuckle. "When has that ever happened?"

"I don't belong here!"

"Just walk."

Shivering, I take a tentative step into the corridor. The floors, walls and ceiling are all made of polished concrete. Thick sheets of steel carve each cell door, fitted with sliding hatches so guards can peer inside.

I've barely taken a step when the first yells ring out. Unlike the wails of whoever occupied the adjoining cell to mine in the solitary wing, this sound is guttural, inhuman. Like someone has pulled the very life from the poor bastard's soul and set it alight.

"While you're out there, pushing our product and creating a steady supply of material for the team to examine, the real work happens down here." Elon shoves me forward. "The rest is just an added bonus."

Half of the cells boast an occupied sign. The sound of someone punching or kicking a metal door reverberates with the continued shrieks. The farther we walk, the louder the cacophony of sounds becomes.

"What is that noise?" I ask fearfully.

"Sounds like Patient Three has been causing trouble again."

Elon stops outside one of the cells where a different thudding sound is leaking through the reinforced steel. He slides back the hatch to give me a clear view inside of the brutal beating taking place.

The woman being pummelled to a meaty pulp barely resembles a human. More like a misshapen, bruised bag of organs, slick beneath a curtain of fresh blood. She doesn't even grunt in pain at the blows being rained down.

"Afternoon, Professor," Elon calls jovially.

Beyond the man delivering the beating, another stands, watching on. I don't recognise him from the clinical staff. With silver-streaked, gelled hair, a thin but strong nose and square-framed glasses, the professor wears a pressed white lab coat over his suit.

Seemingly enraptured by the show being put on for him, it takes him a moment to look up at Elon. The moment he does, his curious smile blossoms, creasing weathered lines and wrinkled skin.

"Elon! What a surprise."

"Just making a delivery. Ripley, this is Professor Craven. Lead researcher of the Z wing here in Harrowdean."

Craven turns his attention to me. "My, my, she is a fine specimen."

Disgust crawls over me. He's looking at me like I'm some five-course tasting menu to be savoured and dissected, dish by dish. I tear my gaze from his ebony eyes and look at his thug, dressed in all black.

"Harrison." Elon nods in acknowledgement.

The man delivering the beating pauses, his vacant gaze briefly flickering up. "Elon."

Harrison uses the back of his black glove to swipe sweat from his brow. He leaves a thick smear of blood across his face, his gnarly features resting beneath a sharp military buzz cut. He seems unfazed as he looks me over.

"Got some fresh meat for us?"

Elon jabs a thumb over his shoulder at me. "Just giving our stooge a little tour of headquarters."

"She still causin' trouble?"

"Not if she'd like to avoid the same fate as Patient Three."

To illustrate his point, Elon flashes me a sick leer. My blood freezes in my veins as his friend nods, casting a critical eye over me again. With a glance at Professor Craven, he ducks out of sight to retrieve something.

"Bring her closer, Elon. This'll teach her not to bite her master."

I'm dragged close to the door before I can think about fleeing. Elon pins me against the steel slab, forcing me to look directly through the hatch and into the dank, padded cell, lined with bloody handprints and deep scratch marks.

I can now see a table of instruments tucked in the corner. Harrison inspects the selection, humming lightly under his breath. When he picks up a medieval looking pair of shackles, the inner circles lined with wickedly sharp spikes, I recoil.

"Fancy those cuffs, Rip?" Elon breathes in my ear.

I gulp hard. "What are you doing to her?"

"Reconditioning."

Harrison nods agreeingly. "The human mind can only endure so much pain before it splinters apart to cope. We reform those shattered pieces and create something new. Something useful."

Booting the semiconscious woman in the stomach, he kneels down and grabs her wrists. She's still conscious despite looking like she got shredded by a violent woodchipper. Something tells me this isn't her first beating.

But when Harrison clamps the torture cuffs around her wrists, the scream it elicits makes me fear for the integrity of my eardrums. The spikes inside the cuffs sink deep into her flesh, causing blood to ooze down her arms.

"Why are you h-hurting her?" I ask despite the boulder in my throat.

Craven produces an amused chuckle. "Ah, it's been so long since we had a new recruit. I forgot how entertaining their naïvety can be."

They all share a laugh.

Fuck you, Professor, I respond mentally.

"Patient Three failed to complete a recent assignment for the corporation." Harrison snaps the cuffs into place. "We don't tolerate such failure in Harrowdean."

A hand slapped over my mouth, I watch in horror as he drags her around the filthy cell by the chains connecting the two halves of the cuffs together. She howls in agony until eventually, she passes out.

Harrison drops her unconscious body like she's trash to be discarded.

He then proceeds to boot her in the stomach for good measure, verifying that she's unconscious.

"How dull."

"Should've paced yourself," Elon snickers.

"She's proven to be a resilient one. But no matter." Harrison shrugs indifferently. "They break all the same."

A throat clears. "Gentlemen. You're keeping us waiting."

Still holding me prone, Elon spins us both to face the scowl I know awaits. I'd recognise the warden's voice anywhere. Here I was, thinking he kept his hands clean and didn't get involved in this side of the business.

"Ah, Miss Bennet." He flashes a PR-perfect smile. "So good of you to join us."

Frozen by terror, I can't make my tongue move to form a response. All I can see is the patient being dragged around her cell, leaving a trail of blood.

Davis tuts like I'm a mannerless schoolchild. "So quiet now, eh? Let's take this elsewhere. The professor has work to be getting on with. Harrison, Patient Five is prepped and ready for you both."

"Sir." Harrison bobs his head.

Moving his hands to my shoulders, Elon pushes me away from the two men watching me like I'm some delicious delicacy to be consumed. With wobbly legs, we follow Davis to the bottom of the corridor.

I don't dare look over my shoulder at whatever Harrison does to that poor woman next. I can hear him talking to Craven, the pair exchanging light-hearted conversation as they continue to inflict a brutal atrocity.

Through another door, we enter a hallway housing several different offshoots. A glimpse into the first room is enough to turn my mouth into sandpaper. I quickly look away and focus on the warden's footsteps.

"Don't fancy a trip in there?" Elon goads. "The submersion tanks aren't so bad once you learn to function on ten percent oxygen. The lungs quickly adjust."

Fear like I've never felt before coils around my lungs. Those huge, two-metre glass tanks were full of murky water and sealed tight with barred lids. It doesn't take a genius to imagine what floats inside. I doubt they've ever been emptied or cleaned.

The next room, to my relief, is an office. But instead of Davis's name on the door, it boasts the initials *SJB*. I'm led inside and roughly deposited in a dark-brown leather, wingback chair.

"No funny business," Elon warns, a deliberate hand on the taser attached to his belt. "I'll happily fry you."

"Now, now." A regal voice emanates from the chair behind the desk. "There will be no need for such unpleasantries. Will there, Ripley?"

With Davis settling in the corner of the office, I'm left to face the elderly figure who turns in the office chair. It takes a moment for me to place his coiffed, silvery hair, wrinkle-lined jowls and lizard-like eyes.

When I transferred to Harrowdean, I made it my mission to understand the truth behind the world I'd entered. It wasn't hard to find the face behind the program. Sir Joseph Bancroft II has a spotless reputation.

Richer than God and arguably more powerful, Bancroft owns a portfolio of companies across the globe. His pride and joy, the infamous Incendia Corporation, has its finger in many pies.

Psychiatric institutes. Private schools.

International conglomerates.

Even… investment firms.

I knew I recognised him when the first news articles popped up detailing his philanthropic work and various charitable endeavours. On the rare occasions when my uncle remembered my existence, he did play the orphaned niece card to his advantage.

As a result, I attended a handful of events put on by his firm over the years. Smile and wave, right? I even met his boss. Not the guy running the daily board meetings and doling out redundancies, but the real boss. The one behind the board of directors.

"Nice to see you again." The same man smiles at me now. "It's been… dear me, ten or twelve years? You're all grown up now."

Play this smart. Stay alive.

"Sir," I return stiffly.

"Always such a polite, well-mannered little thing." Bancroft eyes me. "It's a pity, what happened to you. So much wasted potential. Jonathan was most disappointed by your… predisposition."

Of course, he'd label a chronic, enduring mental illness as an inconvenient waste of potential. Eight-year-old Ripley was already an inconvenience. But bipolar Ripley? She was a problem to be erased.

"Naturally, I offered you a place in our rehabilitative program." Bancroft actually sounds proud. "It's a shame that Priory Lane didn't prove conducive. Though your transfer here was an easy request to grant."

I peel my tongue from the roof of my mouth. "Why am I here?"

"Because, dear Ripley, you were given an opportunity. A chance to be a part of something bigger. But the reports I've been receiving of recent disturbances here are yet another disappointment."

"Perhaps if your men didn't beat us at any available opportunity, the patient population would be more content," I reply without thinking.

He chortles in amusement. "It is unfavourable to resort to such measures. But your control is slipping. Defiance cannot go unpunished."

"I've done my job here."

"Then do better!"

His voice raises several octaves as spit flies across the desk. Behind Bancroft's well-versed speeches and charming smiles, it's clear a predator lies coiled at his centre. I've seen that threat brimming in his eyes before.

"Your job is to keep your peers dependent," he continues briskly. "Those who are dependent are compliant. Those who are compliant... don't ask questions."

The air flowing into my lungs halts. I cast a nervous glance around, but there are no escape routes. Not even a small basement window. This place is a concrete box designed to trap its prey.

"Our recent visitors to this wing asked many questions." Bancroft rests back in his office chair. "I wonder if they knew they were being sent to their deaths. Did you think to warn them?"

"I don't know what you're talking about."

"Cut the shit, Ripley," Davis interjects.

Feeling the weight of their collective gazes searing into me, sweat trickles down my spine. "I had to give them something."

"That wasn't the question." Bancroft smiles again in that creepy, all-seeing way. "Did you think twice before sending those boys to their deaths? Did it even cross your mind?"

Is there any point in lying? I don't need to pretend to be something I'm not here. These three men know the lows I've sank to in order to preserve my own existence.

"No. I wanted to hurt them. Just like they were hurting me."

While Davis looks furious at my admission, Bancroft seems positively thrilled. Like I've somehow ticked a box only he can see. It makes me want to scrub a year's worth of invisible bloodstains from my skin.

"Interesting," he muses, fingers tapping his lips. "Perhaps we still have use for you after all."

"Sir." Davis steps forward to address his superior. "Our program here is compromised enough."

"Which is precisely why it's a bad time to be training a new stooge," Bancroft responds. "I will not add another unstable element into an already difficult situation. We have enough to contend with."

Picking up a stack of folded newspapers from the corner of his desk, he slides them across the gleaming surface for me to take. I reluctantly accept them and begin flipping through the papers.

"Our future is compromised, Ripley." Bancroft rests his chin on his folded hands. "Therefore, your future is compromised too."

The blazing headlines catch my attention, one after another. All of the papers are dated within the last few weeks.

Deadly riot at Blackwood Institute.

Incendia Corporation under investigation by Sabre Security.

Allegations of abuse and malpractice across Britain's six institutes.

"I see a problem for you." I shrug. "Not me."

Bancroft swipes a hand over his silvery coiffure. "Do you think the authorities would agree with that assessment when they hear what you've done on our payroll?"

"I don't get paid. You're the ones profiting."

"Your continued survival is not payment?" he challenges. "You could have been disposed of long ago. But we maintained Jonathan's request to keep your situation quiet and… controlled."

The newspaper judders in my hands. I lay it down, attempting to disguise the fine tremble.

"Ah, now you get it." Bancroft observes my obvious nerves. "Uncle's protection has expired, hasn't it? I am surprised that his patience for your continued disruptions has lasted this long."

"Disruptions?" I repeat.

"If only his colleagues and investors knew that his very own niece was confined to the institute he endorses. Rather embarrassing, isn't it?"

I want to shrivel up and disappear. But I won't give him the satisfaction of humiliating me. So I decide to parrot the disgruntled warden watching our exchange.

"Cut the shit. If you're going to threaten me, get on with it."

"I have no need to threaten you, Ripley. Look around at where you are. If Harrowdean falls, don't doubt that we will all fall with it."

The broken part of me that's endured the cost of surviving the past two years wants to throw open the fucking gates and let the authorities march in here. For the lives I've exploited, I owe them that much.

He's right, though.

The world needs a scapegoat. As humans, we assign an outlet for our rage long before we think of compassion. It'll come down to blame. Incendia won't protect me from the wolves. We will burn together.

I've come too far to let their crumbling empire take me down. Sacrificed too much. I didn't care that a different Ripley would be leaving those gates, as long as I walked out at all. So I wilfully destroyed the person I was to become the person they needed.

The stooge.

The instigator.

The *blame*.

"What do you want me to do?" I grit out.

"Sir, I really must insist—"

"Enough," Bancroft cuts the warden off. "Ripley has proven herself to be an asset despite recent transgressions. These are dangerous times. We cannot squander loyalty."

Gaze catching on the nearest newspaper, I study the mugshot of an escaped detainee from Blackwood Institute. Another chess piece in this eternal game of moves and counter moves.

Staring into the dead-eyed stare of Brooklyn West, the so-called instigator of the riot that engulfed Harrowdean's sister branch, I wonder what this stranger would do in my position. If she'd tell me to let it all burn, even if that included myself.

"Help us weather this storm, Ripley. Control the patient population. Manipulate. Instill fear. Exploit. If Harrowdean survives, you will have your freedom."

"And if I refuse to play my part?"

His wrinkled mouth pulls taut. "You will make an excellent addition to the professor's Z wing program. I do hate wasted potential. But repurposing? Now that's just good business."

I look into Bancroft's eyes. Full of challenge and determination. He isn't afraid—monsters with power and money never are. This world will always be institutionally weighted in their favour. People like us are the foundation of their empires.

I'll be his weapon.

I'll even make it look real.

But the moment his house of cards begins to fall, I don't intend to stick around to bear the consequences. Even if that means shedding the person I am and the life I've fought so hard to resume.

Instead, I'll run.

And leave my soul behind.

CHAPTER 20
RIPLEY
LOVE ABUSER (SAVE ME) – ROYAL & THE SERPENT

"THE NEWS IS SAYING it's a once in a lifetime storm. Half the country is underwater."

Pierced nose pressed against the glass, I study the violent sheets of rain hammering into the ground like machine gun fire. The deep, almost purple clouds that have been looming over several days finally burst open a few hours ago.

"You read the news?" I laugh.

"No," Rae snorts. "I listen to gossip. Other people read the news."

We're standing on the grand staircase, gathered around one of the huge stained glass windows. Several other patients hang nearby to watch the apocalyptic light show of thunder and lightning. Crackles illuminate the night sky, tearing apart the heavens.

Already, the ground is saturated and overflowing with murky rainwater. The quad is slowly turning into a quagmire. We've all been confined to the main building until further notice.

"You think it'll wash this shit hole away?" she asks hopefully. "We can all swim to safety."

"Where's safe, Rae?" I sigh.

"Literally anywhere but here. I saw that dickhead guard, Elon, break someone's nose with that kinky baton thing he loves so much the other day. He fucking laughed."

"Believe me, there's nothing kinky about that baton." I shudder at the thought.

"You're missing the point. He broke her nose!"

I wish that was shocking to me. In any normal hospital or secure facility, it would be big news. A disciplinary matter for sure, maybe even a public scandal. But not here. Not in the shadows.

Remembering Bancroft's words, I force myself to respond. "She should've followed instructions, then."

Rae turns her attention from the storm to gape at me. "You're kidding? No one deserves that."

"I don't know what else to tell you. It's her own fault."

Several of the other patients clustered nearby are listening but keeping their gazes averted. Like if somehow they displease me, I'll arrange a personal nose-breaking of their own.

"Seriously, Rip?"

"Follow the rules, and you won't get hurt. It's simple."

"What the hell is wrong with you?" Rae's head rears back, her brows drawn.

"I'm just saying that we all need to comply."

"They shouldn't be using violence in the first place! You're sick for condoning it."

"Do we have a problem here?" I clip out.

Whatever she sees in my expression causes her eyes to bug out. Rae takes a step back and shakes her head.

"No. Not at all."

"Good. I'd hate to run into a supply issue with your weekly deliveries."

With a blank mask and flat tone that would make my uncle proud, I cast a quick look around at the others listening. Ensuring they all get the message. This isn't the first spectacle I've put on this week.

I push off from the windowsill. "That goes for *all* weekly deliveries."

Rae just stares at me like I'm some alien creature. Ignoring her and the soft murmurings I leave behind, I head downstairs. Exhaustion doesn't begin to describe the extent of my current downward spiral.

But I have a role to play. Expectations to fulfil. No one is paying me to be the hero. Martyrs are romantic in theory, but people forget they have to die in order to make a fucking difference. And I intend to survive.

Like a cockroach.

Holly would be so damn proud.

In the reception, chaos is unfolding. Several members of staff are attempting to block the entrances and exits with all manner of towels, rags and even boxes of paper. Filthy rainwater is spilling inside from the rapidly rising water levels.

Fitting, I suppose. Perhaps we'll luck out, and Harrowdean will be washed away, taking all its evil and evidence with it. We'll be left with nothing but our stories. And no one will ever be interested in those, right?

"Warden?" one of the therapists calls out.

Davis is standing farther back in the safe zone, watching his staff try to keep the place afloat. He eyes the impending disaster, his shirt sleeves rolled up and arms folded.

"What, Doctor Chesterfield?"

"The water, sir."

"Fetch more towels then!"

A sudden rush of water heads towards him and engulfs his expensive leather shoes. He curses and lifts a sodden foot, water now dripping from his trouser leg. I cover my mouth before he catches me laughing.

"Towels! Now!" he screeches.

The sound of his indignation is engulfed by a sudden, ear-splitting crash. Everyone instinctively ducks at the loud smashing sound. Shards of coloured glass slice through the air, catapulted by wind and rain.

Ducked down, I peer out from beneath my arms wrapped around my head protectively. The arched, stained glass window high above the exit doors has been destroyed. One of the rubbish bins from the quad now lies inside the reception.

"Christ!" Davis exclaims.

"Sir, we need to call an emergency lockdown."

"Yes! Now!"

Watching them deliberate, I squeak when a hand circles my wrist and yanks. I'm hauled backwards into the adjacent corridor then slammed up against the wall.

"Where is he?" Lennox hisses in my face.

I shove him away from me. "What are you talking about?"

He pushes my shoulders, causing my spine to slam against the wall again. "Raine! I can't find him anywhere. He's being a stubborn shit, and it's all because of you."

It hasn't escaped my notice that Raine's been sticking to me like glue since he tracked me down. He turns up at my bedroom door most nights and has made a point of ignoring Lennox in particular.

"Raine's decisions are his own," I defend. "It's not my fault you're a shit friend."

"Because I don't support him sleeping with a psycho slut like you?" Lennox seethes. "I've tried to warn him. The son of a bitch is determined to be your next victim."

This hot-headed moron is genuinely deluded. But he makes a good point—I haven't seen Raine all day. He was notably absent from lunch, and with the storm battering us, I need to know he's safe.

"Did you check his room?"

Lennox narrows his eyes. "Great idea. Why didn't I think of that?"

"Ease off, asshole. You haven't got two brain cells to rub together. I have to ask."

"You know what? Forget it. I'll find him myself."

With a final shove, he storms back off into the reception. I hate myself for appreciating the way his tight, white t-shirt bulges over his biceps and the fit of his sweatpants accentuates his perfectly curved rear.

I don't have to like the guy to admit that he's sexy as sin in a rugged, no fucks given kind of way. It's a shame he has to open his damn mouth and ruin that attraction.

That's when the real Lennox emerges. No amount of muscle or delicious stubble can fix that disaster. He's a cruel soul hidden behind a pretty exterior.

Concerned for Raine, I head for the music room. It's outside his usual practise hours, but the list of spaces he feels comfortable and safe in is limited. If something is wrong, he'd seek refuge there first.

In the south wing, it's deserted. Classes have finished for the day, and everyone is taking refuge while the storm rages. I stop outside the pitch-black music room to take a quick glance inside.

"Raine? You in here?"

There's no response, but I step into the darkness regardless, flicking on lights as I go. When I see his ajar violin case, I know the voice screaming in my head is on to something. The case is empty and haphazardly discarded.

"Raine?"

Nothing.

"Where are you? Raine?"

After searching the room from top to bottom, I find nothing. Just an empty case and no answers. Heading down the hall, I slam on the lights in the art room. My canvases and supplies are still in the top corner of the room.

With thunder exploding outside the bay windows, I make my way to the back of the room. Bingo. Raine's sitting on the floor, surrounded by stacks of dry canvases and boxes of oil paint. His violin rests in his lap.

"Why are you hiding in here? You scared the shit out of me!"

Inching closer, I realise his head is lolling to the side. I drop next to him, quickly seizing his hand. It doesn't tighten around mine. His fingernails are blue, matching the strange purplish tint of his lips.

Fuck!

That's when I notice the empty plastic coin bag resting in his limp hand. I haven't seen one of these since I used to help out at my dad's butcher shop as a kid. He'd sometimes let me count the change at the end of a shift.

There's a pale, powdery residue left in the bag from whatever pills were stashed inside. But the more horrifying realisation is that whatever he's taken, I didn't supply it. These aren't the bags we use.

I've been carefully controlling Raine's intake ever since he started coming to me. I never oversell and often reject some of his requests. Plus, the product is safe. Well, as safe as drugs can be. But this bag… it's not mine.

He bought from someone else.

Who the fuck sold this to him?

Shoving the baggie into my pocket to figure out later, I look back at Raine.

"Come on," I plead urgently. "Wake up, Raine."

Withdrawal looks different than this. He's completely out cold. Peeling back his eyelids, I find his pupils smaller than pinpricks. His healed, bruise-free skin is cold and clammy, but he's breathing, albeit in a worryingly shallow manner.

Shaking him several times, I repeat his name, my voice taking on a frantic edge. Not even a twitching of the eye. All I've got is the rapid rise and fall of his chest to reassure me that he's still alive.

I can't leave him. Not like this. If he stops breathing, I'll have to perform CPR. The mere thought is terrifying. Accident or not, I'm certain this is an overdose.

Patting down his pockets, I search for the lump of his smartphone. It's in his jeans and chirps back to me as I stab the buttons, searching his contacts. I have to swallow my pride to press the ring button on Lennox's name.

"Where the fuck are you?" he barks in greeting after two rings.

"It's Ripley."

Lennox pauses. "Where is Raine?"

"Out cold. Looks like an OD. You need to raise the alarm."

"This isn't a funny joke. Where is he?"

"Stop wasting time, Nox! Get fucking help!"

After a beat, there's a loud thud like he's punching whatever available surface is nearby.

"Where?"

"Art room. Next to where he was last time."

"Stay with him!"

When the line disconnects, I toss his phone aside. Raine still hasn't stirred. Pulling him away from the wall, I cradle his head in my lap and wrap my arms around him, attempting to transfer some warmth into his frozen body.

"Why?" I whisper through pooling tears. "I know we're in a world of shit, but you didn't have to do this."

Smoothing sweaty hair from his face, I focus on the whistling of his nose, indicating each breath. Inhale. Exhale. Inhale. Exhale. My world narrows to those two functions, offering me the faintest sliver of hope.

"Please, Raine."

Keeping a hand on his chest, I feel for the thrum of his heartbeat against his breastbone. Seconds pass sluggishly, turning into agonising minutes marked only by the beat of his continued existence.

"You deserve better than this place. I'll let you go if I have to, but I need you to get help and be okay. You'll never heal in Harrowdean."

Holding his hand in a deathly tight grip, I feel the faintest twitching of his fingers. Just a whisper. Enough to convince me that he's heard my voice in whatever drug-trapped hole he's stuck in.

"You had to make me go and give a shit about you, huh?" I laugh wetly. "You couldn't just take no for an answer."

Ducking down, I press a kiss against his clammy, blue lips. My tears drip on his face, absorbed by golden stubble. I hold him close, trying hard not to sob, until the sound of company approaches.

"In here!" I shout.

The door cracks against the wall, mirroring the violence of the storm still raging outside. Lennox is at the head of the group, followed closely by Doctor Hall from the medical wing and Nina, the smart-mouthed nurse who cared for me.

"How long has Raine been unconscious?" Doctor Hall asks calmly.

"I don't know... Ten minutes? He was like this when I found him."

He crouches down, taking the medical bag from the nurse. "What has he taken?"

"I don't know!"

He sighs. "Move aside please."

"No, I'm not leaving him."

Hands slide underneath my arms, and I'm yanked away from Raine. The doctor gently takes his head and rests it on the floor before he begins his examination. I hiss and curse as Lennox drags me backwards, his fingers digging deep into me.

"What did you sell him?" he growls in my ear.

"This wasn't me."

"Where'd he get it from, then? The tooth fairy?"

"It's not my shit. I've been monitoring him."

Lennox keeps me pinned against his front, unable to wriggle free. "I warned you, Ripley. You just crossed the fucking line."

"We've got loss of consciousness and signs of respiratory depression." Doctor Hall straightens. "Likely opioid intoxication. It'll have to be an intramuscular injection."

Nina roots around in the medical bag. After checking the labels, she pulls out two wrapped syringes and begins to prep them. Doctor Hall quickly radios to whoever is listening to request additional help.

We're both transfixed as the nurse lifts Raine's right leg to give the doctor a good angle to approach his thigh from. Doctor Hall holds the first needle at a right angle then inserts it into Raine's thigh through his clothing.

"Naloxone administered at 19:04." He checks his wristwatch. "100 micrograms."

"What are they doing to him?" Lennox snarls.

I struggle against his grip. "It'll reverse the OD."

After waiting two minutes, they check his breathing again before administering another dose. My heart is ready to tear free from my chest, and I can feel how hard Lennox is shaking. He still hasn't released me from his muscled prison.

After several minutes, Raine's breathing is a little less shallow. He still hasn't woken up, but I can see his chest rising and falling with deeper breaths. Nina keeps two fingers clamped tight on his wrist, measuring his pulse rate.

"Is he going to be okay?" Lennox's voice is rough.

"I'm familiar with Raine's file." Doctor Hall disposes of the used needles. "There's a higher risk of acute withdrawal following this treatment in cases of chronic drug abuse."

"Meaning?" Lennox snaps.

"He'll need to be admitted and monitored."

Barely able to see through my tears, I'm not sure when my body stopped fighting to escape and started leaning into the warm embrace of its captor. Feeling Lennox's firm chest at my back keeps me upright as I watch another nurse and two extra guards roll a mobile stretcher in.

"On three. Okay, one… two… three."

It takes two of them to lift Raine's limp body up and onto the stretcher. He's still deathly pale and clammy, those molten eyes sealed shut. Lennox's tight grip on me finally slackens, but I don't leap away yet.

"Please," I whisper. "I want to—"

Disregarding me, they wheel him away. I'm left staring after them, unspoken words hanging on my lips, regret holding me captive now. I can't move. Can't blink. All I can see is Raine's blue lips and slack face. Just like Holly.

She was still hanging when I found her. Tiptoes barely scraping the bedroom carpet. Jeans soaked with urine. Throat crushed. Lips blue. Eyes wide. She was as still as stone and cold as ice.

Worlds coalesce and become one. I'm staring down the barrel of another potential loss while being held by the person who instigated the last. I'm not sure when fate decided to become such a cruel bitch, but I'm sick of the irony.

"Let go!" I erupt.

Seeming to snap back to his senses at the same time, Lennox abruptly releases me like I burned him. "With pleasure."

"We need to get to the medical wing."

"You're going nowhere," he deadpans.

Spinning around, I meet his hard, seafoam glare. "Raine needs me!"

"Raine needs you to leave him the fuck alone!" Neck muscles corded, rage pours from Lennox. "Which you seem incapable of doing. I won't let you sell another fucking pill to him."

"I didn't do this!" I throw out my arms in frustration. "They weren't my pills!"

"You're such a manipulative cunt. I don't believe a self-serving word that leaves your mouth."

"What about the words that leave your mouth?" I shout back. "He deserves better than a *murderer* for a friend."

"Shut the fuck up, Ripley."

But I'm not done.

"Holly wasn't even the first person you killed, was she?"

Lennox recoils like I've slapped him. "Choose your next words carefully."

If I have any hope of getting to Raine, I need to remove this stubborn obstacle. I'll rip out his heart and grind it to a paste without feeling a speck of remorse.

"It wasn't hard to dig in to you. Plenty of news articles out there. The angry, grieving teenager left all alone to piece together what happened to his baby sister."

"Enough," he warns, nostrils flaring.

"What was her name, huh?"

"I said enough!"

It isn't enough. Nothing will ever be enough when it comes to Lennox. For a man who has experienced the deepest depths of grief and despair, he has no concept of the evil he's inflicted in the name of love.

And he expects me to abandon Raine because he says so? Raine is the one who needs protection from him. Lennox is a fucking disease. One that needs to be eradicated, once and for all.

"Rose… Or Iris? No, that's not right."

His chest vibrates with a growl. "Stop."

I snap my fingers. "Ah, Daisy."

Lennox's pale-green eyes swim with intense pain.

"Beautiful kid," I continue spitefully. "It's hard to believe that you didn't know what dear old Grandad was doing to her every night. Not until she killed herself anyway."

The colour has drained from his face. Pulling his innards out for inspection and splattering them all around us has never felt so sweet. His pain is my pleasure. I'll never get enough of this sweet satisfaction for as long as he's still breathing.

I raise a hand, and after years of wondering, lift the silver necklace that hangs around his neck. I've never been close enough to pull it free from his t-shirt before. It's always hidden with the chain peeking out of his collar.

At the end of the silver chain are two military dog tags. My thumb smooths over the inscribed surface. *Alfred Nash.* I recognise the name from the news reports. That doesn't explain why Lennox still wears the insignia of his first victim and sister's abuser, though.

"Did you care for Daisy so little that you'll happily wear *his* name around your neck?"

Grabbing my wrist, Lennox prises the dog tags from my hand. "I wear that monster's name as a reminder to always do what's necessary to protect those I love."

"Like murder?"

Spittle flying, his next words come through clenched teeth.

"I don't care if the world hates me for what I've done, I'll do it all over again. Alfred deserved to die. And Holly was a threat. Now… you."

"And what am I? Another threat to be removed?"

For a flash, I swear I see a hint of remorse in his eyes. The briefest whisper of something akin to enjoyment of our toxic back and forth. However, it's soon crushed and replaced with his signature brand of hatred.

"Yes."

His fist snaps out then slams into my stomach. My bruises have only just healed and faded from Rick's attack. Winded, I double over, gasping for air.

Lennox moves fast, wrapping a burly arm around my neck to trap me in a headlock. I hit him repeatedly, but it doesn't stop him from choking me out.

"By the time Raine wakes up, you'll be gone." Lennox tightens his arm to crush my windpipe. "And there will be no one left to fuck up his life. He'll be safe."

Dragging my nails down his exposed arms, I desperately search for an opening. Even the tiniest weakness. He doesn't flinch at the blood welling beneath my fingers to paint his skin.

The tight, strangling pressure of his headlock is constant. I'm going to pass out. What will he do to me? Panic sets in along with cold, hard survival instinct.

I'm kicking. Writhing. Scratching. Anything to secure the oxygen that my lungs are begging for. But Lennox won't let me escape. Not this time. He's found his moment and won't surrender me again.

"That's it," he encourages. "Shut your eyes."

Everything is growing heavy. Limbs filling with lead and blood flow decreasing. My head feels like a balloon set to burst. I can't stop my eyes from falling shut as nothingness permeates my vision.

His voice is the last thing I hear.

"I'm sorry, Rip."

CHAPTER 21
RIPLEY
CHOKEHOLD – SLEEP TOKEN

WITH THE SOUND *of Xander's shower running, I finally wriggle out of the wrist restraints that have rubbed my skin raw. I can reach down my body to my ankles now. I'm tied with some kind of thin, flexible nylon rope. Fuck knows how he sourced it in here.*

My limbs are like liquified jelly. I'm not sure how they're even still attached after the past few hours. Fumbling with the rope, I'm trembling too hard to even attempt unfastening the expertly tied knots. Xander left nothing to chance.

The glint of black steel catches my eye. He discarded the folding pocketknife once he'd licked my blood from its blade, his tongue an inch away from being sliced open. I was fascinated, watching that twisted display. And fucking soaked too.

Straining as hard as I can, my fingertips brush against its curved handle. I manage to seize the knife then quickly set to work slashing the rope from my ankles. It's tough and doesn't cut easily.

Once the restraints have given way, I try to stand up but crumple instead. I'm weaker than a newborn baby. The ordeal he put my body through, equal parts pain and pleasure, has left me exhausted beyond measure.

Wincing at the sting of bruises across my skin, I can't find the clothes I wore when I nervously tiptoed over here, too curious for my own good. I wanted to know if he would live up to his threats. If I could survive a night in Xander Beck's bed.

Snagging a t-shirt that smells like him—spearmint and something darker, somehow more primal—I quickly dress. My panties are peeking out from beneath the bed. That'll have to do.

I flee before his shower is finished. My mind needs time to process what we just did together. The lines we crossed. His confusing blend of sick fascination for pain and attentiveness for my pleasure. The scarred iceman hides many perplexing secrets.

Those scars weigh on my mind as I creep back to my room. They were everywhere. Littered all over his arms, biceps, stomach, thighs. Not an inch of skin was untouched. And neat, regimented lines too. Some deeper than others. But so clearly self-inflicted.

What internal pain does Xander have that's so great, he has to expel it on to himself? And at what point did that blade stop serving its purpose, and he switched to hurting others instead?

Reaching my door, I realise I don't have a keycard to unlock it. I left it tucked inside my sweats, still lost somewhere in Xander's room. I'm not brave enough to return yet.

Instead, I head for Holly's door. She has a fancy, all-access pass, courtesy of her perks. I can't tell her where I've been. I'll have to find an excuse.

If she knew I'd slept with Xander, she would blow a gasket. But as I lift my arm to knock on her door, my silent plotting halts. Realising that it's ajar, unease swarms in my chest.

For the year that I've known her, Holly has always been paranoid about her privacy. She would never leave her door unlocked. Licking my lips, I gently knock on the door frame.

"Hol? You in here?"

Silence answers me.

"I'm coming in."

My state of undress long forgotten, I creep inside. Light emanates from a lamp deeper in the room. It's as neat and organised as ever. She's particular about her space. But then the broken light on the ceiling with knotted bed sheets looped through the exposed fixture draws my attention.

I look lower.

Squeeze my eyes shut.

Reopen.

Still there.

I'm not sure how long I stand here. At some point, I must start screaming. But I can't feel or hear it. People arrive, and hands usher me outside where I collapse against the wall. Vision unfocused, all I can see is my best friend. Or rather, the remains of her.

Guards arrive. Staff arrive. Medics arrive. Footsteps. Shouts. Barked orders to clear the floor. None of it registers beyond the basic observations of a detached mind. I'm left here, huddled in a ball and gasping for each breath as they take a body bag out.

That's when I look away. Only for a moment. My head turns, allowing me to catch sight of the two patients who haven't been escorted to another floor. They stand at the end of the corridor, shoulder to shoulder. United in their success.

Seafoam rage.

Midnight detachment.

Something fractures inside me. It's almost a visceral thing—the breaking of my sanity. Like an overstretched rubber band that snaps and recoils but never reverts back to its original shape. I watch Lennox's lips lift into a grim smile. Like he's performed a hard but necessary task.

Xander's expression doesn't change a bit.

He just stares.

Transfixed by the sight of my life falling apart at the seams as my best friend's corpse is removed. That's when I start screaming again. I don't stop until the sedatives are administered.

Thunder rumbles.

Deep. Sonorous.

Enraged.

My mum used to say that thunderstorms are just God moving furniture. She was religious in the way that most Brits are—made to endure weekly Sunday school as a kid but never truly committing themselves to the idea of faith. Being force-fed the notion of religion kinda destroys that possibility.

The rumbles continue, each louder than the last. I wonder if the reception is flooded now? I really should go check on Raine. I wouldn't want him to get stuck or hurt.

Raine.

With the distant memories of Holly's death still swimming in my mind, awareness slams back into me. Finding Raine unconscious. Blue and lifeless. The medics taking him away. Lennox's threats. Passing out.

With each mental flashback, my senses trickle back in. The frigid cold hits first, then searing heat in my wrists and arms. Groaning in pain, I force my eyes to open.

It makes no difference. I'm in total darkness. My body is shivering, it's so cold. I can feel that something tight and painful binds my wrists together.

It feels like I'm tied to some kind of metal pipe. The pain in my arms must be from hanging all my body's unconscious weight on whatever binds restrain me.

Attempting to move, I feel water slosh around my legs. The sound of torrential rain echoes all around me in what sounds like a cavernous space. It collides with whatever water I'm submerged in. I'm soaked to the bone.

"Hello?" I call out hoarsely.

The emptiness answers me.

Thick, desolate silence.

"Hello!"

Echoes tell me I'm somewhere spacious. It feels empty. Still. The smell of old chlorine burns my nose, shoving out the last dregs of drowsiness. Kicking around in the water, my foot collides with an unknown object, causing me to yelp in fear.

A sudden burst of lightning cracks above me, illuminating my surroundings for a few seconds. I look around as quickly as possible, ignoring my sinking sense of dread. Then everything falls back into blackness.

Lennox. Fucking Nash.

I'm in the swimming pool.

My rapid look around revealed the zip ties securing my wrists to the bottom rung of the pool's steps. I'm surrounded by discarded furniture and rainwater that pours from the broken windows and ceiling.

Rapidly rising rainwater.

It's fucking flooding.

That twisted, vindictive man couldn't just kill me. Oh, no. That would've been too easy for the bitch who supposedly threatens his precious family, right? Instead, he's left me to slowly drown as the pool floods.

Hysteria quickly sets in. It's human instinct. Inescapable. I scream myself raw and contort my body at every available angle to escape bondage. Muscles burn and protest, but I don't stop.

Nothing breaks the layers of zip ties fastened around my wrists to form an unbreakable plastic chain. He's done his homework. I'm completely immobile.

"Fuck you, Nox!" I yell to the emptiness.

Part of me wishes he'd respond. Even to laugh or bait me. Revel in his victory. Anything but the lonely silence he's condemned me to die in. The lack of humanity is cold, even for Lennox.

By the time my voice gives out, the water has risen a few inches, now up to my thighs. Each flash of lightning reveals its progress. The storm shows no signs of letting up and halting the flood.

Working my wrists back and forth, I'm taken back to that night. The excitement and anticipation I felt as Xander sprawled me out, pinned me down and fastened each limb to his bed frame. All with that predatory gleam in his eye.

It sounds fucked up beyond words. I can admit that in the safety of my own thoughts. But that night, I found a sense of freedom that I'd never had before.

All the money in the world can't buy the ecstasy of handing your autonomy to someone else. Someone who will leverage it to torture you in the most exquisite way. The pleasure he found through hurting me only intensified the satisfaction.

I shove Xander from my thoughts as I battle against the layers of zip ties. My skin splits and bleeds, but I can't stop crying. Not when the freezing cold water is slowly creeping up to my waist.

"Please!" I wheeze uselessly. "Someone help me!"

Rumble. Crash.

All I have is God moving furniture and the ghosts of everyone who has damned me to die like this. Even if I didn't supply the pills swimming in Raine's system right now, I might as well have.

It didn't stop me from doing exactly that to so many others and with the same outcome. Harrowdean's list of victims is lengthy. I've contributed my fair share. Perhaps this is what I deserve. I shouldn't be allowed to go home when they never will.

Villains don't get happy endings for a reason.

How would the good guys cope if they did?

The tears come thick and fast. Tears for Raine. Rae. Everyone I've hurt in order to survive. The other version of Ripley who walked into Priory Lane, deluded enough to think it was her chance to get better. She died like so many others.

Wrists throbbing with each rivulet of blood flowing down my arms, I give up and hang here. Dead weight. Defeated. Powerful Ripley, reduced to a sobbing wreck in an abandoned pool. Without a single soul to miss her.

No one will find me in time.

Not when there's nothing to miss.

Water tickles my ribcage. The shivering has stopped. I'm numb now.

Slowly sinking into the abyss. I won't even fight it, there's no point. Maybe Lennox was right. Raine deserves a better friend than me.

He will be better off without me.

Everyone will.

Letting my head loll, I listen to the violent slam of the torrential rain. It becomes rhythmic. Trance-like. Lulling me into a state of detached calm as my body is engulfed by water, inch by inch.

It feels like an eternity has passed when the crunch of broken glass rouses me. Water laps at my clavicles and forearms as I peer around sightlessly, wondering if I've finally lost it. I'm probably hearing ghosts now.

Lightning flashes again, illuminating the outline of someone at the pool's edge. I blink through my crusted, swollen eyes, trying to discern if I'm imagining things in my desperation.

Another strobe of lightning. Reflections dance off platinum hair and alabaster skin. I've definitely lost it. There's no way he'd be here to save me, not when he's obsessed with bringing about my end.

A beam of light breaks through the obscurity. It's pointed in my direction and moving closer. Squinting, I realise that I'm seeing a phone's flashlight heading towards me.

"Found yourself in a spot of bother?" he utters in a cool voice.

Light shines in my face, making my eyes water. I blink through the haze, waiting as the image of Xander settles. Hair rain-soaked and plastered to his face, his polo shirt is soaked through and jeans mud-streaked.

"You're not really here."

He stops at the pool's edge. "Hearing whispers, little toy?"

Another loud clap of thunder rumbles overhead. The water is tickling the base of my throat now. Even if I crane my neck, I don't have much time left. It'll be in my mouth and nose soon.

"You disappeared." In his phone's weak light, I see him frown. "I dislike losing track of my own property."

"You're normally more focused than that," I rasp.

"I was searching for Raine. Only to find him passed out in the medical wing and you gone. Is this some kind of elaborate suicide plan?"

"I didn't tie myself up!"

His forehead puckers in concentration. "Ah. Lennox was rather cagey about how he discovered Raine in such a state. But it wasn't him, was it?"

Half-drowned and gasping for each breath, icy water kisses my throat and chin. I tilt my neck at a painful angle, hoping to preserve my air supply for as long as possible. Perhaps long enough for someone to follow Xander and find us both.

Watching my predicament, he takes a seat on the tiled edge. Xander studies me unhurriedly, disregarding the rapidly rising water. His eyebrows are pulled together like he can't decipher his own thoughts.

"I suppose he's making a point," he muses. "Drowning his problems instead of burning them alive this time around."

"X-Xander."

"Yes, little toy?"

I can't bring myself to beg. Not to him. Not again. So instead, I suck in each precious mouthful of air left, battling to keep the water level beneath my chin. The rain has to stop sometime. I can still make it.

Xander watches me bob, his head cocked to one side. "I've dreamed of watching your corpse turn blue so many times. In the Z wing, I played out different scenarios in my head while they tortured me."

Funny that.

I've done the same thing for him.

"Then I came here. I started watching you. Following you each day to observe your new routine and patterns. Learning about the person we created, rather than the obsession I once had."

He watches me spit up a mouthful of water that crashes into me in a miniature wave. His stare has hardened from one of intrigue to something akin to concern. If soulless psychopaths can display such emotion.

"I've watched you beat and threaten. Sob when no one is watching. Eat, sleep and take medication. Fuck for the thrill of it. Fall for the one person you never intended to. Hurt those you so clearly care about."

The water sloshes over my mouth and touches my nostrils.

Xander just watches me struggle. "I stopped seeing an object."

Whatever epiphany he's having, I don't want to hear it. Not with my last gasps of oxygen. Water laps at my nose, rising those final few centimetres faster than ever. The panic has come swarming back with a vengeance.

"I want you broken." Xander gracefully draws to his feet. "But I don't want to watch others break you."

Reaching into his pocket, he pulls out a familiar black pocketknife.

The same one I used to free myself once before. Taking a final breath before I'm taken under the surface, I see him frown at the blade.

Then... nothing.

Xander is gone.

I keep my eyes screwed shut as the cold water covers them. That way I can pretend I'm floating out to sea on a blissful wave, content to let the current carry me back to shore when it's time to return.

Chest burning with each passing second, the pressure is a slow build. Lungs seeking to expand once all the air has escaped as dying bubbles. But there's no air underwater. No reprieve from the inevitable conclusion.

Just nothingness.

The watery grave of Harrowdean's whore.

I hear a crash ringing all around me as something collides with the water. When the first bit of water pushes into my mouth and lungs, causing me to gag, I feel hands grasping at my wrists.

Snap.

The plastic zip ties give way. More water spills into my mouth, filling my lungs with each new iteration of panic. Something sharp nicks my wrist as the bindings release, tie by tie.

I feel the last bubble escape my mouth. My throat, chest cavity... everything feels like it's on fire. The snipping of my wrists being set free feels faraway, lost in the expanse of the pool's inky depths.

I hope Lennox is satisfied.

I hope Raine is safe.

I hope Xander learns to feel again.

One wrist suddenly breaks free, floating at my side. I'm too weak to even move it. Sharp nicks from a blade pierce my other wrist, working its way through the plastic trapping me in place.

On the verge of fading out, I feel the last piece of plastic leave my skin. I'm left afloat, sinking deeper into the welcoming nothingness. Until arms wrap around my waist. I'm propelled upwards, through layer after layer of umbra.

Rain showers down on my head as we break the surface. I frantically try to suck in a breath, but the oxygen can't seem to find its way into my airway. Nothing penetrates the blockade of swallowed water.

"Breathe, goddammit."

The voice offers what should be a cold command, but it comes out sounding more like a plea. The desperate call of salvation from the unlikeliest of sources. I wish I could appease that voice. I want to breathe.

Wet clothing slaps against hard ground. Pain radiates up my spine. Hands slip and slide all over me, searching for signs of life. I feel his arms band around my ribcage before I'm jerked—once, twice, three times.

On the third painful manoeuvre, water comes spewing up. It pours from my mouth and nose, burning so fiercely, I may as well have swallowed fire. When the heaving stops, I'm laid back down, and a mouth seals over mine.

Short, sharp bursts of air are pushed past my lips. The five rapid rescue breaths force my airways to reopen and accept sustenance once more. Lips disappearing from mine, I'm free to drag in my first excruciating breath.

In.

Out.

In.

Out.

Each ragged gasp brings life back to my soul. I can feel my limbs twitching and wrists throbbing. I'm flat on my back, still being hammered by rain. But something must be braced above me, protecting my face from most of the downpour.

Fingertips smooth wet curls back from my face. Gentle. Almost tender. The same hand that clasped mine in the medical wing despite thinking I wouldn't remember his momentary compassion.

My eyes flutter open. His face is shadowed but visible. Water drips from his hair and clothing, the continued flashes of lightning revealing what I'd never believe without seeing it myself.

Emotion.

His almost-black eyes are full of it.

"Y-You... saved me."

Xander's features seem to cave, overcome with sudden exhaustion. "You're worth more to me alive."

"But... you h-hate me."

His lids close, as though bracing for impact.

"I thought I did too."

CHAPTER 22
XANDER

DO YOU REALLY WANT TO HURT ME – NESSA BARRETT

KICKING Ripley's door open after scanning my stolen all-access pass, I heave her inside and let it slam shut. Carrying a semi-conscious woman through the quad would've been impossible on any day but this.

I heard the alarms ringing as I resolved to check the swimming pool earlier on, taking a lesser-known guards' exit to avoid being seen. Harrowdean has gone into lockdown. Everyone is confined to their rooms for safety.

It took some stealthy wading through flooded grounds to get back to the manor in the dead of night. And some even stealthier tactics to get upstairs without being spotted. No one can know about this.

Ripley doesn't need the heat.

I'm sure she's already on thin ice.

Telling myself a few months ago that I'd one day worry about her would've been entertaining. That Xander would have revelled in the notion that she'd lose her protection and suffer the same fate that we did.

Her tactics don't work on me. The public displays of solidarity for management and their aggressors. Using threats and manipulations to control an increasingly disenchanted client base. She's playing it well, for sure.

I've studied her enough. Theorised the best ways to break her down and reclaim those pieces for myself. Plotted and waited then plotted some more. While I may feel nothing, Ripley feels the world all too acutely.

But that isn't true, is it?

Did I feel nothing while watching her drown?

Brushing those peculiar thoughts aside, I mentally debate what the fuck I'm doing here, and more importantly, what the fuck I'm going to do with her. We're both drenched, shivering and near-hypothermic.

With the storm still battering against her barred windows, I locate the bathroom and hit the lights. She's breathing normally but still waxy and ashen. Heat. We need warmth. I quickly turn on the walk-in shower.

"Raine," she murmurs groggily.

If the motherfucker wasn't already half-dead in a hospital bed, I'd quickly send him to one for being the name on her tongue right now. She's *my* Ripley. My toy. I've let him have his fun, but I won't be observing from the sidelines anymore.

I carry her into the shower fully clothed then hold her up beneath the warm spray. When she doesn't respond, I inch the temperature higher, watching the steam billow around us.

"Come on."

Ripley jerks in my arms, crying out at the lash of hot water on her frozen skin. Now that she's beginning to respond, I prop her against my front and slowly peel the sopping clothes from her body.

"Easy," I whisper when she struggles.

I'm not certain she knows where she is or who holds her. There's no other explanation for the way she curls into me, seeking some kind of protection from the pain of warming back up. Like I'd ever be the one to protect her.

Turning my attention to her wrists, I rinse off the blood. She's rubbed them raw in an attempt to escape. I even cut her a few times while fumbling in the pitch-black water. My cock unashamedly stirs at the sight of blood drawn by my hand.

A once-white bandage covers her forearm. The adhesive edges are peeling from water damage, with all manner of detritus and filth stuck to the fabric. I pinch a loose edge and begin to peel it off.

When her still-healing stitches are revealed, I try not to get distracted by the sight of her skin held together by synthetic fibres. Only the deeper cuts required treatment. The others have scabbed over in precise carvings.

A risk of infection joins my list of concerns. It was far simpler when I was content to let her suffer. I never anticipated the jealousy that watching others torment my toy would inspire.

Only I'm allowed to hurt her.

Now I have the responsibility of helping her too.

Thoroughly rinsing the wounds, I settle for getting them as clean as possible. I'm woefully unprepared for this task. Lennox is the bleeding heart; he would know what to do here. If only he weren't the one who attempted to kill her in the first place.

"Warmed up?"

Her teeth chatter together. "B-Better."

Sagging against me, I'm forced to pick Ripley up bridal-style to exit the shower.

"Raine… okay?" she asks.

I strip her down to her underwear, wrapping her in a towel to carry her through to the bedroom to be deposited. "Last I checked."

"M-Medical wing?"

I study her steady breathing until I'm satisfied she isn't dry-drowning. At least for the time being. She isn't out of the danger zone yet.

"With Nox."

Gasping, she fists the bed sheets beneath her in an attempt to leverage herself upright. I place a hand on her shoulder and easily push her back down.

"Stay."

"Len-n-nox… I… he…"

"Isn't going to drown Raine in an abandoned pool," I finish her rambling. "If that sets your mind at ease for now."

Her eyes are swollen slits, landing on me. "Why?"

Sighing hard, I perch beside her on the bed. "Why what?"

"Why help?"

Staring into blood-lined hazel orbs, I don't have an explanation for her. Not even a deflection or lie. My reasons for diving into that pool to save her life are as unfathomable as the way she makes my senses come alive.

It's been a long time since I felt the stirrings of a normal human existence. Switching those parts of myself off became a necessity. A means of survival. I endured my childhood that way. Not to mention the years of foster care afterwards.

But I could never turn it back on again. Not with a blade. Not with the cries or pleas of others. Not even as Priory Lane's doctors beat, whipped and tortured me to their heart's content. Cracks formed but failed to split my defences open.

"Lennox wants me dead," she whispers. "You do too."

Her raspy voice wraps around my heartstrings and tugs. Those ancient cracks that I thought I'd plastered over have become deep crevasses that I'm at risk of falling into. The same bleak crevasses that I spent years hiding in to escape what was happening to me.

Whatever darkness Ripley sees brewing in my gaze makes her flinch. She pulls the towel tighter across her chest and swallows hard.

"You should go."

"Is that any way to treat your saviour?"

Her reddened eyes shine with tears. "Thank you for helping me. Now go."

Standing up, I leave a sodden patch behind on her bed. I'm not sure what prompts me to look over my shoulder at her, a single question hanging on my tongue. Seeking an answer I didn't realise I needed.

"Do I scare you that badly?"

Ripley watches me closely. "Versions of you do."

"There is only one version of me."

She swipes escaped tears from her cheeks. "Does that version feel? Or is he still in denial that he's human at all?"

Those words detonate whatever internal defences remain inside me. The ice in my veins solidifies, expands then shatters. Deadly shards rip me apart from the inside out until it feels like I'm bleeding in front of her.

I don't need to be told to leave again. I'm already running as far from this devil woman as possible. Far from her questions and pain-laced stares tugging something free from my soul that I have no intention of giving.

Her door crashes shut behind me. I slump against the solid wood, sliding down until I'm crouched, my knees pressed to my chest. Luckily, the corridor is deserted with no one to witness my ragged breathing.

How dare she?

I dragged her from that pool because only I get the privilege of deciding when it's her time to die. I'm the one who gets to claim that reward after all she's done. No one else. Not even Lennox.

But the even more disturbing realisation is that I don't know if I want that privilege. Seeing her ruthlessness and will to survive firsthand has ignited an obsession too strong for petty revenge to get in the way.

Still breathing hard, I can feel myself vibrating. What the hell is happening to me? My chest is tight. Jaw clenched. Brain whirling. Too many foreign sensations from a time long past are returning.

That conniving bitch is making me fucking *feel* again. I will not go back to being that person. I took the victim I once was and crushed that little kid into a tight corner in my mind. He's been chained there since.

I don't care about others.

I don't care about myself.

I only care about the next target.

Head resting against the door, I know I should leave. She doesn't deserve my concern. If she's found dead by morning, it will be one less concern for all of us. We'll go back to our original plan—taking Harrowdean for ourselves.

Even if she's not in it.

That thought is unbearable.

Banging the back of my head against the door, I savour the dull ache. Pain has always been a means of control to me. A way to check that my bulletproof shields are still intact. Only now, the pain has wormed its way back inside me.

I need to expel it. Purge this spreading poison from my veins and reset my operating system. I can go back to my last safe backup. The uncompromised version of Xander.

Before I ever met Ripley Bennet. Before she sunk her claws into me. Before seeing her in pain made me revert back to that wounded child who endured so much.

The storm rages outside and my own inner tempest grows with it. A battleground has opened up in my mind. The cold logic of removing the malware attempting to corrupt me versus embracing the bug and letting it tear my system apart.

Taking the pocketknife from my still-wet jeans, I spin it in my hands. Considering. Analysing. Reaching the only logical conclusion to end this madness. I've humoured my obsession for too long.

Pulling her from that pool was a mistake. Becoming infatuated in the first place... I never should've been so weak. Allowing hatred and fascination to become so inextricably entwined was only ever going to lead to ruin.

Scanning the keycard, I slip back into her room. The knife is cold in my grip. I follow the path to her bed, lit by lightning flashes. In the time I've spent deliberating, Ripley has passed out in her towel.

I stop a metre or so away, statue still and frozen. She's breathing deeply, sticking it out at this fickle thing we call living. Nothing seems to kill this girl. She's survived far more than I'd ever thought she would.

It would be so easy to sink the knife into her, removing any further temptation. She couldn't survive that, right? Not if I stayed to watch the life fade from her eyes. I'm longing to hear her dying breath.

But my body doesn't respond. Not to move an inch closer, not to lift the knife and not to sink it deep into any available organ. Instead, I'm fixated on the continued evidence of her breathing.

What is she doing to me?

Not even hatred can offer me comfort as she whimpers in her sleep. My stomach lurches, filling with the most unwelcome sense of anxiety. She's afraid. Not in the pleasurable way I want her to be—in actual fear.

I don't want her fearful of the world's monsters. I want her to fear *me*. The real monster. No one else has earned the right to haunt her nightmares. I deserve to be the object of her hatred and revulsion.

If she hates me, this feeling will stop.

I'll regain control.

But still… my body doesn't comply. Not even the slightest twitch of my finger. I'm left staring at the rise and fall of her chest, the scrunch of her dark-brown brows, each vulnerable whimper sliding past her lips.

The cracks are deepening.

I'm being dragged down.

It's several hours before the storm breaks, and clouds disperse enough for a weak beam of sunlight to break through the barred window. I distantly realise there've been no overnight checks from the guards—the situation downstairs must be disastrous.

The faint morning light makes the air sparkle through drizzling rain. I've watched her sleep for hours. Fingers clenching and unclenching around the knife. The morning dawn reveals my predicament. She could open her eyes at any moment and catch me. But doing what?

Watching her?

Or watching over her?

I may be obsessed with her, but in the sickest way possible, it's learned behaviour. I've been the subject of fascination before. If that's even the right word. Stitching the haphazard quilt of my identity back together when I escaped took years. She's going to rip those unhealed stitches apart with her bare hands.

My muscles protest as I finally move. I crawl onto the bed and hang over her, eyes tracing the edge of the towel barely being held in place. Her arms are curled up to her chest protectively, but her throat is exposed.

The moment my blade touches her skin, she inhales sharply. Ripley's eyes flutter open, revealing still bloodshot whites surrounding her greenish-brown irises. It takes a moment for recognition to filter in, her nostrils flaring with a panicked breath.

"I won't let you destroy me, Ripley."

Her throat bobs beneath the sharp kiss of steel. "Please—"

"Begging for your life won't change the outcome. I should've left you in that pool. It would've been simpler."

"Then why didn't you?"

"Human weakness. But I won't be weak anymore."

She blinks, her expanding pupils betraying well-kept secrets. "Is it weak to care?"

"It's weak to feel." I press the knife in deeper. "It's even weaker to want something."

A fat tear escapes the corner of her eye and rolls down her cheek. I watch its path down to her chin.

"Then get on with it. Kill me." Ripley sucks in another short breath.

"Why?"

"Because I hate you, and I hate myself for also wanting something more."

Thin dribbles of blood paint her neck. They coat the blade that could so easily end this for the both of us. All it would take is one swipe. An easy slash.

Her skin would cut like butter, and I could watch her choke on her own blood. My mouth moistens at the thought. I could own her final moments.

"You've fought so hard to survive." I frown in confusion.

She offers a bleak smile in return. "Maybe I'm tired of being the survivor. Look what it's cost me."

Blood speckling the sheets beneath her, Ripley wraps a hand around my arm. But she doesn't attempt to prise the pocketknife away. Her fingers glide over rigid lumps and gnarly scar tissue, tracing each individual scar like she wants to spend hours memorising the exact details.

"What did being the survivor cost you, Xander?"

I hold her life in my hands as I answer. "Everything."

"What would you do to get it all back?"

"Anything." The unexpected admission breaks free.

With the pocketknife still slicing into her neck, I lower my mouth to hers then slam our lips together. I don't care if it hurts. I don't care if she wants me to kiss her or not. I want to taste her fear and see if she's as terrified of this as I am.

Perhaps we're not so different after all. I'm holding her at knife point and taking exactly what I want, regardless of whether she wants to give it. In many ways, she's doing the exact same thing to me.

Hatred and desire collide hard enough to split the fucking atom.

I shove my tongue into her mouth with the necessary force to prise her lips apart. I don't know if she grants me access or simply accepts defeat, but her mouth opens up to me.

Teeth clinking, our kiss is a violent duel. I'm determined to find the answer to my inner turmoil. Even if it means tunnelling my way inside her soul to find those elusive secrets. I have to know why.

Why now?

Why here?

Why her?

Old Ripley was a pleasurable thrill. An intense fuck. Spanking her until she bruised satisfied me. Dragging my blade across her skin and smearing the resultant blood spill enthralled me. Holding her on the cusp of an orgasm made her irrevocably mine.

I broke her.

Claimed her.

Kept a piece of her soul as a souvenir.

Little did I know that she did the same thing to me. All this time, she's been waltzing around with a twisted part of me living and breathing depravity into her too. The girl I broke became the ruthless woman I created.

Perhaps I've broken her enough.

Perhaps now I should worship what I created.

My mouth rips from hers, nipping and sucking from her chin to her throat. Her tiny whimpers make my cock twitch as I slide the knife free and admire the uneven slash it leaves behind. All that glistening blood. Perfectly formed droplets of pleasure.

I lick the crimson beads up. Copper ripples across my tastebuds, far sweeter than any other nectar. Her essence is inside me now. I'll be able to find the control I'm looking for in the metallic tang of her blood.

"Xander," she pants. "I... we can't... Raine. I have to see him."

My temper burns white-hot. "He can wait. You were mine first."

"Please... No. I can't do this!"

Her fresh blood still slicked across my mouth, I grab the edges of her towel and rip them apart. Her now semi-dry panties and bra are revealed beneath the rough, hospital-grade cotton.

Ripley recoils and tries to hide herself, but I prevent her from covering up. She's hidden from me for long enough.

"I don't care what you want," I state fiercely. "I care what you need. What we both need."

Her eyes are gaping saucers. Not even I recognise the raw possession in my own voice. The sheer breadth of emotion and passion colouring each syllable instead of a thick coating of frost.

Blood smears over her collarbones and chest as I trace a path to her breasts. She's struggling to escape, still protesting like I believe a word she says. But as my bloodstained lips clamp around her left nipple, those protests morph into high-pitched moans.

I bite down, sucking the pert bud into my mouth. Hardness rolls between my lips and grazes against my teeth, each suck serving to heighten her arousal, evidenced by panting moans. I grab her right breast and squeeze, adding enough pressure to elicit just a hint of pain.

"Xander!" she mewls. "Please... stop."

Still massaging her breast, I release her now reddened nipple and skate lower still. My lips coast a path down to the apex of her thighs. She whines those pathetic little complaints all while lifting her hips to seek out what her body craves.

I kiss the soft curve of her belly before moving lower. Despite soaked cotton covering the desire she's so frantically trying to hide, I can smell the promise of her wet cunt. All mine. I bring the knife to the elastic holding her panties in place.

"Hold still. I wouldn't want to slip."

"No," she moans.

"No?" I tap her clit through the fabric.

Her hips buck, pushing her clit against my thumb again. She smashes her eyes shut while grinding against my hand. Always so needy. That much hasn't changed.

Sliding a finger beneath her panties, I push it between her awaiting, slick folds. Ripley cries out as I find her molten core and slip inside, burying my finger deep in her enticing heat.

"Still saying no, little toy?"

She clenches tight around the single digit, her pussy spasming in response to the intrusion. Unwanted or not, she's practically dripping on my hand, she's so wet. That's why I'll never believe the lies she tells herself.

"No," she repeats.

"Wetter than a bitch in heat," I observe plainly. "And still telling me no."

Stretching her with a second finger, I love watching her squirm. She wants to hate my touch so badly. Let's see if she feels the same way when my tongue is buried in her cunt instead.

Sliding the knife's edge across her pubic bone, I watch the gooseflesh that rises. My dick swells at the sight. Her writhing abruptly halts when she realises I have a knife so close to her most vulnerable place. Keeping one hand at her pussy, I twist the knife and begin to slice her panties free.

Elastic pings, then the fabric falls away, revealing her swollen nub. I easily sever the strap on the other side, still pushing two fingers in and out of her entrance. Her inner-thighs are already slick.

"Why does your body tell a different story?" I croon.

She gasps as I curl a finger inside her. "I… I… fuck! I hate you so much."

"If that's what you need to tell yourself, then go right ahead."

Pulling my fingers free, I suck them dry. Ripley stares down at me, wide-eyed and trembling. When I bury my face between her thighs, she immediately responds.

Hips bucking, her pussy opens for me so perfectly. I push my tongue inside and lap at her core, sucking up every drop of moisture she's fighting so hard to hide.

Stopping for a short breath, I turn my attention back to her clit as I insert my fingers inside her again. She moans at the pressure of my lips on her tight bundle of nerves.

Licking and teasing with the lightest graze of teeth, I steadily fuck her with my hand, reading her body like it's my favourite playbook. She's clenched around me and panting so loudly, I know she's close to climaxing.

"Does my little toy want to come?" I whisper against her clit.

Ripley huffs in response.

Such a stubborn brat.

Sucking her clit between my teeth, I apply enough pressure to take her to the edge. Then I cruelly rip my fingers from her cunt and sit back up. Her subsequent whine is music to my fucking ears.

"No!" she wails.

"No again, hmm?"

Only this time, she isn't protesting but mourning the loss of what I could give her. What she's too chicken shit to ask for. Smirking, I bring my hand down on her glistening cunt. Hard. The wet slap echoes around us.

"You have to ask for it," I command. "No. You have to *beg me* for it."

"Fuck you!"

I slap her wet pussy again. Ripley's back arches, her lips parting in the perfect O shape. I wonder if I could make her come from doing this alone. She's always had a masochistic need for punishment.

My jeans have become painfully restrictive. I want to strip off and prowl over her so she can see all that she's denying herself. Contemplating the pocketknife, I flip it to hold the blade portion then raise the smooth handle to her lips.

"Suck."

"Go to hell," she seethes.

"Already there, sweetheart. Suck or I'll find another use for this knife."

Gulping hard, she opens wide to accept the slightly curved black handle. I move it in and out of her mouth, letting her saliva coat the surface. Strings of spit stretch from her lips when I pull it free.

"Now, I can't leave this greedy cunt empty. Can I?" Pinning her legs completely open, I run the lubricated handle over her folds. "Keep those legs open for me."

"Xander?" Her voice trembles.

"I told you how this works before, Rip. You're mine to do with as I please. That much hasn't changed."

I push the pocketknife inside her like any other sex toy. Even when I lift my hand from her thigh, she keeps her legs spreadeagled, exposing every last inch of herself to my perusal. Her pelvis must be aching.

"Perfectly safe," I murmur. "As long as you don't move a muscle."

She can't see it from her position, but the blade is a safe distance away. Her fear is delicious, though. I keep an eye on the blade impaling her as I stand and peel off my rain-crusted clothing. Her eyes drink in every pale inch that's revealed.

I've never had trouble baring myself. I'm not ashamed of my scars. Only the secrets behind them. From the feverish gleam in her eyes, she's as dedicated to unearthing them as I am to forgetting.

Standing over her, I wrap a hand around the hard length of my cock. That smart mouth remains clamped shut as I begin to pump my shaft, imagining the glistening heat that will soon be around it.

"Are you ready to tell the truth?"

Her locked jaw tightens.

"I see. We can play this game all day if that's what you desire."

Settling between her legs, I slowly slide the pocketknife from her cunt. It's glazed with her juices. Such a tantalising sight. I raise it back to her mouth then cock a brow expectantly.

"Clean up your mess. This is my favourite knife."

Her rosy lips remain tightly sealed.

"Ripley."

Still being a brat.

"Fine."

I keep the blade pinched but drag the razor-sharp tip across her lips as if I intend to carve her up. She quickly follows my command, letting her mouth open. I push the handle inside and watch her lick it clean.

"Good," I hum. "Not so hard to obey, is it?"

Once the knife's clean, I flip the blade to retake the handle. She can't suppress a terrified squeak when I suddenly stab it into her bed, mere centimetres from the side of her head. Her breaths are sharp and rapid.

"Give me attitude again, and I'll sink it into your heart instead."

Ripley gulps in response.

Perfect.

Kneeling between her legs, I have a great vantage point to study every trembling inch of her. Disfigured ink. Stitched wounds. Trails of dried blood. Odd fading bruises. Every imperfection is its own siren's call.

I don't want her perfect and unblemished. Some of us are brave enough to admit that we find beauty in the twisted and depraved instead. I only wish someone else hadn't touched what's mine to tarnish.

"Poor Ripley. So desperate for relief, yet so willing to deny herself too."

Her tattooed arms are limp at her sides. That won't do. I seize her wrists, above raw abrasions inflicted by zip ties and hand-carved letters, to pin her arms above her. My body knows where to go without needing a map.

Already, my cock is pressed up against her entrance. I nudge it inside a small amount before withdrawing and swirling the head around her moisture again. Each rotation causes her to thrust upwards, a silent beg for more.

"Please," she whines.

"Not until you say it."

"Say what?" Her temper explodes. "That you're a cruel bastard for making me want this?"

There she is.

My furious hellhound.

"No. Say that you want me, the man you claim to hate so fucking much, to fill this sweet cunt up to the brim."

Ripley hisses in frustration as I push inside her again, a tiny bit farther, then withdraw. Such exquisite torture. I'm feeling the pressure already, but I won't relent. Not until she does.

"I told you to beg me, Ripley. Do it now."

When she curses under her breath, I move one hand lower to press against her wounded wrist. The lash of pain soon loosens her tongue, but I squeeze hard for good measure.

"Please!" Ripley gasps.

"Yes?"

"Please… fuck me, Xander. I'm begging you to fuck me. I need you."

How odd it is to be needed.

Satisfied, I surge into her in one fast pump. She takes my full length, but it's a snug fit. Her yelp takes me back to the first night I forced her to beg. Oh, how she wailed when I finally let her fall apart.

I retreat fast then thrust back inside, not giving her even a moment to catch her breath. Watching her blood-streaked tits bounce with each movement is close to godliness. There's no better sight than her submission.

Each time my hips surge and I slam back into her, Ripley moans in such agonising ecstasy. The animalistic sounds burst free, unable to be suppressed for a second longer. She can no longer deny that she wants this.

Wants me. Wants us.

Do I want the same?

CHAPTER 23
RIPLEY
LOVE YOU BETTER – THE HAUNT

I'M NOT sure where my pleasure ends and my hatred for the man gifting it to me begins. All I know is that if he dares to stop right now, I'll surely lose my mind. Analysing what a mistake this is can come after he's fucked me senseless.

I'm restrained tightly by his iron-clad grip and can feel the protest of my wounded wrists. It hasn't entered Xander's awareness. Or perhaps it has, and he simply doesn't care enough to ease up. It's hard to tell with the iceman.

Right now, he isn't that man at all.

This creature is all fury and flames.

My body is nothing more to him than the scorched earth beneath his feet. He'll trample me underfoot to get what he wants. In this frenzied state, I'd probably thank him for it. I'm all sensation, blindly grasping for any opportunity for relief.

His midnight-blue eyes have descended into inky blackness. Each stroke he inflicts makes his jaw tense and wiry muscles spasm. He's built similarly to Raine, lean and agile, but still hiding significant strength. Strength that is marred by scars and pain.

I want to feel guilty. I want to stop this. Walk away. Never look back. Take my rightful place in Raine's hospital room. But selfishness is a powerful motivator, and after what Lennox did, I need this.

I need the safety and control of surrendering to someone else. Someone evil. But I don't know if I can even call Xander that anymore.

His icy nonchalance hides a far more horrifying reality that I've yet to unearth. I don't know who he really is.

The enemy?

The man who saved me?

Both paradoxes wrapped up in one?

Seizing the pain that's setting my mind alight, I focus on my throbbing wrists. It's a wonderful juxtaposition to the way my limbs are turning to mush.

Xander is slamming into me, his tempo inching ever higher. But his attention doesn't waver. After all these months, he's still studying me. Searching for whatever answers he's so willing to sacrifice everything for.

I know I antagonise him. His icy façade can't withstand whatever the fuck this twisted sickness burgeoning between us is. I don't understand it and wouldn't expect anyone else to either.

We're as toxic as all good tragedies are, and that only makes me want him more. Finally accepting that feels like a defeat. This man has brought nothing but grief and misery into my life, but in this moment, that doesn't change a thing.

I want Xander.

I want every emotion he has left.

I want to hurt him back.

Releasing one wrist, he moves his grip to my chin. His short fingernails dig into my skin as he drags my mouth to his. Our lips clash. There's no hesitation on my part this time. I want to bruise him just as badly.

Tongues meeting, his spearmint taste fills my mouth. I bite down on his bottom lip, luxuriating in the blood that wells up to meet me. A deep, satisfied groan rolls up from his throat as I suck the bloodied lip dry.

Taking that tiny bit of control back and hearing his reaction fires me up. I'm already a sweaty mess, clawing ever closer to the edge of a welcoming oblivion. He's tortured me enough. I want to spiral and explode now.

With my freed-up hand, I stroke over Xander's neatly-packed abdominals. The tight lines of muscle are visible beneath layers of scar tissue. Seeing those marks again only reignites the questions I'm too scared to ask.

Years have softened each light-pink laceration but failed to obscure them entirely. He must've been so young when he started cutting himself.

Young enough for the marks to bear witness to all he's done to avoid feeling ever since.

My broken boy.

My twisted, damaged man.

"Eyes on me," he grinds out. "Now."

I drag my attention from his scars. Xander is glowering at me, unable to stand being ignored for even a second. Like somehow I could forget he's making it his mission to command my every thought.

Seemingly appeased, he lowers his face to my breasts. I cry out at the sudden onslaught of his lips. He lavishes each nipple, alternating between kissing, sucking and biting down hard enough to sting. Each sensation makes my nerve endings sizzle.

My legs clench around him, holding his waist in a vice. When he rolls one nipple between his fingers while sucking on the other, I feel an orgasm begging to take over. My nails dig deep into his mottled skin.

"Please," I beg for a release.

"I don't think so," he clips out.

When his lips disappear from my breast, the steely warmth of his cock within me vanishes. I hit a brick wall and ricochet, an unbearable pressure threatening to rip me apart. My orgasm is cruelly snatched away before I can gasp.

Xander holds himself over me, observing each iteration of disappointment. I cry out in shock at the sudden loss, my thighs clenching tight around him, like I can force the clock to rewind and give me the release I need.

"No… Please!"

His grip on my chin loosens. "Hurting, little toy?"

"God-fucking-damn you, Xander!"

"That's more like it." His grin is full of sinister satisfaction. "You haven't begged enough."

Moving to grasp my hips with both hands, he roughly flips me over. I land back on the mattress in a faceful of bedsheets. Fingertips glide down my spine, tracing each curvature as another hand circles my hips and ass.

I brace for the hit I know is coming. His soft touches never last long. When the first spank cracks against my rear, it jolts my whole body. Pain flashes up my spine in time to the exploration of his fingertips.

"You still mark so exquisitely."

Fisting the bedsheets, I swallow a cry. It'll only satisfy the son of a bitch. If he isn't going to give me what I want, then I sure as fuck won't return the favour. He'll have to hit me until I bleed.

Xander strikes my other ass cheek, the force of his smack making my skin tighten and prickle. I can feel blood rushing to the area. My back arches, absorbing the force, still enduring the tease of his featherlight fingers.

Those dancing fingers traverse upwards to wind into my tangled hair. Though it's unkempt and matted from my brush with death, that doesn't stop Xander from fisting the coarse strands.

He wrenches hard, forcing my head to tilt up. I'm suspended, half-upright at a vulnerable angle, breasts jutting out and knees wobbling.

"Is this what you wanted?" He nudges back between my soaked thighs from behind. "Someone to fuck you like the object you desire to be?"

"I'm not your object," I gasp in delicious pain.

"I forgot. You're not mine." He yanks sharply on my curls. "You're Harrowdean's whore, right?"

Before I can snatch the knife from my bed and stick it in his fucking eyeball, he slides back into me. From this angle, his strokes are shallow and fast. A constant drilling that takes me right back to the brink.

I want to wail and rave. Batter my fists against his bare chest and throw him out of this room. But each stroke of his cock inside me silences whatever hatred I'm ready to spew. He owes me this much.

Xander pulls my hair with each pump, merging fierce pain with toe-curling pleasure until tears are pooling in my eyes. I'm too overwhelmed. Overstimulated from every angle. His other hand clasps my hip in a bruising grip.

When that grip slackens, I prepare for the next slap. It's a hard, fast strike against my right ass cheek. Bracing for it doesn't decrease the way my skin burns. With each spank, the fire spreads.

"Still pretending to hate me?" Xander groans.

"Yes!"

His pounding continues, relentless and battering. It's like he's trying to beat the truth out of me. The reason why I sacrificed their lives to get my revenge. He still doesn't get it.

"You... ruined... me," I pant.

"Oh, I know." His breathing is almost as laboured as mine. "And truthfully, I don't blame you for feeding us to the wolves. In fact, I was impressed."

"Why? I wanted you dead!"

"Exactly." His breath teases my ear as he pushes my hair aside. "Look at how formidable we made you."

When his teeth sink into the shell of my ear, I moan again, sparks flying with each sensation. It's all building to the grand finale, but I know he'll make me work for it. Nothing is easy with Xander.

"I hate the person you made me."

"Do you?" he grunts. "Because I find that hard to believe."

I'm climbing a steep cliff, dragging myself up inch by agonising inch. His cock worshipping me shoves me higher up that slope until I can see the tempting fall once more. The edge I need him to throw me off.

This is what he's reduced me to. A submissive, needy wreck, willing to sacrifice my integrity and secrets just to earn his surrender. Just when I thought I couldn't stoop any lower.

"You want the truth?" I grit out.

Xander drags his nails over my skin, leaving scratches behind. "Yes. Admit it."

"Admit that if it wasn't for you… I wouldn't be here at all." My legs quiver as my climax nears.

"More, little toy."

Releasing my hair, he abruptly pushes me down so I'm bent over with my ass high. I turn my head to the side to suck in ragged breaths as his thrusts deepen, finding an angle that pushes me past my breaking point.

"You made me ruthless. You made me cruel." I moan through another punishing spank against my sore ass. "You made me into a monster fit to walk beside you."

"Where." He pumps into me. "You." His cock jerks as I spasm around him. "Belong."

My muscles spasm with the force of my hard-won orgasm. After all the baiting, he finally yields. Xander's roar is a fucking triumph that makes me shatter. I steal his remaining control and plummet with it into the unknown.

My name rolls off his tongue like a lamentation. He's grieving the loss of whatever flimsy protections remained in place between us. The hate that once kept us apart now binds us together in a far more intimate way.

The iceman has finally thawed, and it feels so fucking good to relinquish the fight. That realisation makes my release even more intense. I feel my extremities turn to mulch as Xander pours himself into me.

His body becomes a dead weight above mine. At some point, he collapses next to me on the bed, and we end up entwined. Our limbs are a sweaty tangle as we both search for air, neither able to form a coherent word.

Don't do it, Ripley.

But the voice of reason can fuck off right now. I snuggle up against my enemy's chest and rest my head over his out of control heartbeat. At first, it's like embracing stone. Then a scarred arm curls around me. I feel his nose bury in my hair.

I'm where I belong.

Sleeping with the devil.

"What happens now?" I eventually break the silence.

His buried face doesn't lift from my hair.

"I have no fucking idea."

CHAPTER 24
RIPLEY
DROWNING. – EDEN PROJECT

MY PALMS ARE slippery with anxious sweat as I'm escorted into the medical wing by the on-duty nurse, Nina. This quiet corner hasn't been touched by the water damage that's causing carnage elsewhere in Harrowdean. Half the institute is flooded or trashed after the storm.

Cleanup was unfolding as I picked my way through the rubble earlier to get here—tree branches, waterlogged leaves and all manner of unnamed detritus coating every surface. Patients are being confined to the unaffected areas, but a quiet word with Langley, who was luckily working, allowed me to pass the guards' blockade.

"Is he awake?"

She holds open the door for me. "Yes. He's under observation."

"For how long?"

"Until his blood pressure stabilises. He was in a bad way last night."

Breathing deeply, I follow her to Raine's cubicle. The curtains are drawn. I have a moment to grapple my nerves, letting her walk ahead to pull back the thin blue fabric.

"Raine," she chirps. "Visitor for you."

Propped upright in the bed, Raine rests on several plumped-up pillows. His sandy-blonde locks are uncombed and pointing haphazardly in all directions, while a blanket covers his patterned hospital gown.

Those rich toffee eyes seem to gleam brighter when he breathes in, his lips quirking into a smile. I showered using his favourite body wash before coming. Seeing that grin makes my throat tighten.

His gaze swings around the cubicle. "Hey, Rip."

"Anyone could smell like papaya, you know."

"But no one could smell quite like you."

"I'm never going to be able to sneak up on you. Am I?"

"I wouldn't count on it. Besides, I don't see many other girls queuing up to sob at my bedside. Do you?"

"I don't know. I had to fight my way in here to get past your fans."

He swats a hand through the air. "Feel free to let them in. I'm bored as fuck laying here."

"Perhaps think of that next time, mister." Nina bustles around him, fiddling with his multiple IV lines and frowns at various machines monitoring his vitals. "Ain't nothing fun or interesting about drugs. You worried your girl here."

"Alright, Nina." Raine sighs tiredly like this isn't the first time she's scolded him. "Enough of the lecturing already. Isn't your shift over yet?"

"Behave. I'll be back." With an eye roll, she scurries from the cubicle.

Even with her gone, I can't bring myself to walk over to him. He looks so small and ashen in the hospital bed, an array of needles poking into his arms and the low, steady beep of a monitor measuring each heartbeat.

Part of me wonders if he'd be laying here had we never met. I know this isn't Raine's first rodeo. He's been playing this game for far longer than I know. But I thought things were under control. I thought he was being safe.

"Rip." He pats the bed. "Come here."

I shake my head before realising he can't see it. "I can't do that."

"I need to explain."

"Well, I don't need you to. This... It's my fault."

"Don't do that to yourself. Please."

"It's true. I never should've sold to you in the first place. If you'd gone through withdrawal and maybe gotten clean back then, none of this would've happened."

"Because I'd be dead," Raine deadpans.

"You don't know that."

He fiddles with a clear plastic tube wrapped around him. "I'm here because I was reckless. That's all."

My chest constricts. "Why'd you do it?"

"It was just a dumb mistake." He exhales loudly through his nose.

"Something else must've been cut into the pills I took. I wasn't trying to overdose or do anything stupid."

"It was an accident? Really?"

"I swear, I didn't do this on purpose."

That loosens the pressure on my panic-strapped lungs a small amount. Outrage floods into me instead. I'm in no position to lecture or judge, not after what I've done, but it doesn't stop me from feeling hurt.

"Where did you get those pills? I know they weren't mine. You've been buying from someone else."

His lips pucker then twist. "It doesn't matter."

"No one else is supposed to be selling in here!" My voice raises. "So it does matter. They sold you a bad batch, and it almost killed you. I want a name."

Unseeing eyes gazing over my shoulder, he seems perfectly calm. Like swallowing God knows what chemicals and almost dying as a result is just an average weekday. I don't know whether to kiss him or kill him, I'm so furiously confused.

"Just leave it." He cringes in pain as he shifts his position. "I'm fine."

"Nothing about this is fine. You were blue, Raine! Fucking blue!"

Exhaustion is catching up to me after everything that's happened. Part of me wants to run far away from Harrowdean and all its complications. Three in particular.

Raine.

Xander.

Lennox.

Everything has been spiralling out of control since they arrived. Before then, I had a plan. Less than a year left and I could've walked away. Now I'm in deep waters.

"If you won't tell me who, then tell me why." I stop at the end of the bed. "Why not come to me?"

"Does it matter?" he sighs.

"Yes! I thought you trusted me!"

Raine scrubs a hand over his face and the roughened stubble on his chin. "Please just sit down, okay?"

Still trembling all over, I perch on the end of the bed. Raine moves his covered legs to make space for me. His head is tilted down, eyes unfocused on the hospital sheets.

"You said you're tired of being the bad guy."

I blink several times, certain I've misheard him before the memories of admitting that float back to me. I felt so broken in that moment, tired of being the source of so much pain.

"So?"

Raine shrugs. "I didn't want to be another thing for you to feel guilty about. I figured if I bought elsewhere, it might ease some of that burden."

"So you bought shit heroin from some random to spare my feelings?" I gape at him.

"Erm..." He fights a smile by biting his lip. "Something like that?"

All I can do is stare, stunned to speechlessness by this complicated, enigmatic man with so much damage wrapped up in his pure soul. He really is incredibly stupid but in the most thoughtful way.

"Turns out, you're the only good dealer in this place." He laughs at the irony. "I don't even want to know where those pills were from."

"I really, really want to punch you right now."

"I'm blind and bedridden, babe. That's foul play."

"You want to schedule in a better time for me to kick your ass?" I quip back. "I'll clear my diary."

"It's a date."

Brain still whirling, I'm trying to filter through possible options of who could be smuggling pills in from the outside. It's hard, but not impossible. Some patients have regular visitation.

Raine releases the tube wrapped in his fingers, tentatively stretching out his hand palm up. "So can you forgive me for... uh, almost dying?"

"No! You're so... so..." I slam my eyes shut to try to hold the tears at bay. "I can't do this again. I've lost everyone I have ever cared about."

"I know, Rip. I'm sorry."

The tears escape anyway, trickling down my cheeks with a harsh sting. "Just don't make me lose you too."

"You're not going to. I'm still here."

"For how long?"

"As long as you need me to be," he says confidently.

I open my watering eyes and snatch up his hand, needing the comfort. Our fingers thread together. We hold each other tight, neither of us speaking for a few moments before he chuckles under his breath.

"What?"

"Nothing," he mutters.

That goddamn smirk.

"Spit it out, Raine."

"Just wondering what happened to the whole no commitment thing?" He laughs. "You've changed your tune."

Wiping off my tears, I scoff. "It's complicated."

"No doubt. You know I don't care about labels either way." His playful tone turns serious. "It's nice to be needed by someone."

Chin tucked down, it's almost like he's staring at the place where our hands are joined. This situation is quickly turning into a clusterfuck with two very clear obstacles.

"I thought you'd be here when I woke up." He seems to read my mind. "Where were you last night?"

Shuddering, I hope he can't hear the way my breath catches. Stupidly optimistic, right? Raine immediately sits a little straighter and lifts his head to follow the sharp sound.

"Rip? What is it?"

"I… had a run in with Lennox," I say vaguely.

"A run in?" His brows knit.

"He thought those pills you took were mine and wouldn't listen to me." My voice wavers a little. "Things got physical."

"Jesus." His grasp on my hand tightens. "Are you okay? What did he do?"

Memories of inky rainwater swallowing me whole threaten to take over. I'm just glad he can't see the raw, scabbed-over marks that line my wrists. Nor the slice at my throat from the… well, aftermath.

"I'm alive. It was… uh, Xander bailed me out."

"Xander," he tests the word.

"Yeah. He found me."

"Where, exactly?"

I don't trust myself to speak. Not yet. Not when the memory of Xander is so fresh. So vivid in my mind. That near-death experience was petrifying, but what unfolded with him after scared me even more.

"Bailed you out of what?" he demands.

"It doesn't matter, Raine. Xander helped me."

"It *does* matter. Did Lennox hurt you?"

Gripping his fingers tight, I grimace. "Yes."

"That son of a bitch! I warned him. I told him to stay away!" He breathes heavily.

"If it wasn't for Xander…" I trail off.

"You know he has feelings for you."

Studying his face, there's no hint of anger or jealousy. Raine wears a look of weary acceptance, like he's known this all along. It's startling.

"He hates me," I correct him.

Fucking liar.

"You can want the very thing you hate," Raine states knowingly. "Sometimes, that makes you want it even more."

The unspoken question lingers between us. Since the moment we met, I've made my intentions clear to Raine. I want his friends dead. For a while, that included him too. Until I saw past his affiliations.

But everything is upside down now.

I've lost sight of why this all began.

"So… Xander." He keeps his voice light. "I guess things are complicated."

"This is such a mess. But I still need you in my life, Raine. I know I'm asking for a lot. You didn't sign up for this disaster."

"Not exactly low maintenance over here either, guava girl." He raises my hand to his lips so he can kiss my knuckles. "Besides, I quite like your mess."

"What if it isn't just my mess?"

He hesitates, nibbling on the inside of his cheek. "Then we figure it out."

"How?"

"I'm not willing to give this up because you have a psychopathic… Well, whatever Xander is. That's for him to figure out. But don't expect it to scare me off."

"Maybe it should," I reply jokingly.

"Maybe." Raine relaxes and sinks into the pillows. "But I clearly have no regard for self-preservation anyway."

"Clearly."

Giving a soft cough, I reach into the pocket of my sweats. "Got something for you."

"A hospital gift, huh? I must've been a good patient."

"Call it a loan."

Cupping the back of his hand, I place the folded sunglasses into his palm. They're not the same as his special, blacked-out lenses, but I know he misses the security blanket they provided.

He takes them and begins his inspection, tracing the curved glass lenses and wire arms to map out the shape. I watch him work.

"Sunglasses?" he guesses.

"From my personal collection. Aviators are unisex, right?"

"I've always wanted to look like a fighter pilot."

"Figured it's my fault your real ones got trashed. Will these do as a temporary fix?"

Unfolding the old sunglasses, he fumbles to slide them into place.

"Thank you." His blossoming grin is enough to make my heart flip. "They're perfect."

"Scoot over, would you?"

Shifting in the hospital bed, he shifts over to make a small sliver of space next to him. I crawl into the gap then burrow into his side, my head resting on his shoulder. Raine's head slumps to rest on top of mine.

I bathe in his warmth and citrusy, sea salt scent. Just feeling the steady weight of his body pressing into mine helps to alleviate the terror that's taken root since I found him passed out.

"So what happens now?"

"They've got me on methadone for when the withdrawals start," he murmurs. "But it's temporary. The doctor said I can either detox here or be sent back to rehab. They won't let me out without a plan."

I've never been able to quite pin him down, but I've long suspected that Doctor Hall is one of the good ones. Though few and far between, they're scattered throughout the staff. Anyone else would be releasing Raine without question.

I chew over this for a moment before whispering back. "Do you want to leave?"

"Of course not. If I'm gonna detox, I'll do it here."

"You'd put yourself through that? Detox?"

A short breath sighs out of him. "I've been fucked up for so long, I don't know any different. I'm scared to live any other way. But it's this or go back to square one in some other shit hole… alone again."

The thought of him detoxing alone in some hellish rehab facility hundreds of miles away makes me want to implode. He can't leave. But I also can't ask him to stay and put himself through this.

"Don't freak out on me, but it's different now." He seems to choose his words carefully. "Back then, I didn't have anyone to disappoint when I failed."

My chest warms with emotion. It feels so good to be wanted by someone. But it isn't long before fear slips back in, ever the silent assassin to hope.

"This place… It isn't good, Raine. If you want to get clean, I'll support your decision. But people don't get better in Harrowdean. You deserve the chance to give this a real shot."

"What are you saying?"

"That I don't trust these doctors to keep you safe. None of us are safe. Not here."

His head rubs against mine. "It's this or leave Harrowdean."

"I know."

"I'm not going back to rehab. It's never worked before. But here, I don't know... Maybe I can clean my act up... Ready to make a go of life again when I get out."

The giggle that bubbles up is totally inappropriate. "Raine Starling talking about cleaning his act up."

His chest rumbles with a chuckle. "Shocking, I know. Think the world ended in that storm."

"Mine almost did," I croak.

We both sober, still huddled together in the tiny hospital bed. His breathing is evening out, in time to the drip of the IV feeding into him. I continue to breathe in his clinical hospital scent, savouring those faint notes of summer and seaside.

"Stay?" Raine whispers. "I'm gonna be in for a while yet."

"Rest. I'll be right here."

Within seconds, the light snores coming from his mouth tell me he's fast asleep. Nina returns to check his vitals again, grumbling about our sleeping arrangement before she vanishes.

Listening to the rhythmic beeping of the heart rate monitor, my eyes slide shut. I'm drowsing on the edge of sleep when someone thumps into the cubicle. There's a startled inhale followed by a deep growl.

"You."

Recognising his sonorous bark, my eyes fly open. Lennox stands near the curtain, his chocolate-brown hair tousled and face a lurid shade of red. I quickly slide out from Raine's embrace, my eyes locked on him.

"Come to finish the job?" I goad.

"I should've done it myself in the first place instead of messing around," he spits furiously. "How did you get out?"

"That's the thing about cockroaches, Nox. We always survive."

Stepping forward, Lennox moves towards me. I stand but hover a hand over Raine's shoulder to shake him if needed.

"You want me to wake him up so he can hear you apologise for trying to drown me?"

"I wasn't going to apologise." He stops and crosses his arms. "Raine told me about the pills. Someone else is supplying him."

"You believe me now? Awesome. Thanks for taking my word for it before trying to drown me alive."

"Because your track record is so spotless," he gibes, palming the back of his neck. "Are we going to stand around talking about our feelings, or do you want in?"

"On… what?"

His mouth hooks up at the corner. "I got the name of his dealer."

"Well don't hold me in suspense."

That hint of a smile disappears. "I'll tell you when I have your word that you'll cut Raine off. Stay the fuck away from him. Don't even look at him. You're never going to sell him another pill."

"I told you what they do to nuisances in this place." Tampering my immediate desire to hurl abuse and threats, I summon a sense of calm. "You really think he should detox under Harrowdean's supervision?"

"No, but I don't want to see my friend half-dead again!"

"That's exactly what he'll be if management decides to intervene."

"What's the alternative, huh? Let him kill himself?"

A snore emanates from the bed, prompting us to lower our voices. Lennox spares Raine a glance, my gut twisting when his gaze briefly softens. His protection isn't love. It's control.

"And what about the day he crosses you?" I rebuke. "What about when he displeases you? Will you be the one to throw him in a pool then?"

"I would never hurt Raine."

"You don't know how to do anything but hurt people."

Any hint of softness dissipates the moment I finish my sentence. "Move away from him. You're done."

"I have every right to be here. You're the one who isn't welcome."

"Like I give a fuck where I'm welcome." Lennox scoffs. "I go where I'm needed."

The curtain twitches, silently parting to add another complication. Xander's in a fresh pair of jeans and his usual smart polo shirt, though his hair is still slightly damp. He halts to look between us both.

"I see I'm interrupting."

"Ripley is just leaving," Lennox chides.

"You think I'd leave Raine with you when he's vulnerable?" I laugh at him. "He'll find himself zip tied and underwater the moment he steps a foot out of line."

"That little dunking was just a taster—"

"No," Xander interrupts.

Lennox swivels to stare at his best friend, mouth hanging open slightly. Seeing him gawp in shock is so fucking satisfying.

"Stay away from Ripley," Xander orders unequivocally.

"Xan?" Lennox scowls. "She… What? You know what she's done."

"I know." His voice is ice-cool.

"What the fuck, man?"

"You didn't hear me? Stay away from Ripley."

Lennox looks between us several times. It's almost comical. He's stubborn as a mule but not stupid. Xander's jaw muscles clench, his almost-black eyes glittering like a knife's edge.

"You've spent every single day plotting how to get rid of her." Lennox steps into his friend's space.

"Yes." Xander's voice drips with disdain. "Far cleaner methods than leaving a dead body floating in a pool. That was sloppy, Nox."

"You… helped her escape?"

"I did. She isn't your problem to eliminate."

"Then whose problem is she?" Lennox chuffs incredulously. "Fuck, Xan. Has the bitch made you go fucking soft? Are you deluded enough to think she's *yours*?"

His deliberately impassive expression not wavering, Xander seizes a handful of Lennox's shirt. He drags him close enough for their noses to touch.

"No, she isn't mine. Ripley belongs to herself. But dare to even look at her for another goddamn second, and I'll have your tongue."

"Who the hell are you?" Lennox seethes, his voice rising. "We only have each other, Xan! She's trying to tear our family apart!"

"What family?" Xander claps back.

"How can you even say that to me?"

A third voice interrupts their fight.

"What on earth is going on in here?"

Nina storms into the cubicle with her clipboard in hand. She takes one look at the three of us then jabs her finger towards the door.

"This is a hospital, not a boxing ring!" she adds.

Xander releases Lennox's shirt and steps back. "He was just leaving."

"I want you all out. Right now." She points towards the curtain's opening.

Brushing his wrinkled shirt, Lennox spares a final look at Raine's hospital bed. He escapes the cubicle without another uttered word then vanishes. I suck in a breath, but I still don't look at Xander.

Truthfully, I don't trust him enough not to stop me from what I have to do next. My plan was faulty all along. It isn't enough to break their family. I know Lennox has lost everything before. Ripping his world apart will take far more finesse.

Killing him won't cut it.

I'll feed him to Harrowdean's monsters instead.

CHAPTER 25
RIPLEY

PLAY DEAD (JUST FOR TONIGHT)
– THE MESSENGER BIRDS

WALKING SLOWLY with my arms clasped loosely around my waist, I hold the bulge of contraband inside my sweatpants. With my usual, oversized t-shirt on top, the large bag of pills is well-concealed anyway. I'm just on edge and paranoid.

It's taken me months to build up Noah's stash. Sneaking small quantities from batches here and there, I've had to carefully count each pill, ensuring the plan will work. He's still sure about the desired outcome, and despite the way it makes me internally flinch, I won't let him down.

He's made his choice.

I'm just a means to an end.

Detaching from the reality of my actions has gotten me this far in life. What's one more scratch on the scorecard? No one ever likes to admit that in order to get what we want, or even protect the ones we love, there's always a price to be paid.

I wonder if that's what Lennox told himself before he entered Holly's bedroom that night. Was she simply just another scratch on his scorecard? A price he was willing to pay? I guess that's all we ever are to each other in the end. Pawns to be manipulated and wiped out of the game.

This is my best move.

I'm removing Lennox from the chess board.

The loading bay is deserted. No one else knows it, but the CCTV cameras are always kept on a loop here. Maintaining pretences for the sake of posterity. If anyone was ever to check the feed, they'd see old footage peppered in to reflect normal comings and goings.

But I'm not here to meet Elon today. Instead, I hop down from the dock then head for the collection of wooden pallets clustered in the far corner. Tucked behind them is a small gap in the dock's concrete base. I noticed it while ignoring Elon's scowl during one of our exchanges.

The collection of pills weigh heavy in my hand as I stash them in the gap. After locating a discarded brick to wedge in front of it, they're completely concealed.

I don't know how long it'll be before he can retrieve his pharmaceutical payment, and I can't be caught delivering the drugs. When Noah attacks Lennox, it has to look like any other fight. No one can know I've bribed him to do it.

Brushing my hands off, I quickly glance around before slipping away. The walk back to the quad is quiet. It's been a few days since the flood, but normal business hasn't resumed. The manor itself is suffering from the acquired damage, and we've even had intermittent power outages.

Hired help bustle about the destroyed grounds, loading trucks with broken trees and smashed picnic tables. Several of the institute's stained glass windows have been boarded over, awaiting repair.

The destruction seems to have awakened something wild in the patient population. Violence has been erupting constantly between patients and guards. But now, I see two people creating faux snow angels in the still-wet mud. Their clothing is slowly turning brown, the thick mud covering their hair and faces.

It's a welcome reprieve.

I can't look away from their bright smiles. The sound of laughter sinks into me and thaws something. Even somewhere like this, there's still joy to be found. What I wouldn't give to find some joy of my own.

"Seriously?" a familiar voice gripes. "Come on, guys. Not cool."

The two patients ignore Langley's approach. He stops at the edge of the quagmire and braces his hands on his hips. His round baby blues are filled with aggravation as he contemplates what to do with them.

"You ever consider a career change?" I call out.

His head snaps in my direction. "Got any suggestions?"

"I went to school with this guy, a real entrepreneur type. He used to buy these knock off t-shirts online then sell them for a profit. Last I heard, he's living in a townhouse in Surrey now."

"By selling dodgy t-shirts?"

"Nah. Pretty sure he's a drug dealer now."

With an eye roll, he briefly looks back at the two troublesome patients before crossing the few short steps to join me. I dodge a puddle to meet him in the middle.

"How is Raine today?"

"Still laid up." I shrug absently.

My anxiety for Raine couldn't be more acute. The medical team has kept him in for monitoring. He's on a controlled regimen of drugs and fluids to give him the best shot at making this work.

Each morning that I return to see him, I'm convinced it'll be the day I find his bed empty. I don't trust Harrowdean to do something good for once. They prefer their patients dependent in every sense.

When management hears about his situation, I don't know what they'll do. With the chaos of the storm and subsequent cleanup, no one seems to have realised they have a surplus patient who's ripe for the taking yet.

"Listen, Rip." Langley lowers his voice. "I know you're worried about Raine. Maybe I can help, but it'll require your cooperation."

I blink up at him. "Cooperation?"

"People are paying attention now. Things are changing."

"What are you saying?"

His eyes dart around, checking that we're not being overheard. "Cooperating is your best chance to get him out of here unharmed. You have inside knowledge. We can use that."

My feet inch backwards. "We?"

Langley grabs my shoulder to stop me from leaving. I flinch, my hackles immediately rising.

"All it would take is one phone call, Rip." His voice is low and urgent.

"Take your hands off me. You're not making any sense."

In my periphery, I see Noah's gangly height step into the quad. He glances around, catching sight of me then nodding once. We're on a strict schedule to make this work. I don't have time for riddles.

"We can offer you protection," Langley explains hastily. "But we need your help."

"Who are you talking about?" A hint of suspicion sneaks in. "Wait… Who do you really work for?"

"Just think about it." Releasing my shoulder, he captures my hand

and presses something into it. Langley stares into my eyes for a prolonged second before taking off to deal with the mud-soaked patients.

I slowly look down at the glossy business card he's passed me with a single contact number on it. The organ trapped behind my breastbone does somersaults.

Hunter Rodriguez.
Director of Sabre Security.

Quickly shoving it into my bra before anyone can spot what we've just exchanged, I barely have a second to reel in my shock before Noah jogs over to me.

"Classes let out in a couple minutes."

I shake my head from side to side, trying to focus. "Right. The plan."

"You with me, Rip?"

"Yeah, of course. Payment has been stashed."

"Sure this shit can't be traced back to you?" He scans my facial expression.

My heart is pounding so hard, it feels like it could shatter my ribcage into tiny flakes. Why the hell do those people want to talk to me? Aren't they the same investigators who want my head on a stake? Bancroft warned me what would happen if Harrowdean falls.

I'm culpable too.

I can't trust anyone.

"Ripley!" Noah nudges me. "It's now or never. Are we good?"

"Y-Yes." I rub my eyes.

"So? The pills?"

"There's... uh, someone else pushing product. I put your shit in one of their plastic money bags. Leave it in sight, and it'll lead right back to them."

"Okay." He blows out a heavy breath. "I guess this is it."

Indecision tears at my psyche as I wrestle with the sudden urge to call the whole thing off. I want Lennox gone, but that phone number and all it represents has thrown everything into disarray.

Someone out there wants to help.

Will they still want to if I do this?

Before I can utter a word, Noah tugs me into a hard, fast hug that makes my teeth clack together. I squeak in shock. He quickly releases me then steps away with a small, sad smile.

"Watch your back, Rip." His eyes shine with a weird look of resolution. "You deserve a life outside this place. I hope you find it."

"Noah, wait…"

He's already striding towards the door that attaches to the south wing where classes are about to finish. It wasn't hard to pin down Lennox's routine. Whenever he's done with the maths class he got roped into attending, he always needs to step outside. I suspect it's a habit leftover from his smoking days.

Noah props himself against the brick wall. Right on time, the door bursts open, and patients flood outside. The corridors are being cleaned and repaired after the flood, so there's more footfall heading outside than usual.

Panic takes hold as I scan the crowd, recognising a few familiar faces. The invisible hand at my lungs tightens its grip as I spot his pile of chocolate-brown hair. Lennox's bulky height towers over everyone else.

He's stony-faced as usual in his standard white t-shirt and fitted sweatpants. Walking with big strides, he escapes the throng to stand in the middle of the lawn. The puddles don't seem to bother him.

I watch in morbid fascination as he tilts his head upwards and sighs heavily. His toned shoulders are drooping, reflecting the slump of his posture.

Lennox looks defeated.

Abandoned like the rest of us.

So why doesn't that satisfy me?

Pushing off from the wall, Noah squares his shoulders. I'm carried forward several steps to intercept him before the devil on my shoulder wins out. He's choosing this. I'm just a facilitator. This is the price of war.

If I tell myself that enough times, perhaps I'll be able to sleep at night. But excuses haven't eased the guilt that haunts my nightmares from every other incident I've justified this way. And deep down, I know it won't now.

Noah approaches him then shoves his shoulder. Seeing him facing off against Lennox and his poundage brings home the reality of what I've arranged. Noah's going to get himself killed—by Lennox's rage or the drugs I'm paying him with to provoke it.

If I do this, I'm no better than the monster I've condemned. Lennox hurts people to further his own gains. This right here is me doing exactly the same thing to get what I want.

Holly wouldn't be proud of this. She'd be fucking ashamed. This is wrong. Revenge isn't worth this price. I've been caught up in this twisted game for so long, I've lost my humanity along the way.

It isn't too late.

You can stop this.

As Lennox whirls around and begins to shout, I move. Noah's too far away for me to make out what he's saying, but it doesn't take much to provoke Lennox. Especially since I gave Noah a few pointers. He knows all the pressure points to hit.

Having dragged the patients out of their muddy playground, Langley is occupied by escorting them inside. He hasn't noticed the disaster about to unfold. I have no backup to break apart the impending brawl I've instigated.

Noah shoves Lennox again, hollering something in his face. I watch Lennox slowly turn red, grabbing Noah's shirt and wrenching him forward so fast, he stumbles. His face sails straight into Lennox's fist.

"No!" I screech.

Spitting out a mouthful of blood, Noah laughs as he says something else to Lennox. My yelling doesn't stop the next punch from flying. Only this time, Noah hits back, causing Lennox's head to snap to the side.

Several patients have gathered to watch. I slam into someone's shoulder, desperate to reach Noah and drag him away from Lennox's onslaught. He's still baiting him despite the blood smeared around his mouth.

"Right this way, ladies and gentlemen." A voice rings out across the quad as several pairs of footsteps echo behind me. "You know, we were so delighted to be contacted for this interview opportunity."

Bancroft's gloating is unmistakable. I'd recognise his smug, regal tenor even in a pitch-black room. The old man speaks like we're living in a period drama.

"As you can see, we're pouring every resource into the cleanup effort this week. Here at Harrowdean, we care for our patients."

Horrified, I look over my shoulder. Bancroft is here, with Davis and several guards in tow, Elon included. There's also a leggy blonde with three cameramen. Her bright pantsuit screams journalist.

She points a microphone towards him. "We're here to talk about the investigation."

"There's plenty more for me to show you!" Bancroft quickly deflects. "We have lots of exciting initiatives here."

"Sir, would you care to respond to recent rumours of medical malpractice and violence in your institutes?"

"Violence?" Bancroft shakes his head, a charming smile in place. "No, never. This is a place of healing. We're helping to rehabilitate those in need."

There's a series of bellows before the shouting catches their attention. Surrounded by a gaggle of onlookers, Lennox has Noah on his back, two hands wrapped around his throat as he slams him repeatedly into the ground.

The blonde reporter perks up, instructing her cameramen to begin recording. Bancroft's smile morphs into a look of outrage. To add insult to injury, patients have started cheering the pair on, each body slam eliciting another excited roar.

"You seem to have a security issue," the reporter comments.

Bancroft's enraged gaze bounces over me, his eyes narrowing as he takes in the fracas. I'm running before I can hear whatever crap he's going to spew next. Lennox is going to break Noah's spine on national fucking television at this rate.

This was a mistake.

I've crossed a line.

I should turn around and disappear before I'm incriminated too, but I have to stop this before it's too late. Throwing myself into the mix is probably the stupidest thing I've ever done.

Yet the weight of that damned business card burns against my skin. There's still a world out there, watching this unfold from the outside. A world that would be disgusted by me.

I'm disgusted by me.

"Get out of the way!" I barge past leering onlookers. "Move!"

Close enough to the fight, I can see that Noah's limp but conscious, laying crumpled on the ground. He's given a good defence—Lennox has a split eyebrow that's spilling blood down his face, and his nose is gushing like a waterfall.

"Stop!" I shriek at Lennox.

He glowers over his shoulder at me. "You again. Come to watch the show?"

"Leave him alone, Nox. This was all a mistake."

"Mistake?" Lennox swipes blood from his eyeline. "Did you set this up, huh? Is this some kind of game?"

"Just get away from him!"

"The son of a bitch started it."

Launching myself at Lennox before he can resume pounding Noah into a pulp, I land on his back. My legs cinch around him as I squeeze his neck, attempting to throw him off balance.

He hisses a curse and easily tosses me into the air, causing me to slam to the ground. My bones creak in protest at the hard landing. Teeth gritted, I roll onto my knees and crawl my way back to them.

Lennox and Noah are grappling again, a sea of angry voices spurring them on. But it's the fear in Noah's eyes that hits me like a tonne of bricks. So I throw myself at Lennox again.

This time, he hits the ground from our collision. We twist and roll, sliding through a wet mudslide caused by the flooding. I get in a decent hit before he starts to choke me.

"You have ruined everything," Lennox growls. "Taking my sanity wasn't enough, was it? You had to take my family from me too."

I buck up and down, attempting to throw him off. There's a blur of movement before something crashes into him. Lennox is torn from my body, now tangled up in Noah's long limbs.

Noah's caught him off guard and regained the upper hand. The pair resume beating each other to death as I try to gain enough purchase to intervene.

"Break it up!" Elon's voice booms.

Several guards swarm all at once. Two are holding the reporter and her cameras far back, the combined brawn of Bancroft's remaining men circling the three of us.

When Elon raises his baton, I quickly lift my hands in surrender. He spins around, turning his attention to the two brawling men.

"Enough! Stop!" he bellows.

Noah doesn't seem to get the message. He makes it on top of Lennox, slamming a bloody fist into his jaw. Two guards have to seize his arms to drag him off, but he keeps struggling.

When he manages to punch one of them, a black taser is pulled free.

"Stop!" I shout frantically.

The taser connects with Noah's midsection first. He jerks midair, his knees crumpling as he lands on the muddy lawn with a grunt.

Elon spins to yell at his subordinate. "Stand down! We have reporters here."

I recognise the asshole he's admonishing. It's Kieran, the same one who hit me and groped Taylor without a care in the world.

The red-faced brute completely disregards Elon's order. Kieran hits Noah with the taser again, this time directly in the chest. I watch in horror as his limbs convulse and spit trickles from the corners of his mouth. Teeth bared, Kieran targets him for several painstaking seconds.

Hands clutching his chest, Noah struggles to stand back up before falling backwards onto the ground again. He's bug-eyed and breathless. That's when a vague memory of him mentioning his weak heart slams into me.

"Noah!" I screech.

Elon reprimands Kieran as onlooking patients begin to scream. Eventually, two other guards have to drag Kieran backwards, the taser torn from his hands. In all the commotion, it falls to the ground.

"What are you thinking?" Elon clamours.

"Insubordination, sir!" Kieran splutters, shoving off his co-workers.

Still cowering on the ground, I watch Elon fling his arms around, gesturing wildly in anger. I've never seen him so enraged before.

"He was down!"

"Patient was out of control," Kieran insists.

"You damn knucklehead. We're being filmed!"

Between their arguing and the patients crowded around in every direction, no one is paying attention to Noah. He's clawing at his chest like an elephant is sitting on it, a hiss coming from his throat.

"Hey!" I fume at the bickering guards. "Help him!"

When I try to move closer, Elon reacts. I'm shoved down and pinned with a foot in the centre of my back. My lungs heave, compressed against the wet ground by his bodyweight.

Any sounds I was able to make dry up. Lennox is slumped over while Elon shouts at his men, gesturing around at the chaos. Still, no one pays any attention to Noah. His grip on his chest slackens, and he eventually goes limp.

"You think a good time to get that out is in front of a film crew?" Elon rages on. "You're supposed to be discreet!"

When Kieran spots Noah's limp form, the red flush on his face pales. "Uh, sir?"

"I don't want to hear another word from you!"

"Sir, the patient…"

All eyes finally turn to Noah. Through the sheen of tears bubbling in my eyes, I can see he's now still and lifeless. Elon growls a curse, his foot lifting from my back. He quickly kneels down beside Noah to check his pulse.

"Dammit," he mutters. "Radio the medical wing for support."

I drag myself upright as Elon begins to deliver chest compressions. The other guards are trying to herd patients away from the show, but there's resistance. Everyone wants to see the drama.

Determination fuelling my sore body, I claw my way through gelatinous mud. Noah isn't breathing, curled up at an awkward angle on his side, head twisted and legs splayed. Horror is pouring into me in a relentless wave.

"Come on," I plead.

The panic around us is intensifying. All noise fades into the background as I wait for Noah to take a breath. Elon's grunting with each deep compression, his subordinates anxiously watching.

"Get them out of here," he barks over his shoulder.

All eyes turn to us.

"No!" I protest.

Shuffling away from the armed guards approaching, I'm split between watching them and Noah's still-lifeless pile on the ground. Sweat drips from Elon's face as he continues to administer CPR.

Desperately searching around, my gaze lands on the taser that was dropped in the hubbub. Kieran attempts to block my lunge, trying to retake his weapon, but I slide across the lawn to reach it first.

My hand grasps the black and yellow handle. Kieran stands over me, trying to snatch it from my hands. Teeth bared, I slam it into his cargo-clad thigh and deploy a shock.

"Shit!" he squalls.

Seeing him jerk and thrash before hitting the ground only spurs me on. The other guards react in shock, cursing and trying to reach their colleague. I'm about to hit him again when someone hoists me up from behind, prising the taser from my hands.

"Miss Bennet. Causing trouble yet again."

The warden himself has appeared to grab hold of me, eyeing my dousing of mud with distaste. I struggle, attempting to lash out at him. He swiftly hands me off to his guards.

"Control her!"

I turn feral. Kicking, screaming, throwing out every insult under the sun. Noah still isn't moving. Elon stops trying to resuscitate him to check his pulse again. Sweat dripping down his temples, he swears quietly and resumes compressions.

Kieran is still flopped across the ground, twitching all over as a fellow guard tries to help him sit up. He's keeping a keen eye on Noah.

"Elon?" Davis asks.

He pauses briefly to recheck Noah's pulse. "Nothing, sir."

"Keep going. We have eyes on us."

In the distance, I can hear Bancroft's best imitation of a politician's voice, trying to distract the journalist and her team. They're trapped behind a wall of muscle holding them out of sight.

When the medical team arrives, Elon steps aside, Doctor Hall and his team quickly surrounding Noah to intervene. I get one last look before he vanishes behind them.

His mouth is hanging open, but it's his bloodshot eyes that drag me into a living nightmare. Wide but empty. There's no brimming sadness anymore.

Lifeless.

Gone.

Joining his men in a huddle, Elon looks contrite as Davis turns his hard stare on them all.

"How on earth did this happen?"

Elon wipes sweat from his brow. "Just… a little hiccup, sir."

"A hiccup?" I howl like a banshee. "He's fucking dead!"

"Shut it, Ripley." Elon flashes me a grimace.

"Or what? Are you going to kill me too?"

"Don't tempt me!"

Davis casts a disbelieving look around the scene we've created. "Clean this shit up. The cameras can't see."

His callous tone pushes me to my breaking point. I stomp down on the foot of the guard still holding me then elbow him sharply in the gut. There's a satisfying grunt before the arms banded around me slacken.

I take advantage of the opening and lunge forward. Davis can't duck in time to avoid me. I clutch him by his suit jacket, determined to inflict any amount of damage. But he looks more disgruntled by the mud I'm covering him in than anything else.

"He killed Noah!"

"Enough," Davis replies tersely.

"No! It's not!"

"This is the final straw, Miss Bennet."

Rage consumes me like flesh-eating bacteria finding a tasty new host. I don't care. He can do what he wants. Playing their game hasn't saved me, it's damned me. Along with everyone I've thrown into the line of fire along the way.

"You know what?" I lose all sense of self-preservation as I rant in his face. "The world is going to know what happened here. What's *been* happening here. I'll make sure of it."

"Is that so?" Davis smiles snootily.

"You think I'm scared?"

"Perhaps you should be."

"Well I'm not!"

He dismisses me with a head shake. "Take her away."

Releasing him, I try to duck from the unknown hands attempting to grab me once more, but my wrists are yanked backwards then swiftly cuffed in place. Davis watches on, a seed of a smile playing on his lips.

"Consequences, Miss Bennet." He leans in to gloat. "You've run that loud mouth of yours for the last time. There will be no one to listen where you're going."

I won't let him see even a crack of fear. He'd enjoy the satisfaction far too much. Keeping my head held high, I hold eye contact. Davis clicks his tongue in disappointment.

"Foolish child."

"What about this one?" Elon calls.

Looking away from me, Davis turns his attention to Lennox. He's now been forced to his knees, trails of blood still tracking down his face. Elon forcibly twists his arms behind his back to restrain him.

"Mr Nash." Davis sighs in a distinctly disappointed way. "I should've known when I signed your transfer papers that you'd be nothing but trouble."

Lennox curls his lip in disgust. "You're running a sinking ship, Warden."

"Then I'd better start plugging those holes, hadn't I?" Davis gestures between us. "Take them both down."

"Where?" Elon asks with a slowly blossoming grin.

I can feel the thud of the final nail being hammered into my coffin. It isn't audible, though. The sound boomerangs around in my mind, bouncing from each dark corner, collecting every last scrap of evidence to doom me to this fate.

"There's a cell in the Z wing with their names on it."

CHAPTER 26
LENNOX
ADHD – TWO FEET

THUD. *Thud. Thud.*

The metallic banging repeats on an endless loop. It feels like someone is chipping away at my brain with a jackhammer. Grimacing, I reach for my pillow to hide beneath it. I don't even want to know what Xander's doing to make that horrific noise.

Thud. Thud. Thud.

When I search for my pillow, all I find is cold cement. The aches and pains in my body soon flare to life with that realisation. It feels like I've been violently fucked by a bulldozer. More solid concrete lies beneath me, leaching any remaining warmth from my bones.

Thud. Thud. Thud.

"Don't leave me in here with him!"

I have no desire to peel open my eyes to verify if this is some fucked up, lucid dream or not. I'm no stranger to nightmares, but would my brain be cruel enough to lock me up with that bitch? I'm not that masochistic.

"The feeling's mutual," I mumble groggily.

My muscles relax when her ceaseless banging on the door stops. Colourful cursing precedes the sound of footsteps. I'm unprepared to be kicked in the shin so hard, it makes me grunt. My eyes slam open, and bright lights sears my eyeballs.

"And here I was, hoping you were dead," Ripley complains.

Squinting through my hazy vision, I can make out her silhouette.

She's looming over me, handcuffed wrists curled up to her chest, two furious mossy-brown eyes watching me with revulsion.

Definitely real.

Fucking perfect.

We're in what appears to be a hybrid cell. The floor is made of pocked concrete, boasting too many dark stains that don't bear thinking about, while the walls are lined with scratched, padded material.

Artificial light emanates from a panel built into the ceiling with several air events. This place is ancient. Every surface is scarred and dirty, unlike Priory Lane's more modern facilities.

By contrast, Harrowdean's Z wing feels like a final frontier for the doomed. Not even Incendia can be bothered to maintain this place. I'm sure far too many have died here for them to ever get it clean again.

"What happened?"

Ripley rubs a spot between her brows. "You don't remember them drugging us?"

"Clearly not." I wrestle myself up to rest against the padded wall. "How long have you been making a racket?"

"A while." She shrugs. "You were out cold."

Watching her shuffle to the other side of the cell and sink down against the wall, I try to sort through my fuzzy memories. It's all a blur after some dickhead restrained me.

A quick search of my neck reveals a swollen bump from being needle stabbed. Ripley does her best to ignore me as I silently take stock of my injuries.

Her stupid friend put up a good fight for such a skinny bastard. He sure was determined to get his ass beat. Idiot that I am, I just had to take the bait. Now he's likely dead, and I'm stuck here.

"Was this part of your plan?"

"Winding up in here with you?" Ripley snorts acerbically. "Far from it."

"Either way, it was a pretty stupid plan."

"Almost as genius as drowning someone in an abandoned pool? That sure looked accidental and non-suspicious. You really covered your tracks there, Nox."

Head crashing against the wall, I let my gritty eyes sink shut again. "You have a point."

"Please don't agree with me. It's unnerving."

The last thing I anticipate doing is laughing. But still, the chuckle spills out of me. All these months of threats and counter moves, just for us both to end up buried in an inescapable hellscape. Together. Life's irony really is a son of a bitch.

"Not much need for pretences in here, is there?" I sigh.

"I guess not." She examines her arm, the carved letters pink and shiny with new scar tissue. "Do you think Noah's alive?"

"It sure didn't look good."

I don't have the energy to get up and hammer on the door, but even if I did, it would be a mistake. I made that mistake last time I woke up in a cell. Pissing off the overlords only worsened the next visit they paid.

It took several rounds of near-death beatings to get the message. Resistance is a deadly temptation. You don't survive the Z wing that way. The clinicians and guards only see that as a challenge.

They'll work harder to break your spirit just to grind out any speck of defiance to their regime. The trick is to switch off... To pain. To humiliation. To loss. Everything.

"Fuck."

I crack open an eye. "What?"

Ripley hides her mud-streaked face in her hands. "Fuck!"

"Can you have a mental breakdown quietly?"

"This isn't a game, Nox. Raine is upstairs all alone right now. I haven't seen Xander either. Who is going to keep Raine safe?"

"Maybe you should've thought of that before setting me up!"

Yanking on her cuffs, she tries unsuccessfully to break the chains several times. Even going as far as to wedge her foot between the two halves and attempt to break them apart that way. It's entertaining to watch her struggle.

Ripley winces at the sight of blood oozing down her tattooed arms. Her wrists are a raw mess, still healing from our last altercation. The cuffs are digging deep into the scabbed-over wounds.

"Goddammit," she hisses. "You know what? You're right. I shouldn't have set you up. I'm not a piece of shit like you."

"Debatable. What was the price?"

Ripley glowers at me, lips sealed.

"Come on."

"I don't know what you're talking about."

"He didn't agree to get himself beaten to hell for free. I get it... You provoke me, get me thrown in some dank hole and out the picture. Skip off into the sunset, right?"

"Something like that."

"So. What was the price?"

Licking her lips, she ducks her gaze. "Enough pills to off himself with no questions asked."

I whistle under my breath. "Now we're talking. I guess he kinda got his wish. Still think you're not a piece of shit?"

Eyes squeezing shut, Ripley tilts her head back against the wall. Stray tears break through the thick coating of mud on her face and leave winding trails.

"I wanted you dead… more than I wanted him alive."

"Trading lives, huh?"

"You're one to talk." She sucks in an uneven breath. "I wanted to call it off. Now he's dead anyway. His body will disappear along with his records. There will be no one left to ask any questions."

Her broken hush causes some strange feeling to bloom in my chest. It isn't pity. I could never pity someone like Ripley; she isn't deserving of it. Neither of us are.

I understand what it's like to commit evil in order to survive. To become the villain to keep others safe. It's precisely why I tried to kill her. And why she did the exact same thing back.

"You know…" she trails off.

"What?"

"It's just that… If we'd stopped trying to kill each other and focused on everyone else who poses a threat, we would've had a far better chance of survival."

The bitch just read my mind.

But I won't tell her that.

"Yeah, I prefer taking my chances."

"Stubborn bastard," Ripley chuffs.

"You know me."

"Do you think I want to be locked in here with you? I'd much rather be facing whatever shit they have planned alone. You're a liability."

"Me a liability? You're the reason we're in here!"

"Because you're still not sorry!" she snaps, like the words are a weapon she can wield.

I stare at her. "Sorry for what?"

"Holly was all I had. She became family." Her voice splinters, leaking with despair. "And you took my family away from me to save yours."

For all the sorrow and heartache we've inflicted on each other, I can look at my nemesis and admit to myself that it wasn't worth it. I didn't know what kind of monster my actions would breed.

She has become the threat I never could have anticipated. In many ways, I can see now that I masterminded my own downfall. It was always meant to be her.

Mouth clicking open, I'm not sure what words are forming. Nothing feels quite adequate to summarise the undeniably toxic importance we've come to mean to each other. At least hatred was simple.

But understanding?

Maybe even empathy?

I can't possibly have those things for Ripley. Not for the woman who orchestrated our incarceration and torture. We ruined her life, but she perpetuated the cycle of violence the day she offered us up for slaughter.

Even here, she's continued to destroy our lives from afar—ensnaring Raine in her web then somehow penetrating my best friend's icy shell. We've tried our best to ruin each other without stopping to consider the greater threat.

Before I can figure out what to even say to her, the hatch in the door slides back. Eyes peer in, finding us both awake, before the hatch slams shut. The steel door clanks as it's unlocked.

Shoulders set, a bastard with regimented military hair saunters in, his fingers hooked into his belt hoops. Cruel eyes scan over us.

"Always nice to have new arrivals."

"You," Ripley breathes in fear. "Harrison."

"Nice to see you again, stooge. Or should I say, ex-stooge. Is the accommodation to your liking?"

His voice is lilting and playful in an entirely unhinged way. I've met his likes before. We're in for a rough time if he's in charge of our reconditioning.

"No?" He pulls his lips down in a dramatic pout. "Such a shame. Perhaps we should clean it up in here a bit before the fun begins."

Stepping out of the cell, he huffs loudly while dragging a covered machine in with the help of another guard. This one wears a cap over his short hair, shading slightly effeminate features.

"Bath time!" Harrison exclaims.

Yet another guard enters the padded cell, this one bald and dead-eyed, joining the other one wearing a cap. Harrison leans against the machine, still smiling to himself.

"Strip them."

"Not a chance." Ripley gingerly draws to her feet.

I wobble, trying to stand. "Seconded."

"I wasn't giving either of you a choice."

Each with an approaching guard to contend with, we both find protective stances. I'm still dizzy and can't seem to get my legs to work. Ripley, on the other hand, is ready for a scrap with her knees bent and fists cocked.

I lose sight of her as baldie stalks towards me. He grabs my ankles then heaves, splaying me out on the concrete. Pain reverberates through me. I move to boot him in the leg, but when he pulls out a taser, trepidation causes me to tense.

I'm too weak to stop him from hitting me in the side. Electric slams into me, frying any sense from my struggling limbs. Pausing for a moment, he studies me before doling out another hit.

Jerking violently, spit bubbles spill from my mouth. My eyeballs feel like two overinflated balloons. When the tasing stops, I can't even lift a finger to fight back.

The guard makes quick work of stripping off my sweatpants and boxers. Eyeing my cuffed hands, he reaches for a blade attached to his belt, using it to slice my t-shirt away.

"Excellent." Harrison claps his hands together. "Let's begin."

I get a clear view of Ripley being slammed into the concrete hard enough to split her forehead open. She slumps, the fight draining out of her in time for the guard to strip her too.

We're both left completely bare. It's humiliating. With the help of his two sadists, Harrison uncovers his machine. Dismay unfurls within me as I recognise it instantly. It's a huge water pump on wheels with industrial hoses attached.

Casting Ripley a look, I watch her moan and writhe. Blood is a thick curtain spilling from her forehead to cover her face. She swipes it from her eyes long enough to spot the horror that awaits.

"W-Wait," she pleads.

Harrison waggles a finger at her. "No complaints now. Consider it a welcome spa treatment for our latest projects."

The whirring of the pump's engine fills the cell. Just as feeling re-enters my still-twitching extremities, I'm hit by the first blast of water. It's an immense force, catapulting me back into the wall.

Another hose is unspooled and pointed at Ripley. She cries out at the impact. We're both lashed with icy whips, our bodies battered and frozen by the water's bruising power.

This isn't my first time, so I know not to fight it. Slipping and sliding holds no benefit. It's better to preserve strength for the hours this can go on for. But in typical Ripley fashion, she's struggling.

"That's it," Harrison jeers. "Get nice and clean for your luxury vacation."

Retaining any awareness soon becomes impossible. The constant onslaught is too much for anyone to bear. Pain combined with the cold temperature saps any defiance from me far faster than I anticipated.

I lose track of Ripley and the passing of time. All that exists is the violent hammering of water into my body, leaving bruises that feel bone-deep. A chill has settled in my bones, the only indication that I'm not dead already.

At some point, a familiar sense of delirium sets in. My eyes are squeezed shut to avoid the powerful spray, and behind my shut lids, images start to form. Flashes here and there, forming mental snapshots.

My grandfather resting in his armchair, surrounded by framed medals and family photographs. Daisy proudly handing him her grade three ballet exam certificate to be added to the collection. The way he kissed her head so proudly.

The years speed up.

This time, I see a teenaged Daisy, now stick-thin and sullen. Her pointe shoes buried in the bottom of a drawer. The way she made herself small and invisible in our grandfather's presence. Her certificates disappeared.

I'm not sure when the onslaught of water ceases and a beating begins. Fists pummelling into me feel a lot like the beat of water anyway. Each painful blow fires more disjointed flashes at me as my mind contracts.

Things were blurry after Daisy's death. Glazed-over by grief and shock. It wasn't until I discovered her diary while clearing out her bedroom that I realised why she did it. The note made it clear enough. It's all disjointed from there.

Handcuffs.

Psych evals.

An empty jail cell.

"Lennox. Snap out of it."

Daisy's rosy cheeks.

Seeing my childhood home burn.

Court cases and signed plea deals.

"Get it together, Nox."

Fire.

Screams.

Salvation.

I gradually float back down to reality. It's the same practised routine. A coping mechanism I perfected during months of this same treatment. I'd always come back once the reprieve came.

But Xander?

He never returned.

I open my eyes to Ripley crouched over me, something akin to a look of concern on her bloodied face. Wet hair is plastered to her head, the cut in her forehead still trickling.

She's trembling from exertion, like it took all of her remaining energy to slide over to this corner of the cell. Fresh scrapes and bruises are scattered all over her.

An arm crossed over her bare breasts, she seems to be favouring her left side. My own body aches even more fiercely than before, promising fresh bruises to evidence the onslaught of kicking and punching.

A quick glance around reveals that we're now alone, the machine vanished with Harrison and his grunts. Our tormentors have delivered their welcome gift and left. I really did check out.

"You back?"

I heave a breath. "Yeah."

"Don't die on me yet," she jokes hoarsely.

"You wouldn't like that?"

Ripley sighs, her weight braced on one cuffed hand. "No need for pretence, right?"

Hissing in pain, I breathe through the fire in my ribcage. "Do I look capable of that right now?"

"I guess not. Truthfully, I don't want to die alone in here." She summons a weak smile. "How's that for honesty?"

Coughing wetly, she shuffles her back against the padded wall. I remain curled up in a puddle of water, too limp to lift a finger. There's no concept of time in here. I don't know how long the torture went on for, but we're both drained.

"You kept saying your sister's name." Her voice is a needle in the heart. "And Xander's too."

"It's nothing."

"You can't let them get in your head like that. It's exactly what they want."

"Who survived this shit before?" I wince on an inhale. "Don't lecture me."

"Fine. Be like that."

From the corner of my eye, I can't help but watch her. It's the same sick desire that's brought me into her orbit for months now. A drive I wasn't willing to acknowledge before. Look where that got me.

Disaster follows Ripley at every turn, and I've followed along like a storm chaser on the heels of a promising tornado. In all the plots and schemes, a part of me hoped I wouldn't succeed in destroying her.

Then the chase would end.

And I'd be left with a heavier conscience.

"You need to put pressure on your head," I point out.

"Worried about me?"

"Hardly. Just don't fancy being stuck here with a dead body."

There's an odd rattling sound before a sudden blast of cold air spews from the vents in the ceiling. More is pumped out, over and over, until the cell's temperature has dramatically dropped.

Both sopping wet and exhausted, it doesn't take long for shivers to set in. Ripley hugs her naked body, shaking like a leaf from head to toe. She's curvy but small without a whole lot of meat on her bones to keep her warm.

"What is th-this?" She sits against the wall, her hands wrapped around her knees, appearing to be curled up as small as possible.

"They break you down first, exhaust you mentally and physically." My limbs quiver with each word. "Then they roll out the big guns."

Air vents whistling, there's another quiet click before the lights suddenly cut, and we're plunged into darkness. I focus on preserving any small amount of warmth I have left, but the sound of Ripley's panicked gasps soon filters in.

"Ripley?" I whisper into the dark.

"I c-can't… We're n-never… getting out of h-h-here."

"You need to calm down. They're messing with our heads."

"So c-c-cold," she whimpers.

That fucking sound. I swear, she does it on purpose. Like she knows it makes me feel all kinds of fucked up and confused.

"Focus on something else," I mutter.

"Like w-what?"

"I don't know. The incredible scenery?"

"It's pitch black, dick."

"You still have the pleasure of my voice."

"You know what? F-Fuck you."

"You wish, Rip."

"Are you s-seriously flirting with m-me while we're being t-tortured?" Her teeth chattering is audible.

If it keeps her talking and that goddamn whimpering to a minimum, I'll tell the bitch I love her. Anything to keep those sounds from breaking my fucking heart all over again. Though I'd never admit she has that power.

"Don't tell anyone." I sigh shallowly.

"It isn't necessary t-to be an asshole all your l-life, Nox."

"Really? That's news to me. Thanks for the head's up."

"I hate you s-so much."

"The feeling's mutual."

Unable to hold it back any longer, my teeth begin to clatter too. Anything to maintain what little heat remains in my core. Frigid air is still being pumped into the cell, glaciating our soaked, bare bodies.

It won't be long before hypothermia sets in. If their intention is to make us as weak and vulnerable as possible, it'll be an easy win. We've been tortured, beaten, and now damn near frozen to death.

Lost in thought, I realise Ripley has gone quiet. I can't hear her teeth crashing together or even her snivelling anymore. Just the whistling of more ice-cold air being injected into our cell.

"R-Ripley?"

I strain my ears for any signs of life.

"Come on, Rip. T-Talk to me." I silently pray for a response. "Tell me you h-hate me again."

There's still nothing. I despise the burst of fear that settles in my gut. When did this evil woman come to mean something to me? Or have I just learned to enjoy the sick torture of her presence? I can't tell anymore.

Jaw locked, I fight through the pain as I wrench myself upright. It takes a lot of fumbling in the darkness for my fingertips to catch skin. My cuffed hands skate over her, blindly searching for some identifiable body part.

When I've found what feels like an arm, I tug with my remaining strength. Ripley grunts at the force of being dislodged from her perch against the wall and pulled across wet concrete.

"S-Stop," she moans in pain.

"Don't g-go quiet on me, then."

"No…"

"I'm not dying a-alone in here."

With some awkward manoeuvring, I get her close enough to tuck her into my chest. It takes some serious mental gymnastics to justify cradling her naked body against my chest. It's just self-preservation, right? I can steal her body heat.

Lifting my cuffed wrists over her head, I hold her in a tight embrace. My hands rub up and down her knobbly back to stimulate some warmth. I'm acutely aware of every naked inch pressed up so close to me, it's like we share the same skin.

Any personal space or privacy has deserted us. I can feel each quiet inhale and exhale that tells me she hasn't curled up and died in the dark. Her lungs expanding pushes her soft breasts into my chest each time.

Despite her quivering, body heat is soaking into me due to our extremely close proximity. My teeth stop chattering, allowing me to speak.

"Talk to me," I plead in a painfully neutral voice.

"T-Tired. Cold."

"I know. Me too." I keep rubbing her back, desperately fighting her shudders. "How did we end up like this, Rip?"

"Karma," she jokes feebly.

"I guess we've earned it."

Ripley sniffles in my arms. "I have."

"You've survived."

"So h-have you."

A wave of tiredness washes over me. "I never cared about me. Just them."

"Your family?" she whispers.

"The one I chose."

"Tell me how. P-Please."

I don't know why I comply.

"Xander was an accident. He'd never admit it, but I knew he needed a friend. Then Raine came along. They both just… snuck in. Became important. I'm not sure how."

Silence is a heavy blanket in this freezer, but not a warm one.

Instead, it sucks us deeper into the barren emptiness. A place that lives within us, born of guilt and desperation, used to justify all manner of evils.

"W-Why Xander?" Ripley asks.

"What do you mean?"

"Why d-did he need a friend?"

"The clinicians were always interested in him. I guess I was too. It wasn't hard to break into the office one night and read his file. I wanted to disprove what I suspected so I wouldn't care anymore."

Ripley drags in a shaky breath. "You… know?"

Surprise sparks in me. Xander hasn't even confirmed it to me. Not when I witnessed him thrashing in his sleep for the first time. Not when I questioned his diagnosis. Not even when the Z wing clinicians weaponised his past to break him.

He refused to break.

Or even acknowledge his trauma.

"Do you?"

"Just a th-theory. Someone hurt h-him." She continues to tremble in my arms. "Like y-your sister was hurt."

"Yeah. They did." I swallow thickly. "When I saw his scars, I had a hunch. No one becomes fascinated by pain without experiencing it."

"So y-you wanted to h-help him?" Ripley guesses, her teeth-clacking gradually easing. "To p-protect him."

"Yes, like I couldn't protect Daisy. It's fucked. I know."

"No." She shakes her head in a quick, curt jerk. "It's not. Y-You just wanted to do right."

With nothing but her breath and cold skin to hold me in reality, I can't find the heart to lie. The likelihood of us ever leaving here is non-existent. She may as well know what kind of monster she's dying with.

"I had no idea what was happening to Daisy. It went on under my nose for years." My voice catches. "I didn't protect her. I didn't even see her pain until it was too late. She needed someone to keep her safe."

"It w-wasn't your fault."

"Perhaps not. But failing her was my fault. In a twisted way… I figured that if I could help Xander, if I could be his friend and keep him safe… maybe Daisy would forgive me for letting her down."

"Nox." Her tone enters dangerous territory.

"I know how stupid it sounds. But when I realised that management was interested in Xander's mind... I resolved to do anything to protect him."

She's quiet, no doubt aware of what comes next.

"He has no family, no life or career. It would be so easy for him to disappear into their program. And with that much damage? Xander was an easy target. I needed a way to make him untouchable."

"Like by making h-him a stooge," Ripley finishes.

"Yeah. If we worked for them, then maybe they'd leave him alone. That couldn't happen while someone else held the role. I needed to remove the obstacle first."

It feels so wrong to be justifying why I killed someone she cared about while holding her in my arms. Like I'm giving her no choice but to listen. But the speck of light left inside me wants her to know. *Needs her to know.* This was never about hurting her for fun.

"Holly didn't deserve what I did to her," I admit before I can change my mind. "She was a means to an end. I didn't care that her death would hurt others. I was selfish and single-minded."

"For someone you l-loved," she surmises.

"You don't have to pretend to understand."

"I w-wish I was pretending." Her face is damp with tears against my chest. "When I g-got you and Xander s-sent to the Z wing... I did it for h-her. The person I loved and didn't protect. You were my m-means to an end."

And there we are.

We've been waging a war for the exact same fucking reason all along.

Hatred. Love. Family.

"You know, I can't even say I blame you for doing that to us. I've spent too long consumed by hatred and revenge not to understand the madness it pushes you into."

"The same m-madness that l-love creates, right?"

A short laugh lights my chest. "Right."

The two aren't so unlike after all. We love to hate and hate that which we love. Whoever said humans can't be made of extremes clearly had the privilege of a life without trauma or heartache. The rest of us know that it's a careful tightrope walk between the two.

"I still want to h-hate you so b-badly," Ripley says into my icy skin. "And I d-don't want to understand why you murdered my b-best friend. But... part of me d-does."

"I didn't tell you any of this to change your mind, Rip. I'm not asking for forgiveness… some of us don't deserve it."

"No. S-Some of us don't."

You know what? Fuck it.

I'm tired of the charade. I'm tired of justifying my hatred and looking for the next opportunity to inflict it. I'm tired of being Ripley's nemesis when all along, we were both just collateral damage. The price of surviving Incendia's abuse.

They've taken so much from us.

I want to die with a shred of humanity left.

"But for the record, I am sorry," I say slowly, deliberately. "For all of it."

After a brief pause, she sucks in sharply. "I'm sorry t-too. For all of it."

There's no puff of smoke or sparkling golden gate appearing above us. Redemption isn't a tick box to be checked and filed away. Though we wish it would be, right? Forgiveness would come easier that way.

Hatred doesn't disappear with a few words.

But it does soften and contextualise.

It does *relent*.

"Then I guess… At least we're dying on the same side?" I suggest uncertainly.

"What s-side is that?"

Stroking her wet curls, I let myself savour a split-second of satisfaction. She's in my arms. For tonight, I can pretend she's mine.

"The side of the villains."

CHAPTER 27
RIPLEY

MY NAME IS HUMAN – HIGHLY SUSPECT

I STARTLE AWAKE to the sound of a man screaming. Deep, blood-curdling screams. The kind that only a few are unlucky enough to ever hear. It's a barbaric sound.

My cheek is pressed up against something warm and hard. The earthy smell of burning wood lingers beneath blood and mildew lacing the air. It emanates from the sculpted chest I quickly realise I'm cuddled up to.

Our hips are aligned, legs tangled together and bodies conjoined. Not a scrap of fabric to keep us apart. The fact we survived the night pales in comparison to our current sleeping arrangement. Lennox's face is spooned in the crook of my neck.

Lennox.

Fucking Lennox!

He didn't release me for even a second as we drifted, shivering and near-hypothermic, through hours of misery. When the lights slammed on and the air conditioning stopped, he didn't move to let go, and I didn't ask him to.

We slept like this.

Entwined as one.

Bathing in the body heat of the man who should be my enemy, I let my thoughts stray. Raine is never far from my mind. I'm plagued by the image of him being dragged in here and tortured alongside us.

Xander's almost-black gaze soon sneaks in too. Hardened diamonds of hatred and fascination. For once, he can't follow me. I'm far beyond his reach now. He'll never get the chance to break me—not before the clinicians do.

"Fuck." It sounds like Lennox's throat is coated in gravel. "That hurts."

"No shit, Sherlock."

At the sound of my laughter, he tenses up. "Hey."

"Hi. Comfortable?"

It seems to take him a moment to remember our conversation. The sordid truths we told in the dead of night. Even now, it feels like an immaterial dream. Lennox would never apologise for any wrongdoing.

Only, he did.

Perhaps I don't know Lennox at all.

"Five-star luxury," he grumbles. "I can't feel my legs."

"Be thankful for that."

Every limb feels like it has been dipped in gasoline and set alight. A combination of hydrotherapy, beatings and sub-zero temperatures has left me feeling like a pack of wolves ripped me apart at the seams.

When he shifts, hissing in pain, I expect to be shoved away. Talk of redemption never holds up in the cold light of day—even when day constitutes fluorescent lighting and waking from agony-induced unconsciousness.

Yet the inevitable rejection and return to status quo never comes. Lennox stills, his handcuffed arms remaining curled around me, chiselled muscles contracting as he crushes me closer. I can hear his heart beneath his breastbone.

"We won't be left alone for long," he advises. "Better prepare yourself."

"Why don't they just kill us? It's quicker. Cleaner too."

"While we're alive, we still have our uses. The Z wing repurposes every piece of discarded trash."

I'd rather die than be treated like a lab rat. I don't want to become another one of their creations. An experimental prototype rolled out to the highest bidder.

"What if they hurt Raine?" I whisper in horror. "Or Xander?"

"That's why we have to keep them entertained," Lennox replies like he's given this some thought. "As long as we're here, we have their attention. Our family will be safe."

"Our?"

Breath stalling, Lennox's head lifts from my neck. He looks down at me through vicious bruises. One seafoam eye is swollen shut, while dried clumps of blood are soaked into his thick stubble.

The necklace around his neck is still intact, stark against burnished skin. I'm surprised they haven't taken it. Anything to dehumanise and antagonise. Perhaps that stage is yet to come.

"You care about Raine." His eyes ping-pong between mine

"Yes."

"Do you care about Xander?"

When I don't immediately answer, he lifts a thick brow. Right. No pretences. We have nothing in here but our truth. Last night, Lennox gave me his.

"I… Yes. No." I close my eyes for a moment, drawing in a deep breath. "Look, it's complicated."

It takes him a moment to find the words to respond.

"Family isn't who you're born to. It isn't blood or birth lines or adoption papers. It isn't even a legality."

"Then what is it?"

Licking his plump lips, Lennox's stare bores into me. "It's the people you choose to give a fuck about, through thick and thin."

"You think it's that simple?"

"I do."

Considering this, I study the swell of his inflated cupid's bow. "Then what does that make us?"

Lennox furrows his brow. "I don't know. Probably not enemies."

Don't do it, Ripley.

But not even Holly's whispered warning can stop me.

"How about allies?"

"Allies," he repeats.

"What do you think?"

"I guess… I can work with that."

The corner of his mouth twitches, not quite manifesting into a smile. We're still staring at each other. Suspended in this flux-like state between life and death, our worlds torn apart, and futures gone. There's nothing left to fight for. We both lost.

"Do we have to like each other to do this?" Lennox murmurs.

My breathing halts as his lips near. Lennox holds my gaze until his mouth captures mine, then nothing else matters but the feel of his skin on mine. Only this time, he isn't trying to hurt me. This isn't a punishment.

It's a surrender.

A white flag.

An abdication.

My mouth responds to his without being told. I don't know when hatred transformed into the most acute sense of need, but I couldn't care less. We're facing the unknown together now. At the end of this road, I can accept Lennox Nash for the monster he is.

He pauses to let me answer.

"No," I breathe. "We don't have to like each other."

"Then I guess… allies it is."

His mouth returns to mine, hard and insistent. The man who tried his damndest to kill me is breathing life into my lungs, one kiss at a time. I'm trapped in hell with an enemy, and disaster has never felt so fucking good.

Lips parting, I let his tongue seek passage. He tastes like blood and rage. Hope and fear. The perplexing tale of a man capable of inflicting so much horror in the name of love. But to Lennox, that is love.

Not the half-baked version of love that normal people proclaim. Nothing quite so ordinary or pedestrian. This is a man who will maim and kill to protect those he's deemed worthy of his care. Those lucky enough to be loved in the fiercest of ways.

Not even the intensifying shrieks around us disrupt the moment. While some anguished soul loses his mind, I hand mine over to the devil himself. Yet even the devil once danced with angels. Lennox's evil matches mine.

For we were both forged in the same hell.

And we'll both die here too.

Our kiss breaks at the sound of the cell door being unlocked. Lennox pulls me in close, going on high alert. Footsteps enter before Harrison's sneering voice shatters the morning's relative peace.

"Well, isn't this cosy. Survived the night, I see."

"Afraid so," Lennox retorts.

"Dress, Ripley. We're going for a walk."

When Harrison stomps over to us, I catch a flash of a black weapon before it presses into the back of my head. It takes a moment for the metallic coldness to register.

"Now," Harrisons says tersely. "I have permission to paint your brains across this cell if you disobey."

There's a gun nudging my skull. Not a baton. Nor a taser. It seems that not even Harrowdean's false pretence of being a safe, law-abiding facility can survive the evil of the Z wing. We've all been stripped to our bare selves, guard and patient alike.

"Move, Ripley."

"It's okay," I whisper to Lennox. "Let me go."

"No," he clips out.

"He'll only shoot us both, Nox. Let go."

His jaw set in an unyielding line, Lennox eventually surrenders me. My cuffed wrists held to my chest, I slither towards my discarded clothing, utterly humiliated by the show I'm putting on. Harrison doesn't have the decency to look away as I locate the wet pile across the cell.

"What about me?" Lennox asks.

"You're staying right here, lover boy. Professor Craven will be along shortly."

My blood freezes solid as fear takes root.

"The professor doesn't want to see me?"

"Oh, no. Sir Bancroft would prefer to deal with you himself."

Something tells me I shouldn't be relieved.

With Harrison's leer still locked on me, I pick through the wet clothing. Panties first. He rolls his eyes while watching me struggle with my bra, stepping forward to unlock my handcuffs. The metal chafes my raw skin and rips scabs open as it moves.

"Ouchie." Harrison grins.

I blink away tears. "Had worse."

"We'll see how long that bravery lasts."

Gingerly putting on my bra, I pick up the mud-stained t-shirt to pull on next. Something dislodges from the sodden fabric and hits the floor. The flash of white card captures Harrison's gaze.

"What is that?" he demands.

Terror lashes against my insides. "Nothing!"

"Up against the goddamn wall."

With the gun trained on me, cocked and waiting to be unloaded, I have no choice but to slip the t-shirt on and inch away. Harrison keeps his weapon pointed at me as he squats down to retrieve the business card.

Amidst all the carnage, I forgot about stashing it in my bra yesterday.

The guard didn't notice when he stripped me off, far too preoccupied with being a sadistic overlord. That goddamn card has just stamped my death warrant.

"Sabre Security?" Harrison reads in disbelief.

"I d-don't know… how that got there."

Lennox looks between us, as shocked by the presence of the business card as Harrison is. I may as well have walked myself in front of a firing squad.

Stomping over to me, Harrison grabs my bicep. I struggle against him until he smashes the butt of his gun into my head. Excruciating pain flares through my skull, reigniting the wound from my last act of defiance.

The handcuffs are quickly snapped back in place while I'm still reeling. It's taking all my self-control not to hurl on his freshly cleaned steel-capped weapons of mass destruction.

"Ripley!" Lennox shouts, still bare and bloodied as he finds his feet. "Don't tell them shit."

"Silence!" Harrison barks.

"Rip!"

The bleak acceptance in his pale-green gaze offers the most twisted form of comfort. Lennox knows what's to come. I suppose I do as well. Those two words inscribed on the luxurious card have ensured my suffering.

Lennox shakes his head. A clear message.

Don't let them win.

Harrison tows me from the cell, tugging on the metal chain connecting my cuffed wrists. Each yank causes lava to shoot through my veins. My mutilated skin is now bleeding again, pulsating with heat and pain.

I'm barely able to stand, let alone march down the seemingly endless corridor of cells. He drags me beyond the rooms I last saw, including Bancroft's office, stopping outside another door.

"Good morning," a cheerful voice greets.

Harrison glances over his shoulder. "Professor. Your new recruit is waiting for you in cell seven."

Dressed in a pale-grey suit and white lab coat, Professor Craven nods in acknowledgement. His ebony eyes are lasered on me behind square-framed glasses.

"Pleasant sleep, Ripley?"

I glower at him. "Toasty."

With a barked laugh, he sidles away. "I'll pay your cellmate a visit, then. Please do join us later."

I don't have time to let my dread for Lennox spiral. With a quick scan, the door's lock disengages, and Harrison unceremoniously shoves me inside the unfamiliar room.

"I just have to share your little misdemeanour with the boss. Please do enjoy the facilities in the meantime."

"Wait, please…"

The steel door clanks shut, sealing me in yet another cell, though the walls are white-washed brick this time. It's the sloshing of water and rasping laughter that causes me to tense up.

"Ain't this a sight."

I have the displeasure of knowing who that voice belongs to. Slowly turning around to face the room reveals the deathly pale, almost-blue face of a ghost.

Rick's once olive-toned face is gaunt, his skin sagging and cheeks shallow. He looks half-dead. Starved, bruised and broken.

"You're alive."

"Am I?" He coughs.

The set-up causes my stomach to bottom out. It's a room filled with rusted bathtubs, the four metal shells evenly spaced out and each equipped with shackles at the edges. Rick occupies the nearest one.

He's restrained inside the tub, a black plastic sheet buttoned up to his neck so only his head is visible. From the freezing temperature in the room, I can quickly connect the dots.

Cold water immersion.

An old asylum favourite.

"Christ." A wave of nausea has my mouth filling with saliva. "This is insane."

"Tip of the iceberg." His voice is weak and flimsy. "Didn't think I'd see you down here. Your luck ran out, then."

"Something like that."

Rick's eyes scan over me, taking in the multi-coloured bruises, swelling, deep lacerations and more. His attention catches on the portion of my scarred arm visible through the blood pouring from my wrists.

"How's the brand?" he jokes lamely.

"Sitting pretty. How's the friend?"

"Carlos is dead."

"I hate to say I told you so, but look around you... No one survives this place."

Rick's eyes sink shut. "Then I'm glad you're here."

I'm tempted to dunk him beneath the water and hold him there for old time's sake, but Harrison's return scuppers that plan. His smile seems even wider than before. I cringe as I stand against the wall.

"Change of plan," he singsongs. "We're going to have a little chat while the boss gives your *friend* a call."

"I don't know anything about Sabre or that number," I blurt out. "I never called them!"

"I couldn't care less. Now, Rick here has been cooling down after his last bout of defiance. Shall we reward him with a show?"

I try to run, hoping to somehow duck past him, but I'm easily captured and plucked off my feet. Harrison tosses me like I'm little more than a trash bag to be discarded. My tailbone screams as I hit the floor and roll.

Striding after me, his playful expression evaporates. I hate knowing that Rick is watching as Harrison begins a violent campaign of kicks, punches and slaps to punctuate each deafening question.

"Who gave you the business card, Ripley?"

Kick.

"Answer me!"

Punch.

"Where did you get it from?"

Slap.

The pain is relentless. Blow after blow. Strike after strike. There isn't a part of my body left untouched. Already bruised and battered skin feels like it's ready to rupture and spill organs across the floor.

Harrison's hand grips my chin to wrench me upright. His eyes are a curious blend of amber and chocolate-brown, like volcanic magma trapped beneath the earth's crust. Rage sealed in nerve tissue and skin.

"Did you contact them? Promise to give those nosy bastards all the juicy details?"

"No," I cry out.

"Lies."

With a swift backhand, he drops me again. I collapse, too feeble to even spare our audience a glance.

"Not so loyal after all." Harrison chuckles to himself. "Are you?"

"I'm l-loyal… to myself." I spit out blood.

"So ungrateful. It's a pity, all that wasted potential. But your loss is our gain."

When he boots me in the face, the pain is too unbearable. Finally, my consciousness snaps as I black out. Eventually I come to again, finding Harrison now talking to a suit-clad pair of legs, visible through my unsteady vision.

My mind has turned to soup, but I can make out a few words. Enough to tell me that something is afoot. They sound tense, on-edge. Like troops perched on a hillside, preparing for enemy fire.

"Sabre... video sent... retaliation."

"Phoenix?" a voice responds.

I recognise Bancroft's regal tone.

"Tank," Harrison answers.

"Fine." Their footsteps are muffled. "And her?"

"Nothing, sir."

I hear the shuffle of clothing before a hand strokes over my tangled hair. Peeking through tear-logged eyes, I look up at Bancroft. He's crouched beside me, darkness filtered across his aged features.

"All empires fall, Ripley," he croons softly. "But not this one."

"I d-didn't... The number...."

"Hush, dearest." I want to recoil when he pets me like a dog, but I'm too weak. "It's no matter. They're coming for us regardless now." Bancroft smiles shrewdly. "We have their plaything."

Their... plaything?

"I'm still mightily disappointed in you, Ripley." He sighs dramatically. "After all I've done for you. But it's no matter, your uncle already issued his consent. You're ours to repurpose now."

Desperation barely registers.

"Please." My whisper comes out frail and paltry.

"It's a little late to plead for your life, isn't it?" He tuts under his breath. "You should've thought of that before you betrayed us. I do hate disloyalty."

Straightening to his full height, Bancroft smooths a hand down his front. He casts a critical eye around the room, taking each iteration of horror in.

"Your friend Rick here is learning his own lesson about not sticking his nose where it doesn't belong. But I think we have something more suitable for your level of transgression."

"Sir?" Harrison prompts.

"I believe Professor Craven requested both Ripley and Lennox. Let him have his fun. I am sure she'll be returned as a clean slate, ready for sale."

I groggily watch Harrison unleash a grin. "As you wish, sir."

Bancroft casts me a final look of disappointment. "Goodbye, Ripley."

This time, I'm a lifeless flop in Harrison's arms. I don't even have the energy to acknowledge Rick as we exit. My head lolls, the steady patter of blood dripping from multiple lacerations leaving a trail behind us.

Flashing in and out of consciousness, I startle when the clank of a metal door opening permeates my mind fog. We're in yet another cell. The scent of spilled blood rushes up to meet me, so thick and cloying it makes me gag.

"Ah." Craven's voice is a featherlight tenor. "Right on time."

CHAPTER 28
XANDER
V.A.N – BAD OMENS & POPPY

SPINNING the all-access keycard between my fingers, I study the unfolding scene. A female guard is beating the shit out of a screaming patient, wearing them down while her backup prepares to deliver a sedative. They don't seem to care that we're watching.

It's funny how quickly a façade crumbles once the damage is done. Those spiderweb cracks soon lengthen and multiply. No one can stop the progression of an avalanche once that first clap rings out and the snowfall breaks.

Destruction is imminent.

Who will emerge remains to be seen.

"Take them to solitary!"

The patient bucks and writhes. "No! You did this! We know the truth now!"

It all began when the patient started running from group to group, shoving his phone in every available face. Everyone was sitting outside for lunch, silently stewing after whispers of what happened to Noah spread overnight.

Everyone is furious.

Sick of the injustice.

Ready to revolt.

I didn't bother to collect food, preferring to observe instead. Fury is a necrotic wound eating away at me. Lennox would be proud if he were here. Instead, I had to hear through the fucking grapevine that he was drugged and hauled off.

But not alone.

They took my toy too.

I have no idea where they are. The Z wing seems like a fair guess. But until I figure out where it's located, I can't do shit for them. Powerlessness is a feeling I hoped to never revisit.

As the patient is towed away, I spot Ripley's red-haired friend whispering with a gaggle of others. They were shown whatever played on his phone before security intervened. As they stand up to leave, I also rise.

"You," I shout.

She startles, sparing me a meek look. "Me?"

I search my memory for her name. "Rae. Come here."

Scampering over, Rae stops next to me. She's pale and shaken beneath her auburn hair. Like she's looked evil in the eyes and lived to tell the tale. I loom over her, my voice low.

"What was on the phone?"

"N-Nothing." She avoids my gaze.

"If they want to beat you, the guards will. If they want to kill you, they will. Pretending like you didn't see it won't protect you."

Her throat bobs, working up and down. "It was a video."

"A video?" I frown at her when she finally looks up at me.

"Some grainy phone footage. It's splashed all over social media and the news; not even the internet filters can block it. Looks like it was deliberately leaked from Blackwood Institute."

My mind churns. "What kind of footage?"

"I don't know." Rae raises a slim shoulder, her nose scrunched like she bit into a lemon. "Some kind of basement place. Full of cells and some weird-ass torture stuff. Blood everywhere. I think it's from the riot."

Well, I'll be damned.

"Do you know what that place is?"

"Few do," I reply absently.

If evidence of another Z wing has leaked to the press, this tinder box is about to blow. Rumours are one thing. Video evidence is another, whether or not Incendia plays it off as doctored or part of some smear campaign.

Looking around, I can see all the warning signs. Patients conspiring in small groups. Furtive glances and death glares shot at overzealous guards. A real-life plot is unfolding before my eyes.

"Where is Ripley?" Rae pulls my attention back to her.

"She was taken."

She licks her lips while rocking from foot to foot, clearly uneasy. "Do you think she'll come back?"

Staring down at the wraithlike creature, I study her tell signs. Glistening eyes. Twitching fingers. Lips puckering and red from being chewed. She's battling concern or fear, but I don't know which. Ripley should've never allowed a customer to get so attached.

I shrug her off. "Not a clue."

Rae watches me leave, her tears spilling over. I don't care to offer any shred of comfort. Tension is growing fast. Like an invisible storm, there's an electrical charge in the air and madness in each and every mind. Something is going to erupt.

I stride past gathered patients, trading gossip faster than even management can suppress. Walking inside the reception, several guards are gathered too, nervously glancing from side to side. Snippets of conversation float over me.

"Media shitstorm... press... protest."

"Here?" someone asks.

"Incoming."

I pick up my pace, not slowing until the medical wing is in sight. A handful of cubicles are full, the curtains drawn to conceal their occupants. There aren't any staff behind the nurse's station or in the corridor. Injuries incurred during the storm must still be keeping the medics busy.

Inside Raine's cubicle, he's curled up on his side. A strange pair of aviators are balanced on his nose so I can't see his eyes, but he perks up the moment I walk in. The man's like a damn bloodhound.

"Xan?"

"Yeah, it's me."

Drawing his curtain, I stride over to the small window to the left of his hospital bed. A quick peek outside doesn't reveal much. I may be paranoid, but I feel better, having my sights back on him.

"What's going on?"

"I'm not sure," I admit, studying the institute's grounds. "Some press video is circulating. Everyone is all riled up after what happened to Noah."

"Have you heard from Ripley or Lennox?"

"Still no sign of them."

"Maybe they're just in solitary," he guesses.

"You really believe that?"

I watch Raine rub his temples. He isn't stupid. As soon as I relayed the whispers I'd heard yesterday, it was clear he knew. Both of us did. Neither of them are coming back anytime soon.

"We have to help them, Xan."

"You think I don't know that?"

"Then what are we still doing here?" He winces, trying to sit up quickly.

Rubbing my face, I sigh wearily. "Because it isn't that simple. I don't even know where Harrowdean's Z wing is. No one does."

"Then we have to find out!"

Sitting upright now, he tugs at the needles and wires still attached to him. I grab his wrists to halt his movements.

"You're going nowhere."

"Don't start getting all protective just because Lennox isn't here to do it. We both know you don't care."

"I do care!" I hurl back at him.

Raine freezes, his wrists still caught in my grip. I clear my throat and look away, not that it makes a difference. He can't see the terror that admission has provoked inside me. But he can sure as hell sense it.

"I… I thought I was just a nuisance to you," he admits quietly.

"You are." My stomach flips. "A nuisance I care about."

Raine's mouth hangs open. He doesn't have a response. I don't blame him. I've spent my entire adult life not giving a flying fuck about anyone or anything including myself. This is new for me too.

"That's why you're going to lay back down in the goddamn bed, and let me handle this."

"I can help," he baulks haltingly.

"They both made this mess. But I'm going to fucking fix it."

"Xan—"

"Stay here, Raine!"

Cringing back into his pillows, he summons a reluctant nod. I pluck his plugged-in mobile phone from the bedside table then shove it into his hands.

"I'm going hunting. If any trouble starts, call. Got that?"

"What kind of trouble?" Raine's forehead wrinkles.

"I honestly don't know. But something's coming."

I quickly check around the medical wing, ensuring it's secured. Nina is on-duty again in the small office, preoccupied by her crossword book. She pays me no attention as I stride past.

I spend the next few hours systematically picking the institute apart with my all-access pass. Checking every last locked door, storage cupboard and floor. There seems to be no security around for me to beat any clues from.

After breaking in, I'm picking through the filing cabinets in the warden's office, searching for records of any admissions to the solitary wing, when I hear approaching voices. Slamming the cabinet shut, I duck behind a thick curtain.

"It began as a handful of reporters, sir." Elon's annoying voice is unmistakable. "They're gathering outside each of the remaining institutes across the country."

"The corporation has released a statement," Davis responds.

"It appears the crowds are growing by the hour. The negative response to that leaked video is escalating fast. Security reports a large protest gathering at our front gates."

"Goddammit! Handle this, Elon."

"It's a rather large mob," he says uncertainly.

"I don't care. Send every man and woman we have out there. Go too. I will not be intimidated in my own institute."

"I believe Sir Bancroft intends to address the crowd himself. The leaked video is likely the work of Sabre Security. A distraction technique, perhaps."

"Then Bancroft can clean his own fucking mess," Davis spits.

Trouble in paradise?

The warden sounds less than enthused by his superior's actions. I haven't had the misfortune to run into Bancroft again since he agreed to our release from Priory Lane's Z wing. But I've heard whispers of his presence in Harrowdean.

"What about the patients?" Elon asks. "News has already spread. They're restless."

There's a thunking sound like Davis has slammed his forehead against his desk.

"Hold a skeleton staff back to keep the peace. We'll declare an emergency lockdown for good measure. Send everyone else out to hold the crowd back."

"Yes sir," Elon acknowledges.

When I hear retreating footsteps and the office door close, I peek around the curtain. Davis is sitting at his desk, staring into space. I slide the pocketknife from my back pocket, creeping up behind him.

"Argh!" he startles as I press the blade to his throat.

"Warden. Where are Lennox Nash and Ripley Bennet?"

"Step away from me."

"No. Answer the fucking question before I make this throat a gaping smiley face."

"Think about what you're doing," Davis attempts.

Pausing, I take a moment. "Alright. It's thought about. Now answer."

"They're dead by now!"

Pressing the blade in, I feel his skin begin to part. "You continue to underestimate us all, Warden."

I can feel a weak tremble running over him. The mighty warden of Harrowdean, sweating like a pig in a butcher shop. Men like him shouldn't have power. Yet they always seem to covet it.

"Where is the Z wing?"

"You're on camera," he gasps. "Walk away now, and I won't report this."

"Why didn't I think of that?" I slash deeper into his throat. "Oh, wait. I did. The moment I cut the CCTV camera's power supply."

"Please…"

"Where is it?"

"I can't tell you! I won't!"

"Then what use do I have for you?"

"Please," he tries again, holding up his hands.

"Still begging, Warden?" I lean closer, scenting his sweat and fear. "Didn't you know I have no humanity to appeal to?"

His throat cuts like warm butter left out in the sun for too long. I ensured to sharpen my blade as I plotted overnight, preparing for whatever price finding Ripley and Lennox would demand.

The glinting steel slashes him wide open like a fucking piñata. Warm blood gushes forth in a hot, sticky spray. It pours from the deep wound and splashes all manner of paperwork, framed photographs and incident reports.

No doubt forged documents that are all dipped in the blood of Harrowdean's stuffed suit. His essence now stains the lies he's been paid to perpetuate.

Holding him close despite the spray, I watch every last droplet. Each satisfying spray and gargle. The agonal breath of a dying soul. Holding Davis as he bleeds out stirs some internal bloodlust that only grows.

When I release him, he thuds against the desk with an audible *smack*. Eyes blown wide. Mouth hanging open. Face waxy and a yawning gap where his throat should be. I can't help but stare for several peaceful moments.

The sound of distant shouts breaks my reverie. It floats through the stained glass window, emanating from the institute's gates. From the warden's office, I have a better view of what's unfolding.

A quick look outside reveals something I never expected to see. Elon's description was a gross underestimation.

"Holy shit," I mutter.

He was right about one thing—it sure looks like a protest. Reporters and press vehicles blur with the enraged general public. Placards are being waved, accompanied by shouts and screams.

Harrowdean's security is struggling to hold the protest at bay. Heading down the paved path beyond the gates, I recognise Bancroft's shrivelled form with Elon and a multitude of guards in tow.

He's dolled up in a fine suit, silvery hair slicked back and game face on. The crowd's rage only heightens at the sight of his approach. My attention is pulled from him as the emergency alarm blares.

It shatters the still air of the office and slams me back into reality. Davis's corpse is slowly cooling. But his orders still stand. A lockdown has been called.

Taking one last look around the office and its deceased inhabitant, I duck into the corridor. Emergency lighting flashes on repeat, reminiscent of an epileptic fit. Still, the silence is eerie.

I almost startle when my phone begins to buzz.

"Raine?" I answer hastily.

"What's that alarm, Xan?" His voice is high pitch.

"Everyone's going into lockdown. Hold tight."

"I can hear shouting. Sounds like patients."

"I'm coming now."

Hanging up the call, I keep the blood-slick blade poised in my hand as I enter the spookily empty corridor. Not many staff are around on weekends anyway, but it's deserted now the guards have been directed outside.

As I near the reception, doors are flung open. Chairs upturned.

Brochures scattered. The sounds of screaming and yelling emanate from outside where the witching hour has fallen.

A quick peek outside reveals the growing commotion. With the majority of Davis's men sent to protect the institute's perimeter, few remain to hold the tension at bay. And damn, has it exploded.

All hell has broken loose. At first glance, it looks like Harrowdean's patient population has turned on itself. There are dozens of scraps taking place, fists flying into faces and blood spraying in all directions.

As I squint through the darkness, I can see the true reality. Beyond a few random fights, they're actually targeting the guards. Patients rally together, taking down black-clad brutes and stealing their weapons.

Guards are being tasered and cuffed. Pummelled with fists at every available opportunity. The mob is growing as sides are drawn. In the gloom, violence rules. And it's growing by the second.

This is an uprising.

A fucking *riot*.

CHAPTER 29
RIPLEY
SINNER – OF VIRTUE

"PLEASE!" I beg at the top of my lungs. "Stop!"

Arms shackled to a thick metal ring built into the wall above my head, I strain my shoulders each time I attempt to break free. Hours of agony and I'm still no closer to escaping. Every muscle feels like it's been pumped full of lead and torn to shreds.

It doesn't compare to the pain I've been forced to witness, though. There was a time when I would've enjoyed seeing Lennox scream himself hoarse and pass out. If I could go back to that mental place right now, I would. Anything to escape this.

"The suffering of others is a particularly interesting motivator." Craven's tone is conversational. "Most can have empathy for a stranger. But empathy for a peer? That's far more powerful."

His mouth frozen in an eternal yell that his vocal cords have long since stopped supplying, Lennox strains against his own shackles. He's bound in a similar fashion, but unlike me, the spotlight is all his.

"Again," Craven orders.

His partner in crime, the guard with a cap covering his closely cropped hair, flicks a switch on the battery-like machine placed a few inches from Lennox. It's connected to several wires, each one secured to his bare chest by an adhesive pad.

The moment the lever is pulled, his body jerks. An intense electrical current is being fed into his torso, over and over, the shock far more powerful than a mere stun gun blast. This is brutal, repeated electrocution.

"What do you want from us?" I sob violently.

The professor deigns to look at me, his expression completely void of emotion. "Absolutely nothing."

"Then stop! Don't hurt him!"

"Believe me, I'm being paid a significant sum to hurt him."

When this round of electrocution ends, Lennox's head lolls forward, shining beads of sweat dripping from his skin. He's barely lucid, moaning and swaying during each brief reprieve from the torture.

"Why?" I blubber.

Craven shrugs nonchalantly. "Incendia has orders to fulfil. Machines without morals are in demand, but the mind must break first. Only then can it be wiped."

With that explanation, he crouches beside Lennox. Craven grabs a handful of his greasy hair, using it to wrench his head upright. I can't stop myself from wailing as Lennox's deep-set eyes struggle to open.

"Ready to comply, Patient Twelve?"

"Go f-f-fuck yourself," Lennox moans.

Sighing, Craven lets his head drop. "Again."

The process is repeated. Over and over. Each shock more horrific than the last. Lennox's screams may be silent, but my tears offer a constant soundtrack. I can't feel my own battered body anymore, only the fierce burn in my throat from shouting so much.

"What's your name?" Craven demands.

When Lennox doesn't respond, he nods to the guard who pulls a steel-tipped whip from the rolling table of instruments in the corner of the room. The guard retakes his position, the whip held high.

"Answer me, Patient Twelve."

Still, Lennox doesn't respond.

"Fine." Craven nods to his goon. "Go ahead."

I bellow as the whip strikes across Lennox's lowered face. Blood sprays from the deep laceration it leaves in his right cheek, reaching from earlobe to nose. His tears mingle with the blood, forming a red veil spilling down his neck.

"What is your name?"

He chokes on a phlegmy cough. "L-Lennox fuckin' Nash."

The professor's hands curl into fists. "Wrong answer. We can escalate if you insist on being stubborn."

When the next weapon of choice is unveiled, what little hope I had left in my heart fizzles out. It's a handheld drill, the bit sharpened to a gleaming point. Even the cap-wearing guard seems reluctant.

"Start with his hands and feet," Craven instructs. "That ought to get things moving."

The drill bit is lined up with his shackled left hand. I take the coward's way out. My eyes screw shut as the mechanism begins to turn, the metallic buzz drilling into flesh and muscle. Lennox's voice roars back to life with each ear-splitting scream he releases.

"Lennox Nash is dead," Craven elucidates. "Do you understand?"

It feels like an eternity before the drilling ceases. Ribbons of tears soak my cheeks, leaking from my closed eyes. I don't want to look. I can't. For all his faults, not even Lennox deserves to be unmade.

"No," his sonorous voice wheezes. "H-He's not."

I hear Craven sigh. "Such resilience. Perhaps we should focus on the girl to motivate him."

Daring to look, I find the professor staring at me in contemplation. His goon has halted drilling, leaving Lennox in a bloodied state. I can't even tell if he's still breathing after forcing those words out.

When Craven takes a step towards me, I close my eyes, preparing for whatever comes next. I just hope Lennox has passed out and won't have to watch my torture like I did his.

"Now then…"

The command to inflict more torture that I expect doesn't come. With my eyes squeezed shut, I await my fate. The sound of a heavy blow and body crumpling follows instead. I dare to peek a single lid open.

"What an absolute piece of work." Weirdly, the voice spilling from the guard now holding the drill upside down is light and feminine.

Eyeing Craven, he looks physically repulsed.

"You know what? The world won't miss you, Professor."

The guard repeatedly smashes the drill into the back of Craven's skull. Each collision causes a stomach-lurching crunch, yet the guard doesn't relent.

Thud.

Crunch.

Crack.

Blood pools around the professor's head, peppered with chunks of broken bone. By the time the guard halts, panting for breath, not much remains of Craven's skull but a semi-crushed shell.

He slumps, elbows braced on his knees. "Bastard."

"Y-You," I force the word past my constricted throat. "You killed h-him?"

Breathless, the guard shoots me a glance. "Sorry I couldn't do it sooner. I'm working on someone else's schedule."

Still gaping at him, I feel like I've already fallen into insanity. I must still be mid-torture because there's no way in hell this is really happening. I've hallucinated the whole thing.

"We don't have a whole lot of time." The guard lifts his cap to scratch at his short hair. "I can't fucking think straight in this stupid wig."

With each scratch, edges of dark hair lift, revealing a flash of lurid pink beneath. It *is* a wig. I watch in dismay as he taps a cleverly concealed, flesh-coloured earpiece slotted into his ear.

"Next time, someone else can pretend to be a man and help people get tortured to maintain cover. I do not get paid enough for this."

This isn't a guard at all.

She's a mole.

"Hello?" She taps her ear again. "Come in, Theo."

Seemingly getting no response, she curses. I watch the stranger stand up, tossing the drill aside with a look of disgust. She pulls a set of keys from her cargo trousers then heads towards me.

"Who are you?" I blurt.

"I work for Sabre Security."

"You're… one of them?"

"Unfortunately for me," she replies sarcastically. "I get all the glamorous jobs."

Squatting down, she works on unlatching the shackles holding me in bondage. The moment the metal slides open, I cry out. My wrists and arms have ballooned from all the abuse, so bloated and inflamed, I know an infection is brewing.

"My name's Alyssa," she speaks quickly. "And I'm really sorry, but I'm not here for you. My team is coming in fast, though."

"I d-don't understand."

"Bancroft took one of our own. I'm here to extract him." Alyssa pauses to locate the next lock. "We can offer you both protection, but you have to come with me now."

"Come?"

"Ripley." She frees my other wrist. "I know who you are. This is your chance to choose the right side."

My arms slumping, I lay lifeless as she moves to unshackle Lennox. He's unresponsive now. Alyssa cringes at the sight of his left hand, mangled and seeping blood.

"Sorry." She grimaces. "I had a cover to maintain."

"You h-hurt him!"

"And now I'm freeing him. A fair trade off, don't you think?"

Working fast, she removes his shackles then gives him a nudge. Lennox moans in response, filling me with relief. He's still alive, just completely out of it. Alyssa looks equally as relieved.

"It's time, Ripley," she declares as she stands. "I have to find Phoenix then meet the team for extraction. Come with me if you want to get out."

"I can't leave."

"We can take Lennox with us!"

"It isn't just him," I whisper through falling tears. "I can't leave the others behind."

Staring at me in disbelief, Alyssa shakes her head. "It's now or never. I don't know when we can free the other patients. Bancroft won't give this place up without a fight."

"I know." My eyes move to Lennox's battered state. "But I won't abandon them. Not even to survive."

"So what will you do?"

I watch his chest rise and fall. "Find the others. Then run."

She sighs, reaching into her trouser pocket to flourish a black keycard. I recognise it immediately. It's the same as the one that Elon used to unlock the Z wing's security system.

The matte black rectangle is tossed across the cell to me. Shakily, I take it, stashing the cool plastic in my bra.

"Wait for us to clear out." She bends down to meet my eyes, explaining hurriedly. "This part may get messy. Stay hidden until it's over."

Before she can leave the cell, I summon my voice again.

"Thank you."

Alyssa looks over her shoulder. "Sabre will help you, Ripley. If you make it out… you know where to find us."

Then she's gone as mysteriously as she arrived. The cell door clanks shut but doesn't lock. I eye Craven's practically decapitated body for a second before starting the agonising process of dragging myself across the room.

Traversing his long, powerful legs and the boxer shorts he's been clothed in, Lennox stirs at my touch. I work on detaching the electrodes from his chest, tossing each wire aside. Some leave burned patches of skin behind.

"Talk to me, Nox," I throw his words back at him.

A low groan rumbles in his throat.

"Words, big guy. I need you conscious."

With all the electrodes discarded, I try to wipe some of the blood from his face and neck with my soiled shirt. The jagged slice across his cheek is oozing, his skin flapping open. When I accidentally touch one side, his eyes fly open.

"Argh!"

"That's it." I quickly pull the edge of my t-shirt back. "Wake up."

"R-Rip?"

"It's me."

"Where?" he asks woozily.

"Still in the Z wing. There's some kind of break in happening. We need to find the others and get away from Harrowdean."

"H-How?"

"There must be a way out. Xander will know."

"I c-can't make it…" He hisses in pain. "Leave me."

"Like hell. Thought we were allies?"

"Enemies," he whispers.

"Not anymore, Nox. Not in here."

Struggling to prop him up despite my own throbbing body, I search around the cell for anything I can use. The only items are the table of torture instruments and Craven's body. Biting my lip, I move to the corpse first. Warm blood slips beneath my bare feet.

"He d-dead?" Lennox mutters.

"Yeah. Looks a bit like a smashed egg."

"Good."

Searching his lab coat pockets, I find a folded handkerchief. A quick pat of his suit underneath reveals an old flip phone suitable for a dinosaur like him. Nothing else. This will have to do.

I shove the phone into my bra, stumbling back over to Lennox. He looks like he wants to yell at the pressure I apply to his bleeding face with the handkerchief, but it comes out as a tiny, child-like cry.

"Suck it up." I press down as hard as my own throbbing injuries will allow. "You're bleeding."

"F-Fucking bitch."

"That's more like it. Thought you'd gone soft."

"Not likely."

Lapsing into silence, I let him rest as I focus on staunching the bleeding. It feels like an eternity has gone by before I hear the first incoming noises.

Shouting echoes from the corridor outside the cell. A multitude of different voices. The wet thunk of repeated, frenzied stabbing. Someone grunting with exertion.

"Rip?" Lennox whispers.

"Shh." I hold him tight. "Be quiet."

Gut-twisting screams follow. They sound so close, I wonder what's unfolding just outside the cell we're cowering in. More shouts ensue. The words permeate through the steel door to reach us.

"You're going to fucking die for that!"

It's a female voice. Unfamiliar. I hug Lennox even tighter to me, like I can shield him with my own broken body if the owners of those voices come looking. I don't know if they're friend or foe. We have to stay hidden here.

Bang.

Lennox flinches in my arms at the sound of gunfire. It cracks through the Z wing like an almighty thunderclap. Anguished shrills follow, the shouts all intermingling to form a terrifying mental image of a battle unfolding.

My face hidden in Lennox's shoulder, I tune out the unimaginable sounds. Part of me wonders if we've both died when silence eventually settles what feels like centuries later.

"Are we dead?" he grits out.

"Not yet."

Lifting my head, I strain my ears for any noise. There's a far-off banging. It sounds like cell doors are being systematically opened and closed. Briefly releasing Lennox, I grab the first instrument I can find on Craven's trolley of toys. A scalpel.

"Someone's coming," I whisper.

Lennox grunts, attempting to move, but he can hardly crack an eyelid let alone defend himself. I stand with my back to him, ignoring every last protest of my body. The scalpel rests in my white-knuckled grip.

Another bang.

Another.

Inching ever closer.

"Nox?"

He groans in response.

"If this is it… I just want you to know that I forgive you."

His reply is drowned out by the sound of our cell door flinging open. Three figures step inside, all barefoot and clothed in rags. My eyes bounce from the misshapen caricatures of human faces until I spot a familiar sight.

"Ripley."

Rick pushes past the other two, stepping farther into the cell. Blood drains from my face at the gun clasped in his hands. It sure looks a lot like Harrison's gun, the one he jammed into the back of my head.

He takes one look at Lennox, half-dead and slumped over, then focuses his attention on Craven's caved-in skull. All eyes seem to be locked on that sight with varying looks of satisfaction.

"What are you doing here?" I hiss.

"Getting out." Rick lifts his gaze to me. "Some dude who isn't a dude let me out. You?"

"The same."

"Well, now's the moment. You need a hand with him?"

I tighten my grip on the scalpel. "You'd help us?"

Clothes dripping like he's only just been pulled from his icy tub, Rick shrugs. "The enemy of my enemy is my friend. Ain't that the saying?"

"We aren't friends."

"Doesn't mean we both can't walk out of here," he counters. "No one's stopping us. I handcuffed that sick fuck in the tub when he came searching."

"Harrison?"

"He's taking a little dip now." Rick grins to himself.

"Alive?"

"I didn't care to check. You coming?"

I'm hit by indecision. Even in the best of health, I have little hope of carrying Lennox's massive, over-muscled body alone. But certainly not like this. He's going to take some serious handling.

Resolved to my fate, I reluctantly place the scalpel down then pull the keycard from my bra. Rick lifts a brow.

"I can get us out," I explain.

"Well, no time like the present."

He gestures for the two others to help. Neither speaks nor meets my eyes. I recognise the woman, despite her bruises and sliced-up skin. She's Patient Three. The one Harrison and Craven were reconditioning.

The other patient is male, his hair long and untamed. I don't know how he's maintained his muscles in here, but his arms are corded. Enough to lift Lennox's dead weight with a bit of help from Patient Three.

"You know the way out?" Rick asks me.

"You don't?"

"They pounced before we even had a chance to poke around the building. Never saw them coming. That professor asshole told me the others are already dead."

"How can you be sure?" I limp towards the door.

"I checked. All the other cells are empty."

Looking over my shoulder, I watch the two Z wing patients struggle to manoeuvre Lennox between them. He's breathing unsteadily, his head still limp.

"They got names?" I whisper to Rick.

"Nah. Haven't said a word."

As we step out into the corridor, the smell hits. I should be used to it by now, yet nothing can prepare you for the scent of a bloodbath.

It's everywhere. Covering everything. Walls, floors, cell doors. There are signs that a body has been dragged through the spillage. I have no way of knowing if our mysterious saviour made it out alive.

Not a single soul, though.

We're in a ghost town.

"Where are all the guards?"

Rick picks his way through red spillages, heading where I point. "I don't know. Unless we're missing some secret society party down here, the place has been abandoned."

Not likely.

When I slide on a crimson pool, Rick has to lunge to catch me. My knees are knocking together, I'm so weak. Numbness has swept in as my extremities switch off due to the constant onslaught of pain.

"I'm fine," I struggle out.

"Yeah. You look it."

"No more than Harrowdean's whore deserves, right?"

He clears his throat. "Think we've both paid our dues down here, Rip."

Honestly, he has a point.

We move slowly, barely able to shuffle ourselves towards the concrete staircase leading upward. Tackling each endless step feels like running a marathon on an empty stomach. The thick steel door seems forever out of reach. I can hear the grunts of the pair behind us struggling.

At the top of the stairs, I use the special black pass to unlock the door. My heart threatens to explode when there's no response. I try several times, each failed attempt causing my breathing to hitch.

"Come on!" I hiss under my breath.

Trying one last time, I'm rewarded at last. The security system eventually buzzes, and I could cry from relief. The door clanks open loudly.

A cacophony of sounds immediately filters in, emanating from beyond. Sound can't penetrate the Z wing's fortifications, but it's clear that something is unfolding outside. I hesitate, listening to the distant screams.

"What is that?" Rick's nose is scrunched up, a divot between his brows.

"The reason why there aren't any guards watching us."

With that grim realisation, we inch out of the Z wing and into a lit corridor. The bare bulbs are illuminated, breaking up the nighttime shadows. I don't even know what day it is or how long we were below ground. I've lost all concept of time.

Hanging back, I let Rick take the lead as we break outside. Lennox has roused a little on the way back up, his teeth now gritted for each movement. I swipe hair from his face to check on him, my hand sticky with his blood and sweat.

"You with me?"

"Just about," he grunts.

"We have to find Raine and Xander. I don't know what we're walking into, but this is our chance to get out."

"Following your l-lead, Rip."

He slams his eyes shut as the two patients tow him onwards. I don't know how we'll manage to run let alone walk with Lennox in this state.

We have to try, though. Bancroft won't let our escape go unpunished when the dust settles.

Blazing, bright-white lights temporarily blind us as we're greeted by the night air. Floodlights have been turned on, illuminating the perimeter fence and the manor itself. As we stumble through the trees to reach the quad, the racket intensifies.

"Holy shit," Rick exclaims.

It's chaos.

Violent, deadly chaos.

In all directions, patients run wild and free. Some armed with weapons, others battering the living daylights out of any remaining guards. It goes beyond mere beatings. They're being incapacitated and restrained, then dragged into haphazard lines.

"What is this?"

Lennox lifts his head. "Hostages?"

"What?"

"They're taking the guards hostage." Rick's head swivels as he gapes at our surroundings. "This is like a fucking prison riot."

The five of us huddled together in astonishment, we spend several seconds taking it all in. The still-blaring alarm only adds to the havoc unfolding. With a smile blooming, Rick pulls the gun he stashed in his ragged waistband.

"This is it," he proclaims. "This is how we take them down. If we have hostages… we can make demands. The world will have to listen."

"They're just going to send reinforcements in and kill us all!"

"Not if we barricade the doors." The male patient holding Lennox speaks for the first time. "Secure every entrance and exit."

"We can toss them scraps of dead guards if they dare break our perimeter," Patient Three chimes in.

Looking between the three of them, I'm trying to summon a response when my name rings out. Rae's face is covered in splattered blood, her auburn hair in disarray as she runs towards me.

I warn her off with a raised hand, fearing I won't survive the collision. I'm barely remaining upright as it is.

"You're alive!" she squeals.

"Rae." I lock eyes with her. "What's happening?"

"We're taking over."

"Who is?" Rick interjects.

"All of us." Rae eyes the gun in his hands. "Is that real?"

He nods, clutching his weapon possessively.

Noticing our presence, a handful of other patients have gathered to gawk. We must look like we've swam through a vat of blood. Spotting Rick's gun, a few more converge.

"We're gonna kill the bastards!" Taylor is one of them, a ragged slice marring her brow line.

"No!" someone else protests.

"They deserve it!"

"But we aren't killers!"

Everyone is shouting and arguing, violence still unfolding all around us.

"We need barricades!" Hands cupped around her mouth and voice raised, Patient Three can be heard above the bickering. "Chains! Padlocks! Furniture! Every exit has to be blocked!"

Nodding, Rick waves his gun. "They're worth more to us alive. We can use the guards as bargaining chips."

"Why?" a patient calls out.

"Because if we don't have leverage, they'll kill us."

"Like Noah!" another person screams.

"We're animals to them!"

"I don't want to die in here!"

Rick begins to bark off orders, waving that damn gun around like a lunatic. It's the role he always wanted. A righteous mob at his beck and call. With growing horror, I realise they're all going to get themselves killed.

Backing away from them, I inch towards Lennox. Patient Three quickly surrenders his right arm to me, preoccupied by instructing the horde of patients growing all around us.

"What are you doing?" Lennox groans.

"I'm not sticking around for this. We'll tunnel out if we have to."

"We w-won't get far like this."

"Then we'll take our chances."

"Rip—"

"No! We have to run. Riots only end one way."

Tugging his other arm from over the male patient's shoulder, I'm almost crushed beneath his weight. Lennox huffs, fighting to regain his balance, but he can hardly hold his head upright.

"Ripley," he wheezes.

"Don't start! I'm not leaving you!"

"We can't run forever."

"Fucking watch me."

Half-carrying, half-dragging him, I manage two steps before my knees give out. We go down hard, hitting the ground in a pathetic tangle. Lennox tries to avoid smothering me, but his gargantuan body thwacks into mine.

I'm crushed beneath his bulk, staring up at the night sky with a war waging all around us. I don't even try to fight off the tears, turning cold by the time they drip into my ears. We're never going to get out of here. Not like this. I'm not strong enough.

"Ripley! Hey, someone help me."

Hands grab hold of Lennox then heave, dragging him to the side. I pull in a breath, my entire body wailing. Rae hangs over me, a couple of others helping her position Lennox into a seated position.

"Where are you going?" She kneels next to me.

"Leaving," I cry out. "We have to run."

Her mouth twists into a grimace. "You can't, Rip. There's a protest outside the front gate. We're surrounded. This is our only shot."

"They'll kill us all, Rae!"

"We're as good as dead anyway," she replies tersely. "Come on. We need your help."

"I don't help people," I admit shallowly, pain overwhelming me. "I hurt them."

Offering me a hand, Rae's gaze is oddly steady. "Then start hurting the right people."

In the growing madness, I stare at her hand. At the thick layers of cuts and scars peeking out from beneath her shirt sleeve. A mere glimpse of the evil I've inflicted here. The same evil I'm desperate to run from.

All I've ever done is run.

From memories. From mania.

From demons.

From my own transgressions.

Bloodstained hands clasping, I let Rae tug me to my feet. She offers a tearful smile that I can't return. Not yet. Not until I've earned that privilege back. And she's right—I'll never do that by running. None of us will.

Her eyes shift beyond me. "Incoming."

"What?"

"There!" a familiar voice yells.

Chest aching, I lean on Rae and turn. At the rear exit of the institute, two shadows stare across the quad at us. One in a crimson-splattered polo shirt, the other a hospital gown and aviator sunglasses. Both head towards us.

"Ripley!"

Hearing Raine shout my name is like seeing a tiny ray of sunshine peeking through this hellscape. His arm circling Raine's shoulders, Xander steers him through the half-destroyed quad. His stare flits from Lennox to me, searching both of us.

Fuck me gently.

Xander Beck himself looks bloody worried.

The pair awkwardly stumble closer. Between guards being dragged into line, their cuffs stolen then attached to themselves, and the bark of orders being given, it feels like a battlefield stands between us.

But then I'm in Raine's arms.

Freshly squeezed orange.

Sea salt.

Home.

"Rip," he says urgently. "Are you okay?"

"L-Lennox… He… We…"

Grasping handfuls of his hospital gown, I collapse against him. Raine struggles to hold me upright until Xander intervenes and takes me from him, a hand cupping the back of my head.

"Xan."

"Breathe," he orders. "I've got you now."

Shaking all over, I let Xander gently lower me to the ground. I'm placed next to Lennox, my back resting against his side. He stirs and looks up at his best friend surveying us both.

"Xan."

"Hey, man." Xander's mouth does this strange, curving motion. "Good to see you're… kind of alive."

Lennox blinks rapidly. "Rip… is h-he smiling at me?"

I sag into him. "Yeah, I think he is."

Lennox's mangled, still-bleeding hand finds mine. Xander watches Lennox hold me with a cocked brow. The pair exchange some silent words, their eyes locked for several seconds until Raine interrupts.

"Guys? Plan?"

Lennox hacks up a mouthful of blood. "Ripley wants to run."

"Run where?" Xander replies.

"I... I don't know," I admit.

"The place is surrounded."

We watch the hysteria growing all around us. Rick is gesturing towards the lit-up perimeter fence, directing patients who have stripped the captured guards of all their worldly possessions. Anarchy is spreading like wildfire. But in the pandemonium, I'm not alone.

I have my enemies.

Now... my only allies.

EPILOGUE
EVERYBODY'S DEAD INSIDE – ALISSIC

RIPLEY

Present Day

In the interview room, horrified silence reigns over my audience. I take a sip of my water, some slopping over the edge due to the incessant shaking of my hand. It does little to relieve my throat, raw from hour after hour of talking.

Staring down at his notebook, Elliot is speechless. It's an amusing sight. He brought me here, expecting a story. Boy, has he got one. Perhaps not the tale he thought he'd tell, though. The truth is never simple.

Relaxed against the wall, Hudson stares into space. He hasn't made eye contact once throughout the entire afternoon or evening. I'm sure his own bleak memories of that time are rising to the surface. We all lost something inside the institutes.

Elliot clears his throat. "Well. That was quite the tale."

"I warned you."

"Details of Incendia's experimental program are few and far between. Hearing a firsthand account... It is harrowing."

"The world ought to know. They still see us as monsters. Freaks. Criminals." I curl my lip in distaste. "The ones to *blame*."

"No one blames you, Rip," Hudson croaks.

Looking into his crystalline stare, I ignore Elliot observing us in my periphery. Hudson isn't one for emotions, but so much is simmering behind his blue eyes. All manner of rage and bloodlust.

"I blame me. It took experiencing the true extent of their evil for me to wake up to the truth. To choose the right side."

"You were trying to survive."

"So was everyone else," I refute.

Head hitting the wall once more, Hudson blows out a breath. "The world will never understand what we sacrificed to still be here today, able to tell this tale."

"And that's why we're here." Elliot caps his fountain pen. "So the world will know."

I'm not sure what good it will do, a whole decade down the line. Evil and atrocity continue to this day. Society has a short-term memory when it comes to injustice. What happened back then taught them nothing.

I don't care if anyone watches this interview. I don't even care if it's ever broadcast to the nation. Old Ripley resolved not to run, and this Ripley can't do it for a moment longer either. The ghosts I carry need to be excavated.

Only then can we find peace.

Only then... can I begin to forgive myself.

Elliot stretches his shoulders, chatting quietly to his cameraman. Taking another sip of water, I glance at Hudson who's taking a hushed phone call. He acts like he isn't studying me from the corner of his eye.

"You think I'm done?" I watch Elliot rise.

He startles, looking up at me. "Uh, I just assumed—"

Bitter laughter escapes me.

"That was only the beginning of the story."

"Would you like to continue?" Elliot asks, eyes wide with surprise.

"Well, I'm still here."

With a slow nod, he settles back in his seat. Hudson finishes his phone call then waves to grab my attention. He mouths an apology, stepping outside to let someone else in.

It's almost like he planned it.

Scheming bastard.

Warner takes his place, briefly clasping his arm as they cross paths. Over the last ten years, his dark hair has become peppered with silver. It looks good on him. Glancing around the studio with his attentive gaze, he gifts me a tense smile.

I return it. Somehow, it seems only right that he's appeared to witness the retelling of what came next. After all, it's his story too. We wrote the next chapter together.

Elliot turns to a fresh page, plucking the cap back off his fountain pen. "By all reports, Harrowdean Manor fell into violence. A riot broke out overnight. Incendia kept it quiet, though."

"They were losing the fight. That's why."

He nods, poised to take fresh notes. "Tell us what happened next, Ripley."

"Harrowdean wasn't just my kingdom anymore. It was all of ours." I look to Warner, still here all these years later. "Right, Langley?"

His baby blues twinkle.

"Right."

To be concluded in…
Burn Like An Angel (Harrowdean Manor #2)

BONUS SCENE
XANDER

I choose my marks as soon as I see them.

Their place in my gallery of helpless victims is secured within those first few seconds, and like the proverbial lamb to slaughter, they're none the wiser.

The moment I laid eyes on her—a miniature stack of supple curves, short tawny curls that barely tickled her jawline, and wide hazel eyes that a man could easily lose himself in—I knew she would be my prized possession no matter what the cost.

Ripley.

What kind of a stupid name is that?

It didn't help that she was cosying up to Holly, the redhead currently in our line of fire. Lennox and I have been working on our master plan for months now, plotting exactly how to overthrow the resident stooge and take control of Priory Lane's patient population.

Stroking my hand over my polo shirt, I peer across the tree-lined quad at the buildings. She's in the art room at this very moment. Ripley may be mousy, but she shouts loud through her violent brush strokes.

Admittedly, I've watched her through ajar doorways and misted windows on several occasions. She takes full advantage of the institute's bullshit educational program and spends her days lost in an ink-stained world.

I don't admire her ability to provoke audible gasps and even the odd tear by throwing paint against canvas and calling it therapeutic, though. She feels far too much.

That is a weakness.

One I can exploit.

"Why are you lurking here?"

Drawing to a halt at my side, Lennox's thunderous footsteps betray his presence. He walks like he's trying to shake the earth itself with nothing but his weight crushing the ground beneath him.

"I'm working," I snarl back.

"Holly is outside the cafeteria. You're in the wrong place, Xan."

"She isn't the one I'm looking for."

Stepping up to block my line of sight, Lennox folds his thick, muscle-corded arms over his chest.

"What are you up to?" he demands.

"Wouldn't you like to know."

"Well, we are a team. I should know about any diabolical plans you have."

A cold laugh bursts out of me. "Diabolical plans?"

Lennox doesn't crack a smile. "What are you doing?"

"Just go back to your scheming, and leave me to mine. I'll get us access to Holly."

"Meaning?"

"Meaning go figure out part two of the plan, and stop distracting me."

Rolling his eyes, Lennox unfolds his arms then takes a step back. "Don't fuck this up."

Keeping my gaze fixed on my target, I ignore his snarky comment, and Lennox soon stomps off. The silence is short-lived as lunchtime arrives, marked by the waddle of drugged-up patients through their state-funded prison.

Most will accept a dry sandwich as payment for their obedience and take whatever chemicals the doctors wish to stuff down their necks. They're just happy to avoid prison time for their psychosis-induced crimes.

My gaze catches on a sloppy, half-pinned knot of dense-brown curls, exposing a slender neck that's just begging to be marked by a blade. Ripley lopes down the steps then makes a beeline for the cafeteria.

She's friends with Holly, the patient standing between us and total control of Priory Lane's corrupt system. Ripley is our way to access the institute's ruler. The key to securing the kingdom we're seeking.

But only once she's been fully broken, as all good toys should be, can we access her high-powered protector. Then Lennox will see the merit in my plan.

Adopting a loose stroll, I begin to trail behind her. The helpless lamb isn't even aware that she has a predator hot on her tail. She's far too oblivious for this world.

It will chew her up and spit her right out—so really, I'm doing her a favour by breaking her first.

"Hey, kid! Over here!"

Waving a hand, Holly's tall form stands at the entrance to the main building where the institute's dreary cafeteria is located.

We were watching the day that Holly befriended scared, lonely Ripley in the courtyard. Apparently, offering the sweet candy of contraband enabled Holly to obtain her new sidekick.

"Oh, hey," Ripley calls back in a deep, raspy voice that haunts my obsessive thoughts. "Ready for lunch?"

"Yes. I'm starved."

"Me too." She offers Holly a small smile. "I skipped breakfast to sleep in."

"You ain't gonna grow with that attitude, kid. Let's go put some food in your belly."

"I'm not a kid, Hol."

"You are to me. Come on."

Holly bumps her shoulder into Ripley's in an affectionate way as the pair duck inside together. I hang back, unwilling to let our opponent spot me following her and her little friend.

Once they've vanished from sight, I take the opportunity to invade Ripley's precious safe space. With her gone, the art room is deserted during lunch hour, leaving me to infiltrate its oil paint-scented depths.

I know which work is hers without needing to be told. When I commit to a new toy, I learn everything about them. Every point of entry that may allow me to control them. Break them. Own them.

Her work is striking, I'll give her that. Ripley isn't afraid to spell out every last twisted thought in her mind through the medium of art. This work in progress is a riot of angry reds, greens and melancholic greys.

As much as her propensity for emotion repels me, there is something magnetic about the honesty of her work. I find myself being sucked into its dark, murderous depths as I ponder what fuelled this explosion.

What does she yearn for? What thoughts cycle through her mind when she lays in her uncomfortable twin bed at night, staring up at the blank ceiling? Or does she inhabit the same emptiness that I do?

No, I could never create something like this.

Because she possesses the one thing I'll never have... *Feelings*.

My fingertips trail over the drying paint, smearing a faint shadow of red and green. Sometimes I remember how it felt to be scared. To climb into bed at night and await the inevitable horror that always found me.

When I was the one staring up at the ceiling, plotting my escape. I lived in the deep canyons of fear and the impenetrable valleys of total abandonment. Is that how Ripley feels? Scared and alone?

The rusted latches on a cobweb-shrouded box at the back of my mind groan, rebelling against being pulled open after all these years. I quickly slam the box shut before it can reopen and fill me with memories I'm unwilling to entertain.

I'm not stuck here because of that monster and what he did to me—I'm here because I got caught. Because I allowed myself to get sloppy after years of silently taking what I wanted from those more fortunate.

That's exactly what I must do now. Scheme. Manipulate. Steal. I don't intend to spend my sentence wallowing like the rest of the hapless patients bumbling around these misty grounds. I want to rule. To be in control. To have *power*.

"What are you doing?"

The familiar, raspy voice snaps me out of the mental horrors I'm battling. Clearing my throat, I turn to find the subject of my fascination watching me.

Up close, the fine details of her features are clearer. The slight upturn of her nose, glinting with a silver septum ring. Circles of green that blend with the chocolatey clouds in her hazel eyes. Full, pert lips just begging to be tasted.

Suspicion is written across Ripley's lightly-freckled face. I enjoy the way she looks at me like she wonders if I'm going to snap her in two with nothing but my pinkie finger.

"Considering redecorating," I drawl flatly. "Isn't artwork considered a safe investment these days?"

I'm not prepared for her quick response or the irritated curl of her tempting lips.

"I doubt you have the money or property to warrant purchasing anything. Besides—nothing here is for sale. This is a hospital, not a gallery."

"A hospital, huh?"

"We're patients here, aren't we?" She gawps at me like I'm little more than a fool.

Ripley tentatively inches sideways, giving me a wide berth. It's as if she's afraid of an animal within a cage, snapping its jaws at her. What I wouldn't give to split her limbs between my teeth like a hungry wolf.

"You're Xander," she deadpans.

"That would be my name."

"I've seen you watching me several times recently. Ever since the day I arrived, in fact."

"Only a few times?" I lift the corner of my mouth in a smile. "That's good."

Her eyes widen fractionally. "What do you want?"

"From you?" I shake my head. "Absolutely nothing. That's the point."

Her dark-brown brows furrow together in confusion. "I don't understand."

"You will."

Something flashes in her fear-filled irises, imbued with a hidden fire I doubt she knows is visible. It's the same spark that's kept me intrigued for so long. She isn't as mousy and afraid as she acts.

"I don't want any trouble." Ripley holds up her palms. "I'm just here to finish the program then go home. That's all."

"Oh, that's all. Really?"

"Why else would I be here?"

Prowling closer, I greedily eat up the distance between us, passing other paint-flecked canvases that hold little appeal compared to her masterpieces.

"This institute isn't what you think it is," I reveal casually. "Perhaps I should leave you to discover that fact for yourself."

"What the fuck are you talking about?" Her spine straightens with the rising pitch of her voice.

Ah. There's that fire.

I'm longing to drag her screaming body back to my assigned bedroom to see just how much attitude I can rip free from her sharp tongue. I wonder how she'd react to being displayed like a doll.

"Everything around you… this entire experimental program and all its promises." I gesture around the art room. "None of it is real, little toy."

Her feet have begun to inch backwards, carrying her closer to the wall behind her. I follow intently, refusing to allow her an inch of space. I can only stalk for so long before the chase has to commence.

And all good chases require fleeing prey.

I intend to make her mine.

"Why are you calling me that?" My eyes gravitate to her pierced nose, crinkled in disgust.

"Because it's what I intend to shape you into. By the time I'm done with you, I'll have a new toy for my collection. And believe me… it's an extensive collection."

Her eyes dart between me and the door that leads to her escape. I hadn't intended to skip so far ahead in my plan today, but I don't mind an accelerated timeline. All the more fun for me.

"You are psychotic." Her nose crinkles as she openly appraises me. "I can see why Holly is scared of you."

She's scared?

That's helpful to know.

"Scared is the tip of the iceberg," I chuckle. "Better start running, Ripley. Or else I may catch you first."

For a moment, I wonder if she'll stay to play. If that fire will finally erupt into a burning volcano that will scold us both. I want to see just how far I can push her before she breaks apart.

Her mouth hangs open for a long pause, gathering words to throw back at me, but they never surface. Ripley casts me one last look then turns to dart from the art room.

I give her the relief of thinking she's gotten away. Only for a second, though. I can't have her getting too comfortable. Then I'm in hot pursuit, taking advantage of the still-empty corridors.

"Go away!" she yells over her shoulder.

Her fear tastes so fucking sweet. So satisfying. I want to bottle it like a precious artefact to be displayed. If she's afraid of me, I will forever be the one in control. Just the way I like it.

Ripley squeaks when I catch up to her and slam her into the closest wall. Her short height cowers beneath me, and every last ample curve I've spent weeks studying presses into my front.

The faintest scent clings to her—something fruity and exotic. Her breasts are round and pert, straining the bounds of her t-shirt, displaying some obscure anime reference.

What surprises me is how good it feels to hold her close. The firm pressure of her body seeping heat into mine feels like walking into a warm house on a winter's day. I quickly shake the thought out of my head.

"Leave me alone," she spits out.

"No can do. You have something I want."

Her nostrils flare, betraying her rage.

"And what is that exactly?"

"That information doesn't pertain to you."

"What?" Ripley's confused eyes burn a hole through me. "I don't even know you. Leave me alone!"

Pinning her against the wall, I savour the feel of her round hips pressing into me. Her lips have fallen open, breaths coming in rapid pants. Despite the fear leaking from her, she holds my gaze, her chin raised in defiance.

"I'm not scared of you."

"Tell your body that," I purr back, noting the way she trembles.

Eyelashes fluttering, her breathing hitches. My hands are braced on either side of her head, trapping her. I've wanted to capture her for so long just to see how she would react.

Imprisoning her is a satisfying thrill.

But now… I want more.

Leaning closer, the tip of my nose tickles her short curls. The smell of sweet, ripe fruit is strongest at the column of her throat. I can't stop myself from trailing my nose down her sloping neck.

Her posture changes the smallest amount, enough to give me pause. I realise I can feel her hips pushing back into me. Her spine is curving, gravitating her body closer to mine.

"Ah. I know what you want, little toy."

"Fuck you," she grits out.

"You've been left in here like the rest of us, haven't you? All alone. Nobody cares or even misses you."

My lips brush against her pulse point, stretching and warping the soft skin while displaying the violent beating of her heart. I can hear her gulping hard.

"You don't know me, Xander."

"I know enough to make a reasonable assumption. You want the same thing that everyone does."

"And what's that?"

"To be seen. Loved. Wanted."

Her body moves, shifting against the rock-hard bulge I can feel straining my jeans. Having her in such close proximity is wonderfully torturous.

"You spend your days twirling brushes through paint and longing for a different life, far from this place and the failure it represents. You want someone to save you."

This time, she daren't respond.

"I don't want to save you." I let my teeth graze her throat the slightest amount. "But I can give you the liberation you desire. I'll show you the freedom in giving up all control... to me."

"Why would I give you anything?"

"Because you're bored, Ripley. You're all alone and trapped in a web you don't understand. What do you have to lose?"

Lifting my mouth from her neck, my lips trace the outline of her defined jawline until they hover just above her mouth. Her pupils have grown into cavernous, black holes, swallowing all colour.

I don't force my lips on hers. I'm not that kind of monster. This is a far more intricate game... I want her to wilfully break herself. To bend her morals and take what's terrifying her.

A fast exhale strokes my skin before the inevitable collision arrives. She crash lands her lips on mine, securing my mouth in a hard, angry kiss. A kiss that feels more like a slap than a submission.

My lips rival hers, refusing to form a comfortable mould for her rage. I want her to understand that this is a battle. One she will lose. And I rarely fight fair.

Her mouth rips free from mine, and before I can react, I feel her body jerk. She pulls backwards, then white-hot pain explodes directly between my legs as her foot makes contact.

I double over, releasing her to cup my throbbing crotch. Nausea rises in my stomach and throat, mingling with the agony of being kicked in the damn bollocks.

"You... bitch," I gasp.

She places her foot back on the ground. "Stay the fuck away from me."

Shoving past me, Ripley doesn't spare me a second glance as she flees. I blink past the moisture burning in my eyes long enough to see her vanishing through the double doors that lead outside.

Her kiss still sears my mouth.

Fuck.

The chase is well and truly on.

PLAYLIST

LISTEN HERE:
BIT.LY/SINLIKETHEDEVIL

1121 – Halsey
Punching Bag – Set It Off
Hateful – Post Malone
Dead Or Alive – Stileto & Madalen Duke
I'm Not Yours – The Haunt
All The Ways I Could Die – Arrows in Action
Misfits – Magnolia Park & Taylor Acorn
Meet You At The Graveyard – Cleffy
Devil – LOWBORN
Rain – grandson & Jessie Reyez
Thnks fr th Mmrs – Fall Out Boy
Bipolar Rhapsody – KID BRUNSWICK
Monster – Fight The Fade
Hero – David Kushner
n/A – Bring Me The Horizon
intoodeep. – Dead Poet Society
Start a War – Klergy & Valerie Broussard
Street Spirit (Fade Out) – Radiohead
Pretty Little Devil – Shaya Zamora
Harder To Breathe – Letdown
Love Abuser (Save Me) – Royal & The Serpent
Chokehold – Sleep Token
do you really want to hurt me – Nessa Barrett

PLAYLIST

Love You Better – The Haunt
drowning. – Eden Project
Play Dead (Just for Tonight) – The Messenger Birds
ADHD – Two Feet
My Name Is Human – Highly Suspect
V.A.N – Bad Omens & Poppy
Sinner – Of Virtue
Everybody's Dead Inside – Alissic

BURN LIKE AN ANGEL

HARROWDEAN MANOR #2

TRIGGER WARNING

Burn Like An Angel (Harrowdean Manor #2) is a why choose, reverse harem romance, so the main character will have multiple love interests that she will not have to choose between.

This book is very dark and contains scenes that may be triggering for some readers. These include strong mental health themes, drug addiction, graphic violence, psychological and physical torture, mentions of self-harm, allusions to childhood sexual abuse and suicide.

There is explicit language throughout and sexual scenes involving blood play, breath play, knife play, and orgasm denial.

If you are easily offended or triggered by any of this content, please do not read this book. This is dark romance and, therefore, not for the faint of heart.

Additionally, this book is written for entertainment and is not intended to accurately represent the treatment of mental health issues.

"Speak the truth, even if your voice shakes."

- Maggie Kuhn

PROLOGUE
TWIN SIZE MATTRESS – THE
FRONT BOTTOMS

XANDER

Present Day

Have you heard about those people who poke around abandoned buildings, waving around their bullshit ghost detectors and speculating as to the horrors the decrepit ruins they're violating may hold?

They pay off some cash-strapped security guard to sneak into the site without being arrested, usually by scaling chain-link fences or burrowing through boarded over entrances, carrying backpacks full of flashlights, energy bars and fancy cameras to document their exploration.

And that's where the show begins, right? We're sucked into the fascination from behind our phone screens, hearts pounding and palms sticky, awaiting the next dark twist in the story as they inch forward.

Hook, line and sinker.

I know we all watch those videos.

Not many of us can say that we were once the ghosts to haunt the halls now immortalised on the internet. The flip side of the coin. Part of the fabric of the abandoned husk, and by extension, its story.

Our lives are a mystery that society then monetises and sells off to the highest bidder for entertainment. The human stories interwoven with the tragedy are erased. Written over. Forgotten. That's what happened to us.

Crouched low with the collar of my thick coat turned up to hide my face, I find myself in the paradoxical position of breaking into the institute I was once incarcerated in.

Now I'm the violator. Not the violated. I haven't returned to Harrowdean Manor in the last decade. Tonight is different. I'm saying goodbye for the final time.

Everyone thinks this tale has already been told. The book closed long ago for the short-term memory spans of the disinterested public. Once the uproar died down, the world continued to turn, and Incendia was forgotten.

We were forgotten.

One by one, each of the six private institutes that once fed the wealth and depravity of the corporation have been demolished. It's taken ten years to see the process through, and now Harrowdean is the final institute to fall. It's set for demolition at daybreak.

Most don't know this place still exists. It's kept off the books and quiet for this exact reason—the government and those in charge of the cleanup don't want curious bloggers poking around with their cameras. Instead, the place has been left to quietly rot.

In the pocket of my thick coat, I feel my mobile phone buzzing. I know who it will be without needing to check. Sighing through my nostrils, I answer the incoming call.

"I told you to leave me alone."

"You can't just storm off like that, Xan!" Lennox huffs in his gravelly, sonorous timbre. "We need to talk about this."

"I've made my position perfectly clear."

"Where are you?" he demands. "We're going to sit down and discuss this together. As a fucking family."

"Do what you want. I have nothing else to say."

"Ripley had every right to sit down with that journalist—"

"No," I interrupt him. "She didn't."

Hanging up, I pocket my phone. I may not be the stone cold, level-headed analytic I once was, but I'm not going to sit here and write some shitty pros and cons list to make this decision. I said no.

We've never entertained any interview requests before. I certainly won't be doing it now.

Creeping through long grass that's almost as tall as I am, the loading bay comes into view. Weeds have long overtaken the concrete foundation and brick pillars, cloaking the institute's rear entrance in a coffin-like, green shroud.

I hop up onto the platform, heading for the bolted door where deliveries once took place. My backpack slides off my shoulder and into my hands. After unzipping it, I sift around for the compact pair of bolt cutters I stashed inside amongst my other supplies.

The irony isn't lost on me.

Everyone wanted to escape this hell hole.

Here I am now, breaking back in.

Latching the curved blades around the padlock that secures the bay doors, I position myself then begin to cinch the cutters closed. It takes some manoeuvring, the rusted metal screaming in protest, loud enough to make me flinch.

Eventually, the padlock splits and falls. It thuds against the ancient concrete so loud, it feels like the metallic clank of a guillotine making impact with an exposed neck.

Lip curled, I shake off the thought. No one comes here. The security measures are fucking pathetic. I'm perfectly safe. As I ease the door open, the smell hits me.

There aren't adequate words to describe it... A pungent, stomach-turning concoction of animal waste, mould, burnt-out fires and something inexplicable. Something sinister. Perhaps the stench of long-removed corpses or faded bloodstains.

Stashing the bolt cutters, I swap them for an industrial flashlight then step back into purgatory. My flashlight providing the only guiding light, smashed glass crunches beneath my thick-soled boots, a breadcrumb trail leading me deeper into the suffocating darkness.

All of the evidence of the atrocities committed here was removed when CSI's swarmed, and the infamous Sabre Security picked over the remains. In fact, there's evidence of that—discarded plastic bags, crime scene tape and even the faint sprinkles of fingerprint dust.

The broken pieces of countless shattered lives were left behind, though. A random shoe. Used needles. Broken furniture. Torn books. Graffiti litters every wall with various tags and nihilistic messages left behind by forgotten patients.

One inked tag catches my eye.

WE SCREAM IN SILENCE.

Running a gloved hand over the letters, anger comes rushing to the surface. Strange to think I once felt nothing… until she came along. Now I'm not just angry. No. I'm indescribably, uncontrollably, ire-fucking-futably furious.

We did scream.

Yet all they heard was silence.

Hand falling, I swallow the thick lump that's now clogging my throat and push onwards to the south wing. The damage is worse here. Patients sought safety and refuge wherever they could when the institute fell. Some obviously hid here.

I'm not sure what possesses me to return to the art room at the end of the sagging corridor, now peppered with all manner of animal waste. The door is hanging off its hinges, the room brightly illuminated by moonlight spilling through smashed bay windows.

Gooseflesh rises on my skin, even beneath my heavy clothing. I can feel it prickling and spreading. I numbly realise that I'm staring at a torn canvas, tossed on the floor and covered in stains.

Dirt. Blood.

Who can tell?

I recognise the brush strokes beneath, though. I've spent enough hours silently watching her paint. The way the lurid shades are liberally applied for maximum emotional impact… It's Ripley's signature style.

She doesn't just create art; she creates living, breathing replicas of her motherfucking soul. Each canvas holds a piece, torn directly from her chest then splattered against the material like a bloodied Rorschach inkblot. She paints with her own mortality.

Crouching down, I ignore the coverage of filth to lift the canvas. I don't recognise this one. My leather-encased fingertips skate over the intricate swirls of black, dark-green and crimson, painting a violent maelstrom with three lone figures at the heart of the storm.

It's signed and dated. She painted this not long after we arrived at Harrowdean Manor. I trace the first shadowy figure. She's flanked by two darker shadows, creeping up behind her like prowling wolves.

A low chuckle tumbles from my mouth. I suppose that's exactly what we were back then. Wolves. Predators. Enemies. Which is precisely how we survived. We had to become evil too.

Placing the canvas back down, I forcibly tear my eyes away from the twisted reminder of the past. The rest of the room is a disaster. Work benches are smashed and collapsed, stools upturned, electrical cables hanging from the ceiling. It's a war zone.

The other rooms are no better. My flashlight swings from side to side, illuminating each iteration of the institute's own apocalypse. Weirdly, it's silent. Deathly so. My footsteps are the only sound, not even the clamour of stray animals keeps me company.

The world abandoned Harrowdean Manor.

Much like it abandoned us.

My feet carry me without direction. I don't know what I came here to achieve. Not really. I just knew that I needed to see it one last time—to verify those dark times really happened and weren't some elaborate, fucked up dream.

On the fifth floor, it's a treacherous journey to room seventeen. The door hangs open, partially collapsed. Hoisting my backpack higher, I step into Ripley's old bedroom, the floorboards creaking beneath my boots.

As more moonlight spills through the window, a wave of déjà vu hits me amongst the thick plumes of dust. Like the rest of the institute, the bedroom is trashed. I move slowly and carefully, fearful the floor is going to give way at any moment.

My gaze is locked on the rusted bed springs, littered with scraps of decaying fabric that have peeled off the frame over the years. This is the bed where I held a knife to Ripley's throat, intent on ending the never-ending game for both of us before something stopped me.

She stopped me.

No—It was the way she made me feel.

That cruel vixen brought me to my knees without even trying. I couldn't have stopped her even if I'd wanted to. Deep down, I was always hers to claim. Even in the months I refused to acknowledge that.

Ripley Bennet stole me.

Broke me.

Fixed me.

Fucking *loved* me.

I knew what I was missing out on by refusing to feel or be vulnerable ever again—that's the thing the doctors and psychiatrists could never quite fathom. It wasn't that I didn't feel. Far from it. Rather, I used to feel so much, I instead simply chose never to feel again.

A silent scream.

And an unheard one at that.

But now our screams aren't just being heard. They're being documented. Edited. Cut into palatable soundbites to capture the public's eye. Our stories are being commercialised, swallowed and fucking regurgitated to secure some ambitious asshole's moment in the limelight.

She's enabling it.

Once again, Ripley's signing our death warrants.

I can't allow this documentary to happen. No matter what people's motivations are for getting involved, nothing good can come of dredging up the past. As much as I may hate the way this tragedy has been erased, I won't watch my family suffer the repercussions again.

If the world knows the true story, every last gory detail of what went on in this very manor, we can kiss the last decade of painful peace goodbye. No matter how horrific the long-lasting trauma has made these years. At least we're free.

Ripley's voice may change that.

I have to stop the documentary from airing.

CHAPTER 1
RIPLEY
HELP. – YOUNG LIONS

TEN YEARS EARLIER

I'VE RECENTLY BECOME acquainted with pure agony.

It's not the kind of pain you'd experience from a scraped knee or a sore cartilage piercing. That pain can be buried. Avoided. Numbed. Tucked away into a darkened corner until it grows tired of hanging around and fades.

The pain that's wracking my body now is a whole other level of intensity. Beyond exhaustion or emotional anguish. Survival isn't free— for any of us. It always extracts a toll, one way or another.

Escaping sometimes means leaving pieces of ourselves behind.

I imagine it's the same pain that semi-conscious Lennox is feeling. His injured hand hangs at his side as he's pulled along between Xander and Raine. I watch his bare feet drag against the ground, limp and useless.

"Where now?" Raine asks.

"Straight ahead," I croak.

With a trembling hand, I hold onto his hospital gown, attempting to steer him in a straight line. It's a challenge as we trip and stumble towards the manor, dodging the mayhem unfolding all around us. It's spilling in from all directions.

"Careful," Xander calls out. "Body up ahead."

"Body?" Raine exclaims.

"A guard, I think. Dead or unconscious. I don't know which."

"What the fuck?"

"Be glad you can't see what's going on around us," Xander mutters.

Tightening my grip on his gown, I peer through the haze. "Keep going, Raine. I'll steer you."

Floodlights illuminate the nighttime air, and honestly, I wish they'd just plunge us into full darkness at this point. Then I wouldn't have to see the anarchy we've escaped into. We swapped one hell for another.

After months of malpractice and blatant abuse, the patient population of Harrowdean Manor has declared war. We escaped Professor Craven's sadistic Z wing, fleeing torture and imprisonment only to stumble out into a full-blown riot.

All around us, the madness is spreading like an airborne infection. Patients have turned into wild, almost rabid animals, attacking at will and destroying anything they can lay their hands on.

"Round them all up!" Rick's voice echoes in the distance. "I want every guard cuffed and gagged."

There's a chorus of agreements and various sounds of enthusiasm from the patients choosing to follow him. Most have descended into violence. Some fight, exchanging blows, while others begin smashing whatever they lay eyes on.

Those who've flocked to Rick's call are banding together to capture the remaining guards. Contrastingly, the rest of the patients are cowering or running. Sides have already formed amongst the anarchy.

The organised few—Rick, Rae, Patient Three and her fellow escapee—are doling out instructions as they assume control. They seem to be operating under the delusion that we can pull this pseudo-heist off. Really, it's only a matter of time before the authorities march in here.

Then all our heads will be on the chopping block. I may have decided not to run, but we at least need to give ourselves a fighting chance of staying alive. That starts with getting Lennox help before he deteriorates.

"Ripley?" Lennox moans in pain.

He's unable to lift his head, the way my name slips off his tongue like a sorrowful prayer sending shivers down my spine.

"She's here, man," Raine mumbles back.

"Can't... go... farther."

"Like hell you can't," Xander spits.

"Xan," Lennox gasps. "Stop."

"We're getting you somewhere safe." Xander's usually curt voice carries a disturbing, almost high-pitched edge of apprehension.

Xander is… scared?

No. That can't be right.

"Just leave me," Lennox tries to plead.

"Not this crap again," I cut in. "We're not leaving you, Nox."

I don't miss the curious side eye Xander gives me, a single, midnight-blue orb slicing deep into my skin. It wasn't so long ago when I would've happily left Lennox to be trampled to death in a riot given half a chance.

Now the world has been swept away by a violent tsunami, and we're left to pick over the destruction to find our lives once more. Everything I thought I knew about Lennox, Harrowdean, even myself—it's all gone.

"What?" I snap at Xander.

"Nothing."

"Then stop staring, and get us out of here!"

The corner of his mouth quirks. "Whatever you say."

Dodging the dead or unconscious guard who's sprawled out near the steps leading inside, we head for the rear entrance to Harrowdean's reception. My cooked-spaghetti legs are barely carrying my weight.

We've both been wilfully battered in our time beneath ground, and though Lennox looks in far worse shape, I can feel the steady throbbing of my wrist along with countless bruises and other injuries from the beatings.

My wounds are bleeding, each droplet dripping in time to the rhythmic pounding of my skull. Between the water torture, subsequent beatings and lack of food or sleep beyond passing out, the trauma of our trip to the Z wing is quickly making itself known.

"Inside," Xander orders. "We're too exposed out here."

"How are we supposed to do this?" I ask weakly.

"Take Raine—don't let him fall." He shifts Lennox's weight onto himself. "I've got the big guy."

"I can climb a staircase," Raine grumbles.

Grasping his hand, I hold on tight despite the way it makes my wrists twinge. "We know. Just let me help."

"You're hurt, guava girl. I should be the one helping you."

"You are just by being here."

"I wasn't there to protect you!" His sunglass-covered eyes tilt upwards, like he's praying to the heavens for patience. "I failed you. Again!"

"Cry me a goddamn river," Xander drones with marked exasperation. "Get inside before having a breakdown please."

He tilts his head in the direction of Xander's once again lifeless voice. "Fuck you, Xan."

"He's right," I placate. "We need to hide."

"From who?" Raine shivers in my arms. "The guards? Or the patients?"

Xander releases a dry laugh. "How about both?"

I'm about to drag Raine up the damn stairs whether he likes it or not when a cacophony of screams reaches us through the night, silencing us all.

"Burn, Harrowdean! Burn it all!"

"No more!"

"Burn! Burn! Burn!"

A gaggle of patients are high on whatever riot fever is spreading from one soul to another—eyes wild, fists bloodied, uncaring of who they hurt or why we're pushing back against the oppression at all. When violence takes root, reason soon evaporates.

Their chanting is growing ever closer. We're vulnerable out in the open, our only source of light the now-flickering floodlights that seem to be signalling impending disaster.

"Go!" Xander barks.

Semi-carrying Lennox up the first few steps, we're right behind the struggling pair when the patients catch up to us. It doesn't seem to matter that we're not dressed like guards or even a threat.

"Ripley Bennet!"

Fuck!

Lewis, an idiot from the sixth floor, recognises me. "Hey! Harrowdean's whore!"

Without hesitating, I shove Raine forward, wincing as he trips and falls. But I won't watch him get hurt because of me for a second time.

"Go. Get out of here!"

"Rip!" he yells.

"Move! Run!"

The only way to stop them from pouncing on Raine, sprawled out and disorientated, is to attack first. I fling myself down the steps to Lewis, determined to throw the first punch.

He takes the brunt of the fall. We hurtle towards the hard ground, landing in a tangle and both yelping at the pain of impact. His friends hang back, content to watch us brawl.

"Stay down," I warn. "We're not the enemy here."

"I've heard the whispers," he snarls in my face. "I know you're management's bitch. If we're taking them down… you're going down with them, Ripley."

"Look around you! This chaos only ends one way!"

Lewis grabs a handful of my filthy, bloodstained shirt to wrench me closer. "Yes. We're getting out of here. Not you, though. You're going to die here."

I ignore the sound of Raine's protests on the steps behind us, focused on my attacker. "Back off, man. Final warning."

"Or what?" he challenges.

With a quick glance at the group of onlooking patients, I realise how much of a target I've painted on my own back. They don't see a fellow patient. A victim. A survivor. Whatever bullshit fits the bill.

No.

To them, I'm the enemy.

Harrowdean's whore, right?

I didn't survive this long by making friends or exercising a moral conscience. And I'm sure as hell not going to start now.

"Your mates are leaving you." Lewis nods his head towards the institute where Xander's still struggling to shift Lennox. "I didn't think you had any of those."

Despite the voice telling me that Xander is right to leave me here to die, pain still cuts across my chest. He's here for Lennox. Raine. Not me.

"I don't have friends, and I don't need them."

Drawing back my fist, I deck the stupid son of a bitch. Agony explodes across my knuckles on impact with his square jaw, the vibrations ricocheting up my forearm to my elbow.

"Bitch!" Lewis screams.

His blow comes hard and fast, striking me in the cheek. My head snaps to the side, wrenching painfully. It's a mere drop in the ocean compared to the state of my body, though, and it doesn't distract me.

I use my position above him to my advantage and rain down punch after punch. Not even the wailing of my protesting muscles slows me down. My mind narrows on one thought. Self-preservation.

I've always preferred to rule with words and threats. Most would fear the loss of their precious contraband far more than any physical damage I could inflict. But in a fistfight, I'm still deadly in my own right.

Lewis bucks and writhes, trying to throw me off. Clinging on, I slam my forehead into his as a last resort, a wail threatening to escape from my gritted teeth. Hitting the ground, his skull impacts with a rock, making him go limp.

"Move!" Xander yells distantly. "Now!"

At the sound of shouting, I flick my eyes up to the institute. Raine is still helplessly sprawled out, while Xander's almost inside, but his voice has taken on that disturbingly urgent edge again.

"Move, Nox!" he demands.

"No! Raine! Ripley!" Lennox replies in a weak bellow.

"I can't help them until you're inside, dickhead!"

Distracted by the sight of Xander shoving Lennox inside then rushing to help Raine up, I miss the attack heading my way. The long-limbed patient stinks of cigarette smoke, her face obscured by snarled hair and malevolence.

Air bursts from my lungs as I'm body-slammed, thrown sideways off Lewis's unconscious form. Hands wrap around my throat, finding a tight cinch that cuts off my oxygen supply. I writhe and scratch, frantic to find an escape.

"You used us all," she accuses.

My lungs are burning—filled with white-hot, molten lava that's permeating deeper into my chest. I can feel her blood on my fingertips, her hands seeming to squeeze ever tighter.

"You deserve to be cuffed and paraded around like the rest of them."

Warmth coats my skin from where her nails are slicing my throat. My vision is beginning to haze, awash with bright, white spots.

CLICK.

"Let her go. I'll only ask once."

My attacker freezes, her head raising towards the new voice. The floodlights illuminate her blurry face. Tania. Seems her gratitude for the pink dildo I previously sold her was short-lived.

"You," she hisses at the voice.

"Step aside, inmate."

"You're outnumbered, asshole!"

Peeking over her, I spot the barrel of a black handgun. It's pointed directly at Tania's back. Looking higher, the person clutching the weapon causes shock and relief to blast through me.

"Do I look like I care?" Langley cocks the gun, ribbons of blood spilling down his face from a cut at his hairline. "Move. Now."

I've never heard such raw aggression from him before. The person looming over us both isn't the soft-eyed guard I know. Then again, I had no idea he was secretly working for Sabre Security until he tried to poach me as an informant.

Tania hesitates, her fingertips bruising my oesophagus. "You wouldn't dare use that."

His finger rests on the trigger, twitching in challenge. "Try me."

"It's your job to protect us!"

"Stand up, turn around and walk away."

"There are witnesses!" she screeches.

With a short laugh, Langley casts one of his baby blues around the state of disarray. "Where, exactly? I could unload this entire clip into your skull without anyone saying a word. Now *get up*."

Her eyes now wide with genuine fear, Tania releases her grip on my throat. I splutter violently, sucking in frantic breaths, the rush of oxygen causing my insides to sear. Each inhale feels like drinking fire.

"That's it," Langley says in a flat tone. "Walk away now, and I'll let you live."

"What the fuck is wrong with you?" Tania exclaims.

"I have a job to do. So I'd suggest you get out of my sight, and take your little friends with you."

Langley boots Lewis in the ribs. He's beginning to stir, a semi-conscious groan escaping his mouth. With tears now streaming down her cheeks, Tania gestures for the others to approach and heave him up.

Once they've scuttled away, casting worried looks over their shoulders at the gun Langley holds poised, my surroundings filter back in. I can hear racing footsteps, speeding towards us from the institute.

"You." Xander's cool, clipped voice is unmistakable.

Langley swings the gun around, now aiming it at him. "I don't want any trouble."

"Then step away from her."

"Me?" Langley's dark brows knit into a frown. "Pretty sure she's the one who needs protection from you, last time I checked."

"And why exactly is her welfare your business in the first place?"

Groaning as I sit upright, I massage my aching throat. "Stop. Both of you."

Two pairs of eyes swing to me. Langley's track over me—cataloguing the various injuries, bruises and bloodstains like he's seeing them for the first time. Last time we spoke was before Noah's attack and our trip to the Z wing.

"I heard you were taken," he grinds out. "What the hell did they do to you?"

"No time." I look over to Xander's impassive expression. "Where are Lennox and Raine?"

"Safely inside."

"Then... why did you come back?"

His almost-black eyes make my skin tighten and prickle with awareness. The sheer intensity steals my breath far more effectively than Tania's attempt to choke me.

He's staring at me like it's obvious, but nothing about this complicated creature is ever fucking obvious. We've been playing an elaborate game of cat and mouse for years now, and I still can't fathom the broken mind that lies within his skull.

"You," he deadpans.

My windpipe closes altogether.

"I came back for you, Ripley."

Tucking the gun into his waistband, Langley flashes Xander an odd look. He stoops low to grasp my body. I let him tug me up, too exhausted to do much more than slump into him.

"They did this to you?" Langley grinds out.

"Professor Craven." I gasp in pain. "And... others."

"Jesus, Rip. How did you get out?"

"With a little help." Looking up, I find his concerned eyes scrutinising me. "What are you still doing here? Shouldn't you be running for the hills with the rest of your team?"

"The rest..." He grips his forehead. "How did you... Shit, not now. Can you move?"

Teeth clenched, I nod once.

"Good."

Xander takes one look at me then moves to my other side, a slim, scarred arm wrapping around my waist. "Let her go."

Langley snorts. "You first."

"Not happening."

With them both holding me, neither willing to let go, we awkwardly stumble into the reception. It's dark inside, still littered with debris and water damage from the storm.

That night feels like a million years ago, but from the failing power to the boarded windows and dirt-streaked flooring, the scattered remnants still paint a chaotic scene. The opulence has been destroyed by Mother Nature in all her almighty wrath.

Perhaps the most telling indication of that night's fateful importance has his arm around me. The cold-hearted man with empty midnight eyes who almost left me to drown in a pool.

Xander is my nemesis. The man who vowed to break me and keep the scattered pieces for his collection. Only now he's helping me, limping and half-dead, to safety. I must be delirious.

"I left them down here," Xander mutters in the gloom. "Lennox is in bad shape."

"He... We... They tortured him for hours." I struggle to get the words out. "Water. Beatings. His h-hand..."

"I saw. How did he make it out?"

"I, ah... helped him."

Pausing dramatically, Xander eyes me. "You... helped him?"

"Yes." I hold his stare, defiant.

"You." The word is half-question, half-statement.

"You really want to discuss this right now?"

"Later. But we are discussing it."

Xander leads us into an adjacent corridor leading towards the west wing. It's low-lit from the odd emergency light still working. My eyes adjust, and I spot two outlines slumped against a wall.

"Xan?" Raine's voice calls out.

"It's us."

"All I can smell is blood. Have you got her?"

"I'm here." I wince in pain as we trudge towards them.

Langley takes one look at Lennox, his partially mangled hand still limp at his side, then curses.

"What the hell?"

"You can thank your pink-haired friend for that one."

His blue gaze swings around to me. "What?"

"Alyssa, right?"

The silent bobbing of his throat is all the confirmation I need.

"You have some serious explaining to do," I demand. "Starting with who you really are and what you're doing inside Harrowdean."

Mouth flopping open, Langley's shocked to silence. Clearly, he never expected his cover to be blown so spectacularly. That only makes his betrayal all the more bitter.

"Yeah," he mutters numbly. "I guess I do."

"Shouldn't you be running off into the sunset with your team?"

He draws in a deep breath to gather himself. "It's complicated."

"Then uncomplicate it."

Interrupting our exchange, Lennox groans in pain. How he's still conscious and hasn't passed back out from exertion or blood loss remains a mystery.

"Medical wing," Langley announces.

"Explain yourself first. How can we trust you?"

"There's no time, Rip. I'll explain everything, but not here. We can temporarily secure the medical wing, and Lennox needs looking at."

"We were already headed there anyway," Xander snarkily retorts. "Feel free to fuck off, *Langley*."

"Need I remind you that I'm the one with the gun?"

"You think I need a gun to snap your neck?" Xander counters.

"Good luck getting close."

"I won't need it."

"Yeah? Well, putting a bullet between your eyes will turn around this shitty day. So, make your move."

"Enough!" I chastise them both. "Seriously."

Lennox grunts again before he suddenly collapses. Raine's holding his arm, so he's pulled off balance by the weight dragging him down.

"Shit!" Raine yelps.

Xander releases me to catch his best friend before he hits the floor. He takes Lennox from Raine, throws his arm around his shoulder, then jerks his head to indicate we should all follow.

I steady Raine, taking his hand to steer him along with us. "This way."

"Aren't the guards supposed to be the enemy right now?" Raine whispers worriedly. "We shouldn't trust him."

I spare Langley a glance—stony-faced, his blue eyes darting from side to side, surveying for any threats. His posture betrays a persona I never spotted before. Shoulders square. Feet spread. Always alert and prepared to act.

He's the perfect mole.

Affable. Unsuspicious.

Unseen.

"Langley isn't a guard, Raine."

"What?" His head jerks in my direction.

I tear my eyes from the blue-eyed stranger. "He never was."

We struggle onwards. With the unlit medical wing in sight, I feel my last vestiges of energy dissipate. Xander shoves the door open, manhandling a now-unconscious Lennox inside.

"Anyone here?" he yells. "We need help."

Silence.

"I guess not," Raine murmurs. "Is it still dark? Morning staff probably got stuck outside when everything kicked off."

Jaw clenching, Xander continues to heft Lennox, his alabaster skin now dotted with sweat from the exertion. We limp behind them, slipping inside the deserted wing.

Langley glances at the door standing between us and the war zone. "Patients will come looting soon enough."

"Looting?" Raine repeats.

"Drugs. Weapons. Food. Riots can last days, sometimes even weeks. Survival instincts will kick in."

The reality of the situation hammers home with each word he utters. Hands raised, Raine follows Xander's huffing to help manoeuvre Lennox's now-unconscious body onto a bed.

"If there's no doctor, what do we do?" The concern in Raine's tone is audible.

Langley releases a long sigh. "I was a field medic… Well, in a past life. I'm not an expert, but I can take a look at his injuries."

"What do you need?" Xander straightens, his attention fixed on Lennox.

"A damn sight more than what we have available, I'd imagine." He looks around the deserted wing. "We're going to need some pain relief to start."

Watching them disperse to search, I suddenly teeter on my own two feet. Langley's mumbling is overcome by a loud buzzing in my head. Physical exhaustion coupled with the breakdown I've been holding back at all costs overwhelms me.

Lennox is badly hurt. There's no medical help. We're caught in a riot, surrounded by patients who hate my fucking guts, and have no idea when backup will arrive. Raine's barely recovered and shouldn't even be out of bed, let alone running around fending off attacks.

The odds are stacked against us.

Was this a huge mistake?

Staying here may have been the brave choice, but the violence will only escalate. People will die. Maybe we will too. And all the pain, the suffering, the sacrifice… it will all have been for nothing.

The magnitude of the past few days sucker punches me in the face. The Z wing. Lennox being tortured. Beatings. Sabre Security. Our pink-haired saviour. The bloodied corridor. Professor Craven's broken skull.

We survived.

We escaped.

But the real battle begins now.

"No," I choke out.

"Rip?" Raine cocks his head in my direction.

"W-We… should've… run."

The sight of Raine standing nearby while the other two get to work abruptly blurs. Now he's a pixelated jigsaw of fuzzy limbs and wobbly lines as my energy fizzles out.

"Ripley?" His voice sounds far-off, disjointed. "Ripley!"

Everything turns white. Spinning. Blurring. A hot flush of fever and dizziness sweeps me off my feet and sends me hurtling into the approaching blackness.

CHAPTER 2
LENNOX
MONSTERS – FOREIGN AIR

"I'VE DONE the best I can. I'm not a doctor."

A tired voice filters into my awakening consciousness. It sounds resigned. Perhaps a little defensive.

"Then what do we do?"

This one is flat, cold. Familiar. An iceberg carried to shore by my mind's rolling waves.

"Hope this riot ends fast. He's out of the woods for now."

Their two voices overlap, a confusing tangle of sounds and worried tones that permeate my thick brain fog. I can't drag my eyes open. Everything feels like it's wrapped in fluffy cotton wool.

The drug-induced fog offers me a brief escape from recent horrors. But as I come around, the peace dissipates. Pain comes rushing back in to greet me like an unwelcome house guest.

"Have you seen outside?" The tired voice speaks again. "People are going wild. This isn't ending any time soon."

"Then I guess we're all stuck here."

"We don't even have food!" This time, the second, colder voice sounds different—it's suddenly infected with something. Roughening into a low growl, I can almost taste the underlying fear and anxiety that's thawing the towering iceberg.

"Those patients outside will come looking soon enough."

"Agreed."

"Don't agree with me, Langley."

"I don't exactly like it either."

As the syrupy fog lifts further, I realise they aren't whispering at all. The two opposing voices are deep in a heated argument, their bickering overlapping a cacophony of other sounds that are slowly filtering in.

Screaming. Shouting.

Breaking glass. Loud whoops.

"Guys," a raspier voice interrupts them. "Quiet, both of you. They're right outside."

Banging. Smashing.

Excited hollers. More screams.

Trepidation slithers down my spine. I have no choice but to peel my heavy lids open. The light I anticipated to greet me never comes. Shadows and darkness douse my vision, broken by weak moonlight and blurry outlines.

"Xan," I moan weakly.

There's a shuffle, then a figure looms.

"Here, man. Don't move."

My tongue is glued to the roof of my mouth, a length of scratchy sandpaper that refuses to obey. I will my throat muscles to respond, swallowing repeatedly until I can form words.

"W-Where?"

"Medical wing," Xander answers, holding a bottle to my lips. "You've been out of it for a while. Are you in pain?"

I greedily gulp down lukewarm water, my throat screaming too much to respond.

"He's had the maximum dose," someone else interjects.

"Do you even know what those drugs do?" Xander hisses back.

"I wouldn't have injected him with them if I didn't."

A hand swipes down my arm, tracing a map on my skin. I recognise the rough pads of Raine's violin-worn fingertips.

"Ignore them, Nox." The shape of him sitting next to me becomes clearer as my vision settles. "How do you feel?"

Staring at their faces—Xander, Raine and for some reason, that piece of shit guard who's way too friendly with Ripley—it takes a moment for my brain to catch up. I must've blacked out as we ran.

"Peachy," I rasp. "How long was I out?"

"About… ten, eleven hours." Xander stares at the clock locked behind a metal cage on the wall. "You were sedated while he treated your injuries."

The *he* in question lingers behind Xander, arms folded across his built chest. Langley treated me? I hate that weird guy. He trails around after Ripley like a lost puppy begging for scraps of affection.

"Where is she?"

Xander narrows his dark-blue eyes on me. "What happened in that basement?"

Struggling weakly, I try to sit up in the hospital bed and fail. "Where. Is. She?"

"Lay still, for fuck's sake."

"Xan!"

The corner of his mouth twitches. "You should calm down."

"I will when you tell me where Ripley is!"

"She's in the bed next to yours," Raine supplies wearily. "Don't be a dick, Xan. Show him."

Relinquishing, Xander shifts to show me the view. The other hospital bed is lit by some kind of emergency flashlight resting on its side on the trolley between us.

Deathly pale and hooked up to an IV, Ripley is huddled on her side, unconscious. Her hands are curled up to her chest. In her sleep, she looks like a vulnerable waif, not the ballbuster I've always loathed.

The panic barrelling through my nervous system eases the slightest amount. Thank fuck I don't have the mental capacity to analyse that feeling too deeply right now. Or contemplate why I'm feeling it for her.

"Something to share?" Xander asks slyly.

With a huff, I sink deeper into the pillows. "Fuck off."

"You seem awfully concerned."

Ignoring him, I take stock of my body. Everything feels disjointed, like my limbs have been severed and reattached with makeshift stitches. The pain is a fierce, constant burn, despite whatever drugs I've been shot full of.

"Let me past, Xander. I need to check on him."

Langley is in rough shape. His dark hair stands up in all directions, face streaked with blood and dirt, like he got rugby tackled and punched to shit. It's a pleasing mental image.

I eye him warily. "Don't touch me."

"Easy," he placates with a frown.

Raine lightly squeezes my arm. "Don't be an ass, Nox."

"He's a goddamn guard!"

"Not strictly true." Langley fiddles with the IV line trickling into my body. "And in lieu of an actual doctor, I'm your best shot right now. I've had medical training."

"What training?" I stare at him.

Slender arms folded, Xander flicks his gaze back to the dickhead, a grimace twisting his thin lips. His platinum blonde hair is also a mess—shoved back, peppered with blood. In fact, he's covered head to toe.

"Care to elaborate?" Xander asks icily. "We've been patient."

Satisfied by his inspection of the IV, Langley turns his attention to me. "Just trust that I know what I'm doing right now."

I bite back a sarcastic response, letting the man go to work checking me over. As my limbs wake up, there's far too much pain wracking my body to protest any further.

"You're lucky that was a flesh wound." Langley nods towards the bandaged club resting across my chest where my left hand should be. "I can't be certain without an x-ray, though."

Looking down at the thick swathes of cotton, I internally wince at the memory of the drill digging into my hand, parting my flesh like butter. The entire limb feels completely numb, causing worry to flare up.

"Anaesthetic." Langley seems to read my concern. "I flushed the wound with saline and stitched you up. It'll hurt like a motherfucker soon enough."

"Can't wait," I drawl.

"Someone beat the shit out of you," he observes. "I can't rule out internal bleeding, but that's above my pay grade. You want to fill us in on what made that mess?"

He gestures to my bandaged club.

"Drill," I supply.

"A… drill? Like a fucking power tool?"

"The electrocutions didn't work." I hiss at the pain that attempting to shrug causes. "I'm stubborn."

"Fuck me." He scowls.

Xander remains silent, observing our exchange. I can see the memories dancing in his twilight-hued eyes. This isn't our first bout of torture. That's probably why my sanity is still semi-intact.

"You'll have a pretty scar on your face." Langley cracks his neck, trying to regain his composure. "Just pray the wounds don't get infected."

Suppressing a shudder, I force back the memory of the steel-tipped whip slashing into my face, parting skin and flesh. The bitch pretending to be a guard didn't have to go so hard, did she? The facial bandage feels huge and uncomfortable.

My gaze wanders back to the adjacent bed. "What about her?"

Ripley's face is swollen and misshapen. Slithers of her badly bruised body are visible around the sheet she's tangled up in. Her pale complexion makes the inked foliage on her arms stand out like dark thunderclouds.

With black-lined eye sockets, mottled purple bruises circling her throat and countless cuts and abrasions, she bears the evidence of all we endured beneath ground.

Bile burns the back of my throat as indignant rage threatens to take over. Those evil motherfuckers almost broke us. The pain-warped memories were real. It's a small miracle that we survived at all, let alone escaped.

The memory of fleeing Craven's house of horrors are blurred. Pain-laced fragments that no longer fit together in a neat patchwork.

"Similar story." Langley's forehead wrinkles with concern. "She's resting now, but her wrists are infected. You guys were chained up?"

"Shackled in a concrete cell."

"You were together?" Xander asks sharply.

Not trusting myself to speak, I merely nod. His pale-blonde eyebrows are furrowed, likely attempting to piece events together. I'm sure no one expected to see Ripley dragging me of all people out of the basement.

Langley visibly swallows. "I've cleaned her wounds and hooked her up to IV antibiotics. She'll recover. Now we wait."

Raine hisses through clenched teeth, appearing angrier than I've ever seen him. "What happened, Nox?"

A bubble grows and lodges itself in my throat. We've dealt with this kind of evil before. In Priory Lane, I saw the devil's face and lived to tell the tale. That gave me the strength to survive again.

But seeing Ripley, bare and battered as she fought to stay alive? Hearing her soft cries and whimpers while we clung to life? That did something to me. Something irreversible. Something far more crippling than their torture sessions. And I don't know if I can fucking fix it.

"Trust me." My voice is an aching rasp from all the screaming. "You don't want to know."

"Pretty sure we have a right to, though," Raine argues, his slender shoulders fraught with tension. "You both disappeared!"

"How long were we gone?"

"A couple days," Xander supplies.

Raine's grip on my arm tightens once more. "We were worried sick."

The panicked feeling is back. Breeding. Metastasising. In my head, I can hear Ripley's cries ricocheting, ping-ponging around the internal cavities of my skull. My own pain doesn't feature in the flashbacks—just hers.

Her body scrunched up, protecting itself from the battering water. Freezing-cold skin, snuggled into my chest, covered in gooseflesh. Her feeble whispers as she wrapped her fingers around the fleshy strings of my heart and ripped it clean out to keep it for herself.

If this is it... I just want you to know that I forgive you.

I didn't deserve those words. Hell, I didn't even know I wanted them. But now that she's given me her forgiveness... Lord, fucking help me. It's like an invisible dam has burst, and a torrent of guilt and self-loathing is spilling out.

Hatred has kept me safe. Protected. Immune. With that stripped away, I'm at risk of feeling things I've spent years trying not to feel. At least not for anyone but the family I chose in Priory Lane.

"Why didn't Ripley just leave you down there?" Xander stares at me like he's trying to figure something out.

"What?" I snap out of my musings.

"You tried to drown her alive, Nox."

The guilt building inside me explodes, spewing in all directions like an erupting volcano. "I'm aware."

"Then she used Noah to try to frame you." He shakes his head. "But what I can't figure out is why you're both lying here, and she didn't just leave you to rot or vice versa."

Now leaning against the wall, Langley is tuned in to Xander's interrogation. Raine's golden-haired head is cocked, demonstrating his attention, latching onto every hitched breath and note of hesitation.

My scalp prickles, a hot flush of awkwardness washing over me. I'm not telling them shit. Not about this.

"That was... before."

"Before what exactly?" Raine questions.

"Before everything."

"Everything?" Xander repeats drily.

The truth swirls through my mind. I can't explain. Not when I've barely wrapped my head around the whispered apologies we shared, the feel of her skin on mine, her soft lips and velvet tongue or bare breasts pressing into my chest…

"Nox!" Raine grips my arm, demanding an answer I can't give. "Well?"

"Raine," Xander cautions, reading something on my face.

"I have a right to know, Xan. She's my… She's… We… Fuck!" He pauses to blow out a frustrated breath. "Look, how can I help her if I don't know what happened?"

"You can't help," I snap back. "Not with this."

"I care about her. Far more than you do!"

Self-loathing quickly morphs into molten anger—the noxious fumes poisoning my thoughts. How dare he presume to know what I'm thinking or feeling? He doesn't know shit about what we just survived.

"And?" I scoff.

"And whatever game you're playing, stop. You can't keep me from being with Ripley."

"That's not what I'm doing," I quickly deny. "Well… anymore."

"Then what is this?" he challenges fiercely. "You despise her. What's changed?"

The pressure inside me boils over, a foaming, caged beast snapping through my veins as it breaks free.

"Everything!"

My voice carries, seeming to ricochet in the medical wing's gloom. Glaring at Raine like he can see the warning on my face, I breathe heavily, a tight ball of tension burgeoning in my chest.

"Take your hand off me."

Raine gapes at me, the borrowed aviators sliding down his nose. I watch his shock filter into defiance—mouth creasing, fists balling, his shoulders squared like I'm challenging his claim or some dumb shit.

"This conversation isn't over," he warns in a low tone. "Hurt her again and I'll kick your ass, blind or not."

Adjusting his sunglasses, Raine moves over to Ripley's bed. I watch him run his hands over the thin mattress, feeling for a spot to perch next to her. His hand moves to rest on top of her lifeless one.

My stomach clenches.

Get your fucking hands off her.

I swallow the words begging to spill out, imprisoning them instead in an imaginary steel box. Of course, he gets the right to touch her. I sure as hell don't. Not after all I've done.

The awkward silence is broken by the sound of more glass smashing outside the medical wing. Hoots and screams float through the windows, permeating the heavy air.

I glance at Xander, his attention now focused outside. "What's going on out there?"

He shrugs. "They've been securing the institute for a few hours. Barricading, bolting doors. The front gate's been chained shut to hold the authorities back."

Langley sighs, his attention focused on the bag of fluids hanging above me. "That isn't gonna keep management from sending a tactical unit in to retake control. There will be casualties."

"Are we safe in here?" I wince at another wave of pain.

"As safe as anywhere. You're both hooked up to IV antibiotics and need to rest. We can't risk moving yet."

"I'm perfectly fine."

With an eye roll, Langley finishes fussing over me. "You look it."

"Once the fatigue and hunger set in, the novelty of rebellion will wear off," Xander inserts. "Sides will form. They'll soon forget the enemy and turn on each other."

"Well... shit," I deadpan.

If Incendia were planning on sending in the cavalry to stamp out any resistance and retake control of Harrowdean, they would've done so by now. We must have enough hostages to stop them from storming the place.

We're on our own.

And I can't lift a damn finger.

"We should all get cleaned up," Langley suggests. "Then we'll make a plan."

"Help me up."

He shoots me a scathing look. "Fuck off, Lennox."

"What's your problem?"

"My goodwill only extends so far when it comes to assholes."

"Mind telling me what exactly I've done?" I ask caustically.

"Where should I begin?"

Temper flaring, I glower at the prickly son of a bitch. "By all means, from the top."

"Believe me, there aren't enough hours in the day to cover all the reasons why you deserved to be dragged into that basement. Ripley should've left you there to rot."

"Then why help me?" I fire back.

His gaze briefly strays to Ripley before he looks away. "I'm not here for you."

Turning away, he moves to pick through a cupboard of medical supplies on the opposite side of the room. Xander turns away from the window, frowning at Langley before he looks around the empty wing.

"They must keep spare clothes here for discharged patients."

"You could use some yourself." I jerk my chin, indicating his bloodied state.

Xander plucks the hem of his soiled shirt with a look of distaste. "He did bleed rather a lot."

"Who, exactly?"

"Davis," he answers casually.

I stare at my best friend, mouth hanging wide open. "Davis?"

"Yes. He's dead."

Xander drops the shirt hem then resumes scanning the medical wing. He doesn't spare my stunned expression a second glance.

"Did he say Davis?" Raine whispers from the other bed. "Like… Warden Davis?"

"You know any other Davis in here?"

"Fucking hell. He has to be kidding."

Watching Xander pick around the room, searching for clothing, the punch line never comes. He doesn't crack a smile or yell *gotcha!* For each second that trickles past, the dread blooming in my chest grows wings and takes flight.

"I don't think he is," I grumble.

"The warden, Nox?" Raine hisses in disbelief. "Xander… he… he wouldn't do that, would he?"

Honestly, there's no limit to the fucked up shit that Xander would do. He's just a hell of a lot quieter about it than the rest of us. That's how his evil so often goes undetected.

Ducking his head inside a tall cabinet, he pulls out a handful of second-hand clothes from a labelled laundry sack. Xander begins searching for the right sizes.

"I'm not kidding," he clips out.

A conflicting maelstrom rushes through my mind—disbelief, shock, fear. But for the life of me, I can't summon the humanity to pity the dead warden. As long as Xander isn't at risk, I'm glad he's dead.

"Was it an accident?" Raine inquires hesitantly.

Xander laughs under his breath. "Most certainly not."

Watching the colour drain from Raine's face, I refocus on Xander. "What happened?"

He yanks out a bundle of tangled clothing. "We had words."

"And?"

"And none of his were what I wanted to hear."

Dipping back into the bag to search for more suitable clothing, he halts as his eyes stray to Ripley. The man who doesn't bat an eye while telling us he killed the fucking warden now appears… uncertain.

What in the ever-loving fuck?

"He wouldn't tell me where you were." Xander's throat undulates as he quickly looks away. "Where either of you were."

"Were you seen?" I grit out.

"Of course not. The riot took care of that."

"Where…?" Raine pauses, swallowing audibly. "Where is he?"

Attention focused on sorting the clothing, Xander holds up an oversized t-shirt, seeming to consider the size. I watch his eyes flit back to Ripley's unconscious form, comparing her size to the shirt he holds.

"Office," he replies.

Nodding robotically, Raine now looks a little green. "So… he won't be found for a while."

"I suppose not."

Raine's been with us for long enough to know how Xander's bizarre mind operates. The boundaries of human emotion that fail to apply to him. Yet he's never quite accepted or even understood it.

Xander doesn't care. Not in the way normal humans do. He's destroyed his own ability to do exactly that. I've often wondered what he feels for us—his surrogate family. It can't be love. He isn't capable of that.

I didn't think I was either, but I'm fooling myself if I think I shared my body heat to stop Ripley from dying of hypothermia just for the company in hell. And I've deluded myself enough in the past.

That's how I lost everything.

I won't lose it all again.

We broke each other, and for good reason. But those reasons feel irrelevant now in the cold light of day. If it wasn't for her, I'd still be rotting in that basement, shackled and bleeding out in a padded cell.

Sinking into the hospital pillows, fatigue and weakness crash over me. I have enough energy left to turn my head to the side, giving me a direct view of the adjacent bed.

Raine's hand is still clasped over Ripley's limp one, his head tilted back as he contemplates. I can't help but stare at them. The familiarity. The intimacy. His palpable fear and clear devotion to her.

What I'm not prepared for is the piping-hot burst of emotion that stabs into me, over and over in a relentless assault on my damaged sanity. It isn't anger. That I can recognise, utilise, *control*.

It's… jealousy.

Well, fuck.

I'm jealous of Raine, sitting there like a goddamn guardian angel, holding the hand of the bitch who saved my life. He's earned her trust. Her love. Her vulnerability. That's why he gets to touch her and I don't.

That realisation only magnifies the feeling tenfold until I'm choking on the barbed wire lodged in my throat, taking the razor-sharp edges deep into my oesophagus and letting them shred apart my insides.

I want to shove him aside and take his place at her side. Ripley would certainly reject me. Deathbed forgiveness doesn't mean she's ready for all the thoughts running through my mind. I need to play this safe.

She's given me a second chance.

Now I have to earn her forgiveness.

CHAPTER 3
RIPLEY
UP IN FLAMES – RUELLE

HANDS BRACED on the edge of the bathroom sink, I stare into my hollow hazel eyes. Bloodshot. Lids drooping. Wrinkles pronounced. The brown and green swirls are overshadowed by black bruises and swelling.

I study my reflection, seeing a scared girl raising her hand, fingertips lightly dancing over each purple cloud and crusted laceration. Her eyes swim. The tears brim over, spilling down her cheeks in glistening ribbons.

"Rip?" There's a gentle tap on the door. "Everything okay in there?"

Sucking in a breath, I quickly scrub the tears aside, ignoring the way it makes my skin ache.

"I'm f-fine, Raine."

The door between us feels like an endless ocean, the raging torrent stopping us from clinging to each other to stay afloat until rescue comes.

"Can I come in?" he asks softly.

"I… I don't know."

There's a thud, like his forehead connected with the door. After straightening my septum piercing, I fill my hands with water, sloshing it over my face in an attempt to clean the blood. Dark, russet streaks cling to my skin.

"You don't have to do this alone," Raine coaxes. "But if you really want to be alone, then I'll go."

I stare at my reflection again. The water hasn't helped. I'm a fucking mess. Being confined to a hospital bed may have replenished my energy levels, but my entire body is now technicoloured with bruises.

I woke up to darkness after passing out then remained silently curled up for several more hours while the others bickered about what to do. It wasn't until the shouts and cries from a nearby fight roused me that I resolved to move.

"Rip? Are you listening?"

My mouth opens.

Shuts.

Nothing comes out.

I hear Raine sigh. "Alright, loud and clear. I'll go."

Chest spasming, an invisible fist tightens around my bloodstained clothing and seems to drag me towards the mirror. Closer. Closer. I'm spiralling back into the numbness, the detachment. Staring at a girl I don't even recognise.

No. I can't let myself fall into that dark, downward spiral. There will be no way back up. My mind is too fractured and exhausted to protect itself right now—I have to hold it together.

"Wait," I force out.

"Yeah?"

"P-Please…" My voice catches.

"Tell me what you need, Rip."

Head lowering, I squeeze my eyes shut.

"Please don't leave me."

The door clicks open and shut. I hate being vulnerable. Weak. Dependent on others. It goes against everything I've worked so hard to build here.

Hurried footsteps approach, then hands find my shoulders. Raine searches me with his hands, banding his arms around my torso from behind in a tight embrace. A sudden, unwelcome sob tears at my chest.

"Never, guava girl," he murmurs. "Let yourself fall apart for once. You're safe with me."

Behind my closed lids, all I can see is blood. Slicked across the corridor in the Z wing, evidence from a dragged body. The gore spilling from Craven's broken skull. More blood spraying from the drill tearing into Lennox's hand. My own blood seeping from my wrists.

"Raine," I whimper.

"Shh, babe. I'm here."

"N-No… We're not safe! None of us!"

"Breathe, Rip. Come on."

One hand splayed over my belly, he raises the other to rub my arm in slow, comforting circles. His face is buried in the nape of my neck. Each time he exhales, I feel his breath tickle my skin. It feels warm and comforting.

Heart pumping.

Lungs expanding.

Tense muscles loosening.

Each small detail offers me something to focus on. It's a trick an old therapist suggested years back when I was first diagnosed. I haven't struggled to scrape myself together like this for a long time.

"That's it. Focus on me."

"You nearly d-died from the overdose." The air escapes my lungs like a popped balloon. "And for what? We're going to die here anyway."

"I just fancied a little getaway to the medical wing," he jokes quietly. "You get to stay in bed all day, you know? They even bring you food. It's like an all-inclusive resort."

Another choked sob breaks out of me. "Seriously?"

"Bad joke?" Raine chuckles into my hair. "Come on. The OD is old news now. I'm getting clean."

"It's not old news to me."

"You're deflecting, Rip."

My shivering body melts into his, seeking the reassurance of his sea salt and freshly squeezed orange scent. Raine smells like beachside breakfasts and sunshine, the perfect accompaniment to his golden boy persona.

Not many people get to see what lies beneath that deliberate façade. He's been blind since he turned eighteen. The honeyed jewels he keeps hidden behind specialist lenses, and now my borrowed sunglasses, brim with his secrets.

Raine plays the confident jokester, but deep down, he's broken like the rest of us. Uniquely traumatised. Lost. Clinging to vices to make him feel alive. That used to be drugs until he overdosed.

"Right now, I'm stable," he asserts calmly. "The meds are working. So let's focus on you and get cleaned up before Langley blows a gasket."

"Did he send you in here?"

Raine's head lifts from mine. "No, he's changing Lennox's dressings. And Xander's looking for food."

I wish the mention of their names didn't cause my heart to sputter like a faltering engine. Raine knows what complications are facing us. Xander's obsession almost killed me not so long ago, even if he did save my life before he held a knife to my throat.

What we shared that night has thrown everything into doubt. Our feud. The hatred between us. Years of resentment and violence. But now, after the Z wing and shivering in Lennox's arms, not knowing if we'd live to see morning… well, complicated no longer cuts it.

"I can't get the blood off," I admit.

Slowly turning me around, his fingers trace a path upwards, finding my wet face. "You're using cold water, babe. This crap is too dried on for that to work."

"Am I?"

Raine's full, thick lips quirk in a smile. "Yes."

"Oh. I… uh, didn't notice."

"Here, I can help."

Resting my tailbone against the sink, I let him take over. Raine has excellent spatial awareness, using touch and context to decipher his surroundings. I wait for him to locate the tap then test the water until it turns warm.

"Is there soap?"

Shaking my head, I realise my mistake and clear my throat. "No."

"Hang on." Raine inches backwards to fumble the door open. "Xander? Can you find soap? Or medical wash of some kind?"

A clipped voice responds, the seconds trickling past until footsteps near. Raine mutters a thanks, closes the door then returns to me. He's moving carefully without his guide stick in the small space.

"Let's hope this goes better than the time I shampooed your face instead of your hair." He cracks another blinding smile. "You should've just told me."

"I wanted to let you figure it out."

"Enough to let me shampoo your mouth?"

Sniffling, I bite back a grin. "I guess so."

"That's some serious love right there, guava girl. I'm swooning."

"Pack it in."

"Or what?" he challenges.

"Or you won't live to ever swoon again."

Locating a stack of paper towels, he begins to systematically wet each folded square. His smile widens until he's flashing pearly-white teeth.

"Ouch. I'm terrified."

"You're such a dumbass." A chuckle bubbles out of me.

"There's the laugh I was hoping to hear."

Dumping most of the medical wash everywhere but his intended target, he lifts a wet paper towel to my face. I direct him to the bloodiest areas. Raine begins to wipe, the scent of antiseptic permeating the bathroom.

Gasping, I blink aside tears when he hits a sore cut above my eyebrow.

"Sorry, sorry." He momentarily pulls his hand away, chewing on his cheek. "This would be easier if I could see your face."

"Not your fault."

"Isn't it?" His easy smirk falls away. "I should've been there to stop this from happening in the first place."

"Raine—"

"Instead, I was laid up in a hospital bed for making a stupid choice. You had no one there to protect you."

The memory of Lennox's body fitted to mine flashes back through my mind. His warmth seeping into me, holding hypothermia at bay long enough for the torture to end. The asshole kept me alive.

"I wasn't alone," I blurt.

As soon as the words have escaped, I wish I could take them back. Raine's hand freezes, his head cocking ever so slightly, like he's attempting to read the clues my body is giving him.

"You hate Lennox."

My heart rate thunders. "Yes."

Raine rolls his lips together as he thinks. "You tried to frame him for beating Noah up."

"Yes."

"The Z wing is exactly where you wanted him to wind up."

"Yes." My voice catches on the word this time, forcing me to gulp hard. "But I didn't plan to end up in there with him."

"Yet… You weren't alone." He resumes cleaning, swapping out for a new paper towel. "So what? You're glad he was there?"

"I… I'm not… I don't know." I watch him toss a used, crimson-stained towel aside. "I don't know what I feel."

"Well, by the sounds of things, neither does he." His voice is painfully neutral.

"This isn't what you think it is."

"What do I think it is, Rip?"

The bruises ringing my throat throb, feeling a pair of hands squeezing the life from my lungs. Only this time, there's nothing choking me. Nothing but emotion—confusion, exhaustion, fear. This isn't the time to be figuring our situation out.

"We had to look out for each other." I try to focus my exhausted mind to explain coherently. "They tried to break us. If Lennox wasn't there, I wouldn't have survived."

He tosses another used paper towel. "Does that mean all is forgiven?"

"I didn't say that."

"Sure sounds like what you're *not* saying, though."

Eyes burning, the brewing tears return. I've never been much of a crier, but the barbed wire I've wrapped myself in for all this time isn't keeping me safe from feeling anymore.

Now the razor-sharp barbs have turned inward, and they're cutting deep into my soul. Tearing. Shredding. Scarring. My hatred and determination enabled me to survive Harrowdean… until now.

At the sound of my wet sniffling, Raine sighs. He ditches the last paper towel then tugs me back into his arms. I let him cradle me to his chest and stroke my back.

"I'm sorry," he whispers, pecking my temple.

"Don't be. This is all my fault."

"No, it's not."

"Noah… Nox… The Z wing… I made this mess!"

"Stop, Rip." He plants soothing kisses against my hair. "Have we all made mistakes? Sure. Plenty. I'm not blaming you for anything. I just don't want you to get hurt again."

My face hidden in his hospital gown, I let the relentless tears pour free. It's a battering waterfall, wave after wave of uncontrollable hysteria, obliterating my defences.

Years of pent-up emotion seems to be taking advantage and escaping before I can close myself off again. Raine doesn't say another word, holding me against his undulating chest as I fall apart.

It feels like we've been standing here for an eternity, wrapped up in each other's arms, when there's a hesitant tap on the bathroom door.

"Everything okay?" Langley's voice carries through.

"Fine. We're coming," Raine replies croakily.

"Xander's sorted clothes for everyone. I'll leave yours out here."

Pulling myself together, I breathe deeply as I raise my head from Raine's chest. There's a huge, wet patch on his hospital gown where I've sobbed my eyes out. I swipe a hand over it, biting my lip.

"I'm a bit damp." He smiles lopsidedly.

"Sorry."

"It's okay. So, ah… are we good?"

Raising my hands to grasp the aviators I lent him, I slide the frames off. Raine's molten caramel eyes are unveiled, darting side to side in the unfocused way that betrays the fact that he can't see at all.

"Was it ever in doubt?"

His cheeks flush adorably. "Maybe."

"Why?"

"I guess it feels like I've got some competition now… Maybe you want to upgrade to someone with two working eyes."

An amused smile tugs at my lips. "I'll pass."

"Sure?" He summons a tiny grin. "I wouldn't be offended."

"Positive. Your eyes work just fine for me."

Leaning in, I move my mouth against his in a hesitant brush then retreat. Raine's hand skates back up my shoulder, following his mental map until he cups the back of my head.

"You call that a kiss?" he teases.

I'm quickly pulled back to him, our lips crashing together. Raine's mouth is hot on mine, his lips moving to a fast beat as his tongue pushes its way inside. He's lit with a visceral passion that takes my breath away.

Burying a hand in his golden locks, I kiss him back just as furiously. Teeth clicking. Lips massaging. Our tongues touch and tangle in a feverish waltz. In each touch, I taste his fear, desperation, and need to fix what's been broken.

He can't, though.

No one can.

A hot flush of toe-curling need sweeps over me. With the pain I'm in, I didn't think it would be possible. Yet the feel of Raine pleading with his mouth is enough to set my core alight.

Gripping his hair, I take control of the kiss. Raine backs up into the bathroom wall, trapped by my dominance. Fuck casual. Fuck whatever the hell we've spent months doing. I want him. I need him. I fucking *missed* him.

The low moan from his throat tells me just how much power I hold over him. All this time, I thought giving in to my feelings for Raine would make me weak. That allowing him to matter would expose a vulnerability.

I didn't stop to consider the possibility that having people who care about you does entirely the opposite. It isn't a weakness to love or be loved. Those connections are actually what make us strong.

Breaking the kiss, I press our foreheads together. Raine catches his breath, nose nudging mine as he chuckles lightly.

"Now that was a kiss."

I huff out a breath. "Smug, much?"

"Always, babe."

"Alright. Enough of that."

"Just reminding you that I was here first." He gently kisses me again, his citrus scent caressing me. "And I meant what I said before."

"Which part?"

"That I'm not going anywhere."

Leaving me reeling, Raine tentatively moves to the door to retrieve the clothes left for us. I suck in a breath at the thought of the two complications sitting in the medical wing. They may have something to say about Raine's promise.

I can't begin to fathom what either of them want from me. Xander hasn't exactly made his intentions clear since we slept together. Not to mention the clusterfuck that's me and Lennox.

"I can't tell what's yours and what's mine," he complains.

"Here. Let me look."

Taking the bundle from Raine, I search through the detergent-scented clothes. There's a pair of well-worn jeans and a t-shirt that looks around Raine's size, then some stretchy leggings for me with a man's shirt.

"Guessing you don't fancy second-hand yoga pants?"

He scoffs under his breath. "I reckon I could pull them off."

"No one needs to see that."

"Don't you think this ass would look good in Lycra?"

Biting my lip, I silently laugh as he strips off his medical gown, exposing slender limbs and tightly-packed abdominals that make my throat seize. He's slimmer than the others but no less attractive.

Raine clumsily steps into the jeans, refusing to ask for my assistance. They're much looser than his usual, tight style. Rips and scuffs mark the old denim.

"The leggings would look better," I comment.

"Stop being a shit stirrer and strip."

With a blonde brow cocked, he stretches out his hands in offering. I snort, stepping into his space so he can help me ease off the filthy shirt I'm still wearing. The way it clings to my skin makes me want to hurl.

Langley may have cleaned and bandaged my wrists before he hooked me up to the IV, but apparently, he didn't dare to strip me off. I'm thankful there's still some boundaries left between us.

"I'd kill for a shower right about now."

"You need another sponge bath?" Raine offers.

"I need a scourer and a bottle of bleach, I think." My gaze travels, cataloguing the bruises covering every inch of me. "At least the blood is off."

"The hot water seems to still be working. Maybe we can find somewhere to hole up that has a shower."

"Maybe."

Turning back to the mirror, I study the bird's nest on top of my head. My short, tawny ringlets are matted with sweat and blood. Cursing, I lean into the sink and transfer water from the tap onto my head.

It takes several minutes of scrubbing before the brownish stains stop swirling down the drain. Squeezing water from the semi-clean strands, I call it quits, picking up my share of the borrowed clothes.

"Be glad you can't see me right now."

Raine lounges against the wall, my aviators in place. "I still have my imagination. Though in that, you're lying naked on my bed."

"Behave."

"Why?" he drawls.

"This is kind of a life and death scenario right now."

Raine snickers to himself. "Is my dirty fantasy distracting you from our imminent doom?"

"Little bit, yeah."

Pulling on clothing, I grab the scuffed pair of Converse last and shove my feet into them. I feel infinitely better after getting dressed. The monumental problems facing us feel less intimidating with clothes on.

"Ready?" Raine checks.

"Yeah. As I'll ever be."

He clicks open the door, holding it ajar for me to step back into the now-lit medical wing. Combing my hair with my fingers, I move my throbbing limbs, keeping my gaze averted from Langley's stare.

While Lennox rests with his eyes closed, Xander has cleaned up too. His thin lips, exaggerated cheekbones and stony expression are now free from blood. He looks odd in old jeans and a too-big t-shirt.

"Feeling better?" Langley breaks the silence.

The cut on his forehead is now closed with Steri-Strips. His headful of thick, dark-brown hair is damp, hanging over his tanned face and fuzz-covered jawline.

Tucking wet curls behind my ears, I nod. "Yes. Thanks."

"Listen, Rip—"

"Who are you?"

His aquamarine eyes dart over my face, brimming with secrets. "You really want to do this now?"

"I think I'm owed some answers."

"Ripley, look—"

I can practically see the excuses he's preparing to roll out. My temper flares back to life. He has no idea what he's done.

"Are you familiar with Harrison?" I interrupt angrily. "Bald dickhead, works for Professor Craven in the Z wing?"

Langley hesitates before answering. "We've… met."

"Well, he found that business card you gave me. I had it stashed in my bra before they stripped us both to torture us with hoses. We were nearly frozen to death overnight… Then that damn card."

Xander halts searching through a box of snacks, hands freezing and head snapping in our direction. I ignore our audience as I stare into the face of a man I thought I knew. Perhaps even considered a friend.

"He dragged me into another cell and beat me with his fists until I blacked out. I refused to tell him where I'd gotten the business card from."

Head lowering, Langley stares at his laced boots. "I'm so sorry, Rip."

"I don't want your apologies. Why did you give me that card?"

"To help," he rushes to explain. "That's all."

"Is giving me cryptic half-truths helpful? I thought…"

Teeth clenched, I choke off my next words.

I thought we were friends.

Our roles didn't matter—patient and protector, faceless employee and stooge. He was still the only guard to treat me like a human being. And I came to see him as something akin to a friend.

"I gave you that business card because I work for Sabre Security."

"Wait." Xander straightens, hands flying to his tapered hips. "The people investigating the institutes?"

Scrubbing a hand over his face, Langley sighs wearily. "We're a private security firm specialising in criminal investigations."

Raine shuffles on his feet behind me. "Shit. You're really not a guard."

"I was given an assignment in Harrowdean last year to gather intelligence." Langley anxiously cracks his knuckles. "We've been investigating Incendia for a long time."

Vindicated, I glower at him. "I was right. You're one of them."

He nervously glances at me. "Yeah."

"Why are you here?"

"My job is to collect evidence. Flip key players. Line up potential informants. Anything to pin down the truth behind these institutes."

A hot burst of sickness twists my gut. "So you've spent all this time pretending like you care? It was all an act?"

"No! I… I thought if you trusted me, I could turn you against management. Convince you to be our witness instead. But as time went on, I realised that you weren't the villain in this place."

An incredulous scoff emanates from Xander's side of the room. I deliberately ignore him.

"You played me." The sense of betrayal sinking into my pores practically coats my words. "I'm no saint, but you pretended to care so that I'd trust you."

Panic flashes through his azure eyes, darting from side to side as if searching for some excuse to offer. Sure, I've treated him like shit. I know that. I'm not excusing or even denying it. But I never once lied to him.

"It wasn't like that, Rip. You needed a friend."

"And you needed a lead for your investigation!"

"No," he balks, widening his eyes. "I wanted to help. I still do."

Angrily swiping at the moisture that's dared to grace my cheeks, I look away from his pleading expression. It's pulling at goddamn heartstrings I didn't realise I still have.

"I don't need your help."

"Our team can—"

"No!" Uncontrollable rage and hurt spike through my veins. "How can I ever trust a word you say?"

He steps closer, what appears to be genuine concern shadowing his eyes. "Because I care."

"You just admitted that you manipulated me to score yourself a star witness. Bet it came with a juicy bonus from the boss too, right?"

Focusing on anything but Langley, my gaze collides with two seafoam orbs daggering into me from across the room. The pale, blueish-green hue is as captivating as the arrogant son of a bitch daring to look at me.

Lennox is awake.

He screams something unheard without ever opening his mouth. Any remaining air is sucked from my lungs as we communicate silently, the horrors we endured together snapping between us in lingering looks.

"We can still help each other," Langley attempts.

I forcibly tear my eyes from Lennox, pulling in a deep breath. "Forget it."

"Listen to me, Rip!"

"Never again."

Inching away from him, I'm suddenly itching for an escape. Somewhere to hide, far from these men. Their newfound kindness and concern expose the raw fault lines cracked across my fractured soul.

"The riot will end, and Incendia's days are numbered," Langley continues urgently. "You need to cut a deal while you still can."

"Numbered?" Xander repeats. "Do you know something that we don't?"

Langley seems to beg with his eyes. "Sabre will expose the corporation. You've heard what happened at Blackwood. Now this? It's only a matter of time."

"Good." I hold back a violent sob.

"Who exactly do you think they'll blame, huh?" Langley shakes his head. "I know the truth, but that won't stop Incendia from taking down everyone with them when they go. Stooges included."

"No one could ever blame Ripley," Raine protests.

"You think that'll matter to them?"

"It should!"

"We've all done things we're not proud of." Lennox speaks for the first time, his voice flaying my soul down to its bare bones. "Are you saying all our necks are on the line?"

"This will turn into a blame game very fast," Langley confirms in disgust. "My team is already working with a group of ex-patients from Blackwood. There are criminal charges on the table."

The white walls of the medical wing bend and contract, creeping ever closer like the bars of a prison cell slamming shut for an eternity. Terror curls in my lungs, filling them with acrid smoke.

"They're going to bury me," I whisper in horror.

"Not if you cooperate with us," Langley says emphatically. "We can offer you protection."

"She's not going anywhere without us," Xander announces.

His words have the impact of a killer blow to the solar plexus. I feel like I've been shoved into a freefall. The shock of his declaration only accelerates my rapid plummet into the bottomless pit I hoped to avoid.

I've gotten this far by compartmentalising the real Ripley into a deep, silent part of my mind. That mental prison is failing now. The unstable walls are collapsing with each realisation.

Worst of all? I hate how the sick tendrils of Xander's obsession wrap around me, forming a safe cocoon. I'm not alone in this. We're all implicated and caught in the firing line.

"Pretty sure that's her choice." Langley scowls at him. "Not yours."

Xander glares back, unfazed. "You think we're giving her a choice?"

"What the fuck is wrong with you?"

"Plenty." Xander shrugs. "Ripley stays with us. End of story."

"So you can have another shot at killing her?" Langley says incredulously. "I don't think so."

"Why don't you back off?" Lennox cuts in to defend his best friend.

Langley scoffs in disbelief. "I'll be doing her a favour by getting her away from you both."

"Because you're so perfect?"

"Oh, I'm sorry." Langley narrows his eyes on Lennox's prone form. "Says the guy incarcerated for burning his grandfather to death. I've seen your file."

Raine inhales sharply, whispering a curse.

Lennox's face is partially obscured by the thick dressing covering his cheek, but I can still see the angry red haze filtering over him. My attention catches the silver chain he never removes from his neck.

The military dog tags rest against the hospital gown he's been clothed in. After the raw emotions we shared in the Z wing, I finally understand why he's willing to wear that disgusting heirloom.

It's a reminder.

Lennox will do anything for those he cares about. Anything at all if it protects them from the same fate his baby sister suffered because of their grandfather's abuse.

Beneath the rage and hatred, his modus operandi is powerful, unconditional love. Lennox beats the world bloody so it doesn't have the opportunity to hurt his loved ones. That's how he shows that he cares.

"Congratulations," Lennox drawls sarcastically. "You can read words on a piece of paper."

"Just saying. You're in no position to talk to me about being perfect."

"Keep running your mouth," Lennox warns. "Go on. I dare you."

"What are you going to do from a hospital bed, huh?"

"Uh, guys?" Raine tries to interrupt.

Lennox acts like he didn't even hear him, too busy trying to escape the various lines tangled around him. Xander steps in to place a hand on his shoulder then shoves him back into the mattress and holds him there.

"Stay, Nox."

"No! I'm going to pummel his fucking face!"

"You think you're such a big man, don't you?" Langley goads. "And now you can't even get out of bed."

Still struggling, Lennox flushes red despite his sickly pallor. "I don't appreciate assholes sticking their noses where they don't belong."

"Guys—"

"I care about Ripley," Langley defends hotly. "Far more than you do. I'm trying to help her."

"By lying to her?" Lennox laughs.

"By doing my job!"

On a good day, even Langley's physique would be no match against Lennox's oversized bulk, packed with hardened muscle. His injuries are the only thing stopping him from beating Langley into a pulp.

Beyond the sheer size advantage he has in most fights, Lennox's deep-lidded eyes, round jaw smothered in unshaven stubble and slightly upturned nose give him a rugged, wild-like aura of threatening power.

"Guys!" Raine's worried voice cuts through their bickering. "Shut up for one moment and listen."

The room is quiet enough to hear the distant echo of voices humming through the early morning light outside. Langley moves to the window to assess the surrounding grounds.

"What can you see?" Xander questions.

"Well, everyone's awake," he replies. "Patients are gathering outside the institute."

"Why?" I frown at him.

"They're marching the guards out. Got them all tied up. Some look half-dead already."

Straining in his hospital bed, Lennox shoves Xander's hand away. "What are they doing with them?"

"Lining them up in front of the locked gates. I can't see who's watching beyond the barricades, but it looks like a fucking parade." He blows out a leaden breath. "Fuck. Harrowdean is crumbling."

Trembling all over, I glance down at my borrowed Chucks, trying to get a handle on my emotions. The buzzing noise is back and louder than ever, a cacophony of shrill decibels cutting into my brain like miniature knives.

The guards were first to fall.

They'll come for me next.

The sound of the guys conversing is swallowed by my foggy brain, a spiralling cyclone dragging me into the depths of destruction with it. Fisting my wet curls, the sense of acute panic rises with Langley's words on repeat.

Harrowdean is crumbling.

I'll be crushed beneath the rubble.

He's right; the riot will end. When it does, everything will implode. The regime I've enabled was already hanging by a thread. If Sabre Security really is investigating, that means the institute will fall.

I may not be the monster behind this program, but I'm sure as fuck no angel either. I'll burn for their sins. There's guilt in culpability, and for every drop of suffering my fellow patients endured… I benefitted.

My gaze swings around, searching for an escape route. Reason dissipates as the instinct to run takes centre stage.

"Ripley."

His ice-cool voice laden with an odd softness, Xander abandons his best friend to follow my retreating steps. Each time I move, he closes the distance between us.

The look on his face could almost be described as concerned. But that can't possibly be right. I must be imagining the curve of his pale brows, the creases marring his marble forehead, all indicating fear.

"You need to stop and take a breath," he advises, studying me intently. "This isn't the time to make a rash decision."

"A rash decision?" I huff out.

Head tilted, his throat bobs. "I'm not letting you run away from us this time."

Features hard with determination, his thin lips press together. Each minuscule clue points to a far more petrifying reality beneath his stoic expression. It's pouring through the cracks in his mask.

"You want to talk to me about rash decisions, Xander Beck?"

He opens and closes his mouth, eyes swirling with a confusing maelstrom of ice-cold detachment and red-hot anger. For once, he has no smart retort or threat to levy. Not this time.

"I became Harrowdean's stooge to make myself untouchable. To protect myself. To honour the woman who became my family when my last relative abandoned me. I did this for her."

I can't tear my eyes from Xander, the slight twitches and near-invisible tells offering a glimpse of the man behind the machine. His human alter-ego, not the soulless psychopath who runs the show.

"Why did I have to do that?" Tears spill freely down my cheeks. "Because of your *rash decision*." I gesture to Lennox to include him. "Because of what you two did to survive. Because you killed her."

"Rip–" Lennox tries to intervene.

"Do you know what the worst part is?" I cut him off.

Both men stare at me, waiting for the guillotine to slam down on their necks. They're willingly giving me the fatal blow. Only this isn't a victory. Not for me. The time for revenge has passed.

This admission is a soul-destroying defeat.

My greatest failure.

"I can't even blame you." Acceptance dampens my words into an almost-whisper. "Not anymore. Not after the things I've done with the exact same justification."

I turn away from them, my prickling skin pulling tight with the urge to run. The next words hurt to utter.

"I wish I hated you both, but I don't."

My fate seals, setting ablaze the last crumbs of my self-respect. I flee towards the exit, unable to look at any of them for a second longer. Overlapping voices chase after me.

"Ripley!"

"Wait!"

"Rip! Stop!"

Their concerned shouts fail to slow me down. All I can focus on is the foul taste of humiliation coating my tongue, reminding me of all I've sacrificed... for absolutely nothing.

They still won.

And I'm as broken as they intended.

CHAPTER 4
RIPLEY

YOU'VE CREATED A MONSTER – BOHNES

HARROWDEAN MANOR IS IN PANDEMONIUM.

Hellish, uncontrolled, fatal fucking mayhem.

In my haste to get some space, I failed to consider what danger I'd be running headfirst into. After all, this place is my home. My kingdom. Nothing can surprise me, right?

Wrong.

All bets are off now.

Corridors littered with ripped antique paintings, scattered belongings and all manner of detritus stretch before me as I speed walk into the unknown.

I don't care where I'm headed. As long as it's away from them. My weakened body protests with each footstep, but I ignore it. The throbbing aches, mind-numbing pains and infection in my searing wrists aren't going to slow me down.

Morning light illuminates the carnage that's unfolded. Clearly, we've been holed up for long enough to allow our familiar surroundings to transform. The opulent hallways no longer represent the extravagance and corruption I've come to hate.

My footsteps slow as I turn a corner, the sound of pleasured grunting quickly reaching my ears. I'm close to the reception where two patients are taking full advantage of the chance to indulge.

"You like that, baby?"

"Yes… Fuck… More!"

Her pasty ass on full display, a new girl I vaguely recognise from the sixth floor is bent over with her clothing wrapped around her ankles. Eyes screwed shut, she fails to notice me watching.

I'm shocked to recognise one of my regulars behind her—Luka. I've been selling him laxatives for months. He's ploughing into her like a man possessed. Damn. A twisted part of me wants to clap him on the back.

I race past them, keeping my eyes averted.

Light also reveals the dank mess and water damage. The flood that preceded the violence engulfing the institute trashed this area.

Adding to the destruction, patients have gone to town, smashing every available piece of furniture. I have to stop for a second to take in the sheer devastation. It gives me a sick thrill.

Windows shattered. Paperwork discarded. Computers broken. What looks like some kind of condiment from the cafeteria has been used to scrawl on the walls.

Chilled gooseflesh rises on my skin as my eyes follow the letters, spiky and rushed, seemingly written by any means necessary. An artefact left behind in the devastation for the world to read.

THE SYSTEM HAS FAILED US.

Staring at the words, the script screams the hard truth that nobody has ever dared to acknowledge. I want to trash anything left untouched in this false paradise. The emotion flooding my system isn't anger. It's pure rage, born of total powerlessness.

My attention strays to the entrance doors—somehow still intact but swinging in the spring breeze that comes from outside. The sound of voices and activity are carried in.

I look back at the words. Feel the rage. The defencelessness. Every debilitating second caught in this state-funded trap, protected by an uncaring world's wealth and indifference. And I don't want to fucking hide.

They can hate me.

But we share a common enemy.

Fists clenched, I slip between the swinging doors into the new dawn. The entrance to Harrowdean Manor is usually heavily guarded by security, but it currently stands unprotected.

I can still remember being frogmarched past the gates and up the winding, cobbled driveway to the manor. The view looking out to the surrounding woodland has drastically changed since then.

On all sides, the same imposing cloak of juniper and birch trees remain as silent sentries. I can see the wrought-iron gates in the distance, embellished with the institute's crest.

"Get them in a line!"

Rick's voice booms over the hum of patients swarming all around me. A crowd has gathered to watch the unfolding circus.

"On your fucking knees!"

One by one, a group of eight or nine guards are being roughly shoved onto their naked knees. Daylight illuminates their exhausted faces, bruised and dirt-streaked, others bloodied.

They've all been stripped, mud covering their shivering bodies. I quickly catalogue their terrified expressions, making a mental list of who isn't here. Apparently, not all the guards were present when the institute fell.

Each one is chained to the next using interconnected handcuffs, forming one linked line of humiliation. Positioned execution-style.

Behind them, Rick prowls up and down, examining his handiwork. Beyond the barricaded entrance, cameras flash on repeat. Reporters are baying for blood behind the iron bars holding them back.

Harrowdean's gates are bolted shut from our side, keeping their desperation at bay. The chains may as well be flimsy cobwebs for all they matter, though. They won't keep us safe for long.

The hostages are lined up for their photoshoot, imprisoned like livestock and posed for the country's media to capture. Riots end fast without leverage, and Rick was quick to secure his. The guards.

"We have a message for the world." Rick's voice carries through the suddenly still air. "You don't know our faces. You don't know our names. That's because to you… we don't exist."

Microphones are thrust through the bars to capture his shouts. For every beady eye latched on to us, my stomach twists into a tighter knot. They aren't here out of concern. Our rebellion is nothing more than clickbait for them to utilise.

"And that's exactly how Incendia Corporation sees us!" Rick shouts angrily. "As commodities. Specimens. Fuel for their sick experiments."

Reaching out a hand to Patient Three who stands nearby, my heart convulses at the sight of the gun Rick took from Harrison in the Z wing. Raising the weapon, he aims it at the back of the first guard's head.

"What if we treat you like commodities too?" Rick screams. "What if you're the specimens this time? Will you remember our names then? Does that grant us the right to exist?"

I watch the guard's shoulders shake with petrified sobs. It's hard not to feel a shred of sympathy, but I quickly crush it. His sliced-up, bare chest is on display, a miasma of lurid bruises stark against his flesh.

Humiliated and hurt.

Just like us.

Scanning the crowd watching Rick's performance, I realise what's been gnawing at the back of my mind. What's missing from this picture is the reinforcements. Other guards. Elon. Bancroft. His goons.

The flashing blue lights accompany the sizeable police presence, but looking closely, they aren't even focused on us. The officers are supervising the crowd of reporters. Keeping *them* safe. They aren't here for us.

We've overtaken the property, seized their guards, publicly shamed management for all their misdeeds. And still, nobody cares. None of the missing guards or clinicians are here to plead with us. We're alone.

I heard Raine and Lennox's whispers as I came to earlier on. Warden Davis is dead. By all accounts, Xander was the one who took his life. Does Sir Bancroft know that? Has he declared Harrowdean a lost cause?

No.

I quickly discount the theory. That snake would never cut and run. He isn't the kind of man to walk away with his tail tucked between his legs. So this scene must be deliberate, luring us into a false sense of security.

He wants us to feel powerful. Vindicated. That'll make it all the more satisfying to storm in here and crush the riot with unfettered violence. Any bloodshed will simply be written off as a tragic accident.

"We will not surrender our hostages until Harrowdean's shut down and everyone is set free!" Rick proclaims, the gun still poised. "Those are our demands."

The surrounding patients shout and cheer, commending his words. When Rick turns to smile at them, his eyes sweeping over the substantial crowd, he catches sight of me lingering far behind.

We lock gazes.

Rick fucking *winks*.

He spins around to continue shouting. "If anyone attempts to penetrate the institute, we will begin killing hostages. Report that."

Pulling the gun back, Rick pauses to scan the baying crowd. I'm not the only one who gasps when he whips the weapon up so it collides with the side of the unsuspecting guard's head, eliciting a scream.

He slumps over, blood splattering his shoulders and back. Rick gestures for Patient Three and the other silent Z wing patient to step forward. They begin pounding on the fallen guard, kicking him until their target is a bleeding, unconscious lump on the ground.

"We will be heard!" Rick roars.

The panicked shouts of the other guards being tugged by their colleague's body makes my palms twitch. I want to march over there, take the gun then unload every last bullet in its clip into their heads.

Their little display over, Patient Three and her friend stumble back. They're both panting and sweaty from doling out the beating.

"Get them back inside," Rick orders curtly. "Show's over."

I look away from the guards being rounded up, their purpose now served, to find Rae's gaze on me. She looks unkempt, her voluminous, auburn curls frizzy and unbrushed.

My senses are on high alert as she approaches. I trust Rae, but there's still plenty of anger and tension floating in the air, and I'm not looking to get nearly strangled to death again.

"Rip!" She rushes at me. "Where have you been?"

I gingerly accept her hug, keeping a wary eye on the others. "Um, unconscious."

"Fuck, doll face. Are you okay?" Rae pulls back to skim her eyes over me. "Stupid question. You look like you had angry sex with a woodchipper."

"Then I look better than I feel."

Her dark-brown, almost black eyes catch on my throat. It still feels enflamed and tender after Tania's attack.

"I guess I've made some enemies in here." I try to force a smile, but it feels alien. "You may not want to be seen with me."

Lips pursed, she looks around at the crowd dispersing to head back inside. "Rumours are swirling. Rick's been telling anyone who will listen the truth."

"Does that include you?" I ask tightly.

She hesitates, letting several people pass us. "I don't care where you got the contraband from. You didn't judge what I did to survive each day, so I'm not going to judge you for the same thing."

Heart sputtering, I can't swallow her forgiveness. She's a prime example of all I've done here. All the reasons I deserve to be punished for my role in the conspiracy. I enabled Rae, fed her addiction and reaped the rewards.

"How long do you think this can last?" I gesture towards the energised crowd.

"As long as it takes. We won't stop until we're treated like actual human beings. We're going to be set free, Rip!"

Her wide, excited eyes and the grin stretching her lips only intensifies the lead weight settling in my gut. She's as deluded as the rest of them, running around thinking this is some kind of pre-release party.

"Why do you think there aren't any reinforcements outside the gates?"

Rae sucks her bottom lip between her teeth, suddenly appearing nervous. "Because… they've given up, right? We won?"

Gripping her shoulders, I shake her roughly. "Wake up, Rae! They will never give up! This is just the calm before the storm."

"But we have hostages!"

"You think management cares about a few worthless guards?" I scoff. "They'll cut their losses just to get their operation back up and running. Guards *and* patients alike."

Tears have filled her eyes, sparkling swells hanging on the tips of her eyelashes. She looks from side to side, cataloguing the roar of the nation's media trying to regain our attention as everyone disperses.

"I thought you wanted to take them down too."

"I want to walk out of here alive," I correct. "Do the smart thing, and keep your head down, Rae. Or you're at risk of losing it when this all ends."

Releasing her, she takes a big step back, rubbing her arms. We stare at each other as the shouts and hollers amplify, a group of hooligan patients running past with boxes of paperwork they're emptying out on the lawn.

Two others heave bundles of broken furniture between them, the polished mahogany now splintered into perfectly sized kindling. Adding them to a rapidly building pile, the addition of paperwork reveals their plan.

"Patient 2185," one reads from the thick file. "They didn't even give us names."

"Burn it! Burn it!"

In the distance, cameras are still rolling. I can imagine the madness sweeping over various newsrooms as they rush to report on the latest developments. Not even Incendia can suppress this story.

I recognise one of the instigators, yelling her head off with such gleeful rebellion, you'd think she was a kid on Christmas morning. Taylor hasn't even stopped to clean herself up, a curtain of dried blood still cascading from her sliced forehead.

Fingers pinched around a lit cigarette, she watches the pile of furniture and discarded paperwork grow. The hysterical crowd is emptying out the reception, adding anything flammable to the stash.

"Here!" someone shouts. "We raided the groundskeeper's storage."

I hear Rae curse next to me as a canister of fuel is paraded above their heads like the fucking holy grail. The kind of fuel you'd use to fill a lawnmower, I think.

With the canister emptied all over the broken wood, Taylor flicks her cigarette into the pile of kindling. The patient files scattered throughout quickly crisp and blacken, growing into a fireball.

"Yes!"

"More! More!"

The chorus of celebration fills the smoky air. Heat and acrid fumes pour from the bonfire, growing larger and more vicious by the second as it greedily consumes the destroyed furniture and files.

Smoke rises.

Patients cheer.

Harrowdean is burning.

CHAPTER 5
XANDER

SINCERELY, FUCK YOU – PARDYALONE

FLASHLIGHT SWINGING from side to side, the beam illuminates my path through the pitch-black night. The emergency lighting that offered a little reprieve has now failed, plunging Harrowdean into total darkness.

Ripley didn't come back.

The fucking disobedience.

Trembling with a feeling I can't put a name to, I left the medical wing after growing tired of listening to the others' fretting. Even the meathead himself, Lennox, seems worried about his so-called least favourite person.

They both wanted to join the search party, but neither would've been able to navigate the war zone I've encountered while looking for Ripley. After only a handle of days, the institute is unrecognisable.

I didn't think I shocked easily. Watching patients physically fight over food, scratching eyes and pulling out clumps of hair is the least of what's unfolding. We knew it was coming. They're turning on each other.

Scanning my eyes over the crowded cafeteria, I peer through the gloom at various faces scattered all around. Patients shout and threaten, arguing over whatever scraps of food from the kitchen are left.

Nothing.

She isn't here.

"Woo!" A dirt-streaked blur goes screaming past me. "We're free, bitches!"

Turning away from the cafeteria, I watch the girl stagger off, quickly deducing that she's wasted. Alcohol is a less popular form of contraband—too easily spotted by staff. Now, along with raided nurse's stations and riot fever, it's fuelling the carnage all around me.

I already had to punch some delirious guy a few hours ago when he came at me with a chair leg, screeching at invisible voices. I have no clue who he thought I was, but I wasn't hanging around to find out.

Sure, anarchy is fun. It's a romantic idea. Then reality sets in, and the delirium isn't so cute after all. The whole intoxicated, frat party atmosphere rife with explosive, unmedicated violence won't last much longer.

I'd usually enjoy the chaos. It provides ample opportunity to blend into the shadows and stalk my next plaything. Oh, the fun I could have right now while no one is watching.

It'd be easy to find something soft and vulnerable to slice. A pure, untouched specimen, ripe for the taking. Someone who would cry and beg. Vocalise their pain in a sweet symphony of desperation.

I haven't touched a soul since that night.

When *she* slept curled up in my arms.

Saucer-like, hazel eyes, brimming with tears. Tangled snarls of mousy-brown hair. Plump, perfectly proportioned lips, begging to be bitten. Her insults and protests turning into whimpers of submission.

My fantasies now have a face.

The woman I hate has become… What? Beyond fascination. Beyond obsession. Beyond everything I thought I knew and wanted from one of my targets. She's no longer just a toy.

Ripley Bennet has drilled her way into my bone marrow, infiltrated my blood cells and set up shop like a parasitic infection. My interest in her felt different than this before. Intense but under control. She was a collection of cells trapped beneath my microscope.

When she snuggled up to my bare chest, pressing the tip of her nose into my skin, tickling me with each relaxed exhale… my entire existence shifted. It happened so fast, I didn't see it coming.

I've never been touched like that—with gentle care and something akin to tenderness. In my experience, touch only brings pain. Humiliation. Degradation. I torture others to hold that agony at bay.

Without warning, my mind plummets into the black pit I never allow it to linger in for long. A place reserved for pathetic emotions. The weakness of a younger, smaller, more damaged version of the man I've become.

Walking faster, I head back in the direction of the medical wing, ignoring the way my lightly-trembling hand causes the flashlight's beam to shake. The institute's messy chaos is interwoven with lifelike memories exploding all around me like inkblots.

Mummy's asleep, Xander.

Don't wake her up. I'd hate to hurt her.

Revulsion writhes beneath my scar-striped skin at the voice accompanying my vivid flashbacks. I can still see the yellowing carpet adorned with a lumpy, striped mattress. The cracked, still functioning lamp lying on its side where I tried to fight back.

I always slept with that light on, terrified of what would happen in the darkness. It allowed me to stare at the newspaper cutouts of the latest 90s computer model tacked on my bedroom wall.

I loved computers even back then. I'd stare at those clippings through it all. Every second, minute and hour. Every night. Dreaming of the possibilities that my fingertips touching a keyboard would bring.

Technology intrigued me. I dreamed that if I could find a way to make money, I'd be able to run away. Or erase myself like the elusive secret agents I saw in crappy spy movies. I would never fucking return.

Shut up, brat.

I warned you what happens to boys who cry.

Over time, swallowing the sobs became a form of self-preservation. Clamping down on my wails. Extinguishing any protests. By the time my eighth birthday rolled around, I'd perfected the art of detachment.

Lost to the dark miasma clouding my thoughts, I trip over a length of bloodstained carpet that's been ripped up. I brace myself for a hard impact, dropping the flashlight and sending it spinning.

"Fuck!" I smack a hand against the floor. "Fuck, fuck, fuck!"

The whole world is tilting. Morphing. Crimson-dipped and filtered through a furious lens. I don't know how to hold this burden inside—the weight of thinking, feeling and caring about another human being. It hasn't happened since I switched all those vulnerabilities off.

Wait… Fucking caring?

Is that what this is?

Sprawled out, the most ridiculous details enter my awareness. The hunger pains in my stomach. How stray pieces of shattered glass have embedded in my palms. The coppery scent of a nearby blood spill.

My carefully constructed world is splintering apart. I've built it to the highest degree of perfection. Organised. Controlled. Emotionless. A shackled reality, the impenetrable bars of my indifference keeping me safely imprisoned from the entire world.

"We have their attention now. I want all the mattresses thrown outside next."

"From the windows?"

"Perfect. Wait for daylight so the cameras capture it."

Voices snap me back to the present moment as effectively as being dunked in ice water. I force a blank expression over the torment twisting my features.

Their footsteps crunch through the corridor's debris until they reach me. I peer up at the small group of patients holding flashlights. How fortunate. Perhaps I'll have an outlet for all this distracting emotion after all.

"You," I spit out.

Rick contemplates me through facial bruises and filth, his smile full of stupid confidence. "Xander, right?"

The son of a bitch beat the shit out of Raine not so long ago. If he hadn't been shipped off to the Z wing, I would've arranged a convenient little accident for him instead. He got off lightly.

"Correct. I was under the impression you were dead."

He shrugs casually. "Not quite."

"How unfortunate."

Sneering, he shares looks with his two friends. "Unfortunate?"

"For you, yes."

I don't recognise the patients with him, though the visible signs of torture and the dead look in their eyes are familiar. More of Incendia's little experiments. Ripley and Lennox clearly didn't escape the Z wing alone.

I know what this asshole did to her. So why didn't she leave him there to die? Yet another detail she's failed to share. Rage crystallises into an ice-cold shard that slices through my chest.

"Where is she?"

"Who?" Rick laughs.

Jump. Slice. Stab.

The temptation is strong.

"Ripley." I force a calm tone.

The amusement written across his face causes my teeth to grind in irritation. He can smirk all he likes. It won't change the satisfaction that slitting his throat will give me.

"Why do you assume I would know?" he retorts.

My blood boils. "Did you enjoy carving those marks into her?"

Rick's eyes flash with surprise. I knew Ripley wouldn't admit who hurt her; she has too much pride for that. The truth was easy to pry out of Raine's mouth, though.

"I'm far too busy cleaning up Ripley's mess to follow her around like the rest of you." His nose wrinkles in derision. "Look at you. Didn't take much for her to wrap you around her finger."

"What gave you that impression?"

He waves a hand over me, visibly dishevelled and sprawled out. "Not your best look."

Teeth gritted, I climb to my feet. "Perhaps go have a shower before commenting on my appearance."

I narrow my eyes at the male patient on Rick's right side who is eyeing me like a piece of meat he'd happily pummel.

"You want to call your attack dog off?" I gesture to him.

"Oh, don't mind him. He's just... focused." Rick casts his friend a smile. "We all want the same thing. You included."

"And what's that?"

"To see the institutes and Incendia burn," the female patient supplies. "Starting with Harrowdean."

Laughter rips out of me. "Why would I want that?"

All three of them gape, their silence punctuated by the loud chaos unfolding all around us. Anarchy has resumed, peppered with smashing glass and screeching.

"You think this means anything?" I gesture around at the people running wild. "This little rebellion of yours won't last."

"Is that what you want?" Rick's lip curls. "You think Ripley will return to her seat of power once we've all been eliminated? Maybe she'll toss you some scraps of attention, huh?"

"I have no interest in what Ripley does when this is all over."

Lies.

Swallowing my tongue to keep my composure, I stand firm as he runs his disgusting eyes all over me. The black shirt I located is short-sleeved, revealing layers of shiny scar tissue that he openly peruses.

"I suppose I did her a favour," he muses. "Her scars match yours now. You two freaks can compare notes."

"You touched something that doesn't belong to you," I spit venomously, my hands balled into fists by my sides.

"No, I simply made sure she'll never be able to forget what she did here."

My brain misfires with the surge of scorching-hot anger that barrels through me. I find myself leaping into his personal space before my common sense comes back online.

We're chest-to-chest with nothing but anger and violent threat trapped between us. All I see is red, causing my momentary calm to implode.

"For every mark you left on her skin, I'll break one bone. Would you care to choose which?"

Whatever Rick reads in my expression causes him to falter. He looks around for support, but his new friends don't jump to his rescue. Both look intrigued. Seems like loyalty only runs so deep.

"But… she—" he splutters.

"Never mind," I interrupt.

"Wait!"

"Too late. Dealer's choice."

My curled fist snaps outward to connect with his face. I lavish the sight of his nose exploding into bloody fireworks upon impact. The lurid red splats coating his shocked face are mesmerising.

I wonder what the blood would look like spilling from his broken skull. Shards of bone and soft, squelchy tissue floating in the remains. He wouldn't lay another finger on Ripley then. Not without his head intact.

Bringing my knee up to smash into his stomach, I wait for his pained wheeze before punching him again. Over and over. The pain slicing across my knuckles is an exquisite shot of pure adrenaline. Heavenly.

His friends stand there, shuffling their feet like they're stuck watching an uninteresting theatre performance. Neither moves to intervene.

"Tell me, did you scream and beg for mercy when their experiments began?" I ask conversationally.

Punch. Crack. Ooze.

"Perhaps you prayed for someone to come to save you from the big, bad doctor."

Smack. Crunch. Splat.

"Truthfully? You should've stayed down there." I laugh loudly. "It would've been safer."

Thwack. Grind. Squirt.

His attempts to fight back are feeble at best. Inconsequential. I've switched gears and slotted into a less-visited corner of my mind. The primitive part that embraced violence and strength to endure the same torture he did.

The pain of each blow is insignificant. My tired muscles protesting. Stomach growling. Head pounding with exhaustion. Human weakness wasn't allowed in Priory Lane, so I quickly learned how to block it out.

Pausing, I hold him by the throat, watching the crimson rivulets spill over his cheeks. "At least down there, you were safe from me."

With a final, bone-grinding hit, I toss his unconscious carcass to the floor. Rick rolls through debris and sharp glass, a wet rattle pushing past his lips. Disappointing. I'd hoped he would beg before passing out.

As satisfying as it would be to bleed the bastard dry, a part of me is curious to see how many pieces Bancroft and his organisation will cut him into as punishment for leading the riot.

I look up at the two patients standing there watching the show, a single brow raised. Still neither moves to attack.

"This piece of shit is going to get himself killed when the authorities decide to intervene. Unless you'd like to join him, I suggest you consider your options."

"Options?" the female patient repeats. "We're here to fight."

"We know the truth about the real experimental program. Incendia will target us first when the riot ends."

"You weren't with us." She pulls her head back in confusion.

"Not in Harrowdean," I correct with a shrug. "But every institute in the country has a Z wing program."

Her eyes widen as she seems to view me in a new light. Even her close-mouthed friend seems thoughtful. Regardless of our choices, we're facing the same threat. Total fucking annihilation.

"This is bigger than all of us." I look between them. "Your pathetic riot means nothing to a multi-million pound corporation."

Colour drains from the female patient's face, making her bruises and visible injuries stand out. Her bravado is vanishing faster than our chances of survival.

"Do you really think we'll be rescued and released like this asshole is saying?"

"Well... The others... He..." she struggles. "We have hostages!"

The woman is as stupid as the rest of these morons, skipping around with their unearthed contraband and makeshift weapons, thinking this is some kind of game. It's laughable.

"The only reason management hasn't stormed Harrowdean and wiped us out is the media attention. When that dies down, they'll bring in the bulldozers."

Their posture changes—both seeming to shirk away from the writhing bag of organs at my feet.

"Or are you dumb enough to think Harrowdean will change?" I roll my eyes. "Perhaps they'll listen to your demands? Or let you skip off into the sunset and rebuild your lives?"

The more I speak, the further their unease seems to spread. Even Mr Silent is glancing at our surroundings and shifting on his feet. My words have made an impact. Good.

"Do what you want. It makes no difference to me." I draw my leg back to boot Rick in the ribs for good measure. "But think twice before throwing your weight behind this scum."

Dismissing them with a terse nod, I continue on to the medical wing to regroup. I've scooped up my dropped flashlight and taken a few steps from Rick when I set sights on her.

My lungs twist and knot. Oxygen collects in my oesophagus, burning hotter than trapped lava. Resting against the wall, Ripley is watching the interaction from afar, safe and fucking sound.

Relief swims through me.

Sweet, blissful relief.

My blood doesn't freeze solid in my veins like it used to at the sight of her. Those sad doe eyes and teeth-baring hisses used to be the equivalent of a cold plunge in liquid nitrogen. Enough to send my soul running for the hills to make way for my blood thirst.

Vulnerable. Lonely. Angry. Hate-filled. The most perplexing combination of something so delicate and breakable yet reinforced with a pain-forged strength. I longed to break the last of her resolve.

Just like *he* once broke mine.

But not now.

Now… I want to bathe in her strength and formidability. To wipe the horrors from her gaze and soothe the pain that others have inflicted. She's mine to hurt. Mine to own. Mine to fucking cherish.

Standing on opposite ends of the corridor, we stare at each other.

Two predators, sizing the other up, calculating the possibility of a quick kill. But… no, that isn't right at all. It isn't hatred I see burning in her eyes.

With long strides, I close the distance between us, halting with our noses mere inches apart. Her eyes are wide and glimmering through the dark bruises ringing them, fading from black to lightning-streaked purple.

"Where have you been?" My voice seeps with frustration.

"Why do you care, Xan?" she replies smoothly. "Worried I'll make a rash decision?"

Rather than strangle her black-and-blue throat like I'm longing to do, I brace a hand either side of her head. Seeing her whole and unharmed allows me to draw my first full breath since she disappeared.

I'm sucked into her orbit. Tumbling through a bottomless wormhole into the unknown emptiness beyond my line of sight. If I'm not careful, I'll lose myself along the way. Perhaps that would also be a relief.

"I didn't begrudge your rash decision the night we slept together."

"You restrained me and held a knife to my throat," Ripley snarks.

"Yet my little toy still shivered at my touch and begged for more."

I lean into her space, dragging the tip of my nose up her throat and neck. She shivers against me, a whispered moan daring to break free when I trace the tip of my tongue behind her left earlobe.

"In fact, I think you begged me to fuck you." My lips follow her ear's curvature, leaving a featherlight trail. "Tell me, do I have to beg you in return now?"

Her body arches against the wall, pressing her round curves into me. "Hmm. The great Xander Beck begging?"

Sucked into the bottomless, hazel pits peering up at me, I don't bother to cushion the inevitable fall. I'll crash land in the innermost parts of her being and happily break every bone in the process. As long as I can stay there.

Seeing her disappear into thin air reacquainted me with an old nemesis. Fear. And fuck if the idea of losing whatever we are now feels far scarier than the emotions she's reigniting within me.

I lick my lips. "Yes. I'd beg for you."

"Me?" She drags in a shaky breath.

"Your acceptance." Blind hope forces me to keep going. "Maybe even your forgiveness."

Searching my face for any hint of deception, Ripley's brows crinkle. "You think I could ever forgive you?"

I raise a hand, vaguely noting the way she no longer flinches in my presence. Not a single hint of revulsion as I trace my pointer finger across her lips to map the kissable swell.

How would it feel to be touched by her?

Held by her?

Perhaps… even loved by her?

I don't know what that's like. My mother loved her bottles of cheap, supermarket liquor far more than she ever loved me. I doubt she even loved the monster she allowed into our home. And there was certainly no love in the string of foster homes that came after.

Before Ripley entered my life, I'd never been gently touched. Held. Cherished. At least not without the expectation of pain. I have no clue how to earn her affections rather than plotting how to cause her pain.

"I doubt Lennox would be alive now if you hadn't forgiven him," I point out. "Why else did you save his life?"

"Because I'm not you."

A smile pulls at my mouth. "Perhaps we're not the people you think we are either."

Still pressing into me, whether consciously or not, she speaks a thousand words with her body language alone. Her grimace deepens as she wrestles with the words she doesn't want to say aloud.

"I want to believe that," Ripley finally admits. "I want to stop seeing the triumph on your face when they wheeled my best friend's body away. I want to forget."

"Can you forget?"

Her lips pucker and roll. "I don't know."

Flush with anticipation, I can't stop myself from acting on pure instinct. She's slipping through my fingertips. I can't have that. Whether she accepts it or not, Ripley Bennet belongs to me. She has for longer than either of us realised.

My mouth strikes hers without the pleasantries of a gentle reintroduction. I don't intend to entice her with some long, elaborate scheme—I want her to fucking submit. To accept the sick bond that's grown between us and join me in the torment.

I still want to own her. Break her. Shatter every last recognisable piece. But I also want to help her put those pieces together again. Her pain is no longer my obsession; instead, her will to survive against the odds is.

She hesitates for a moment before responding to my kiss. I wouldn't begrudge her punching me. Last time I touched her, we collided violently. Her response is no less rough as she bites my bottom lip.

I lift a hand to her short curls and seize a handful. Ripley moans into my mouth when I sharply tug, positioning her head to devour her at a deeper angle. Her lips take the brunt of my determination, smacking together with each kiss.

Her body writhes against mine, trapped between my onslaught and the hard wall with no room to escape. I grind into her soft curves, my cock hardening at the feel of each rounded angle.

Gripping her ass tight, she's pinned to my chest. I want her to feel the effect she has on me. A mere taste and I'm harder than steel. The sight of her crying out in ecstasy the night I saved her life has haunted me since.

I want that again.

I want her.

I'm ready to admit that.

Her desperate moans increase as I thrust my tongue past her lips, branding her mouth as mine. Our teeth clang. Lips wrestle. Breath intwines. The institute and all its madness fades into the background.

BANG.

Screams follow the loud crash. Ripley tears her mouth from mine, immediately on high alert. Two bickering patients race down the corridor, chasing each other to continue trading blows.

"Shit." She touches her swollen lips, stained an exquisite shade of cherry red. "We should move."

All I want is to bend her tight little ass over and roughly plough into her sweet cunt until she cries out my name in surrender. I swallow deeply and force myself to breathe instead.

"You're probably right."

"What about him?"

Ripley studies Rick's unconscious body in the distance. His companions have deserted him already. I wonder if her mind is chewing over whether she could forgive him... Whether she could forget.

Would his death appease her? If I find a sharp instrument to carve out his organs with, will I earn her forgiveness? Will she curl up in my arms again? All she has to do is say the word.

"Would you like me to go back and finish the job?" I ask plainly.

Her teeth seize her inflamed bottom lip. I'm calculating the best place to dissect the bastard, limb from limb, when she shakes her head.

"He'll get what he deserves. We have bigger concerns."

Stepping back from me, she crouches to pick up the bag at her side that I didn't notice. I move the flashlight to illuminate the backpack, noting that it's bulging as Ripley swings it over her shoulder.

"Some food I scavenged," she explains quickly. "And the last of my contraband stash."

"That's some survival kit."

Ripley jerks her head towards the medical wing. "We have mouths to feed."

"You're done running from us?"

"I'm done running. Period."

To my surprise, she stretches out a hand in offering. I stare at the tattoo-wrapped limb, uncertain how to respond. What is she offering me? Does she want me to... hold it? How do I even do that?

"Just take the hand, Xan."

Her palm is warm as it slots into mine.

"That wasn't so hard, was it?" she jibes.

Our fingers tightly intertwine, and she gives a barely-there squeeze. From the corner of my eye, I watch her frown at our connected grips.

Ripley tugs me onwards, leaving the bloody mess behind us. Illuminating our path to the medical wing, I let her guide the way as I keep a wary eye out for any more patients.

Creeping through the darkness, I'm so focused on our surroundings, I almost smack into her back when she suddenly halts. The door leading into the medical wing is hanging off its hinges.

"Shit," she mutters softly.

I move fast, stepping in front of her. "Stay here."

"Forget it." Ripley quickly drops my hand. "Raine is in there!"

"Rip! Wait!"

Running after her, we race into the darkened wing, picking our way over smashed detritus. Gloom from outside and the swinging flashlight reveals a catastrophic mess.

Furniture overturned. Cabinets raided. Medical supplies scattered. Lennox's bed is empty, lying on its side with the sheets tangled on the floor. My gaze lands on a puddle of congealed blood smeared across the floor.

"Hello?" Ripley shouts frantically.

Her voice echoes—a panicked reverberation bouncing off the walls and vaulted ceiling. Its high-pitched tenor fades without a response.

The wing is abandoned.

They're gone.

CHAPTER 6
RIPLEY
FREEDOM – YOUNG LIONS

THE SHOWER SPRAY is freezing cold as it hits me square in the face. Whatever hot water remained when I woke up in the medical wing has petered out along with the electricity. We're truly cut off now.

Scrubbing myself with my papaya body wash, I continue to survey my mental map of Harrowdean, considering possible places where Lennox, Raine and Langley could be hiding.

Xander and I searched until the sun rose and our exhaustion refused to be ignored any longer. He was already dead on his feet when we started looking. We had to stop and find somewhere to get some rest.

I turn off the cold spray, teeth chattering as I step out into the chilly bathroom. My bedroom has been turned over, much like everyone else's on the fifth and sixth floors. The thieves didn't find anything, though. I'd already retrieved my stash.

As I set the makeshift shank made from a toothbrush and razor blade on the bathroom sink, a low-pitched whimpering echoes from the adjacent room. I left the door open a crack in case any wayward patients decided to surprise us with another sweep.

The noise stops before I can figure out what it is.

After hurriedly drying off, wincing at the pain of my aching body, I stand poised. It's silent. The floor is pretty much abandoned—during our searching, we found most still-lucid patients congregating in communal areas where light sources can be shared.

A smaller, almost incoherent group was attempting to break into the pharmacy to raid the medication stash when we passed. Unsuccessful, of course. The store is locked behind a reinforced steel cage that wouldn't budge.

Everyone's going cold turkey.

More fuel for the fire.

I pull clean leggings and my favourite oversized anime tee on, thankful to be back in my own clothes. The butter-soft, over washed fabric doesn't irritate my lingering injuries. It feels so good to be clean.

"No… S-Stop… Please."

My hands freeze while pulling the t-shirt down. The whispered pleading is barely audible. Confused, I glance around the bathroom, convinced my several missed doses of medication are taking effect.

It's definitely coming from the bedroom where I left Xander resting alone. I wasn't about to climb into the tiny, twin-sized bed with him, despite the kiss we shared. Surely, he isn't the one crying out?

"No! Leave m-me alone!"

Oh, shit.

It is Xander.

The sheer terror in his voice seizes hold of my heart and wrings the blood from it. I creep into the bedroom, now bathed in late afternoon sunlight leaking through the barred window.

My bed is occupied by a sprawled out Xander, his legs sticking out from the twisted sheets and arms flailing blindly to ward off something I can't see. In his fist, he holds a familiar pocketknife.

I should remain at a safe distance, but his mouth is frozen open in a silent scream for mercy. I can't just watch. He's keening like a frightened child, thrashing and kicking.

The powerful iceman is battling invisible demons and crying out to be saved from his own mind. Equal parts fascination and reluctant empathy carry me towards him.

Beneath his whimpering, I can almost hear the fissures in my heart cracking wide open. Hatred spills out in a violent geyser, leaving space for something else. Something unnerving. Something a lot like… understanding.

Xander Beck isn't only a monster.

He's a survivor too.

Just like me.

Resting on the edge of the bed, I tentatively place a hand on his cold, bare shoulder. He stripped out of his shirt and jeans to sleep, exposing the pale, defined ridges of his packed abdominals and pectorals.

While ganglier than Lennox, he's still wiry and muscular. His marble-like skin stretches tight across each chiselled tendon. The old, silvery scars that cover his arms and biceps also adorn his flat stomach and lower still.

"Xan," I murmur gently. "You're safe."

At the sound of my voice, the tension drains from his posture. Xander slumps on the thin mattress, a sigh whistling from his nostrils. I trace circles on his skin with my thumb, whispering under my breath.

"That's it, Xan." My throat thickens as my conflicting emotions battle it out. "You're safe."

The urge to climb into bed with him and hold this fragile version of the psychopath I thought I knew is overwhelming. In this moment, he looks so lost. So alone. So irreparably broken.

I know what that's like.

I've been so alone it physically aches.

Xander is evil, capable of inflicting incomprehensible cruelty. I know he craves pain and humiliation. To him, love is degradation. Power. Control. It's all he knows, and that's why he targeted me.

Being evil doesn't mean the person is all bad, though.

We contain multitudes.

There are a million reasons why he deserves to be left to battle his nightmares alone. Anyone saner would take one look at the terrifying brutality inside him and run away. But… fuck, there's something comforting about his capacity for violence.

How would it feel to have that power on my side? I've been alone for so long, I don't know what it's like to be defended by someone. To have the protection of another human being—even one who once hurt me.

When I try to put some space between us, a low moan rumbles from Xander's throat. His eyelids move, and before I can pull away, his weapon-free hand snaps out to capture my wrist in an iron-tight grip.

His long fingers tense, digging deep into the barely-healing wounds that ring my wrist. The hot throb of pain makes my breath catch, and at that tiny noise, his eyes suddenly fly open.

"No!" he shouts.

"Xan! It's me!"

Unseen ghosts haunt his shadowy cobalt orbs as the knife flicks out and swoops towards my face. I duck before he can stab me, trying to capture his attention so he can see it's me.

"Xander! Stop!"

Panting hard, he looks at me. The palpable fear warping his face into a child-like caricature morphs into surprise when he realises I'm the one touching him.

My chest expands with relief when he lowers the pocketknife. For the first time, he stares back at me with no defences intact.

Holy. Shit.

The truth is plain as day, written in blinding lights. He can't hide his secrets in this state. In his uncertain stare, I can see the tormented reality he hides behind cold smiles and indifference.

"Let go," I whisper in a small voice. "You're hurting me."

"Ripley?"

"It's me. You were crying out in your sleep. I thought…"

Not sure what to say, I purse my lips. He's still clasping my wrist, blinking hard to clear the sleepy fog from his mind.

Xander licks his lips. "You heard."

"Does this happen often?"

He looks away, blinking several times before answering. "Sometimes."

"What were you dreaming about?"

"Nothing," he replies flatly.

"That didn't look like nothing. You nearly stabbed me."

I wouldn't have put it past the old him to use physical violence, though that's more Lennox's style. Xander prefers mind games and careful manipulation.

The physical change is clear when he transforms back into the lifeless droid I'm used to. The fog clears from his gaze, and he wipes any trace of vulnerability away, smoothing a cool smile into place.

"Are you concerned?" Xander asks dryly. "I can assure you I don't need your pity."

"Fine, be like that," I snap in frustration. "I'm not the one who's scared to feel anything at all."

"Scared?" He laughs.

"Yes!"

"I don't get scared, Ripley. You should know that."

"Bullshit. I think you're fucking terrified."

His amusement makes my teeth grind. I finally see his cruelty for what it really is—a defence mechanism. The world shaped Xander into the psychopathic monster he proclaims to be. He wears it like a cloak.

"Fear is for children," he spits out.

"Is that who was crying out for help?" I lash back.

"I wasn't doing that."

"Bullshit! Tell me, who hurt little Xander?"

He physically recoils like I've slapped him. It brings me a shameful sense of satisfaction to see the hurt my words inflict. I'd rather he feel that pain than nothing at all. As long as he's feeling, there's hope.

When he releases my wrist and tries to wriggle away from me, I act quickly. Xander falls back on the bed with a huff as I pull myself on top of him, straddling his waist in a position of power.

I don't care that he still holds the pocketknife. He can lash out again if he so pleases. I'll take the blade and sink it into his chest to make him understand. This is our breaking point.

"Ripley," he warns.

"What? You're allowed to make demands and take my choice away from me, but I can't do the same?"

"Enough."

"No. It isn't enough, Xan."

Beneath me, his chest rises and falls in a fast rhythm. I trail my hand between his defined pectorals, over his breastbone and down his sloping abdominals. My fingertips catch on raised, puckered scar tissue.

His breath catches. "Stop."

"No. Not yet."

I watch indecision and torment flicker over him, breaking his act. My thumb strokes across a deep, jagged groove beneath his belly button, the shiny mark faded with time.

"I think the truth is… you feel too much."

Xander remains silent, so I plough on.

"It's why you bear these marks. It's why you hurt others to feel in control. And it's why you won't open up to me. You're consumed by fear."

"That's… That's not true," he splutters.

"Then you won't mind if I walk away right now. I can't forgive or forget without first understanding the man demanding so much from me."

Climbing off him, I leave Xander looking startled. My gut burns with frustration and regret. For a brief, pathetic second, I dared to believe that he could be more. That *we* could be more.

I'm searching for my shoes to storm out when I hear movement behind me. Pale fingers wrap around my bicep.

"Stop."

I'm spun on the spot, forcing me to look up at Xander as the blade presses deep into my throat.

"Don't go," he croaks.

"You're threatening me to get me to stay?"

The pressure slicing into me is a silent bid for control. I don't think Xander knows how to communicate without threatening death in one way or another.

"I... I can't... I don't know how to do... this," he mutters awkwardly. "Talk."

When I try to pull away, his grip intensifies, holding me prone. He's clothed in nothing but form-fitting black boxers, his hair wild and eyes darting around like he's hoping to pluck the right words from thin air.

This Xander isn't in control.

"I was dreaming about your voice," he blurts abruptly. "Telling me I'm safe. No one told me that when I was a kid. No one... cared."

Holding still so he doesn't cut me, I carefully lay my hand over his. "Safe from what?"

Inhale. Frown. Exhale. Blink.

"Let me in, Xan."

"I... don't know when it started."

"Did someone hurt you?" I coax.

He licks his lips, avoiding my gaze. "You could call it that. I was too young to understand, I suppose. The memories are blurred, but the dreams about him are vivid."

Blood trickles down my neck, leaking from the shallow nick I can feel he's inflicted. If he needs to do this to feel in control, I'll take the punishment. A scar is a small price to pay for Xander's bared soul.

"So you were dreaming about... him?"

Watching his reaction, I'm unsurprised by his terse nod.

"Who was he?"

I've been able to deduce some of Xander's past from my conversation with Lennox. When he revealed the truth about his sister's suicide, he made it clear that he believes Xander was a victim of sexual abuse too.

"He was my stepfather," Xander grits out.

My stomach rolls. "Fuck."

"I never knew my real father. Mother spent my childhood at the bottom of a bottle. She almost died from liver failure when I was six. He was my only real parental figure."

My hand tightens on his, more blood sliding down my neck. Xander blows out a long breath and lifts his gaze to mine.

"He came most nights. I suppose Mother was too inebriated to hear or notice anything. We never spoke about the… the assaults. He just snuck in, left before dawn and always returned the next night. Every day for as long as I can remember."

His throat moves with a hard swallow.

"I was eight when the police came. I didn't say anything, the damage was done. He was actually arrested for assaulting a young boy in a park, nothing to do with me."

"That's so incredibly messed up."

"I guess he couldn't help himself." Xander eases the knife slightly, keeping it held at my throat. "The authorities took one look at Mother and sent her to rehab. I was taken into foster care. That's it."

Processing, I try to make sense of his words. "You never told anyone?"

Xander laughs humourlessly. "I didn't have to."

"Why?"

He drags his other hand over his weary face. "The bastard admitted it all. I wasn't the only person he hurt. He was charged with multiple counts of sexual assault and died in prison four years later."

Emotion boils behind my eyes, matching the white-hot sensation his blade is inflicting. I don't pity him. He doesn't need that. Yet the truth tears at my soul regardless.

"What happened after?" I ask in a guttural voice.

"I bounced between foster homes until I aged out of the system a decade later. No one wanted to adopt the antisocial kid who liked to cut himself. I scared off every potential adoption."

"Your mother never came back for you?"

Lowering the pocketknife fully, his shoulders slump. "No. I never saw her again. She could be dead for all I know and care."

Watching him breathe heavily, I can't comprehend how any mother could abandon her son like that. Sure, she was sick. But to never come back for him or make contact? After everything? It's plain cruel.

"When he…" His voice falters as he looks down. "When he used to hurt me, I'd cry and plead with him to stop. He warned me about what happens to little boys who cry."

"Xan. You don't have to keep going."

"I need to say it," he explains with a newfound fierceness.

I close my mouth, waiting for him to continue.

"After years of his nightly visits, it was easy to switch off to the pain, the fear, the confusion and disgust I felt… and feel nothing at all. He told me not to cry. So I stopped."

"He threatened you?"

My voice is barely a whisper, fraught with horror for that poor little boy, alone and scared, who found a sense of safety in not feeling at all.

"Me… Mother… His threats were indiscriminate. Crying wouldn't save me. If I laid there silently, the time passed quicker. The less I cared, the less it hurt each time he came back for more."

The broken person standing in front of me hardly resembles the white-haired demon I met in Priory Lane. The same man who tried to scare me into submission. Who kept me busy while his best friend ensured Holly's demise.

Xander scoffs, his gaze focused on the floor. "I never cared about anything ever again."

My attention latches on to his visible scars. I wondered about them for months in Priory Lane.

"These look old."

"It started in foster care."

"Can you tell me why?"

Xander pauses for a long moment, searching for the right words. He flips the pocketknife in his hands, uncaring of my sticky blood coating the surface.

"No matter how many times I sliced my skin until I ran out of space, I felt nothing. But I loved the act of doing it. The pain became a way to prove to myself that I'd never be vulnerable again. As long as I could confirm that the numbness was still there… keeping me safe."

I can't help but think of Rae. Her own addiction to pain. But for Xander, he wasn't cutting to feel something. He did it to check whether he still felt nothing at all.

His need for pain suddenly makes more sense. Not just his own, but the pain he inflicts on others. It's all a test of his control. A way to ensure his own survival. If everyone else is hurting, then they can't hurt him.

"That's why I didn't care about Holly." Xander finally looks up at me. "I didn't care how much it would affect you either. I was willing to push her over the edge."

"Because it was necessary?"

He shakes his head. "I know how it sounds."

"The amount of times I've told myself the same thing." I laugh at the insanity of it all. "I guess nobody survives with their morals intact. Desperate people do desperate things."

Lips parted, Xander cocks his head. "Do desperate people forgive others' shitty choices?"

Even with a fresh wound, I'm twisted enough to actually consider it. Old Ripley would've left him, naked and humiliated. Lord, I'm fucking tempted. It would be no less than he deserves.

That was before I experienced for myself the true cost of survival. The evil that breeds when you're existing in a world forever weighted against you. We can all be a little monstrous when we're desperate.

"They try to." I touch the slick mess at my throat. "Even when it isn't easy or quick… they can try to make progress."

Stepping closer, I admit defeat and curl my arms around him. Xander shudders against me, his skin chilled and goose pimpled. He hides his face in my hair then grips my hips.

"For what it's worth," he says into my curls. "I'm sorry for the pain we caused you. For all that you suffered through because of our choices."

"I know, Xan."

"I mean it. We put you through hell."

"Well, yes." Pain prickles my throat at the admission. "But I suppose I did the same to you. You were tortured because of me."

Xander chuckles against my head. "It was no less than we deserved."

"As true as that may be, I don't want to hurt you anymore, Xan. I want us to be more than that."

A long pause is filled with the sound of his rapid breathing.

"I thought I knew what I wanted. What… I needed. Now I'm not so sure."

I tilt my head up to look at him. "What do you want right now?"

"Right now?" His tongue darts out to swipe across his bottom lip. "You."

CHAPTER 7
RIPLEY
FIXED BLADE – TRADE WIND

XANDER'S LIPS CAPTURE MINE. The anger that drove our kiss yesterday is absent. Instead, I'm overwhelmed by the urgent intensity his mouth embodies. He isn't punishing me; he's pleading with me. Begging for understanding.

Searching for a way to comprehend what he feels, Xander tattoos a frantic prayer against my lips. The voice that once screamed at me to never let this creature into my head has been beaten into submission.

He pulls my leg up so it hooks on his hip. I'm flush against him, the cold from his naked skin seeping through my t-shirt. His mouth massages mine before he sucks my bottom lip between his teeth to bite down.

I gasp as slick copper seeps between us. The piping hot flow seems to ignite something within Xander. When he squeezes my jaw tight enough to crack bone, the spark of danger makes my soaked core clench.

Stopping for a breath, Xander pushes his thumb through the blood dripping from my lip. He inspects the stained pad before taking his thumb into his mouth to suck it off.

"I want to earn it," he says emphatically.

"Earn what?"

His hand lowers, moving to clasp my injured throat. My mind can't keep up with the rapid fluctuations, a desperate man pleading for forgiveness as he squeezes the wound he inflicted.

This is how he surrenders. Xander could never tear down his

defences without maintaining some control. The pressure at my windpipe demonstrates his internal struggle, fighting to shed his old self.

"You," he repeats. "Your trust."

Releasing my throat, he allows me to suck in a breath. Forcing me to trust him. To believe that even when he holds my life in his hands, he'll give it back to me in the end.

This isn't control.

This is trust.

When his grasp loosens completely, I grab his wrist, encouraging him to do it again. Xander's eyes blow wide. I finally get it. I know what he needs. And right now, I want him to hurt me. I want to give him the pain he needs to inflict.

"You want me like this?" he murmurs, eyelids falling to half-mast.

I nod, my chest searing.

"I'm not a good person, Ripley. I've hurt a lot of people. You included. Why are you still begging for more?"

Controlling my breath, he holds me in suspense until spots appear in my vision. I blink rapidly, unable to form words. The overwhelming pain of being choked feels good in the sickest way possible.

Xander releases me, allowing a short breath. "Well?"

"B-Because… I want y-you."

"How could you possibly want this?" he spits in disgust.

His choking hand caught between us, I lean in to press our foreheads together. "Because I'll always be safe with a villain on my side."

The molten determination that's replaced his icy stare steals my voice. I can handle cold Xander. Calculating Xander. Obsessed Xander. But angry, emotional, fucking *possessive* Xander?

He's a different beast entirely.

A beast I'm longing to tame.

"I'll be your villain if that's what you want."

I nod in total compliance.

"No one is going to lay another finger on you," he promises menacingly. "Not if they want to keep that finger attached."

His expanding pupils are bleeding into his irises, spelling imminent attack. Xander's unfettered attention is an intense force, one that once terrified me. Now it feels fucking magnetic.

He's a powerful riptide holding me captive, repeatedly dunking me beneath the ocean waves, filling my lungs and nose until I'm reliant on his mercy to suck in a single breath.

Abruptly releasing my throat, Xander drops to his knees in front of me. He lifts my oversized tee to seize my waistband. I don't protest as he wriggles my leggings down over my hips and thighs.

Neither of us speaks. Not as he takes his pocketknife to my panties' elastic. Nor as the sliced cotton hits the bedroom floor. And not when his head lowers between my thighs.

His mouth travels from my hip to my public bone, planting wet kisses. I shove my fingers into his hair, fisting the strands tight. His teeth scrape against my sensitive inner thigh, teasing me.

"Xan… please."

"Hush."

My knees are practically knocking together with each second he fails to offer me relief. I'm lightheaded and trembling, the warring sensations inside me too much to hold.

"Be still," he demands.

His mouth descends exactly where I want it, his tongue licking the seam of my pussy. I hold back a shudder, terrified he'll stop if I move an inch. His tongue slides over me before he sucks my clit between his teeth.

"Oh God!" I moan.

Lavishing attention on my sensitive bud, he feasts on my core like a starving man shown a three-course buffet. I buck into his face, silently pleading for more as electric tension coils inside me.

Xander halts, glancing up at me. "I told you to stay still."

"You try to stay still."

Finding his feet, he eyes me with a knowing smirk. "Such a brat."

I yelp when he bends over to grab hold of my bare legs. I'm tossed over his shoulder, carried back to my own rumpled bed. Xander deposits me on the mattress with a huff.

Splayed out on my back, I'm exposed from the waist down. Xander drags his gaze over me, his boxers already straining from a large bulge. He discards the pocketknife on the bed.

The way he's looking at me while he strips is intoxicating. Every inch of Xander is on display for me to drink in. Whenever I see him naked, I learn something new. This time, I study his defined hips, guiding my eyes down to his cock.

He's many things, but shy isn't one of them. Nothing Xander does ever carries a hint of embarrassment. Particularly in the bedroom. He's made no secret of his proclivities, and a wanton part of me loves that.

"Open your legs for me," he commands. "Show me what you want, little toy."

That sick fuck with his stupid nickname.

Holding eye contact, I tug off my t-shirt to reveal my chest. I didn't bother to pull a bra on after my cold shower. My nipples are hardened spikes, tingling under his attention.

Squeezing my right breast, I feel my mouth quirking as I spread my legs wide open. The power I hold over him without a single touch is enough to get drunk on. Far more potent than any drink or illicit drug.

I was his obsession.

Now he watches me like I'm his god.

Playing with my nipple, I twist and tug, moaning with each painful jolt. I can feel the warmth pooling between my thighs, on full display for him to observe. Just his hungry gaze is enough to excite me.

Xander approaches, certain and purposeful. As he braces himself on the bed, moving to taste me again, I lift my leg high. My bare foot connects with his face, pushing him back so he can't lay a finger on me.

"I'll show you," I croon. "But right now… You have to stay still."

Keeping him a length from me, I dip my hand down to my dripping pussy. Xander curses under his breath as I circle my clit, coating my fingers in slick moisture. Holding him back is only making this power play hotter.

When I thrust a finger deep into my cunt, heat sizzles down my spine. I work myself over, stretching my pussy wide before pushing another finger inside. A moan spills from my mouth.

"Fucking hell," Xander rumbles quietly.

"Problem?"

He pushes his face against my foot, trying to get closer. I add more pressure, effectively shoving him backwards. I love humiliating him. Xander winces but doesn't try to move again.

"Stay." I grin broadly.

My hand moves faster. Pulsating back and forth, my walls clench tight around the wet fingers I'm taunting him with. I swipe my clit with each oscillation, using my spare hand to roll my nipple.

"You get to stand there and watch me climax. That's all you're allowed."

He breathes heavily. "Yes."

"Watch me fall apart, Xan."

"Yes." The word sounds like a plea.

"Stand there and watch, knowing how much I love seeing you get a taste of your own medicine."

"Fuck, Ripley… Yes."

I've always sought out a quick fuck during my sexual manic episodes, but I still know how to get myself off. My pussy clamps tight around my fingers as my orgasm explodes through me.

Spine curving, I let my release take over. I'm trembling too hard to stop Xander from wrapping a hand around my ankle.

He's focused on me—every shaky breath, the slippery warmth wetting my hand, my breasts shuddering as I pant for air, blood still leaking from my throat. I've become a filthy mess for him.

"My little toy likes to play games," he purrs, releasing my ankle. "I suppose turnabout is fair play."

Lowering my foot, I brace myself upright on my elbows to scrutinise him. His hand is wrapped firmly around his cock, pumping the veiny steel. It makes my mouth go dry.

"You're damn right it's fair." I trace my tongue over my lips. "Now, why don't you come here and fuck me?"

"I'm allowed to move now?" He quirks an eyebrow.

"Yes. But don't push your luck."

Xander prowls farther onto the bed. "Now, where's the fun in that?"

I shuffle backwards so my head rests on the pillows. He kneels between my legs, his thigh muscles bulging. But he doesn't move. The man hovers stiller than a statue and wears a goddamn smirk.

He scours every inch of me like he's seeing me for the first time. Or perhaps seeing me differently now that our rivalry has been thrown into question. The wait for him to finally snap and take charge is excruciating.

"Xan…"

"Something you want? You seemed quite content to deny me and satisfy yourself a moment ago."

Hissing, I stare up at the white ceiling. "You're a fucking asshole."

"As advertised."

The air displaces around me as I feel his hands seize my body. I'm quickly flipped, so fast I've barely sucked in a shocked breath before my face hits the pillow.

Xander lifts my hips to pull my ass up high before white-hot pain crackles across my left butt cheek. The smack is hard and fast. Fiery tingles spread, bringing a surge of pleasure with them. When he hits me again on the other cheek, I can't hold back a loud moan.

The constantly-shifting dynamic makes me feel raw and untethered. I know damn well that's his intention. He wants all the control for himself. Despite all my bravado, I'm far too ready to give in.

"I want to fuck your beautiful little cunt while I hold your life in my hands," he admits in a rough growl.

Twisted anticipation explodes through me.

"Yes," I mewl. "Do it."

Xander's heated skin brushes against my pebbled nipples as he reaches behind me. Cool metal kisses the side of my neck, behind my jaw. I don't need to see the knife to know that's what it is.

Xander strokes my skin with the razor-sharp edge. "So beautiful."

"I'm not afraid of you." I stifle a groan.

"Maybe you should be."

My body tightens as need pulses between my thighs.

"There are a great many arteries in the human neck," he says conversationally. "Internal and external carotid. Jugular. Vital muscles and branches. So many fragilities."

It shouldn't turn me on to hear his unhinged musings. The man could end my life with a single slash. Once upon a time, I would've been sobbing in terror, convinced he'd do just that.

The pleasure spawns from knowing that he won't. Not now. This Xander wants to hold my still-beating heart in his palm, just so he can put it back behind my ribcage with the memory of his touch.

It aggravates my healing bruises and injuries to be bent over, but the moment his fingers press against my slit, pain is overtaken by near-animalistic need. His finger swirls over my pussy in a cruel taunt.

"So wet," Xander marvels before spanking me again, the jolt causing the knife to shift. "Is all that from putting on your clever little show?"

"Xan... Fuck."

"Or is it the threat of death that gets you so wet?"

"Please, just..."

"Just what?" His palm crashes into my ass so hard, it rattles my bones.

Hiding my face in the pillow, I cry out. Each hit blends agony and ecstasy in an excruciatingly perfect way. I could climax from his punishing spanks alone, I'm so wound up.

Xander slides two fingers into me, stoking the furnace with each deliberate pump. I rock into his hand, desperately trying to relieve myself.

"You asked me to fuck you." He tuts and withdraws them. "So behave."

Fucking behave?

"This is how it's going to work." Xander inserts his fingers into me again and resumes pumping. "I'll give you whatever broken excuse of a soul I have left. In exchange, I want you to make the pain inside me stop."

Fisting the anti-ligature bedsheets, I want to scream at the top of my lungs. Beg him. Plead with him. Use his fucking pocketknife to carve out my heart and offer it to him on a silver platter if it means he'll relent.

"How?" I gasp.

"By giving yourself to me. All of you."

"I... I don't know how."

"You do. It goes like this."

His fingers vanish, but before I can yell out in frustration, I feel his cock plunge into me. He doesn't inch in with any grace or patience. Xander buries himself to the hilt and waits for me to scream out.

The moment I do, he withdraws then slams back home with a loud grunt. He's blasting past my limits and fucking me as roughly as I'd hoped he would.

The room is filled with the sound of our bodies slapping together and my gasps each time his knife slices into me. Feeling every shallow nick is enough to keep the exhilarating danger ever-present. He knows exactly how to push my limits, and my body is addicted to the adrenaline rush.

Melting into a puddle of pure sensation, days of anxiety from watching our world erupt disappears. The fire he's injecting into my veins becomes my whole existence.

Now I'm the one burning.

Happily.

And he can keep the fucking ashes.

Xander keeps me suspended on the edge of the highest cliff as he holds me at knife point, moaning with each flex of his hips. He pulls out almost to the point of withdrawal before surging back in each time.

When he spanks me again, the blow makes his length spasm inside me. We both groan at the same time, overwhelmed by the deep, penetrating vibrations that ignite every last nerve ending.

"You did this to me," he accuses angrily. "You made me care, Ripley. You made me give a shit when no one else could. How?"

I'd laugh if I wasn't terrified of slitting my own throat. Even like this, he's hung up on where the true power lies. He has to be the most obsessive creature I've ever met.

"I don't know," I whisper.

Xander's thrusts gain momentum, becoming deeper and rougher. "Neither do I. That's what terrifies me—not knowing how this stupid, goddamn useless organ in my chest works."

His heat pistoning into me abruptly disappears. I choke back a sob when the knife vanishes from my neck, totally overwhelmed by emotions. Relief. Frustration. The thrill is mind-boggling.

I'm on the verge of shouting at the sadistic son of a bitch when I'm flipped over. My back meets the bed, leaving me sprawled out in front of Xander.

Hovering over me, his sweat-dotted skin betrays how much his control has frayed. He can be passionate, but he was always clinical. There's no sign of that cold fascination right now, though. Obsession, sure.

But it feels personal this time.

Hunger has overtaken him.

Raw, famished, cannibalistic hunger for all the emotion he's never been allowed to feel. Every taut muscle shows how it's overwhelming him. I place a hand on his chest, easing him backwards.

He lets me guide him until he's on his back. Inelegantly manoeuvring myself on top, I ease the bloodied knife from his grip. He's had his fun. Now I want to have mine.

Bracing one hand on his shoulder, I lift the other to my neck. Xander's pupils blow wide as I collect the red spill, smearing it over my palm. His mouth falls open when I seize his cock, smothering it in my blood.

"I've given you all of me," I tell him. "My submission. My trust. My life. Isn't that proof enough that I want you?"

I guide his steel inside me. Xander's eyes roll back in his head when I sink down fully, allowing his bloodstained cock to stretch my internal walls. The crimson lubricant creates a silky mess.

"Goddammit," he hisses out. "Yes. It's enough."

"Then you will give yourself to me. Every day. I want this Xander by my side, not the detached man who felt no remorse for his actions."

Adjusting, he leans back on his hands. "I'm scared, Rip."

Part of me expected a fight, even wanted one. But I think I'm enjoying his vulnerability even more. The scales flipping back in my favour gives me an energy boost, numbing the pain from my aggravated injuries.

I begin to move, lifting my hips and pushing down on him in a steady beat. At this angle, he's breaching me deeply, his cock nudging the sweet spot inside me.

"You should be scared," I say between moans. "If I wanted to, I could take that stupid, goddamn useless organ and shred it to ribbons. But I won't, Xan. You need to trust me."

"I don't... trust anyone," he rasps.

"That's the problem." My nails dig into his shoulders, leaving crescent-shaped grooves. "Even if we can't forgive or forget immediately, we can learn to trust."

Riding him at an increasing pace, I batter my words into him with my body. We're a sweaty mess of limbs, both nearing the edge. The orgasm that's been slowly building is on the cusp of overwhelming me.

Xander drops a hand between us to find my clit. Extra sensitive, all it takes is one swipe through smeared blood to push me into the abyss. I throw my head back, calling his name.

His face buried in my neck, I can feel him finishing too. His body quakes beneath mine, and heat surges into me, creating an irreversible brand. Satisfying heat pulses through me as our essences mix.

The aftershocks continue, burst after burst, fireworks pulling at my skin. My entire body is weak and spent. It's all I can do to collapse against Xander's chest.

My head slumps onto his shoulder, too heavy to hold up. Warmth seeps between us as he catches his breath. Completely drained, we don't move for a long time.

I can't summon a protest when Xander lifts me from his lap to separate us. He lays me down on the bed then curls up beside me. Any hatred I had left dissipates when he lays his head on my stomach.

"Trust is hard for me," he whispers faintly. "I've gotten this far alone."

Stroking through his unkempt hair, the usually silky-soft strands are coarse, in need of a wash. My heart is still hammering relentlessly behind my rib cage. It feels as badly bruised as the rest of me.

"You're not alone, Xan. You have Lennox and Raine."

His palm splays across my belly, leaking warmth. "What about you?"

"I guess I've got this far by myself too."

"You don't have to anymore."

"Don't I?"

"You're not alone now," he explains drily.

"I still feel it. Even when I'm surrounded by people."

"People like us?" Xander queries.

Uncertain, I lick my lips. "Sometimes."

"Well, people care about you. And Raine… I don't want to come between you two. He deserves happiness."

I don't dare speak, unnerved by this new, thoughtful Xander.

"And whether he's ready to admit it or not, Lennox wants something from you too," Xander muses tiredly. "You've managed to ensnare my entire family."

"Should I be apologising for that?" I ask honestly.

His spearmint-scented breath licks my skin. "No. I think it will take all of us to escape what Incendia has planned next."

"They won't go down without a fight." Trepidation crawls through me at the mere thought. "The gates will be blasted open soon enough."

"I agree. When that time comes, we'll need each other."

He falls silent, seemingly lost in thought. Harsh reality is crashing into our post-sex bubble. Violence and threats still surround us on all sides as an invisible clock ticks down to the unknown.

"Perhaps we're meant to be a fucked up family." Xander trails his hand up and down my back. "Maybe that's how we live."

"Together?"

"Exactly," he responds, tracing small circles with his fingertips. "Together."

My heart balloons to absolute breaking point. I want to tell it to brush his exhausted comment off, but that damned, sticky hope can never release its clutches on me. No matter how hard I try.

Family.

Could he possibly mean that?

I'm not sure I even deserve one.

CHAPTER 8
RAINE
SAID & DONE – BAD OMENS

MY ENTIRE BODY is wracked with violent shaking as damp claws sink into me. I'm overwhelmed with sounds, tastes and smells. None of them good. It's making it hard to focus on breathing through the nausea.

Mildew.

Old chlorine.

Floodwater.

Rotten wood.

Each individual scent helps me paint a picture of the place Ripley once brought me to. Only this time, the storm damage has worsened the swimming pool's state of disuse.

"Nox," I choke out.

"Coming. Shit, where are the pills?"

A scuffle betrays his frantic efforts to sort through our supplies. We weren't able to grab much when we fled the medical wing. A horde of patients came searching for food, drugs or weapons. They weren't exactly calm either.

Another burst of nausea causes pain to build behind my eyes. My stomach revolts, and it takes all my self-control to hold my meagre breakfast of stale cereal bars down. I can't afford to waste the food we scrounged up.

"For fuck's sake," Lennox hisses, clearly in pain.

"Be careful. You're still hurt. I can wait for Langley to get back."

"You need your damn pills, Raine. You look like shit."

I'd send him a glower if I knew where he was standing, searching through our two bags. I can hear his movements, but with all the dripping water and sporadic breezes, my spatial awareness is being thrown for a loop.

"Gee, thanks. You're always so complimentary."

"And you're a fucking idiot for waiting this long to take your dose," he hits back. "You know it takes the edge off the withdrawals."

"I'm trying to ration the pills. They're all I've got."

Another worry to add to the ever-expanding list. The longer the riot drags on, the more desperate our situation is becoming. I had one bottle of pills prescribed by Doctor Hall when it all went to hell.

No refills.

Without the methadone to manage my withdrawals, I don't want to consider what state I'll be in. Getting clean from several years of opioid use won't be an easy fix. I feel shitty enough even with the pills.

The sound of tablets clashing against plastic brings sharp relief. I hear Lennox's faint *aha* before his slow footsteps approach. He's up and moving but still in considerable pain, judging by his laboured breathing.

"Got them," he announces. "We'll find more."

"Where from, Nox?"

"I don't know, but we will," he insists. "I'm not watching you suffer. We both know that going cold turkey could kill you without help."

"But—"

"Take your fucking pills, Raine."

I suppose it's ironic, really.

I'm going through this self-inflicted torture to kick my addiction for the last time. But to do that, I'm dependent on a handful of synthetic pills. I can't truly escape the power they still hold over me.

"Here, man." Rough fingertips touch my hand where I'm crouched against the wall. "How many do you need?"

"I'll do it. Pass them here."

"You need water?" Lennox asks.

Nodding, I close my fist around the pill bottle dropped into my palm. Lennox shuffles away, still trying to hide his pained grunting, and quickly returns with the sound of crackling plastic.

"Thanks."

"Yeah," he acknowledges. "Please just tell me next time? You look paler than a ghost. I could've found the pills hours ago."

Counting out my dose, I knock back the handful then let my head rest against the cold, cinder block wall. I doubt the pills will help my aggressive shivering. It's freezing cold in here.

Langley went searching for the other two and more food. Ripley and Xander have been missing since she stormed out. In this strange, lawless period, two days is a lifetime.

"That dickhead has been gone all night." Lennox loudly slumps back down. "You reckon some idiot's captured him for ransom?"

"Don't say that, Nox."

"I mean, it's possible. He is a guard."

"Apparently not. What's the deal with his… I dunno, colleague? The woman Ripley mentioned? Sounds like she works for these Sabre people."

His breathing catches. It always does anytime the topic of the Z wing or their escape is broached. Lennox plays a good game, but I've learned to read his unconscious tells. What he saw down there has left its mark.

"I don't know," he deflects.

"What happened?"

Lennox shuffles on the hard floor. "Some pink-haired bitch pretending to work for Incendia was torturing me. Maintaining cover, I guess. She admitted she was undercover and offered to get us out."

"Like… out of Harrowdean?" I enquire.

"Yeah. Ripley told her to leave us there."

"Why?" Confusion sits heavy in my voice.

"She refused to run without me." He clears his throat, sounding like he was barely able to utter the words.

I'd give anything to see his expression right now. To have even the smallest clue to the secret feelings he's harbouring. I've long suspected there's more to his hatred for Ripley, but recent events have made the situation ten times more complicated.

"That's why she helped you escape." I nod in understanding. "Ripley couldn't leave you there to die."

Lennox doesn't respond.

"Because… she cares about you."

Nothing but a sharp inhalation.

Come on, stubborn bastard.

"And you care about her," I add.

He still won't say it.

Not even to me.

Bizarrely, it frustrates me more than it angers me. I'm not even jealous. I just want him to admit it. Until then, we can't make any decisions on how to proceed.

"You can't avoid this conversation forever, Nox. Like it or not, the three of us are in neck-deep with this girl. I need to know where you stand."

"I…" He pauses. "Don't know."

"You don't know?"

"Ripley and I… It's complicated."

"You don't say," I mutter sarcastically.

"I know, alright?" he snaps in exasperation. "We've spent months trying to kill each other, for fuck's sake. Then in the basement… Well, things changed. Now I'm fucking lost."

"What does that mean, exactly?"

"I don't know!" Lennox exclaims. "What's with the third degree?"

"Oh, I don't know. May have something to do with the fact you tried to kill the woman I'm in love with! Did that ever cross your mind?"

My words drop with the impact equivalent to a street-level explosion, holding the power to blow our entire lives apart. I can feel them reverberating in the chlorinated air as my confession lingers.

"You love her," he deadpans.

My throat aches with unspoken emotion. "I wouldn't get clean for just anyone, Nox. I want a future. One with Ripley in it."

The sound of his teeth grinding is a loud bullet in the silence. "Does she know?"

"It's complicated," I throw his words back at him. "She made it clear we were just casual for a long time. Then everything happened… Now I'm not so sure what we are."

"And the fact that Xander's got some fucked up claim on the woman you apparently love doesn't bother you?"

"Does it bother you?" I counter.

Teeth grinding. A sharp breath. More grinding.

"Who Ripley chooses to spread her legs for is none of my concern," Lennox replies flatly. "And frankly, she can do whatever the fuck she wants."

"Right. Because you don't care."

"Right," he repeats.

For all his fierce loyalty and commitment to his family, Lennox can be a thick-skulled bastard. This ridiculous denial phase is doing none of us any favours.

"I have no idea what your problem is, but you need to figure it out. Fast." I take another drink from the plastic water bottle. "I won't stand for you hurting Ripley ever again."

"If I wanted her dead, she would be," he says ominously. "We made it out of that wing together."

"Then fucking get over yourself!"

I want to get up and storm far away from him, but even if I could see to navigate the destruction we're hiding in, I doubt my shaking legs would hold me. The pills haven't kicked in yet.

Instead, I rest against the wall, focusing on anything but the pain fracturing my skull in two. I'd kill for a line right now. Even a single hit. Enough to take the edge off.

The awkward silence wraps around me like a blanket as Lennox stews. I have no concept of what time it is. The sharp hunger pains intermingling with my constant nausea are the only indications that several hours have passed.

Slipping into a trance-like state of deep concentration in an effort to manage my sickness, I startle back to reality when a loud bang permeates the building. Lennox curses, disturbing something as he moves.

"We've got company," he announces.

"Nobody knows about this place but us."

"Maybe that asshole Langley has given up searching?"

"Doesn't seem likely," I reply worriedly. "He was determined."

Bracing myself on the floor, I try to push myself up. I feel a little stronger though still shaky and weak. My spine doesn't leave the wall as I slide upright, trembling like a leaf.

Distinct footsteps are growing closer. Multiple pairs. Hope flares in my chest, but the very real possibility that more unruly patients looking to pick a fight have found us is acute.

"Just give them what they want," I whisper-shout. "You can't fight anyone off with one working hand, Nox."

"No one is stealing our shit. I'll crack their spines first."

"It doesn't matter!"

Between the two of us, one injured and one barely able to stand, we can't put up much of a fight if people are here searching for supplies. That's precisely why we abandoned the safety of the medical wing.

A resounding voice ends our bickering.

"You could've left a damn note!"

"A note? Seriously?"

"Well, I don't know! Anything but vanishing!"

The voices quickly burst the fearful balloon that's expanded inside me. Part of me was terrified I'd never hear her razor-sharp tongue chewing someone out ever again.

"It's them," I breathe out, letting myself slump in relief.

Lennox sighs, though I can't hear him moving to greet the others. The voices are nearing, exchanging heated whispers. Langley, Ripley and Xander. They're all safe. Thank fuck.

The door to the swimming pool slamming open announces their return. Taking a deep breath in, I feel myself smile. Papaya. The tropical fruitiness is like a homing beacon guiding me back to her.

"Raine!"

I could collapse from relief. "Guava girl."

"Did you show them my secret hiding place?"

Her rapid steps magnetise her to me. The familiar scent I've come to know and adore envelopes me as Ripley pulls me into her arms. I snuggle into her chest, getting a face full of fruity curls, but I couldn't be happier.

"Nah," I murmur.

"So how did you find your way back?"

"My idea," Lennox rumbles from far-off.

"I should've known," Ripley mutters acidly.

Squeezing me tight enough to ache, I feel Ripley running her hands all over me. Two small hands cup my cheeks, bringing warmth to my cold, clammy skin. She feels like a blissful furnace.

"You're pale and sweaty," she worries. "Withdrawals?"

"I'm fine, Rip."

"Nothing about you looks fine. Aren't you taking the pills Doctor Hall prescribed?"

"Under protest," Lennox supplies. "He looks better now than he did a few hours ago."

"Raine! You have to take them."

"I forced them down him," Lennox adds.

"Good." Ripley squeezes my hand.

I'm not sure how I feel about being the only thing these two agree on right now.

Using the memory of Ripley's body, I eventually find her jaw and begin searching it with my fingertips. Her face still feels swollen and a little hot to touch. My fingers coast over her neck, stopping when I feel several crusted cuts on her skin.

"What are these?" I ask, panic riding me hard. "Are you hurt?"

"It's nothing," she rushes to assure me. "I was coming back to find you guys when I found Xander. We holed up overnight to rest."

Oh.

Perhaps I shouldn't pull at that thread. I'm not about to judge how the pair sort their shit out as long as she… erm, consents. Then it's fair game, I suppose. Ripley is her own woman.

The sound of huffing follows something heavy hitting the floor.

"You lot were supposed to stay put."

I jolt at the sound of Xander's voice. "We had no choice."

"Let's agree not to split up again," Xander suggests.

A throat clears. Langley. "Well, about that."

Pulling away from me, I sense Ripley turn around to face the others. I snag hold of her t-shirt to keep her within touching distance.

"What does that mean?" she asks suspiciously.

"I need to re-establish communication with my team," Langley explains. "My mobile phone was in the staff lockers when the riot broke out. If it's still charged, I can use it to contact the others."

"Why didn't you check while you were out searching?" Xander asks.

"Because I was preoccupied by looking for you two," he claps back. "I do have priorities."

Xander has the good sense to stifle any response.

"Sabre can tell us what's unfolding outside," Langley continues. "We need to know when the authorities will move in. Perhaps we can still cut a deal."

"Perhaps?" Ripley barks. "You made that sound like my only option!"

"It is, Rip."

"Like hell it is."

"Look, I can't keep you safe if I'm hiding here, waiting for the fucking SWAT team to move in and start handcuffing everyone to be shipped off. It needs to be done now."

"You can't go out there." Ripley attempts to pull away from me.

Tugging her t-shirt again, I haul her back to my front. I can feel her trembling in the pointed nodes of her spine. Regardless of her anger, Ripley does care for Langley. And right now, guards are far more at risk than any of us.

"I have no choice," he justifies. "And I can take care of myself."

"What if you're taken hostage too? You didn't see Rick out there. He was waving around a stolen gun like a lunatic and threatening to shoot! This is serious!"

"Out where?" Lennox chimes in.

Ripley vibrates with a long sigh. "There were journalists outside the gate, filming us all. I watched Rick parade the guards out to make his demands to the world."

"Rick won't be making any demands for a while." Xander's tone belies a hint of pride. "Though I wish it were permanent."

"Don't pretend you beat the shit out of him to stop the riot," Ripley challenges. "He was unconscious at your feet before you found me."

"You're right," he submits without hesitation. "That's not why I did it."

Xander's reply is silky smooth. Utterly shameless. Judging by Ripley's sharp breath in, a hell of a lot more happened while they were *resting*. I'm weirdly satisfied by Xander's clear possessiveness.

The more people looking out for Ripley, the better. Having Xander on her side is the equivalent of having a fanatical cult running headfirst into war for you. He'll do anything to defend those he deems worthy.

"The point is," Langley draws the conversation back to him. "If I can make arrangements with my team, we can find a way out of here."

Chuffing rudely, I can almost taste Lennox's mistrust. But Ripley doesn't give him a chance to speak for her.

She presses herself into me, seeking reassurance. "It can't go on for much longer. Something has to give."

"All the more reason for me to go now," Langley argues. "While we still have a chance."

"What would a deal entail?" Xander queries.

"Full cooperation in exchange for protection. You know we've done it with other inmates. If Incendia moves in first, I can guarantee that you will all disappear."

Wrapping my arms around Ripley's midsection, I hold her close. She's in their firing line, but Xander and Lennox aren't exactly innocent either. Hell, I'll be guilty by association. We'll all be erased.

"Go then," Ripley whispers.

"Rip—"

"No." She speaks over me, her voice gaining volume. "Go make contact. We'll wait here. But I want protection for everyone—Xander, Lennox and Raine. I'm not doing this without them."

Not even Lennox has a comment to make as he processes her words. The magnitude of her request keeps them both trapped in silence.

"I never should've viewed you as a mark to be flipped," Langley says in a low voice, footsteps coming towards us. "I'm sorry for that. I'll make this right, Rip. I promise."

"You were doing your job," she eventually replies. "Just like I was doing mine."

"That doesn't make what I've done right."

"Well, me neither. But we all make mistakes." She pulls free from my arms. "Please be safe."

From the ruffling of fabric, I think they embrace. Ripley steps back into me shortly after as Langley clears his throat.

"There's something else," he begins with a hint of uncertainty. "I guess the time for disguises is over, right?"

"Langley? What is it?"

"That's not my name." His feet retreat, crunching over debris. "My name is Warner. You deserve to know that."

Bombshell dropped, he hastily leaves. The silence stretches on until the sound of the exit door slamming shut breaks it. Ripley is leaning so heavily into me, I wonder how she's upright at all.

"What now?" Ripley murmurs.

"Now we wait. And try not to die."

"Fuck," she whispers back.

Yep. Fuck indeed.

CHAPTER 9
RIPLEY
GOD NEEDS THE DEVIL – JONAH KAGEN

ROLLING OVER on the folded cardboard box I'm using as a mattress, I tighten a stolen green parka around myself, ignoring the pain from my shoulder and hip digging into the hard floor.

Even if I were comfortable, I'm too agitated to sleep. The invisible fire ants are back. After a week since my last medication dose, it's inevitable. I'm surprised it took this long to set in.

I've managed to keep the signs to myself so far. Shaking hands. Agitation. Rising anxiety. I thought I'd adjust, but if this is an impending manic episode, I won't be able to keep it quiet.

The sounds of sleep around me offer a small sliver of comfort. Raine and Lennox are both napping while waiting for daylight. We've been taking refuge around the abandoned pool for the last two days, living off odd snacks shared between all four of us.

Warner hasn't returned.

Each passing hour is excruciating.

I can only assume that something went wrong, but when I suggested I go look, it was met with a resounding chorus of denials. Even from Raine. Xander stormed off to skulk around the abandoned building when I raised it again a while ago.

When did I sign up for three possessive men to tell me what I can and can't do? Even if I did barter for their lives, it doesn't give them the right to start this controlling shit. Our truce won't last long if this continues.

"I can practically hear the gears in your brain grinding," Raine whispers into the early dawn light. "Did you sleep at all?"

"How am I supposed to sleep?" I growl back.

"Typically, it involves closing your eyes, getting comfortable, dreaming about a stunningly attractive, blind violinist who can make your wildest dreams come true with his tongue…"

"Ha. Someone thinks highly of himself."

"That's not a disagreement. So you do love my tongue."

Huffing, I awkwardly turn over to face him. Raine is sleeping next to me, less than a metre between our cardboard boxes. Lennox opted to sleep beside him, still keeping a safe distance from me.

Raine is curled up on his side, the rich caramel of his unfocused eyes gleaming in the morning light. Beneath his golden locks sticking up in all directions, his gaze bounces around haphazardly.

"We can't just lay here and wait forever," I hiss under my breath. "What if he's been captured by Rick's merry band of idiots? Or he's injured? Or…"

"Rip," Raine interrupts. "Time out. Langley—or Warner—he's a big boy. He can look out for himself. You going out there is a shitty idea that we've already proven sucks."

"He needs our help!"

"We need to help ourselves," he disagrees. "That starts with laying low until we have a decent plan. The longer this goes on, the worse it's going to get."

Deep down, I know Raine's right. The nightly screams now bleed into daytime. From our hiding spot, I've heard bonfires crackling outside at all hours, the smoke leaking in through the broken roof and windows.

For the last two nights, we've been plunged into darkness to preserve our waning flashlight. The pitch-black cloak only intensifies the awful sounds all around us.

I've startled awake to wailing and sobbing several times. Sounds of people being assaulted. More brutal fights. Starving patients are turning to desperate measures to ride the riot out.

Something has to give. If Incendia's plan is to wait this out, it isn't working. Exhaustion and hunger aren't starving out the violence; it's just fuelling it. And Harrowdean's patient population has plenty to be angry about.

"How long was the longest prison riot? Like, ever?"

"In this country?" Raine questions. "I dunno. A couple weeks, maybe?"

"We've been trapped in limbo for almost a whole week now. It won't last much longer, surely?"

Skin prickling with trapped energy, I begin to scratch at my arms and neck, savouring the bite of pain. My injuries are healing well as the evidence of our torture slowly disappears. The memories remain just as raw, though.

I've seen the shadows in Lennox's eyes. He blinks them away when he catches me staring and always averts his gaze. We've woken up to the sound of him thrashing about in nightmare-filled sleep multiple times too.

The back and forth of my ping-ponging thoughts is only worsened by the physical symptoms I'm trying to ignore. I scratch my arms to the point of bleeding, watching the blood vessels burst in bright-purple streaks.

"Rip," Raine croons.

Ignoring him, I keep scratching. Harder. Rougher. My skin stains red from abrasions. The thick, gnarly scars beneath my touch are a harsh taunt. *Harrowdean's whore.* I've memorised each letter by touch alone.

Look at her now.

I'm a fucking coward.

With each second ticking away, I can feel the devil breathing down our necks. But in this case, the devil has a human face. One that now infiltrates every restful moment I manage to find.

Bancroft won't let me go unpunished. My uncle told me enough stories about his associate long before I experienced his cold calculation firsthand. He rules the corporation with an iron fist.

Now he's out there. Plotting and moving his chess pieces into place. I'll never take his silence for defeat. It's deliberate. The calm before a violent storm that destroys everything in its path.

Is my uncle helping him now?

Will he cheer Bancroft on when I'm sacrificed?

"Rip! Come here."

The sharp snap of Raine's command interrupts my downward spiral. I look over at him, sitting up and wearing a concerned frown that's directed in my vicinity.

"Now," he adds.

Blinking hard, I move robotically. My stiff body protests as I crawl over to him on quivering limbs. Raine grunts when I slam into him, climbing onto his lap and banding my legs around his waist.

"Shit, babe. You're shaking."

He strokes my back, letting me plaster against his chest like a fucking limpet. I want to crawl inside his skin and hide there until this is all over. I don't have to be brave around him.

"I'm scared," I admit shakily. "I can't hide it anymore."

I've spent years burying my fear, pretending to be some formidable badass, when deep down I'm just fucking terrified. I trust Raine to understand and protect that vulnerability.

"Breathe, Rip. I know how hard this is. We have to sit tight."

"Breathe?" I laugh. "We're going to die!"

"We're not going to die."

"Says who?"

"Says me," Raine insists fiercely. "You need to calm down."

Rocking back and forth, his attempts to soothe me fall on deaf ears. I may not be thinking logically, but my sudden urgency to be anywhere but here makes complete sense to my overwhelmed mind.

My head feels like it's on fire. The slow burn of rising hysteria only needed acknowledging for it to take full control. It's rushing in now, setting aflame anything in its path and gathering speed with each second.

We're running out of food. Freezing cold and constantly soaking wet. No medication. We have just a single flashlight with very limited life remaining. No plan for rescue or escape. Even Raine's withdrawal meds are running low.

My big, grand decision not to run is going to get us all quietly killed. That's how they'll keep our stories silent, and there's nothing I can do to stop it. We'll be forgotten. Erased. The slate wiped clean like it always is.

"Ripley," Raine urges. "Come back. I'm here. You're safe."

"We are not safe!"

"From the world? Fuck no." He chuckles bitterly. "But you'll always be safe with me."

I want that to be enough. It *is* enough. All I've ever wanted, beneath the role I've played, is for someone to make me feel safe in a world determined to prove otherwise. But I want Raine safe too, and that won't happen here.

"Come on, babe." Sliding a hand into my hair, he gently massages my head. "Focus on my voice. Can you feel my breathing?"

"Yes," I gasp.

"Good girl. Pay attention to it. I want you to block everything else out. It's just us."

Squeezing my eyes shut, I focus on the feel of his body pressing into mine. The lines I've memorised over the weeks and months. Soft angles. Muscled ridges. The smell of fresh oranges and tangy sea salt.

In a terrifying world, Raine is a solid constant. The confident, smirking jokester hiding a lifetime of trauma behind blacked-out lenses. Everything about him defies the odds. He's living proof of human resilience.

It's what first intrigued me, back when he was just another patient, sniffing around for contraband. The silver-tongued flirt with all the right words. Every syllable interwoven with deep, irrecoverable pain.

"Don't let the fear win, Rip. We're all afraid. Defeated. Exhausted. That just means we're winning the fight—because we're still alive to feel all those things."

"For how much longer?" I squirm on his lap.

"That I can't say. But I think every single one of us has proven that we're kinda difficult to kill. We've all survived shit beyond most people's worst nightmares. We can survive this too."

His fingers pressing into my skull causes me to flinch. My body is wound so tight, every small sensation is agonisingly intense. I don't know if I need to fight, fuck or flee. I'm longing for the oblivion of sedatives.

"Tell me what you need," Raine begs.

I can't possibly answer him, and the stirrings of another prevent me from having to confess.

"What's going on?" Lennox asks groggily.

With his long limbs stretched out, it takes him a moment to sit upright. He blinks rapidly to clear his seafoam eyes. Spotting me in Raine's lap, his spine stiffens.

"What is it?"

"She's okay," Raine replies in a gravelly rasp. "Just… struggling."

"Struggling?" I let out a strangled sound.

"You're supposed to be breathing, Rip. Not arguing."

"While we're sitting here waiting to be slaughtered? And Warner is out there risking his life! This is fucking stupid!"

When I try to climb off Raine's lap, determined to do what's necessary to abate the storm brewing beneath my skin, I find myself trapped.

"Stay." His arms imprison me in a steel cage, pinning me to his chest. "You're not going anywhere until you've calmed down."

"You can't fucking make me, Raine! I need... I can't... I..."

Running out of words, tears hit me hard and fast. The wave of mental torture rises from a deep well, a poisonous smog that gains speed until it's sweeping over me in a pyroclastic cloud.

"She's losing it." Lennox narrows his gaze on me.

"No shit, Sherlock. You want to try?"

"Isn't she your problem?"

The cruel bite of his words lashes into me, slashing skin and bone. Turning my tear-blurred gaze on Lennox, I want him to see just how much power the heartless bastard holds.

The power to heal.

The power to break.

The power to end it all.

"I c-could've run and left you to die," I snarl at him. "I could've been f-fucking free and safe right now."

"Maybe you should have gone," he replies softly.

"Is that what you want, Nox? To be rid of me?"

Sitting up straighter, he scrubs his hand down his face, careful to avoid the gauze on his cheek. Frustration quickens my pulse when I don't get the answer I want.

The old Lennox was as cruel as he was sadistic. That in itself was safe. Predictable. Not this weird, introspective in between who runs so hot and cold.

"Answer me!" I thrash in Raine's arms.

"If it means you're safe, then yes!" Lennox suddenly yells back. "That's what I want! You... gone!"

The tears filling my eyes run over like burst riverbanks, the hot dribbles coating my cheeks and jaw. For once, Lennox stares back without flinching. A turbulent hurricane swirls in his conflicted gaze.

"Nox," Raine scolds. "Shut up."

"She asked for an answer."

"You didn't have to give that one! Fuck!"

Looking at Raine, the mental assault only intensifies. I'm surrounded by my failure on all sides. The man I saved who doesn't want me and the one who wants me so much I've ruined his life.

"I'm going to find Warner." I wipe my tears aside.

"No." Raine refuses to release his grip. "You're staying right here."

"Let me go! Now!"

"He doesn't speak for me, guava girl. I'm selfish enough to admit I want you here, even if it means you're in the firing line with us. At least we're together."

Raine's head lowers to my chest, the only place he can reach as I continue to fight his hold. I'd expect this from one of the others, but not my Raine. I hate how this horror show is changing us all.

He kisses my chest and clavicles exposed by the loose t-shirt's neckline. The small, simple touches are an attempt to distract me from spiralling.

"I know you're scared," he breathes into my skin. "But you didn't make a mistake by choosing to stay. You chose us."

Each kiss he lavishes me with drives his words home. I hate that Lennox is sitting right there, witnessing our intimacy, yet I'm also glad he's forced to see what he'll never have.

"Let us choose you back," Raine pleads. "Let us carry the burden with you. Let us help you get through this."

Lips coasting up my neck then skimming my jaw, I pour all my focus into the feel of his touch. Each gentle, delicate kiss. I home in on the way it contrasts the hatred I still feel pouring from Lennox's glower.

"Raine," I whine. "We have company."

"Ignore him, babe. Let the asshole see exactly what he's missing because he's being too stubborn to change."

Then his lips meet mine—plush and attentive. Raine pushes his mouth on mine to drive out every last horrid thought causing me to fracture. The kiss is passionate, demanding, full of desperation.

Pressure sears into the side of my head, intensifying Raine's firm kiss. I know Lennox is watching intently. What I don't know is how he's going to react. Not anymore.

Hysteria turns red-hot and liquifies as it fills my veins. Treacle-like heat pumps through me, warming my extremities even in the building's chill. I can feel every solid inch of Raine beneath me.

His tongue glides into my mouth, exploring every corner in his bid to pull me back from the brink. The fire ants morph into tiny, pleasurable explosions that cause my hips to shift.

I think I hear Lennox choke on a breath. Yet I couldn't care less. Not when Raine responds in kind and bucks up into me, the heat from his growing erection hitting my core.

"Rip," he breaks the kiss to rasp. "Let's... just take a minute. You're upset."

"Shut up, Raine."

Glancing to the side, I lock onto Lennox's hard stare. The column of heat stirring the still waters in his eyes encourages me to slam my lips back on Raine's mouth.

Fuck him.

He doesn't want me?

Fine. Raine does.

I don't care if it's the adrenaline talking. If a week of barely sleeping has frayed my sanity and I'm on the verge of an unmedicated breakdown. I need this release. Just the thought of it is already loosening my lungs.

Grinding on his hardening cock, I enjoy each toe-curling spike the friction brings. A groan builds in Raine's throat as he kisses me back, painting a bruise onto my lips.

His grip has slackened so he can clutch my hips, giving me room to touch him. I drag my hands down his chest, stopping at the waistband of the borrowed jeans he still wears.

I make short work of unclasping the button and pushing a hand inside. Lennox can continue watching if he likes. He can also fuck off to kingdom come for all I care.

Shifting backwards, I guide Raine's length free from his jeans. He groans when my hand clasps around his velvety cock, stroking the shaft in a slow tease.

"Watch your friend fuck my throat, Nox," I taunt brazenly. "Watch what I let him do to me. Watch what you could be doing... if only you cared."

Kneeling in front of Raine, I drag my tongue across his entire length, from tip to base. His cock jerks in my hands in time to his hissed breathing.

I don't spare Lennox a single glance as I suck Raine deep into my mouth. When his tip nudges the back of my throat, I lift my head, swirling my tongue back up to the end before taking him deep once more.

"Goddammit," Raine grinds out. "You're going to be the death of me."

Not him.

Just his asshole friend.

With each suck, I rotate my head to lick around his engorged cock. The light scrape of teeth causes Raine to curse again. Hearing him moaning in pleasure only spurs me on.

I'm going to make him fill my mouth with his seed just so Lennox can see me swallow it. If he wants to play mind games, I can give just as good as I get.

Raine fists a hand in my short hair, using his grip to guide my movements. Each time he pushes me down, his hips lift to glide in deeper. I happily let him fuck my mouth.

Each thrust makes moisture gather in the corners of my eyes. I don't mind his roughness, though. I want Raine to feel good, to let go even if only for a second. For the burdens he's carried for me, he deserves no less.

"That's it," he encourages in a low rasp. "You take me so well, babe."

The burn of each pump is oh-so-satisfying. I love that he's completely disregarding Lennox and taking exactly what he wants. Something tells me Raine is just as mad as I am at the stubborn bastard.

Each tug on my short curls makes warmth pool at the apex of my thighs. I'm already clenched tight with need. At this rate, I'll let him strip me bare, bend me over and fuck me on full display.

In my periphery, I can see Lennox is unmoved. The man's frozen to the spot. He doesn't even have the shame to look away. I feel fucking powerful, yet I hate myself at the same time for even caring.

"Rip," Raine moans languidly.

His jean-clad thighs are tensing beneath my palms, telling me he's close. Increasing my speed, I'm determined to wring every drop of bliss from him. I want his complete and utter surrender.

"I'm going to pour myself down your throat, guava girl."

His cock jerks in my mouth, spasming with the force of his orgasm. My pussy quivers at the sensation of driving Raine to the brink. I don't stop sucking until he groans loudly, the hot spurts of his seed hitting my throat.

His painfully tight clasp on my hair loosens. Stilling, I slowly pull my mouth from Raine's cock, wiping at my bottom lip with a single finger. He's a panting mess beneath me, his liquid gold gaze burning bright.

I tilt my head to see Lennox. Eyes narrowed. Lips wet. Two wide pupils melt the skin from my bones with the violence of an acid attack. He doesn't blink as I make a show of swallowing Raine's come.

"Are you still here?" I ask bluntly.

Lips parted, Lennox sits stock-still. Stares. Falters.

"You may want me gone, but I'm right where I belong." I refuse to look away from him. "You're the one who should go if you don't want this."

His mouth opens and closes, like words are forming on the tip of his tongue. His facial expression twists and transforms, rapidly shifting between anger, lust and... Is that jealousy? Oh, fucking perfect. He's pathetic.

Squirming with need, I'm tempted to let Raine return the favour. Would that cause Lennox to relent? Seeing me ride his friend's face? I want to know just how far I can push him before he breaks.

"Rip." Lennox's lips form a narrow strip of anger. "I—"

The doors to the swimming pool being tossed open cuts him off. Xander runs in, his face flushed. He skids to a halt as Raine quickly rights himself, zipping up his jeans.

"Helicopters overhead," Xander rushes out.

"What?" Raine gasps.

"I was on the roof. I counted dozens of men, armed and wearing protective gear. The journalists have all been cleared out. Their weapons... I saw bullets."

"Bullets?" I repeat.

"This isn't a rescue mission. They're going to storm the institute and clear it out by force. No cameras, no witnesses."

"Shit." Lennox gapes at him. "What do we do?"

"We need to move. Now."

Focusing on me, Xander's face is grave.

"Incendia is coming."

CHAPTER 10
RIPLEY
OUT OF STYLE – KID BRUNSWICK & BEAUTY SCHOOL DROPOUT

I'M ALWAYS PREPARED.

Harrowdean was my grand master plan.

Shoving dirty clothes, half-filled water bottles and the last of our scavenged supplies into my backpack, I realise how far I've fallen. My grand fucking plan lies in tatters. Along with my entire life.

I thought I had it all figured out. For a whole year, I made myself untouchable. Above reproach. An object of terror and fascination. That power was heady, but now I'm paying the ultimate price.

We're fleeing for our lives.

Lost, traumatised and alone.

"Pack faster!" Xander barks. "We need to move."

I accidentally drop the last remaining bag of sweets we have in our stash. The bag hits the floor, but before I can scoop it up, a bandaged hand grabs the bag for me.

"Here," Lennox mutters gruffly.

Snatching the sweets from his grasp, I shove them in the backpack. "Where the hell are we going to go?"

"I don't know."

"Then we shouldn't be running at all!"

"They're not coming in peacefully," he states plainly. "Weapons and riot gear hardly spell out a calm, orderly evacuation."

Avoiding looking at him, I continue shoving everything I can lay my hands on into the bag. Terror has condensed into laser-sharp focus. Adrenaline has a way of simplifying even the most complex emotions.

"Has anyone seen my guide stick and glasses?" Panic drips from Raine's words.

"Go help him." I gesture wildly.

Lennox straightens then moves to help Raine locate his belongings. After the show I just put on, being thrown into a life-and-death situation with him feels like a bad joke.

"Are we ready?" Xander questions.

"Warner's still out there." I zip the backpack and toss it over my shoulder. "We need to find him."

"There isn't time." He grimaces, shifting on his feet. "They'll breach the gates at any moment. We have to leave now before it's too late."

"And go where?" Raine asks timidly.

"I don't know... but if we stay, we'll be killed. Therefore, we run."

"This isn't a time for your stone-cold logic, Xan!" I snap at him. "Rick and the others swore to kill the hostages if anyone entered Harrowdean."

"I'm aware."

"If they've captured Warner... he's as good as dead."

"How is that our problem?" Xander throws his hands in the air.

"He's my friend!"

"Your friend didn't come back," Lennox interjects. "Perhaps his priorities lie elsewhere."

I flash him a furious look. "I'm not leaving without him."

"Would you prefer to stay here and be shot between the eyes when those men storm the institute?" Xander clips out.

"Obviously not!" I explode. "But... fuck! Where can we run? We have nothing. No money. Nowhere to go. We need Warner."

"Incendia's men are here to get the hostages out alive," Xander reasons. "If Warner has been captured, he'll be rescued. If he's in hiding, he'll be safe soon enough. Unlike us."

He's lying through his fucking teeth right now. There's no guarantee Warner will make it out alive, even if reinforcements have arrived. I don't even know if his cover is intact or if Incendia will kill him too.

"Xander's right." Lennox taps Raine's hand to pass his located items. "If we stay, we'll be dead by nightfall. Either way, we can't help him from here."

"So what? We make a run for it?" I laugh.

"I'll die running before I die on my knees." Xander picks up a bag and swings it over his shoulder. "They're storming the gates. No one is watching the perimeter."

Raine unfolds his guide stick as Lennox takes a final look around. We're running dangerously low on essentials. This plan sounds a lot like suicide. I don't know if we can even get beyond the perimeter fence.

"Let's move." Xander casts a final glance around. "No splitting up, no one gets left behind. Remove anyone who gets in the way."

"No!" I protest. "We said we'd stay and fight. I'm not running scared!"

Tapping his way over to me, Raine clasps my face. He softly strokes my cold skin, his sunglass-covered eyes reflecting my own terror back at me.

"We can't fight this if we're dead," he says quietly. "I want to see Incendia taken down too. Of course, I do. But this isn't the place to do it."

"But—"

"Please, Rip. We have to go. I need you to be safe, not killed by Harrowdean's thugs or captured by the authorities investigating them. Then we can fight this war until the end."

Strangled by miniature knives cutting into my lungs, I can only nod. The words refuse to surface. Xander turns to leave as Lennox claps Raine on the shoulder.

"I'll take the rear," he announces. "Xan, help Raine."

Throwing me a loaded look, Lennox waits for me to step past him before slipping in behind. Xander leads the way out of the main swimming pool room with Raine, through the mould-ridden corridors and outside.

We step into the crisp dawn air as a group, all on high-alert. This part of the institute is always quiet, shrouded in mist and ominously swaying willow trees that obscure the outside world.

The abandoned swimming pool is surrounded by older, disused buildings separate from the main manor. I'm not surprised there aren't any other patients hanging around, though signs of destruction litter the grounds.

"Jesus," Lennox grunts behind me. "Did they leave any furniture inside?"

Eyeing a nearby smouldering bonfire with a blackened bed frame still intact, I choke on the cloying ash that hangs in the air. The destruction has gone beyond a defiant PR stunt now.

Loud humming rings above us through the interlocking birch trees. We're still tucked into the dense foliage that hides the abandoned building, giving us a precious few seconds to take in the scene.

"Our best bet is the rear fence on the south side of the property." Xander studies the landscape. "Farthest away from where all the attention is right now."

"What if they're patrolling the perimeter?" Raine whispers fearfully.

"We can handle it," Lennox answers.

I snort in amusement. "With your one working hand?"

Before Lennox can snark back, Xander intervenes. "Focus. We don't have much time."

We form a makeshift human chain, picking through the barbed shrubbery. Above us, spinning rotors seal our fate. We all knew the riot would end, but this doesn't sound like a resolution.

It's a massacre.

The last act of a crumbling regime.

The corporation has the power and reach to spin the narrative. It's the same game they've been playing for decades to cover up their brutality. All the world will hear is how they liberated Harrowdean and saved the innocent hostages.

Keeping close to Xander and Raine, my head is on a swivel as we creep forward. Far-off shouts pierce the sound of helicopters flying low overhead. It isn't long before we find our first group of patients.

Instantly, I spot Luka and his corridor hook-up among them. They seem to be searching for a hiding place, all wearing matching expressions of pure terror.

In the distance, the sound of metal screeching as entry is forced indicates the countdown to anarchy. Harrowdean's gates are being wrenched open. The cavalry has arrived.

"They're coming!" Kitty, one of the younger girls, wails in a panic. "We have to hide!"

Despite being adults—though some barely—they're too young to be caught in this situation. Doomed to endure violence and persecution simply because their brains work differently.

"Over there!" I yell at them, pointing to my left. "There's a building hidden by the trees! Hide inside!"

His gaze colliding with mine, Luka gulps hard. We're not supplier and customer anymore. Now we're just two petrified humans, tied to the same deadly train tracks. I nod at him, and he dips his chin in respect.

They disperse to hide, allowing us to continue fleeing. Raine puts his total trust in Xander as he runs without using his stick, guided by the elbow he's gripping hard.

We've passed several buildings and found the path that leads to the southern side of the grounds when the first shots ring out. Undeniably real. My pulse ratchets—we're being fired at in broad daylight.

"Fucking guns?" Raine shouts. "What are they thinking?"

"They don't care anymore!" Lennox yells behind me. "Go, go, go!"

The world whizzes past me in a blur of fear and shock. As more patients pour out of the manor, fleeing into the grounds to escape the onslaught, I catch a flash of auburn hair from a distance.

"Rae!" I shout helplessly.

Before I can skid to a halt, I'm shoved forward.

"Don't you dare stop," Lennox barks into my ear. "I'll throw you over my shoulder if I have to!"

He pushes me again, forcing me to continue running. The brief sighting of Rae vanishes as we're swallowed by dense trees. Harrowdean's gothic outline melts into the forest's shadows.

"The perimeter is through here." Xander slows a little to help Raine dodge a tall juniper tree. "Stay close."

Not even the forest that encases the institute in mist-soaked mystery can silence the sounds of destruction. Shouts, screams and distant cries for help still reach our ears, carried by a cold wind.

"They can't just kill patients indiscriminately." Raine puffs in exertion. "Surely?"

"Who's going to dispute the lies they'll spin?" Xander replies curtly. "The corporation has total impunity. It always has."

"Not anymore," I pant back. "We are going to shout the truth so loudly, the world will have to listen to us."

I'm so focused on Raine and the death-grip he holds on Xander's elbow that I don't see the huge tree root jutting out of the ground until it's too late. My foot catches, sending me tumbling forwards.

Before I can smash face first into the mossy forest floor, two strong iron bands capture me from behind. I hang suspended, cinched tightly by tanned biceps. There's a low, disapproving rumble from behind me.

"Watch your step."

Lennox pulls me upright, setting me back on my feet. He doesn't release me at first. Instead, his arms squeeze tighter, holding my back to his broad chest. I feel his breath stirring in my hair.

"Thanks," I mutter. "You can let go."

In all the madness, his scent still registers. It's rare that I'm close enough to drink in its intoxication. Lennox smells like summer campfires and musky, burning wood, carried into my senses like curling smoke.

His one unbandaged hand is balled into a fist above my stomach, making the scar tissue that disfigures his knuckles stand out. He twists the front of my t-shirt before blowing out a tense breath.

"You need to be more careful."

Releasing my t-shirt, Lennox's arms vanish. I immediately miss the firm press of his steel-carved muscles around me. The same arms that held me close the last time we faced death.

"Come on!" Xander bellows at us.

I look up at Lennox, his vast height towering above me. Two pale-green orbs stare back, the ever-present, burning hatred now awash with more concern and mind-bending tenderness than I can fathom.

"Look where you're going," he grumbles. "Now move."

With a far gentler push, Lennox encourages me to continue following. There isn't time to consider my actions. I reach down and grab his huge hand, forcing his fingers to wrap around mine.

Nostrils flaring in surprise, he glances at me. I stare back for a prolonged moment, allowing him to see my warring emotions.

Perhaps this is all we'll ever be.

Simply each other's means of survival.

Rushing to catch up, we find Xander and Raine as the trees begin to thin out. The cloudy morning sky emerges once more, penetrating the thick canopy overhead. With it comes the sight we've been searching for.

Glinting barbed wire. Sharp spikes. The metal monstrosity stretches at least ten feet tall, topped with deadly razor points and an array of security cameras. I don't have time to worry about whether they're working.

"Shit." Lennox comes to a halt.

"Yeah," Xander replies tersely. "It's high."

"Can we even climb that?"

"We have no choice," I answer them. "Be thankful it isn't electrified with the power still out."

"Hate to be the voice of doom and all," Raine vocalises. "But I can't climb shit. Not without being able to see it."

Glancing between us and the fence, Xander taps his lips, falling into deep concentration. Our options are limited. We climb or stay. Run or surrender. Die falling or die kneeling. That damn fence can't stop us now.

"Xander goes first with Lennox." I eye the towering fence. "He's still one-handed. Then I'll support Raine on this side. Xander guides him down the other, and I'll climb last."

"Forget it," Xander snarls.

Lennox glowers at me like I just suggested something utterly insane. "We are not leaving you standing here alone."

"Agreed," Raine parrots.

"We don't have time to argue!" I look around the circle. "This is the only way it'll work. So climb!"

They exchange grim looks. Raine remains silent, but eventually, Lennox and Xander both stiffen as they seem to reach the same conclusion. It's this or nothing; we don't have time to find another solution.

Xander's subsequent choice of curse words raises even Lennox's eyebrows. Resolving himself to this decision, the iceman goes first, peering up at the individual chain-links and looming spikes.

"Wait!" I quickly pull off my green parka to hand over. "Tie this around your waist. You can cover the spikes."

He accepts the thick coat, quickly looping it around himself. Xander hoists the backpack higher on his shoulder then begins to deftly hoist himself up, link by link, causing the fence to groan.

At the top, he drops the backpack over the other side. It lands with a hollow thunk. Xander braces himself in place to spread the parka over the spikes, offering some minor protection.

"Alright," he calls down. "Nox."

Stepping up, Lennox follows his lead. It's a torturously slow process, heaving himself up each inch with his bad hand curled into his chest. I internally panic each time he falters, almost losing his grip.

Halfway up, Xander stretches out a hand, intending to grab him. Lennox tentatively raises his injured limb, allowing Xander to snag his wrist above the bandage and pull.

"What's happening?" Raine asks anxiously.

"Xander has him. They're almost over."

The pair tackle the top together, Xander guiding Lennox over the spiked barbed wire, now hidden beneath feather-filled fabric. Lennox grunts when a sharp tip pierces through the coat and catches his inner leg.

"A few steps down then jump," Xander advises from his perch. "I've got Raine."

Knowing that's my cue, I nudge Raine forward. "You're up."

He folds his guide stick then tucks it into his waistband, taking small steps forward. I help him hook his fingers into the criss-crossed metal and locate his first foothold.

"Go slow. Xander will grab you, alright?"

"Sure," Raine chirps. "Fucking brilliant."

"I'll catch you if you fall."

"I'd crush you, guava girl."

"I'd let you do that too."

With a tiny, forced smile, he starts to move. The process of feeling out each slot to nudge his foot into is painstaking. Raine has to blindly locate each metal link all while finding where to put his hands.

"Higher," I call to him. "Left foot."

"Almost there," Xander adds, still teetering up high.

When Raine's foot slips and he begins to fall, the scream trapped in my chest surges to the forefront. My vision narrows to the sight of him plummeting.

"Not so fast!"

Grabbing a covered spike for better balance, Xander swoops his top half low to reach Raine. I watch his mouth contort in an agonised grimace. He just manages to grab the scruff of Raine's t-shirt to steady him.

"Raine!" Lennox bellows.

He dangles for a horrifying split-second until his feet miraculously find a hold. Raine flattens himself against the security fence, gulping down air.

"Move," Xander shouts in a strained voice. "Now!"

I can see blood pouring from Xander's palm from here, the bright-red spill trailing down his forearm and elbow in swirling ribbons. He's clutching a spike to stop Raine from falling.

Lennox's face drains of colour as he watches in clear horror, unable to intervene. We can only stand and fret as Raine resumes climbing, step by treacherous step.

"Are you bleeding?" I hear him exclaim.

"Climb over, dammit."

"I can smell your blood, Xan!"

"Just hurry!"

At the top, Xander braces Raine to allow him to hook a leg over the barbed wire. My throat closes up as I watch both of them teetering, narrowly avoiding any further cuts or injuries.

My attention is dragged away from them by the sound of raised voices, leaking from the woodland directly behind me. It sounds a lot like orders being screamed.

"Incoming!" I cry out. "Get down, now!"

Encouraging Raine to drop down the other side, Xander watches him descend then drop to the grass beside Lennox. He barely spares his bleeding hand a second glance as he starts to descend after Raine.

"Ripley!" he thunders.

"I'm coming!"

I secure my backpack tight, already climbing up the same route the others took. The fence flexes and bends beneath my weight, the metal protesting at the violation. This is harder than it looks.

My fingers ache, pain slicing into my joints from the pressure caused by gripping such thin, inflexible metal. It's slick too, making me slip several times, barely clinging on for dear life.

"Faster, Rip," Xander calls from the bottom. "I see movement."

"I'm coming! Go take cover!"

"Take Raine and run!" Lennox shouts at him. "I've got her."

"No," Xander roars back.

"Go! You need more time to guide him!"

Xander reluctantly grabs hold of Raine and makes a beeline for the woodland that surrounds the institute. Raine tries to fight against him, shouting my name, but fails to break free.

Reaching the top in record time, I swing my legs over the barbed wire then toss the torn parka down to Lennox. He catches it, checking to verify that Xander and Raine have made it to safety.

"Go!" I scream down to him.

"Not without you! Shift your ass!"

I quickly drop the backpack to free up my movements. Just a few more steps down and I can jump the rest. Preparing to move, my blood freezes into a solid mass in my veins when a voice calls out.

"Ripley Bennet!"

Teetering, I almost lose balance at the sound of the familiar sneer. I find my next footing, risking a look over the other side of the fence. Four men have broken free from the forest.

Elon's smarmy grin hasn't changed. It still sits proudly on his face beneath gunmetal eyes that hold no mercy and his stern, military-cut hair. The sick fuck's even freshly shaven for the occasion.

He cups his hands around his mouth. "Long time no see, inmate!"

The three men with him are all dressed like something out of a prison escape movie. Thick, padded black clothing and stab proof vests. Holsters loaded with weapons—batons, tasers and guns. They came prepared.

"You look awfully uncomfortable up there," he jeers. "Fancy hopping down to have a little chat with me and my friends?"

My grip on the chain-links tightens. "Alternatively you could go join your other friend, Harrison, in the Z wing. I heard he's floating in a tub down there!"

The smirk wipes clean from his face. Elon clenches his stubbled jaw, a hand resting on the gun slotted into his holster.

"Fun's over, Ripley. I have one job today and not a whole lot of time to do it. You're on my list of loose ends to clean up."

Below me, I can see Lennox still lingering. He should've run to safety and joined the others. Instead, he looks up at me imploringly, his hands spread wide in a clear message. I watch his lips move.

Jump.

The metallic click of a gun causes my head to snap back up. Elon has released his weapon and holds it aimed at me. His lascivious smile makes his intentions crystal clear.

"I'm under no obligation to bring you back alive," he gloats. "Though I'm sure the boss will be disappointed that he won't get the chance to deal with you himself."

Looking back and forth, my options are shitty. Fall and pray that Lennox catches me. Stay and get shot. Surrender to Elon and his sycophants. Karma is truly kicking me in the ass with these choices.

"Come on, Rip," Elon cajoles. "You know we will always find you, no matter where you run."

"Good luck with that, asshole!"

"You're a part of this. The world wants your head too."

"Don't listen to him," Lennox clamours.

It's too late to stop the seed of doubt from blooming. We may be jumping from the frying pan into the flames. The outside world holds no more safety than Harrowdean's crumbling ruins.

I'm their enemy too. Society will never understand the horrors we've endured. We don't fit into their cookie-cutter reality. Staying here to scream our innocence until we're quietly killed isn't happening, though.

"You're right!" I reposition myself, legs spread apart and shoulders squared. "I'll be labelled as a monster when the truth comes out. The world will burn me right alongside the corporation."

My grip on the chain-links loosens.

"But the least I can do is destroy the evil I've enabled before that day comes. I can atone."

Trees, clouds and four shocked faces become a fast-moving blur. I'm airborne. Free-falling. The ground rushes up to meet me, approaching in rapid flash frames.

BANG. BANG. BANG.

The feel of a bullet whooshing past me registers in drunken slow motion. Rushing air. Loud popping. Something else sails past me. But the third and final bullet doesn't miss.

I don't process the fierce bite of being shot at first. Not until the burning sensation becomes a deep, excruciating laser beam carving into my flesh.

The thin air doesn't cushion my fall.

Something else does.

Our bodies audibly smack together. Faintly, I hear someone bellow loudly in pain as we both crumple. I should feel the impact more, but all that exists is the radiating agony in my inflamed thigh.

More vision-blurring pain slams into me as I'm jostled in a pair of thick arms, the muscular cushion beneath me attempting to shift. Crackling bonfires and woodsy smoke filter into my nostrils.

Lennox.

"Fuck," he wheezes. "That hurt."

Yelling voices feed back in. We need to move, but for the life of me, I can't lift a single limb. Not with my body succumbing to weakness. I'm barely able to hold my eyelids open as adrenaline pours out of me.

"Xan! Help us!"

Reality keeps flashing in and out. Lennox's body trapped beneath me shakes, attempting to wrestle his way up with the new bruises I've given him. When the world reappears, I feel myself being lifted.

"Give her to me."

"No." Lennox's tone is strained. "I'm carrying her."

"Nox—"

"Let's move!"

More darkness. An inky pond pulling me into its all-consuming depths. Light eventually filters back in, and this time, I can tell we're running fast.

Wind whipping and voices bellowing. More bullets. Distant shouts. Crunching footsteps. Birch trees reappear all around us.

I'm cradled safely into a firm chest.

Broad. Warm. Adorned with military dog tags.

I'm... safe.

"Hold on, Rip," Lennox whispers raggedly. "I've got you."

CHAPTER 11
LENNOX
IN YOUR ARMS – CROIXX

RIPLEY'S round curves are featherlight in my arms. She's too small. Dainty. A delicate, tattooed shell holding so much beautiful fury. The same fury I've tasted first-hand.

I still wonder how such a tiny body can hold all that rage. What I wouldn't give for her to peel open her angry, hazel eyes and curse me out right now. I'd take any insult she wants to lash me with.

She can beat me black, blue and every shade of the fucking rainbow if she so pleases. As long as she's awake. As long as she's alive. Then we can go back to hating each other. I'll give her that.

"Is it clear?" I heave in exertion.

Xander peers through a dirt-streaked window, the thick cobwebs obscuring our view of the other farm buildings we stumbled across. We must've walked for miles before exiting the forest and finding signs of life.

"Helicopter still overhead."

"The same one?" Raine asks tiredly.

"Looks like it. They're circling the area."

Cradling Ripley close, I keep my uninjured hand clamped on her upper thigh. The bleeding has slowed to a sluggish trickle. Xander tore up one of our spare shirts to tie a tourniquet before bandaging his own hand.

She's still lost a considerable amount of blood, enough for her to keep dropping in and out during the hours we've been stealthily moving. I can feel it sticking to me, saturating my already filthy clothing.

"It's been hours." Raine rests nearby, keeping a hand on Ripley's pulse. "They'll give up soon."

"You think Incendia cares about a private helicopter bill?" Xander ridicules. "That wanker Elon said it himself. We're loose ends."

Back pressed against the wall, I glance down at Ripley again. Her sweetheart-shaped face is ashen. Waxy. The bullet passed straight through—I found the exit wound. That doesn't make blood loss any less deadly.

It's a miracle we escaped at all without catching another bullet. They sure fired enough of them after us before attempting to scale the security fence. I caught a glimpse of an over-confident guard falling on his ass before we made a run for it.

I have no doubt they eventually followed. On foot as well as in the air. The near-impenetrable woodland that keeps Harrowdean Manor secure from the outside world did us a favour. It was easy to lose their tail.

But now that we need to find safety? Not so great. We also need food, water and medical attention. Our varying degrees of mud-streaked skin, unkempt hair and drawn faces will scare anyone off.

"We need to find a doctor. A pharmacy. Anything," I fret anxiously. "Her wound needs treating."

Xander abandons his watch to approach us. The juicy vein throbbing at his temple betrays his anxiety, even if he's plastered his steely mask back in place for the sake of remaining calm.

He isn't fooling me.

Tension he can no longer suppress pulls his skin tight across sharp angles and defined bones. While he uses his ethereal looks to his advantage when hunting prey, he looks more like a starved ghost than a model right now.

"We're in the middle of nowhere." He studies Ripley's slack face. "Harrowdean is deep in the countryside, miles from the nearest town or city."

"Yeah, no shit," Raine drawls.

I jerk my chin towards the odd buildings scattered outside. "Someone must live nearby. Or there's another farm close. It can't be that much farther."

"You're forgetting that we're fugitives now," Raine interjects. "Who would help us? They'll just call the police."

"We don't know what the public's been told," I reason, trying to cling to some calmness. "Blackwood already fell before the riot. Now Harrowdean. People know we're victims now."

"Do you really believe that?" Xander laughs coldly. "No one gives a fuck about us."

"Now is not the time to debate hypotheticals, Xan. No one knows our faces or our stories. We can use that to our advantage."

"What about Sabre Security?" Raine shifts uncomfortably against the wall.

I want to facepalm even though he can't even see me to appreciate the sentiment. This is where our levels of optimism differ greatly.

The asshole Ripley thinks is her friend either got himself killed or abandoned us to die. I'm not about to bet anything on this mysterious company coming to our rescue any time soon.

We're all quiet while deep in thought. The sound of beating rotors seems to be moving farther away, giving me a small sliver of hope. They're searching a wide radius. The woods stretch on for miles behind us.

"We keep moving," Xander decides in a firm tone. "If Incendia's searching for us, they haven't been dismantled yet."

"And we're still in danger," Raine concludes.

"As long as they're operating, we will never be safe. I'm all for running, but unravelling criminal conspiracies can take years. We'll have to stop running sometime."

"Says who?" I retort.

His icy-blue eyes flash to me. "Be realistic."

"I am! We are not surrendering to those bastards!"

"Nobody is suggesting we surrender." Raine fidgets with his folded guide stick. "Right, Xan?"

"Not to the corporation," he clarifies. "But if Sabre really is investigating and planning to shut down all the institutes, cooperation may be our only chance."

My mind whirls as I catch on to his plan. Warner didn't come through for us. So what, Xander wants to contact his team himself? We'll be feeding ourselves to the wolves—just under a different guise. I don't trust any of these corporate suits.

"We need to get back online." Xander sighs wearily, buckling under the weight of the day. "I can swipe some phones if we find a town or city."

"You can?" Raine wonders aloud.

"Sure. Easy."

I know a little about Xander's criminal past. He was sent to Priory Lane for some elaborate embezzlement scheme, and he's happiest with his fingertips touching a keyboard. I know he has a talent for theft. The rest is a mystery, much like the man himself.

"I don't trust anyone but the people in this room." I blow out a leaden breath. "We're not surrendering, cooperating… whatever the fuck you want to call it. We keep running until it's safe to stop."

Our gazes locked, Xander seems determined to freeze me out. The way he glowers at me chills my internal organs. But I'm not afraid of him. The time for him to call the shots is over. We all have a stake in this.

I look back down at Ripley.

Her.

Even if I've done a terrible job of showing my intentions so far. Every time I see her, I just get so wound up. She knows exactly how to push all the right buttons to drive me fucking insane.

"I can't hear the helicopter anymore." Raine tilts his blonde head, listening closely. "Are we clear to move?"

Xander drops his stare then returns to the window. I shift Ripley in my arms, cracking my neck to loosen the kink that's formed. Her dried blood pulls at my skin, adding to my unease.

"I hate this," Raine mutters. "We're sitting ducks."

"Me too. How's her pulse?"

I watch his fingers tighten on her wrist.

"Thready but strong. She's exhausted and lost a lot of blood. I think it's normal for her to dip in and out. You need to keep her warm, though."

"Yeah, I'm on it."

His thumb circles her skin in a loving, affectionate caress. We're facing life and death, but I can't stop my mind from flashing back to the moments before we ran for our lives. It's seared into my memory.

The powerful look on her face as she drove my friend to ecstasy with her filthy mouth. The way Raine flexed beneath her, so perfectly in tune to her body. Ripley swallowing his load before proudly licking her damn lips.

I've never considered the possibility of sharing a woman before—no matter how much I love the family I found in the shittiest of times. Fuck, I never considered touching Ripley until recently. At least not consciously.

But in that moment, it took all my self-control not to bend her over Raine, strip her tight ass bare and sink into her cunt while he fucks her smart mouth. I wanted to take that powerful look she wore and obliterate it.

Needing to earn Ripley's forgiveness is one thing—I can chalk it up to a guilty conscience—but this possessive need to protect her, to love and to hold her… That's something I never anticipated. Not even when we kissed in the padded cell.

I thought if I kept my distance, used cruelty to hide these strange new impulses… they would go away. My secret would be safe. But the longer we're trapped in this together, the harder it's becoming to battle my desires.

I want her.

Us.

Any tiny fucking scrap she'll give me.

"Nox!" Xander snaps me back to reality. "We're moving."

"Right. Coming."

Shifting Ripley higher against my chest, I push off from the wall. Raine may own her heart right now, but I have something he doesn't. Something he'll never have. And that feels so fucking good.

Their love will never compare to the addictive intoxication of our hatred for each other. I have the real power here. Namely, the sole ability to fix what I once broke. Only someone intimately familiar with her pain can ever hope to ease it.

I'll happily be her enemy.

Her own personal monster.

As long as I can also be the one to keep her safe. Perhaps even hold her the way that Raine does. Touch her. Comfort her. Fucking *matter* to her.

"This way." Xander leads us outside.

The late afternoon sunshine has broken through the thick cloud coverage. We plough on in a loose formation, Raine walking independently behind Xander with his stick swinging.

My leg muscles protest as the miles trickle by. I fall into a rhythm, my attention focused on the skies above and the path ahead. I almost startle when I feel ice-cold fingers pressing into my face.

"You don't suit the white knight stereotype, Nox."

A pulse of adrenaline shoots through me when I find Ripley's semi-open eyes. "You're awake."

"Is that what this feeling is?" she groans in pain. "Feels a lot like hell to me."

Her hand lowers, fastening on my shirt collar instead. She fists the bloodstained fabric, tiny whimpers slipping past her lips with each step.

"Sorry for ruining your t-shirt."

"You owe me a new one."

"Add it to my bill," she gasps.

"You've lost a lot of blood. Please don't die in my arms before settling up." I pause to enjoy her look of surprise. "Plus I don't want to be responsible for burying your body."

"Ever the charmer." Ripley rattles out a laugh. "Or should I say asshole?"

My mouth twitches in a smile. "More appropriate."

"Where are we?" she wheezes.

"We're going to find some help."

"In a field?"

"You're in no position to complain."

Xander suddenly halts, his exhausted shoulders straightening out. He's spotted something ahead. We've been passing fields of bleating livestock for at least an hour now. Perhaps we've finally escaped the farmland.

Barren fields have shifted to cobbled-stone pathways turn and wind-stripped fences, the grass massively overgrown. When I spot the first dated-looking structure ahead, the urge to laugh bubbles up in my chest.

"Seriously, Xan?" I call to him.

He glances over his shoulder. "You got a better idea?"

"What is it?" Raine taps his stick in a wide circle.

"Imagine the most British holiday you can think of."

"Uh… pass." He chuckles to himself. "My parents were a bit too concerned about shooting up to take me on holiday."

We're approaching a run-down resort, the front gates leading to rows of retro mobile homes. The place appears to be deserted in the late spring sunshine. We stop in front of the peeling welcome sign.

Golden Oaks Holiday Park.
Open July through November.

"Anyone against a little breaking and entering?" Xander asks after finding the gate locked.

There are no complaints.

"Good. Keep watch."

He pokes around the entrance, locating a loose, round stone on the roadside. Xander returns to the gate, contemplating for a moment before slamming the stone into the rusted padlock.

After three hits, the busted lock hits the ground. He pulls off the chain, allowing the gates to creak open. We all shuffle forward, tentatively entering the desolate park.

"Does this place look as spooky as it feels?" Raine whistles.

Squeezing Ripley close, my head swivels from side to side. "Pretty much."

"Kinda glad I can't see it, in that case."

Surveying the vacant homes, Xander guides us to the very back of the resort. The silence is fucking eery.

"This will do," he decides, gesturing ahead.

Shaded, net curtains hide the interior of the mobile home he's chosen. The garden is a wild jungle, indicating the months of closure during off-season.

"I'll see if there's a park office or something. They must have first-aid supplies. Can you get us in, Nox?"

"Leave it to me."

Xander nods, vanishing to keep searching. I approach the mobile home then crouch down to lower Ripley onto the moss-speckled, plastic steps. Her pained grunting cuts deep into my chest.

"Easy," I murmur.

She hisses, releasing my t-shirt. "Son of a bitch."

"You're welcome."

With Ripley safely deposited, her leg stretched out in front of her, I check Raine is at a safe distance then look around for something to use. The door is made of two frosted-glass panes. If I can smash the top one, perhaps I can flip the inside lock.

"You reckon these things have alarms?"

Ripley grimaces. "Doubt it. This one looks ancient."

Buried in weeds and grass tufts, I spot my target. A stone garden gnome covered in crusty fungus. I pick it up with my good hand. The ugly bastard will do the job nicely if I get the swing right.

Backing up to a safe distance, I swing the gnome hard, letting it sail into the glass pane. The resultant crack pierces the silence like a gunshot. A huge split marks the pane in complex spiderweb patterns.

"Shit, Nox," Raine shouts from below. "Could you make more noise?"

"Feel free to come do it yourself, dick."

Still using the lump of slick stone, I repeatedly smash the cracks I've created to chip away the glass. With the pane destroyed, I'm free to reach in to feel for a lock. My fingers catch on smooth metal.

"Gotcha," I whisper. "Please work."

Click.

Thankfully, the lock is cheap and crappy. It flicks open, allowing me to flip the handle. The door swings open, granting us access to the mobile home. My momentary relief dissipates as I move forward uneasily.

"Let me check to make sure it's clear."

Ripley attempts to shift, her teeth gritted. "Need backup?"

"You're in no state to help."

"I can walk," she protests.

"No. You can't. Just sit still."

"But—"

"I mean it," I cut her off. "Sit fucking still."

Relieved when she deflates, not daring to protest more, I step inside. Stale air and dust register first. Then the stench of old, musty furniture. Anyone coming here for a holiday better have low expectations.

I check each room—a cramped living area, peeling kitchenette, single bathroom and two bedrooms with matching double beds. The old linoleum squeaks with each step I take, mirroring my rapid heartbeat.

"Nox? You good?"

Following Raine's voice, I step back outside. "It's clear. Probably best you can't see the '70s shag carpet and bright-orange kitchen. This thing is old as fuck."

"Awesome," Ripley quips.

"Raine? You good to follow?" I study him.

He waves my concern off. "I've got this. Go first."

Helping Ripley stand, I throw her arm around my shoulders. Raine follows us in, using his stick to feel his way up the narrow steps. I set Ripley down on the kitchen counter, outstretching her leg on top.

"So much dust." Raine wrinkles his nose in disgust. "I can literally smell the '70s grandma vibes in here."

"I'd like to think '70s grandmas had more style than this," I reply distractedly. "Who buys an orange refrigerator?"

"If it meant I could see it, I'd take a neon-green kitchen. Count yourself lucky."

"Buy a green kitchen, and I'll disown you."

"Well, that's you uninvited from the housewarming," Raine snarks.

"Thank fuck for that."

"Pack it in," Ripley snaps at us. "It's a roof over our heads."

Creaking footsteps interrupt our conversation. We all startle before Xander's dirt-flecked face quickly appears in the doorway.

"Room for one more?" He sighs.

"Welcome to the five-star hotel," Raine jokes.

Slapping a turquoise box down on the table, rattling the contents, Xander deposits his backpack next. He's practically sagging with fatigue, still covered in dirt and grass stains from our escape.

"First aid kit." He rubs his face tiredly. "There was a small shop in the office too. No CCTV cameras. They're not concerned about security out here."

"Anything good?" Raine folds up his stick.

"Some long-life cereals, a bag of peanuts, a few chocolate bars and a cheap bottle of whiskey."

"That's a gourmet dinner." Ripley winces when she tries to laugh. "No pain relief?"

"Nothing." Xander shakes his head.

"Then someone crack open that booze."

"Hand it over," I offer.

Xander passes me the backpack. "I'll sort out the medical supplies."

With my bandaged hand, I fumble with the zip until I get it unfastened and locate the sealed bottle inside. Once I've cracked the seal, Ripley immediately snatches it from me.

"Woah." I pull the bottle back to stop her chugging. "You haven't eaten or slept, and you nearly bled out. Go easy on the hard liquor."

"Fuck off," she retorts, reaching for the whiskey.

"Nice try." I pull the bottle behind my back. "We agreed you wouldn't die on my watch, remember?"

"I don't remember that." She grimaces, a pained whimper slipping past her gritted teeth. "My leg feels like it's on fucking fire."

Reluctantly handing her the bottle, I watch her take another few mouthfuls before I intervene again, managing to wrestle it back. She pins me with the stink eye, a red flush already creeping into her cheeks.

"We need to do this now." Xander clicks open the first aid kit to search inside. "Bring Ripley here."

One arm sliding around her waist, I decide to take advantage and lift her off the counter by her ass. "My bad."

"Don't use your mangled hand as an excuse to grope me," she hisses out. "You're still on my shit list."

"Then I'm good to grope you, right? If I'm already on the shit list."

"Good luck getting off it with that attitude."

I carry her over to the kitchen table, gently laying her down across the tacky surface with her bleeding thigh on Xander's side. He takes one look at the mess and begins rifling through the box.

"Jeans off," he orders.

"Raine," I call out. "Come help me."

"You're both going to strip me?" Ripley asks incredulously.

I'm not sure if it's the booze or an actual blush staining her cheeks now. Raine laughs under his breath. I swear, the motherfucker knows exactly what's running through my mind.

"Any scissors?" I ask with forced neutrality.

Xander scours the kitchen, banging drawers and cabinets. "Nothing."

"Great." I study her splayed-out form. "Alright, this isn't gonna feel great."

With my good hand, I pick at the knotted t-shirt to untie the tourniquet before tugging her jeans down as gently as I can. Raine slowly pulls the denim over her ankles.

"That hurts," she spits through gritted teeth. "Go slow."

I try my best to carefully ease the denim down when we reach her thighs. The jeans are stuck to her skin and take some manoeuvring, each inch causing her to curse bloody murder.

"God-fucking-dammit!" Ripley lashes out. "I am going to put a bullet in Elon's fucking face. Fuck!"

"I think cheap whiskey breaks her cuss filter," Raine mutters.

"Did she ever have one?"

"Fair point."

"I can hear you both!" she bellows. "Fucking assholes."

Raine smirks to himself. "Case in point."

With the jeans removed, an inflamed, ragged mess is revealed.

Thankfully, the thigh wound itself is small, maybe five or six centimetres wide. She's lucky they only had handguns.

"Lift her leg." Xander snaps on a pair of blue medical gloves. "I need to check the exit wound."

Slowly raising her leg, I avoid looking at the agony that's carved into her clammy features. Xander moves fast, ducking low to inspect the back of her thigh before straightening up.

"Clean shot, minimal damage. We need to flush the wound then pack it."

"Stitches?" I frown at him.

"Not yet. Got to rule out an infection first. Re-evaluate in a few days."

"A few days?" Ripley croaks.

"You're going to rest while we scout the area." Xander keeps his instructions clipped, leaving no room for argument. "We're secure here for the time being."

I lower Ripley's leg back down. "What about a hospital?"

"Right now, we don't even know where we are. We'll get her stabilised then make a plan."

Lining up sealed packs of bandages and swabs, Xander quickly scans the label on a bottle of clear liquid. Behind me, Raine is shifting on his feet in clear agitation.

"Ankles," I order him. "You can hold her legs straight."

"You sure this is a good idea?"

"Have you got a better one?" Xander asks distractedly.

"Just feels a bit back-street clinic, you know?" Raine gnaws on his cheek.

"We're not giving a false name and paying in cash." I move up the table to stand at Ripley's head. "Make yourself useful."

Both moved into position, Xander unwraps several packs of cotton gauze. He uncaps the liquid, leaning over Ripley's injured body while wearing a displeased expression.

"This may sting," he advises with a quick glance. "We don't need company."

"Meaning?" Ripley grates out.

"Try not to yell too loud."

Without ceremony, he douses her leg in antiseptic. I watch the clear liquid run red, filling the bullet wound before spilling over in a crimson flow. Ripley's back arches as a shrill scream erupts from her mouth.

"Fuuuuuck!"

"Nox," Xander barks. "Cover her mouth!"

Cursing rapidly, I slam a hand over Ripley's O-shaped lips. Her tortured howls now muffled, she bucks and writhes on the table like we doused her in petrol then lit a flame.

"Stop it, Xan!" Raine frets in a high-pitched screech. "You're hurting her!"

"Less than a blood infection will," he hits back. "Let me do my job."

Using cotton gauze, Xander begins to dab and clean, his jaw locked tight. I can feel the tears pouring from Ripley's eyes soaking my hand. The huge, green-brown pits stare up at me like I'm responsible for carving her heart out.

It's a sight I once craved. Dreamed about. Fantasised over. I wanted her tears, freshly spilled and bottled like nectar. Her grief and heartache helped ease my desire for revenge after she had us thrown in the Z wing.

Considering all the regret I feel now, that craving has packed up and left the fucking planet. My sick need for revenge drove me to the brink of insanity.

I'd do all manner of insane things to protect my family—she can attest to that—but somewhere down the line… my brain moved her into that same category. *Fuck!* When did that happen?

"Stop!" she shrieks behind my hand.

Xander tuts under his breath. "Not yet. We have to clean the wound."

"I'm sorry." The words tumble freely from my mouth. "I'm so sorry. Just hold on."

When Xander douses the gunshot wound again, her wails intensify, chest pumping and body trembling beneath a sheen of glistening sweat. I lift my hand so she can gulp down shuddering breaths.

"P-Please." She swipes at her wet cheeks. "Take m-my mind off it."

"How?" I ask desperately.

"Anything… Tell m-me something… A story."

Now finished flushing the wound, Xander resumes swabbing it to remove any debris. If that vein in his forehead throbs any harder, I'm worried it's going to explode. He fucking hates this too.

"I… I don't know any stories."

"Your sister," she whines through her pouring tears. "Tell me about her."

My gaze snaps to hers. "Uh, now?"

Slamming her mouth shut, Ripley shrieks again through tightly sealed lips. Raine looks on the verge of passing out too, his face white as a sheet as he continues to hold her legs straight.

"Shit, okay," I rush out. "She... She practiced ballet. Some free program for ex-service families. Our grandfather signed her up."

Ripley's eyes screw shut. Her skin has lost its alcohol flush and turned almost translucent. Determined to stop her from shutting down, I search for something happy amongst heart-wrenching memories.

"Every single day after school, I'd take the A7 bus to pick her up from class. It was a rattling hunk of junk. If I had enough money, we'd stop for an ice cream cone on the way home."

She mumbles weakly, her eyes flickering. "Ice cream?"

"Yeah, that boring vanilla kind. Bright-yellow and full of additive shit. But she enjoyed that damn cone so much. I loved seeing her smile, even if I had to scavenge pennies just to make it happen."

Tossing aside bloodied handfuls of gauze, Xander locates fresh bandages next. He nods to me in encouragement.

I smooth sweaty hair back from her forehead. "One time, the shop closed early. Daisy stared up at that closed sign, and the look on her face fucking killed me. I hadn't realised how much our little ritual meant to her."

Ripley's eyes flutter open and lock on mine. Her tears are pearlescent rivers staining her skin. Skimming her cheek with my thumb, I wipe them away.

She lets out a thready breath. "What d-did you do about it?"

"You know me too well."

"Yeah." Her laugh is weak.

"I snuck around back and broke into the storeroom. Stole two tubs of that shitty ice cream then took it home. Daisy had a bowl every night until it ran out."

Directing Raine to lift her injured leg, Xander packs the wound with sterilised cotton then begins to tightly bandage it. Ripley's vibrating so violently, I wonder if she'll pass out again. I seize her shaking hand.

"Hey," I bark at her. "Eyes on me."

Her muddled gaze flicks back to my face. "I h-hate vanilla."

"You want to know a secret?"

She nods loosely.

"Me too. I only ate it to make Daisy happy. I don't have a massive sweet tooth. Though if pushed, I'd go for chocolate every time."

Xander applies medical tape to hold the bulging bandage in place. Panting roughly, Ripley interlocks her fingers with mine. I run a finger over her knuckles, studying each laboured breath.

"I went back to the ice cream shop after she died," I blurt before I can stop myself. "I guess I wanted to feel close to her again. All her stuff at home was gone by then, and it felt like she never existed."

Lowering Ripley's leg, Xander casts a critical eye over his handiwork before nodding. He starts to clean up the medical detritus. There's blood and bandage wrappings spread everywhere around us.

I didn't get the chance to hold Daisy's hand like this. I couldn't give her the love she needed. The protection of her big brother—the one person in the entire world who was supposed to keep her safe.

I failed her.

But I'll never fail my family again.

"It was gone." The truth is a raw whisper that I can hardly vocalise. "Boarded up and gutted. Some little shits even graffitied the exterior. Daisy died, and everything she loved died with her."

"Not you," she replies weakly.

"The Lennox she knew did. He was weak. Blind to the truth. Pathetic. He didn't protect her."

I ignore the other two paying close attention to our whispers. I'm focused solely on Ripley's face, wrinkles smoothing out and muscles relaxing. Her septum piercing is crooked again.

I gently straighten the silver ring. "Rest, baby."

She mumbles an unintelligible protest.

"It's okay, Rip." My vocal cords spasm, causing my voice to break. "I'm right here. I promise I'll keep you safe."

Because that's what family does, no matter how much they beat, bruise and hate each other. There's no stronger bond on Earth than that. Not all of us are lucky enough to have biological family left.

But the connections we create can be stronger than shared DNA.

We're living proof of that.

Ripley demonstrated her worth to me the day she avenged her best friend's death. She was defending her family. The family we took from her. Beneath all that goddamn beautiful rage, we're just alike.

Together, we could be unstoppable.

Our rage will burn the whole fucking world.

CHAPTER 12
XANDER
ROSES – THE COMFORT

THICK BLACK HOODIE flipped up to offer me protection, I stare straight ahead at the bald guy in front of me. He's distracted, intently studying the coffee menu on the wall while flipping his car keys in his hand.

Clueless.

The perfect mark.

Spending the better part of a decade in foster care teaches you life skills. Just not ones that are necessarily advertised. When you're competing with twenty plus kids for basics like clothes and toys, the art of stealing becomes second nature.

"Next!" a haggard barista calls.

Before he's even moved to place his order, I've already pulled my hand from his back pocket. I stuff the loot into my hoodie and quickly turn to leave. The sour-faced teenager wearing headphones behind me pulls a face.

"Changed my mind." I shrug at her.

The trick is to walk away slowly—with confidence and like I have all the time in the world. Baldie's in for a shock when he attempts to pay for his overpriced sludge. The idiot shouldn't stash his valuables in his back pocket.

I melt into the morning crowd, happily going about their daily routine. Dog walkers. Postmen. Delivery drivers dropping off boxes of newspapers and fresh produce to the numerous corner shops. The picturesque scene makes me fucking sick.

I'm headed for the outdated internet cafe two streets over that I spotted earlier on. None of us escaped Harrowdean with our belongings, let alone mobile phones. We've been totally cut-off from the world.

Using a walking map I pilfered from the holiday park's office, I volunteered to find the nearest town and get us back online. We already needed food, clothing and more medical supplies—requiring me to swipe some cash.

Before I set my sights on greater targets in my early twenties, I honed my skills as a street thief. I don't care what kind of person that makes me.

The rich take from the poor all the livelong day, and we don't kick up a fuss. Why shouldn't it work in reverse?

"Morning." The cafe's owner waves me in. "Just here for coffee, or you want internet?"

I adjust the heavy backpack on my shoulder. "Two computers. Half an hour should do."

The fact that this place exists at all speaks to the elderly demographic in the town it took me two hours to find. I haven't heard of anyone using internet cafes like this in the last decade. I was convinced I'd be stuck using the public library.

"Two?" he repeats.

Nodding to his plugged in phone, I slide an extra note over. "Your charger as well."

His grey brows raise. Sighing, I add another note. He palms the crisp twenties, any further questions drying up. I accept the charger then follow his pointed finger to the back of the cafe. Two monitors sit next to each other.

Sinking into the chair, I fish the two phones I've managed to lift from my hoodie. Baldie wasn't my first mark; I had already targeted a distracted parent wrestling two kids from her flashy Range Rover outside the supermarket. It was easy to lift her phone and cash.

I keep the screens angled slightly to prevent any prying eyes. It's child's play to commence a hard reset on both phones. I snap the SIM cards in half before sliding in new ones I purchased earlier.

Two working phones.

We're in business.

While the phones reboot, I pull up the search engine on my second computer. Ripley and Lennox were itching to join me, even though she can barely walk. The least I can do is report back with news.

I quickly tap in *Harrowdean Manor* then watch the breaking news stories populate. We holed up for two nights, until the food ran out. That's long enough for word to spread.

As I suspected, the official story is vague in the extreme. Details are sparse enough to satisfy the public's demands for action but conceal the truth about how the riot came to an unceremonious end.

> **Deadly riot at psychiatric institute ends in violence.**
> **Hostages rescued, multiple casualties reported.**
> **Sir Bancroft II to make a public statement as criminal investigation gathers speed.**

Scoffing under my breath, I scan through the final story. The silver-haired son of a bitch will soon charm the media. He always does. Even with the evidence pouring out of Blackwood, it took Harrowdean revolting to get the world talking this much.

Yet he's still a free man.

And there's still no justice.

The mention of Warner's employer, Sabre Security, catches my eye. I don't expect a full breakdown of an active criminal investigation, but these Sabre people seem to be kicking their feet.

There's some crap about cooperating witnesses from Blackwood but nothing more. It's infuriating. Why do we accept the existence of evil so quickly but discount the truth just as fast when it stares us in the face?

Because it's uncomfortable.

It's a mark of failure as humans.

We treat the truth with contempt when it doesn't tell us what we want to hear. It's far easier to turn the other cheek, to pretend like suffering doesn't exist all around us. We keep scrolling, drinking down the easy to stomach content we're drip fed instead.

At the bottom of the article, there's a number for a tip hotline. I type it into the first now-unlocked phone then study the half-empty cafe while waiting for the line to connect.

"Sabre Security," a perky voice chirps. "You've reached Operation Nightshade's tip line. Tara speaking."

"Tell them to print the truth," I whisper angrily. "Some of us don't have time for your investigation to gather speed."

There's a brief pause.

"Who am I speaking to?"

"And tell your idiot boss to look beneath Kingsman dorms."

"Sir, if I can just—"

"Each institute has a Zimbardo wing. You need to tear them all apart."

Loaded silence. I've got her attention.

"Priory Lane. Blackwood Institute. Harrowdean Manor," I lay them out, one by one. "All gone. You have the evidence you need to shut the remaining institutes down before Bancroft decides to clean house."

A scrabble on the other end makes me pause before hanging up. They're probably tracking the call. No matter, I'll be gone soon enough.

"This is Theodore Young," a new voice announces. "Your call has been escalated to me. Tell me, what might we find beneath Kingsman dorms?"

"Ask the pink-haired bitch who tortured my friend. She knows all about it."

The sudden intake of breath is curious. I have no clue who the woman that saved Ripley and Lennox is, only that she works for the prestigious security firm. We only have jagged pieces of a much larger puzzle.

His breath rattles down the line. "We've had plenty of hoax calls. Prove to me you're trustworthy."

"Trustworthy?" I check to ensure that no one is listening. "What about the trust put in a faceless corporation to protect the unwell? Or the trust put in you to bring them to justice? Don't talk to me about fucking trust."

"I'm in a position to help if you have information," he tries to placate. "This is a fast-moving situation, and I understand several patients from Harrowdean remain unaccounted for. Are you one of them?"

"What, amongst the dead bodies Incendia has piled up?" I laugh hollowly. "They're hunting us with helicopters and guns. How do I know *you're* trustworthy?"

His sigh stretches across several seconds. Bad day at the office, clearly. If Theodore is looking for a shred of sympathy, he better not hold his breath. I'm willing to cooperate, but only for the right price.

"We can offer protection," Theodore replies. "Will that earn your trust?"

"Empty words won't. We've heard this spiel before, and it amounted to nothing in the end. I need assurances this time."

"I'm not sure I can give that to you over the phone. We should arrange to meet at a rendezvous point. My superiors will want to hear your testimony."

"So you can hand us over to Bancroft and take his hush money? I'll pass."

His voice drops to a low whisper. "Off the record, that evil bastard Bancroft is going to get what's coming to him. I'll personally see to it. The pink-haired woman? She's dead. He's going to pay for that."

Ah. His reaction is an emotional one. Curious indeed. That would've repulsed me before. Now I find myself wondering how I would react in similar circumstances. If Ripley's death would impact me so viscerally.

Agony constricts my lungs at the thought.

Grief? Fear? Regret?

It's exhausting, telling all these emotions apart.

"I have others who deserve to be included in this decision," I eventually concede. "We will discuss your offer. How can I reach you?"

Theodore rattles off a phone number, different from the public line I found online. I quickly tap it into the spare phone and end the call before he can utter another word. Another SIM card snapped and discarded.

Shoving everything into the overflowing backpack, I haul ass to leave the internet cafe. If he's committed to earning our trust, Theodore won't follow the location my call inevitably gave his team.

I make it back to our hideout far quicker than my trek into the nearest town, skin prickling with the need to lay eyes on the three people I left behind.

Shoulders aching from the weight of the goods I'm hauling back, the holiday park is still deserted when I arrive. It will be for another month or two. Even though we boarded over the smashed window with several cardboard boxes I found, we can't stay much longer. It's too risky.

I knock on the door three times then twice more. There's a wait as footsteps move inside. The curtain twitches, showing Lennox's tired face before he clicks the lock to allow me inside.

"Fuck, Xan. You've been gone for hours."

"It's not exactly around the corner," I grumble while stepping in.

"We were getting worried."

In the cramped living area, Ripley lays on the retro, flower-print sofa with her legs stretched over Raine. He's fiddling with those ridiculous sunglasses he wears, the pair clearly mid-conversation.

"Xan," she breathes a sigh of relief. "All clear?"

"Yeah, no trouble. Just a long walk."

"Did you find what you need?"

"Enough to restock and get us online."

I reach into the full backpack to pull out a grease-stained paper bag. Ripley squeaks when the paper bag sails through the air and collides with her chest. The smell of baked goods permeates the cramped space.

"What is this?"

Avoiding her stare, I resume pulling items out. "For you."

I lay out more bandages and gauze. Pain relief. The phones and charger. A few clean shirts and miniature toiletries. Sanitary towels. And as much food as I could feasibly carry.

"Wait." Raine holds up his hand. "It's... Hmm, I smell sugar. Fresh dough. Maybe icing? Oh, I know! I know!"

"Cream-filled doughnuts," she tells him. "Good guess."

"Good nose," he corrects.

Ripley pulls out a golden doughnut, casting me a very suspicious look. "Apparently, Xander is an excellent guesser too."

I clear my throat, organising the packs of dried ramen. "No idea what you're talking about."

Lennox leans against the bright-orange cabinets, looking between us both. "What am I missing?"

"Apart from the fact that this man has made it his mission to stalk me relentlessly ever since he arrived at Harrowdean? And probably months in Priory Lane before that?"

My mouth tugs up in a satisfied smile. I wasn't sure she'd realise my choice of flavour was deliberate.

"I hate doughnuts," Ripley explains. "Apart from one kind."

"Cream-filled?" Lennox guesses.

With everything laid out on the table, I finally level her with a look. "Your choice of doughnut flavour is relevant information to me. And I dislike the unknown."

"Is that the stalker's manifesto?" Raine smothers a laugh.

"I'd say so." Lennox rolls his eyes.

Ripley sighs. "I suppose I've heard worse justifications."

Her voice is laced with sarcasm, but the tiny, reluctant smile tugging at her mouth screams of amusement. It makes my thundering pulse do all kinds of strange things.

"There weren't even any doughnuts in either institute." Raine frowns at the bag placed in his hands. "So how did you find that stupidly specific information out?"

"Trade secret," I deadpan. "Check the *manifesto*. I'm sure it's in there."

They all burst out laughing. Unable to stop myself, I join in. It's an odd feeling—one that pulls at my belly and abdominal muscles in an unfamiliar way. I haven't used those muscles for this purpose much.

"Xander's worrying tendency to overstep every boundary known to man aside." Raine pulls out a doughnut. "Did you find anything out?"

I take a seat at the kitchen table. "It's as we thought. The story's all under wraps. Whispers about the investigation but nothing solid. Bancroft's still preening for the cameras and spouting shit."

"You lifted these?" Lennox gestures to the phones.

"Yeah, wiped and ready to go. There are more SIM cards in the bag. Cash too."

Nodding, Lennox takes one of the phones to start fiddling with. "Good."

I removed the thick bandages around his hand yesterday, applying a lighter pad with gauze instead. The dressing on his face is gone too, leaving a fresh, pink slash across his cheek behind.

"I called Sabre Security."

My words cause Raine to drop his doughnut. He curses to himself while Lennox sets the phone down so he can give me his full attention.

"Why?" he growls.

"Testing the waters. We need to know what our options are."

"Xan, I thought we agreed—"

"I didn't cut a deal or make any agreements with them. The person I spoke to offered a secure rendezvous to exchange information. The same protection offer. I've got his contact number."

"Who was it? The director?" Ripley asks.

"No, someone called Theodore."

"Theo?" she repeats, eyes narrowed. "I know that name."

We all wait for her to cycle through her thoughts. Ripley dusts off her sugar-speckled fingertips, the doughnut now discarded.

"In the Z wing…" She shakes her head. "The woman, Alyssa. She was communicating with her team. I heard her call his name. Theo."

"So he's legit," Lennox concludes.

"Seems so." I focus on Ripley. "She's dead."

Ripley's eyes snap up to mine. "What?"

"The pink-haired mole. She died." I shrug nonchalantly. "Sounds like this Theodore character has some personal stake in taking Bancroft down. He seemed committed to helping us."

"I bet he did!" Lennox explodes in frustration. "You know that Incendia has their claws in everyone! Government. Private companies. Investors. They're probably bankrolling these Sabre pricks too!"

"No." Ripley turns to face off against Lennox. "Warner works for them. I trust his judgement."

"Some anonymous guard who ditched us? Great plan, Rip."

"I'm telling you, he's on our side, Nox!" she argues back. "Would it kill you to have some faith for once?"

"Yes! It could kill us!"

Anger tattooed into every line of his expression, Lennox pushes off from the kitchen cabinets and disappears deeper into the mobile home. I wait for one of the bedroom doors to slam shut before speaking again.

"That was a rather short honeymoon period."

"Fuck off, Xan." Ripley clenches her eyes shut. "His trust issues are going to get us killed."

I'd like to point out the irony that she's demanding trust from the man she tried to frame, but something tells me it wouldn't go down well. Besides, the pair seem to be putting their differences aside, if Lennox's heartfelt display in the kitchen was any indication.

"He has a point," Raine says quietly. "You of all people know how deep the corporation's ties run. We should be cautious."

Ripley stares down at her bandaged leg, the white cotton revealed by the long, oversized tee she wears with panties.

"Care to fill me in?"

Raine's head tilts in my direction, but he doesn't answer. I wait for Ripley to gather herself, watching her chest rise as she takes a deep breath.

"Bancroft. Incendia's president."

I nod in response. "We were acquainted in Priory Lane."

"Well, I met him before the Z wing." Her nose scrunches with a look of revulsion. "Incendia Corporation controls a huge portfolio of assets. Including two major investment firms in London."

I'm aware that her richer than sin uncle is an investment banker. Apparently, he's embroiled in all this too. He dripped with entitlement and wealth during his trip to the medical wing when Rick carved her up.

I overheard his brutal disownment speech. The man holds no love in his heart for the orphaned, mentally ill niece he was lumped with. Something inside Ripley broke that day when he walked away.

"You're sure he's involved?"

"I know he is," Ripley confirms, rage forming lines that bracket her mouth. "After Harrison beat the shit out of me over that business card… Bancroft paid me a visit. Told me he had my uncle's consent to repurpose me."

"Repurpose?" Raine asks breathily.

"It's what the Zimbardo program does." I swipe a finger over an old stain on the table. "Dehumanise, manipulate and torture until the mind breaks. Then it can be reformed."

"To what end?"

"Incendia creates mindless killing machines by destroying the vulnerable, one brain cell at a time." My lip curls at the thought. "Then they sell their creations off to the highest bidder."

Raine grows even paler than Ripley. "Jesus Christ."

We've shared enough of our past for him to understand. It was never a secret—hell, he was our customer once. But the real purpose behind the institutes is a tough pill to swallow.

"If I can't even trust my own flesh and blood… I can't trust anyone." Ripley pinches the bridge of her nose. "I hate it, but Lennox is right."

"Don't tell him that. It'll go straight to his head."

"Not funny, Xan. What the hell are we going to do?"

Staring at the phone left behind on the table, I can confidently say I have no fucking clue. We're completely alone out here with nothing but the clothes on our backs and the truth we carry with us.

Telling it may just set us free.

But it may also get us killed.

CHAPTER 13
RIPLEY

SAILOR SONG – GIGI PEREZ

RAIN HAMMERS against the mobile home's thin roof, creating a deafening roar. It's like we're trapped in the belly of a moving aeroplane. I stare up at the ceiling, unable to sleep. Each falling droplet too closely resembles the patter of gunfire.

It doesn't matter that we're taking turns to keep watch while the others sleep. Nor does it matter that we've seen no signs of life in the holiday park for the last few days while recuperating and weighing our options. It's as secure as anywhere for now.

That doesn't eliminate the fear, though.

There are still targets on our heads.

Carefully rolling over, I study Raine's face. Even though it's the middle of the afternoon, he's asleep. I have no idea how with his hypersensitivity. Even I have a headache from the pounding rain.

I run my finger down his straight, perfectly proportioned nose. There are slight indentations on either side that I never noticed before, evidence of him constantly wearing glasses. He still wears the aviators everyday like they're his proudest possession.

Without them on, I can see his thick black lashes, framing the brilliant, honeyed orbs that he keeps hidden from the world. I trace my fingertip over his cupid's bow, the defined dip exaggerating his full lips.

We're running dangerously low on his withdrawal medication. He puts on a brave face for our sakes, but I see the constant trembling, cold sweats and how he barely eats anything.

The methadone alleviates most of the withdrawal symptoms but not all of them. Without it, there's no telling how he'll react. Getting clean from years of opiate use is a long and extremely difficult process. Not to mention the impact his returned cravings would have.

With all the attention on Raine and his dwindling supply of pills, I've managed to keep my own ticking time bomb quiet. I know Xander sees everything, but out here, there's nothing he can do to help.

The insomnia can be explained away. We're all stressed and bone-deep tired. It's the constant agitation and unmanageable mood swings that are taking me to a dangerous place.

I screamed at Lennox yesterday for eating the final stale doughnut before bursting into violent sobs when he offered me the last bite. It was safest to barricade myself in the rear bedroom until I could think straight again.

"Rip?" Raine mumbles.

"You're supposed to be sleeping."

"As are you."

"How do you know I'm not asleep?"

"Besides the fact that we're talking?" He cracks a yawn. "Your breathing. Short and fast. Not exactly conducive to REM sleep."

"I don't think I like it when you spy on my body with your weird, Batman hearing."

"Sorry."

Moving my fingertips to his closed lids, I stroke the soft skin, following the curvature of his eyes. In the small bedroom, filled with late afternoon sunlight filtering through net curtains, it's easy to pretend we're the last two humans alive.

Part of me likes the idea of Raine having no one else, no matter how fucked up that is to admit. He'd never be able to abandon me if we were the last two humans. Not like everyone else has. I'd be his sole reprieve.

Love didn't stop my parents from dying, leaving me an orphan. It didn't stop my uncle from keeping me at arm's length until he cut all ties with me. And it didn't stop Holly from following them all on a fast-track course out of my life.

"You were sleeping so peacefully," I whisper.

"I think I was dreaming."

My soft touches still. "Can I ask you something personal?"

"Are we still at the stage where we ask for permission?" He smiles gently.

"I guess not. Think we've moved past all formalities at this point."

"So what's the question?"

I smooth the light creases around his left eye. "Can you still see in your dreams?"

Raine runs a hand over my curled-up body. "Sometimes I see visual images. Memories from before I lost my sight. Other times it's flashes with more sensory input like smells, textures, even tastes."

"What does that look like?"

He thinks for a moment, his caramel eyes now open and bouncing around. "I guess… a messy, colourful patchwork quilt."

The fact that he explains such a complicated concept with open-hearted honesty is what I admire the most. Raine has his demons, but he also has something not many can relate to.

The purest of souls.

That's a rare commodity.

"Can I ask you something else?"

"What is this, question time?" he jokes.

"I can stop."

"It's fine. Lay it on me, guava girl."

Snuggling closer, I take a deep breath of his salty, citrus scent. "Can you see me in your head?"

"I… have an impression of you." He cups my cheek.

"How?"

"It's made of fragments pieced together from touch. I guess I can tell you how your appearance feels to me. The image is a little more unclear, though. It's half imagination and half my best guess."

Equal parts confusion and curiosity draw my brows together. "So it's not an actual image?"

"Probably not in the same way you see me in your head. Images look different to me now. More textured and amorphous."

His inability to see me doesn't take away from the intense bond we've formed. Raine was the first person to worm his way inside my heart in a very long time. He did the impossible.

"Does it bother you?" he asks worriedly. "The fact that I can't see?"

"God, no!" I rush out. "Of course not."

"Then what's on your mind?"

"It's just… I thought it was safer to be alone. That's why I kept you at arm's length for so long. I feel like I wasted a lot of time by doing that."

"And now?" he urges.

"Now I'm glad we're in this together. It makes no sense, given what we're facing… but I've never felt safer than when I'm with you."

Raine listens intently, but his silence fires my uncertainty.

"Am I going insane?" I laugh.

"No." He tenderly brushes a hand through my short curls. "You're not."

"I want us to work, Raine. I want everything I was scared to even consider before. That fear has gone. We could be killed or thrown in prison at any moment, and I'm tired of wasting time."

The smile that blossoms on his lips is breathtaking. I just wish it didn't make my stomach curdle when my thoughts stray to whether I'll ever see a smile like it on Xander or Lennox. If they're even capable of it.

"But…"

"But… the others," he finishes for me.

"They're important to me. Even if I don't understand how or why, I know that much."

"You still don't get it. Do you?" Raine asks after a beat.

"Get what?"

Shifting closer, his nose brushes mine as he crowds my personal space. "I've accepted their place in your life."

"You… uh, have?"

"Because I don't have an image of your looks, and I don't need it. I'll never need it."

"I'm not sure I follow—"

"Just listen," he interrupts

I seal my lips, waiting for him to explain.

"I know your soul, Rip. I know your voice. Your scent. Your breathing patterns. Your intonations. I have the incredible privilege of seeing intimate, invisible, even unconscious details about you. I'll never have to share that privilege."

Numbly, I wonder if he can sense my heart soaring right now, racing at breakneck speed. Raine's self-satisfied smirk tells me he's all too aware of what his confession is doing to me.

"That's why I don't care how Xander obsesses over you," he continues. "Or how Lennox can't even comprehend the depths of his feelings because they're so overwhelming. I don't care if my brothers love you too because what we have will always be unique."

My toes curl when his lips press against mine.

"They can own their individual pieces of your heart, but what we have is just ours. And that's enough for me."

Too shocked to respond, I let his kiss linger. It's deep and passionate, our mouths familiar enough to fall into a tempo that feels natural. Raine kisses the hell out of me then rests our foreheads together.

"You… love me?" I murmur.

He chuckles. "Is that the only part you heard?"

"I mean, it kinda stood out."

His sigh sweeps across my face. "Yes, Rip. I love you."

"Can you say it again?"

"I love you so fucking much, I'm willing to give you this because I know you need them too. And hell, they need you. We all do."

A loose tear trails down my cheek. That single droplet encapsulates a lifetime of grief and loneliness. All the hope for a different life I imprisoned long ago when I realised that love was unrealistic. It dies and life goes on.

I didn't think I wanted it.

I didn't think I needed it.

But for the first time, I feel like my heart is beating wholly in my chest. I'm not just the lonely orphan, misunderstood by the world, finding solitude in her oil paints and immoral choices.

I'm loved.

Raine actually loves me.

Slanting my mouth back over his, I pour all that grief into my kiss. Every sleepless night spent sobbing into a pillow. The hole in my heart that formed as I grew up without a parent's love or touch. The rejection and self-hatred my condition created.

Sometime during those empty years, I stopped waiting for someone to love me. I stopped trying to love myself. It was enough to escape this world through my art, longing for the next life… where someone might love me instead.

Feeling his lips move against mine, I wonder how I made it this far on my own. Sheer determination and will to survive alone, I suppose. For the longest time, it was enough.

Not anymore.

I don't want to just survive by any means necessary. To live a solitary existence, taking comfort in the inanimate and protecting my heart from any further hurt. I want the whole fucking world. A future. A goddamn life. And they're all in it.

Fingers fisting in his sandy-blonde hair, I take it all. Every last drop of commitment and devotion his kiss has to offer. He lets me push my tongue into his mouth and taste each dark corner, needing to commit this moment to memory before it floats away.

"Ripley," he gasps into my lips. "Fuck, babe. I want to touch you so badly, but these walls aren't exactly soundproof."

"I don't care if they hear."

"The guys—"

"Can mind their own business," I finish his sentence.

After pushing him onto his back, I sit up, tugging my baggy shirt over my head. I'm left in panties and the slightly thinner bandage on my thigh that Xander applied last night.

"You're still hurt." He worries his lip.

"Not enough to change my mind. I need to feel you inside me."

"Rip…"

"Just strip."

Shimmying my panties off, I watch him deliberate before eventually tossing his clothing. He was sleeping in boxers and one of the clean shirts Xander brought back, his jeans nearby in case we need to move fast.

Raine lays back on the bed, a hand pumping his stiff length. For a second, I leisurely watch him. How his muscles clench and pull taut. The smooth curves of his pectorals. Flat stomach and tapered hips.

"I can feel you watching me," he teases.

"That isn't actually possible, you know."

"I can assure you it is."

"Well, sue me. I like the view."

He smirks proudly. "Bring your gorgeous ass to me. Just go slow, alright?"

I carefully lift myself on top of him, keeping the weight off my leg. "How would you know my ass is gorgeous?"

"Call it intuition."

His touch skims over my hips and waist, each teasing brush electrifying my nerves. When his hands move to cup my breasts, I arch my back to push my chest into them. Raine makes a low, satisfied noise in his throat.

He squeezes my mounds, his thumbs sliding over my aching nipples.

Each brush causes them to harden into sensitive points. Everything is tender, heightening the twinges of pleasure.

I grind myself on him, feeling his shaft sliding against my pussy lips. It feels more intimate somehow, now that we've laid all our cards on the table. This isn't just sex anymore. We've become more than the shallow labels I insisted on.

"I can feel how wet you are," Raine marvels, lightly pinching my nipple. "Were you soaked when Lennox watched us the other day?"

"Yes," I admit.

"You wanted to make him jealous, didn't you?"

Sliding a hand down my body, he locates my pulsating clit. I gasp when his thumb circles the sensitive bundle of nerves, causing my skin to tighten with pins and needles.

"Ripley," he says sternly. "Answer the question."

Between his length sliding back and forth in a torturous taunt and his thumb pressing down on my clit, I have no hope of keeping the truth to myself. It spills out in a low whine.

"Y-Yes."

"I bet he was dying for a taste of your sweet cunt." He grins wolfishly. "And furious when he couldn't have it."

Pleasure rolls over me. I love the thought of driving Lennox insane with lust. Especially when I'm touching Raine. He spent so long trying to tear us apart, it felt right to tease him with his failure.

"You know, I imagined what it would be like if he joined us," Raine admits as he flicks and circles my bud. "How I'd feel if he touched you while I rode your mouth."

The mental image is enough to make the heat within my core boil over. I push myself against him, begging for any amount of friction. All I want is for him to sink inside me and ease the hollow ache.

"Can you imagine it, Rip?"

"It crossed my mind," I whimper.

"Did you imagine him bending you over and pushing inside you? How would it feel taking us both, do you think?"

"Fuck, Raine." My pussy clenches, weeping with unmet need. "Please."

"It's not something I've tried before. I wonder if he has."

The dirty-minded bastard is going to kill me off with all these mental images. Sure, I wanted to piss Lennox off. Perhaps I even considered what it would feel like, having them both inside me. But Raine's bringing the fantasy to life with each filthy word he whispers.

Reaching between us, I seize his shaft, tired of playing games. He's hot and pulsing in my palm, a bead of shining pre-come gathering on his tip. I slick the moisture with my thumb, watching his breath catch.

"You want to know what I imagined?"

"Fuck yes, babe. Tell me."

I languidly work his length up and down. "I imagined Lennox bending me over while your cock was deep in my throat. He'd be rough. Angry. Determined to prove himself."

Raine breathes raggedly in time to each squeeze. I don't care if it's messed up to be talking about his friend while straddling him like this. None of us have to answer to anyone. If it feels right, I'm doing it.

Circling my entrance with his tip, I hold him at the precipice of satisfaction. An inch from heaven.

"I imagined him shoving himself inside me," I tease breathlessly. "Taking me hard and deep like he wants to fuck the fight out of me. You'd ride my mouth while he fills me from behind."

"Such a dirty little angel," he groans. "Why does this turn me on so much?"

"I think you have a sharing kink, Raine."

Nudging him inside me, I slowly sink down, inch by excruciating inch. He stretches me so perfectly, filling me to the breaking point as he bottoms out. I watch his golden eyes roll back in his head.

"Shit, babe. I think you're right."

Gasping at the intensity, I savour the burn. "I'm all for exploring it. Keep that in mind."

Lifting my hips, I push back down on him. It's an awkward manoeuvre that tugs at my thigh wound, but in the heat of the moment, the pain only amplifies my acute pleasure. We've talked ourselves into a frenzy.

I move slow and steady, taking him deep with each thrust. His cock pushes against the sweet spot buried within me that makes stars burst behind my eyes. Already, I feel overwhelmed with sensation.

"You feel so fucking good, babe. So good."

He ruts up into me, matching each stroke with one of his own. Raine's always been acutely in tune to my body. His ability to see the unseen comes into play when we fuck. He's as attentive as he is passionate.

We're perfectly synchronised, reading each other's needs without words. Each time I press down on him, Raine slides up into my cunt with a low groan. I clench tight around him, my walls hugging his length.

Footsteps halt outside the bedroom, making my heart patter harder. My ears straining, each clash becomes harder, more frantic. Raine's muscles clench, his burnt-toffee orbs swallowed whole by expanded pupils.

"Please," I mewl, letting him slam into me. "I need to come."

"Take it, babe. Show me how well you fall apart."

Hands splayed on his chest, I throw my head back. I'm close to exploding. My climax hangs on the cusp of overwhelming me, magnified by the knowledge that those halted footsteps haven't moved away.

When Raine finds my clit again, lightly tugging the tingling bud, all rational thought vanishes. My release hits hard and fast. I don't know if it's exhaustion or the imbalanced chemicals swamping my brain, but the orgasm is blisteringly intense.

"Yes!" I moan loudly.

Raine eases to a slow roll, his hips shifting up into me. He's breathless too, but I haven't felt him finish. He's still thick inside me, holding my climax in suspension as aftershocks move in.

"You're bleeding, Rip."

"Hmm?"

His movements slow. "Your leg."

Glancing down, I find the thin bandage speckled with blood. I didn't even feel it. We ruled out an infection when Xander stitched the wound yesterday, but it's still tender.

"We should stop."

"No!" I writhe on top of him. "Don't you dare."

Grasping my hips, Raine gently manoeuvres out of me. I cry out at the sudden loss. I'm about to chew him out when he lays me down, feeling for my legs then spreading them wide so he can settle between them.

He doesn't say a word as he slides back into me, assuming the position of power. I greedily accept his forceful thrust, my blood pumping like liquid caramel through my veins after my first release.

"You drive me insane, Rip. I want to take care of you, but instead, I'm fucking you senseless because you don't know when to take no for an answer."

"You're right. I don't." I stare up at his unfocused expression. "So shut up and fuck me senseless, Raine. Give me what I want."

"So demanding."

His grin tells a different story. Secretly, he loves it. The explosive way our bodies collide. The sense of control it gives him in a world determined to take his autonomy away. With me, he can take a piece of himself back.

As he begins pounding into me faster, it feels like Raine is determined to prove a point. I've given him free rein, and he's damn well going to take it regardless of who may be listening nearby.

My mind fantasises about the possibilities. I know Xander has no respect for boundaries, that's old news. He'll happily munch his popcorn while listening to us if he so pleases. The man doesn't care about social graces.

Lennox… He's the question mark.

Our dynamic is changing, morphing from raw hatred to bitterly reluctant infatuation. I don't know if the new, softer Lennox would dare interrupt our privacy. He's an unknown to me.

Raine's continued thrusting shows how little he cares too. He hasn't just accepted the others' place in my life; I have a sneaking suspicion he actually fucking loves it.

"I want you to give me one more, babe."

With lust snaking through me, I fist the tangled bedsheets. "Yes."

"That's it. Give me everything." He urgently ruts into me, chasing his own climax. "Show me that you love me too, Rip. I need to feel it."

I'm sure I don't imagine the barely audible curse emanating from outside the bedroom door. I don't have the mental capacity to question it as Raine ducks down to kiss my chest, sucking a nipple in between his lips.

The cramped bedroom is a blur all around me. Raine's silhouette fills my vision, dappled with sparkling sunlight. Stray hair falls across his slick forehead, the sunshine accentuating every taut muscle in his neck and shoulders.

He licks and sucks my nipple, his teeth scratching against the peak. His playful bite sets off sparks in my mind that catch alight and spread, filling my whole body with delicious heat.

"I can feel you clenching around me," he marvels. "I know you're close, babe. Let go."

"Oh god," I whine. "Raine!"

"Let them hear you scream my name."

The heat inside me reaches its apex. Everything seizes, my nervous system knotted so tightly, it's just begging to be unravelled. All he has to do is shove me into that downward spiral.

Raine draws my breast into his mouth, pulling on my skin so firmly, I know it'll leave a bright mark. An indelible reminder of all we've shared. I still can't quite believe it.

He loves me.

And… I think I love him too.

I know I do.

My second climax hits harder than the first, the blistering cloud of pure euphoria sweeping everything else out. I'm a sputtering wreck, my entire body shattering into a thousand unrecognisable shards.

Raine bellows in time to me crying his name again. I feel him judder inside me, his release filling me up with a rush of heat. The feeling stretches out my orgasm until it's echoing on in tortuous waves.

Slumping, he hides his face in my neck. I can feel how violently his heart is beating through his skin. Raine breathes hard, his hair tickling my face as I pant for air too.

When my brain decides to function again, I realise how much my thigh is screaming at me. The discomfort didn't matter in the moment. Now I know I've pushed myself too far. Worth it, though.

"Raine," I whisper throatily. "I need to go clean up."

He groans, half-awake. "Are you okay?"

"Yes. More than okay."

Lifting himself off me, he collapses to the side so I'm free. I move stiffly, grimacing at the blood-soaked bandage around my thigh. Xander's going to chew me out if I've popped a stitch.

Raine catches my arm. "You're not okay."

"It's just a bit of blood. Stay here."

"I can help—"

"I've got this."

Teeth gritted, I stand up. I'm headed for the door to find the bathroom when something stops me. I look back at Raine in the bed, his attention fixed on me, even if his eyes aren't.

"Raine?"

"Yeah, guava girl?"

I smile at the silly nickname. "For the record, I love you too."

A stupid grin spreads across his face, softening his pink-flushed features. I leave him smiling like an idiot. Limping out of the bedroom, I'm thankful the corridor is empty. Our voyeur has vanished.

I'm so focused on avoiding being spotted in my naked, messy state, I don't look up as I enter the bathroom. The sound of harsh breathing and low, guttural grunts only filter in when I've closed the door.

"Oh," I squeak.

One hand braced on the sink, Lennox has his jeans around his ankles, the other hand fisting his thick, vein-streaked cock. My eyes bulge at the sight, cataloguing not only his ridiculous size but the blazing desire written all over his face as he jacks off.

"Am I interrupting?" I ask slyly.

Jaw locked, his gaze swings to me. Touching everywhere. My breasts. Raine's love bite. My swollen pussy, slick with our come. Lennox rubs his cock faster, hand flashing up and down, unashamedly drinking me in.

And I let him.

It's a liberating sight.

My feet carry me forwards without command. I hold his stare as I reach in to push his hand away. Lennox sucks in a ragged breath when I take over, cupping his shaft and delivering a slow squeeze.

"Did you like listening?"

His tongue darts out to wet his lips. "I wanted to break the door down and take you for myself."

"What makes you think I'd let you?" I rhythmically stroke his cock.

"I know you feel it too, Rip." His stubble-smothered throat bobs. "I know you're struggling to fathom how the person you once hated most can become the very thing keeping you sane."

"You drive me insane," I correct.

"Which one of us looks insane right now?"

My lips spread in a satisfied smirk. "You."

"Exactly."

"Since we're being honest, I enjoy the thought that I've driven you to this. I want that power. In fact, I want you on your knees, begging for the chance to fuck me like Raine does."

"That's what you want?" he grits out.

"Yes. I want you grovelling on your fucking knees, Lennox Nash."

"Then when the time comes, that's what I'll do."

Grabbing a handful of my hair, he pulls my mouth to his. Lennox kisses me above the hot flush that Raine left behind. His lips are firm, devouring the memory and replacing it with a brand of his own.

I can feel them both on me. Claiming. Marking. Possessing. But in my mind, they're distinct. Even Xander has his own little patch of neurons dedicated just to him. There's no competition.

Working Lennox's length over, I call the final victory. His huge cock jerks in my hand, mirroring his sudden grunt into my mouth, and I feel sticky ribbons hit my lower belly.

We separate, his lips rapidly pecking mine when I steal a final taste. I love how closely his pale-green eyes resemble a seaborne storm right now. Unruly and uncontrollable.

"I look forward to it," I purr, releasing his dick. "Preferably away from prying ears. My roommates seem to have no sense of privacy."

Snorting, he looks down in embarrassment. That's when he notices the saturated bandage on my thigh, now leaking thin trails of crimson.

Lennox pierces me with a glower. "What the fuck?"

"Erm… it was an accident?"

"Raine!" He pushes me away from him even as I start laughing. "I'm going to fucking kill him!"

CHAPTER 14
RIPLEY
HATE ME NOW – RYAN CARAVEO

TIME PASSES DIFFERENTLY when you're running for your life.

It's broken flashes.

Disjointed. Rapid.

Staring out the window at the dreary, grey sky hanging over the hotel, I breathe a matching cloud onto the glass and watch the condensation drip down. The droplets fall slowly, sluggish and tiresome.

It's a total contrast to the energy burning me from inside out. I thought it would've fizzled out after several sleepless nights in the crappy hotel we moved to. That usually does the trick. But not this time around.

The door beeps on the other side of the double room before it clicks open. I recognise Lennox's thudding footsteps. He stomps around like he's determined to shake the earth with his weight alone.

"That son of a bitch turns my stomach," he hisses as the door slams shut.

I turn around to check him over. There's a hollow ache in my stomach that triples at the sight of the food bag clutched in his hands. Lennox offers me a tense smile, pulling his healing facial cut.

He heads for the small table opposite the bathroom. "We're lining his fucking pockets just to keep his mouth shut."

Focused on the newspaper clasped in his hands, Xander lounges on one of the double beds. He spares Lennox a dismissive look over the lines of typed ink that have held his attention for the past hour.

"We're paying over the odds in cash for the hotel's discretion. No IDs and no questions asked. Suck it up, Nox."

"The owner is rinsing us for every goddamn penny!"

Xander shrugs. "We can cover it."

"With more stolen cash?" he retorts.

"If you'd like to offer an alternative solution, be my guest."

With that, Xander disappears back behind his apparently fascinating newspaper. The man's living on a different planet if he thinks the answers to all our problems are printed in that thing.

The media is still acting like we're the bad guys for inciting the riot. All the limited coverage we've seen has been unfairly biased. Apparently, unstable patients overtook Harrowdean. Unprovoked and with the intent to cause maximum destruction.

What's worse is the fact that people are actually swallowing it. Even with rumours of medical malpractice and abuse running rampant. The narrative that we're the instigators is a more palatable truth.

There's been no mention of Rick, Rae or the others in the media. The official public line is that all remaining detainees in Harrowdean have been secured and transferred elsewhere. I'm sure Rick didn't make it that far, though. Like us, he knows too much.

Lennox drops the paper bag on the table. "I know we had to move on at some point, but holing up so close to the city feels like an unnecessary risk. We should pack up and leave."

"Derby is twenty miles away." Xander remains focused on the newspaper.

"Close enough! What if we're recognised?"

"By a greedy hotel owner? Or his half-deaf cleaner?" he harrumphs. "Doubtful."

I turn back to face the window. They've spent the better part of the last week bickering. As the days have passed, it's been harder for me to decipher exactly what about. Something to do with a phone call, I think.

The running shower halts in the attached bathroom. Raine must be nearly done. He's having a rough day, barely able to keep food or water down between fitfully sleeping.

"How is he?" I hear Lennox ask.

"Spent an hour throwing up. I've located a public library with decent computers. So I can forge a paper prescription slip given enough time to fabricate the details and a false ID."

"You can get that stuff on prescription?"

"I've done some research. Rehab patients take it in the community too. I should be able to make something convincing enough to get refills."

Tuning them out, I focus on my breathing. In and out. Chest expanding. Oxygen spreading. If I break the process down in my head, I can fool myself that I'm still the one in control.

My hands shake at my sides, shattering the illusion as quickly as it's able to form. Too much is going on. My defences are shot to pieces right now. I can't control the haywire thoughts invading my mind like I usually can.

I've been turning over what superpower I wish I had for the last ten minutes or so. If I could go incognito, I could slip past the men eyeing me like a ticking bomb and run free. Invisibility would be a cool power.

It would feel so good to run as fast as my little legs can carry me. Strip off my clothes. Sprint into the threatening rain. Or perhaps oncoming traffic. I can see the main road to the city from here.

I wonder if my incognito powers would kick in to stop me from becoming a human pancake if I were struck. I'd like to try—I bet they would. Not even fast-moving cars can slow me down.

Don't they know who I am? I'm Harrowdean's whore. The ultimate stooge. I'm untouchable. Invincible. Not even a high-speed, fatal crash could stop me from running for the hills right now.

"Rip!"

A touch on my shoulder is an unwelcome shock. I jump out of my skin, quickly falling into fight-or-flight. Grabbing the paw-like hand, I tug hard, throwing my assailant forward.

They don't even fight back, allowing me to floor them in record time. How dare they touch me? I don't belong here. Not in this shitty room. Not with these people. Not on the run. This wasn't the plan.

What was the plan?

I can't quite remember.

"Ripley! Hey!"

"I'm invisible!" I roar angrily. "You can't see me!"

Kneeling on the cheap hotel carpet, Lennox peers up at me with concern. "It's me, Rip."

Blinking rapidly, I stare down at him. Lennox Nash. Funny to think he scared me once. Both he and Xander did. I'm not sure why since I can turn invisible. Perhaps if I try hard enough right now, I'll disappear in front of him.

"Talk to me. What's going on in your head?"

"Can you still see me?" I ask in frustration.

Lennox blinks, still on his knees. "Uh, yes. I can."

"Goddammit!" I tug at my hair. "Why isn't it working?"

His newspaper discarded, Xander stands up to approach us. "Why isn't what working, Ripley?"

"I hate it when you look at me like that," I snap at him. "I'm not a zoo animal."

Eyebrows drawn together, Lennox stands up. "No one is looking at you like that, baby. You're not eating or sleeping. What's going on?"

At the mention of food, an embarrassingly loud growl erupts from my stomach. I slap a hand over the offending organ. Why is it making such a fuss? I ate… hell, a few days ago. Maybe?

It doesn't matter. I don't have time to eat or sleep while I'm plotting my grand escape. I'll never master my new superpower if I'm too busy resting like they're always insisting upon.

"Have you ever seen her like this?" Lennox whispers.

Xander shakes his head. "Not to this extent."

"What do we do?"

"No idea. I'm not a damn psychiatrist."

See, this is exactly what I'm talking about. I may as well be invisible. They're talking about me as if I am. Unless… Has it finally happened? I look down at myself, pinching my tattooed forearm to check.

"Stupid!" I hiss impatiently.

Someone is touching me again—Xander. Cursing him out, I attempt to peel his fingers from my bicep. He's trying to direct me over to the bed. I don't want to lay in that again.

"Don't touch me!"

"Ripley," he scolds. "You need to rest."

"I'm not tired. I need to keep working!"

"On what?" Lennox follows us.

"My superpowers, obviously. You can still see me. How can I disappear if you can see me? I have to disappear!"

Lennox's shoulders slump as he turns back to his best friend. "I think we need to forge more prescriptions. How did we not see this coming?"

"I did." Xander exhales. "The signs have been there for a while."

"Why didn't you say anything?"

"We've been a little busy running for our lives, Nox."

I'm still trapped by his grip. It feels like he's scalding me. When I pull free, Xander bands his arms around me, cinching me tight like a straitjacket. I'm strong-armed, bucking and protesting, over to the bed.

"Xan, I don't think—"

"I'm trying to get her to rest," he justifies.

"You shouldn't physically restrain her, though!"

"Do you have a better idea? I'm all ears."

The bathroom door opens on their continued arguing. Spotting Raine, damp and redressed, I cry in relief. I know he'll understand. Maybe he'll help me practise my invisibility.

Raine is safe. Warm. Familiar. He never hurt me like these two did. I didn't have to forgive him because he's been nothing but genuine and respectful towards me since day one.

"What happened?" He tilts his head, listening closely.

Lennox clears his throat. "We're concerned Ripley's having a manic episode."

"Help me, Raine!" I blurt out in panic. "He's trying to make me sleep. I don't want to sleep."

One hand outstretched to feel for obstacles, Raine follows the sound of my whimpers. I sob in pure relief when he eases me from Xander's imprisonment and wraps me in a warm, citrus-scented hug.

"It's okay, guava girl. No one is going to make you sleep if you don't want to."

Arms thrown around his neck, I break down in hysterical tears. Raine lets me cling to him, covering his fresh shirt in moisture. If I could share my invisibility, I'd extend it to him. He can run with me.

"What were you thinking?" he mutters above my lowered head. "She needs to feel safe and supported. We have no idea what's going on inside her head right now."

"I'm trying to help!" Xander booms.

"By scaring her? Great plan."

"I just thought…"

"No, Xan. She's a person. You can't take her choice away even if you think it's for the best."

I'm grateful when they all shut up. The frenzied voices yelling in my head are making it difficult to focus.

"Come on," Raine coaxes, clutching me tightly. "Did you know I had panic attacks for months after I lost my sight?"

"N-No," I stammer.

"My sensitive hearing made it feel like the entire world was screaming at me. The trauma centre assigned me a therapist. He told me to picture a giant ocean wave crashing over me when I was panicking."

"I'm not… This isn't… I'm not panicking! I just don't want to rest!"

He rubs up and down my back. "I know. You don't have to. But I do want you to try and calm down."

His fresh scent is seeping into me, drawing me into the dream of a warm summer's day on the beach. Sipping orange juice and dipping my toes into the salty ocean. Content. Invisible. Free.

"The waves I imagine sparkle in the sunlight," Raine murmurs soothingly. "And I sometimes picture dolphins dipping in and out of them."

"Dolphins?" I whimper.

"Why not? It's my imagination. You can picture a massive pink unicorn swimming along if that's what you want. Give it a try."

Ignoring the sounds of heavy breathing and moving footsteps behind us, I desperately yank together my mind's frayed strands. I can do this for Raine. It's just a silly game.

Hands fisting in his t-shirt, I screw my eyes shut. The blackness of my closed lids fades as my vision takes shape. Shimmering, aqua waves, topped with a light-white froth. Gleaming sunshine. Squalling seagulls.

"Let the wave roll over you," Raine encourages just loud enough for me to hear. "Feel the water. The bubbles. The current carrying you along."

"W-What if I drown?"

"You won't. It's perfectly safe to let yourself bob along, floating on the water. Let it crash over you and wash everything else away."

The sobs ripping out of me slowly begin to ease as I picture calm waves falling over me. The water feels like silk. It kisses my skin and warms my bones, pushing out the intense energy that's been tormenting me.

"That's it." Raine strokes the back of my head. "Deep breaths. Did you see the unicorn yet?"

"A whale," I breathe out unsteadily. "Beluga."

"Okay, we can work with that. Keep going."

His hand moves rhythmically over my spine. Each stroke mirrors the waves that have filled my head, swelling up and undulating with the swirling current. White, pearlescent whales pop their head up and squeal.

I'm not sure how long we stand there for, lost in our heads and ignoring the entire world. Long enough for terror to set in when I realise how out of control I'm feeling right now.

"I... don't f-feel so good," I hiccup.

"I know." Raine blows out a long breath. "Tell us what you need."

"I want to go. We have to run."

"We're going to keep you safe, Rip. I promise."

No. Nobody can.

The sound of the other two talking filters back into my awareness. They're exchanging urgent whispers elsewhere in the hotel room.

"How long will it take you to forge a prescription? And do you know what she takes?"

"Of course, I do," Xander responds. "Stay here."

"Take a phone. Be careful."

Hearing Xander grab something and leave, I immediately pull away from Raine. He can't leave. I didn't mean it. I'll share my invisibility with him—he shouldn't go out alone. It isn't safe.

"Rip!" Lennox calls out. "I brought something back I think you'll like."

Skidding to a halt, I look between him and the door. "But, Xander..."

"He'll be back soon," Raine rushes to assure me. "I smell food. Are you hungry?"

I shake my head, reluctantly turning away from the door. Lennox has started emptying the bag he brought back, laying out takeaway cartons. That gnawing in my belly is back. Tiny ravenous butterflies.

"Come and eat something," he encourages.

"I don't have time to eat!"

"Then I can't show you the other thing I got." Lennox raises an eyebrow. "Food, Rip. I need you to eat something."

Tiptoeing closer, I follow Raine over to the table. "What's the other thing?"

"Something that will help. But food first."

"Come sit with us," Raine adds with a smile.

They both sit down, passing plastic cutlery between them before digging into their food. The salty, savoury scents assault my nose. Spices. Herbs. Something rich and fragrant. The butterflies are going berserk now.

"Mmm." Raine chews his mouthful. "Sure we can't tempt you, Rip?"

I stare at them, conflicted.

"This is so good," he continues with exaggerated enthusiasm. "We've been living off crap for so long, I forgot what real food tastes like."

"Enjoy it while it lasts," Lennox responds, though he keeps an eye on me.

I've inched within touching distance of a carton. I can see herb-studded rice and a vibrant sauce with chunks of meat. My mouth waters. All the fizzing energy that's distracted me narrows in on that carton.

Nudging a plastic fork closer, Lennox moves it to the edge of the table. I have my hands on the carton and the fork in my mouth before I can draw a breath. Exotic flavours explode on my tongue.

"S'good," I moan.

Lennox looks down at his food, smiling to himself.

Finishing in record time, I snag a few triangles of bread then move back to the window to munch in peace. Their attention in the past few days has been suffocating. It's why I wanted to disappear in the first place.

The sound of eating dissolves as I zone back out. The clouds have broken now. Big, fat raindrops hammer down from the sky. It obscures the busy road running alongside the budget hotel.

A woman with auburn hair rushes to safety from the falling rain, holding a soaked magazine over her head. The bright-red waves linger in my mind, taking me back to our final moments inside Harrowdean.

Is Rae alive?

Did she make it out?

The bread in my mouth turns to ash. I abandoned her. All of them. People I hurt to bolster my own position. People I equipped to hurt themselves. Rae deserves to be free, not me. She's the innocent one.

"Ripley?"

Lennox stops next to me without touching me this time. He peers at my face, a frown forming between his dark-brown eyebrows.

"You're crying again."

I numbly touch my cheek, finding it wet. "I don't deserve to be invisible."

"What's that?"

"That's why my superpowers aren't working. The world wants me to be punished for what I did in Harrowdean. It won't let me disappear."

"Oh, Rip." He shakes his head. "Can I touch you?"

When I don't reject him, Lennox moves closer. He clasps my cheek in his huge, calloused hand, the rough skin making my face itch. His thumb travels through my falling tears in a wide arc.

"You've been punished enough," he whispers emphatically. "Just being locked up in there was a punishment. You did what you had to. The world could never begrudge you that."

"But… I left Rae behind."

His gaze fractures with sympathy. "You barely escaped with your life. That's a bit different."

Eyes closing, I lean into his touch. It feels more welcome this time. I know it's Lennox. Not the Lennox that exists in my memories, but the Lennox I recently discovered. Protective. Loyal. Firm but gentle when needed.

"Now, I can't help with this superpower issue." He strokes a thumb over my parted lips. "But I have something that may take your mind off it. Want to come see?"

I nod, reopening my eyes. "Okay."

He releases me to take my hand. Raine still sits at the table, surrounded by their empty takeaway cartons. Lennox guides me into his vacated chair as he locates the backpack he also brought back.

"Found a small art shop on the walk back to the hotel," he explains while reaching inside. "It's been a while, right? I heard this helps you cope with stuff."

Lennox stacks two sketchbooks, a pack of charcoal pencils and a miniature watercolour set with sealed brushes in front of me. For several astonished seconds, I just gape. It's been so long since I saw paint or brushes.

"These are for me?"

"Well, yeah." He shrugs, his teeth digging into his bottom lip. "If they're not right… I can go back."

With still-shaking hands, I pick up the watercolours, clicking the tin open to inspect the colours. The familiar scent of paint feels like walking into my childhood home and accepting a perfume-scented hug from my mum.

Tears well back up. "I don't know what to say."

"Reckon you could show me some of those famous skills while we wait for Xander?" he requests, locating a bottle of water to fill a glass. "I haven't seen much of your art before."

Flipping open the sketchpads, I run my fingertips over the paper. It's good quality, thick and well-grained for watercolour work. The charcoals are all perfectly sharpened. He chose these supplies thoughtfully.

"Just like old times in the studio." Raine laughs before quickly sobering. "God, I miss my violin. I really hope she survived the riot."

Lennox takes a seat, pushing cartons out of the way. "We'll get you another."

"Not the same. She was perfect."

Ignoring their conversation, I dip the flat brush into the water he poured and begin mixing colours. Just seeing the brilliant swirls kickstarts the creative fever that always sets in when I sit down to paint.

It's a living, breathing thing, stirring deep inside my gut. The world just fades away. I've never felt more at peace than when I'm creating. In these moments, I can control the emotions running rampant in me.

I test each brush and colour, familiarising myself with the equipment before sketching an outline with a thin charcoal. The image comes out of nowhere.

My hand steadies with each stroke and flick. The excruciating energy that's kept me on the verge of a breakdown since we escaped pulls tight inside me. I'm uncoiling it, taking back control from the violent force and stretching it to breaking point.

Vivid blacks. Deep, burnished greens. I mix red and blue to form bubbling, purple storm clouds around the landscape that's spilling from my brush. Using my pinkie finger, I blend the paint to create the perfect, fluffy shapes.

The persistent ache in my neck tells me hours have passed when I finally sit up, looking down at the scene I've crafted. It's not the image I thought I was painting. Somewhere along the way, it changed.

When I look at Lennox and Raine, both slumped in their chairs, I realise I'm no longer shaking. I can breathe again. Think again. The coil has snapped and withered, leaving me to float back down.

I push the sketchpad over to Lennox so he can take a look. He picks it up, his expression neutral as he studies the scene closely for several long seconds.

"What is it?" Raine asks curiously.

Sliding the sketchpad back to me, Lennox keeps quiet to let me answer. I look back down at the watercolour sketch. Stormy, threatening skies. Smoking ruins. The destruction entombed in a woodland sarcophagus.

I've recreated the institute we fled. Harrowdean Manor in all its grandiose monstrosity—stained glass, gothic stone, the wrought-iron gates and ivy-wrapped crest pronouncing the letters *HM*.

Only the manor no longer stands.

Harrowdean has been demolished.

I refocus on Raine. "The future."

CHAPTER 15
LENNOX
BLEED – CONNOR KAUFFMAN

PACKING the supplies we've gathered over several cautious trips, I set the third and final backpack at the end of the double bed. I'm straining my ears for any sign of Xander and Ripley's return. They've been gone for two hours.

We decided to take the plunge and test his counterfeit skills before moving on. Raine collected his medication yesterday without issue. Now it's round two.

After working tirelessly to forge fake IDs and prescription slips, Xander has taken Ripley to collect her medication today. It can't come a moment sooner. She's been semi-lucid since the first manic symptoms manifested.

"They've been gone for too long." Raine folds and unfolds his stick, obviously agitated. "How long does it take?"

"He's taken her to the pharmacy in the next town over. We don't want anyone asking questions about Xander's forgery."

"How long can we continue hiding like this? Living off scraps and stealing to survive?" He sighs. "We need help, Nox."

"We're not trusting those Sabre people."

"Then who can we trust?"

"Ourselves." I glance over the packed supplies again. "We just need to keep moving. I'm not letting any of us get taken back into custody or worse."

"And if this situation rumbles on for years to come? If the

investigation doesn't find Incendia at fault or clear our names? What happens then?"

Ignoring him, I perch on the bed and watch the door. When they get back, we'll set off. Xander found a sleepy bed and breakfast in a small town farther east. It's a mammoth trek, but we can't risk public transport right now.

"Lennox! I'm talking to you!"

"I don't know, alright?" I bark at him. "I have no idea how this ends. My concern right now is getting through each day. We can't think beyond that."

"We can, and we should. This is untenable."

"What do you suggest, Raine? Hand ourselves over to the authorities? Let them quietly execute us? I suppose you'll be okay. They may ship you off to one of the other institutes and just kill us three."

He slaps his folded stick down on the bed. "That's not fair. We're in this together."

"Are we? I don't remember you dealing contraband, killing the fucking warden or breaking out of the Z wing."

"No," he replies hotly. "I suppose I just *accidentally* tagged along on this little trip, right? The same way I *accidentally* chose to go all in with the three of you. I do hope they let me off easy."

Head bowing, I press the heels of my palms into my eye sockets. Escaping Harrowdean feels like a lifetime ago, yet the infinite nightmare has also passed in a terrifying flash. None of us can live like this much longer.

"I'm sorry," I croak. "That wasn't fair."

"You're damn right it wasn't fair."

"I said I'm sorry, alright?"

"Don't turn on the people who love you most." Hurt laces his words. "Not when they're all you've got left."

Regret swamps me, provoking a burst of honesty. "I just feel so powerless."

The bed shifts as he shuffles to the end to sit with me. Raine bumps his shoulder into mine.

"You're doing the best you can."

"It sure doesn't feel like it."

"Look, I know you don't trust these people. I don't think any of us do. But we're running very low on options right now. This could be our last play."

"We can't risk ending up back there, Raine."

He whooshes out a sigh. "Bouncing from place to place, hoping we're not spotted or tracked down, isn't exactly a long-term plan either."

Lifting my head, I look down at my mangled hand. It's healing, a shiny, puckered scar forming. The discoloured skin reminds me of the horrors we escaped every day. And what I'll do to keep my family from enduring them again.

"Footsteps," Raine announces.

"Jesus, man. Your hearing really is creepy."

"You're starting to sound like Ripley."

Right on cue, the woman in question storms into the room. Xander follows behind, a baseball cap tugged low to cover his ash-white hair. We decided he needs to be more inconspicuous, given how many supply runs he's been making.

Ripley doesn't even spare us a glance as she marches straight to the bathroom and slams the door shut, the lock snicking into place. Pulling several medication boxes from his hoodie, Xander tosses them on the bed.

"Well?" I prompt.

"We got everything." He gestures to the boxes.

"Then... what's the issue?"

"We need to get moving. There was a slight complication."

"Slight?" Raine repeats apprehensively.

Xander runs a hand over his pale face. "Ripley was a bit agitated and got upset. The pharmacist took her into a side room. I wasn't allowed in."

Dread blooms in my gut. "Why?"

"Concern for her safety, I guess. We had to play along."

"Then what happened?" Raine asks.

"She won't say. All I know is we left behind a pharmacy tech with a broken nose on the phone with the police. I managed to swipe the meds before we hauled ass."

"Shit!" I exclaim. "Were you followed back?"

"No. There was CCTV, though."

Frowning at the soft vibrating coming from his pocket, Xander pulls out one of the stolen phones. I walk over to the bathroom door and tap, my ear pressed against the wood to hear Ripley's response.

"Rip? Are you okay in there?"

"Go away," she fires back.

"What happened?"

"Leave me alone, Nox!"

"Please, open up. Let us help."

Silence.

Shit, this isn't good. She's been hanging on by a thread. If this tech did something to trigger her paranoia, it's lucky they didn't get worse than a broken nose.

"Raine. Can you talk to her?"

Turning around, I find him tuned in to the voices emanating from Xander's phone. They're both totally immersed. My scalp prickles uneasily as I stop at Xander's side to look over his shoulder.

"What is it?"

"Another press conference," he mutters. "I just got the notification. But it's not Bancroft dolling out more professional lies this time."

"Then who is?"

Bloodthirsty journalists gather on the live feed. It's being shot against a professional backdrop, the pedestal and microphone set up next to an oversized easel with a board positioned on it.

The floor falls away beneath me when I realise whose face is printed on that board. She's younger. Hazel eyes filled with innocence. Smiling. Arms tattoo free. Tawny-brown curls pinned back with two criss-crossed paintbrushes. No septum piercing in sight.

Ripley.

"What is this?" I gasp.

"Some kind of missing persons' appeal?" Xander laughs without humour. "This is a new low."

The hum of voices on the live feed falls silent. Striding over to the pedestal, a broad-shouldered man takes the stage. His smooth skin is tanned, like he's been sunning himself on a tropical island recently.

Dark-brown hair that doesn't seem to match his age belies an expensive dye job. Even his beard is well-trimmed without a hair out of place, complementing his crisp, pinstriped suit.

Businessman, clearly. From his confident walk to the way he holds his head high with self-importance, his entire persona screams extravagant wealth and power. Already, I hate him.

"Who's the suit?"

Xander exhales loudly. "That… is Ripley's uncle."

"Oh, shit," Raine mutters.

On the screen, journalists lean forward in their chairs, notepads poised and questions ready. This is another staged show for the world's media to gulp down. I have a bad fucking feeling.

"Good afternoon. My name is Jonathan Bennet."

"Weren't her mum and dad married?" I question. "He's the maternal uncle, right?"

Raine braces his elbows on his knees, listening closely. "This dickhead made Ripley change her surname when he took custody. I gather he was more concerned about his public image than being a parental figure."

"Be quiet," Xander orders.

He turns up the volume on the phone. We all lean closer.

"I'm appealing for information about the disappearance of my beloved niece, Ripley Bennet. She was undertaking a rehabilitative program at Harrowdean Manor until the recent violence broke out."

Jonathan actually manages to look concerned. It makes my skin crawl.

"Ripley is unwell and has serious, long-term, mental health needs that require ongoing treatment. She's vulnerable. I'm very worried about the delinquents my niece has gotten caught up with."

I guffaw at his choice of words. "We're delinquents now."

"Been called worse," Xander grumbles.

"Delinquent is a damn compliment for what you are, Xan."

"Hey, idiots," Raine redirects our attention. "Why is he going public now? Minimal information has been coming out of Harrowdean for weeks."

Xander studies the asshole wiping away his fake tears. "He's Bancroft's new mouthpiece. It's probably just another tactic to hunt us down. They're getting desperate."

"Ripley, please." Jonathan bleats emotionally. "The riot is over. You don't need to run from us. Let us provide the help you need."

"He's actually convincing." I shake my head. "Fucking hell."

"I know you didn't mean any harm... Please come home. We only want to help."

"This piece of shit never wanted to help Ripley," Raine viciously snarls. "He's treated her like damaged goods ever since she was diagnosed. The man disowned her!"

"But now his investment is in danger." I watch the journalists throw up their hands to ask questions. "This is the performance of his career."

The first journalist takes hold of the microphone. "How does a renowned investment banker and respected public figure like yourself justify bankrolling a criminal enterprise?"

A nasty, red flush creeps up Jonathan's neck, spilling from his pressed collar. "I have full faith in the important work Incendia Corporation is doing in the private medical sector."

"That's a non-answer, Mr Bennet. Does that work include illegal human experimentation and abuse?"

"Most certainly not." Jonathan's sneer is a very brief crack in his façade. "You shouldn't believe everything you hear, Miss Moore."

He turns his attention to the next journalist, his picture-perfect smile back in place. The slick bastard's been media trained to within an inch of his life. Though I recognise a snake when I see one.

"Sir Bancroft announced the death of Harrowdean's warden, Abbott Davis, in his latest update. Does the disappearance of your niece and several other patients relate to his passing?"

"Son of a bitch." I roll my head over my tense shoulders. "I can't believe they dared to ask him that."

Xander keeps his lips sealed shut. Cool as a cucumber. The warden's death was publicly announced not long ago—we caught that news while moving to this location. So far, no information is being released as to the circumstances.

Xander assured me he wasn't seen and the killing can't be traced back to him. I'm sure all manner of violence that took place during the riot is being investigated, like the multiple guard deaths.

I can't help worrying that this will come back to haunt us. We're being drip-fed updates while management scrambles to make sense of the destruction we left behind. That doesn't mean there won't be consequences.

"Warden Davis's death is a senseless tragedy," Jonathan replies calmly, his fingers steepled in front of him. "One that is being actively investigated. I am confident that justice will be served."

The questions keep coming, prying for any updates into the riot, Harrowdean's now closed doors and the increasingly serious allegations facing Incendia. I watch Jonathan's cool, PR-perfect mask falter again.

"Ex-patient of Blackwood Institute, Brooklyn West, has publicly accused the corporation you support of medical malpractice and negligence. Tell me, has your niece fled for the same reasons?"

"Oh, killer." Raine excitedly pumps his fist. "Please tell me the asshole is melting into a puddle right now."

"More like a purple-faced ogre," I respond.

"I will not be commenting on media speculation and the false accusations of unwell individuals." Jonathan keeps his reply curt. "I'm only interested in locating Ripley and bringing her home where she belongs."

"How can he say that?" Xander spits in disgust.

"Because he only cares about the money."

We all turn at the sound of Ripley's flat voice. Focused on the screen, we didn't hear the bathroom door reopen. She stands in the doorway, chest heaving and eyes shining, her hands curled into white-knuckled fists.

"Ripley." I start towards her.

"Uncle Jonathan would throw his own mother under a bus if it scored him a pretty penny." She steps past me, heading for the medication.

The press conference wraps up as Jonathan stalks off. Apparently, his patience for uncomfortable questions has expired. The comparison to other escapees was the final straw for him.

Xander tosses the phone aside, turning his focus to Ripley. She's unpacking various boxes, checking over the names and dosages. We watch her line up a handful of different pills—methodical and oddly calm.

I grab a bottle of water to hand over to her. "Got it all figured out?"

"I wasn't always locked up in a fucked up psych ward run by corrupt maniacs," she replies dryly. "I know how to organise my own medication."

Ripley takes her pills, one by one. It's the calmest I've seen her all week. I guess part of her understands she has to do this, the same way a type one diabetic takes Insulin every day. Mental health is no different.

Repackaging the boxes, she neatly stacks them up. It almost seems like a calming ritual. I thought we'd have to beg her. She's been fluctuating up and down faster than a goddamn yo-yo recently.

"You want to talk about what went down in the pharmacy?"

She shudders. "I just got muddled up, that's all."

"On what, exactly?"

"The woman was asking me all these questions. I couldn't think straight."

"Did you hit her?"

Ripley frowns, glancing down at her fist. The knuckles are red, marked with a shallow abrasion. She studies the evidence, her brow crinkling.

"I just wanted to get out of that room." She exhales slowly. "It felt like the walls were closing in on me. I couldn't see Xander. I was scared it was a trap."

Honestly, it's hard to tell where the manic paranoia ends and legitimate concern for the insanity we've found ourselves in begins. If we weren't running from a criminal conspiracy, I'd be concerned about her justification.

Taking her hand, I trace her swollen knuckles. "It's time to move."

Ripley glances between the three of us. Her freckle-dusted features are filled with apprehension. Biting down on her lip, she seems to think something over.

"What is it?" Xander prompts.

"Are you sure you want to take me with you?" Her chin drops, eyes pinned to the ground. "I'm a proven liability. The police could be on their way here this very second because I couldn't keep my shit together."

This fucking woman.

I'm such an idiot for ever making her doubt us.

I want to crush her to my chest and forcefully strangle it from her mind. Her demons aren't liabilities. We started this journey together, and we're going to finish it together.

Before I can do just that, Xander strides over to us. He snatches Ripley from her chair, trapping her chin between his thumb and forefinger. I watch her visibly gulp as his darkening gaze bores into her.

"You are not a liability, Ripley. Say that about yourself again, and I'm going to take you over my knee."

Her mouth opens, and he promptly clicks it shut.

"Priory Lane. Harrowdean. On the run. Dead in the ground. I don't care where we are. You will stay right by our sides. Where. You. Fucking. Belong."

Something about Xander's emotive growl feels so right. Ripley has become our nucleus without even trying. She's transformed the chaos and suffering we've endured together into an opportunity.

A chance to belong.

A twisted, toxic, perfect family.

Releasing her so she can respond, Ripley sucks in a breath. "I want to stay with you. I just... I don't want anyone else to get hurt because of me."

"That's our choice," Raine speaks up. "We're choosing to stand by each other. Whether we get hurt or not is irrelevant. It's our decision to face the danger as a united front."

I nod in agreement, gaze locked on her. "If we get hurt, then we do that together too. It wouldn't be the first time."

Ripley flashes me a knowing look. We've witnessed far too much of one another's pain. Caused plenty of it too. My motivations are different now, though. We're standing together on the right side of the line this time.

I swore to myself that I'd make right on all the damage I've caused. If she thinks I'm giving up so soon, she's in for a real surprise. We're only just getting started. I'm going to stick around and fix what I've broken.

"Let's go, then." Her lips lift ever so slightly.

Picking up his stick, Raine unfolds it. "That's our girl."

CHAPTER 16
RIPLEY
SEE YOU IN HELL – BEAUTY SCHOOL DROPOUT

THE CHECKOUT IS fast and impersonal. Our favourite hotel owner barely spares us a second glance now that he's milked us dry for an extortionate hush fee paid in cash. We step out into the daylight and follow Xander's directions.

Each one of us has dressed to blend in, wearing dark colours and casual t-shirts. Raine is unrecognisable beneath his aviators and the indigo hoodie he pulled on. Don't get me started on Mr Polo Shirt now wearing a baseball cap. Xander's sleek style is long gone.

Tensions are high as we leave the town behind, walking along a concrete underpass that snakes beneath the main road. We're moving away from the Derby vicinity now that we have supplies and medication.

Xander doesn't release my hand as the miles sluggishly trickle by. He's holding onto me so forcefully, I wonder if he thinks I'll float away like a helium-filled balloon. Or start rambling about my incredible invisibility again.

The time between holing up in the holiday park and the hotel is worryingly disjointed. My episodes often leave me confused and left to pick up the damaged pieces my manic self has scattered around me.

It's an exhausting cycle.

Not many stick around afterwards.

Part of me can't believe they're all still here and didn't take me up on the offer to leave me behind. I wouldn't have blamed them. I'm an unstable element. A liability. No one wants that on their team.

"About the press conference." Xander draws my attention.

"It doesn't matter, Xan."

"Doesn't it?" He quirks a brow. "That snake is still your uncle."

"Trust me, I've long stopped believing he's going to wake up and suddenly give a shit about me. That was just further proof of how little he cares."

My words are bitter and caustic.

"You don't need him," Xander spits out.

That was never the issue.

It wasn't a need. It was a *want*.

As we walk, our surroundings filter between rundown council estates to half-empty high streets. Families pass us on the way home from the school run, carrying bicycle helmets and glittery book bags.

The scene makes my heart ache with loss. I never had that. A chauffeur handled the school runs throughout my childhood while the housekeeper my uncle employed performed the role of caregiver.

I didn't have the normal, workaday familiarity of a warm family home. I'm sure some kids would trade their lives for the luxury and privilege I had, but to me, it was nothing but hollow grief. A reminder of all I'd lost.

All my life, I wanted a family.

I wanted to be loved.

All I got instead was sickness and disgust.

"We'll make them pay, Rip." Xander keeps his voice down. "All of them."

"How?" I laugh quietly. "We're penniless and on the run. Up against wealth and corruption the world barely believes. Not even the authorities can see the truth."

"Then we make them see."

"We both know it isn't that simple."

The destruction we left behind wasn't the smoking gun Harrowdean's patients hoped it would be. It won't be that easy to dismantle the lies pushed by money and privilege.

"Comfort break?" Raine taps his stick in an arc. "We've been walking for ages."

"It's been two hours." Xander scoffs. "Suck it up. Daylight's fading."

"Not a problem for me. You seeing folk may struggle, though."

I resist the urge to smack him upside the head. "Do you want us to get lost?"

"Isn't the human satnav leading the way?" Raine retorts.

Xander flips him the bird over his shoulder. "I have a name."

It takes me by surprise. I never thought I'd see the day he loosens up enough to laugh and joke with us. Raine chuckles when Lennox translates the gesture to him.

"Up yours too, Xan. Ripley's leg is still healing, you know."

"I'm fine," I splutter.

"No thanks to the stitch you caused her to tear," Xander adds acerbically. "I didn't think you had it in you, Raine. It must've been some spectacular sex."

Fucking kill me.

"Hey!" Raine cuts over him, visibly incensed. "I've said I'm all for this weird dynamic we have going on, but don't insult my ego, man."

"Not sure your ego was his target," Lennox claps back.

"I was aiming for his sexual prowess." Xander's tone is matter-of-fact. "I've always assumed you were a vanilla pushover, not a closeted freak in the sheets."

Bursting into laughter, I can hardly walk straight. Lennox yelps at the hard smack delivered to his arm. His blow delivered, Raine lowers his guide stick back to the ground, lips smashing in a grimace.

"What the hell did I do?" Lennox whines.

"You encourage him! Did I get your head?"

He rolls his eyes at us. "Not even close. Better luck next time."

"I never want to hear Xander say the words *freak in the sheets* ever again."

"Honestly, me neither," I agree.

We pass a sign denoting our destination, informing us that the small town of Keyworth is still six miles away. We've graduated back to narrow country roads, the winding bends sandwiched by drystone walls and fields of munching cows.

As the last of the sunlight fades, Xander pulls a flashlight from his backpack. They stocked up on batteries on the latest supply run. The yellow beam lights the road ahead, leading us deeper into the countryside.

"How much farther?" Raine groans exaggeratedly.

"Probably two or three more hours." Lennox pulls a cereal bar from his coat pocket. "Here. Eat this."

Raine stretches out his hand for him to place the food in it. Lennox almost drops the bar when the sound of a rumbling engine breaks the quiet nighttime. We haven't seen a car for miles now that we're back in the sticks.

"What's our excuse here?" I scan the road ahead. "Out for a pitch-black hike?"

"We haven't seen a local for ages," Xander replies. "Let's take cover."

Snagging Raine's sleeve, Lennox guides him over to the side of the road. We deftly scale the wooden fence, one by one. The field beyond is completely dark, pierced by the occasional mooing sound.

The distant rumbling grows louder. Safely ducked inside the farmer's field, Xander clicks off the flashlight, plunging us into complete blackness.

"It sounds like a van," I whisper.

A huge, familiar hand engulfs my leg, offering a reassuring squeeze.

"Delivery truck maybe?" Lennox guesses.

"In the middle of nowhere?" Raine replies.

Headlights illuminate the thick rows of hedges we've ducked behind. The engine slows, idling for a second before crunching tyres pull up. I hear Xander quietly curse as heavy-sounding doors slam.

Come on. Please.

Be here for someone else.

Lighting the flashlight but covering the beam with his hand, Xander gestures for us to creep after him. He keeps down, ducked close to the wet grass before he begins crab-walking as silently as possible.

"Stay low," Lennox murmurs.

Grabbing hold of Raine's hand, their grips interlock, ensuring he won't get lost in the shadows. Xander moves ahead with us following, away from the road. With any luck, it's a taxi driver taking a leak.

I almost falter and faceplant when another door slams and high-pitched sobbing permeates the night. Xander looks back with a questioning look, also searching for the source.

"Go ahead, sweetheart." A familiar, male voice rings out. "Call for your friend."

Ice blooms deep within me and crystallises in my bloodstream. The darkness must be playing tricks on me. There's no way that voice has followed us all the way out here, far from the subterranean hellscape we left it in.

"Do it!" he thunders.

Stretching to his full height, Xander motions for us to run. "Go!"

But paralysing fear holds me captive. A clammy chill sweeps over me, causing beads of cold sweat to trickle down my spine. My breath comes in short gasps as I hear the weeping voice scream out again.

"N-No! I won't do it!"

"Rip," Xander hisses under his breath. "Move!"

Lightning cracks through the night, causing us all to startle. Only it isn't an electric crackle but a gunshot. The boom disturbs sleeping birds and livestock, echoing endlessly in the nothingness all around us.

"Next shot won't be a miss," the man yells. "Do it!"

The sobbing intensifies.

"Ripley! Rip!"

Realisation comes in an awful trickle, burying its pincers deep in my chest. I know that voice. Xander pulls off his backpack to search inside. He then tosses something shiny and metallic to Lennox.

"Here," he mouths.

Lennox catches the folded switchblade. It has a stainless-steel grip, the slightly curved blade flicking out with a deadly snick. Xander locates his own pocketknife. A surviving relic from our Harrowdean days.

"We're not here to mess around!" the deep voice rattles through the air. "Let's make this quick and easy, shall we? It's been a long few weeks for us all."

Xander tsks. "Is this joker for real?"

"Come on, stooge. Show yourself. I don't think you want Red here to take a bullet."

Red?

"No," I whisper in horror, my suspicions confirmed. "Please, no."

"It's the one who tortured us, isn't it?" Lennox stares at me imploringly. "Harrison?"

"He's… He's got her."

"Who?" Xander demands.

"Ripley!" a petrified wail answers his question.

Tossing my head back, I clench my eyes shut. "It's Rae. He has Rae."

"Show yourself, Ripley!"

That evil bastard can't be here. It isn't possible. Excruciating memories rush to the surface before I can staunch the traumatic flow.

Harrison's fists and feet delivering each punishing blow, beating my organs into a paste in an attempt to find the truth. Him tossing me around like a bag of bones. Being cruelly stripped and hammered with freezing water.

It is Harrison.

He's here.

The sadistic motherfucker is supposed to be dead. Rick told me himself—he left him floating in an ice-water tub. Stupid me dared to believe Harrison was dead. He must've been down there for the whole riot.

Who survives that?

"Next bullet's going in her stomach!" Harrison shouts gleefully. "There's no one around to hear your pretty friend's wails as she bleeds out."

Dropping my backpack, I snatch the flashlight from Xander's hand. "I'm getting Rae."

"Ripley, stop!" Lennox bellows. "He'll kill you."

"She doesn't deserve this! I'm not letting anyone else get hurt because of me!"

Silent and deadly, Xander pounces on me. The flashlight is knocked aside as he weighs me down in the damp field, the pocketknife an inch from my eyeball. I recoil from the cold determination on his face.

"I'll knock you out and throw you over my shoulder if that's what it takes," he warns starkly. "Don't test me."

"Xan! Please!"

"No, goddammit!"

Bucking wildly to throw him off, I freeze dead when another shot rings out. The resultant howl sets my teeth on edge as hot tears prickle my eyes. All I can picture is the blood pooling around my friend.

"No! Rae!"

She's screaming in agony... because of me. All I've ever done is put her through hell. She's going to bleed out on the side of a fucking road because I'm too weak to save the people I care about.

"Who should get the next bullet?" Harrison calls out.

I want to face the son of a bitch who hurt my friend head-on. But Harrison's next threat causes sense to win out.

"Your little blind friend?" he cackles. "Or one of his two guard dogs?"

"Screw that." Lennox pulls Xander off me. "Let's fucking move!"

My breath escapes me when I'm plucked from the ground and

shoved forward. The paralysing numbness that's seeped in prevents me from fighting them. I can't watch Raine or the others get hurt.

"There!" someone screeches. "They're running, sir!"

Xander snatches my hand. "Go!"

Lennox is half-dragging Raine, the pair hot on our heels. We're straying deeper into the field, slick grass quickly turning into tall, ripe maize stalks.

As shouts pursue us, the world narrows into rapid snapshots. Crops whipping our arms and faces. Flashing lights carried on the breeze. Pain pulsing from my still-sore thigh, matching the stitch forming in my stomach.

Tears blur my vision as an arctic defeat settles in my heart, turning my entire body to ice. We're running into literal blackness with a futile hope of escape.

"There they are! Fire!"

Voices overlap more gunshots. Bullets sizzle past us in a fast stream as we all duck low to avoid being hit. Lennox hisses a curse, pulling Raine with him, the pair taking cover amidst swaying crops.

"Stop! We need her alive!"

During a brief pause in firing, we throw ourselves forward. Evil is snapping at our heels. Fleeing for your life is a horrifying pressure like none other. I can almost feel death breathing down my neck.

"Argh!" Raine howls.

Tripping over, he flies onto the dirt ground. Lennox is pulled down with him, the pair landing in a tangle. I tug Xander to a halt, my pounding heart on the verge of spewing from my throat.

Yelping in pain, Raine grabs fistfuls of dirt. "Shit!"

"What is it?" Lennox picks himself up.

"My ankle." He tries to stand and immediately falls. "Fuck it. Leave me!"

"Never!"

Scooping him up, Lennox throws Raine's arm around his shoulders to carry him onwards. We've lost precious seconds. The pounding footsteps sound closer than ever as light swings above us.

I shriek Lennox's name when a red beam slices through the crops, marking a target in the dead centre of his chest. Noise is exploding all around us, creating a dizzying effect. I've lost track of direction completely.

"Lennox!"

He skids to a halt, looking down at the red glow. "Oh, fuck."

"Move another muscle and the big guy gets it." A balaclava-clad figure emerges through the stalks, carrying an assault rifle. "You're done."

Two others follow with flashlights while the third carries a small weapon. None of us dare breathe, let alone take off. That red dot hovers just above Lennox's heart, his gaze fixed on the man threatening to end him.

Xander steps forward, his hands spread. "Let's talk about this."

"Silence!" the assailant snaps. "We're here for the girl."

"You've got me!" I throw my hands up. "Lower the weapon."

"And let you take off again? I don't think so."

Breaking through the maize forest, a face I never thought I'd see again emerges. Harrison is sweaty, an ugly flush reaching his buzz cut. His once-bulky frame has slimmed down since he delivered me to Professor Craven.

He still wears an unhinged grin that promises all manner of ungodly sins. If he didn't have a screw loose before, it's safe to say his entire brain is untethered now. He's looking at me like I'm a fucking Christmas present.

"As much as I enjoy a chase, I promise to shoot the next person who moves a muscle." He smiles maniacally. "It's over."

"How are you alive?" I blurt.

Harrison lifts his arms, showing off welts and healing abrasions that circle his wrists. "Courtesy of our mutual friend."

Looks like Rick was telling the truth about shackling him in the same barbaric tub he'd been imprisoned in. The sick fuck survived the riot, handcuffed in the darkness. I don't want to imagine how.

"I'm afraid to say Rick's dead now," Harrison chortles without remorse. "A little apology present from the boss for all that I endured."

"You didn't suffer enough for my liking if you're still alive and breathing."

"Charming." He hooks up an eyebrow. "It felt like Christmas had come early when I heard you'd been spotted in a pharmacy. It wasn't hard to track you from there."

Harrison flicks his eyes to Lennox, lip curling in a sneer. I take the chance to make eye contact with Xander who shakes his head infinitesimally. *Don't move.* We're outnumbered.

"I'm surprised this tool survived Craven's lair." Harrison chuckles derisively. "Perhaps I underestimated your plaything, Ripley."

"Fuck you," Lennox seethes.

"I have no qualms about shattering your skull, Mr Nash. Your life is forfeit now. Watch your mou—"

"What's the play here?" I cut across him. "A quiet little execution?"

"Originally, yes." Harrison sniffs in mock disgust. "A waste if you ask me. However, my orders have changed. You should be glad."

"Changed?" Xander parrots.

"Our management structure is rather complicated right now. I'd hate to bore you with the details. Suffice to say, for the trouble she's caused, the price for Ripley's safe capture has tripled."

In my periphery, I can see Xander clenching the pocketknife in his palm. He keeps his hand angled so it's tucked out of sight, allowing him to finger the blade. Rage radiates off him in waves.

"Where is Rae?"

"The redhead?" Harrison smirks. "I'll take you to see her body if you'd like. She may still be alive."

Nausea flushes over me, setting off light-headed prickles. Harrison's lying. He has to be. Surely, they haven't stooped so low as to shoot innocent people in plain sight. Not in public, at least.

"Surrender, and we'll kill your other friends quickly."

"She's going nowhere with you!" Raine shouts back.

Harrison casts a withering eye over Raine, Lennox and Xander. "You're protecting a monster, boys. Think about it. The Z wing program wouldn't run if each institute didn't have a willing stooge."

"Because you're so much better than me?" I snarl at him.

He shrugs, grinning ear to ear. "I'm just doing my job. It's a generous pay cheque. What excuse do you have?"

The lunatic actually thinks he has the moral high ground. This is the same man I saw attaching spike-laden handcuffs to Patient Three. His fucking pay cheque is saturated with spilled blood.

"Ripley stays with us." Xander strokes his blade.

"Is that your final answer?"

"Yes!" Lennox roars.

A sinister grin curls Harrison's lips. "Very well. I played nice."

Clicking his fingers, Harrison gestures for his men to advance. I'm preparing to throw myself in front of the rifle's scope to protect Lennox when Xander strikes.

Like a coiled python going in for the kill, he glides through the air with graceful precision. The pocketknife strikes faster than a whip as he jams it into the first assailant's shoulder.

The scream that spills from the man's lips is ear-splitting. He drops the rifle, the red glow spinning out of control. Xander pulls the blade free and sinks it into his exposed neck before the others can react.

Lightning fast.

Savage.

Deadly.

Blood erupts in a tidal wave, spitting out of the wound and spraying across his face. Xander continues to jab over and over. Wet, stomach-turning stabs that turn smooth skin into shredded flesh.

"Take them!" Harrison jumps into action.

Stepping in front of Raine, Lennox holds his own glinting blade. He faces the two men coming for him, elbow cocked and switchblade poised. His wide shoulders hunch in preparation.

I can't step in to help him before I'm faced with my own attacker. Harrison has set his sights on me. Perfect. I'll be the one to kick the shit out of him this time around. Retribution for the beating he doled out.

"Afraid to face me now that I'm not handcuffed and half-dead?" I taunt.

He pulls a baton from his belt. "On the contrary, I'm going to enjoy this. I don't mind losing a few thousand for turning you over in bad condition."

Ducking the baton's swing, I surge at him. Harrison grunts when I slam into his midsection, throwing him backwards.

It's easier than anticipated to throw Harrison off his feet. Being confined in his own filth has dissolved much of his strength. I follow him down, my fist cracking across his gleeful face.

Blood and spit somersaults from his mouth. My pleasure is short-lived as he rolls us, the inflexible metal of his baton smashing into my back, sending pain shooting up my spine.

As the breath flees from my lungs, he rolls to crush me beneath his weight. The baton sails towards me, but I dodge at the last second, causing him to strike the ground.

Frantically searching for anything to defend myself with, I seize a handful of wet dirt. He curses when I throw it in his eyes, buying me precious seconds to punch him in the throat.

"You should've died in that basement!"

Harrison clutches his throat, gurgling beautifully. I shove him off me, searching around for the others. The gloomy night clamours with punches, cursing and yelps.

Raine is still on the ground, cupping his ankle. In front of him, Lennox is able to put one guy in a headlock while the other rolls around at his feet. I follow the heavy scent of blood to the culprit.

Oh my god.

Xander is doused red, locked in a hand-to-hand knife fight. He discards the still-bleeding corpse of the first man he disarms, turning his focus on gutting his current opponent.

I'm dragging myself up to intervene when a hand latches around my leg. Yanked backwards, I fall on my chest, nails painfully digging deep into the ground. Grunting tells me who's got me ensnared.

"Little bitch." Spittle blasts past Harrison's lips, his amusement spent. "You never could obey."

Something sharp slams into the middle of my back. Any retort dies on my tongue at the instant rush of blistering pain. My entire body is gripped by a violent electrical current, causing every muscle to lock up.

I'm being stabbed by a thousand needles all at once. The convulsions take over, assaulting me with rapid bursts of excruciating electricity. My heart threatens to explode as disorientation sets in.

"That's better." Harrison relinquishes the taser from my back. "I prefer you like this. Whimpering like the pathetic stray you are."

My silent howls wrap around me. I'm trapped by aftershocks, each spasm causing more tears to leak from the corners of my eyes. For good measure, Harrison stands and boots me hard in the stomach.

Heat radiates through my belly. I cry out, unable to move a muscle or curl in on myself. His steel-capped boots strike over and over, sending me plummeting back into the past.

I'm back in the Z wing, stripped bare in a padded cell. Covered in my own blood. Tears. Sweat. Taunted by his cackling while beating me to a semi-conscious pulp. This time, he'll kill me.

"S-Stop," I beg.

"Now you want to behave, huh? Where was that attitude when I held a gun to your cute friend's head?"

Blood bubbles in my mouth, forming a hot, foaming pool. I feel it streaming from my lips, mingling with stinging tears. Everything around me is swimming in the dropped flashlight's glow.

I couldn't save Rae.

I can't even save myself.

"Step back." The command is delivered in a monotone voice. "I'd prefer not to cover Ripley with your innards."

Peering through cracked lids, I can make out the shadow looming behind Harrison through a beam of light. Lanky. Blood-streaked. Hair unkempt and eyes cold. Harrison sucks in a surprised breath.

"Now." Xander nudges the back of Harrison's head with the rifle. "I quite fancy testing out your friend's gadget. You can be my guinea pig."

Slowly, Harrison raises his hands, the baton clattering to the ground beside me. I watch his gaze harden, but my lips won't move for me to warn Xander. They're still numb and slippery.

"You know how to use that thing, son?"

Xander sighs in a long-suffering manner. "I'm disappointed at your lack of confidence. Though I appreciate the chance to make good on my threats."

With the speed of a trained thug, Harrison snatches a sheathed knife from his belt. The black-handled blade slashes in a circle as he spins. I'm powerless, forced to watch everything unfold in slow motion.

The knife.

His secret smile.

Xander being sliced wide open.

Only the blow never comes—just in my petrified imagination. Before Harrison can land his shot, the thunderous burst of the assault rifle marks his fate. The muzzle flash temporarily blinds me.

I have to squint through my tears to take in the aftermath. Terror grips me at the sight of the body sprawled out amongst crimson-soaked crops. Except he doesn't have bright-white hair and calculating eyes.

The corpse is Harrison.

Mouth open in an eternal scream. Chest caved in from a bullet delivered at point-blank range, tearing straight through his heart. His cruel eyes stare at the night sky, empty and lifeless.

Teeth bared, Xander drops the gun. "Ripley!"

He looks like an avenging angel, saturated in our enemies' blood as he steps over his final victim to reach me. Xander falls to his knees, yanking out the taser darts then sliding an arm beneath me to lift me into his lap.

"You hurt?"

"I hate tasers," I cough out. "Fuck, my ribs."

His almost-black stare bores into me. "I'm sorry."

Blood trickles from my mouth. "Why?"

"I promised no one would hurt you again." His neck muscles spasm. "Yet the son of a bitch laid his hands on you."

My eyes stray to Harrison's body. "He p-paid the price."

"I'll tear his corpse limb from limb!" He wipes the blood from my chin.

With a heavy thump, Lennox spits out a curse nearby. He's got the final perp subdued, a knife pressed against his jugular. The three other men are dead, watering the earth with their life blood.

"One move and I'll give you a new smiley face." Lennox digs the switchblade in deep. "You wanna join your friends?"

He's rewarded with a groan.

"That's what I thought." Lennox looks over at us. "Rip?"

Breathing deeply, I force my lips to move. "I'm okay."

"Jesus, Xan. Did you have to go full Hannibal Lecter?"

"We need to get out of here." Xander eyes the bloodbath all around us. "Can you walk, Raine?"

"I think so," he utters quietly. "Christ, all I can smell is blood."

Struggling to his feet, Raine winces as he puts weight on his ankle, but he manages to stay upright this time. His stick has vanished somewhere in the melee. All of our supplies are scattered in the dark.

"What should we do with this one?" Lennox nods to his captive.

"Kill him." Xander isn't fazed.

"W-Wait," I stammer. "We can use him."

"For what?" Lennox frowns.

Raine catches on, looking panicked at the thought of even more death. "Leverage. He works for Incendia."

Sighing in disappointment, Lennox lowers the blade to tuck it in his pocket. "Pass me the gun."

I work on flexing my muscles, attempting to regain control of them while Xander tosses the rifle over. Lennox trains it on our new prisoner's back, ensuring he knows the deal.

"Let's get you up." Xander pulls me to stand with him. "Easy."

I cry out at the throbbing heat wrapped all around my middle. The entire area is tender, pulsing with deep, shooting pain. Xander braces me against his side, a hand clasped on my waist.

"Can you move?"

Lips smashed shut, I nod curtly.

"Let's get the fuck out of here, then."

"What about the bodies?" Lennox asks.

"Leave them for Bancroft to find."

With each step, the internal fire roars hotter. Still, it falls short of the fear knotting my windpipe at the thought of what we'll find. Or rather *who*. We ran into the night while Rae was still screaming.

Retracing our steps is a harrowing dance in the dark, hobbling along in faint light, all panting and exhausted. Lennox still guards his stumbling prisoner.

"Hear anything?" Xander asks apprehensively when the road comes into view.

Raine tilts his head, still favouring one foot. "Ticking engine up ahead."

"I'll go first with this one." Lennox digs the rifle into the man's spine. "Just in case."

Blood surges in my ears, creating a vehement roar. Xander has to help me over the fence, his face crumpling as he struggles to remain stoic. The still-running van's lights illuminate the deserted road.

Hesitating, Raine's steps slow. "Rip... maybe you shouldn't look."

I can already hear the words he doesn't want to say. He can sense what lies ahead. Shrugging off Xander's support, I stumble towards the vehicle, a relentless fist locked around my lungs.

There's a delusional slither inside me that hoped I'd imagined it. Maybe Harrison found a way to trick us. Those sounds were recorded, or he used someone else... Or... Or...

No.

Life isn't that kind.

It's hard to tell where her vibrant auburn hair ends and the puddle of blood spilling from her stomach begins. A crimson river paints the tarmac, glistening in the headlights. Surrounded by her deathly halo, Rae lays still.

The discomfort from slamming to my knees fails to compute. Her blood is still warm as it slides across my palms. I wade closer, uncaring of the mess. Rae feels boneless in my arms when I hug her body close.

"No," I weep helplessly. "I'm so fucking sorry, Rae. I'm so sorry."

All I want is for her arms to hug me back. She could crack a smile or drop one of her sarcastic jokes. Tell me I'm forgiven for leading her to this place. But that doesn't happen. It's too late.

She's dead.

And it's all my fault.

Sobbing senselessly, I cuddle her close until I have nothing left to give. Not a single tear. Soul-destroying grief boils into smouldering rage. It hits hard and fast, sweeping in and obliterating my self-control.

I slacken my grip to look at her face. Ashen. Waxy. Slack. Blood smears across her freckled skin as I stroke her hair back, lowering my lips to her forehead.

"I'll make it right, Rae," I vow fiercely. "All of it."

"Ripley." Raine awkwardly crouches down near me. "She's gone. You need to let her go."

"It's my fault. She didn't deserve this."

"I know," he whispers sincerely.

"I was so cruel to her, Raine. Unnecessarily. She just wanted to be my friend, and I kept pushing her away. I was scared to let her get close."

"She didn't see it like that, babe." His voice is thick with emotion. "Rae wanted to be your friend. She knew you needed one."

"And where did being my friend get her?"

His nostrils whistle with a long sigh. "You can't take the blame for all the world's evil. This isn't on you."

Smoothing her red waves a final time, I gently lay Rae back down. My fingertips leave two matching streaks on her eyelids as I slide them shut. Like this, I can convince myself she's asleep. Peaceful and safe.

By the time I look up, my decision is made.

"No more running scared," I declare firmly. "We're taking the fight to them."

"How?" Raine questions.

Looking up at Xander, I implore him with my gaze. "Call Theodore. Tell him we have a hostage for them. I want a rendezvous by dawn."

"Rip," Lennox attempts.

One look in his direction silences him. I'm kneeling next to my friend's corpse, covered in her blood. Death and defeat are scattered all around us. We've fled. Schemed. Bargained. Killed.

Enough.

No more cheap hotels or breaking and entering. No more stealing cash to buy enough food to keep us alive. No more hiding our faces and praying death doesn't come knocking. I'm done being scared.

"Make the call." My words come out steadier than I feel. "That's final."

Xander pats his pockets, searching for the stolen phone kept on his person at all times. A startling ringtone erupts before he can find it, only the noise isn't coming from him. We all glance around in shock.

Our captive moans weakly. Eyebrows knitted, Lennox reaches into his bulletproof vest, pulling out a clunky-looking burner phone. He frowns down at the lit screen.

"Boss," he reads.

The ringtone halts, leaving us in crushing silence. It quickly starts up again with a second call.

I lift a trembling hand. "Here."

Lennox pauses, clutching the device. "Sure you want to do this?"

"Yes."

His mouth pursed, he tosses the phone underhand towards me. I numbly catch it, stabbing down on the green button before holding it to my ear.

"Why is no one else answering their phones?"

My hand tightens into a vice, creaking the cheap plastic.

"Hello? Is it done? Do you have her?"

Summoning my voice, it sounds alien to my own ears.

"Hello, Uncle Jonathan."

CHAPTER 17
XANDER
JERK – OLIVER TREE

PRESENT DAY

THE SHINING lights of Central London blur all around me in the drizzly morning rainfall. It paints a saturated, kaleidoscopic world, busy with suit-clad workers, dawdling taxis and bright-red tourist buses whizzing past.

Normality is a thin veneer painted over the truth I know lies within. A transparent film, invisible to the naked eye, concealing the reality that few are unlucky enough to ever uncover and live to tell the tale.

London—the heart of power and corruption in a lawless land.

I hate this fucking city.

It's not so much the people. I've learned to tolerate them. And I only truly pay attention to those I care about. Like always, everyone else is irrelevant. Inconsequential. Undeserving of my limited empathy.

No, my qualms with this dirty, sweaty hellhole are far more pertinent. It's the secrets this city holds so dear. So much exploitation, hiding in plain sight behind glittering tourist attractions and gilded palaces.

What if those in power cared?

Would we still have suffered back then?

Even if the bigwigs behind the corporation that stole our lives from us harboured a mere speck of humanity, we earned our places in

Harrowdean Manor. Perhaps it's only fair that we bore the brunt of their scientific curiosity.

No.

That isn't true at all.

Sure, some of us earned our place there. You only have to look at the long list of convictions that were quickly doled out when the world started the lengthy process of assigning blame for what unfolded.

Not everyone deserved to be hammered with society's hatred and disgust, though. Regardless of what they did, and the innocents they harmed, to ensure their own survival. Which is exactly why I'm here today.

"Mr Beck?"

Wrenched from my musings, I look over my shoulder. "Mr O'Hare."

His morning coffee in hand and a tan, leather satchel slung over his shoulder, Elliot O'Hare blends into the crowd on his morning commute. I've memorised his routine well enough. The investigative journalist is a creature of habit.

"What are you doing here?" He jostles on his feet to keep warm.

I push off from the wall. "Waiting for you."

"You're alone."

Staring at him, I lift my shoulder in a shrug.

"Changed your mind about that interview?" Elliot fishes.

The anticipation gleaming in his eyes turns my stomach. I've denied enough media requests over the years. None captured more than a split-second of my attention. But I'm not here for me.

It isn't selfishness that's led me to lurk outside his place of work at eight o'clock in the morning, waiting for the nosy reporter to show his face. I swear, the fucking lengths I go to. Yet I'm labelled obsessive and controlling.

When I don't immediately answer, he scans his security fob to open the door. "How about a cup of coffee?"

Fuck yes, you leech.

Nodding, I follow him inside the fancy skyscraper, escaping the lightly-misting rain. Elliot has a quiet word with the security guard manning the entrance before he's handed a visitor's pass that's then passed to me.

My body clenches tight with paranoia as I watch the guard absently wave us past. His eyes are glued to his morning newspaper. Thank fuck he didn't insist on doing a search.

"Right this way," Elliot chirps. "I'm glad you're here, Mr Beck."

I have to grit my teeth to maintain my blank expression. He thinks he's scored a big fish. To get to where I need to go, I have to keep it that way. Lips pursed, I follow Elliot over to the elevators and we ride upwards.

"What changed your mind?" he asks.

"Irrelevant."

Elliot chuckles softly. "Believe it or not, we're on the same side."

"And what side would that be?"

"The side of the truth."

Welcome rage swirls in my chest, a vortex spewing sulphuric ash that quickly heats my veins. "No one has ever cared about that."

"Well, I do."

"I'm sure."

Slipping the lanyard over my head, I smooth a hand down my pressed, white polo shirt, tucked into plain black jeans. In my periphery, I can see Elliot trying to subtly look at my toned forearms.

Pale skin stretched over corded muscles, both arms are layered with years' worth of meticulous horizontal lines. They haven't faded since I first inflicted the marks as a sullen teenager, fascinated by the pain that accompanied seeing myself bleed.

I'm not ashamed of the silvery lines covering me. In fact, I never have been. Why should I? It's my body. My blood. My pain. If I wanted to take myself apart to study the pieces, that was my prerogative.

Now at thirty-six years old, those marks have evolved to mean something more to me. Not evidence of my experimentation with cheap razor blades as a child. Nor a survivor's badge of honour, even if the battle was fought against my own mind.

No.

These marks are a reminder.

A reminder of who I once was—and who I'll never be again.

Because of her.

My eyes ping-pong as we weave through desks bearing half-awake employees, camera gear, desktop screens and steaming cups of coffee. I'm surprised by the size and gravitas of it all.

This is an industrial-scale operation, filming episode after episode of documentary footage, ready to be churned out. When it airs… I predict a toxic media frenzy. And I refuse to see that shit play out again.

"What are you trying to achieve here?"

Stepping into the studio, Elliot holds the door for me. "There are still many unanswered questions about Harrowdean Manor and the other institutes. The world needs to know."

"You're reporting on them all?"

"Yes, we're unravelling the whole story. This documentary series has been in the works for the last decade." He smiles proudly. "It will be my life's work."

Inside the studio, two folding chairs sit in the centre of the room. It's clear I've caught him with his pants down—lackeys rush in to begin setting up tripods and cameras, and an assistant is urged to make fresh coffee.

Elliot flips through several stacks of notebooks. I get a glimpse at the covers while he searches for the correct files. Each is carefully labelled with the names of the interviewee attached to their relevant institute.

They've spoken to a whole pool of people. Countless names I recognise. I've followed the lengthy criminal investigation and subsequent years of media reports ever since those horrific days.

My eyes brush over the labels denoting the five other institutes until he lands on *HM*. Harrowdean Manor. The sixth and final institute. We got our own file. How organised. But beneath those letters? There are names.

Ripley Bennet.
Lennox Nash.
Raine Starling.
Xander Beck.

"Ah, here." Elliot hums as he plucks the file free. "Truthfully, I didn't think you'd come around to this interview. You've caught me rather unprepared."

"Clearly."

My gaze is locked on that file. I want it. The tapes. Notes. Documents. Photographs. I want every fucking scrap of salacious gossip he's got piled up in there so I can build myself a nice little bonfire.

The truth isn't some ray of light shining on those who've spent their lives downtrodden. How could it be? Nobody values truth anymore. Not even when it's printed, played or publicised. We're wilfully ignorant as a species.

That doesn't mean I will allow our lives to be sold off for profit. I don't care how healing this bullshit is supposed to be. Some stories shouldn't be repeated, and ours is one of them.

"We've been given a great deal of information from Miss Bennet. Perhaps you'll be able to fill in some gaps for us."

Jaw clenching, I fight to keep my voice even. "Of course."

Elliot casts me a look. "She was rather tight-lipped about what became of your… uh, relationship. I wonder if you'd care to shed some light on that."

"Alternatively, you could mind your own fucking business."

Elliot grimaces, his crow's feet deepening with the movement. "I don't get paid to mind my business, Mr Beck."

"Or to respect people's privacy, it seems."

"Unfortunately, not in this line of work."

The coffee appears right on time, carried by a bumbling, early-twenties lad who seems eager to impress. Elliot appraises me while I accept the hot drink.

"You know, we had journalists stalking us for years," I state casually. "Hacking into our email accounts, accessing medical records, reading therapy notes. Even picking through our trash. We were hunted."

"Harrowdean was a sensational story." He shrugs like the lifelong invasion is a mere inconvenience. "It still is."

"And this tell-all documentary series… That's going to settle the score, is it?" I chuckle. "You're going to create public spectacles of us all. The last decade will have meant nothing."

Elliot takes his own coffee. "I believe the public reaction will be one of sympathy."

"When have they ever been sympathetic to people like us, Mr O'Hare?"

He opens his mouth to answer but can't find a response.

"The ignorance of the world is the reason Incendia Corporation and its six institutes went unchecked for decades." I stare at him without mercy. "The public is culpable here, not us."

His gaze ducks to my white-knuckled grip on the coffee mug. There's a flash of apprehension in his eyes, like he can tell I'm wrestling the urge to dump it over his head.

Did no one else give him a hard time? I have no idea how many people he's sat down with. Only one matters to me. One I made a promise to protect ten long years ago. I intend to keep my word.

"Excuse me?" A dawdling employee sneaks into the room. "Elliot, security would like a quick word. It seems you have another visitor."

"Of course." He clears his throat. "Mr Beck, make yourself at home."

Placing his notebook down, Elliot scuttles from the room, taking his lackey with him. Pathetic. It shouldn't be this easy to play him, but I've never had much trouble bending the will of others.

He's so desperate for his scoop, he'll do anything to capture our stories on tape. Including letting the wolf into the sheep's pen. I have to stop this. He'll regret ever dragging the past back up.

Setting the untouched coffee down, I know I have to move fast. This place is prestigious enough to have a full security team and countless levels of staff, offices and more. I won't have long.

Scanning the room, my determination hardens, steeling my muscles with staunch focus. This has to be done. I'm the only one who sees this exposé for the threat it really is.

Opening my jacket, I pull the canister of lighter fluid out. I'll have to aim for the important stuff. Documents, cameras and records. Anything that can be used against us. Secrets that should never see the light of day.

My foot connects with a tripod, sending it flying. I douse the motherfucker in fluid then turn my attention to the other cameras. It's easy enough to pop the memory cards out, each marked with date stamps.

RB. Interview Three.

Seeing Ripley's initials causes a lump to lodge in my throat. She's done a brave thing. I want her to find peace. Salvation. Whatever the fuck she's still looking for after all these years. This just isn't the way to do it.

But she chose this.

Can I take that from her?

Unable to burn the memory cards, I tuck them into my pocket. I'm not chickening out. These files will remain in the one place they'll be safe: my possession. I'll protect Ripley's secrets with my life.

The cameras are smashed then added to the pile of metal gathering in the room. I don't have long before the dickhead returns. There's still so much to destroy before I can calmly rest again.

Grabbing as many of the labelled notebooks as I can hold, I toss them into the mix, dousing everything in fluid. One lands on top, spelling out another recognisable name written beneath the words *Compton Hall*.

Colour me surprised.

I never thought they'd get that nutcase to sit down.

Not even I would risk that conversation.

The pungent scent is thick in my nose as it fills the room. I've turned the studio into a tinder box. I take a moment to enjoy the scene before pulling a cigarette lighter from my jeans.

Elsewhere, Harrowdean is being ripped down for the final time. Bricks pummelled and secrets burned. I'll burn its legacy here and finally set us all free. We need to forget. It's the only way to start living.

Flames leap from the lighter's tip. All emotion drains away as I drop it onto the pile of rubble. The effect is instantaneous.

Fire engulfs the stacks of evidence, setting noxious fluid alight in bright-blue flames. Black smoke curls from the smouldering pages, setting off multiple fire alarms.

Yet not even the blaring racket can rouse me. I've zoned out, staring deep into the flames, watching our history vanish for the last time.

I thought I'd be relieved.

Defeat settles like ash instead.

I can't burn the memories. Years of suffering. Lives destroyed, by our own hands and theirs. Indelible scars left behind on skin and soul alike. Truthfully, nothing can erase that lifelong trauma.

"No!" The studio door cracks open. "Stand back!"

I'm manhandled from the room, now billowing with thick smoke. Bodies swarm, and footsteps pound. The screeching alarms add to the escalating panic, and in the mayhem, I summon a smile.

"You!" Elliot stops in front of me, spitting with anger. "You did this!"

"Correct." I seize fistfuls of his cheap dress shirt. "Our story is not your life's work. It never belonged to you."

Grabbing my hands, he tries to prise free. The alarm on his face is enough satisfaction for me. I haven't hurt anyone for a long time, but that side of me is still in there. I can bring it forward if he doesn't let this selfish pursuit of fame die.

"Xander! Put him down immediately!"

My scalp prickles, a flush racing all over me. I release Elliot, setting him back on his feet, and look over his shoulder at the lilting voice spelling my name out with utter disbelief.

Ripley stomps closer, her weary, hazel orbs trained on me. "You had no right."

I lick my suddenly dry lips. "I had every right."

She looks between the fire being tackled with extinguishers and Elliot scuttling away from me, shouting down his phone at an emergency responder. My little toy's anger still tastes the sweetest.

"This was my choice," she screams at me.

"I'm protecting you! You have no idea what this will unleash!"

Ripley stops in front of me, our faces almost touching. The years have softened her sweetheart-shaped features and lightly-freckled skin. She still wears her septum piercing after all these years.

"I'm choosing to unleash it." Ripley's furious eyes scour my face. "I need to speak up. I can't spend another year hiding in the flat, painting the pain away until it returns come daybreak."

Hand spasming, I take her cheek into my palm. Despite her fury, she leans into my touch, a ritualistic behaviour that's stood the test of time. Years haven't diminished the intensity between us.

"It's killing me," she whispers. "I want to live, but I can't until I face the past."

Unwelcome guilt infects my cells. "Don't make me watch you get hurt again, Rip. We barely survived."

She rests her hand over mine. "And we're still not living. Not really."

Foreheads meeting, I push my lips on hers. Each time we kiss, it's like the first time all over again. Back then, I was manipulating her. Ensnaring the touch-starved orphan with the attention she craved in order to achieve my own goals.

Yet another story I'd like to erase.

One the world won't get.

So much of our history doesn't bear dredging back up. I wish our family had been forged under better circumstances. That we hadn't spent so long hurting each other or found our strength when it was too late.

No one will understand. Love like ours isn't fit for public consumption. They'll judge our shared darkness. Ridicule the bond we formed. I didn't want to silence her—I just wanted to protect her. To protect all of them.

"I need to do this." Ripley releases my hand. "Burn whatever you'd like. I'll keep doing these interviews until the truth is out there for everyone to hear."

She steps to the side, giving me a view of who's behind her. Of course, she didn't come alone. None of us have been that for a long time. Harrowdean took everything from us. But it didn't take our family.

Gripping his white guide stick, Raine stares off to the side, listening to the whooshing extinguishers. Lennox loosely holds his bicep, exchanging urgent whispers with our mutual friend, Hudson Knight.

"Come home, Xan," Ripley pleads.

I look away from her to the mess I've made. The fire has been extinguished. Elliot stands in the doorway, shaking all over as he studies the destruction. His staff are scattered in varying states of shock.

"You should give him these." I reach into my pocket, reluctantly pulling out the memory cards. "I kept them for you."

Shaking her head, she takes the small handful. "One day, you'll stop being the obsessive psychopath with no boundaries who made me fall in love with him."

"Is that really what you want?"

Peering up at me beneath her lashes, a small smile curves Ripley's lips. "I wouldn't still be here cleaning up your messes if I did."

I watch her walk over to Elliot to hand over the remaining memory cards. He's gesticulating angrily, losing the professional persona that makes him so slyly amicable. This wasn't a total waste, then.

Strolling over to me, Hudson pulls a cigarette from tucked behind his ear. "If you'd like tips on how to be a successful psycho boyfriend, I offer private tuition."

The black-haired bastard pins me with a hard stare. I bite back an eye roll. Like that's ever worked on me.

"Fuck off, Hud." I punch him in the shoulder.

"The offer stands. It's an art I've perfected over the years."

Hudson snakes an arm around my neck to lock me in a playful headlock. Snarling, I knock the unlit cigarette from his hands.

"This was your plan?" Lennox shakes his head, approaching with Raine in tow. "Great plan."

"I did this for her." I lower my voice. "For us. Nobody knows how our story ends. Do you really want them to find out like this?"

"Of course not! But it's Ripley's decision!"

"We did what we had to, Xan." Raine's eyes shift behind his round, blacked-out lenses. "It's nothing every other person in our situation wouldn't have done."

I hope the world sees it that way.

Because surviving cost us everything… Including our souls.

CHAPTER 18
RIPLEY
STRAY – JXDN

TEN YEARS EARLIER

OAKHAM AIRFIELD IS NESTLED between a smattering of sleepy villages in the rural midlands. By some miracle, there are no passing motorists on the quiet roads. I've no doubt anyone who spots us would run away screaming.

We're all filthy, struggling to walk and utterly exhausted. Even after doing his best to clean with water and old napkins found inside the van, Xander is covered in bloodstains.

The others haven't fared much better. Lennox has a rapidly swelling black eye while Raine limps with a bad ankle that we've concluded is sprained rather than broken. I'm covered in Rae's dried blood. We're all done.

After a lengthy debate, we decided not to risk driving the van straight up to the private landing strip, allowing us to be tracked. Leaving Rae's body behind with our captive when we parked the vehicle miles back was devastating.

Xander holds me braced to his side. "The airstrip is coming up."

Hobbling along, Raine clutches Lennox's sleeve. "See anything?"

With his guide stick still lost somewhere in a maize field, he's reliant on Lennox to move safely. We couldn't locate any of our supplies either before we had to flee, leaving a bloodied graveyard behind.

Lennox scans the distant buildings. "Not yet."

"Theodore said to meet here," Xander grumbles unhappily. "He better turn up."

"He will," Raine croaks.

I'm leaning almost all my body weight on Xander. Hours of sleepless travel have made an already pitiful situation worse. I haven't stopped to look, but I can feel how badly bruised my tender stomach and ribs are.

If the mysterious Theo doesn't show up, I'll march down to London and tear down Sabre's front door myself. No matter what happens, the running ends today. We've already lost too much.

"Ripley?" Lennox calls my name. "You still with us?"

I feel Xander peer at me, his arm curled around my back. I've been silent since my beloved uncle swiftly hung up the phone upon hearing my voice, leaving us stranded with several corpses and a half-alive hostage.

"She's okay," Xander answers for me.

I'm grateful. I don't have any reassuring words for them right now.

"Raine's ankle is the size of a fucking balloon." Lennox guides him forward. "We can't go much farther."

"The airfield should be just up ahead," Xander replies.

In the rising dawn, our rendezvous point is eventually revealed. It's an exclusive, members-only landing strip in the middle of upper-class suburbia. Probably home to all manner of sleazy politicians' private jets.

Bonus? It's deserted.

Sabre chose carefully.

The office buildings appear empty at this hour, but the two blacked-out, armoured SUVs pulled into the car park make my hackles rise. Our desperation doesn't make this last-ditch effort any less risky.

We've been alone since escaping Harrowdean. Pinning everything on total strangers is a tall order after everything we've endured. But regardless of the lies Warner previously told, I trust his intentions.

"Eyes open," Xander orders curtly. "Two vehicles parked up."

"This is a shitty idea," Lennox mutters.

Raine hisses in pain. "We're out of options."

"Doesn't mean I have to like this."

"When do you ever like anything, Nox?"

Tentatively approaching the car park, we linger outside the gates. The two SUVs are tinted, concealing their occupants. Birds chirping is the only sound for several tense seconds. No signs of movement.

It feels like we're locked in a tense Mexican standoff. Someone has to make the first move. I shrug off Xander's support, swaying on my feet for a moment before steadying.

Xander creeps behind me with each step I take, refusing to let me move more than an inch from his side. He hasn't let go of me since we clambered into the van and fled for our lives.

A car door cracks open, two booted feet hitting the gravel. My pulse races at lightning speed, almost knocking me straight off my feet. When the heavy door closes, I recognise the face that appears.

Thank god.

Overwhelming relief makes my knees knock together. It takes all my mental resolve to hold still instead of melting into a puddle.

"Ripley!"

I stare into Warner's rich baby blues. "Hey."

Hand braced on a gun holster, he rushes across the car park to meet us. I've barely managed a step before I'm pulled into his arms. Not even my smarting ribcage can stop me from hugging him tight.

"You have no idea how good it is to see you."

"Yeah." My throat is thick with emotion. "You too."

Leaning back to examine me, his mouth turns down in a grimace. When his gaze travels to the other three standing nearby in varying degrees of distress, that grimace morphs into a look of abject horror.

"What on earth happened?"

I wave for Xander and the others to approach. "Long story. We have some catching up to do. What happened to you?"

He shrugs with a strained smile. "Even longer story. I got caught up in the violence and had to hide so I didn't get taken hostage like the real guards."

"Well, I'm glad you're alive."

Warner squeezes my shoulder. "I'm sorry we got separated. I searched for you once the authorities moved in, but you were already gone."

"We managed to escape."

"So, what happened?" he repeats.

I brush his question off. "Later. Is your team here?"

"Yeah, we're all here." He shakes his head in disbelief. "I couldn't believe it when I heard you'd made contact. Thought I'd never see you again."

"We contacted Theodore a while back, but things have escalated."

"So I can see."

Surveying the guys, Warner offers them a tight nod. I shoot Lennox a glare, silently urging him to behave. He's glowering at Warner like he can melt the skin from his bones with his mistrustful stare alone.

The sound of more car doors slamming interrupts our reunion. We all tense as several figures emerge from their SUVs and stroll towards us. Every single eye is locked on our motley group.

Walking ahead, a truly intimidating mountain of a man leads the way. He's built like a fucking house, exuding strength and aggression. I try not to gawp at his massive frame, stacked with corded muscle.

The moment his glowing, amber eyes land on me, the most peculiar shift happens. This terrifying, raven-haired beast… offers me a little smile. Peculiar. Though it does soften his harsh features.

Behind him, a slimmer man walks fast to keep up with his colleague's strides. He's hugging a laptop to his flannel-covered chest like it's a safety blanket. His messy blonde ringlets are denser than mine.

They're flanked by security—two men and one brown-haired woman, all wearing holsters and matching black clothing. I count several weapons, though I have no doubt more are concealed.

"Warner," the giant rumbles deeply. "Care to introduce us?"

"Right." He steps back to wave them forward. "This is Ripley, Xander, Lennox and Raine."

"The missing patients." Blondie looks up at us.

Past the wire-rimmed frames he wears, intelligent blue eyes several shades lighter than Warner's hold deep apprehension. I recognise his voice from Xander's earlier phone call. This is Theodore Young.

"That's close enough." Xander inches in front of me. "Who are you?"

"Bloody hell." The woman's eyes are wide as saucers. "You walked here looking like that?"

If looks could kill, she'd be adding her blood to Xander's splattered state with that comment. He looks none too pleased about her attitude.

Warner clears his throat, gesturing to the huge man first. "Enzo Montpellier. Second in command of Sabre Security."

Scanning us up and down, Enzo narrows his bright-amber eyes. "You're all looking rough."

"Charming, aren't they?" Raine snorts to himself.

"Trust me," Lennox whispers back to him. "If you could see us, you'd agree with them."

Enzo gestures to his glasses-wearing colleague. "You've been speaking to Theo. Head of Intelligence." He turns to wave a hand at their security detail. "This is Becket, Ethan and Tara. Warner's teammates."

With pleasantries exchanged, I run out of patience. It takes a moment to moisten my mouth enough to form words.

"There are bodies behind us," I rasp. "Just outside Keyworth. Look for the maize field."

"How many?" Enzo doesn't even bat an eye, his attentive stare still locked on me.

"Four." Xander eyes him suspiciously. "And another in the van we ditched several miles back. An unconscious hostage all trussed up too. He works for Incendia."

Murmuring to each other, Warner's teammates seem to be formulating a plan.

"Rae." I glance at Warner, vision swimming with burning tears. "They killed Rae."

"Oh, Rip." His gaze fractures with sympathy.

"Harrison shot her. He tracked us down in the middle of the night." My voice cracks. "We ran for our lives. They had weapons… an assault rifle. We barely escaped."

"Are you injured?"

I contemplate our sorry states. "A little. Raine has a sprained ankle. And all our stuff is gone… Meds, clothes, everything. We lost it all."

"Don't worry; we can sort all that out and arrange immediate medical attention. What about Harrison? Is he alive?"

"Not anymore." Xander lays a possessive hand on my shoulder.

I push past my grief, sucking in a deep breath. "Rae's body is in the van. I couldn't just leave her in the field. She deserves better."

Cataloguing that information, Warner nods. "I'll take care of her, Rip. I promise."

He turns to his teammates. Weirdly, Warner defers to the older blonde guy, Becket, who seems to be presiding over the small group. I reluctantly match the smile he shoots me.

"We can locate the vehicle," Becket assures me. "And it's… contents."

Theo clutches his laptop. "You'll need help disabling the tracking software. I'll accompany you." He looks at Enzo. "Are you taking them back to HQ?"

"Hunter has a safe house lined up," Enzo responds. "Brooklyn and the others are still at HQ. We'd like to keep witnesses separate to avoid evidence contamination."

I perk up at the familiar name. The escapee from Blackwood. She's still working with them. These people seem to be collecting Incendia's strays faster than we can escape.

"Just hold on a minute." Theo and Becket turn back at Lennox's deep timbre. "Why should we trust you?"

"Nox," Raine chastises.

"In the last twenty-four hours, we've been hunted down, shot at, threatened, beaten and damn near killed. I respect Ripley's choice to make this call, but I still want assurances that my family will be safe."

My head jerks in his direction, a swarm gathering in my stomach. *Family.* Lennox fucking Nash wants his family to be safe—including me.

His pale-green gaze snaps up as if he can feel my surprise. For a breathless second, we're alone. Isolated by our locked eyes. Hatred bled into attraction a long time ago, but right now, it feels like something more. A destructive force.

The kind that ruins people.

In the best possible way.

"Unravelling Incendia's complex criminal web is painstaking work." Enzo sizes him up. "It may not look like it from the outside, but we've been battling these people for years."

"Are you expecting some kind of praise?" Lennox laughs.

"No. Just a little faith."

Whispering a curse, Xander tilts his head up to the sky like he's searching for patience. The analytic in him doesn't ascribe much to faith. Every move he makes relies on cold, hard logic.

"We will make a move on Incendia Corporation and its assets soon," Enzo proclaims, his gaze fixed on me. "When we do, your testimonies will join the countless others we've helped."

"To what end?" Xander growls.

"You'll have the chance to earn your freedom."

They may not be able to have faith right now, but I can. I don't have much choice. I've got nothing else to give. Pulling Xander's hand from my arm, I move to Lennox.

His deep-lidded eyes are pinched with tension, watching me approach. "Don't even start—"

"Can you give us a moment, Raine?" I speak over him.

Raine releases Lennox's sleeve, taking a limping step away. "Sure."

"Thank you."

I stop in front of Lennox, laying a hand on his broad chest. He paces backwards, putting some distance between us and everyone else. His expression is caught somewhere between apprehension and intrigue.

"Ripley, I'm just—"

"I can't run anymore," I interject. "Not from this. We need to take a stand."

"I know," he agrees. "But I need you to be safe."

Newfound warmth curls around my heart. Not the same warmth that Raine's honesty and soft affection provoke. Nor the toxic warmth I hold for Xander and all his complexities.

This feeling is different. It's been there for a while, escaping in brief moments ever since our shared trauma in the Z wing. Even when he's driving me insane or I'm plotting his death, I still feel it. The inescapable draw.

Lennox brings out the worst in me. I want to taunt him. Punish him. Break his mind the same way he broke mine. Yet I also want to reassure him. Gain his trust. Put the broken pieces in his brain back together.

"Don't look so surprised." Lennox smiles wryly. "I'm aware that I fucking suck at… well, this. I've never felt the need to fix my mistakes before."

"Must be nice."

"It was." His teeth pierce his bottom lip. "Until you."

This isn't the time or place, but honestly, we need to lay it all on the table. We almost died last night with all this unfinished business.

"And now? What do you feel?"

"I've been trying to figure that out." Lennox shifts from foot to foot.

"When we go with these people, I don't know what's going to happen. What they'll demand from us. We have to be able to trust each other… fully."

Seeing him so uncertain would be funny if it didn't take us almost dying to get here. I suppose it couldn't have been any other way. Only facing pure evil could force us to put our old hatred aside.

"You flipped my entire world upside down in that basement." He pauses for a breath. "I finally understood your actions. We hurt your family."

"And you were protecting yours."

"I'll always hurt someone else before I let the people I love suffer. I want to protect you, Rip. I want to make up for all the cruel shit I've done. The pain I've caused you."

In the spirit of honesty, I gather my courage.

"We've almost died more times than I can count, but these past few weeks... Fuck, I've never felt so whole, Nox. Even while on death's door. You all make me feel that way."

My hand still resting above his heart, I can feel how out of control it is right now. Stuttering with each hard pound, the organ is pleading with me. Begging for this clean slate.

"That's why I'm willing to have faith right now." I smooth his bloodstained shirt. "Because I know you'll protect me. Just like you'll protect Raine and Xander. I trust you."

Reaching up, Lennox pushes a matted curl behind my ear. "You do?"

"Perhaps against my better judgement."

His mouth quirks. "I've learned to ignore my judgement. It's led me down the wrong path too many times."

"And now?"

"Now... I think it was wrong all along. I'm where I need to be." His knuckles gently stroke down to my jaw. "I'll spend every waking moment ensuring your trust isn't misplaced."

I take Lennox's hand from my face, his grip firm and reassuring. It feels right clutching mine. His fingertips dance over my skin, leaving butterfly kisses that raise my gooseflesh.

"Ready?" I ask him. "They won't wait forever."

"No. I'm not ready. Not yet."

Grip tightening on my jaw, he leans in to touch his lips to mine. It doesn't matter that we're standing in broad daylight, surrounded by strangers. Coated in blood. Beaten and broken down.

Because Lennox is kissing me.

He's holding me close.

Giving himself to me.

Unlike previous kisses, this one is tender. A slow, delicate touch of the lips. He's hesitant at first, mouth lingering on mine before he pecks me again. Harder. Breathing vulnerability and hope into the vacant space I've carved for him in my heart.

Everything about Lennox is intimidating. His harsh demeanour. Acid tongue. Propensity for violence. Inability to forgive. But I'm starting to realise this isn't the real Lennox at all. Like Xander and Raine, he played a role.

We all did.

It's how we survived.

This is the real Lennox. Kissing me so softly, I almost wonder if the man who knocked me unconscious and left me for dead in a flooding pool ever really existed. Back then, I was just another threat.

The kiss ends, and I gulp down air.

"Now I'm ready." He plants a final kiss on my forehead. "Let's go see what these fuckers want from us for their stupid protection."

"You don't have to sound so thrilled."

"I'm struggling to contain my enthusiasm, really."

"I can tell."

Fingers interlinked, we turn to face the others. Xander's holding Raine upright to relieve his bad ankle, while Warner's team is pouring over a map pulled up on Theodore's laptop.

Enzo glares around with his thick arms folded. The hard-faced grump can't fool me. I saw that smile earlier and all it entailed. He's a fucking teddy bear.

We walk over to Xander and Raine. Standing as one united front, even in our pathetically dishevelled state, I've never felt so powerful. Perhaps we can do this. Face the evil hunting us and end it, once and for all.

I want the future I became the stooge for.

And I want it with them.

CHAPTER 19
RAINE
PULL THE PLUG - VOILÀ

SHAKING the pills from the plastic bottle, I count out each dose. I'm determined to do this alone, hands sliding over each sleek kitchen cabinet as I search for a glass.

I've barely familiarised myself with the two-bedroom apartment we were deposited in by Warner and his superiors. They instructed us to get cleaned up and rest while they handle the fallout of the mess we left behind.

After being driven down to London and checked by the doctor waiting, we were ready to pass out. First, we had to wait for medications to be delivered. Sabre must have serious money if they can summon controlled substances with a click of their fingers.

They left quickly, promising to return with updates and more essentials. Warner assured us that security would remain outside for our protection. They're taking no chances after our close call.

Feeling something cool knock against my fingers, I feel for its texture. Curved edges. A glass. Triumphant, I pluck it from the cupboard. With the pills in one hand, I can attempt to locate the sink.

Clang.

My foot smashes into a hard piece of furniture, causing my still-painful ankle to flare. The sudden collision unsteadies me, and before I can stop it, the glass slips from my hand.

"No," I yelp, trying to catch it.

The shattering blast of it smashing on the kitchen tiles will certainly draw attention. Sighing hard, I rest against the sink, my fist curling around the pills.

Bloody useless.

This is why I always kept my room precisely organised, down to the inch. I hate new environments. It always takes time to adjust. And right now, I don't even have a guide stick.

"Raine! Where are you?"

"Kitchen, Xan."

Hurried footsteps bang through the apartment. I don't bother attempting to move. Xander announces his arrival with a loud exhale.

"Ah."

"Yep." I pop the P exaggeratedly. "Figured you'd slept enough."

Cracking a yawn, he steps closer. "You should've just woken one of us up."

"It was just a dumb mistake. I hit my ankle."

"Alright, stand still."

I remain frozen while Xander cleans up the broken shards then fills another glass with water to hand over. Knocking back the pills, I swallow the powdery mouthful then hand the glass back to him.

"How long did we sleep for?"

I hear the glass make an impact when Xander deposits it in the sink. "Fifteen hours. Must've needed it."

"Christ. Those guys will be back soon to start taking statements."

"Yeah." He sounds groggy and half-awake. "I'll get Lennox up. Can you find your way back to Ripley's room?"

"Erm…"

Xander chuckles. "We'll get you another stick. Come on, take my arm. You shouldn't be walking on that ankle."

"It's fine, the swelling is down."

Gratefully accepting his elbow, I let him steer me through the unknown space. Once I commit the layout to memory, I'll be fine. In the meantime, I despise being so dependent on others.

"Good luck with the snorer."

"Thanks," he drawls sarcastically.

"I'll wake Ripley up."

Easing the door open, I keep a hand stretched out to avoid any more collisions. Ripley's stirring in the bed. She was exhausted when we arrived, passing out immediately once the doctor cleared her and she'd showered.

Finding the double bed, I crawl back underneath the cheap, scratchy duvet. Being roused by turbulent shaking and nausea twisting my gut wasn't a pleasant awakening. She slept through it, though.

"Mmm," Ripley moans.

Snuggling up to her back, I hold her in a close spoon. "Just me."

"Where did you go?"

"To take my meds." Her scent is an unfamiliar perfume, not the papaya fragrance I'm used to. "I don't like the shower gel you're using."

Laughing sleepily, she presses her back into me. "It was a bar of soap. This place is sparse."

"What's it like?"

"Bare." Ripley pauses to yawn. "Kinda like a cheap London rental but unfinished. I don't think anyone's been here for a long time."

"I guess safe houses aren't supposed to be luxurious."

"At this point, I would take a cardboard box on a street corner if it's safe." Her back vibrates with a laugh before she curses. "Ouch."

We all heard the doctor declare her stable, though she'll be multicoloured for a while. Thankfully, there's no permanent damage from Harrison's beating and the brutal tasing she received.

"How are the bruises?"

"Delightful," she groans. "I can't believe that bastard didn't break a rib."

"You got lucky."

"Some didn't."

Ripley falls silent, and I know she's thinking about Rae. Whenever I interacted with the girl, she was open and warm. I liked her energy.

"I'm sure Warner's teammates have taken care of Rae."

"I don't even know if she had family," Ripley replies thickly. "I know what type of razors she liked. How often she'd reorder. What she was willing to pay. Nothing actually important or meaningful."

Unable to alleviate the guilt she's overwhelmed by, I do the only thing I can. I hold her close, her spine aligned with my chest as I rock her gently. Her sobs are barely audible when they take over.

"How did Harrison even know we were friends?" she weeps. "It's my fault. I let her get close. He used Rae against me."

"Stop, Rip. Her death isn't on you. Letting people get close doesn't mean you're sentencing them to death."

"Doesn't it?" She releases a miserable-sounding laugh. "I let her matter to me, and she's dead."

"Because a lunatic killed her. Did you ask him to?"

"No," she whimpers.

"Did you want her to get hurt?"

"No, of course not!"

"Are you happy she's gone?"

Ripley shrugs away from me, awkwardly twisting in the bed. "What the fuck, Raine?"

"I'm proving to you how the rest of us see it. Rae's death is a tragedy. She didn't deserve what happened to her, but that doesn't mean it's your fault. You have to stop taking on all this guilt."

"But—"

"No buts, Rip. It stops now."

Finding her shoulder, I slide my hand up and behind her neck to knead her skull. Ripley draws in a heavy breath, curling up into my chest. I can feel her tears sliding against my skin with each hiccup.

"It's okay, babe. Let it all out."

In many ways, I feel lucky to experience this side of her. Not many people know the real Ripley. The fact that she's willing to let herself fall apart in front of me is a privilege I'll never take for granted.

Holding her tight until her sobs turn to quiet sniffles, I let Ripley work through her grief. Sometimes, words are unhelpful. Providing a safe space to acknowledge the grief and let it come pouring out is far more powerful.

"Did you go into the kitchen naked?" She breaks the silence after a long time.

"I have boxers on."

"What about the smashing sound?"

"Erm, I dropped a glass. Need to map the place out in my mind."

Her hand splays across my lower back. I tune into the rhythmic strokes, each touch taking me to a familiar place where I don't need sight. Not with her. With Ripley, I feel perfectly whole.

We drift for a long while until the sounds of stirring echo from outside our bedroom. Kissing the top of her head, I gently peel her from my chest.

"Ready to face the music?"

"Not really." She sighs.

"We can hide here if you need more time."

"As much as I appreciate that, we can't. We'll have company soon."

"I'll happily barricade the door for you."

Ripley pecks my cheek before I feel her sit up. "I love you."

I never thought three simple words would mean so much to me. Perhaps I never thought she'd say them back. In a matter of months, my entire existence has shifted. It used to revolve around the next hit.

Now, it's her.

A far more intoxicating drug.

Dragging myself from the bed, I feel around to locate the sweats and crumpled t-shirt I discarded before climbing into bed. They hang loose on my frame, but for clean clothes found in a pinch, I won't complain.

Ripley uses the bathroom then pads back out, the ruffling of clothes being pulled on evidence of her stiff movements. She clasps my arm, leading me from the room.

"How's the ankle?"

"It feels a lot better. The ice pack helped." I hesitate, sniffing the air. "Oh, smooth."

"Huh?"

"Xander's demonstrating his obsessive knowledge once more."

As she pulls me into what I think is the open plan living and dining area, I hear Ripley gasp. It's a weirdly happy sound. That alone makes me smile.

"Is that…"

"Not me," Xander volunteers. "The snorer was already up and dressed."

I sense movement accompanying Lennox's signature heavy thuds. I'm convinced he's incapable of walking quietly. He fiddles with something before approaching us.

"Joint effort," he explains. "Xander knew your coffee order."

Ripley snickers. "Of course, he did."

"Here. Macchiato, right?"

The satisfied groan she releases can only be described as sexual. Seriously, I'm concerned about what she's planning to do with that coffee.

"You went out?" Ripley takes a loud slurp. "Oh, holy shit."

Lennox laughs under his breath. "Yeah, I wanted to check out the security we've been assigned. There's a coffee place across the street."

His rough fingertips brush my hand, passing me a Styrofoam cup. I won't tell Ripley that I'm a tea before coffee kinda person. She'll probably decapitate me with her macchiato in hand.

"Security still outside?" I take a hot sip.

"Five of them."

"Armed?" Ripley asks.

Lennox sniffs loudly. "Yeah."

Seems they're taking the meagre information we've offered seriously. Warner and his colleagues don't even know half the story yet.

We all listen to Ripley make increasingly disturbing sounds as she drinks. You'd think the woman hasn't tasted decent coffee in years… Which isn't far from the truth, thinking about it.

"Here." There's a rustle before footsteps near. "Eat before your heart gives out from all the caffeine."

"Xan," Ripley warns sassily. "Touch my coffee and I'll drink it from your skull."

A choked cough comes from Lennox. "He'd probably enjoy that."

"No." Xander is quick to protest. "I wouldn't."

"That's an outright lie." I savour another sip.

"It's not!"

"You totally would enjoy it."

"Raine's right." Lennox harrumphs in disdain. "Tell the truth."

An audible sigh.

"For fuck's sake… Yes. I would probably enjoy that."

Xander joins our laughter—begrudgingly, from the sound of it—as he helps me walk over to what feels like a kitchen table. Measuring the space between the chairs with my foot, I begin to form a mental image.

Lennox passes around breakfast pastries crammed full of thick, sugary jam. I recognise the taste and texture on my tongue. We eat peacefully, sipping our drinks, until he breaks the silence.

"Do you think he meant it? That Enzo bloke?"

"Meant what?" Ripley chews loudly.

"What he said about cutting the head off the snake," Lennox clarifies. "Are they going to make a move on Bancroft?"

"Are we even sure he's the real threat anymore?" Xander slurps his drink. "Harrison hinted at management changes. Then there was that phone call."

I hear someone put their food down.

"You can say it. My uncle."

"Yes. He clearly sent those men after us," Xander says, blunt as ever. "Your uncle put a hit out on us."

"That goes a bit beyond mere disownment." I wince at my own words. "Sorry, Rip."

"Don't be. We can't tiptoe around this." She sounds resigned. "I think his role goes beyond being an investor. He's more deeply embroiled in the conspiracy than I realised."

"We have to tell them," Lennox chimes in. "Bancroft is still a threat, but they need to get eyes on Jonathan. Perhaps he's pulling the strings while his boss is under fire."

"That seems likely," Xander agrees.

Finishing up our breakfast, we remain at the table, gulping down our hot drinks. Ripley's leg pushes against mine underneath the table—she's sitting on my right side. I drop a hand to her thigh.

"So we tell them everything." She covers my hand with hers. "In exchange for what? Protection?"

"We need to negotiate for immunity," Xander responds. "For the riot. The contraband. All of it."

"You really think we'd face prosecution?" Nausea spikes through me.

"Warner told us criminal charges were on the table for other escapees."

My mouth pulls down in a grimace. "And if Sabre doesn't have that power? Or won't help us avoid charges?"

Xander doesn't answer. Fantastic. That really gives me a vote of confidence.

"Shit, Xan." Lennox breaks the long pause. "You can't tell them about… You know…"

The silence is frustrating. I strain my ears, trying to understand what's happening.

"Lennox is miming," Ripley whispers to me. "Throat cutting, to be specific."

"Thanks. Can we really keep that a secret?"

"Nobody saw me," Xander says nonchalantly.

"Are you absolutely certain?" Lennox counters.

His silence is telling. Nope. He's not.

"Then lie!"

There's a loud boom, and the table shakes as Lennox must slam his fist down onto it.

"Tell them what happened, but say the warden threatened you. Anything. It'd be your word against a dead man."

Something has really gone wrong if I'm sitting here, trapped in a safe house, discussing how best to cover up a grisly murder one of my best friends committed. It's a far cry from my old life.

"We aided and abetted the experimental program by selling contraband." Ripley changes the topic. "I doubt the law will look upon that leniently."

"Then we have a bargaining chip." Lennox snaps his fingers. "Our inside information will fast-track years of investigative work. We can tell them everything. We sell them on that."

Someone drums on the table's surface. I can taste the boiling tension. We've sided with the good guys, but that doesn't mean we're off the hook. The world doesn't work that way.

"And if it's not enough?" Xander eventually asks. "Lennox, we both have criminal convictions. Who's to say we won't be sent to an actual prison this time?"

"They wouldn't do that, surely?"

Just the thought has anxiety vibrating beneath my skin.

"This will turn into a blame game. Throwing us in jail with a nice guilty label will be an easy win."

The thought of them being ripped away from us is too much to bear. While a violent episode landed Ripley in Harrowdean Manor, I know she was never charged. Like me, she was among the percentage incarcerated without a criminal conviction.

The rest—patients like Lennox and Xander—took their rehabilitative sentence to avoid prison. That's not to say their mental health wasn't a deciding factor. Ultimately, no one in the institute was altogether sane.

I rub my aching temples, a headache forming. "Why does it sound like we're screwed either way?"

"No." Ripley's leg presses harder into mine. "We just have to play this smart until the investigation concludes with Bancroft and his associates behind bars."

"Or six feet under," Xander adds.

Lennox makes an agreeing sound. I trace circles on Ripley's loose sweats, the cotton rough and cheap. No matter what role he's played, Jonathan is her last living relative. She has to be struggling.

"I know he's your uncle, but…"

"He won't stop," she finishes for me. "Jonathan is relentless. Focused. If he wants something, he'll pull every trick in the book to get it."

"In business," I point out. "This is different."

"I was always a business transaction to him. It's no different now.

He's a core investor in Incendia Corporation, and we're a threat to that. To his entire livelihood and reputation."

Her words hang ominously. She's right. To him, we are a threat. An erasable one. That's why he sent those men to capture or kill us. Jonathan is far more than the heartless bastard we all took him to be.

He's dangerous.

And we're on his hit list.

CHAPTER 20
RIPLEY
ANOTHER ONE – TOBY MAI

TAPPING a ballpoint pen against his notebook, Enzo Montpellier stares me down. His attention is a precisely-aimed blowtorch, intending to incinerate any lies he detects. He's terrifyingly perceptive.

I'm holding my own against his harsh glare, even after several hours of his carefully worded questions. The others were removed from the apartment under protest to be interviewed separately.

Xander had to be threatened several times to get him to leave for his own interview. It took a lot of pleading for him to eventually relent for the sake of getting this done.

"Why do I feel like you don't trust me?" Enzo deadpans.

Shifting, I fold my legs. "Because I don't."

"We're on the same side."

"No one is on our side, Mr Montpellier. Ever."

"Enzo is fine," he tells me for the fifth time.

Piercing amber eyes sweep over me. We've been talking for hours, running through every single detail. Years of information from my first day in Priory Lane to scaling the security fence at Harrowdean.

I never thought I'd be laying out my life story in brutal black and white for a total stranger. One whose job is to judge whether I'm deserving of his help. After all I've done, I wouldn't be surprised if Enzo threw us back out on the street.

When you're drowning, it's easy to justify pushing other heads beneath the water so you can stay afloat. It's necessary, right? They'd do the same to you. Only in the aftermath does the price of evil come knocking.

"I have one more question." He snaps his notebook closed, placing the pen on top.

"Shoot."

"Why'd you do it? Become their stooge?"

"Do you ask all Incendia's victims this?"

"Most of them were admitted into the program by force." His mountain-sized shoulders lift in a shrug. "I have one guy who even worked for them before he was imprisoned and tortured for several years."

Acid swarms in the back of my mouth. "So I'm the bad guy for choosing to do what I did?"

"Do you deny it?"

Focusing on the coffee table, I avoid his stare. "No."

"Why, then?"

"I've done things I'm not proud of." I lace my hands over my roiling stomach. "A lot of people have gotten hurt because of my actions."

Looking down at the battle wounds decorating my arms, I struggle to find the right words. The events that have led me to this sofa, recounting a tale too harrowing for most to fathom, feel alien.

Did I do all those things? I hold the memories. Bear the scars. It must've been me.

I spent so long detached from my morals, I didn't care who I was hurting. At least part of me didn't. Peddling management's agenda became second nature. I fanned the flames so they could study us all.

Sick, right?

I'm under no illusions.

It's an old cliché. Hurt people, hurt people. Is it the same for those who've been abandoned? Do we dole out cruelty to ensure our own survival at all costs because no one else is coming to save us?

No one has ever helped or been there for me. Not since Holly. I've done everything myself, starting with getting revenge. Leveraging my grief into power was nothing more than a calculated business move.

"Every time I sold pills to an addict or blades to a cutter, I knew what I was doing." I swallow the lump in my throat. "It was just… inconsequential. I needed the power. The control."

Listening attentively, Enzo doesn't look judgemental as I expected.

The gentle look of understanding is back, crumbling his gruff exterior. I'm surprised he hasn't run for the front door yet.

"Their pain guaranteed my freedom," I try to explain. "Doing things that made me sick meant I would live when Holly didn't get to. It was a desperate trade off."

He nods in acknowledgement. "In my experience… desperation is the source of most evils."

"Don't excuse what I did."

"I'm not." Enzo smiles sadly. "Perhaps it was simply an inevitable side effect."

How this towering pillar of strength can hold so much soft-hearted concern, I can't quite understand. He isn't what I expected from Sabre's second-in-command.

Despite his tactics, I hold the full, unfiltered truth back. Enzo is playing the good guy, but I've fallen into that trap before.

"I'll take your testimony back to our director, Hunter."

"Warner mentioned others were facing criminal charges." Panic flutters behind my breastbone. "I need to know what I'm looking at."

He appraises me, the crinkles around his eyes making him seem conflicted. "I don't know, Ripley."

"That isn't good enough."

"We're negotiating charges with the Serious Crimes Unit. Your cooperation will help your case."

"I have more information. Inside knowledge that can help you dismantle their entire operation."

"If you're all willing to cooperate with the investigation, perhaps a plea deal can be made. Hunter will take your case to the authorities to make a decision."

"He doesn't want to speak to me himself?" I ask in surprise.

"He's… preoccupied right now." Enzo worries his bottom lip. "We lost a member of our organisation recently. Someone important to us."

"Alyssa?"

The muscle in his neck twitches. "Yes."

"She freed us from the Z wing."

"So I've heard."

"What happened to her?"

Enzo releases a world-weary sigh. "The night we entered Harrowdean, we were undertaking a rescue mission. Alyssa lost her life in the crossfire."

"If it weren't for her, we would be dead or worse. I'm sorry."

"Yeah." He clears his throat. "Me too."

Feeling like I've poked a sore spot, I decide to look away. "What happens now?"

"You'll remain in protective custody here at the safe house while we take this information away. The security detail won't let anything happen to you."

"Bancroft will plough straight through your men."

Enzo gathers his things, rising to his full height. "Bancroft won't be a problem for much longer. Until then, we will keep you safe."

"You're not going to tell me anything else. Are you?"

Humour sparkles in his molten eyes. "No."

Frustration burns through me, but I hold it at bay. We've barely survived a few weeks in the firing line. This man helps run a multimillion-pound business that operates under enemy fire. This is his fight.

Before showing himself out, Enzo glances back at me, looking like he wants to say more.

"What?" I prompt.

"You remind me of someone. She's feeling guilty right now too."

When he pauses, I wait for him to gather his thoughts.

"I told her healing is hard."

"Why do you say that?" I can't hold the question in.

"Well, it's a constant battle between your inner child who's scared and just wants to feel safe… your inner teenager who's angry and wants justice… and your current self. The one who just wants peace."

Gaping at him, I'm too surprised to form a response. Enzo drags a palm down his rugged face, his gaze now averted.

"I don't know if that helps. Good to meet you properly, Ripley. We'll be in touch."

With that wise pearl delivered, he turns and leaves. Enzo Montpellier could rival Lennox with his aggressive stomping around, but I doubt anyone could match the heart of gold he seems to have.

Silence drapes over me, broken by the distant ticking of the clock hanging on the wall. Now that I'm alone, all the shameful secrets I've just revealed leave me feeling dirty.

Perhaps the different parts of me have been fighting all along. Orphaned Ripley. Angry, grieving Ripley. Abandoned Ripley. Now tired

Ripley. In that battleground, I lashed out, creating so much collateral damage.

A layer of blood and tears coat my soul, and short of digging the thing out with a rusty spoon, I'll never be able to get it clean. Not after all I've done to be sitting here today.

The invisible fist in my chest squeezing, I head for the shared bathroom, quickly stripping off the clothing I was given to wear. More essentials and toiletries were delivered this morning.

Studying my bruised torso in the mirror, I poke the sensitive flesh. It could be worse. The pain meds are working. I locate the new shampoo and shower gel we were given before stepping into the shower.

Not so long ago, I stood in a shower and scrubbed the memories of Xander and Lennox from my skin. Life has changed so much since then. I feel lost without the guys all around me now.

Head ducked, I brace my hands on the tiled wall. Water sluices over me, and in the spray, I fail to realise I'm not alone until the bathroom door clicks shut.

"Wha…?"

My exclamation dies on my lips. Leaning against the bathroom door, Lennox watches me through the steamed-up glass. A million warring emotions dance in his eyes beneath ruffled, thick-brown locks.

"You're done?"

He shrugs. "That Ethan guy didn't have any more questions. I guess the other interviews are taking longer. Xander and Raine aren't back yet."

"I see."

Continuing to wash myself, I lather my body with foaming shower gel. Lennox's throat bobs beneath dark stubble overdue for a shave. His chest stretches the bounds of his shirt, the defined muscles making my toes curl.

"What did you tell Enzo?"

"Enough to take to the authorities." I tip my head back to rinse my hair. "Kept some details brief."

"Like?" Lennox challenges.

"Like you zip tying me in a swimming pool, for one."

His gaze lowers, flitting over me unashamedly. "I see."

A column of heat gathers between my legs, the long slow burn gathering into a raging furnace. I like the way he looks at me. Powerless and hungry. Like he'd beg for a mere touch.

After washing the shower gel from my body, I turn off the spray and step out. Water clings to me, trailing over my curves as I disregard the towel I laid out. The sore bruises and bright-pink gunshot wound on my thigh suddenly feel inconsequential.

Lennox holds stock-still, watching me pad towards him. I stop mere inches away, completely bare. His attention dips to trail over me, greedily drinking in every inch.

It isn't the first time he's seen me naked, but we're not imprisoned in a cell now. He can do whatever he likes.

"Don't you want to know what I told them?" he asks thickly.

"Not right now. No."

Nodding, Lennox's tongue darts out to lick his bottom lip. "So what do you want?"

Pent-up desire has emboldened me. We've exchanged heated whispers and the odd kiss since escaping. Yet he refuses to take that next step. I'll take it for the both of us if I have to.

"For you to keep your word."

"My word?" He tilts his head.

"I recall you promising to do something."

His eyes widen in understanding. "I thought you were injured."

"And I wouldn't be asking if I couldn't handle it."

Without touching me, Lennox holds eye contact as he steps away from the door. I watch him sink to the bathroom floor and land on his knees.

The almighty Lennox Nash is fucking kneeling in front of me. My hand knots in his soft brown hair, giving it a hard tug.

In this position, I feel utterly invincible. The man who vowed to ruin me is cowering on his knees, a million miles from the person he once was.

"Is this what you want?" he purrs.

Feeling brave, I lower my other hand between my legs. My fingers meet slick warmth. I'm wet, my swollen clit aching. Lennox watches me push a hand over my folds, spreading my arousal.

I slide a finger in my pussy, my thumb rotating above my clit. His rapt attention on me is exhilarating. He hasn't even touched me. This is all about surrender after months of our futile war for revenge.

"Yes," I answer breathily. "This is what I wanted."

"What if I tell you that you are the most infuriating, confusing, frustrating person I've ever met?" He hesitates, nostrils flaring. "But also the most beautiful woman I've ever laid eyes on?"

Slipping in another finger, I scissor the digits inside me. My back arches, pushing my cunt closer to his face. Still, Lennox doesn't move an inch, determined to give me all the control.

"And for the longest time, I was terrified of admitting how drawn I felt to you. How you infiltrated my dreams. My thoughts. My fantasies. I was scared to love the very thing I hated."

Working myself over for his perusal, I fist the hand still knotted in his hair. "Are you still afraid?"

I watch Lennox nod, pulling in fast breaths.

"Of me?"

"No. Now I'm scared of losing you."

Triumph fills my every cell.

"I want you to forget it all, Nox. Everything we've done to each other. And I want you to prove to me how much you want this. Right here, right now."

Anticipation blazes in his seafoam orbs. "Are you sure?"

"I won't break. I need you to touch me."

The tentative Lennox dissipates. All it took was that verbal admission. He knocks my hand aside, sliding my fingers from inside me. Hunger pulses between my legs when he sucks the glistening digits into his mouth.

Lennox swirls his tongue over my fingers, sucking them clean. Then he lowers his mouth to the apex of my thighs, dead set on one target. Placing my other hand on his shoulder, I buck into his face.

When his lips meet my core, I mentally rejoice. The man who tried his best to kill me is now on his knees, worshipping my body. I've taken his hatred and turned it into pure lust.

He devours my pussy like a starving man, his tongue dragging over my tingling clit. I continue rocking against him, encouraging each lick. Sparks are zipping up and down my spine in fast succession.

"I can't wait to feel you, baby."

When he thrusts a finger into me, I can't help but cry out. Lennox fucks me with his hand, mouth fastened on my bud with each pulse. The combined effect has my knees weakening.

He pauses for a breath. "You taste so fucking good."

"Is that all you've got?"

"Fuck no. I'm dying to fill this sweet pussy, but I need to prep you first." His heated gaze flashes to mine. "I don't want to hurt you."

I suppress a smirk. The eyeful I got of his package in the bathroom was intriguing. He's far bigger than any man I've been with, matching his stacked height. Part of me wants to push my own limits.

"I want you to come for me, Rip." His fingers pump into me, hard and fast. "I'm begging you to give me an orgasm. Cover my hand in your juices."

"Yes," I moan.

"You like that, huh? When I beg on my knees?"

Squirming, I ride the hand driving me wild in time to his ministrations. My climax is approaching, making my skin tighten and tingle like I've been wired with electrodes.

"God, Nox. I like it."

"What if I beg to throw you on the bed and spread your legs wide open so I can see your glistening, pink cunt?"

"Yes! Oh, fuck. Yes."

"And what if I beg to sink my cock inside you and stretch this tight little cunt to breaking point?"

"P-Please."

My vision swims, an electrifying wave washing over me. His dirty words are heightening my arousal to the point of being overwhelmed. I'm going to explode if he keeps going.

"And what if I beg to fill every inch of your spent pussy with my seed? Just so I can see it dripping out of you and trailing down your legs?"

All it takes is a final thrust and I'm erupting all over his hand. My orgasm hits all at once, core spasming and body trembling. I dig my nails into his shoulder, riding out the wave.

Removing his hand, Lennox ensures I'm watching as he slowly sucks each soaked digit, just like he did to mine. His expression is downright predatory. I wonder if I'll even survive his begging.

"Such a perfect girl," he croons. "May I stand up now? I'd like to do everything I just said and more."

Christ.

Everything clenches tight.

"You may," I pant, my heart galloping. "Take me to your bedroom. Right now."

Finding his feet, Lennox sweeps me into his arms. I grunt when I'm tossed over his shoulder, the pain flaring through my stiff body only serving to heighten my arousal.

His palm smacks against my bare ass as I'm carried from the bathroom to the room he's sharing with Xander. The king-sized bed has been neatly made. God forbid the iceman ever leaves a single thing out of place.

As soon as he places me on the mattress, he's yanking his t-shirt off. I lay back, thighs pressed together to alleviate the intense pressure his words have created.

Naked Lennox is a sight to behold. Barrel chest carved with stacked muscles, his abdominals, pecs and shoulders resemble chiselled marble. Unlike Xander, his skin is bronzed and smattered with dark hair, a trail leading into his sweats.

"Spread your legs, baby. Show me everything."

I follow his instructions, spreading myself wide open so I'm utterly on display. Lennox's piercing attention scours over me, drinking in the view as he strips off the rest of his clothes.

The faintest crack of doubt inches in at the sight of him. As I remembered, he's fucking huge. His shaft is thick and girthy. I'm doubting whether he'll even fit.

Lennox fists his cock, slowly pumping it. "Don't look so scared, Rip."

I squirm on the bed. "Are you going to hold me in suspense?"

Prowling closer, he kneels on the bed above me. The anticipation is heady. I wasn't ready to give myself to Lennox before, but now I want him to take everything. All I have left to give.

He braces himself over me, moving down to plant open-mouthed kisses across my chest. His lips lock around my right nipple, sweet pain flashing through me when he pulls it deeply into his mouth.

Releasing my nipple, he sucks and bites a path to my left breast, leaving a constellation of red marks. I wriggle beneath him, pleading for any amount of friction.

"So impatient." His words warm my already scalding skin.

"Nox," I whine.

"Easy, baby. I want to take my time with you."

Hasn't he waited long enough?

Playing with my nipples, he seems determined to cover every part of me in tiny bites. I don't know if it's some kind of branding in his mind, a statement to the other men allowed to touch me. I think I like that idea.

"Please," I try again. "Stop teasing me."

Lennox lifts his head. "How can I get you to shut up?"

My mouth falls open in protest.

"Ah." He quirks a thick brow. "I know."

Pulling me upright, he sits back on his haunches between my legs. Lennox threads his hand through my hair, pushing my head down towards his proud cock.

"I'll fuck your throat if that's the only way to teach you patience."

He pushes himself past my lips, holding my head in place. The rough handling only makes me hotter. I take his length deep into my mouth, bobbing up and down on his shaft.

His grip on my head guides my moves, allowing him to set the pace. Lennox doesn't deny himself, pushing down fast so he can roughly ride my mouth. Each time he hits the back of my throat, tears spring up in my eyes.

"That's it." His praise is guttural. "Get me nice and wet so I can slide into that dripping cunt."

Tongue swirling over the velvety tip, I suck him deep once more, feeling moisture springing from my eyes. I can't take all of him—he's too big to fit into my mouth even while relaxing my jaw.

"Yes, Rip. Perfect. Let me fuck that mouth, baby."

I could fall apart from his enthusiastic praise alone. It's making my pulse thrum, struggling to hold the excitement building within me. I had no idea he'd be so vocal.

He ruts into my mouth, over and over. Pushing deeper each time. Forcing me to suck down more of his huge length until I'm gagging on his cock and loving every intense second.

"God, how I want to pour myself down your throat. You are everything, Rip. Fucking everything."

Before he can finish, Lennox eases himself from my mouth. I sit up with streaming cheeks, my chin soaked by strands of saliva.

"Lay down," he commands. "Now."

I'm shaking so hard, it's a relief to slump back on the bed. He retakes his position, pushing my thighs farther apart until my bones ache to fit his wide frame.

The head of his dick slides through my folds, swirling heat and moisture. He teases my slit with it, only entering me the smallest amount before withdrawing and sliding himself around my entrance again.

"More!" I beg shamelessly.

Each slow tease is torture. I want him to surge into me and take me as roughly as he did my mouth. We may not be enemies anymore, but I'd happily let him fuck me like we are.

"Please… Oh god. Please give it to me."

"Are you this demanding with the others?"

Writhing beneath him, I don't answer. Lennox bares his teeth and pushes farther into me, his girth straining my walls. We both groan at the same time.

"So goddamn tight."

He withdraws before I can fully adjust, sliding out before nudging back inside. The agonising dance goes on and on with him giving an extra push then snatching it away each time.

My mind is starting to fray. He's barely entered me, and it already feels like too much. I'm not a shrinking violet. I've slept with my fair share of guys. None that rival Lennox, though.

Giving me more of his cock, he rocks into me. The shallow thrusts make me stretch to accommodate him. I couldn't take him if I wasn't so frenziedly turned on right now.

Each time he pushes forward, I take a little bit more. Adjusting to the pressure is excruciating in all the best ways. It feels like my mind is set to split in half before I can orgasm again.

"Nox," I whimper, overwhelmed.

"It's okay, Rip. You're doing so good. Can you take a bit more, baby?"

He moves faster, retreating and thrusting back in enough to make me moan loudly. It's too much. I'm so full. Stretched to my limits. Lennox is filling every part of me, mentally and physically.

"Just like that," he hums. "Good."

"Oh f-fuck. Nox!"

"That's it. You can take me. I know you can."

When he bottoms out, we're both struggling for air. Lennox shifts his hips, finding the perfect angle to glide into me with steady strokes. I'm over-stimulated, my skin slick beneath his weight above me.

"You're so fucking perfect."

Lennox palms my breast, squeezing tight as he jerks into me. The burst of pain is welcome. It cuts through my mind's fog and gives me something to latch onto amidst all the warring sensations.

He pistons into me, switching between shallow thrusts that stoke my building climax and deep pounds, delaying my release each time it nears. Just as I feel it within reach, he slows his pace, holding me on the brink.

It's like he can read my body, translating each tremble and whimper to determine exactly when to restrain himself. Lennox is determined to break me open and take my shattered pieces for himself.

"You take me so well," he grunts in exertion. "So damn well. It's like you were made for me."

I gasp and moan, my body slick with our combined sweat. I wonder if the others have returned and they're listening to everything Lennox is saying. Their friend's mouth is filthy.

Feeling my core tense, I'm ready to finish. My bruised body is taut, desperate for relief. The cusp of my orgasm rises, on the precipice of consuming me, when Lennox abruptly pulls out.

"Not yet."

I scream loudly, slamming my clenched fist against his chest. "Fuck! Lennox!"

"You know, Xander warned me you're a little brat. I may have begged, but now, you're going to come when I say so."

"Goddamn you!"

"And not a moment sooner," he adds, ignoring my outrage.

He stands, seizing my ankles to pull me to the mattress edge. I'm a boneless pile as he turns me over, my stomach meeting the bed and face burying in the warm sheets.

Lennox lifts my hips, positioning me like I'm a limp doll. When he surges inside me from behind, I come back to life. My hands twist in the sheets, needing something to hold on to.

I distantly hear him spit before it hits my ass, sliding down into my crack. I startle at the impact, surprised by his fingers pushing the saliva farther down until he's circling my asshole.

My whines reach a fever-pitch.

"Have you ever taken a man here before?"

I'm not going to tell him about Raine finger-blasting my rear while he fucked me during a depressive episode. We need at least some boundaries.

"I was jealous, watching Raine ride your mouth." Lennox's fingertip enters me. "But I also wanted to join in."

He pushes in deeper, listening to my muffled wails. I'm already full to the brim. Just when I think I can't take anymore, he finds a new limit to test.

Working his finger in and out of my backside, Lennox resumes fucking me. His timing is perfect, breaching each hole simultaneously. My stolen orgasm comes soaring back within reach.

"Easy, baby. You're tensing up."

"Because you won't let me come!"

He chuckles behind me. "Do you have any idea how long I've waited to do this? You can hold out a little longer."

Digging my nails into the bed, the room is filled with the sound of our bodies smacking together. It's reaching intolerable levels. I'm far too full to cope with his thrusting much longer.

"I hate you!"

Pain sizzles across my scalp as Lennox seizes my wet hair. He manages to twist the short curls around his fingers, forming a tight leash. My head is wrenched back, pulling my torso upwards.

"Say that again," he hisses. "I dare you."

I'm suspended mid-air by his grip on my hair alone, his cock still plunging into me. It's a dominating move, inflicting pain to silence me while he's still fucking me into oblivion.

Breasts pushed out, I think he's going to finally relent. Only for him to still again when I don't respond, denying me right before I can fall apart. My throat is raw from crying out.

"Well?" Lennox tugs on my hair.

Panting, I can't string a response together. Lennox slides his finger from my asshole to deliver a punishing spank. It leaves a fiery brand on my skin, already sensitive from his constant teasing.

"Do you hate me when I've got my cock in you?"

"No," I moan helplessly.

"Then don't lie. Or I'll keep you hanging for an eternity."

"Please... Nox. Let me come. Please."

He swats me again, right above my soaked asshole. "No."

"Please!"

My ass is still tingling from his penetration, the feeling intensified by him striking me. Shockwaves roll over me, exploding in every limb.

"I want something from you."

"A-Anything," I whimper.

Lennox pushes back into my slit, nudging the hidden spot inside me that makes stars burst behind my eyes. A strangled sound erupts from me. I can hear how soaking wet I am from so many denials.

"I told you how I feel, Rip." His voice is rough, like he's trying desperately not to finish. "Now I want to hear it from you."

Another hard slap causes his grip on my hair to tense. The white-hot pain blurs with everything going haywire inside me. It sends my system into a cataclysmic meltdown.

"Hear what?" I bleat uselessly.

Lennox swaps to a slow roll, his hips jerking. "I heard what you said to Raine. You love him. I won't begrudge you that, Rip."

He delivers another loud smack, causing me to cry out his name.

"But I'm a selfish bastard. I need proof that you've forgiven me."

His tempo increases again, slapping our bodies together. I'm going to slide off the bed in a boneless puddle if he doesn't stop this game.

"I want to hear that you love me."

The son of a bitch.

He's trying to tear the truth out of me. Fuck me until I have no fight left to give and steal my affections before I can change my mind. But worst of all?

I want to give it to him. He wants proof. Fine. I'll hand over the signed confession he needs to finally move on. We've come too far to stop before the final hurdle.

"Lennox." The six letters strain my vocal cords. "You're a sadistic motherfucker."

Spank.

"Argh! Fuck! But I do... I do love you. God, I fucking love you."

Spank.

"Again!" he commands.

"You insane asshole! I am in love with you!"

Spank.

The sheer intensity has tears saturating my cheeks. I can no longer tell exquisite pain from pleasure anymore. I've melted into him, too weak to withstand his onslaught.

Spank.

"Now," Lennox orders. "Come all over my cock, baby."

It's all the permission my mind needs. It splinters apart, the individual lobes rupturing behind my skull. The howl pouring from me doesn't sound like my own. I've become something unrecognisable.

My climax is so intense, I faintly wonder if I'm going to black out. It feels like too much to hold inside. Every part of me is quivering, exhausted by his relentless teasing.

The hot burst of his release surging inside me makes my own deep pangs roll on and on. Lennox roars through his climax, hands clamping on my hips so he can pour every last drop into me.

"Take it all." He thrusts furiously. "Milk me dry, baby."

"God! Yes!"

I shout out through each iteration of blissful agony. I've fallen flat onto the soaked sheets, unable to hold myself up any longer. Lennox pulls out and slumps, lifting me so I can rest on his chest.

Beneath my head, his heart rate is a racing symphony. Warmth slicks between us as our essences mingle. I feel utterly spent, every part of me wrung-out.

"Fuck," he gasps.

My eyes are sealed shut. "That was… intense."

A hand drags up and down my sweaty spine, rough fingertips pausing on the healing punctures left by the taser.

As we both struggle to catch our breath, I hear the faint words he forces out. It takes all my strength to raise my head to look up at him.

"What?"

Blazing lake water eyes flick over me. "Nothing."

"I heard you, Nox. Just say it again."

His mouth crooks in a tired smile.

"I love you."

Lowering my mouth to his, I press our lips together. Lennox kisses me passionately, his tongue gliding over my lips to seek entrance before filling my mouth.

He's everywhere. Tongue brushing mine. Hands wrapped around my hips. Chests glued together. For a man who once couldn't stand the sight of me, he's now practically living in my skin.

"I love you," I reply simply.

"You meant it?" His smile is wide. "Not just a mid-sex confession?"

"I mean, you did torture it out of me. But that doesn't mean it isn't true."

Resting our foreheads together, I feel the final pathetic wall stacked around my heart crumble to ruin. The inevitable destruction feels like fucking nirvana.

I've opened my heart to them all. Accepted the possibility of grief for the chance at something more. A future without emptiness and heartache. Perhaps a happy ending.

I'll do anything to get that.

Even if I don't deserve it.

CHAPTER 21
LENNOX
SPIT IN MY FACE! – THXSOMCH

EARLY SUMMER in London used to be my favourite time to visit the city. I grew up east of the capital in a working-class town but visited on occasion. Once for my grandfather to collect his military pension.

Now the glass skyscrapers, towering office blocks and crammed tourist buses glisten in the warm sunshine. Through the window of the tinted SUV, I watch the morning chaos go by undisturbed.

It's funny how even when your own life is hanging by a thread, the world still turns. Oblivious and undisturbed. People stroll past stacks of newspapers, emblazoned with headlines that lose impact after a while.

"Headquarters is up ahead." Warner indicates to move into a different lane. "The SCU have already arrived—they're interviewing other witnesses today too."

"They took long enough to decide what to do with us," I grumble.

In the passenger seat, Xander nods in agreement. It's been a tiresome week, hiding in Sabre's safe house, uncertain of our own fates while the SCU deliberates over our fates.

After our interviews, Enzo and his team agreed to negotiate any charges. We're not so worried about Raine. He was little more than a bystander. But for myself, Xander and Ripley, all bets are off.

Each of us have aided and abetted Incendia's criminal activities over the years. Then there's the grisly murder that Xander owned up to, though he claimed self-defence. Not to mention the altercation in the maize field. We've racked up a list of possible charges.

"Yours are the first to be agreed on." Warner huffs. "The Blackwood inmates are still being questioned. So be glad it didn't take months."

"Why is it taking so long for the others?" Ripley frowns.

"Their situation is a little more complicated."

The curved point of Ripley's jawline clenches tight. I know that in her mind, we deserve whatever lies ahead. She's feeling the guilt of all we've done to make it this far. I see things differently.

For every bad deed we've done, we prevented the suffering of our loved ones. Sometimes ourselves. Evil is justified if it's to stave off something worse for those you want to protect, right?

While I don't relish what we did to Holly, I also don't feel guilty. She was a stooge too. Culpable and heartless in the name of her own survival. But I do regret what it did to the woman who's fast become ours.

"What about Bancroft?" Raine speaks up from between us. "We can't hide in a safe house forever."

His lips sealed, Warner remains silent.

News reports appear daily about Incendia's worsening legal troubles. Aside from that, we've been kept in the dark. The evidence appears stacked against them and calls for the remaining institutes to close are growing.

Ripley rests her head on Raine's shoulder. "We swapped one prison for another."

"You're safe, fed and have around-the-clock security." Warner stares at her in the rearview mirror. "That's a damn sight more than those trapped in other institutes or transferred from Harrowdean."

"Hey," I snap at him. "She's allowed to feel frustrated."

"We're doing the best we can. This is a complex investigation."

"You need to do better."

The dick doesn't deign to respond.

Merging through the dense traffic, we're deep in the business district, surrounded by cloud-kissing buildings on all sides. Bystanders wear pressed business suits and carry extortionately priced coffees on their morning commutes.

It's places like this that gave birth to Incendia Corporation. All the country's wealth and power concentrated into a handful of streets and buildings. Millions of lives dictated by the select few privileged enough to rise to the top.

"Jonathan's firm is half a mile from here, in Canary Wharf," Ripley observes.

"My team is monitoring your uncle personally," Warner attempts to reassure her. "If he steps even a toe out of line, we'll know about it."

"Comforting," Xander chuffs. "Because none of these people have done anything criminal under scrutiny before, right? They'll stay on the straight and narrow now."

His sarcasm aside, Xander makes a good point. Surveillance isn't enough. We've warned them about Jonathan Bennet and his connections to the conspiracy they're attempting to unravel.

"Look." Warner sighs audibly. "We're up against decades' of corruption here. This conspiracy goes right to the top of the government. You need to be more patient."

The monstrously huge building he drives up to silences our conversation. I'm gawping at the sky-high slab of polished steel and impenetrable tinted glass as the SUV slows to pull in.

Countless burly security officers surround the building, all wearing dark sunglasses and visible earpieces to match their stern expressions. Warner waves to one as he stops for a retinal scan before entering the underground parking garage.

We all pile out together on high alert. Raine unfolds his new white guide stick then takes Ripley's arm with his spare hand. Resting a hand on her lower back, I follow Xander and Warner over to the elevators.

The ride up to discover our fate is fraught with nail-biting silence. We're all balancing on a razor's edge, instinctively closing ranks in the small space. Ripley and Raine end up sandwiched between us.

I have no idea how many witnesses are cooperating with their investigation but given that we haven't been hauled in front of the authorities until now, Sabre must be combing through countless interviews and testimonies.

"What if they want to prosecute?" Raine whispers.

Considering his question, I study the back of Warner's head. It'd be easy enough to knock him out. I doubt we could take his whole team or their reinforcements, though I'd give it a damn good shot.

"We handle it." Xander's voice is impassive, betraying nothing. "Like we always have."

Translation—he goes full feral and butchers anyone standing in our way. Xander's ability to switch his humanity off would terrify anyone else. For us, it's like having our own personal army.

"Great plan." Ripley scrubs her face.

"I'm aware."

"Sarcasm, Xan. You need to rein in the stabby attitude."

I snort at her words. "Like that's gonna happen."

The floor we arrive at is brightly lit with plush carpets and numerous rooms off the long corridor, hidden by frosted glass. Warner gestures for us to follow him, tucking the special black pass he scanned in his pocket.

We're taken to an empty conference room fitted with a long, wooden table and several chairs. Ripley steers Raine to the nearest seat, glancing up to ensure we're following. I brush her shoulder as I pass.

"Wait here." Warner ducks from the room.

Arms folded, I lean against the wall, unwilling to relax. Xander moves to stand beside the window, studying the impressive skyline beyond. We're high up, enough to see the wispy clouds.

"What's the play here?" I question. "I'm not seeing anyone get taken to prison."

"That won't happen." Ripley somehow sounds certain.

"You trust these people that much?"

"I trust that they know an opportunity when they see one. We have inside information. The only way to get us to cooperate is to guarantee our freedom."

"Think they'll go for that?" Raine wonders.

Ripley huffs out a tense breath. "They have to."

Remaining silent, Xander stares into the distance. He's been characteristically quiet. That never leads to anything good. It's the kind of silence that precedes a violent explosion.

We're not held in suspense for long. The door reopens, allowing two suits flanked by Warner and Enzo into the room. I recognise the final person from the newspapers—Hunter Rodriguez. Director of Sabre Security.

He scans two dark-chocolate eyes over our group, his steely frown pulling a scar bisecting his eyebrow taut. Tall and well-muscled, he wears an expensive, three-piece suit and a flashy watch that befit his position.

"Let's begin." Hunter's tone is smooth and impersonal. "Please take a seat."

The two suits, one male and one female, sit at the other end of the table. Hunter moves to take a seat opposite Ripley and Raine, sparing them both curt nods while Enzo leans against the wall beside me.

"This is Agent Barlow." Hunter gestures to the female suit. "And Agent Jonas. Our representatives from the Serious Crimes Unit."

None of us offer a greeting.

"Well, then." Agent Barlow clears her throat. "Let's not beat around the bush."

"Our clients have provided written testimony to my team," Hunter explains crisply. "They have invaluable information that will aid your investigation. And they're willing to cooperate."

Agent Jonas laughs coldly. "Undoubtedly to save their own skins. This is quite the rap sheet of crimes you've compiled for us."

"Our clients are under no illusions about their culpability. Regardless, they're willing to act as cooperating witnesses. Their knowledge could shave years off the criminal investigation ahead of the SCU."

Drumming her nails against her chin, Agent Barlow stares straight at Ripley. I hate the way she's making her squirm under the spotlight. I move to step forward, but Enzo rests a hand on my shoulder, giving a head shake.

"Ripley Bennet."

She looks up at the female agent. "Yes?"

"You stand accused of severe crimes. It won't be hard to trace back the history of patients' deaths in Harrowdean's custody resulting from your dealings."

"Ripley was just doing her job," Raine protests hotly.

"Hurting people?" Agent Jonas counters.

"The real monsters are those manipulating desperate patients into doing their dirty work! Those profiting on exploitation and abuse!"

"Raine." Ripley touches his shoulder.

"No. You can't be blamed for this!"

"It's okay."

"Nothing about this is okay."

"I know what I did was wrong, and I'm prepared to accept the consequences. But there are people out there still trapped and suffering. They need our help."

The two agents listen to their exchange, both seeming to contemplate the best path forward.

"You're barely keeping the media on our side right now." Xander turns from the window to address the agents. "Government incompetence has allowed an exploitative regime to torture and experiment on the mentally unwell for profit."

A smile tugs at my mouth.

Here he is.

"We have plenty of uncomfortable details that we'll happily take to the press. Gory, unpalatable information that will impede your efforts to tame this raging fire. You don't want us as enemies."

"You're threatening to go public?" Agent Jonas laughs. "Why would that impact us, son? We're not Incendia."

"Perhaps not, but I'm sure the names of government inspectors who were paid a tidy profit share to ignore our dealings would cast an unpleasant light on a public-funded department such as yours."

The agent's smile quickly morphs into a glower.

"In fact, I saw a rather fetching photo of Sir Bancroft accepting his knighthood after a quick online search not so long ago. Plenty of politicians and public figures in attendance."

Xander's musings are silky-smooth. Even my hairs are standing on end. The entire room is focused on him.

"Perhaps we could talk about the man who watched us being whipped, beaten and psychologically tortured then ordered us to become his stooges when we refused to break. A man you've failed to catch."

"Making the media storm worse doesn't benefit you either." Agent Jonas draws his silver-grey brows together. "You'll be dragged over the coals."

"Less than you will be for allowing this to go unchecked. Bancroft's out there right now, getting his feet rubbed by countless political heavyweights and business leaders. That's on you."

"What do you want?" Agent Barlow intervenes.

Xander shrugs. "We're not asking for clemency, we're demanding it. Agree to a plea deal, and we'll cooperate. Prosecute and we'll cause the biggest public outcry you've ever seen. Enough to make your jobs hellish."

Leaning back in his chair, Hunter looks mildly impressed. He scrapes a hand over his trimmed, chestnut beard, seemingly appraising us in a new light. I doubt any other witnesses have been so bold as to make threats.

"We can tell you everything." Xander lands the final blow. "Supply routes. Contraband stashes. Key players in the institute's power structure. Criminals you'll never prosecute without our testimony."

"With all due respect—"

"Prosecute and you'll never hear a word from us again," Xander cuts the male agent off. "Not so much as an ID verification when you round up a few culprits after decades of investigative work."

Their stunned silence causes Enzo to chuckle under his breath. "He drives a hard bargain, doesn't he?"

"This bullshit calls for it," I whisper back.

"Not disagreeing with you, Mr Nash. I don't believe anyone should be blamed for the fucked up stuff that went down in the institutes."

"We'll need a moment to discuss and call our superiors." Agent Barlow rises. "Excuse us."

The pair shuffle out, their heads hanging. I can't believe our futures are being decided by a pair of government stuffed suits. Ones who didn't see rampant corruption staring them in the face all this time.

As soon as they've left, Hunter turns his attention to us. "Bold move, Mr Beck."

Xander glares back, unrepentant. "If you had bothered to interview us yourself, you would know that we'll do anything to protect each other. No one is going to prison."

I bite back a laugh. The look on the famous Hunter's face is like he's bitten into a sour apple and spat the innards out. The man clearly isn't used to his authority being challenged.

Stepping into the room, Theo's familiar face causes everyone to release their held breath. He offers a two-fingered wave with his laptop in hand, the door clicking shut behind him.

"All wrapped up with Hudson?" Enzo asks.

Theo nods. "His final interview is done."

"Tell Brooklyn and the others I'll be out soon," Hunter tells him.

Anger curdles in my gut. We've spent all week locked behind bolted doors, fearful for our lives. Not so much as a goddamn whisper about when this nightmare will end. I've had it.

"I suppose some witnesses are more valuable than others, right?" I look between Theo and Hunter. "While we're being left to fend off fucking prosecutions for surviving something unimaginable."

"Nox—" Raine begins.

"No! Enough of this! Why are we being treated differently?"

"You're not," Hunter replies flatly. "But your cases are vastly different."

Ignoring his shitty excuse, I stare at Xander. "I told you we shouldn't trust these people."

Enzo attempts to grab my shoulder. "Look here—"

"Lay a single hand on me, and it won't be attached for much longer. I'm getting my family out of here before you pull out the cuffs."

Marching over to Raine and Ripley, I'm hellbent on yanking them both up when the conference room door opens again. Agents Barlow and Jonas sidle back in with matching grim expressions.

Nope. Fuck this.

If we can get out of here, they'll never see us again. We never should've come here. They're going to take my fucking family from me, just like all the other times I've lost the ones I love. This is all my fau—

"You have a deal."

The panic dies a sudden death within me.

"For all of us?" Xander asks.

Sighing, Agent Jonas wrings his hands. "Full clemency for Ripley Bennet, Xander Beck, Lennox Nash and Raine Starling. No charges relating to the contraband, deaths or riot."

My breath is still held, waiting for the punchline.

"In exchange, you'll give us absolutely everything you know about Incendia Corporation's dealings. Names. Dates. Locations. The lot. You'll remain as cooperating witnesses until we deem your roles fulfilled."

"And if the investigation takes years?" Xander pushes.

His shoulders rise dismissively. "Then you'll certainly earn your freedom, won't you? When this is over, you can have it."

Lips parted, Xander looks at each of us. Weighing our reactions. We're talking about signing our souls over to the authorities for an undefined period of time. Snitching on every last person doing dirty dealings in Priory Lane and Harrowdean.

But we'll be free.

We could have a future.

Her fingers clenched tight around Raine's hand, Ripley does her own sweep over us all before facing the two agents. Hunter, Enzo and Theo all keep quiet. None dare to speak for us.

"We want witness protection until this is over," she calmly demands.

"Our lives are already at risk. This will paint an even bigger target on our backs."

Agent Barlow looks over to Hunter, communicating something silently. I watch the formidable director nod once, signalling his agreement. Neither Enzo nor Theo protests the decision.

"Do we have a deal?" Agent Jonas drones.

This is my chance to protest, but I don't say anything. No matter the mistrust and paranoia brewing inside me. I trust Ripley, and if this is her decision, then I'll respect that choice.

She rolls her shoulders, looking at the agents without fear.

"Yes. It's a deal."

CHAPTER 22
RIPLEY

AGAIN – NOAH CYRUS (FEAT. XXXTENTACION)

WATCHING the breaking news slogans filter past on the TV screen, I'm only half-heartedly paying attention. Balled-up, failed sketches are scattered all around me. I can't focus long enough to create anything decent despite my return to a medicated equilibrium.

We had the chance to request items via Warner and his colleagues. I've since learned they're one of several investigative teams within Sabre Security. He's part of the Anaconda team, who've now been assigned to us.

The charcoal pencil clenched in my hand leaves a black smear, staining my fingertips. I shouldn't be watching the news. If Xander were here and not having his brain picked at HQ, he'd unplug it at the wall.

"Incendia Corporation's president, Sir Joseph Bancroft, had this to say to our reporters this morning."

The exaggerated voice of the newscaster catches my attention. I can hardly stomach seeing Bancroft's wizened, wrinkle-linked face and sagging jowls take up the screen.

He wears a fine, navy-blue suit, the deep silk accents showing off his diamond tiepin. Behind him lies a disgusting display of wealth. His vast, old money estate is hidden deep in the Cheshire countryside.

"Blackwood Institute will be open again soon after significant refurbishments to repair the damage. We hope to return to normal operations at Priory Lane and Harrowdean Manor in the near future too."

Pain lances my hand. Startled, I look down and find the charcoal pencil snapped, the sharpened tip digging into my palm. Unclenching my fist, I flick my eyes back up to the TV.

The obnoxious flash of reporters snapping photos fills the screen as Bancroft climbs into the back of a fancy town car. Their yells are unanswered. He doesn't address the accusations thrown at him and the chauffeur service drives him away.

I attended a lavish fundraiser at his country estate once, forced into a hideous velvet gown by my uncle's stylist. The thirty-bedroom monstrosity was bustling with famous faces and well-lined pockets that night.

It turned my stomach even then.

Now it's fucking intolerable.

A click draws my head up as the news report switches off. Standing behind the sofa I'm curled up on, Lennox peers at me in an assessing way. He places the remote control down.

There's something different about him today. He looks heavier somehow, a sad kind of darkness making his pale irises appear dull in a sharp contrast to the shiny, vibrant pink scar on his face.

"Are you okay?"

Rolling his lips, he glances over me. "Would you come somewhere with me?"

"Like… go out?"

Lennox nods.

"Is that allowed?"

"I've cleared it with the team. Warner's guy, Ethan, will drive."

Unlike Xander, Lennox doesn't lock his emotions away when he doesn't want anyone to see them. He's always been an easy read, it's just the only story his face ever told before was one of gut-punching anger.

Now there's a tale of grief written across his slumped facial features and bag-lined eyes. Even his clothing is gloomy today, an all-black shirt and fitted sweatpants combination that makes his golden skin stand out.

He has washed and styled his hair, though, like he wants to make some effort. The messy brown locks are pushed behind his ears in a semi-tidy pile, revealing the silver ring in his left ear.

"What's going on?"

"It's… my sister's birthday today." He slowly trails a finger along the back of the sofa. "I've never been able to visit her on her birthday. Figured I may go."

"I'm so sorry. I had no idea."

Canine sinking into his pillowy lip, Lennox looks away. "I just don't feel like going alone."

Setting my sketchpad and charcoals aside, I sit up on the sofa so I can lean over and reach him. Lennox keeps his gaze averted as I wind my arms around his neck to tug him closer.

"You don't need to be scared to ask, Nox. If you want me there with you, I'll be there. No questions asked."

Daring to make eye contact, he appears relieved, the tense lines around his mouth evening out. I stroke a hand over his trimmed stubble, trying to wipe away any doubts.

"Where is she?"

"About an hour or so from here." He pulls my hand into his. "You sure? We've all had a lot on our minds since that meeting."

"Yes, I'm sure. Let's go."

He pulls me up, leaving the failed sketches behind. We call out to Raine, washing the city off himself in the shower. He was escorted out to see Sabre's medic for a check-up and meds refill earlier on.

"Be careful!" he yells back.

Escaping the apartment together, one of Sabre's blacked-out SUVs is parked on the curb outside. Ethan leans against it, studying the quiet neighbourhood.

The safe house is surrounded by copy and paste apartment blocks with little character. We're far enough from Central London to grant us some privacy from the usual hustle and bustle.

"Hey." Ethan offers us both a professional smile. "Ready?"

Lennox opens the back door for me. "Yeah. Did Warner give you the location?"

"He did. I've got a couple extra security officers following in a second vehicle to be safe, but they'll keep their distance. The rest will remain here with Raine."

Nodding to him, I climb into the SUV. Lennox joins me in the back and clips my belt in place for me without thinking. The small gesture makes my cheeks warm.

"Where did you grow up?" I pull his hand into my lap.

Lennox settles into his seat. "Near Colchester."

"I don't know much about your childhood."

"There isn't much to tell. We were raised by my grandfather. You know he was a retired army vet. Mum died shortly after Daisy was born from birth complications. Neither of us had dads we knew about."

The silver chain peeking out of his t-shirt collar is even more visible against the black fabric. I've never seen him without it. Even when we were running for our lives without a single belonging, he kept it safe.

"You've never been to see her? Daisy?"

"I was arrested not long after her burial. You know why. I haven't seen her grave since."

It's no secret that Lennox was facing a hefty sentence for first-degree murder before he took the plea deal to attend Priory Lane. He burned down his childhood home with his abusive grandfather still inside.

I can't imagine the pain of burying a sibling, let alone in those circumstances. It was hard enough saying goodbye to my parents. Throwing dirt on your baby sister's coffin must be a whole new level of agony.

Holding his hand tight, the journey passes fast once we escape London to find the main road heading east. The cramped apartment blocks shift into vast green fields with clustered neighbourhoods.

Lennox doesn't speak again until we turn into a small town just outside Colchester, but I can feel his legs quaking underneath our linked hands.

We wind through twisting streets sandwiched with in-bloom summer florals to reach the graveyard. It's tucked away in a quiet spot, the church car park empty when we pull in with another SUV loosely following us.

"We'll remain here in the car park, but don't wander too far," Ethan announces, turning his head to us. "We're not taking any chances."

I offer him a tight smile. "Thanks, Ethan."

"Of course. Take your time."

Dragging Lennox's silent self from the car, we face the graveyard together. His feet seem rooted in the gravel when I try to encourage him to start walking. He's eyeing the scene with a look of mild panic.

"I left her alone for all this time," he croaks.

"That wasn't your choice."

"None of this was, Rip. Doesn't change the fact that I haven't been there for her."

Linking his arm with mine, I squeeze tightly. "You're here now. And you aren't alone."

Taking a deep breath, he nods and begins to walk into the graveyard.

Sunshine beats down on us, bouncing off polished marble headstones adorned with dried and fresh flowers.

We walk all the way to the back where the newer graves are located. Lennox's tentative steps slow beneath a tall apple tree, laden with unripe fruit. He stops in front of a moss-speckled stone, third from the left.

My eyes water as I read the inscription.

Daisy Nash.
Our beautiful angel.

The dirt streaks on her headstone and lack of flowers break my heart. There's been no one to visit Daisy for a long time, not while Lennox has been serving his sentence. Her grave is unadorned.

I release Lennox's arm. "Wait here."

At the base of the apple tree, a cluster of wildflowers have sprouted. They aren't much, but I gather up the colourful pops of indigo blue, yellow and vibrant purple.

He raises an eyebrow when I walk back over. "Here."

"What are they for?"

"You can lay them on her grave."

Taking the picked flowers from me, Lennox studies the makeshift bunch for a moment. He then splits them into two halves and passes one back to me.

"Do it with me?"

I take the flowers, my chest twinging. "Of course."

Together we lay the tiny bunches in front of Daisy's gravestone. The natural sprigs immediately brighten up the sad scene. Lennox remains kneeling while I shuffle back to give him space.

"Sorry I haven't come by for a while, Dais. I... uh, made some choices. Got myself in a bit of trouble. I'm okay, though. Don't worry about me."

He runs his hand over the inscription, tracing her name.

"Happy birthday, squirt. I miss you every day. I'd give anything to feel you yanking my sleeve and begging to go for ice cream one last time. I never should've taken those moments for granted."

Lennox's head lowers, shielding his face. I can hear his quickening breathing, matching each time his shoulders shake. The remains of my heart splinter at the sight of him crying for his baby sister.

I've come to realise it's a misconception that bad people don't feel pain or regret. Oftentimes, those who've been forced to make the most awful decisions do so from a place of immense pain.

Lennox is no different.

All his choices, even the most morally questionable ones, have come from such deep-rooted trauma, it's a wonder he's alive at all. His fierce protective instincts have led him to many dark places.

"I don't blame you for what you did, but I wish you'd talked to me." His sonorous voice breaks. "I'd have gotten you out, Dais. I would've protected you from him."

Kneeling beside him, I wrap an arm around Lennox's broad back. His head presses against my shoulder, the sound of his quiet sobbing filling the warm breeze. There's nothing I can do but hold him.

"I failed her," Lennox whispers brokenly.

"No. This cruel world failed Daisy. Not you."

"She needed someone to save her, Rip. I didn't do it."

The silence stretches on. Helpless tears prickle my eyes.

"I fucking failed her," he rasps. "I'll never forgive myself for that. What good was my revenge when she's still lying dead beneath the ground?"

Licking my lips, I decide to speak my mind. "I know I'm not supposed to say this… but you did right by her, Nox. You got rid of the monster who hurt her so badly. And that man can't hurt anyone else now."

"It was too late for her."

"Yes, it was," I agree sadly. "But it isn't too late for you to start living your life for her. She wouldn't want you to carry around all this guilt forever. You have to live in her name now."

He vibrates with barely silenced sobs. "How?"

"However you want—that's the point. She'd want you to be happy, living a life you've chosen for yourself. Not one full of regret for something you didn't choose and can't ever change."

Holding him tight, I let him cry it all out. The grief. The guilt. Every toxic emotion and traumatic memory that's carved Lennox from immovable steel into the complex man he is today. A man borne from pain but holding so much capacity for unconditional love.

My muscles are protesting from sitting frozen for so long by the time Lennox lifts his head. I trace my thumb across his cheek, smoothing the faint, silvery trails that have soaked into his stubble.

"Better?"

He puffs out a long sigh. "Yeah. Thanks."

"It's okay to rely on others too, you know. I get that you want to protect us all, but we care about you. And you can lean on us when the burden gets too heavy as well."

With a faint smile, he presses a kiss against my hair. "I'll bear that in mind."

"Please do. I'm a mess half the time anyway. I'll happily share that title with you."

"How generous."

Rising, I offer him a hand up. "That's me. Such a giver."

Lennox clambers to his feet, clutching my hand in his huge paw. We both look back down at Daisy's grave. He curses, leaning down to clean the stone with the hem of his shirt and remove the moss speckles.

"I should book one of those grave cleaners." Lennox brushes off his tee. "You know, when we have actual lives and freedom again. She deserves for it to be sparkling clean."

"We'll make it happen."

"Ripley!" someone bellows. "Lennox!"

Both startled, we turn simultaneously to look back at the car park. Another tinted SUV has pulled in, the interior shaded from sight. No one drives vehicles like that around here without having a good reason.

Terror blooms inside me, quickly growing into a spiky ball that fills my stomach. Ethan's backup is another man I don't recognise, and Tara, the brown-haired agent we first met.

They've both pulled out their weapons. The guns are aimed at the driver's side, but it's the passenger door that opens to release an occupant.

My breath catches. "Shit."

"Is that…?"

"Yes."

Brushing off his smart trousers and designer polo shirt, my uncle casts a withering glare at the agents training their guns on him. It's rare he's seen out of a full suit. Apparently, he views this as a social call.

I watch the agents reluctantly lower their weapons, though they are kept drawn. Right now, Sabre has no jurisdiction to threaten my uncle. Harming him would cause a huge scandal.

Lennox keeps me slightly tucked behind him as we walk back to the cars. Their voices grow louder. Three men exit the SUV behind my uncle, all stacked with muscle and wearing fearsome scowls.

"I'd just like to speak to my niece." Jonathan shows his palms placatingly. "There's no need for weapons."

"That isn't going to happen," Ethan retorts.

"Now now. Your hostility isn't required."

"Jonathan," I call out, approaching the tense scene. "What are you doing here?"

"Ah, Ripley." He trains a picture-perfect smile on me. "I thought it's time we had a chat. You've been laying low for some time now."

"Keeping an eye on me?"

"Much like you've been monitoring me, I assume. Your new friends didn't spot us coming today?"

Ethan's eyes connect with mine, full of apologies. I shake my head at him. They can't be expected to follow his every move, twenty-four hours a day. Not when his team is spread thin like it is today.

"Can we talk?" Jonathan's request draws my eyes back to him.

"You had the chance to talk before you ended that phone call. Now I have nothing to say to you."

He audibly sighs. "Always such a difficult child. Come on, Ripley. Spare me a few minutes."

"Like you spared my friend's life when your men killed her in cold blood?"

"That was not their instructions," he explains like it's obvious. "These mercenary types... They do get carried away, I'm afraid. The girl's death was unfortunate."

"Unfortunate?" I glare at him.

"We've all made some regretful decisions of late. I'm here to simplify matters."

Lennox cinches his arm around me. "She isn't going anywhere with you."

"Ah, Mr Nash." Jonathan turns his attention to him. "You know, my niece can do a lot better than a filthy criminal such as yourself. Do release her before I'm forced to take action."

Laughing hard, Lennox doesn't budge. "You're funny. I see Ripley didn't inherit anything from you. Thank fuck for that."

His eyes hardening into cold diamonds, Jonathan takes a step forward. The lowered weapons all around him suddenly raise, again pointed at him. In turn, each of his men pull their own guns, aiming them at Ethan's team.

Great.

We're all going to die.

"See, this is the fuss I hoped to avoid." Jonathan huffs with a head shake. "Ripley, walk with me. No one needs to get hurt."

Releasing Lennox, I try to inch away from him only to be held back by his thick arm. He stares at me with fierce disapproval, his glower firmly fixed in place. Damn. I haven't been on the receiving end of that for a while.

"Not a chance," he growls through his teeth.

"Would you prefer for us all to get shot in some bullshit Wild West standoff? Come on, Nox."

"He's playing us!"

"And killing me in broad daylight would be just as bad for his public image as Sabre shooting him would be. We're out in the open. I'll be fine."

Cursing colourfully, Lennox eventually surrenders me. I pat his arm before gesturing for my uncle to follow. He orders his men to remain behind and follows me into the churchyard, away from Daisy's grave.

Once we're far enough from prying ears, he slows his steps.

"You're looking well, Ripley."

"Cut the shit. What do you want?"

"Am I not allowed to check in with my beloved niece?"

"I didn't feel very *beloved* while running from assassins in the dead of night. We almost died."

"Unfortunately, desperate times sometimes call for a blunt instrument. I can assure you, it was merely a business decision to round you up and prevent any further damage to our operations."

Laughter spills out of me. "In that case, I do apologise for foiling your plan. I'm sure it would've been more convenient for us to die in a maize field."

We circle several crumbling statues of well-known saints, coming to rest at a wooden bench. Jonathan gestures for me to take a seat. Eyeing him, I reluctantly sit down.

"I'm seeking a quiet resolution to all this bother, Ripley. It's bad for business."

"I have no idea what you're talking about."

He sits down next to me. "I'm sure the plea deal you signed with the authorities to act as their informant has already slipped your mind."

How the fuck does he know about that?

Jonathan waves dismissively. "Before you ask, I'm not inclined to reveal my sources. You've squandered the trust I once had in you. Now you've become a problem."

In the distance, I can see Lennox keeping a wary eye on us, pacing with his arms folded in front of him. He looks ready to bolt over here and pummel Jonathan into the ground if he dares to try anything.

"I want you to come home, Ripley."

I jolt in shock, staring at my uncle. "Excuse me?"

"You've proven your point. Good show, very dramatic. But we both know you're knee-deep in this. Your new friends cannot be trusted. I'm offering you a lifeline."

I thought he was just a stone-cold, power-hungry asshole, but I'm starting to wonder if my uncle is certifiably insane.

"We can weather this storm together," he continues, laying on the faux concern. "I'd hate to see you blamed for all that has transpired. Let me help you."

"Help me?" I scoff. "You can't even help yourself! You're backed into a corner along with your dickhead boss, Bancroft, and all his associates. Silencing me won't save any of you."

"I raised you to make smart decisions," he tries again. "I'm offering you a chance to avoid any further bloodshed. Take it."

Unable to stand our close proximity for a moment longer, I quickly stand, turning to shoot daggers at him. Jonathan remains seated, a leg casually crossed over and his hands clasped.

"You didn't raise me, Jonathan. An endless parade of hired help did. I've been alone ever since Mum died."

"Always so ungrateful. I took you in!"

"And treated me with disgust and contempt for my entire life!" I don't bother trying to remain calm any longer. "You hated me before I was diagnosed and couldn't stand the sight of me after."

Creases form on his forehead as he pinches the bridge of his nose. "You had a chance to rule in Harrowdean, dear niece. Who gave that to you?"

"I sold my soul to survive an evil regime you helped fund."

"And were you not safe? Protected? Able to live a privileged life behind bars?"

"You're fucking insane! Nothing about that was privileged!"

He tuts condescendingly. "You're still a child. Spoiled and selfish. I've given you everything, and this is how you repay me?"

"No, this isn't." I take a breath, unclench my fists then stare into his clear gaze. "I'll repay you by tearing down Incendia Corporation and ensuring the trail of money leads straight back to you. Then we'll be even."

"Careful," he warns.

"Or what?"

"Or your position as my niece won't keep you safe from what's to come, Ripley. I've been gracious thus far."

In my periphery, I can see Lennox jogging over to us. He's run out of patience. I'm glad—this was a huge mistake. Every second spent entertaining Jonathan's psychosis is just wasted breath.

"I don't care how long it takes for the investigation to tear your empire down," I lash out. "I'll give them every single detail to ensure you rot behind bars for the rest of your life."

Instead of fear, Jonathan merely smiles. Cold and unaffected.

"Very well. You've made your choice."

"I have." I inch away from him. "We won't speak again."

His fake smile remains fixed in place. "If that is your wish."

When Lennox skids to a halt, eyes scouring over me in search of any signs of harm, he's red in the face. Jonathan rises to his feet, but his attention is now fixed on Lennox.

"You've tied yourself to a sinking ship, Mr Nash. I'd advise you to get far away from my niece before she takes you down with her."

Lip curling, Lennox casts him a look that would terrify even the most steadfast of men. I know something has well and truly broken in Jonathan's brain when it only makes his sick smile widen farther.

"I count my blessings that your niece even gives me the time of day," Lennox replies unequivocally. "Threaten her and you'll have a hell of a fight on your hands."

Jonathan snickers. "Why should I be afraid of a scumbag convict like you?"

Approaching him, Lennox's shoulders pull back, his head held high. Not a single flinch or hint of embarrassment for his past.

"Because I've proven the lengths I'll go to for my family. That includes Ripley now. Consider the kind of people you're threatening before running your mouth."

I relish the look of surprise on Jonathan's face when Lennox snaps his curled-up fist out. The punch hits him square in the nose, a powerful blow that elicits a loud crack. Jonathan shrieks in pain.

Lennox shakes his fist out, knuckles now covered in fresh blood. My uncle is doubled over, cupping his bleeding nose.

"Us *convicts* aren't afraid to play dirty to win the game," Lennox hisses. "Enjoy explaining that at your next board meeting."

Still dripping in my uncle's blood, he seizes my hand. I let him tow me away, wrapped up in his campfire-scented warmth. This time, I'm walking away from Uncle Jonathan. Leaving him afraid and alone.

And I'll never look back.

I don't need him anymore.

CHAPTER 23
RIPLEY

VIDEO GAMES – GOOD
NEIGHBOURS

SUMMER RAIN PATTERS against the bedroom window, blocking out all light. The storm rolled in overnight, ending the brief hot spell that's encapsulated England's capital city. London sucks in the heat.

I'm grateful for the reprieve while tucked up in bed, limbs laden and immovable. Despite being stabilised on medication prescribed by the doctors who attended to us, it doesn't stop the inevitable cycles from continuing.

Soaring highs and crushing lows. At least in this state, I'm not rambling about turning invisible. I've had stranger delusions during manic episodes, but even for me, that was a weird one. It could've ended far worse.

"Rip?" Raine pokes his head inside the room.

I peek out of my blanket pile. "Yeah?"

"You're awake. Reckon you can try getting up for me?"

Burrowing deeper into the snarled-up covers, I ignore his pleading. "I'm fine, Raine."

"We all want to help, guava girl. I hate seeing you like this."

"It'll pass. Just leave me alone."

I hate crushing his hopefulness, but when the depressive episodes that keep me immobilised hit, it's easier to wait them out. Their lingering around and attempts to force food down me are wasted. I want to rot alone.

"Come on, babe." He steps into the shaded room, stick in hand. "Don't you remember the agreement we made before?"

"No."

"I know you do. Don't give me that crap." Raine stops next to the bed. "We agreed you'd give me a signal on the bad days. I need to know what I can do to help."

God, that feels like ages ago. Raine dragged me out of the eternal misery I was drowning in when my uncle left me in the medical wing in Harrowdean. He refused to let me wallow.

"We never did agree on a code word." I sigh tiredly.

"How about papaya?"

"That's ridiculous."

"Ouch! Shot down. You're bad for my ego, Rip. Papaya it is."

The brief smile that touches my lips feels like seeing sunlight after a long, dreary winter. Snagging his shirt sleeve, I stroke my thumb across his forearm, the small touch offering me an anchor point.

"Raine?" I murmur.

"Yeah, babe?"

"Papaya."

Straightening, he pulls his arm away. "I'm on it."

Tapping his way from the room, Raine disappears into the corridor. I can hear voices conversing. The other two left me in peace after we returned from our latest interrogation with the happy twins—what we've started calling Agents Barlow and Jonas.

At this point, we're barely scratched the surface of gory information. They're methodically picking through every last detail, documenting our inside knowledge for the investigation. We're being fucking dissected.

When Raine returns, I can hear footsteps leaving the apartment. We've been granted a little more freedom now, though security still follows us everywhere. He returns to the bed to tug my covers off.

"Arms around my neck, babe."

"Where are we going?"

"I'm going to take care of you while Xander and Lennox gather some stuff. Then we'll ride this out together, alright?"

Reassurance trickles through me. "Okay."

I wind my arms around his neck. Raine lifts me from the bed, holding me curled up against his chest. He taps a path to the bathroom, only stubbing his toe once while carrying me.

Thrusting the stick out, he maps each bathroom fixture until he locates the tub. It echoes with a hollow thunk. Raine carefully deposits me on the edge, tossing the stick aside so he can feel for the taps.

"You're going to have to read the bottles for me." He laughs to himself. "Unless you fancy a shampoo bath."

While he adjusts the flowing water, I read the various products lined up on the bath's edge. I wonder which member of the Anaconda team purchased marshmallow-scented bubble bath.

"Who do you think went shopping for us?"

"Why?"

"Just curious. These scents seem very specifically chosen."

Raine runs his hand beneath the stream of water. "That Ethan dude is a total softie. I heard him chatting to some guy called Ryder on the phone the other day. They were flirting like crazy."

"Do you think it was his boyfriend?"

"Early days, I think." Raine shrugs. "Sounded like a long distance love affair."

"That's kinda cute. I pegged him for the bachelor, secret agent type."

Uncapping the bubble bath, I hand it over to Raine and gape when he dumps the whole bottle in. He raises an eyebrow at my chuckle, but I don't dare tell him. Not when he's making an effort to help.

Once the bath is three quarters full and overflowing with bubbles, I reach over to turn off the taps. The last thing we need is to flood the bathroom. He kicks off his jeans and tee then reaches for my shirt.

"Oh," Raine chortles. "Mind if I come in?"

"Looks like you've already made that decision."

"Sorry." He smiles cheekily. "I just assumed."

"It's fine. Some company would be good."

I let him help me out of the baggy t-shirt I've worn for the past few days. I'd feel embarrassed, but I know he isn't judging me. If I could choose otherwise, I wouldn't be this way.

"Hop in, Rip."

"Can you help me?"

"Of course, I can."

Letting him steady my trembling legs, I climb into the steaming bathtub. The sweet smell of marshmallows curls around me in the rising steam, inviting me deeper into the warmth.

I sink down in the middle, leaving space for Raine behind me. He runs his hands along the edge, estimating how high he needs to lift his legs before clambering in. I shift to let him settle at my back.

"This feels like a lot of bubbles."

I hold back a laugh. "You were pretty generous."

"Well, shit."

Slender arms slide around me, pulling me flush against him. Raine places gentle kisses along my shoulders, pushing matted curls aside to reach my neck. I lean into him, taking the comfort he's offering.

"You haven't spoken much since Lennox took you to the graveyard."

"There's nothing to say," I reply quietly.

"You don't need to pretend, Rip. I'm sure the situation with Jonathan is painful. If you want to talk about it, I'm here to listen."

"He's made his choice. That's it."

Raine doesn't respond right away, pouring water over my arms and chest. "Okay."

"Okay?"

"I'm not going to pry. If you've come to terms with it, then I trust you'll reach out if you need to. Just know I'll be here if anything changes and you need to vent."

I relax at his easy acceptance. He knows when to push but also when to back off. That's a skill most people aren't capable of.

"Shift forward and lean your head back." He gently nudges my hips. "I won't shampoo your face this time."

"Promise?"

"Now, I wouldn't go that far."

Smiling, I do as told and give Raine access to my head. He takes the shampoo I place in his hand, wetting my curls with bathwater and lathering them up. His touch is slow, coaxing. I always feel so revered in his arms.

"Can I ask you something else about your trip with Lennox?"

"Like what?" I feel my muscles tense up.

"Xander told me he's stopped wearing that necklace. It's vanished."

"Wait, what?"

"Yeah." Raine begins rinsing my hair with handfuls of water. "He took it off."

In the depths of my latest episode, I hadn't noticed that detail. Lennox has been curling up in bed with me each night, pleading with me to eat small bites of food or watch a movie with him.

It's a gentler approach than Xander's threats to hogtie me in a kitchen chair and shove food down my throat if I don't look after myself. I'm sure that comes from a place of love, just Xander-style love.

"Has Lennox said anything?" I ask him.

"Nah, nothing. He seems different, though. Lighter, I guess. Whatever happened at the graveside has changed something."

Weirdly, it gives me a slither of pride to think that I helped Lennox put some stuff aside. Even if it's the tiniest amount. He's carried this burden alone for so long, I want to help him.

After conditioning my hair, Raine takes his time washing my limbs, even as I protest. He completely ignores me, reaching around me to lather up my arms and legs, ensuring I'm clean.

"Does that feel better?" he asks once done.

"Yes. Thank you."

"I'll soap you up anytime."

We relax in the water for a while, enjoying the comfortable silence. I feel better after getting cleaned up, but his touch is making the real difference. I wouldn't have peeled myself from the bed on my own.

The water is almost cold by the time I feel more like myself. The internal smog is still there, but it's receded enough for me to see the light shining through. Raine has dragged me back to the surface.

"Is that them?" I listen to the apartment door opening.

"Most likely. Shall we climb out?"

"Not yet. I want more time with just us."

Raine presses a kiss to the top of my head. "You can have as much time as you need, guava girl. Forever if you want it. I've got no plans."

My heart rate spikes. "Do you think about forever?"

"Sure. Who doesn't?"

"I guess we haven't had much time to plan the future, between dodging bullets and escaping psych wards. When this is all over... I don't know what I'll do."

He smooths wet hair from my neck. "You know we'd all follow you anywhere."

"I can't expect you guys to do that. You have lives."

"Sure, we do." Raine laughs shallowly. "Mine is laying in my arms right now. And if you think Xander or Lennox are going to let you out of their sights, you're in for a shock."

Relief settles behind my breastbone, silencing the rapid beating that fills my ears. For so long, I was focused on getting out of Harrowdean and returning to my life. That doesn't feel so important now.

My home isn't a stale apartment in Hackney, full of dusty belongings. It isn't the paint or canvases I replaced human connection with. Nor the state of quiet existence I'd made my peace with long ago.

I feel at home curled up in Raine's arms. Breathing in his citrus, sea salt scent. Arguing with Lennox. Drowning in his watered-down green eyes. Touching Xander and dragging a smile from him on the days he closes himself off.

Somewhere along the way, they became my home.

I don't have to be alone anymore.

It doesn't feel terrifying to rely on them. Raine has proven he'll love me through my depressive episodes. Xander's communicating more, opening himself up to me. Lennox has relented, and now I can't seem to get rid of him.

We've gone to hell and back together.

While our current arrangement isn't ideal, and it's exhausting to continually relive our pasts, this will buy us a future. One where we can start living instead of just existing.

"Raine?" I vocalise.

"Hmm?"

"When this is all over, I want forever too." Certainty steels my words. "The four of us. I don't care where, but I want us to be together."

"Took you long enough, babe."

Turning my head, I reach up to press my lips to his. The kiss is sweet and simple. An honest declaration. It causes the numbness that's fallen over me to recede the last few inches.

When that darkness feels overwhelming, I know I won't have to face it on my own. It's easy to forget that until they remind me. My illness still hasn't scared them off.

Raine fervently kisses me back, his lips moving against mine in a tender exploration that still makes butterflies erupt inside me. I'll forever be falling for the tortured musician I found in the dark, stroking his violin strings.

He didn't just heal me.

Raine brought *them* back to me.

He's the glue holding us all together. The positive ray of light in a band of broken individuals. Without his determination to worm his way into my heart, I don't know if we'd all be here today.

I pause for a breath. "Have I mentioned that I love you?"

"Once or twice. I'm always happy to hear it, though."

"Forever, right?"

He kisses between my eyebrows. "Forever."

Resting our foreheads together for a moment, we hold still, embracing each other tightly. The sound of banging in the kitchen indicates the others are up to no good, and we should probably intervene.

"I'm turning into a prune."

"My entire body feels shrivelled up." Raine chuckles. "And I'm cold. Let's move on to phase two."

Climbing out the bath on legs that feel significantly stronger, I pluck a towel off the hook. "What?"

Raine stretches to his full height, accepting the towel I hand him. It's a struggle to keep my eyes averted. I could drink in his gorgeous body all day long without getting bored.

"Get dressed and find out."

"Suspicious much?" I ask sceptically.

"That's us."

We both return to the bedroom to throw on clothes. Pulling on one of Xander's spearmint-scented shirts I stole from his room, I finger-brush my dripping curls into some semblance of order.

Raine takes my hand, leaving his stick behind. I guide him down the corridor into the open plan living room where voices exchange conspiratorial whispers. An odd scene greets us.

Xander is obsessively arranging something on the coffee table while Lennox supervises. The pair are trading arguments, their entire attention focused on whatever they're doing.

"Guys?"

At Raine's prompt, both snap upright, wearing sheepish looks. It's a change after Xander's aggressive approach to caring for me. They've drawn the curtains and lit a handful of cheap tea lights throughout the room.

"Um, ta dah?" Lennox spread his muscular arms wide.

Xander smacks the back of his head. "Have a bit more showmanship, for fuck's sake."

"You want to take over?"

Clearing his throat, Xander gestures around the room in a weird, awkward way. "Well, we realise that none of us had a real first date with you."

I take in the candles, the dimmed lights and an array of different snacks that have been laid out. Including several of my favourites and a multipack of chilled beer. An old sci-fi movie is already loaded on the paused TV.

"This is a first date?" My hand flies up to cover my mouth.

"Safe house edition." Lennox shrugs. "We realise it isn't much."

I'm too surprised to fathom a response. Xander curses while studying my reaction. Raine shuffles on his feet. Hell, Lennox's chest is heaving so hard, it looks like he's on the verge of a fucking panic attack.

"You hate it. Shit, Xan! She hates it!"

"I told you to get the double chocolate chip cookies, not the plain kind!" Xander snarls at him. "You had one job, Nox."

"You're the one who chose the shit movie!"

"You're both useless." Raine shakes his head.

"Hey! We got beer!"

"Guys!" I shout above them, trying hard not to laugh. "This… This is everything. It's the best first date I've ever seen."

Their arguing halts, all fixing their attention on me. Xander visibly relaxes. Lennox runs a relieved hand down his face. Raine chuckles, nudging me forward with a touch to my lower back.

"My idea," he whispers proudly.

I take a seat on the sofa before they can start bickering again. Lennox hands out cracked open beers, fighting to hold back a grin. I study his neckline, finding his silver chain is indeed absent. It really is gone.

"Guys?" Raine clears his throat. "The first date gift?"

"Fuck." Lennox fists his hair agitatedly. "Xan!"

"Chill out. I've got it."

Plucking a small box off the coffee table, Xander presents it to me. Eyeing him, I accept the wrapped gift, feeling all kinds of confused. They're really not the type to go in for grand gestures.

"We figured flowers are average," he says with a slight smile. "And not your style."

Looking down at the box, I slip the lid off. Inside rests a delicate, black bracelet made of miniature chains welded together. I finger the smooth metal. It's lightweight and totally unique. I've never seen a bracelet like it.

"This is for me?"

Lennox stares at me. "Do you like it?"

"Yes." I lift the light chain, finding it's the perfect size. "This is so beautiful."

Xander snags the seat next to me, a huge pile of snacks stacked in his arms. He dumps them on the side of the sofa, finding a comfortable position where he can lay his head in my lap.

"Want me to fasten it?"

Nodding, I hold out my wrist for him. "Please."

The chain slips easily around my wrist, fitting like it was made for me. I'm still a little flabbergasted. No one has ever bought me jewellery before, and this is exactly my style.

"Perfect." Xander fastens the small catch. "Now you're shackled to us for life."

"Is this some kind of proposal?" I laugh.

"No." He rests back in my lap. "Just a reminder."

Smiling to the others, I murmur my thanks. They both take seats, their expressions pleased. I bury my fingers in Xander's hair, gaze focused on the unique present.

The simplest of gestures mean even more coming from him. It was worth getting out of bed just to see his features soften and his eyes slide shut now that I've approved of his gift.

Sighing as he relaxes, it's clear that Xander is perfectly content with me touching him. Lennox watches his best friend's behaviour with a perplexed look.

"Well that's just fucking bizarre."

Eyes still closed, Xander flips him off. "Fuck off."

"Since when did you become a cuddler, Xan?"

"Since now, shithead."

I try not to disturb Xander with my silent laughter, accepting a beer from Lennox. He and Raine are sharing the other sofa, clinking their beers together.

"I'm not sure when I last had a drink." I lift my own bottle. "This is going to taste so good."

"You literally doled out contraband for over a year." Lennox frowns at me. "You never drank any of it?"

"Well, no."

Raine sighs in pleasure as he sips his beer. "Seems like a waste of power to me."

"Agreed." Lennox nods.

"Neither of us should be drinking on medication," I point out.

Raine swallows his mouthful. "I don't care right now."

Taking a long draw, I savour the lightly fizzing liquid. I've never been much of a drinker, but something about this feels triumphant. Like we're celebrating living long enough to share a pack of beers.

"Did you get the sour cream pretzels?" Raine asks.

Without answering, Xander plucks them from our pile of snacks and tosses them at Raine. They hit his chest. He hums happily, tearing into the snacks with gusto.

"So freaking good," he mumbles around a mouthful.

Lennox wrinkles his nose. "That's the worst flavour."

"Then I don't have to share with you. Win-win."

Lennox starts the movie, but I'm too focused on the silky-soft tresses weaving through my fingers. I comb through Xander's hair before repeating the action, measuring and studying each platinum strand.

Having him so relaxed around me feels like a privilege. A couple of nights ago, he even slithered into bed with Lennox and me. The three of us tangled together without uttering a word. It felt so natural.

"Have you ever been on a first date before?" I whisper to him.

"No."

"Ever?"

"Do I look like much of a dater, Ripley? Not exactly the relationship type."

"You never... ah, romanced your toys before?"

"I'm sure they didn't need romancing after being referred to as toys," Lennox butts into our conversation. "Who wouldn't fall for that?"

"Watch it, swimming pool. You aren't winning awards for romance either."

He falls silent, glowering at Raine when he starts laughing. I tune them out, focused on Xander.

"I never wanted more than a brief physical connection before," he explains slowly. "I didn't care about their feelings or wellbeing. This is all new for me."

"Well, I'm glad to be your first date."

Candlelight flickers in his navy irises, highlighting the varied tones of blue melting into a dark, inviting hue. Xander lifts a hand to run his fingers over my chin.

"Me too."

The sounds of the movie play in the background. Lennox is explaining it to Raine, describing the dystopian future where robots have taken over and all but eradicated the human race. The pair are laughing together like idiots.

"So you're a sci-fi fan?"

"Does that surprise you?" Xander is still watching me.

"It seems fitting. You love technology."

"I like computers. That's all."

"Right. I heard you've been making friends with Theo at HQ."

"He showed me his set-up in the intelligence department." His pitch lightens, seeming to radiate excitement. "You wouldn't believe the tech they have in there. Incredible."

He's so touchy about admitting he enjoys something, but the clear passion in his voice reveals the truth.

"Did he let you touch his computer?" I tease.

"Not yet. I'll convince him, though." He looks away, deep in thought. "Or offer to break his skull."

"You can't manipulate everyone with threats of death or violence. I'm happy you're excited, but we should perhaps talk about managing these new feelings."

"What's to manage?" Xander sniffs. "I'll simply befriend the flannel-wearing nerd and convince him to let me use his tech. That or I'll find a new home for my pocketknife in his gut."

I stifle the urge to facepalm.

Xander is a work in progress.

CHAPTER 24
RIPLEY
HIGHER – CROIXX

I WAKE to weak morning light, far too warm and comfortable to move. Credits roll in the background, accompanying the sound of heavy breathing and snores. I must've dropped off after the fourth movie.

Something hard and wiry is sprawled out beneath me. I've turned Xander into a human mattress, my face tucked into the crook of his neck, legs spread either side of his waist and chests flush together.

On the other sofa, Raine is resting in Lennox's lap. Both fast asleep. None of us survived the sci-fi marathon we ended up undertaking after watching the first movie Xander put on.

"No, stop," Xander begs beneath me.

I quickly sit up to shake him. "Xan. Wake up."

"No… Please."

"Hey, hey. It's me."

"S-Stop."

"Xan!"

With enough shaking, he finally rouses. "Argh!"

The sleepy fog that fills his eyes whenever I wake him from a nightmare clears faster than usual. Xander looks over me then the room, verifying his surroundings. He hasn't had a dream like this for a while.

Throat bobbing, he slumps back on the sofa, drawing in uneven breaths. I push damp hair from his face. He's feeling clammy and looks even paler than usual.

"You okay?"

"Yeah," he pants. "Fine."

"Just take deep breaths. You didn't wake the others."

He works on breathing slowly while I continue smoothing his hair.

"You're safe with me, Xan. You can come back."

It takes time for him to calm down, his eyes now at half-mast. The dawn sun splatters across his porcelain skin, highlighting curves and angles sharp enough to slice me wide open.

Xander hides his face in my chest, his hot breath warming my skin. I keep him close until the sound of birdsong leaks into the living room, and my neck aches from holding it at an odd angle.

I'm not sure if he's gone back to sleep. We've been cuddled together for what feels like forever. When I try to move, his hand quickly bands across my back to hold me in place, answering that question.

"Xan," I whisper. "I need to stretch."

His only reply is a low moan of protest, face tucked into my throat. I squirm at the feel of his lips teasing my neck, skipping higher until he finds my pulse point and lightly nips.

The arm keeping me trapped against him tightens, flattening me on his chest. My breasts are pressing into him, the baggy shirt I stole from his stash riding up to reveal my hips and thighs to the air.

A hand sneaks down my body, coasting lower until he slides it into the back of my panties. I gasp when Xander grabs a handful of my right ass cheek and squeezes hard.

"I could get used to you waking me up from bad dreams looking like this," he purrs into my throat.

His tight grip on my rear causes me to buck, accidentally pressing into his growing erection. I want to stand and move away, knowing what woke him up, but he won't release me.

"Xan, wait—"

"Keep squirming," he rasps. "I'm not letting you go."

"We shouldn't…"

"Shouldn't do what?"

His hips press upwards, rocking his hardness into me. I'm straddled right above his crotch, giving him the perfect position to rub himself on me. I can feel how my body on his is affecting him.

The hand infiltrating my panties cinches again, making my skin burn. He's squeezing my backside like he wants to flip me over and take out all his emotions on my body.

"The others," I gasp.

"Trust me, we've heard about Raine's sharing kink," Xander murmurs back. "He's discussed it at length with us."

"Oh."

He chuckles beneath me. "Surprised?"

"A little. Do you guys… erm, discuss what we do together?"

"No, never. But Raine wanted to broach the subject. I was surprised by how on-board Lennox was. He's changed his tune, hasn't he?"

That may have something to do with the mind-blowing sex we had during their interviews and the multiple times he's made me shamelessly beg for an orgasm since. The man has a passion for edging.

"Want to test the theory?" Xander teases.

Simmering heat pools between my thighs, created by his hard cock pushing up into me. Each move makes my skin tighten and constrict. I feel like I want to tear myself apart just to get more friction.

"How?"

"You're going to follow my instructions, little toy. Word for word."

Hips surging upwards, his hard bulge meets my clit. It throbs beneath my panties, the thin cotton quickly becoming soaked.

"I want to watch them fuck you." Xander's lips touch my ear. "And I want you to keep your eyes on me when they fill you with their cocks."

"Fuck, Xan."

"You like the sound of that, don't you?"

More warmth swirls through my veins. "Yes."

"Go on, then. Wake Lennox up with your mouth. I know he'd like that."

Releasing his arm, Xander pushes me away from him. I slide off the sofa to find my feet, drinking in his desire-laced gaze. He actually wants me to do this.

Fine. I'm not scared to take what I want.

Padding over to the other sofa, I kneel in front of Lennox. He's asleep in an odd position, almost seated normally but with his head laid back and Raine's head resting on his left leg.

I stroke a hand up his other leg, feeling each rigid muscle in his bulging quads and thighs. When Lennox stirs, I halt briefly, my eyes locked on his face. His breathing evens out, and I continue upwards.

Lifting Lennox's shirt, I place featherlight kisses along his abdominals. My lips leave a light trail, causing his already firm bulge to grow. He's sporting morning wood.

Easing the front of his sweats down, I splay a hand over his lower belly and use the other to rub his cock through his boxers. His huge length strains against the fabric, barely trapped inside.

"Are you staring at it?"

The quiet voice almost scares me until I realise it's coming from Raine, his head resting inches from where my attention is focused. His eyes are still closed.

"No."

"Then do as Xander asked, babe."

"You really want to hear this?"

"Fuck yes, I do."

I slip Lennox's dick from his boxers, taking it in my hand. The thick steel fills my palm, hot and throbbing as a deep sound rumbles from his chest.

In their own ways, both Xander and Raine are observing me now. Neither moving nor speaking. Ducking my head, I pull Lennox into my mouth, swirling my tongue over his smooth head.

Muscles tense beneath my other hand. I draw his cock in deep, bobbing up and down on his length to coax him awake. Lennox stirs with a groan, his hand moving to rest atop my head.

"Wha…? Rip?"

Hearing his voice, I suck hard, taking him to the back of my throat. Lennox's fingers tighten in my hair. Easing back, I tease his shaft with my tongue and move my eyes up to his.

Yep. He's awake.

Wild-eyed with surprise, Lennox stares down at my mouth latched around his dick. Raine hasn't moved, though his unfocused, golden eyes are now open, and he's breathing a little harder.

"Raine," Lennox says gutturally. "Get off me so I can fuck our girl's face right now."

Raine pulls himself upright. "Be my guest."

I watch his hand move to cup the straining bulge between his legs as Lennox repositions himself, his grip still firm on my hair.

"Whose idea was it to wake me up like this?"

I blink up at him innocently.

"I have a few guesses." Lennox looks at the two others. "Do we all want to do this?"

When there's no complaints, he ruts up into me, pushing his cock deeper into my mouth. His thickness skates against my tongue, nudging my throat until I make a faint choking sound.

"Shall I show them how rough we like to play?" Lennox strokes my head.

God, I have no idea how either man will react. Xander loves to mix pleasure and pain. Raine's game for just about anything, but Lennox smashes past my limits like it's a personal vendetta.

I let him set the pace, using my mouth as if I'm little more than an inanimate doll. It's freeing to let Lennox take control and be rough, even with his friends in the room.

When he yanks on my hair to lift me off his cock, I gulp down air, feeling thick strands of saliva pull from my mouth. Lennox glances to the side before refocusing on me.

"Raine," he grumbles. "Get down there, and tell me how wet our girl is for us."

Raine pulls himself off the sofa to land on the floor next to me. He uses his hand to feel for my position, identifying where I'm placed on the carpet before I sense him settle behind me.

He lifts Xander's loose shirt to locate my panties, gliding the elastic over my hips but leaving it around my knees. Air kisses my bare backside and pussy, now exposed to the room.

I'm bent over to reach Lennox's cock, leaving me wide open. Violin-roughened fingertips dance across my hips, back and ass cheeks in a taunting rhythm. When he slides them over my wet folds, I can't hold back a moan.

Lennox's nostrils flare. "Quiet, Rip."

He silences me by shoving his cock deeper into my mouth, cutting off any further noises. I swallow down his length, still focused on the feel of Raine torturously circling my entrance with two fingers.

"Our dirty girl is fucking soaked," he announces, running his thumb over my aching clit. "She likes being watched. Don't you, Ripley?"

I'm unable to defend myself with Lennox rocking into my mouth, filling it at a steady cadence. Each nudge against my throat makes the backs of my eyes burn.

"Taste her," Lennox demands.

A wet tongue slides over me, clit to pussy, making me spasm. Raine sucks my bundle of nerves into his mouth, applying just enough pressure to make my spine curve.

"Focus, Ripley." The knot of desire in my core tightens at Lennox's commanding tone. "You have a job to do."

Tightening my lips around him, I move in time to each of his upward thrusts. Saliva runs down my chin, causing wet, sliding sounds to spill from where we're connected.

Hearing his throat clear from across the room, my eyes dart to Xander. He's still watching, now sitting up on the sofa, one leg braced on the other. Yet he doesn't touch himself. All his attention is on me.

I whimper when I feel Raine's tongue spear my slit, pushing inside me. It's a welcome intrusion, causing my pussy to pulse and contract. I can imagine how his face looks, smeared in my juices.

"Problem, Rip?" Lennox fists my hair tight. "Is he fucking you with his tongue?"

Blinking up at him, my eyes are swimming. Raine pulls his tongue from my entrance long enough to push two fingers in, circling them inside my cunt. I let them both fill me, keeping my gaze locked on Xander as power unlike anything I've ever felt floods me.

Eyebrow cocked, he gestures for me to move. I know what he wants to see. This is all a tease. Pushing against Lennox's hand, I remove him from my mouth.

"Xander wants a show," I explain shakily.

Breathing ragged, Lennox looks at his best friend. "Is that so?"

Xander shrugs. "She has her instructions."

He looks between us then back at Raine, still positioned behind me. He's pulled his fingers from my pussy, now resting at my backside and awaiting his next order.

"Well, I wouldn't want to get in the way of that." Lennox snickers, tongue dancing slowly along his bottom lip.

I kiss his inner thigh before shuffling around to face Raine. After pulling off my panties the rest of the way, he lets me push him down to the carpet in the space between the sofa and the coffee table, putting him on his back.

Grabbing the waistband of the pyjama pants he pulled on yesterday, I tug them down, pulling his boxers with them. Raine braces a hand behind his head, content to let me take control.

Each guy has their own dynamic with me. We trade power in unique ways in the safety of the bedroom. I'm not sure what the combined result will be, but my quivering pussy is ready to find out.

Settling above Raine's hips, I keep my attention fixed on Xander as I seize hold of his cock to position it at my entrance. Raine grunts beneath me, his hands finding their way to my hips.

"What are you waiting for?" Xander asks impatiently.

I narrow my eyes at him. "Nothing."

Then I push down on Raine's steel, allowing him to bottom out inside me. I don't need any more prep after having his fingers and tongue. I'm itching to feel him stretch me open.

He groans loudly, fingertips digging deep into my skin. I've found the perfect angle to take him fully inside me. Still, my focus is split between all three of them.

Xander's stare. Lennox watching me take Raine. The moaning violinist caught in the middle, letting me ride him. Even outnumbered, I feel in control. They're all here for me.

"Shirt off," Lennox orders. "Let us see those perfect tits bounce."

Pulling it up and over my head, I toss the shirt at him. "Here."

He catches the balled-up fabric then throws it onto the sofa. With my free hand, I seize my breast and squeeze, adding to my own pleasure. Lennox watches me flick and twist my nipple until it stiffens.

"That's better. Now ride him, baby."

I hungrily slide up and down on Raine's shaft. He's still gripping my hips, allowing him to drive into me each time I thrust down. The result has me moaning loudly, over-sensitised by all the eyes on me.

I've no idea how Xander is still just sitting there, drinking in his fill. Lennox is pumping his cock as he watches us perform in front of him. But the iceman is content to observe for now.

"Yes, babe." Raine surges into me, his blazing caramel eyes darting in all directions. "God. You feel so fucking good clenched around me."

Pinching my nipple tight, I throw my head back, rising and falling on him at a quickening tempo. My breasts jostle with each move, the heavy mounds pushed outwards for their perusal.

"Fucking gorgeous," Lennox praises. "Right, Xan?"

He nods in approval. "She is breathtaking."

"She feels it," Raine adds throatily.

Their compliments only make me feel bolder. I drop a hand to my pussy, working my clit in fast circles in time to Raine surging up into me. He's panting on the carpet, chasing each movement to make our collision even more intense.

In my periphery, I can see Lennox rising to circle us. Anxiety prickles my body. I can't possibly take them both—not with Lennox's size. I have a feeling he'd be all too happy to try, though.

When he halts on my right side, hand curled around the base of his cock, I know what he's seeking. My mouth opens, accepting his length back. Lennox glides past my lips to fill me.

"That's my perfect slut." He cups the back of my neck. "Taking us both so well, aren't you?"

My only response is a hum from my chest, barely audible.

"I'm going to fuck your pretty throat while you make Raine come." Lennox slams into my mouth, over and over. "Let him fill your cunt up, baby."

I'm already clenching around Raine's length, hugging his cock in a vice. Between all the stimulation, I'm ready to climax. But I want Raine to fill me first. I want them to see me dripping in it.

Controlling my sucking with his hand on my neck, Lennox quickly drives into my mouth. Each hit pushes my tolerance to the limit. I can feel the moisture sliding down my cheeks from his roughness.

"Come for me." Raine replaces my hand with his so he can strum my clit. "That's it, babe."

The feel of him jolting inside me is so exquisite, I let myself fall apart. My orgasm hits in an intense rush, rolling in with little warning. My muscles pull tight, holding me in suspension between them.

"Fuck!" Raine bellows.

Heat rushes into me, spilling from his cock. I slow my movements, undulating my hips in a circle to pull every last drop of pleasure from him. He grunts underneath me, thumb stilling on my clit.

Lennox pulls out before he can finish, rubbing his thumb over my bottom lip. Seeing that Raine is spent, he slides his hands underneath my arms to pluck me up like I weigh little more than air.

"Sorry, man. You wanted to share, though."

"Fair." Raine wipes a bead of sweat from his forehead.

I'm carried to the sofa, but Lennox doesn't deposit me on it. Instead, he bends me over the curved armrest, nudging my legs open with his knee. He lifts me by the hips so he can access every part of me.

"Look at all this mess," he grumbles roughly. "Your perfect cunt is glistening, baby. I hope Raine didn't tire you out."

"Not yet," I gasp. "Please... More."

"You beg so beautifully for me. I love the sound of it."

I cry out when he nudges against my entrance, teasing my sensitive slit. I'm not sore after riding Raine, but I know I will be by the time Lennox is through. He loves to make me work for it.

"Easy, Rip. We both know you can take me, and Raine's got you all relaxed."

He clearly doesn't care that I'm soaked in another man's fluids. Noted.

"That's it," Lennox praises, nudging himself inside me. "Legs open for me, baby."

Bent over the armrest, I have a perfect view across the room of Xander. Still unmoved. The strain tenting the jeans he slept in must be uncomfortable. Why won't he touch himself?

Holding his eyes, I let him see every iteration of bliss that having Lennox inch into me creates. Just when I don't think I can take anymore, he withdraws and slides back in, pushing me that little bit further.

I feel the moment he's fully sheathed, his balls slapping against me. Hell, it's intense. Even after an orgasm from the man still sprawled out on the floor.

"Dammit." Lennox moves behind me, our skin slapping together. "You've already got me so worked up."

It's a hedonistic thrill to know that Lennox is struggling to hold it together. I don't know if he can feel my satisfaction, but the harsh spank he delivers feels more like pleasurable punishment than praise.

"You like taking us all, don't you?" he grunts. "Letting three men fuck your sweet pussy."

"Yes." I can't suppress the loud moan that escapes me.

"After all this time… You got what you wanted. We're all gone for you, Rip."

Contracting around him, I love the way it makes Lennox turn feral. The first time we slept together, I could hardly sit down afterwards, he'd hit me so hard.

I loved feeling the bruises twinge each time I moved. Even if I was already black and blue from Harrison's beating, it felt good to have Lennox's handprints on me, erasing the unwanted touch.

With each pump into me from behind, Lennox spanks me hard on the ass. Fire ants race over my skin, making me cry out at each impact. His strokes are long and broad, sparing no time.

I catch sight of Xander moving the slightest amount. He unfolds his legs, tongue darting out to wet his lips. The psychopath still hasn't touched himself. Not a single stroke.

"Patient, isn't he?" Lennox puffs. "Half the pleasure is watching you like this. Sweaty and stripped bare, covered in our come."

"Oh, Nox."

"Should we relieve him? He looks rather lonely sitting over there."

Slapping my ass hard, Lennox abruptly pulls himself out. I shout his name louder, feeling myself overflow with trickling warmth. The sudden change sends me reeling.

I'm lifted from the sofa, my midsection burning from being bent over the stiff fabric. I let Lennox carry me, taking a second to look at Raine. He's upright now but still on the carpet, listening.

When we stop in front of Xander, something is silently communicated between them. Xander shifts on the sofa to strip his bottom half off. Lennox holds me mid-air, planning something unknown.

"You're going to ride him backwards," he murmurs into my neck. "Fold your legs beneath you then lower yourself onto him."

"I can't—"

"Yes, Rip. You can."

Lowering me onto Xander, Lennox gives me a moment to fold my legs. I end up kneeling on the sofa cushions, a leg either side of Xander's thighs so I'm braced above his prominent erection.

Lennox stands in front of us, his dick at eye-level with me. He fists his length and begins to stroke, jerking the shaft in fast pumps.

"Take him." He tilts his head towards Xander. "I want to see what it looks like."

My core clenches tight, loving the remaining boundaries between us being smashed down. Xander's hand stroking up and down my spine leaves gooseflesh. He takes hold of my breast and twists, causing pain to hum through me.

"Shy, little toy?" His soft purr sweeps over me.

I find my balance over him. "I'm not fucking shy."

"Prove it."

Finding his shaft, I guide him inside me. Xander slots in like lock and key, taking full advantage of my sweat-slick state. I'm a mess, but he doesn't complain. Not when I accept his full length without protest.

"Good." Lennox continues to work himself over. "That's perfect."

"You like watching me take another man?"

His eyebrows draw together. "Surprisingly, yeah. It's hot as fuck."

Despite my burning thigh muscles, I lift myself on Xander and ease back down to take him inside me. I have enough energy to see this filthy game we've begun through.

It takes some adjusting, riding Xander from this position. I can't see him or gauge his reaction, but in some ways, that makes it hotter. All that exists is the pressure of him pressing into me.

Teeth sink into my shoulder, causing me to yelp. Xander presses his canines down, breaking skin. He ignores my whimpers. I can feel warmth trickling from where he's drawn blood.

"Help Lennox." His tongue glides over my skin, licking up the red spill. "Now."

Biting my lip, I reach out to cup Lennox's balls. His teeth are gritted, face flush with exertion. I know he's close. Massaging the softness beneath his shaft, I help him towards the finish line, watching for his reaction.

"Open your mouth," Lennox growls out.

Still fondling him, I spread my lips. He fists his cock, inching closer to hold the engorged head over my mouth. When his eyes screw shut, I accept the hot strands of come that shoot onto my tongue.

He shifts after a second, letting his fluids cover my face too. I can feel stickiness hitting my cheeks and parted lips, leaving me stained with his juices.

"Christ." Lennox gapes, wide-eyed. "That's a fucking sight."

Watching him, I lick my lips and swallow the seed that made it into my mouth. Lennox smirks through his laboured breaths, squeezing his cock as he wrings out his climax.

I'm still rolling back and forth on Xander, letting him slide deep inside me. Seeing my task is complete, his mouth lifts from cleaning the wound he's inflicted to touch my ear.

"Such a good toy," he whispers indulgently. "Next time, I'll let him finish inside you while I fuck that beautiful mouth of yours."

"Xan…"

"Yes?"

"P-Please… I… I need…"

"What do you need, Ripley?"

Between all of them, I don't know which way is up anymore. They've all marked me in some way. The salty fluid all over me and blood streaming down my shoulder are evidence enough.

"I hate it when you make me guess." Xander's slim arm circles me. "You're to answer when spoken to."

The hand that finds my throat isn't even a surprise. I may be on top of him, but Xander will only entertain my desire to control him for so long. His grip on my throat proves his patience has fizzled out.

And I let him. He can do as he pleases. They all can. I'll let them live out their fantasies with my body while I relish in mine. That's what trust is. We surrender ourselves to the mercy of those we love most.

I drag in a deep breath, prepared for his hand to close. He's gripping my throat, fingertips piercing my skin with each stroke of his cock. Every time I push down on him, Xander's hold tightens.

"I'll give you the air to answer me, little toy. But this time, I want to hear words."

Frantically, I bob my head.

His hand loosens, granting me a precious sliver. "Speak."

"I... I—"

"No." He doesn't let me finish. "Too slow."

Unable to cry out in frustration, I'm forced to succumb once more. Xander chokes me again, his short nails cutting into my skin. While Lennox observes with parted lips, Raine listens intently to each small sound.

What did they expect?

Xander fucks exactly how he loves.

Intensely and all at once.

My lungs sear, lit with invisible fire. The room is blurring, morning light piercing my vision. Still I ride his length, pushing past the pain to seek the release I'm so desperate for.

"Try again." Xander quickly lets go of my throat. "What do you need, Ripley?"

"To c-come."

"Good. Now ask me nicely."

Sadistic fucking bastard!

Eyes streaming, I work myself on his cock, chasing my climax with each rough surge of his hips. My body is on the verge of giving out, but I need a release for all the tension coiled inside me. It's becoming unbearable.

"Please, Xan. P-Please let me come. Please."

"I can see the appeal in making her beg," Xander comments to his best friend, still watching us with saucer-like eyes.

"Told you," Lennox retorts.

Lowering his hand from my throat to my swollen nub, he pinches it hard. More pain crackles over me, setting alight numerous nerves that are already stretched thin.

Xander circles my clit, rubbing it over in a rhythmic pattern. He pistons upwards from the sofa, grinding into me when I begin to falter. I've reached my limit. I want to fall into oblivion in his arms.

"You can finish," he finally relents, slapping into me. "Show them whose cock you love the most."

The evil son of a bitch's whispered command travels directly into my mind, pulling the trigger on an orgasm that's been threatening since Lennox bent me over. I screw my eyes shut, head thrown back and lungs constricted.

The release barrels over me. Eruptions inside me sap all my strength, adding it to the fire that's crisping my insides until it feels like I'm being burned alive.

Xander announces his own climax with a roar, holding me clamped on top of him. If it wasn't for him, I'd slump over in a lifeless pile. My body is beyond exhausted and awash with sweet pangs.

His forehead connects with my shoulder blade, soft hair tickling my skin. I sag backwards into him, letting Xander take my dead weight.

It takes great effort to peel my heavy lids open to take in the scene. Still on the carpet, Raine is repeatedly opening and closing his mouth, trying to find appropriate words.

"Um, in case anyone is keeping tabs… I definitely have a sharing kink. That was so fucking hot, I think I came twice."

"Gross," Xander mutters breathlessly.

Lennox shrugs, legs crossed to cover his manhood. "Raine called it. Hot as fuck."

"Oh my god." I let my head fall back onto Xander's shoulder. "You're all insane."

CHAPTER 25
XANDER
BRAIN STEW – GREEN DAY

WE'RE SITTING SILENTLY with morning coffee when the news comes in. Our entire group has been on tenterhooks since we received word that Sabre is making its move on Bancroft. Just in time for his grand reopening of Blackwood Institute.

It's been splashed over the airwaves for days now, deafening any other news reports. His last-ditch PR effort to fix Incendia's public image is a newly refurbished institute with reformed measures and security practices.

What a crock of shit.

Naturally, Enzo and his team kept details limited, citing unearthed concerns about the SCU's trustworthiness. Not like we hadn't figured that out long ago when Ripley's deadbeat uncle knew far more than he should.

Nursing my black coffee, I watch Ripley fret over the commentators tearing the story to shreds. Overnight, hours' worth of interview footage was leaked to blow the cover off Incendia's lies once and for all.

"This is insane," Lennox grumbles. "I can't believe this has all been leaked."

Remaining silent, I watch the reports drag on.

None of us have been mentioned, but the elusive inmates from Blackwood feature in all the snippets we've seen. The blonde-haired ex-patient, Brooklyn West, is being ripped to pieces live on air right now.

Another short video clip rolls.

"Blackwood and all the other institutes like it harbour a dark secret." Brooklyn's slate-grey eyes stare dead into the camera lens. "One bought and paid for by this country's wealthy elite."

Newscasters flick back on to the screen, dissecting every word and tearing apart Brooklyn's recorded testimony. It's a character assassination. This leak has rocketed the investigation back into public awareness but at great cost.

"This is what they'll do to us in time," Ripley mumbles lifelessly. "Drag up our pasts, throw every last mistake we've ever made in our faces and tell us to be silent once more."

"They're just chatting shit for the views." Lennox is trying to placate her, though his voice lacks any hope.

"We can never go public."

"Rip…"

"No matter what I threatened my uncle with." She ignores him. "If we aren't silent for the rest of our lives, we'll face the same public lynching as these patients."

None of us can offer Ripley any comfort. Not when the irrevocable proof of what she fears is staring us all in the face. The regime that ruined our lives is falling apart at this very moment, but it changes nothing.

We're still outsiders.

Misfits. Rejects.

That's all we'll ever be.

"Do you think we'll be free now?" Raine changes the topic.

Sitting next to him, Lennox is pushing cold toast around his plate. "That seem likely to you?"

"Well, I don't know. Bancroft is the head of the snake. If Sabre is apprehending him, the rest of his empire will follow, right?"

"It isn't that simple," I butt in. "We have other enemies."

"But if the truth is being dragged into the light, they can apprehend everyone who funded Incendia's evil for so long," Raine states like it's simple. "Including Jonathan."

In theory, that's how it should work. Yet we all know the wheels of justice turn slowly, and in the case of mass-scale corruption and decades' worth of high-level bribery, they turn even slower.

Laying a hand on Raine's arm, Lennox's stare is fixed on Ripley. She's twisted in her seat at the table to see the TV better, her charcoal-stained fingers drumming nervously on her folded arms.

We're all on edge, but she's worryingly calm. Her only anxious tic is the twitching of her fingers. It's like she's waiting for the other shoe to drop. I don't trust this supposed ending, but Ripley trusts it even less.

Hours pass sluggishly without an update. Lennox cleans up from breakfast, wasting time making endless cups of tea and coffee that sit untouched while Raine has coaxed Ripley onto the sofa to rest.

"Now let's take a look back at the history of Britain's privately-funded psychiatric care, commencing in 1984 with the opening of…"

"Enough," Lennox snaps, grabbing the remote. "We can't listen to this crap all day long."

"Stop!" Ripley shouts at him.

"Come on, Rip. This isn't healthy."

"What else do you expect me to do? Sit here and wait for news?"

"I expect you to stop digging yourself a mental hole!"

Knocking pounds on our front door, making us all collectively freeze. The loud banging comes again. Louder. More frenzied. Someone is trying to break our goddamn door down.

Lennox drops the remote, his posture stiffening as he launches into battle mode. I shove back the kitchen chair to stand, my eyes focused on the corridor leading out of the apartment.

"Stay with Raine," I bark at Ripley. "We'll see who it is."

She moves to Raine, fists clenched. "Be careful."

I bend over to roll my jeans up, pulling the stashed pocketknife from its hiding place. Lennox raises an eyebrow before quickly moving to pull a meat cleaver from the kitchen block.

I gape at him. "Are you for real?"

"What?" He shrugs.

"This isn't a horror movie. Why the cleaver?"

"Shut up, Xan. A knife's a knife!"

Together we creep through the apartment, following the sound of the obnoxiously aggressive knocking. When Lennox leans in to check the peephole, his wide-set shoulders still don't relax.

"It's Warner."

I remain poised, mirroring his suspicious stance. "Alone?"

"Yes."

Ripley trusts him far more than we do, and if recent accusations are anything to go by, Bancroft has moles planted all over the place. Warner hasn't earned my unequivocal trust yet.

"What do you want?" Lennox yells.

Warner braces a hand against the door. "Let me in, Nox. It's urgent."

"Then tell us urgently."

"Not here."

"Then we're not opening the door," I fire back.

"For fuck's sake! Let me in. I think your location may be compromised."

We exchange glances, both wavering. I make a fast judgement call and open the door, allowing Warner to step inside. His eyes blow wide at the sight of us clutching weapons, but he quickly nods.

"Good. You're prepared."

"Prepared for what?" Lennox demands.

"Where are Ripley and Raine?"

I gesture down the corridor. "Kitchen."

"Let's talk together. Hurry."

We return to the living area where Ripley is still standing in front of Raine. He's been backed into the corner beside the TV. She visibly relaxes at the sight of Warner, red-faced and jittery in our doorway.

To be fair to him, my least favourite agent looks rough. His blue eyes are bloodshot, face sagging with tired lines and his clothing rumpled. Even his gun holster is fastened lopsidedly.

"Warner!" Ripley rushes towards him. "You're okay."

He waves her concern off. "No time. Sabre raided the Blackwood reopening last night. Bancroft is dead. His known associates are being arrested as we speak."

Surprise stiffens my muscles, holding back the barrage of questions I intended to hit him with. Bancroft. Dead. The man who hurt us all so badly and forced us to flee for our lives… is gone.

Why don't I feel relieved?

This is what we wanted. But the emotion never comes. It can't be me because I'm still feeling all kinds of fucked up about what's driven Warner to our door. My brain is trying to tell me something.

Bancroft's death may have kicked the hornet's nest. There're plenty more below the head of the snake. Far more harrowing secrets will come to light now that he isn't here to hold them back.

"That's… good, right?" The uncertainty in Raine's tone is palpable.

"It was." Warner swallows hard. "Until I got word that Jonathan Bennet's bank accounts, the legit and offshore holdings we've identified, were emptied at eight o'clock this morning."

I connect the dots faster than he can explain. "Shit."

If Jonathan is shuffling funds, he's planning to disappear. With the amount of money that bastard holds, he could vanish off the face of the planet in no time.

Something tells me he isn't the type to cut and run without tying up loose ends. Especially not after his altercation with Ripley and Lennox. He knows we'll keep talking. The authorities will never stop hunting him.

Even if he can escape, tuck himself away on some bought and paid for tropical island under a false identity… he'll live the rest of his life as a fugitive. It's far from the luxury he's used to. That won't do.

"You think he'll come for me," Ripley surmises.

"I think he's going to be angry and desperate." Warner shifts on his feet. "He made it clear that he's had you under surveillance. To be safe, I want to move you to a new location."

"Move us?" Lennox glares at him. "That doesn't sound safe at all."

"It's a necessary precaution."

Warner doesn't seem like a man who'd act as a mere precaution. Moving risks exposure, but if our location is compromised, staying would be far riskier.

"Why are you alone?" I ask, the hairs on my arms standing at attention.

"The teams are dealing with last night's raid." He fidgets again, failing to contain his nerves. "Sabre is preoccupied right now. Everyone's guards are down."

"But not you." Lennox scrutinises him with his head inclined. "You came to get us."

"Just call it a hunch, alright? I'm worried about the timing. Jonathan isn't the type to scuttle away with his tail between his legs. I need to make sure you're safe."

Observing him, I decide to heed his warning. Warner didn't have to come here. It would be stupid to ignore his instincts, even if I still loathe the bastard.

"Pack your bags," I order them all. "We're leaving."

"But Xan—" Lennox starts.

"That's final."

Mouth slamming shut, he throws his hands up in frustration then stomps off towards our room. Raine presses a kiss to Ripley's cheek and leaves the room too, a hand outstretched to feel for the layout he's memorised.

Crossing my arms, I level Warner with a stare. "What else happened last night?"

For a moment, I don't think he'll respond.

"Bloodbath," he eventually admits, pinching his nose with his thumb and forefinger. "There were multiple casualties including Bancroft. Enzo, Theo and Hunter are all safe. The other witnesses too."

"How did he die?" Ripley asks.

Warner kneads the back of his neck. "Does it matter?"

My temper flares. "He hurt us both. It matters."

"His… ah, throat was torn out, I believe."

Whistling under her breath, Ripley's mouth spreads in a smile. She looks up at me. I'm trying to puzzle out the thoughts I can see dancing in her eyes… Relief, satisfaction, maybe disappointment?

Did she want the kill for herself?

Our lives are inextricably interlinked by the monster who ensured our paths would cross. I can understand her thirst for revenge. That man caused untold damage to so many people.

"Good." She nods.

Appearing uncomfortable, Warner's eyes flit around the apartment. "We should move."

"I'll grab my things."

Leaving Ripley to find Raine and pack her essentials, I don't budge. Warner flicks me a glance.

"You're not packing?"

"I've got all that I need." I toss the pocketknife effortlessly up and down in my left hand. "Where are you taking us?"

"We have another safe house far from London. Closer to Oxford."

If Warner is a mole, he would've turned us over to Bancroft long ago. Or be fleeing to hide from the inevitable convictions that will now be doled out. Perhaps it's time I gave him some due credit.

"Listen, Warn—"

CRASH.

Glass daggers hurtle towards us as the living room window shatters. A projectile flies through the air, carrying sharp daggers. Warner lunges to shove me to the floor, landing half on top of me.

We hit the rough carpet with a thud, the impact jolting my spine. His weight pins me down, azurite eyes lit with concern. The brief second of silent shock doesn't last long.

CRASH.

A second projectile hits the carpet closer to us in a pile of scattered shards. It takes a moment for the round, dark-green object to register in my mind. Then terror sets in faster than I can bellow a warning.

"GRENADE!"

Warner kicks the grenade across the room before a flash blinds us. The detonation causes an almighty roar of crumbling bricks and broken glass. Smoke quickly fills the open plan space.

It's all we can do to cower. The explosion ripped a hole in the apartment, causing an almighty racket. When I lift my head in the thick plumes of dust that have filled the room, I spot the first projectile.

Another grenade, but it hasn't detonated. I'm not taking any chances. Reason doesn't pierce the surface of my determination. We can't take another hit. Protecting those around me becomes my only thought.

"Xander! Stop!"

Warner hollers when I pick up the grenade and aim it towards the window, hoping it sails through the smoke to reach outside. For an awful second, I'm standing there with it in my fucking hand.

"Run!" I scream at him.

Thick, noxious smoke is billowing from the hole blasted in the side of the apartment. The first grenade flies through it, vanishing into the black cloud. I momentarily look at my hand. Huh. It's still attached.

"Go!" Warner bellows back. "Now!"

Dropping low, I follow him out into the corridor. The hollow smash of an exploding bottle reverberates throughout what's left of the room behind us. Crackling flames and the stench of ignited fuel chase us out the kitchen.

Is that..?

"Fire!" Warner roars.

Molotov cocktails.

We're being firebombed.

I point for him to find Lennox while I head towards Raine and Ripley's room, my panic narrowing into a pure adrenaline rush. We need to get out of here.

"Xan!" Ripley pulls Raine into the corridor, their bags forgotten. "What's going on?"

"No time! Out, now!"

They run for the door, leaving me to find Warner and Lennox. The pair stumble through the rapidly-increasing smoke, billowing from the burning kitchen. More cocktails must've been thrown in.

Grabbing Lennox's wrist, I hold onto him as Warner guides us to the exit. Raine and Ripley hang in the stairwell outside, waiting for us to follow. Throughout the building, fire alarms are wailing.

"We can't just go out there," Lennox shouts over the sounds of destruction. "We're under fire!"

"Service exit." Warner draws the weapon from his gun holster. "Second floor. Car's outside. Go, go!"

All clinging together, we race down the levels, passing other startled residents battling to escape. Chaos is fast unfolding. The apartment block is huge with countless lives now caught in the crosshairs.

Ripley almost trips in her hurry to get downstairs as fast as possible. I lunge to catch her before she can go flying down several flights of steps. She steadies in my arms, barely able to breathe.

"Shit," she wheezes in panic. "Xan!"

"Keep moving, goddammit!"

My grip on her bicep doesn't relent. We escaped the dense black smoke and flames only to run into herds of people flooding out, heeding the warning to find the nearest exit. I can't risk losing her in the melee.

"This is insane!" Ripley shrieks. "Why attack so blatantly?"

"Figure that out when we're secure!"

Warner darts ahead, waving for us to follow when we reach the second floor. While everyone else heads for the main exit below, we wind around the staircase to head deeper into the building.

Lennox is now hauling Raine each step, ensuring he doesn't hit anything. We follow closely, keeping a wary eye out for anyone who decides to infiltrate the building.

"There." Warner points towards a service door marked with a sign. "Should be steps leading down to the back of the building."

He wrenches the door open, ducking his head outside for a cursory glance. After a beat, Warner takes a tentative step outside with his gun raised, ready to fire off a round into the first person who stops us.

"It's clear. Follow me."

I hold Ripley back. "Bring up the rear behind Lennox and Raine. I'll go first."

"So you can get shot first?" she hisses back.

"If necessary, yes! Don't argue!"

Shoving her behind me, I step in front of them and follow Warner. Ripley has the good sense to heed my instructions, moving to the back of our group.

I step outside, surveying the concrete slab wrapped around the apartment block. It's littered with communal bins and broken down cardboard boxes that are piled up, set to be recycled.

Not a single assailant.

For now.

Warner gestures towards his SUV, clicking the key fob. "In! Now!'

The exit steps are made from thin, inflexible metal sheets. This door is clearly only used for building maintenance. It's a tight squeeze to fit us all as we rush to reach ground level.

"Let me help you!" Lennox insists, pulling Raine down the steep steps. "We don't have time."

Reaching the ground, we take a split second to check each other over before racing towards Warner's parked car. The sound of erupting glass and raging fire is deafening.

A quick glance up reveals that the flames have spread, now consuming several apartments surrounding ours. Our attackers didn't seem to consider the collateral damage of their firebombs. Or they simply didn't care.

"In the back!" Ripley throws open the door for Lennox. "Hurry!"

They both help Raine into the car. I climb into the passenger seat, all my focus fixed outside. Still nothing. Distant sirens are now wailing, adding to the mayhem rattling my brain.

Warner clambers behind the wheel, stashing his weapon in the door. He throws the car into gear then takes off in a squeal of tyres, causing us all to be slammed back in our seats.

"I didn't think Jonathan's surveillance was that sophisticated," he mutters to himself. "We should've moved you days ago, before the raid went down."

"You think?" I counter.

"We fucked up, alright?"

"No! It's not!"

"Stop, Xan," Ripley gasps. "This isn't his fault."

Warner drives like a man possessed, attacking sharp turns without an ounce of hesitation. Other motorists blare their horns, narrowly avoiding being mowed down.

"Shit." Lennox stares out the back window.

Black smoke billows into the sky behind us even after the apartment block vanishes. It must be visible for miles around. Their reckless attack is eating through the building's cheap cladding without mercy.

"All those people." Ripley stares out of the window numbly. "God, what about casualties?"

"Emergency services are en route." Warner hits the handsfree, pulling up a phone number. "We can't worry about them right now."

Ringing fills the car as he manoeuvres his way through the traffic winding out of London. The line connects to heavy, panicked breathing.

"Warner!" Becket's crisp voice booms. "What the fuck is going on? We're getting reports of a fire at the safe house."

"We need backup. I got them out. Track the car."

Curses spew down the line.

"We're half an hour out from your location. Goddammit!"

"Just find us, Beck. I'll keep them safe."

"Be careful."

The line disconnects. Gaze locked on the rearview mirror, I study the huge, black Range Rover swerving through other cars to catch up to us.

When it passes several cars to catch up, my suspicions grow. It can't be a coincidence. The windows are tinted too, showing a hint of multiple passengers.

"Behind us," I call out. "We have a tail."

"Bollocks." Warner bangs a fist on the steering wheel.

We almost careen straight into the back of a rusted minivan as Warner slams his foot down on the accelerator. This road is cluttered with traffic. Horns blare all around us.

Swerving dangerously, the Range Rover gains on us. Warner spits another choice curse word, his eyes fluctuating between the road ahead and his mirror.

There are only two cars acting as a buffer between us, holding the Range Rover back from a hard collision. At this rate, they'll be hot on our tail in seconds.

"You know how to use a gun?" Warner glances at me.

I have the inappropriate urge to laugh. "No! I just guessed what to do with that damn assault rifle before."

"Well, you're gonna have to learn on the job. Those bastards are coming for us fast."

Gingerly accepting the weapon he passes me, I familiarise myself with the metal grip. Running a one-man, international embezzlement scheme from my keyboard didn't exactly call for much firearms practice.

"Aim for their tyres!" Lennox suggests, gripping Ripley's leg. "We need to get them off the road."

"Civilians!" Warner exclaims. "Hang on."

The engine revs, pushing the car to the max. We pull out in front of a dawdling estate car, taking a left to find a dual carriageway. The press of traffic thins out, leaving us to advance ahead in the fast lane.

I roll down the window, peeking out to evaluate how far the speeding car is behind us. I've no doubt they're also armed. I don't exactly fancy getting my head blown off while trying to defend our vehicle.

"Now, Xander! Fire!"

Aiming as best as possible, I squeeze the trigger. Pain ricochets up my arm from the kickback. The bullet hits the smooth tarmac then bounces off, missing its target.

"Shit." I blow out a tense breath.

"Again!"

Shifting my aim higher, I fire off another shot. This time, I'm prepared for the force that pulling the trigger creates. The shot lands in their front bumper, leaving a smoking, black hole.

My head smacks into the door's frame when Warner is forced to turn, the lanes merging into a narrower road. More cars sandwich us, forcing me to retreat so I don't hit anyone around us.

"Take the wheel," he instructs, clicking the car into cruise control to free up the pedals. "And pass me the gun."

"Seriously?"

"Yes! Now!"

I lean over the console, steadying the steering wheel. Warner takes his weapon and shifts closer to the window. Ripley screeches his name in alarm, watching him leaning outside to find his aim.

Before he can pop off a shot, something hard slams into us. The impact jolts the SUV to the side, shaking us all. Warner grabs the seat to steady himself, preventing himself from falling out of the fucking car to become a human pancake.

"There!" Lennox cries out. "Blue transit van."

A faded blue vehicle is swinging between lanes like the driver was mainlining heroin before deciding to drive. It swerves deliberately, bringing it back within range. The front rams into us, causing another rough impact.

"Xander!" Ripley screams in alarm.

I lose grip of the wheel, causing the SUV to slam into the railings. Sparks fly. Metal grinds, causing a horrific screech. Warner retakes his seat, abandoning his attempts to fire at our pursuers.

"Incoming!" Ripley shouts, trying to hold steady. "Swerve, swerve!"

But we're sandwiched against the railings, the blue transit van trapping us in place. With the Range Rover creeping up behind us, there's nowhere to go but forwards.

"Brace for impact!" Warner yells.

SMASH.

More screams come from the back seat. We're rammed repeatedly, each slam causing the tyres to slip. Warner pulls us into the middle lane before another impact can land.

"Hang on," he warns.

It's futile. Our pursuers ram their front bumper into the back of the car. It propels us forward, giving the van the perfect chance to hit us at an angle.

SMASH.

My stomach lurches when our tyres leave the tarmac. Reality slows to a crawl, hitting me in horrific jolts. The car is airborne. Warner desperately flails. We're going too fast to prevent the inevitable.

BANG. BANG. BANG.

Each time the SUV hits the road, flipping us over in a death roll, agony crashes over me. It feels like my bones are being pulled out and ground into a fine dust, unable to withstand each hit.

Blood pours down my face. Hot. Slippery. Something burns. The pain... It's overwhelming. Something else cracks. Distant wails sound dull in the weightlessness.

Head smashing on a surface, everything blackens. The crying and pained howling all around me feels like it's happening above surface while I'm sinking to the bottom of a frozen lake.

Forcing my eyelids to lift, all I can see is smoke. Crackling flames. Shattered glass. Twisted, unrecognisable metal. I think... I'm upside down. Pinned by the seat belt making my ribcage wail.

Beside me, a crimson-soaked lump of meat is trapped at an unnatural angle. Head slumped. Leg pinned. Warner's breathing is uneven, matching the sobs coming from somewhere behind me.

I dip in and out, too tired to hold myself in the present. The flashes return. Shouts. Car doors. Barked orders. Crunching footsteps. Someone is prising the back doors open.

"Ripley," I slur semi-consciously.

Hands grab her. Slicing seat belts. Wrenching her struggling limbs. No matter how much I shout internally, I can't get my body to respond. It's shutting down on me.

The sound of her screaming our names is the last thing I hear before the world disappears.

CHAPTER 26
RIPLEY

END OF A GOOD THING – CORY WELLS

I'M TRAPPED IN A NIGHTMARE. A terrifyingly realistic, lucid dream. One pulled from the depths of my traumatised memories. That's the only explanation for this scene. There's no way it can possibly be real.

Wrists chained above me, I battle to clear the fog from my struggling brain, hoping my surroundings will change once I wake up. I must be on death's door to be imagining this place.

A scratched, ancient, padded cell.

Blood streaks marking the concrete floor.

Dusty air vents high above me.

Alone and shackled.

Slamming my eyes shut, I will the nightmare to be over when I reopen them. It's no good. Nothing changes but the worsening ache in my head. It feels like it's on the verge of rupturing.

Small details filter in like trickling tar. Like the fact that I'm wearing the same clothes I had on while watching the news reports spill in over morning coffee. It's tacky with dried blood now. I'm covered in it.

Wiggling my toes, I try to decipher any injuries. The steady throbbing in my skull sure feels like a concussion. I can remember my head smacking into something hard when we flew through the air.

Fuck!

Realisation hits in a heady wave.

The car crash. Being rammed. Flipped over until our armoured vehicle was little more than cotton wool. Lennox slumped over me. Raine's shouting. Smoke and fire all around.

I was conscious when a balaclava-wearing figure wrestled me from the wreck. My neck aches as I shift, testing my theory. It's a familiar pain. The result of being jabbed with a syringe.

"No," I whimper in pain. "Fuck... Xan! Lennox! Raine!"

My shouts are pitiful, barely permeating the old padding that wraps my cell. This can't be happening. There's no way I'm back in Harrowdean, locked in a cell. The concussion is fucking with my head.

Yelling their names at the top of my lungs, nothing but abandoned silence answers me. The padded cell absorbs my cries, playing them back to me in a sickening taunt.

When I notice the tally marks that have been painted on the cell walls in crusted blood, my sobs turn to screams. This isn't the same cell I was previously in.

It's dirtier, scarred from years of battling to escape by any means necessary. Each day trapped in hell marked in mortality. Perhaps the same cell Patient Three and countless others were held in.

I cry myself to the point of almost throwing up, falling into petrifying hysteria. Any comfort that surviving my last trip here should offer is short-lived. Escaping the Zimbardo wing was a miraculous feat.

One I can't repeat.

And this time, I'm alone.

For a long time, I simply float. Exhausted and riddled with pain. When I find the energy to rouse myself again, I tug on the shackles pinning my arms above me at such an awful angle, it feels like my shoulders are being ripped from their sockets.

Solid. Immovable.

My tear-logged eyes catch on the black, chain bracelet still secured around my wrist. I haven't taken it off since that night—our makeshift first date. Not even to shower. Seeing it only increases my hysterical panic.

I have no idea if they're alive.

No. They have to be.

I don't want to live if Xander, Raine and Lennox aren't in this world with me. Not after all we've seen together. I'd die right here just to be with them before taking another step alone.

Time holds no meaning in the cell. Like before, it could be passing in minutes or hours, and I'd have no concept of it. I don't even have Lennox here to keep me sane this time around.

All I can think about is their twisted, broken bodies trapped inside that wrecked car. Lifeless and bleeding. The thoughts become reality in my solitude until I'm convinced the guys are dead.

Gnawing stomach pain degrades into nausea, but it fails to rival the fierce burn in my throat. I'm painfully dehydrated—the only measurement of time passing. My arms have gone numb too.

When the door to the cell opens, I don't move. I can't summon an ounce of will to defend myself against whoever has come to greet me. Revulsion stirs in me at the sneering grin worn by my captor.

"Isn't this a familiar scene?" Elon saunters into the cell. "Nice to see you again, Ripley."

Not real. Not real. Not real.

He crouches down in front of me. "You're looking a bit peaky. Can I get you a refreshment? Glass of champagne? We do like our guests to be cared for."

"E-Elon," I somehow manage.

"Yes, stooge?"

Licking my crusted lips, I draw saliva into my mouth. "Please…"

"Ah, the begging stage. Perfect. Please what?"

"P-Please…"

Smiling maniacally, he slaps me across the face. A dull throb radiates across in my jaw, causing my eyes to water. I blink aside tears to look into his cruel eyes.

"Do spit it out," he commands impatiently.

"P-Please… go f-fuck yourself."

His grin pulls down. "Always such a disobedient bitch. You never learn."

This time, he punches me in the face. My neck snaps to the side, wrenching agonisingly. The pain increases tenfold, racketing through my bones and teeth, making tears spill over.

Elon watches my reaction, his knuckles red from hitting me. The look of satisfaction on his face is fucking repulsive. He looks genuinely thrilled by my tears.

"You've been a monumental pain in the ass, Ripley. Running away to join the super spies like that… Tut tut. Poor choice. They couldn't keep you from ending up back here."

Rising back up, he brushes off his jeans and shirt. Seeing him out of his all-black uniform is unnerving. This isn't Elon the overpaid thug. I could handle him.

Now I'm dealing with Elon the rogue ex-con. Unhinged and without a master to answer to. All bets are off.

"Killing Harrison was a low blow but rather impressive, I'll give you that." He inspects the cell with a look of disgust. "Never thought I'd see that tough bastard get snuffed out."

"Like your b-boss," I cough out.

"We have your new buddies to thank for that. Though we all saw it coming. Bancroft got sloppy; he allowed too much evidence to slip past him. We were prepared for his demise."

"W-We?"

He nudges my leg with the tip of his boot.

"Turns out, there's far more profit in protecting the underdog. It's easy to sit atop an empire and dictate the world. But the real power lies in those who fund the man on top."

Dread sinks into me faster than a knife into butter. I knew we were in trouble the moment Warner turned up at our door. Blood is irrelevant when decades of wealth are burning all around you.

My uncle has millions tied up in this investment. There's no way he'd let all that money simply go up in smoke. To him, this madness is just another business decision.

"The boss wants you quiet and secure like a good patient for the plane ride." Elon sighs exaggeratedly. "If I didn't need this job, I'd happily slit your throat and call it done."

Pounding roars between my ears.

"P-Plane ride?"

Elon grins down at me. "We're all going on a trip."

"I d-don't understand."

"Killing you would create a martyr. Another evidence trail. You're going to take your medication and be a docile little freak."

With a sudden adrenaline rush, I buck and fight, attempting to reach him. If I can just slip these shackles, I'll fight my way out of here. Kick. Punch. Stab. Anything to escape.

Watching me struggle, Elon simply laughs. "You'll spend the rest of your life in a drugged-up haze until your brain cracks open like an egg. He needs you complacent, Ripley. Silent."

"No!"

"Now, now. No need to make such a fuss. I'll get your meds, hmm? That'll make you feel better."

Strolling from the cell, Elon hums a tune under his breath. The shackles tear into my wrists, reopening old scar tissue in my desperate attempt to pull free. Even if I have to dislocate my limbs to do it.

Blood trails down my forearms, joining glass shards buried deep in my skin, dirt and ashy streaks. The words carved into my skin are obscured, the eternal brand covered by my fresh blood.

"Lennox! Xander! Raine!" I wail helplessly.

Elon returns, a zipped pouch in his hand. "Oh, they're dead. Nasty wreck that was. I did tell my men to be gentler."

"You're a fucking liar!"

He rolls his eyes. "Again with the yelling. Let's get those lips sealed tight."

Elon unzips the pouch, pulling out a glass vial and hypodermic needle. I can't read the label through my swimming vision.

He moves onto one knee beside me, pinching the skin above the veins at my inner elbow. That goddamn humming. It's like nails scratching my brain apart as Elon draws clear liquid into the syringe.

"Stop," I beg uselessly. "Don't do this."

"Ah, now she changes her tune. It's too little, too late."

"No! I'll be good, I promise. I'll keep my mouth shut. Just… Please, don't do this."

"We have a long way to travel to meet your uncle, Ripley. This was just a pit stop. And I don't want to listen to you for the entire ride."

I scream out at the pressure of the needle slipping in, plunging deeply into my vein. Blood wells up, spilling around the entry wound. Elon doesn't bother to be gentle.

"You know, Craven once told me this is the good stuff," he says conversationally. "Trialled and tested by his colleague, Professor Lazlo. An old friend, I heard."

Elon depresses the plunger.

"Let's give it a go, shall we?"

I watch in terror as the clear liquid is pushed into my body, a chill quickly spreading through my vein. He squeezes out every last millilitre then tears the needle from my arm.

"No," I moan, my lips thick and rubbery.

"We may as well make use of their stash now that the institutes are toast." He stands back up, rezipping the pouch. "Consider it payment for your role in destroying all our hard work."

I frantically try to fill my lungs. For every second he watches me, I can feel my bodily functions slowing. Woollen numbness is rushing through me faster than a heart attack.

He squints while watching me. "How interesting."

My fingers soon stop responding. Not even a twitch. Then my legs and toes. My tongue becomes an immovable mass, trapped in my mouth. Even breathing shallowly feels like it takes great exertion.

"I believe the drug has a paralysing effect," Elon muses. "You can hear and see everything… but you're powerless to move. Can't even say a word. How fascinating."

No, I want to scream.

But my vocal cords have been severed.

Pinching my chin between his fingers, Elon peers into my eyes. Whatever he sees causes satisfaction to stretch his smile into a clown-like caricature.

All I want is to claw that fucking sneer from his face and leave him in fleshy ribbons. The will is there, but nothing responds. I can hardly blink.

My body has been stolen from me and locked in a mental cage, the key dangled out of reach. He could do anything. I can't fight back.

"I enjoy seeing you like this." He trails a finger along my jawline. "Immobile and trapped in your own mind."

Vomit swells in my belly and throat, unable to expel itself. Not even at the nauseating feel of his touch coasting over my face.

"No one is coming to save you. Harrowdean is abandoned, and believe me, it's low on the list of priorities right now. We'll slip away while the world is busy arguing over blame."

The drug hasn't paralysed my tear ducts which seem to function perfectly well. Stinging rivers stream down my cheeks, making my skin ache where he punched me. Elon catches a tear and lifts it to his lips.

I watch him lick up the moisture, tongue flicking out to taste the proof of his victory. My stomach lurches again. I'd take choking on my own vomit over going anywhere with this maniac.

"I think we're ready to go."

His laugh bounces around the cell.

"This all could've been avoided if you'd just kept your mouth shut."

CHAPTER 27
RIPLEY

BURN IT TO THE GROUND – NICKELBACK

THE RUMBLING engine is my sole companion in the blackness. Discomfort long since stopped registering after my third hit of Elon's favourite weapon. Each time the numbness begins to lift, he doses me up again.

I've been carelessly tossed between vehicles every time he stops. The two men travelling with Elon seem determined to throw any potential tail, changing vehicles multiple times.

During our most recent stop, I didn't even open my eyes. My limbs had started to tingle and wake up, but I remained a limp rag doll. Enough to avoid another dosing to keep me placid.

Every part of me is still weak albeit coming alive. As the engine roars and infinite time slips by, more feeling returns to my extremities. I can make my fingers twitch now. I'm basically deadly.

No, Rip.

You're basically screwed.

In the pitch-black din of the car boot I've been tossed in, I construct a mental portrait of the faces I left behind. Adding brush strokes here, splashes of colour there. Creating realistic texture and nuance. Adding voices, touches, familiar scents.

God, I fucking miss them.

Raine is sunshine. Warmth dappled on my face. Summer barbecues on the beach. Orange juice freshly squeezed in the morning. All things love and light in a world awash with such despair.

By comparison, I see Xander as all dark. The violent, bubbling storm clouds that roll in when that summer day comes to a close. Yet it's still beautiful—all that destructive threat. Complex and purposeful. Storms are a necessary part of nature.

I'd paint Lennox as the undulating lake that lives in his seafoam eyes. That's the reality beneath his angry façade. A bottomless pit of water with a whirlpool at the centre. Holding us all firm.

The painting I first created of them in Harrowdean couldn't be further from the truth. I thought they were my demons. The villains lurking in the background, creeping ever closer with their foul intentions.

Now... I'd take the monsters I first encountered over whatever lies ahead of me. Given the chance, I would rewind the clocks, return to Priory Lane and do it all over again.

Every second of heartache and anguish. All the trauma, the grief, the regret. I wouldn't change anything. Even if it leads me right here.

If they're dead... I would know, right? I'd feel it in my bones. Gravity would shift, and the world would dim into everlasting night. I've waited so long to find a place to belong, and now it feels like it's being torn away with each mile that passes.

This can't be it.

I didn't survive all I did for it to end like this.

Ears straining when I feel the vehicle pull to a halt, I listen for any clues as to our whereabouts. These assailants are incredibly skilled. Jonathan must be expending a small fortune to secure my safe capture.

I don't know why he doesn't just kill me. Sure, it would play into the villain narrative that will form against him. He'd be forced to hide underground for the rest of his life. But isn't this far more effort?

Car doors slam, causing the boot I'm encased in to jolt. I close my eyes, forcing my tingling limbs to loosen. I'm far from being able to run for the hills, but I won't take another hit of those damn drugs.

"Sir," someone greets.

"Any problems?" a clipped, all-business tone responds.

"None. We're clear."

"Good. Get her inside."

Fresh nighttime air rushes in when the boot clicks open. Hands grab hold of me, lifting my torso and ankles between them. It takes all my self-control to keep my eyes shut.

My body is jostled between two people, the hands beneath my

armpits carrying me a short distance. Multiple footsteps follow. I dare to crack open a lid the tiniest amount.

Black tarmac marked with stripes and landing strips. Curved metal fuselage. Circular windows. Spinning rotors. Golden embossing spelling out a familiar company name.

Langdale Investments.

I'm being carried onto a private jet.

If I try anything now, I'll be drugged and incapacitated again before I can get far. The pins and needles are still spreading, bringing sensation with them.

"Leroy will meet with us in Rio De Janeiro."

Uncle Jonathan. I recognise his voice.

"Very good, sir."

That motherfucker, Elon. I'll kill the son of a bitch.

"You'll be compensated for your assistance, Elon. I understand it has been a trying time, but we'll recover from recent setbacks and rebuild."

"Sir." Elon hesitates, shuffling his feet. "Is it wise to keep her alive? She's a proven risk."

Jonathan chuckles. It's a flat, ugly sound. A true reflection of the man who lies within his carefully choreographed exterior, clothed in luxury and false smiles to schmooze his clients.

"My niece can do far more damage in death than she'll do subjugated by my side. I will not allow her ramblings to destroy what assets we have left."

"But—"

"That's final," Jonathan cuts him off.

Elon sighs audibly. "Very well, sir."

I'm roughly deposited in what feels like a leather seat. Terror grips my lungs, almost causing my act to slip. I can wriggle my toes now. When my body obeys me, I'm going to tear these monsters apart.

Noise bustles all around me. Bags being heaved. Men huffing. Pre-flight checks accompanying the hum of the engine warming up. I sense someone stop in front of me before cool lips briefly touch my temple.

"Dear, dear niece. It didn't have to be this way."

"Please take your seat, sir. We'll be ready to depart soon."

His presence moves away, taking his expensive aftershave with him. The smell of it makes me want to gag. All the things that made my uncle seem like such an impressive deity when I first arrived in London as a scared kid are laughable now.

It was all a sham.

One I swallowed for too long.

His rejection and disgust used to hurt me. Enough to leave wounds that impacted every relationship I had since. But I didn't hate him. Not fully. Not until he showed his true colours and harmed those I care about.

Now I'm ready to end this, once and for all.

Bloodlines be damned.

Holding my eyes open as slits, I can safely peer around. I'm sitting at the back of the jet, an incapacitated prisoner kept out of sight. Elon is barking at his guys, disregarding my unrestrained state.

Always so cocky. He hasn't even bothered to cuff me or fasten my body into the seat. The wanker clearly thinks I'm still dosed to my tits on his drug cocktail. I'll show him.

"In the distance! Headlights!"

Before I can move, shouts pour in from outside. Jonathan stiffens in his seat, sternly calling out for answers, but Elon waves him off.

"Stay seated, sir."

"Who is it?" he demands, angrily slamming a fist down on his armrest.

"Those Sabre pricks have tracked us down!"

I don't allow the blast of dizzying relief to change my mind. These men have harmed me for the very last time. I'm not going to wait to be rescued this time.

I carefully test my limbs. Still shaky. My legs respond, pressing my feet into the plush aeroplane carpet. Hands balling into fists, I can just about move my arms. It'll have to be enough.

My plan is simple—I have no fucking plan. Nothing but a last-ditch attempt to escape whatever unthinkable fate my uncle has cooked up for me this time.

I finally get what Xander meant as we fled Harrowdean. I'd rather die on my feet than on my knees. Even if that means throwing myself at the mercy of a suicide mission in order to escape this jet. They can shoot me on the runway before I let it take off with me onboard.

Numb fingers latching onto an empty crystal tumbler on the beverage cart next to me, I lift the leaden weight. Elon has moved to the front of the jet to continue yelling at his men, hurrying them along for take off.

My legs are like trembling spaghetti underneath me. I can hardly hold my own weight. Each step forward towards my uncle's occupied chair feels like running into the middle of a battlefield with a high probability of being shot.

He's watching the exit for any hints as to what's coming, sitting on the edge of his seat. Elon hasn't returned. It's now or never.

I lift the glass as high as possible, swinging it in an arc to meet the back of his head.

"Argh!" Jonathan cries out.

He slumps forward, falling from his seat. I react fast before we have company. My body protests at the sudden movement, carrying me to his fallen form.

"Fuck you!" I hit his head again, causing the glass to smash.

Crystal scatters between us, cutting his shocked face and forehead. Jonathan writhes on the carpet, trying to peer through the blood now pouring from the wound under his hairline.

"Ripley, stop!"

Instead, I launch myself on top of him, willing my fists to respond. The punches are feeble, borderline pathetic, but I pour all my will into each strike. Raining down every last scrap of fight I have left to give.

We wrestle each other, two opposing forces, both on the wrong side of the law. I may have earned this fate, but I learned to be bad from the best. He sank his evil into me long ago.

"Little bitch!" he screams out.

My fist slams into his cheek, causing spit to fly from his mouth. "You did this!"

"I saved you!"

"No." I hit his barely-healed nose. "You fucking doomed me!"

Shouts are fast approaching. I'll be tossed aside by his men soon. Snagging a crystal shard, I grip the sharp piece, raising it high above Jonathan's face. His eyes bug out, but he doesn't dare move or provoke me.

I don't think I've seen him afraid before. It's a pleasant sight. Empowering. For the first time, I hold the upper hand over him. I'm no longer a petrified teenager, handing over her diagnosis for his perusal.

"Ripley," he splutters. "We're… We're family."

"You were my family," I howl at him. "You were all I had!"

"Stop this!"

"Did you stop those doctors from torturing us? Experimenting on us? Killing without consequence?"

"You can still walk away," he pleads, eyes locked on the shard.

Years of hatred boil into a concentrated poison in my veins. Rage has been injected into my heart's muscle, pouring fuel on a fire that's long burned within me. The same fire that drove me to avenge Holly's death.

Injustice.

Pure abandonment.

Cruel, senseless fucking grief.

It all stares back at me in his terrified eyes.

I won't allow the world to hurt me ever again. I've given up enough. I don't need Jonathan's threats hanging over me any longer. I'm more than the orphan he beat down with his negligence.

"I don't want to walk away. I'm right where I need to be."

Jonathan bellows when the shard sails towards him. I numbly register that I'm screaming as I slam the pointed tip into the side of his throat, just below his jawline.

The glass easily tears through his flesh, parting skin and muscle like it's little more than butter left out on a summer's day. It buries deep inside him, slicing vital arteries, and I know I've paid the final price.

My soul.

It's truly broken now.

Pulling the weapon free from his throat, blood squirts from the wound and splashes all over my face. Beneath me, Jonathan's eyes are wide as saucers, a crimson spill pouring from him at an astonishing speed.

Still straddling his chest, I relax my hand, letting the crystal shard hit the carpet. Watching the life rush from him, taking with it a man who did nothing but hate the child he was supposed to love.

"You didn't silence me." I stare into his petrified eyes. "You just made me desperate. I'll never let you take my voice from me again. *Never.*"

Jonathan tries to clamp down on his throat to staunch the blood, but it's futile. I easily capture his wrist and pin it above him, stopping his efforts to save himself. I want to watch him die.

The guilt never comes.

Not as the light inside him begins to dim. Nor as the last remaining member of my family slowly fades before me, growing weaker with each second blood gushes from his neck wound.

He isn't my family.

Not anymore.

This monster doesn't deserve that title.

"You fucking lunatic!"

Movement over my shoulder is the only warning I get before Elon launches himself at me. I'm tackled to the side, thrown off Jonathan. We roll together in between the leather seats.

"Goddammit!" Elon's spittle wets my face.

Plastering on a smile that hopefully rivals his, I'm caught underneath him. "Did I foil your great retirement plan?"

"You killed him. Your own fucking relative!"

"No!" I screech back. "I killed a stranger!"

Surging my head forward, I slam my forehead into his face. Elon yelps in pain, knocked off kilter by the hard blow that reignites my head wound. Before I can launch another attack, he lands a fast punch to the cheek.

The strike makes my teeth grind together, metallic blood bursting on my tongue when I accidentally bite down. I turn feral, bucking against his body and acting on pure instinct.

"Help me restrain her!" Elon roars over his shoulder.

Yet no backup comes.

When his men fail to make a reappearance after several long moments, he hisses in frustration, attempting to pin my wrists above my head so I can stop trying to claw his face.

"Stay still, whore!"

I'm pinned on the carpet, running low on viable options. I don't have the strength to buck him off or attempt another head butt. The glass shard is out of reach beside my uncle's still-gurgling body.

"I should've snapped your fucking neck when I had the chance." Elon's neck is mottled with red spots, a sheen of sweat shimmering above his lip.

"You should have," I snarl back.

"You've ruined everything!"

Bullets spray against the side of the jet, causing him to startle. He releases one wrist, trying to reach for his weapon. The split-second opening allows me to lash out, aiming my nails towards his eyes.

I don't have time to hesitate. It's a last ditch move. A final, desperate act. My fingers connect with his eye sockets and begin digging, tearing through wet mulch.

The wails that spill from his mouth feel like they're going to shatter my eardrums. I push past my revulsion, scratching deeply until blood soaks into my fingertips.

Oh, how he screams.

So fucking gloriously.

Elon clasps his hands over his bleeding face and falls backwards. I wipe my fingers off, ignoring the ruckus echoing from outside. Bullets have been replaced by stern shouting.

I'm hardly able to stand, bracing myself on a nearby seat. Elon lays flat on his back, writhing in pain. Too exhausted to smile, I loom over him, debating whether to slit his throat from ear to ear.

"People like you are the reason evil exists." I boot him in the stomach as hard as I can. "You enable it. Profit from it. Fucking create it. All from the sidelines."

A strangled howl is his only defence.

"I could kill you, but when the dust settles, the world will forget. You'll be wiped away. And I need everyone to remember what happens to snakes who profit from others' pain."

Curled up like a despicable worm, it's hard to imagine how this man spent a year taunting me. Forcing me to push product and hurt everyone around me. Ferrying innocent lives down to Craven and Harrison to meet their inevitable end.

He's a failure now.

The final pawn to fall.

Falling to my knees, the rush of extreme exhaustion almost drags me under. My adrenaline is waning fast. I have just enough energy to crawl back over to my uncle's body, lying deathly still in a puddle of blood.

His eyes are frozen open, pupils expanded to cavernous pits. Mouth slack. Tongue lolling. Throat gaping open. I reach over to slide his eyes closed, forever silencing his evil.

Footfalls clang against the jet's steps, indicating multiple arrivals. But my muscles can't hold out any longer. I lower my head to Jonathan's shirt-clad chest, forehead resting above his still heart.

That's how Sabre finds me.

Bloodied and limp.

"I'm sure I'll meet you in hell someday, Uncle Jonathan," I whisper into his chest as my strength wanes. "Hold the gates open for me."

CHAPTER 28
LENNOX
SPEYSIDE – BON IVER

THE INSCRIBED military dog tags weigh heavy in my hands, tossed from palm to palm. Back and forth. Over and over. The nervous tic mirrors my rapid heartbeat. I need something to focus on while we wait.

Sitting opposite me in a shitty hospital chair, Raine fiddles with the Velcro brace that encases his wrist. He's lucky to have escaped the wreck with minor injuries, mostly cuts and deep-purple bruises.

We were partially shielded in the back, leaving the front seats to take the worst of the impact. By the time I roused after being knocked unconscious, Xander was unresponsive. Warner screaming in pain. Raine yelling for help.

And Ripley… was gone.

All I felt was pure fucking terror.

The same terror that sunk into me and set up shop the day I found my sister's corpse. Blue and lifeless. I was too late to save her. Trapped in the back of that SUV, I couldn't save my family from this either.

The terror didn't abate even when we were cut from the twisted, smoking wreckage and blue-lighted to the nearest hospital. Nor did it ease when a still-unconscious Xander was rushed away to receive a CT scan.

"I hate this," Raine grouses, snapping the Velcro strap back into place. "We should be in there."

"We're not family, Raine."

"Bullshit! We are!"

As much as I agree with him, my last conversation with the medical team resulted in them offering to call the police to have me thrown out on the street. Apparently, violent threats aren't acceptable in hospitals.

Who knew?

We both fidget and stew until the sour-faced ward manager, Doctor Kilton, eventually makes a reappearance. He's a miserable fucker, far too old to still be working the midnight shift in a chaotic place like this.

My bones protest as I tap Raine's shoulder then rush to stand, tucking the dog tags into my pocket. Countless scratches, sore scrapes and bruises make my movements stiff. Raine stretches out the cheap blue stick the hospital lent him.

"Well?" I demand.

Doctor Kilton huffs at my sharp tone. "She's awake and ready for visitors."

"We should've been in there hours ago," Raine snaps at him.

"You are not listed as next of kin."

"Because she has none!" I try to retain a sense of calm. "Just take us to Ripley."

Waving tiredly, the weary doctor leads the way into the mixed ward. We both raced to the ward as fast as our battered bodies would allow when news of Ripley's arrival by helicopter filtered down to us.

We're escorted past several occupied rooms, accompanied by the sound of beeping machines and nurses bustling all around. It's a busy emergency department, taking the most severe triages from across London.

Doctor Kilton gestures towards the final room. "In there."

I don't bother to thank the old bastard. He could've bent the rules for us hours ago. We all know Ripley has no relatives or emergency contacts to call. He was just deliberately being difficult.

"You want to go first?" Raine asks me.

I snag his arm. "Together. Come on."

The frosted glass door clicks open, granting us access to a private booth. Hearing a fluttering heart rate monitor causes me to stride faster with Raine in tow beside me. We quickly round the corner to enter the room.

That's when the terror dissipates.

At last.

Sitting upright in a wide hospital bed, Ripley's propped up on several fluffy pillows. She watches us run in through one eye, the other blackened and swollen to the point of being closed shut.

Like us, she's covered in cuts and scrapes from the car crash, the deeper ones closed with stark white strips. I survey her body, searching for any other injuries. She's pale and rumpled, her septum piercing off-kilter, but she looks whole.

"Lennox. Raine."

"Rip," I gasp.

We both stop at her bedside, searching for anywhere to touch her. Raine finds one of her hands while I feather kisses across her mouth and face. Ripley's here. Safe. Alive. Fucking breathing.

We made it.

The sound of her crying reaches into my chest and rips out what's left untouched inside. There isn't much of me she hasn't sunk her claws into, but I'll happily surrender the rest to her now for the relief she's giving me.

"Oh god," Ripley hiccups, her face burying in Raine's chest. "You're both okay."

"Us?" I look at her quizzically. "What about you? Fuck, Rip. You were kidnapped!"

"I thought you were all dead."

She's sobbing, hands fisting Raine's shirt.

"We thought you would be too!"

Stroking her hair, Raine plants kisses on top of her head. "Nobody is dead. Everyone take a breath. We're all here safe."

Jolting in his arms, Ripley pulls back to look around behind us. The frenzied look in her one working eye matches how we've been feeling for the last fifteen hours, waiting for any updates from Sabre's teams.

They tracked us down as soon as emergency services attended the crash, assuming jurisdiction to prevent any further public spectacles. By then, Ripley was already gone. They were too late.

"Xander?" Her head hurriedly swings back to me.

"Hush," Raine soothes, still stroking her hair. "He's fine, Rip. Just had some sense knocked into him."

"What? Where is he?"

"A couple of floors above us being fussed over by nurses he keeps threatening to stab." I smile broadly. "Slight skull fracture, but unfortunately, still alive."

Tears well up and streak down her bruised cheeks, causing me so much fucking pain, I don't think I can take it. I gently ease her from Raine's arms to swipe the moisture away.

"It's okay, baby. We're all fine."

"I was so scared, Nox."

"I know. I'm so fucking sorry, Rip." The apology spills out of me in a jumbled rush. "I hate that you were taken from us."

Ripley's breath shudders, causing her gown-covered body to shake between us. We both sandwich her closer, offering gentle reassurances and touching her wherever possible.

It's a while before she can suck in a full, unobstructed breath again. The machine she's wired up to eventually calms, her heartbeat evening out and returning to a healthier, only slightly elevated rate.

"Are you hurt?" I study the fluids hanging above her bed.

Ripley leans back to shake her head. "Elon was injecting me with some drug cocktail. The doctors are just making sure it's all flushed from my system. I was pretty dehydrated too."

"Any other injuries?" Raine frets.

"Concussion." She winces at the sight of her bandaged wrists. "And rubbed myself raw trying to escape the shackles Elon put me in. No permanent damage."

"I can't believe he took you to Harrowdean." White-hot anger is a bitter weight inside me, causing my body to tense up. "What a fucking nut job."

"You heard?" Ripley glances up.

"The Anaconda team debriefed us," Raine explains, sitting on the bed. "They're the ones who caught up to you. Ethan, Becket and apparently some big, scary dude called Hyland from another team."

"Those were Enzo's words," I point out.

"Isn't he big and scary?" He laughs.

"I'm not answering that, Raine."

"That's a yes. You were intimidated."

"I was not!"

Ripley smiles, sinking into the pillows. "I don't remember any of that. I was fading fast by then."

Trying to gauge her mental state, I decide to rip the Band-Aid off. "Your uncle is dead, Rip."

"I know." She screws her eyes shut. "I... I killed him."

"It was you?" Raine arches a blonde brow.

"Yes. I stabbed him."

We're both silent for several seconds, processing the confirmation of what we suspected. The description of the crime scene on that private jet, mere seconds from taking off, didn't leave many other explanations.

I still wasn't sure she had it in her. Ripley is many things, but I know she's never taken a life before. Even if she's ruined plenty of them. Taking that step extracts a different kind of mental toll.

She shakes her head, bloodshot eyes flicking back open. "He wanted to keep me drugged up like some kind of zombie prisoner. I had no choice."

Raine clutches her hand tight. "You did what you had to."

"Does that make it right?" Her bottom lip wobbles.

"No," I reply honestly. "It makes it necessary."

"I've justified a lot these past couple years using that line." Ripley sighs with what appears to be bone-deep exhaustion. "I don't think I want to be that person anymore."

"We're free," Raine reminds her. "You can be whoever you want to be now."

"It's really over?"

I take her other hand, careful not to disturb the IV line feeding into it. "The investigation will rumble on, and we'll still have to cooperate… but the corporation is being dismantled."

"The institutes are all closing," Raine adds with a hopeful smile. "Everyone will be transferred to real facilities. No more experiments."

The back of my throat burns. Honestly, we haven't had time to process the news. Not while anxiously waiting for updates. There's still so much to be uncovered, but this is the first step towards eradicating Incendia's rule.

I'm not stupid enough to believe we'll be left in peace. Not after the deals we've all signed to act as informants to avoid any prosecution for our actions. Freedom has come at a steep cost.

"What about Elon?" She swallows hard.

"Alive," I answer. "Not sure he'll ever see again, though. He's been remanded into custody along with his men and countless others."

A relieved breath whooshes out of her. "Good."

"Did you really gouge his eyes out?" Raine scrunches his nose up.

"Um, a little bit."

"Damn. I feel like I shouldn't approve of that, you know?" He gestures to his own honeyed eyes. "But honestly, if anyone deserves to suffer, it's that son of a bitch."

"Seconded," I grumble.

"I half-expected it to be the police when you guys walked in," Ripley admits, chewing her bottom lip. "What's going to happen to me?"

Raine shrugs. "Jonathan's death was self-defence."

"With no witnesses?" she challenges.

"You've got a massive black eye, a concussion and were kidnapped after a hit and run," I list off. "I don't think there's a court in the world that would prosecute after all that."

"Fair point."

"Enzo says we're all free to go as long as we hold up our end of the deal." Raine caresses her bruised knuckles. "We won't be transferred with the other patients or taken back into custody."

"Fuck." She looks up at me, a glimmer of hope in her one good eye. "Seriously?"

"Seriously. The SCU will honour their word."

"We really are free." Ripley shakes her head. "I can't quite believe it. What now?"

Lifting her hand, Raine presses a kiss on it. "You remember that future we talked about?"

I look between them, eyebrows raised.

"It rings a bell," Ripley hedges.

"Well... perhaps it can be more than a far-off dream now."

"Am I allowed to ask about this inside joke?" I nudge Raine's shoulder playfully.

"Not an inside joke." Raine tilts his head in my direction. "I told Ripley that when this is all over, we'll follow her wherever she wants to go."

"Xander and Lennox may not want that." Ripley looks down at her legs, covered by the thin hospital sheet.

Aghast, I stare at the most insane woman I've ever met. The vengeful bitch who jeopardised our lives. Instigated our torture. Stole our power. Then... our fucking hearts too.

"Nox?" Raine sighs. "Help me out here."

"I'm struggling myself."

"Then use your words! Fucking hell."

Releasing Ripley's hand, he picks up his new guide stick and walks away from the bed to give us a moment. I wait for him to tap his way to the window, weighing up my words.

For a moment, I just look at her. The one person I never expected to feel something so incredibly strong for beyond stone-cold hatred. For so long, I fucking loathed her.

My eyes catch on the black bracelet still secured around her wrist, above the bandages covering where she must have been shackled. Again. This time without me there to hold her close.

Fuck.

We almost lost her.

I can't lose her ever again.

"We had an unconventional journey to get here, didn't we?"

She chuckles under her breath. "Is that what we're calling it?"

"Sure."

"Then I guess we did."

"Six months ago, I never would've thought we'd be here. I had every intention of paying you back for the pain and torment you put us through. I wanted you dead, Rip."

"I'm aware."

I lick my lips, searching for the right words. "But I wouldn't change any of it. Do you know why?"

Ripley meets my gaze through one open eye. "Yeah, I think I do."

"Then you know what I'm about to say. All that grief, trauma, unthinkable torture… it led me here. To this crossroad. Staring at the most incredible woman in this fucked up world."

My voice has turned raspy, forcing me to stop for a breath. I'll scream in her face until I'm hoarse if that's what it takes for her to hear me. To believe what I know to be true deep in my soul.

"A woman I love," I add emotionally. "And who I hope will let me join her on this future train she's taking far away from all this heartache. If she'll have me."

"How could you even doubt it?" Her tears overflow, making her bruises shine. "You know I love you, Nox. Our future is what all this has been for."

"Then I guess I'm following you, baby."

Hands braced on the bed, I lean in to press a kiss onto her lips. Ripley responds fervently, proving her words with mere touch alone. There's no lie in the way she kisses me like I'm her life support machine.

Little does she know… she's mine. Always has been. Even when we despised each other and traded blows from afar, both determined to eradicate the other. That hatred kept me alive so I could love her to death now.

"Where are we going, anyway?" I laugh into her lips.

"You have a preference?"

"I don't exactly have a home to go back to. Hell, none of us do."

"I suppose we can figure it all out," Ripley decides with a tiny, hope-filled smile. "We've got our whole lives ahead of us."

Turning away from the window, Raine taps a path back over to us. "Now that's taken care of... how about a snack? I'm fucking starving."

"I saw a vending machine down the corridor." I consider him. "Need help reading the buttons?"

"Nah." Raine waves me off. "I'll leave it to chance."

Ripley snags his arm before he can leave. "Wait. How did Sabre find me so fast? Elon changed vehicles like a thousand times."

A hot, guilty flush creeps up my neck. I roll and pucker my lips, unable to provide an immediate response. Raine looks like he wants to laugh. He's barely holding it back.

"What?" She frowns at us both.

"Yeah, Nox. What?" Raine breaks out in laughter.

I rub the back of my neck. "Look, if we hadn't done it... We never would've gotten you back. Remember that."

"Done what?" Ripley asks suspiciously.

"It was just a precaution... Sabre helped set it up! Blame them!"

Chortling, Raine squeezes his stick between his hands. "Oh, this'll be good."

"And it came from a place of love," I add, feeling my panic spiral. "Nothing else."

"Seriously, Nox. What the fuck?"

My eyes skid back down to her bracelet. The one we gave her on our impromptu date. She looked so confused when Xander handed it over out of the blue.

I clear my throat. "Ahem. There's... erm, a tracker in your bracelet."

Ripley is silent for several seconds. It seems to stretch on endlessly. I'm preparing my escape plan before she can throttle me with her IV line when she finally spits out a response.

"You gave me a fucking tracking device as a fake gift?"

"Technically, it was a real gift," Raine jumps in. "And for the record, I knew nothing about it. All I suggested was flowers or something."

"Oh, let me guess!" she shouts in a rage. "I know exactly who's goddamn idea this—"

Click.

The door to her room swooshes open. Wheels roll across the tacky linoleum, preceding the appearance of a chair being pushed by an aggravated-looking orderly.

His ghostly face set in a scowl, Xander is seated in the wheelchair, demanding his carer hurries up. When they round the corner, his tired midnight eyes snap over to us.

The doctors decided that surgery wasn't required after his emergency CT scan showed a hairline fracture in his upper skull from the wreck. Much to our collective relief. Xander simply bitched about being kept on the ward against his wishes.

Before he can say a word, Ripley points a finger at him.

"You! Xander fucking Beck! What kind of psychopath gives his girl a damn concealed tracker on their first official date?"

Thin lips pressed together, he turns to look up at the orderly. "Turn me around and run, would you?"

The middle-aged woman snickers, parking him up right next to me.

"You've dug your hole, son. I could use a break from your complaining while she rips you a new one."

CHAPTER 29
RIPLEY
VIOLET HILL – COLDPLAY

AN OBNOXIOUSLY LARGE bunch of sunflowers clasped in my hands, I follow the signs to the male ward. I left Lennox and Raine in Xander's room while his discharge papers are signed and went on a hunt for flowers.

I know I'm in the right place when I spot two familiar figures outside a hospital room, both with crossed arms and hard scowls. Neither look like they've slept in days.

Ethan sees me first, arms dropping so he can wave. "Ripley?"

I adjust the flowers in my arms. "Hi."

At the sound of my name, Enzo straightens. I expected the rest of the Anaconda team to be here, but from what I understand, the whole of Sabre Security is facing months of evidence collection and investigating. They must be overwhelmed.

"Hey, guys."

"What are you doing here?" Enzo looks over me.

"Here to see the patient."

"It's good to see you in one piece." He smiles reassuringly. "Been discharged?"

"Not with a clean bill of health, but yes. I'm free to leave."

"You need a ride somewhere?" Ethan offers.

"Are you still our protection detail?"

"For the time being. While the investigation is ongoing, you'll have security."

Unease filters into my bloodstream. "Are we still in danger?"

"The main threats have been eliminated. We believe you're safe."

"Consider it a precaution," Enzo adds with a wink. "We're already working with the authorities to round up suspects based on your evidence."

"I'm not taking any more risks after what happened." I glance between them, offering a genuine smile. "So thank you."

"You gave us a scare," Ethan admits. "The car wreck was a complete disaster. And finding you passed out on that damn jet shaved ten years off my life."

"Sorry?" I pose it as a question.

"It's us who should be apologising. I'm sorry it took us so long to get to you."

"Apparently, I have the guys to thank for my rescue." Cool metal slides along my arm, reminding me of the bracelet I'm still wearing. "But thanks for coming to get me."

"Sure thing."

"Is Warner awake? Lennox told me he's here. I want to see him before we leave."

Enzo rolls his shoulders, working out the tension. "He's pretty heavily drugged right now. His surgery is scheduled for the morning."

"Surgery?" Anxiety explodes inside me.

Looking down at his feet, Ethan flinches. "His leg was crushed in the wreck. It cut off the blood circulation. The doctors have tried all they can to save it, but…"

"No," I whisper, horrified.

"It'll have to be amputated," Enzo finishes. "There's nothing else they can do."

"Shit. I'm so—"

"Don't apologise." Ethan cuts me off. "This isn't your fault. We understand the risks in this business, Ripley."

"Still, his leg?"

"He'll recover and live. Nothing else matters now. In time, he can return to work if he wishes."

Throat thick, I can't find anything else to say. I hitch the flowers higher in my arms and give them both nods. Ethan holds the door open for me to step inside the room filled with ticking machines.

Warner rests in a bed on the far side of the room, surrounded by countless machines. He's hooked up to several monitors with bags of sedatives and pain relief suspended from a hook above him.

I quietly pad closer, placing the sunflowers on the folding table pushed away from his bed. Above the crisp, white sheets, his injured leg is secured in a brace, holding the doomed limb prone.

It's hard to see through the stitched cuts and grazes that cover his face. I didn't recognise myself when I stumbled to the bathroom to shower, but Warner looks even worse. He took the brunt of the hit.

"Hey." I lightly touch his arm, scared to hurt him. "It's Ripley."

His eyes don't open.

"God, I'm so sorry." Guilt strangles my lungs. "All you wanted to do was help us. If you hadn't come to the apartment... I don't know if we'd still be alive. And look what thanks you get."

Beep. Beep. Beep.

"I heard about the surgery. We're all going to be here when you wake up, okay? I promise we'll help you through this. Just like you helped us."

Adjusting the covers, I smooth the wrinkles out, making sure he's securely tucked in. There's a stray lock of hair hanging in his closed eye, the dark-brown hue stark against his sickly pallor.

I swipe the hair away, pushing it back from his face. "Thank you for being my friend. Even when I was hurtful to you and determined to make it on my own. You didn't have to care about me."

Beep. Beep. Beep.

"I have the chance for a life now. I'm hoping you'll be a part of it. I could use a friend."

Determined not to start crying again, I take one last look at his face. For a whole year in Harrowdean, I took Warner for granted. Even when he did his best to provide the help I desperately needed.

I'll never do that again.

I'm not afraid to care now.

Connections are what make us strong, and if he wants a friend, I'll spend forever repaying him for doing his best to help. That's the kind of person I want to be. Not someone who hurts others for selfish means.

Someone who helps.

The kind of person my parents would be proud of.

―――

"Stop here."

Pressing the brakes, Ethan pulls up at the curb. Aside from taking a phone call from his long-distance boyfriend in some faraway town, he's been silent the entire ride into Hackney.

I look over my shoulder. "You guys okay?"

Xander, Lennox and Raine are all seated in the back of Ethan's car. We're all a sorry sight, wearing donated clothes from the hospital, our bodies bearing the marks of all we've endured.

"Tired." Raine smiles sleepily.

"Cramped," Xander grouses.

Lennox elbows him. "Stop moaning."

"Ow. I'm injured."

"I'll give you a fucking injury if you complain one more time."

"Get him, Nox." Raine yawns.

Convincing them to get back in an SUV took some pleading on Ethan's part. I was busy fighting my own internal battle after making the decision that we would return to my home for now.

None of us have another place to go. It was this or a hotel. I have money tied up in various accounts, but Uncle Jonathan took charge of my affairs when I was shipped off to Priory Lane. I don't even know where my purse is.

"I called Theo," Ethan informs me. "He sent a team in to fit new locks and check the place for anything Jonathan may have installed. It's clear. You should be able to get in."

"Thank you."

"Pretty sure he also installed a security system with CCTV cameras." He casts me an unrepentant grin. "Sorry."

"Am I going to have secret agents turning up at my door every time someone dodgy walks past?"

"I'll keep them in check. Don't worry."

Placing my hand over his, I squeeze tight. "Thanks for everything."

"I'll be back tomorrow to take you all into HQ to be debriefed."

"Got it."

Ethan nods. "Theo told me he had the team leave a couple phones inside from the company stash. My number is programmed in if you need anything."

"Is this dude giving Ripley his number?" Lennox murmurs.

Raine huffs. "Did you miss him flirting with a guy on the phone?"

"Irrelevant," Xander quips. "Can I rip his spine out of his throat?"

I turn around in my seat to scowl at him. "Xander! Jesus!"

He tilts his head, deadly serious. "Is that a yes?"

"No!"

"Too bad." Shrugging, he glares at Ethan. "Well, the offer stands."

"Ripping out people's spines is not a proportionate response in any circumstance, and most certainly not when Ethan is trying to help us."

"See that's where we disagree," he deadpans.

Popping the door open, I clamber out before he can threaten to kill anyone else. The guys all follow with Lennox helping Xander to straighten. Ethan offers us a wave then pulls away from the curb.

With a calming breath in, I turn to face my building. It's an old, converted warehouse, swept up in London's gentrification. I bought it when I moved out, so I've owned the loft apartment for several years now.

"Home." I wave awkwardly. "Top floor."

"This is your flat?" Lennox asks, surprised.

"Yeah, there's an art studio combined with the living space. And I have a spare bedroom. Should be enough space for us all."

Leading the way up the slick stone path, the entry door swings open after I tap in the security code. Thankfully, it hasn't changed. Climbing the concrete stairwell proves to be a challenge for all of us.

As promised, my front door is unlocked, fitted with shiny new locks and a blinking camera strategically placed outside. I hesitate before pushing it open, feeling a sense of trepidation.

"What is it?" Xander drops a hand on my shoulder.

"I just… I'm not the person I was when I lived here. I don't know who I'm coming back as now."

"You're still you, little toy."

"Am I?"

His nimble fingers sink into me, providing a reassuring pressure. "Sure. Perhaps just a little rougher around the edges. A bit more scarred. But also a hell of a lot stronger."

Twisting my head, I look up at him. "I lived here alone for a long time. I'm coming back with something else too. Three something elses."

"That a problem?" His mouth hooks up.

"No." My hand moves to rest on top of his. "I love you, Xander. I want you to know that even if you can't say it back."

His star-speckled, navy eyes flick over mine. Considering. Processing.

We've come a long way, but I know he's still learning to let people in. I don't expect him to return the sentiment.

"My chest feels strange when I'm with you," he rumbles. "It has for a while. Is that what this feeling is, Rip? Love?"

"Is that what you think it is?"

Xander peers away, his bottom lip clamped between his teeth. "I'm not sure. I haven't felt it before."

I look briefly at the other two. "Does your chest feel like that when you think about Lennox or Raine?"

"Yes." He clears his throat. "But in a different way. They're my brothers."

"Because you care about them."

"Yes."

As much as I want to drag the words out of him, I leave Xander with that realisation. His mind takes time to pick the world apart and translate it into terms he can understand. I trust that he'll get there.

Pushing open the apartment door, my nose wrinkles at the stench of thick dust and disuse. A massive pile of unanswered mail has been neatly stacked on the console next to the front door by whoever checked the place over.

The guys tentatively follow me into the vast, open plan space. Vaulted ceilings stretch all the way to the rafters, lined with huge steel beams. Light spills in through floor-length windows built into the brick.

I divided the space into two—living on the right side with the two bedrooms, a shared bathroom, glistening steel kitchen and restored, antique dining table. It's all still the same beneath inches of dust.

On the left, my studio space is separated by rows of drying racks and a bookshelf full of art books. Years worth of old canvases are stacked in piles, exactly how I left them.

"Bedrooms are over there." I gesture to the right. "I've no idea how clean any of the linens or towels will be."

"How did you pay the bills?" Lennox queries.

"I'd accumulated enough from selling art over the years." Dust particles tickle my nostrils. "Everything gets paid automatically each month so I knew the place would be okay while I was gone."

Leaving them to explore, I walk into the living area. Behind the table, I have a smattering of different coloured armchairs, all thrifted from my local antique dealer. I've always loved objects with history.

At the console table next to one of the windows, I flick on the

Tiffany lamp, illuminating a collection of framed photographs I kept on display. My parents' wedding photo. A shot of me, all red and scrunched up, swaddled in my dad's arms.

The final frame holds one of me and Uncle Jonathan—my graduation from art school. I wore my robe with my hard-earned diploma clasped in my hands. But I can see the strain behind my practised smile.

It fucking hurts to look at him now. Younger but still immaculate in his charcoal suit and blue tie. Those same clear eyes, filled with schemes and secrets. I was still trying to please him back then.

Lifting the frame, I throw it at the brick wall and watch in satisfaction as it shatters. The smashed glass hits the floor, shredding the photo imprisoned inside.

"Ripley?"

"I'm fine!" I call back.

Someone stops behind me, breathing hard. I feel arms wrap around me, a firm chest pressing into my back. Spearmint washes over me, a refreshing comfort in all the stale air.

"Didn't like that one?" Xander whispers.

"No. Not anymore."

His lips press into the side of my head, cool and dry. Every clenched muscle relaxes at the feel of Xander holding me. Pulling me back to the present, where that man can no longer dictate my life.

"My chest hurts again," he murmurs. "I think I love you."

Laughter spills out of me.

"Fuck. Hell of a way to declare it, Xan."

"Want me to take it back?"

Pulling his wrists, I turn in his arms so I can see him. My swollen eye is still a badly bruised mess, but I don't need twenty-twenty vision to recognise the jagged angles and alabaster skin I've memorised.

"No," I whisper.

His mouth is drawn to mine, landing softer than I expected. The kiss is everything Xander isn't. Gentle. Tentative. Exploratory. All the traits I couldn't possibly ascribe to the man who thinks it's perfectly acceptable to gift me a tracking device.

I don't give a fuck, though.

Xander is perfect the way he is.

I'm so wrapped up in his lips, it takes Lennox shouting our names several times for us to separate. There's an odd ringing emanating throughout the apartment. Taking Xander's hand, I walk over to the front door.

The security system that Theo had his men install is demanding my attention. Next to the door, a small screen has been installed, offering me a view of the outside pavement and our floor.

"Someone pressed the buzzer." I study the image. "Do you think it was a mistake?"

Xander leans closer to study the four men standing outside the apartment building, all carrying shopping bags. His finger hovers over one—tall, raven-haired and radiating danger.

"That's Hudson Knight. He was in HQ when we first went. I saw him in the corridor afterwards."

"The Blackwood inmate?" Raine asks behind us.

"Wait, I recognise him too." My attention narrows on the guy wearing a pressed shirt and glasses, his pearly-blonde hair slicked back. "He was on those tapes that got leaked."

"Kade Knight," Lennox supplies. "Brothers, I believe."

"What are they doing here? Who are the other two?"

Jabbing his finger on the intercom, Xander offers a friendly greeting. "This isn't Blackwood. Fuck off."

"Smooth," Raine mutters.

The preppy-looking one, Kade, steps up to answer. "Uh, hello. This is a bit weird, but I kinda swiped this address from Theo's computer while he was busy."

My eyebrows feel like they've met my damn hairline.

"We just want to chat," he rushes to add. "Nothing sinister. This is my brother, Hudson, and our friends, Eli and Phoenix. We're unarmed and come in peace."

"What the fuck?" Lennox whispers. "Is this a joke?"

"He seems genuine."

"I don't trust genuine," Xander replies, hitting the speak button again. "Why are you here?"

"We have a peace offering." Kade lifts the white, plastic bag in his hands. "Thai takeout."

Looking at each other and silently deliberating, we leave them hanging. Hudson seems to say something to his brother, a stormy scowl carving his features as they both turn to face the others. Collectively, the group starts to leave.

I push past Xander to jab the button. "Wait! Come up."

"Ripley," Lennox hisses.

Ignoring his protest, I press to give them access to the building.

"Okay, then." Raine jostles on his feet.

The guys disappear from the camera as they walk inside. Lennox and Xander are both bitching while I wait for them to reappear on the second camera outside. They appear before a knock echoes on the door.

"Ripley," Xander warns.

Ignoring him, I pull the door open. Two friendly hazel orbs meet mine. Kade can't be much younger than us, though the dark circles beneath his black-framed glasses seem to age him.

"Hi."

"Hello," I reply timidly.

"Kade." He gives an awkward wave. "From the intercom."

Xander's shoulder pushes into mine, forcing his way in front of me. "Can we help you?"

A pierced, black brow cocked, Hudson gestures to the takeout his brother is holding. "We brought dinner."

"Why?" Lennox barks.

There's a snort from the blue-haired guy behind them, holding the hand of the fourth member, who avoids looking at us altogether.

"This is going about as well as expected."

"Phoenix," Kade scolds before turning his attention back to us. "You don't know us, but we've heard about your stories. You've probably heard some of ours. I figured we should all meet."

Looking between them, I'm filled with confusion. "What about... uh, Brooklyn? Brooklyn West?"

The silent, curly-haired one at the back flinches. That must be Eli. He's staring down at his shoes, a pair of ancient-looking Chucks, and seems deliberately secluded from the world around him.

When he finally looks up and I get a full view of his startling, rich-green eyes, I know he's hurting. Whatever they've been through to get here, it's left them battered and scarred. Just like us.

I offer him a tentative smile.

After a beat, Eli smiles back.

Phoenix is holding his hand in a white-knuckled grip. The pair seem glued at the hip. By comparison, Hudson and Kade feel like the team leaders, both standing shoulder-to-shoulder.

"She isn't with us." Hudson's stubbled throat bobs. "It's kind of a long story."

Nodding, I hold the door open for them.

"We've got nothing but time."

EPILOGUE

WHEN WILL WE BE FREE? – YOUNG LIONS

XANDER

Present Day

With Ripley's parting words describing that first encounter over Thai food, the documentary credits roll. I close my laptop, leaning back on the bed to blow out the breath it feels like I've held for an eternity.

The full, unfiltered truth is out there now.

Being seen is an odd thing.

Perhaps one of the most divisive opinions among humans. Some will sacrifice everything for the chance to be heard. For the world to know their name. No price is too high for fame.

Then there are those who stick to the shadows. Who thrive on invisibility. Striving to be forgotten by the sands of time. History erases us all in the end, but some make it their mission to expedite that process.

I never cared strongly enough about either before. Other people's opinions weren't exactly my concern—not when I lacked the emotions to care about their scorn or praise. I simply lived for the next thrill, the endless chase for the most exquisite pain.

Life looks a little different now.

I can't say I regret the road that led me here.

Stashing the laptop in the cluttered desk drawer, I catch sight of the faded military dog tags stuffed at the very back. Lennox never did quite summon the strength to toss them, but he hasn't searched for them in years.

He doesn't need that reminder anymore.

His family is right here in front of him.

Walking into our spacious living area, the three mismatched sofas we soon replaced Ripley's sparse armchairs with are fully occupied. Phoenix and Eli dominate one, trading whispers with their fingers intwined on their crossed legs.

Everyone arrived while I poured over my laptop, unable to stand another second without answers. None of the others wanted to watch with me. Not even Ripley.

"You know, Kade's winning the best husband contest," Eli grouses, his gaze fixed on the TV. "We need to outsmart him."

"How?" Phoenix moans.

"We get the others to have Logan and take Brooklyn out for sushi. You know it's her weakness."

"You hate sushi, Eli."

The green-eyed recluse shrugs. "I'll grin and bear it for her."

"We should rope in Jude when he finishes work. He can help us conspire."

"Late shift tonight," Eli replies. "He'll be a while yet."

Casting my gaze around, I spot Raine plucking the violin in his lap while sitting with Hunter, his younger brother, Leighton, and Theo. The men have a warm, healthy glow from their time in the Australian sunshine. It's rare that we see them.

They're back visiting England with Enzo and their newly minted fiancée, Harlow. The past decade since Sabre's business exploded after Incendia was a bit complicated. They went through hell, but that's a whole other tale.

"Come visit us after your concert in Melbourne?" Hunter suggests, a tumbler full of whiskey in hand. "We'll put the four of you up for a couple weeks."

"Oh, awesome." Raine adjusts his rounded, black lenses. "I've got another show in Sydney the week after. I can get you all backstage passes if you want?"

Theo fiddles with his phone, engrossed in something. "Anywhere away from the crowds would be great."

"Consider it done."

"Xan?" Raine's head cocks, his nostrils flaring. "I know you're standing there. Can you get time off from work?"

"Haven't exactly got a boss to answer to while I'm freelancing," I reply easily. "As long as no major projects come in, it should be fine."

"You can code software on an aeroplane, Xan. Just say yes."

Sighing, I decide to humour him. "Yes, Raine."

"Perfect!" He grins broadly.

Turning away from them, I head for the kitchen where Lennox is arm-wrestling Hudson and failing miserably. Who the hell would challenge that massive oaf? It's giving Enzo and Kade some decent entertainment, though.

"Prepare to pay up," Kade boasts.

Glowering, Enzo watches them intently. "Never gonna happen."

"Double or nothing?"

Clasping his hand, Enzo shakes firmly. "You're on. Hudson's got this."

I halt while passing. "Did you bet against your own brother?"

Kade shrugs, unrepentant. "Hudson needs his ego checked every once in a while."

"Heard that!" the man in question grunts. "Fuck, dude. How are you so strong?"

"It helps to own a gym." Lennox strains to hold his position. "I have to look the part."

"I've got twenty on Lennox," I declare.

He flashes me a smirk. "Is that a vote of confidence? I'm flattered, Xan."

"Don't get cocky."

It's only another thirty seconds before I lose the bet. Hudson slams Lennox's arm down into the kitchen counter, much to his chagrin. With a series of imaginative curses, Lennox concedes defeat.

"How?"

Hudson grins smugly. "Wait until you're chasing around after a kid all day long. It does wonders for your stamina."

"Not sure that it's on the cards for us." Lennox chuckles, taking his hand to shake. "So I'll take your word for it. Good match."

"Come on then, Hud." Enzo takes a seat at the counter. "Let's see how you fare against a pro."

Hudson rolls his eyes. "Whatever, old man."

"Less of that. I'm in my prime."

Lingering against the stove, I watch the next few rounds. Hudson loses his winning streak. A short-lived challenge by Kade only intensifies Enzo's bragging. I decline a match, already certain of the outcome.

"That man's biceps should be fucking illegal." Lennox stops next to me, slurping a beer. "Like, shit. Reckon that's what Australia does to you?"

"Enzo's always been huge."

"Not that huge."

"You should take him down to the gym tomorrow. I'm sure he'd like to see the place."

"You think?" Lennox arches a dark brow.

"Yeah. Last time he was in the country, you were still extending the new weightlifting section."

"That's true." He nods to himself. "Alright, I'll take him."

"Good. Have you seen Ripley and the others?"

Lennox gestures towards the art studio. "Looking at some paintings, I think."

Slapping his shoulder, I head for Ripley's attached studio. These days, it's more like organised chaos. The space gets messy when she's having a bad week and can't stop. That and the times she doesn't have the energy to even move.

When those episodes hit, I come in and reset her workspace for her. We both work from home while Lennox is often at the gym he part-owns, and Raine makes use of a rented studio a few streets over to rehearse in peace for his upcoming tour dates.

Through the drying racks, I can see Ripley standing with Brooklyn and Harlow. Logan, Brooklyn's chubby toddler, bounces on her hip. Both women are a few years younger than Ripley, but they became fast friends.

She learned to love Brooklyn through the friendship we formed with her guys while she was gone. What began with an awkward drop-in and Thai food slowly blossomed through bonding over our similar experiences.

As for Harlow and how she ended up in our extended family, that's a whole other story. But having survived her own ordeal, she slotted into the close dynamic we've all formed over the last decade.

"How do you feel about the documentary airing?" Brooklyn asks.

A finished canvas clutched in her hands, Ripley stares down at the swirls of paint. "I'm glad the footage was salvaged from the memory cards."

"That's not what I asked."

Harlow runs a hand over her shoulder-length ringlets. "It's okay to have mixed feelings. This is a huge step."

"No... I'm relieved." Ripley chooses her words carefully. "I knew I'd never feel at peace until I told our version of events. We never had that closure."

Brooklyn coos over her little boy. "We just want you to be happy, Rip. Even if I didn't do an interview myself, I respect your decision to sit down with the journalist."

"You do?" Ripley glances at her.

"Of course."

"I was a bit worried about your reaction."

"No need to be." Brooklyn flashes her an easy smile. "You have to do what's right for you. We all heal in our own ways. I know I did. You've waited a long time to find your peace."

"I don't know if I've found it yet." Ripley hikes up a curved shoulder. "But this feels pretty damn close. I needed to purge myself of all the things I did back then."

"Are you worried about backlash?" Harlow asks fretfully. "I know firsthand how cruel the media can be."

"You know what? I'm not. What can they possibly do to me that's worse than what we went through?"

After Ripley puts the canvas back in its place, the three women embrace, all squishing Logan between them. He squeals loudly at all the attention. Brooklyn swipes under her silver-grey eyes when she steps back.

"I'm proud of you, Rip."

"Thank you."

Harlow rubs Ripley's arm, a warm smile making the burn scars that cover her neck wrinkle. "The world needs your voice. I'm proud of you for using it."

Letting them all hug again, I wait a second before interrupting.

"For the record, I'm proud too."

Her head lifting, Brooklyn points an angry finger at me. "You! Who the hell sets fire to a damn recording studio?"

Harlow bites her lip while Ripley just smiles exasperatedly. I keep my distance so Brooklyn can't slam her fist into my face. It's happened once or twice. She has the firepower of a fucking nuclear arsenal.

"Erm, me?"

"What were you thinking?" she demands.

"I was... feeling some stuff." I shrug it off. "Lots of stuff."

"Lots of stuff," Brooklyn repeats. "God help you, Ripley. You must have the patience of a saint to deal with this one's emotional vocabulary."

"Says the woman married to five men." Ripley giggles.

"Point taken. Speaking of..."

Winking at me, Brooklyn hoists Logan on her hip then tows Harlow from the studio, giving us some privacy. I linger by the door, feeling uncertain.

I haven't found the words to say since the documentary aired a few days ago. Hell, it took me this long to watch it myself. The backlash has been pretty fucking horrific. We've all had to turn off our phones to stop getting calls and emails.

But did the planet implode when the truth was laid bare for public scrutiny? No. Did armed assailants break our door down to throw us in some off-grid prison for escaped delinquents? Also no. The world did not end.

I can handle some assholes on the internet spouting half-baked opinions about things they'll never understand. They're irrelevant. Frankly, I don't need them to like what we did or even understand it.

All I need is for Ripley to be okay. We coasted for a long time, struggling to find our feet in the aftermath of what we survived. It took a long time to establish a semblance of normality before starting to rebuild our lives.

But she never quite got there. Her artwork has always given her some solace, and for years, I feared it became a cocoon. One she could hide in when the memories and guilt became too much to bear.

She's finally torn down all her barriers.

Ripley has told her truth.

Why did I ever doubt her motivations?

"Xan," she coaxes, a finger crooked. "You can come here."

"Wasn't sure if I'm forgiven or not yet."

"For running away from us to break into an abandoned building? Stalking a journalist? Or attempting to sabotage my interview?"

"All of it?" The words come out as a question.

Ripley rolls her green-brown eyes. "You're forgiven. We all make stupid choices when we're scared, right?"

"Apparently."

I step into her arms, letting my face hide in the crook of her shoulder. Ripley cups my neck, holding me close. She smells the same as always. A fresh, tropical thunderstorm. All things sweet and fruity.

"Thank you for organising this. It feels good to get everyone in the same room."

Abruptly straightening, I check my watch. It's past eight o'clock.

"We're short by a couple, but I've seen to that."

"Huh?" Ripley frowns at me.

"Come and see."

Taking her hand, I pull her from the art studio.

"Xan—"

"Just wait."

Logan is now snuggled up in Eli's lap, eating something he definitely shouldn't be while Brooklyn bemoans her husbands. Enzo has dragged the others in from the kitchen to gather the whole group.

Tucking Ripley into Lennox's side so he can hold onto her, I head for the front door. A flashy company SUV has pulled up outside the building. They're already headed up to us.

I open the door before Warner and Jude can knock. Both look at me in surprise.

"You're late by three minutes."

"Hello to you too," Jude remarks. "Where are my wife and son?"

Gesturing over my shoulder, I wave him in. He slaps me on the back as he passes, pulling off his medical lanyard to tuck it away. Warner follows him in, walking with a new, slight limp.

"You alright?"

He shrugs. "New prosthetic. Had a mishap with the last one."

"Do I even want to know what happened to it?"

"Probably not."

Smiling, I tug him into a hug. "You need to be careful."

"Bullets just seem to like me, Xan."

"Ripley won't buy that bullshit."

Admittedly, it took about six years for us to reach the touching stage. His steadfast presence in Ripley's life cemented my trust for him, though thick-skulled, younger Xander should've appreciated his actions long ago.

"What's kept you so busy?"

Warner releases me. "New client. Bit hard to explain. We're wrapped up in some messy shit."

"Sounds about right."

"We'll handle it." He flicks his hand dismissively. "How did the doc airing go?"

"As expected. We need to give you our new numbers."

He bites back a laugh. "That bad, huh?"

"It'll die down."

Guiding him into the bursting apartment, I watch for Ripley's reaction. Warner is her confidante. They talk regularly, but his work at Sabre pulls him in all directions.

Their most recent case—some complex, human trafficking situation—has led him to be absent since her interview. He had to undertake a long-haul trip to Mexico as part of the ongoing investigation.

"Did I miss the party?" Warner calls out.

Her head snapping up, Ripley turns to gape at us. "You're back!"

"I couldn't miss seeing this lot altogether in one room."

Ripley rushes to pull him into a hug. "I'm so glad you made it."

"Nothing could've stopped me, Rip."

I catch Lennox's gaze across the room. He's smiling at the sight of our girl, happily surrounded by everyone we care about. People we didn't know existed when we first set upon the road to this moment.

"Did I miss the live show?" Warner jokes, his eyes on Raine still plucking the violin in his lap.

"No." He shakes his head. "No live show."

"Oh, come on," Enzo cajoles. "Give us a preview. Then we'll all have bragging rights that we heard the great Raine Starling's latest hit first."

There's a chorus of agreements. Silencing them with a raised hand, Raine grins ear to ear as he stands up in front of the room. Sobriety agrees with him. His career has hit the damn stratosphere in the last few years.

"I have something, but it's rough," he explains, placing the violin under his chin. "I'm not sure if it counts, but I wrote this for the anniversary of our first date, Rip."

Sliding her arm around Lennox's waist and kissing his cheek, Ripley perks up at her name. She immediately looks down to the black chain bracelet she still wears, even though the tracker broke about five years ago.

"You remember the date?" She chuckles.

"Well, it's a rough estimate."

Raine lifts the bow, coaxing it over the violin strings with precision that will never fail to astound me for a man without sight. He plays like the instrument is an extension of himself—a living, breathing body part.

It's a complex song, layered with low, mournful notes that sound like deep sorrow. Then he flicks the bow with masterful expertise and adds lighter segments, blending the two contrasts into a seamless melody.

Light. Dark.

Hopeful. Devastating.

All of life's vast complexities.

Perhaps this is actually the most divisive opinion. Whether we can contain these multitudes at once. Hold evil and redemption inside us simultaneously. Strike with love and hatred in the same blow.

Raine's music is honest. Raw. Painfully realistic. A jagged blend of the two extremes. Just like Ripley's artwork. Both of them have immortalised our stories in their purest forms. Our voices will live on.

For many, we were the villains.

But we fucking deserve this happy ending.

The End

BONUS SCENE
RIPLEY

It feels fitting to begin this chapter on the sixth anniversary of leaving Harrowdean Manor. It's been far from smooth sailing, but after spending years working hard to reach this point, Lennox has finally achieved his dreams.

Picking up the stretchy, Lycra hoodie emblazoned with his new gym's name—*Flex Fitness*—I run my finger over the embroidered logo. My chest is bursting with so much pride, I wonder how I'll contain it.

"Do you like it?"

I lean my head against Lennox's shoulder, still fingering the logo. "It's perfect."

"Phew." His chest rumbles with a deep laugh. "I certainly don't want to go back to the drawing board for the sixth time."

"How does Lincoln feel about the logo?"

"Lord knows. The man doesn't give much away."

Snorting, I peer up into Lennox's seafoam eyes. He seems to have a love-hate relationship with his business partner, despite the pair becoming friends while training in a different gym a few years back.

They've worked hard to get here—scoping out locations, securing loans, investing in equipment. The pair have spent many long nights imagining the perfect venue for their gym, and it's all about to pay off.

"Well, I think it looks great. Clear, simple and effective. The launch is going to be perfect, Nox."

A long sigh blows from his nostrils. "I really hope so."

"You've worked your ass off for this, haven't you?"

"Yeah."

Placing the hoodie back on our kitchen table, I lift my hand to his face. Lennox's chin is heavily stubbled these days, his chocolatey-brown hair so long it's curling around his ears.

"Then trust that it will work out. You've got everything under control."

His large hands moving to cup my hips, Lennox spins me to face him fully. I have to strain my neck to look up at him, looming far above me and casting a shadow equivalent to a deadly mountain peak.

His thirties have been generous to him, gifting smile lines where unmarked skin lived, gratitude in his pale-green eyes and the added bulk of a relaxed lifestyle, though he's still corded with muscle.

I love seeing him content, even if the last few years haven't been without hardship. It took a long time for the heat from Harrowdean Manor's implosion to die down.

For years, we've been hounded and ridiculed by journalists and the public alike. Nowhere was safe. Not even our trash was safe from being picked through. But we survived the abuse and constant surveillance as a team.

Our skin thickened overtime, and amidst the demons that forever seem to follow us, we carved out our own piece of happiness. A space large enough to fit my unlikely family and all the love we share.

"Your faith in me is astonishing," he whispers tenderly, his fingers threading into my curls. "And I love you for it."

"Why wouldn't I have faith?"

Lennox shrugs, his lips rolling together.

"After all these years, do you still doubt how I feel?"

"No." He shakes his head.

"What, then?"

"I just... I don't know what I'm doing or if this is going to work, yet you've still shown up every single day to encourage me. I don't want to disappoint you if the gym fails."

"It's not going to fail. Besides, I'm pretty sure it's my job to be there for you."

His lips twist ruefully. "Nobody asked you to do it, though."

"And I didn't need to be asked. I love you, Nox. That's enough reason for me to be standing by your side today when you cut that ribbon and realise your dream."

"There's no one else I'd rather have at my side, baby."

His forehead touches mine before our mouths meet in the middle. Lennox still kisses me as roughly as he first did all those years back, our bare bodies entwined in a frigid Z wing cell while we battled for our lives.

But I'm glad he hasn't lost his hard edge. The man I fell in love with was as brutal as he was passionate. Protective and vengeful in the same fell swoop. That fascinating paradox still lives within him today.

It's the reason why his love is so all-consuming. I know exactly the lengths he has and always will go to for his family. Lennox's devotion is the reason we've made it this far.

"I realised my dream the day I made you mine," he says into my lips. "And there isn't a day that goes by when I don't think about how ridiculously lucky we all got."

"Well, I am pretty fantastic."

He snorts, lips softly pecking mine. "Shut up, Rip."

"Make me."

Letting his mouth hungrily move against mine, I lose myself to his demanding touch. Sometimes, I wonder how we managed to shift from one extreme to the other. For a long time, all I felt for Lennox was utter hatred.

That couldn't be further from the truth now. The memory of hating him feels like a distant dream, the shadow of a time long passed. He's proven himself to me a million times over since those horrific days.

I let my hands crawl up his corded, barrel chest, tracing lines I've memorised across many evenings. I used to spend my nights dreaming about how to end his life as painfully as possible. Now I spend them curled up in his arms.

A shiver slips over me when I feel heat at my back. Someone's hand slicks up my spine, pushing curls over my shoulder to expose my neckline. Teeth graze my earlobe, leaving an imprint.

"Where's my invite?" Xander's voice is silky-smooth behind me.

Of course.

He's never far away.

"Open invitation," Lennox replies.

"Don't I get a say in this?" I joke.

Lennox's lips fasten back on mine for another breath-stealing kiss before he releases me. "No. You surrendered that right the day you gave yourself to us."

"Asshole."

"He is," Xander murmurs into my hair. "And this asshole is late for his own party. So stop distracting him."

Pain sizzles through me as his hand smacks into my jean-covered ass. I arch my back, pushing myself into Xander's tall body. The scent of spearmint is a comforting musk wafting off him.

"He kissed me," I whine in a low voice.

Chuckling, Lennox squeezes my hips. "Didn't realise it was illegal to kiss my girl."

"It's not. But tell your best friend that."

"Both of you need to get your asses in the car." Xander sighs. "We're already late, and we still have to pick Raine up from the studio. Let's move."

With a warning pinch delivered to my still-tingling butt cheek, Xander steps back, leaving me to roll my eyes at Lennox. I take the hand he offers, then we follow Xander out of our apartment, down to the awaiting muscle car.

Leaning out of the driver's window, the black-haired owner himself is smoking a cigarette while leaning obnoxiously on the car horn. He lets up when he spots us emerging.

"Took long enough!" Hudson yells. "I don't have all fucking day."

Lennox opens the rear door for me to climb inside. "Calm down, Knight. We're hardly late."

"Tell that to Brooklyn because she's been calling me non-stop for thirty goddamn minutes."

"She's your girl, not mine."

Hudson silently shakes his head in exasperation.

"Hi, Hud," I call to him.

"Hey. Hurry up and get in, will you?"

Climbing into the back seat, I'm sandwiched in the middle between Lennox and Xander. Both lay possessive hands on my thighs. I'm barely able to breathe with their bodies tightly packed around me.

"Are Hunter and the others coming?" I ask Hudson. "They didn't RSVP."

"They're still in Costa Rica." He flicks his cigarette then shifts the car into gear. "This ongoing serial killer case is a fucking nightmare."

"So we've been hearing." Lennox tightens his grip on my leg. "The news talks about nothing else."

"Yeah." Hudson sighs. "Sabre Security is going through it right now. We're just trying to stay afloat."

"Anything we can do to help?" I ask hopefully.

"Nah. But thanks."

"You know where we are."

"I know, Rip." He smiles in the rearview mirror.

Lapsing into silence, the drive to Raine's nearby studio passes fast. It's only a few streets over so he can travel there independently when he wants silence to rehearse and compose.

I spot him lounging outside the frosted glass door, his guide stick passing back and forth in his hands. Hudson blares on the horn to alert him to our arrival and shouts his name out the window.

Running a hand along the Mustang's wide bonnet, Raine manoeuvres his way to the passenger seat, folding his stick as he climbs inside. I lean between the front seats to clasp his shoulder.

"How was your day?"

His glasses-covered eyes turn in my direction. "Better now you're in it, guava girl."

Grinning, I drop a heavy kiss on his cheek. "Missed you too."

"Mmm, you taste good. Why didn't you come to the studio with me?"

"Because you needed to work, and the last time I came, we broke the coffee table."

"Ah." He hums contently. "That was a good day."

"Alright, alright," Hudson grumbles. "Enough of that."

"I've seen you stick your tongue in Brooklyn's mouth enough times." I shove his shoulder. "Suck it up."

Weaving through traffic, we head into East London. Located in a popular neighbourhood, the gym isn't far away, but it takes time to battle through the capital's traffic.

The closer we get to the venue, the harder Lennox grips my thigh. He's staring straight ahead with his plump lips set in a hard line. I haven't seen him this tense for a long time.

Pulling into the car park, several vehicles have already snagged spots close to the entrance. I recognise Kade's flashy SUV. His brother refuses to let any of the guys drive his precious Mustang.

"They beat us here," I observe as we pull in.

"Like Kade would ever risk being late for anything," Hudson mutters scornfully. "Bet he even came out of his mum's womb fucking early."

"Gross," Raine mumbles.

"True, though."

Climbing out first, Lennox slams the car door a little harder than necessary. I wince at the sudden movement then follow Xander out, snagging Raine's hand once he's unfolded his guide stick.

Flex Fitness is an industrial style building carved from red brick with black railings and huge, criss-crossed windows that offer a view of the newly-renovated interior. I can see the sparkling equipment from here.

As soon as Lennox leads us inside, the roar of conversing voices greets us. The reception area smells freshly painted, while the new flooring is squeaky clean beneath our feet.

A desk sits before the lightly-tinted, double glass doors, sealed behind a thick, glistening, red ribbon just waiting to be cut. In front of that, a large group has gathered.

"Rip!"

The flash of ash-white blonde hair alerts me to Brooklyn racing towards us. She's intercepted by Hudson stepping up to sweep her off her feet, spinning her in a small circle.

"No hello for me?" he teases.

She swats his shoulder until he releases her. "I'm still mad at you."

"Come on, blackbird. I didn't blow off our date for any old reason. You know what work is like right now."

"Whatever. You owe me sushi and a movie, Hudson Knight. Until then, I'm not talking to you."

"Ouch. Love you too."

"Whatever, dickhead."

Shoving him with a laugh, Brooklyn pulls me into a hug. Admittedly, it took her a long time to warm up to me. We first met her three years ago when she joined Hudson, Kade, Eli and Phoenix in their London home.

While our shared trauma allowed us to quickly bond with the men from Blackwood Institute, Brooklyn was a tougher nut to crack. We both share a mistrusting nature, but over many late nights and takeout meals, she eventually started to soften.

"If one of the guys bailed on date night, I'd be killing them too," I whisper to her. "Make him work for your forgiveness, Brooke."

She winks at me. "I always do."

We turn with matching smiles to watch all the guys begin to greet each other. Phoenix insists on lifting me into a cuddle while Eli squeezes my shoulder and Kade offers me a wave.

Jude simply nods, standing in a quiet corner to avoid the crush. With everyone acquainted, I notice a few other familiar faces. Warner is notably absent, too busy fighting fires back at Sabre's HQ.

Lennox is chatting to Lincoln and their newly recruited receptionist, Poppy, in front of the desk. When she hands him a pair of scissors from behind the desktop monitor, his eyes quickly find mine across the room.

With his spare hand, Lennox crooks a finger towards me. I check that Xander has his eyes on Raine then make my way through everyone to reach the desk.

"Hey, Lincoln."

The stormy-eyed gym nut gives me a smile. "Rip."

"Congrats. The place looks great."

"Wait until you see the equipment area."

"Shall we?" Lennox asks, offering me his arm.

"You don't want to do it?" I glance at Lincoln.

"Nah, this one's all his. You two go ahead."

Accepting Lennox's arm, I follow him to the ribbon-wrapped doors. Everyone falls to a hush at seeing us position ourselves. I meet Xander's gaze and grin, loving the smile that spreads his thin lips.

"Ready?" I ask quietly.

Lennox pauses for a moment, staring through the clear glass doors at the pristine gym equipment. "I've been thinking about this day for the last two years. Didn't think it would actually arrive."

"You deserve this, Nox."

"Do I?" He looks down at me. "I'm not so sure."

"Then I'll be sure for the both of us. This is your day—own it. We're all so proud of you."

Gently smiling, he drops a kiss on my cheek. "Thank you."

"Always."

Holding him close, we turn to address everyone together. The faces of our friends and loved ones stare back at us, full of excitement and huge smiles. The bubble of pride burgeoning in my chest reaches a fever pitch.

"Speech, speech!" Phoenix catcalls.

Huffing, Brooklyn pinches his arm. "Shh."

He throws an arm around her shoulders and tugs her close to kiss the side of her head. It's strange to think that the people we once heard terrifying stories about have become our family in so many weird and wonderful ways.

"Thanks for coming," Lennox begins, his voice strong and even. "I'm grateful to have you all here for this special occasion. Today, we officially open Flex Fitness for the first time."

Lifting a hand to his mouth, Xander's eyes crinkle at the corners. I think the iceman is actually getting emotional.

"It's been a long journey to get here," Lennox continues. "One that began the day we left our old lives behind and dared to imagine what our future could look like. This was my dream."

Looking up at him once more, I feel tears spring to my own eyes.

"I couldn't have achieved it without my business partner, Lincoln." He offers the man a smile. "And my brothers, Xander and Raine, who helped us design this gym from scratch."

Loosely holding Xander's elbow, Raine is grinning so broadly it's a wonder his face doesn't split in half. He's tucked his blacked-out lenses into his shirt pocket, allowing his golden eyes to absently dance around the reception.

"But most of all, I want to thank my partner in life and crime... Ripley."

Turning his full attention to me, it feels like the rest of the room fades away. All I can see is him. My enemy. My saviour. My ride or die.

"I wouldn't be the person I am today if it wasn't for you pushing me, day in and day out. You encourage me as much as you drive me crazy. All of this is for you, baby."

Moisture spills from my burning eyes and douses my cheeks. "Love you."

"Love you too." Lennox wipes my tears aside with his thumb. "Let's cut this damn thing together."

"Nope."

"No?" His chin jerks as he does a double take.

"This is your achievement to claim. Go ahead."

Releasing his arm, I take a couple of steps back to encourage Lennox to stand alone. He laughs at me, his hand clenching around the scissors as he faces the sealed doors.

We all watch with bated breath as he snips the bright-red ribbon clean down the middle. It flutters to the ground while Lennox pushes the release button so the doors swing open.

"Congrats!"

"Whoop! Whoop!"

"You did it!"

Roaring applause echoes all around me. Eli, Kade and Phoenix step up to shake Lennox's hand while Hudson claps Lincoln on the shoulder. Brooklyn has made her way to Jude's safe corner to exchange a tight hug with him.

Letting everyone head inside the gym ahead of me, I linger behind to await the final two members of my family. It doesn't take long for two slender, scarred arms to wrap around me from behind while Raine's freshly squeezed orange and sea salt scent halts at my side.

"How does it look?" he asks.

"Um, shiny. And… energetic."

"Energetic?" Raine laughs, his fingers tangling with mine. "You're always so eloquent, Rip."

"I dunno, I'm not exactly a gym person. But it looks like they've done an awesome job."

"The equipment is all the best money can buy," Xander explains while snuggling me close. "Word is already spreading. New memberships doubled this past week."

"Damn." Raine shakes his blonde head. "This place will be buzzing soon enough."

"It's going to be a hit," Xander agrees.

With both of them holding me, I'm content to watch on. Lennox throws his head back, reacting to a joke that Phoenix tells him. The group is all belly laughing, filling the gym with the light, hopeful sound. Even Lincoln has cracked a rare smile.

I remember the first day I set foot in Harrowdean Manor. It's a feeling I'll never forget—the sense of total despair and loneliness. Even with the promise of a sparkling new position as Harrowdean's stooge, I felt so fucking alone.

I didn't ask for a family. Hell, I didn't even ask for friends. My hatred and rage were enough to keep me warm during that empty, grief-stricken year before the guys were transferred.

Who knew that the monsters responsible for so many of my bleakest moments would become my sole source of happiness? The reason I continue to get up, every goddamn morning, and fight to survive this cruel world.

We hated each other so deeply.
But that just made our love stronger.
And now… No one will break us apart ever again.

PLAYLIST
LISTEN HERE:
BIT.LY/BURNLIKEANANGEL

Twin Size Mattress – The Front Bottoms
Help. – Young Lions
Monsters – Foreign Air
Up In Flames – Ruelle
You've Created A Monster – Bohnes
Sincerely, Fuck You – Pardyalone
Freedom – Young Lions
Fixed Blade – Trade Wind
Said & Done – Bad Omens
God Needs The Devil – Jonah Kagen
Out Of Style – KID BRUNSWICK & Beauty School Dropout
In Your Arms – Croixx
Roses – The Comfort
Sailor Song – Gigi Perez
Hate Me Now – Ryan Caraveo
Bleed – Connor Kauffman
SEE YOU IN HELL – Beauty School Dropout
Jerk – Oliver Tree
STRAY – jxdn
Pull the Plug - VOILÀ
Another One – Toby Mai
SPIT IN MY FACE! – ThxSoMch
Again – Noah Cyrus (Feat. XXXTENTACION)

Video Games – Good Neighbours
Higher – Croixx
Brain Stew – Green Day
End of a Good Thing – Cory Wells
Burn It to the Ground – Nickelback
S P E Y S I D E – Bon Iver
Violet Hill – Coldplay
When Will We Be Free? – Young Lions

WANT MORE FROM THIS SHARED UNIVERSE?

The timeline of Harrowdean Manor runs parallel to Blackwood Institute. Learn more about Brooklyn, Hudson, Kade, Eli and Phoenix by diving into the dark and twisted world of another experimental psychiatric institute.

mybook.to/TwistedHeathens
mybook.to/SacrificialSinners
mybook.to/DesecratedSaints
bit.ly/BIBoxSet

Dive into Sabre next. Set in the same shared universe, the Sabre Security series follows Harlow and the hunt for a violent, bloodthirsty serial killer. Featuring cameos from all your favourite Blackwood Institute characters.

bit.ly/CorpseRoads
bit.ly/SkeletalHearts
bit.ly/HollowVeins
mybook.to/SSBoxSet

Follow Willow's story next as she flees an abusive marriage and takes refuge in the small mountain town of Briar Valley, assisted in her hunt for justice by Sabre Security.

WANT MORE FROM THIS SHARED UNIVERSE?

mybook.to/WBWF
mybook.to/WWTG

Read Warner and the Anaconda Team's story in an upcoming, dark why choose trilogy featuring a desperate heroine fleeing untold horrors and the complicated, morally grey security team who rescue her.

mybook.to/FracturedFuture

ACKNOWLEDGEMENTS

Ripley's story is one that many of us can relate to. I remember writing a blog post for a mental health magazine not long after receiving my diagnosis in 2019, admitting that I wished I could tell my loved ones it was something simpler and less enduring.

The stigma surrounding bipolar disorder is still prevalent, and helping to shed some light on how it impacts so many lives is something I feel deeply passionate about.

For anyone out there who feels alone, misunderstood, or abandoned — You are seen. You are heard. You have a voice. Please use it.

I'd like to thank the incredible people who support me with every book I write and release. My partner, Eddie. Lilith for making me smile, day in and day out. Kristen, my wife from across the pond. Zoe who deals with the random tasks I send her through ranting voice notes. And Kaya for her endless love, enthusiasm and passion for all my books. Thank you all for your unconditional support.

Thanks to my fabulous editor, Kim, for working her magic on this book baby. And I need to say a huge thank you to my publicist, Valentine, and the whole team at Valentine PR for supporting me with this release.

Finally, I'd like to thank you. The reader. I would be nothing without my loyal fans, showing up for every book I write, shouting about the shared universe, and recommending my stories to anyone who will listen. Thank you for inspiring me every day to continue showing up and telling these dark tales.

See you next time.
Stay wild,
J Rose xxx

NEWSLETTER

Want more madness? Sign up to J Rose's newsletter for monthly announcements, exclusive content, sneak peeks, giveaways and more!

Sign up:
www.jroseauthor.com/newsletter

ABOUT THE AUTHOR

J Rose is an independent dark romance author from the United Kingdom. She writes challenging, plot-driven stories packed full of angst, heartbreak and broken characters fighting for their happily ever afters.

She's an introverted bookworm at heart with a caffeine addiction, penchant for cursing and an unhealthy attachment to fictional characters.

Feel free to reach out on social media. J Rose loves talking to her readers!

For exclusive insights, updates and general mayhem, join J Rose's Bleeding Thorns on Facebook.

Business enquiries: j_roseauthor@yahoo.com

Come join the chaos. Stalk J Rose here…
www.jroseauthor.com/socials

ALSO BY J ROSE

Read Here:

www.jroseauthor.com/books

Recommended Reading Order:

www.jroseauthor.com/readingorder

Blackwood Institute

Twisted Heathens

Sacrificial Sinners

Desecrated Saints

Sabre Security

Corpse Roads

Skeletal Hearts

Hollow Veins

Briar Valley

Where Broken Wings Fly

Where Wild Things Grow

Harrowdean Manor

Sin Like The Devil

Burn Like An Angel

Anaconda Tales

Fractured Future

Standalones

Forever Ago

Drown in You

A Crimson Carol

Writing as Jessalyn Thorn

Departed Whispers

If You Break

Made in United States
Orlando, FL
12 June 2025